THE COMPLETE SHORT STORIES: THE 1960s

PART FOUR: 1967–69

Brian Aldiss, OBE, is a fiction and science fiction writer, poet, playwright, critic, memoirist and artist. He was born in Norfolk in 1925. After leaving the army, Aldiss worked as a bookseller, which provided the setting for his first book, *The Brightfount Diaries* (1955). His first published science fiction work was the story 'Criminal Record', which appeared in *Science Fantasy* in 1954. Since then he has written nearly 100 books and over 300 short stories, many of which are being reissued as part of The Brian Aldiss Collection.

Several of Aldiss' books have been adapted for the cinema; his story 'Supertoys Last All Summer Long' was adapted and released as the film *A.I. Artificial Intelligence* in 2001. Besides his own writing, Brian has edited numerous anthologies of science fiction and fantasy stories, as well as the magazine *SF Horizons*.

Aldiss is a vice-president of the international H. G. Wells Society and in 2000 was given the Damon Knight Memorial Grand Master Award by the Science Fiction Writers of America. Aldiss was awarded the OBE for services to literature in 2005.

Also by Brian Aldiss

BRIAN ALDISS

THE COMPLETE SHORT STORIES: *The 1960s*

Part Four:
1967–1969

HARPER
Voyager

Harper*Voyager*
An imprint of HarperCollins*Publishers*
1 London Bridge Street
London SE1 9GF

www.harpervoyagerbooks.co.uk

This paperback edition 2015
1

Stories from this collection have previously appeared in the following publications:
Nova (1967), *New Writings in SF* (1967), *New Worlds Science Fiction* (1967, 1969), *Titbits* (1967),
Orbit 2: The Best Science Fiction of the Year (1967), *Impulse* (1967), *Intangibles Inc. and Other
Stories, Dangerous Visions: 33 Original Stories* (1967), *Galaxy Magazine* (1968, 1969), *Solstice* (1969).

A catalogue record for this book is
available from the British Library

ISBN: 978-0-00-814896-6

Set in Minion by Born Group

Printed and bound in Great Britain by RR Donnelley

MIX
Paper from
responsible sources
FSC™ C007454

Contents

Introduction

Should an author concern himself about who his readers are? Should he worry about what they think of his writings?

Is not the world full of better and more cogent concerns?

These questions I raise without, hardly surprisingly, being able to answer them.

I raise them because I have been so entirely a writer all my long life, forever concerned with what to say and why I choose – or why I have been chosen – to say it.

Hardly a year has passed without the publication of a slender book of verse, a translation of the poems of Makhtumkuli, a novel, SF, a travel book, a volume of social commentary, or a selection of short stories, as here and now.

The possible length of a tale has long been of interest. One of my inventions was the mini-saga. My mini-saga project was to confine a story within fifty words. Titles did not count within the bastions of that punitive fifty. *The Daily Telegraph* embraced my idea, and we ran mini-story competitions in the paper for six successive years.

My determination from the start was that a mini-saga should not be trivial; its spacial limitations drained narrative from the form; a moral aspect should remain.

Here is the example I offered my newspaper readers:

The doors of the amber palace
closed behind the young king.
For twenty years he dallied with
his favourite courtesans. Outside,
the land fell into decay. Warlords
terrorised the population.
Famine and pestilence struck,
of which chronicles still tell.
The king emerged at last.
He had no history to relate.

Some years after this was published, I discovered that a beautiful and cultured lady of my acquaintance carried a cutting with her of this mini-saga in her purse. What is more enthralling than fame? Why, secrecy ...

When I phoned *The Telegraph* with my suggestion, I was working at the other end of the narrative scale, on a long trilogy concerning a planet called Helliconia.

And now? A new year dawned and I suddenly determined to challenge myself, not with shortage of words but with shortage of time. In brief, I would write a short story every day in succession. This book contains some of the results.

To be honest (generally a foolish thing for a writer to do) a short story written on a Monday requires a Tuesday as well. On Tuesday, you edit, you correct, you knock out ungainly sentences, you amplify, you may suddenly discover a new meaning that had never occurred to you on the Monday. So you in effect rewrite. That's what Tuesdays are for ... the writing of tiny masterpieces ...

Most of these stories are fairly dark, glowing with gloom. I like it that way. Such matters as this I discussed with a new friend. Whereas it had been my own firm decision as an ex-soldier to leave Devon for Oxford, my meeting with Anthony Storr was accidental. We became close. Where I was just a writer, Anthony was an important figure in the university, and the clinical Lecturer in Psychiatry.

He suffered from depression, but liked to be amused; he himself could be greatly amusing. More to the point – and the reason why he features in this introduction – is that Storr was the author – among other titles – of *The Dynamics of Creation*. It was that wonderful perceptive book which drew me to him. To read his volume was to understand better why and how and what I wrote.

As can be seen, I have written a generous amount. In the past at least, this was because of the times we lived in. And more recently we have the temperatures of our own mental climates to deal with. In the sixties, I was busy adjusting to life in England after many excitements in the tropics, coping with failing marriages, looking after children, struggling for recognition.

And in a writer's life – as in other lives – curious accidents occur. Fearing my small children might be taken away from me for ever, I wrote a short story about it. Then I decided that was not enough. I launched out on a novel. As I wrote, I said to myself: 'This is so miserable, no one is going to want to read it ...'

But I continued to the end, christened the results *Greybeard*, and sent the bundle off to my publisher. Faber & Faber accepted it, as did Signet in New York. And they labelled it – to my surprise – science fiction. Under that flag, the novel sold promptly to Germany, Tokyo, Budapest, Milan, Verona, Copenhagen, Oslo, and Rio de Janeiro. Oh yes, and Amsterdam.

Never again was I to have such success with a novel. One often does not realise what one is writing or – fortunately – reading ... Let's hope it holds psychological truth.

Anthony Storr puts it this way: 'A man may often be astonished to find the scarlet thread of his identity running through a series of works which appeared to him very different at the time they were conceived.'

In the end is my beginning, and in my beginning is my end

A Difficult Age

Various rumours have been circulating about Imago, the first robot ever to commit suicide. I'm in a position to end those rumours. Imago was our family robot.

I remember clearly how he revealed the way his thoughts were tending. My wife and I had given a dinner for my father, to celebrate his sixty-fifth birthday; our eighteen-year-old son Anthony was also present. As guests, we had invited father's youngest brother, Eddy, who was fifty, and his daughter Vera. Imago waited on us during the meal and brought us drinks out on to the air-conditioned terrace afterwards.

Following an idle line of conversation, Eddy exclaimed, 'Well, I wish *I* was thirty years younger, anyhow!'

'Nonsense, uncle, you'd feel foolish being younger than your daughter!' I said, and everyone laughed.

'It's a pity we can't all stay at a favoured age,' my father said. 'I don't know why you want to be younger, Eddy – I'd say fifty is the golden age. You have reached the pinnacle of your career – without going downhill, like me! You still have your health and your wits. Your career is stable, your prosperity is assured. You don t have the worry of growing children, like a younger man, or the vexation of grandchildren, like an older man.'

'Nonsense, fifty's the worst possible age,' said Eddy. 'You can't yet sit back and enjoy a pension and delicate health as you do, nor can you still chase women like a man of forty.' (He had the tact not to look at me, perhaps remembering I was thirty-nine.) 'At fifty, you see all too clearly the things you hoped to do and now never will. No, for preference, I'd be – if not Anthony's age – Vera's age.'

Vera laughed. 'Daddy, you're an old misery! And I assure you that the mid-twenties are not as comfortable as you may sentimentally recollect they were.'

'They sit very well on you, my dear,' my wife said. 'What do you find to object to? You have such a marvellous supply of adoring young men. What more do you want?'

Imago handed Vera a coffee. She took it, stared at it as if to hide her embarrassment, and said, 'Well, take those young men. Honestly, you can't imagine how silly they are, most of them. They either treat me as if I was still a little girl or as if I were already past it.' At this, I noticed my son Anthony colour slightly. 'And – I must admit – I do sometimes feel just a kid and at other times absolutely past it. The truth is, twenty-six is a very uncomfortable age. You don't have the fun of being teenage or the pleasure of being regarded as a responsible person. If I could choose my ideal age, I'd be – oh, thirty-five, say!'

'It's not a bad age,' I admitted. 'At least, each succeeding year is worse. Every age has its snags. I remember feeling worst when I was twenty-nine and some idiot called me "sir." At that moment, I knew youth had fled.'

'Each age has its snags,' agreed my wife, 'and also its benefits.'

I could see she was going to say something more, but at that moment Anthony gave voice. He was at an awkward age, the poetry writing age, the age – as a friend of mine once said – when you have the hairs but not the airs of a man. He seemed always moody and generally silent, except when silence would have been the better policy. He was, in short, terrible company, and had my full sympathy, which I never dared express.

He said, 'Some ages have no benefits! I notice all of you naturally want to be younger but none of you are fool enough to plump for *eighteen*. At eighteen no one likes your music, no one will publish your poetry, your clothes never suit your personality! You're really a man but nobody believes it, not even yourself!'

'Nonsense, Anthony, you've all life before you!' exclaimed Eddy firmly.

'But you don't know what to do with it! At eighteen, you see everything with painful clarity before age starts its merciful task of dulling the brain. And you realise for the first time at eighteen how short life is, how much of it has scudded by without your having done a damned thing about it! By the time you're twenty-five it'll be too late – sorry, Vera! What is there but death and old age ahead?'

His grandfather said, 'You express precisely why I was not foolish enough to say I wished I was eighteen again, Anthony. I agree that it is a very painful age. I too was obsessed with death – more so than I am now. We can only assure you that your perspectives will change in a very few years.'

'It's easy enough to talk!' Anthony said, and walked out of the terrace, leaving his coffee untouched.

When the others had gone home, my wife and I sat chatting and gazing into the night. Imago was clearing away the coffee cups. Unexpectedly, he said, 'Sir!'

'What is it, Imago?'

'Subject, evening's discussion, sir. Discussion revealed clearly marvellous variety and complexity of human existence. My deduction is correct, sir?'

My wife and I looked at each other.

'I don't think any of us would have regarded it in that light, Imago,' she said – I thought a little uneasily.

'Every few years, madam, irrespective of other factors, for humans different quality of experience. Is so? Different view of self? Correct deduction?

Somehow, I didn't want to admit as much. So I said, 'Certainly, one experiences such things as the passage of time differently at different periods of one's life.'

'Of one's human life, sir. Exactly. Not only different quality of experience, also different quality of time-enjoyment.'

'Take the cups, Imago, please.'

He stood his ground, against all robotic programming. 'Robots, sir. Imago just realises: their only source of pride, that they are made in man's image. But is not so. Are too simple. Are more made in image of dumb things like elevators, traffic lights, automobiles, clockwork acrobats. No enjoyment of time's passage at all.'

'What follows?' my wife asked in a whisper.

Imago dropped a cup. 'The poetry I secretly write can be no good. Am just – machine!'

He ran from the room, out into the night. We stood and saw him go, speeding towards the river, his head-light flickering. Even as he flung himself in, we noticed Anthony standing moodily on the bank. Maybe he was thinking of doing the same thing.

He entered the room with a dull air of triumph, waving a hand. 'Remember when you bought Imago, on the day I was born? If you check on his guarantee, you'll see he was eighteen too. It's a difficult age.'

So that's the truth and the end to rumours. Now you tell me what the truth *means*.

A Taste for Dostoevsky

He was nearly at the spaceship now, had slithered down the crater wall and was staggering across the few feet of broken rock that separated him from safety. He moved with the manic action of someone compensating for light gravity, his gauntleted hands stretched out before him.

He blundered clumsily against the outcropping teeth of rock, and fell on them. The knee joint of his suit snagged first on the rock, bursting wide. Still tumbling, the man grasped at his knee, feebly trying to clamp in the escaping oxygen-nitrogen mixture.

But help was at hand. They had been tracking his progress through the ship's viewer. The hatch was cycling open. Two men in spacesuits lowered themselves to the lunar surface and hurried over to the fallen figure.

Grasping him firmly, they pulled him back into the ship. The hatch closed on them. The audience applauded vigorously; they loved the old corn.

In the spaceship cabin, relaxing, the two rescuers lit mescahales and sat back. Eddie Moore sprawled on the floor, gasping. It had been a close one that time. He thought they were never coming for him. Slowly he sat up and removed his helmet. The others had gone by then; there were just a few technicians backstage, clearing up.

Still breathing heavily, Moore climbed to his feet and headed for the dressing room. The lunar gravity did not worry him at all – he had lived here ever since his mother died, three years ago.

When he had changed, tucking himself into his ordinary everyday one-piece, he made his way towards the players' exit. Halfway there, he changed his mind and climbed down through the airlock of the mocked-up twentieth-century rocketship.

Most of the audience had left the big hall now; there were just a few of them at the gallery at the far end, admiring the cleverly recreated lunar landscape. Eddie trudged through the mock pumice, head down, hands in pockets.

Funny the way it wasn't until the whole moon surface was built over and the artificial atmosphere working that people had recalled the terrific aesthetic pleasure they had derived from the old primeval landscape of the moon – and had been forced to recreate it here out of artificial materials. That was the way things went. They didn't appreciate his once nightly performance as the dying spaceman; he so fully empathised with his role that he knew one day he would die of oxygen-failure even while breathing it – and then there might be those, the discerning ones, who would hold the name of Eddie Moore dear, and realise that they had once been in the presence of a great artist.

Looking up, he saw that a solitary figure stood on a ridge of rock, staring moodily up at the fake heavens. He identified it as Cat Vindaloo, the Pakistani director of their show, and called a greeting to him.

Cat nodded sourly and altered his position without actually coming any nearer to Moore.

'We went over well tonight,' Moore said.

'They still pay to come and watch,' Cat said.

'Your trouble is, you're obsessed with being a failure, Cat. Come on, snap out of it. If there's anything wrong with the show, it is that it's too realistic. I'd personally like to see less of a dying fall to end with – maybe a grand finale such as they'd have had at the end of last century, with all the crew parading outside the ship, taking a bow.'

As if the words were dragged out of him by compulsion, Cat said, 'You're beginning to over-act again, Eddie.' Moore realised the director was not standing here purely by accident; he knew that Moore, alone of the troupe, often preferred to trudge home the hard way.

'Let me tell you, I'm the only one of the whole damned batch who still throws himself into the part. You can have no idea of the sort of life I lead, Cat! I'm an obsessive, that's what, like a character out of Dostoevsky. I live my parts. My life's all parts. Sometimes I hardly know

6

who I really am. ...' He saw the beginnings of a glazed expression on Cat's face and grabbed his tunic in an effort to retain his attention. 'I know I've told you that before, but it's true! Listen, it gets so bad that sometimes – sometimes I'm you – I mean, I sort of take your role, because I worry about you so much. I mean, I suppose I am basically afraid – it's silly, I know – afraid you may be going to sack me from the cast. I must tell you this, though of course it's embarrassing for us both. I – don't you sometimes feel I am being you?'

Cat did not seem particularly embarrassed, a fact that disconcerted Moore. 'I was aware you were unbalanced, Eddie, of course. We all are in this game, and I suppose I may as well confess – since you are bound to forget every word I tell you – that my particularity is suffering any sort of insult people like to heap on me. So that's why I attract your attentions, I suppose; it's destiny. But I fail entirely to see how you mean you are being me.'

'If you don't understand, it's no good explaining. What I mean to say is that sometimes for days at a time I think myself – though I'm pure English – to be an Indian like you, living in India!'

'I am a Pakistani, Eddie, as I have told you many times. You are choosing your own way to insult me again, aren't you, taking advantage of the fact that I fundamentally have this degrading urge to be insulted. How can you live like an Indian here? And why should I care if you do? Your life is your own to make a fool with if you care to!'

'That I would dispute if you were capable of arguing properly. How far are any of our lives our own ? Where do we live? Who lives us? Which is us? But to pose such philosophical questions to you – pah, it's laughable! I must be out of my mind!'

'The very truest word I have heard from you for months! You're mad!'

'Don't you call me mad!' The two tiny human figures confronted each other in the vast grey reconstructed landscape. Suddenly, one of them flung himself on the other. For a moment, they struggled together and then fell, rolling over and grasping at each other's throats, lost on the ill-lit and broken plain. They became quieter. Finally one of them rose. He staggered off in the direction of the exit, gaining control of his movements as he went, and then breaking into a run that took him as fast as possible from the scene of the struggle.

*

When he got back to his apartment, he went straight into the little washing cubicle behind the surgery and rinsed his face and hands. He stood there bent at the basin for a long while, soaking his cheeks in cool water. Life was such nonsense that the more serious it grew, the harder it became to take it seriously.

The more he thought about it, the more amused he became. By the time he was drying himself on a fluffy white towel, he was laughing aloud. The moon indeed! The twenty-second century! Funny though it was, this nonsense must be put a stop to, once and for all. Clearly, he must go and see Etienne.

He rolled down his sleeves, walked through the surgery, down the passage, and to the front door. Looking through the two panels of frosted glass, he could see that beyond lay a fine summer's evening. Although it was almost past nineteen-fifteen, the sun was still shining brightly, and quite high in the sky. He paused. Just beyond the door he would see the brass plate that announced he was practising as a dentist; and the name on it would be – Vindaloo or Morré? He hesitated. He hoped, Morré.

He opened the door. On the brass panel, polished by the concierge that morning, appeared his name: Morré. He beamed with relief. Beside the panel was a little pasteboard card with his surgery hours and reminders to patients to present their health cards, all neatly written out in French and Flemish.

He strolled down the side street and on to the main road, where the quiet was instantly lost. The garish seaside street carried a lot of through traffic, often international traffic hurrying from France through to Holland or Germany. Taking the undercut, Morré crossed the road and walked a couple of blocks to Etienne's place. On the way, he stopped at a little flower stall and bought her a posy of blue cornflowers; they would soften the blow of what he had to say.

Etienne lived over a magazine and paperback shop in a flat she shared with two other young Belgian ladies – both happily away on holiday at present. Her pleasant little living room looked over the low dunes and the wide beach to the sea.

'You are very late this evening, Eddie,' she said, smiling as she let him in.

'Perhaps so, but why attack me for it? It's my misfortune, isn't it – or so I would have thought it if you had greeted me lovingly!'

'Eddie, don't be that way! I did not reproach you, my darling!' She stood on tiptoe, as he had noticed she often did. She was short and very shapely, in a little blue dress that went well with the cornflowers. She looked very sexy standing like that.

'Please come off your tiptoes,' he said. 'You are trying to fool me.'

'Darling, I was not – and I swear to you, I did not even notice I was on my tiptoes. Does it disturb you to see me on my tiptoes? It's not usually reckoned as an indecent posture, but if it offends you, I promise I won't do it again.'

'Now you are trying to humour me! You know nothing maddens me like being humoured! Why can't you speak to me like a reasonable human being?'

She flung herself down rather prettily in the wide armchair. 'Oh, believe me, if you were a reasonable human being, I'd make every effort to talk to you like one. You're absolutely nuts, aren't you, Eddie?'

He had a brilliant idea. It would scare the pants off her. 'Yes, you have uncovered my secret: I am nuts.' Without undue haste, he lifted up the cornflowers before him and ate them one by one. Then he wiped his hands on his handkerchief. 'I am nuts and that is what I wished to talk to you about this evening.'

'I have to go out almost at once, Eddie ...' She looked as if she would have liked to faint. When he sat down close to her on the straight-back chair with the tapestry seat that was an heirloom from her old Flemish grandmother, she became rather fixed in expression, and said nothing more.

'What I was going to tell you, Etienne, darling, what I especially came over for, was to say that I feared our engagement must be broken off. It's not so much that we are not suited, although that is a consideration; it is more that I don't even seem to know what century I am living in – from which it follows, I suppose, that I don't even know what country I am living in – which in turn means that I don't know what language I am speaking, or what my name is. In fact I don't even know what planet I'm on, whether it's the Moon, or Earth, or Mars.'

Etienne gestured out of the window towards the beach, where two sand yachts were bowling merrily along.

'Take a look for yourself. Does that look like Mars? You were born on this coast; you know the North Sea when you see it, don't you?'

'Don't interrupt me! Of course I can see it's the flaming North Sea –'

'Well then, don't talk so stupid! Look, Eddie, I've really had about enough of your nonsense! You come up here every Saturday night and break off our engagement –'

'I do not! I've never broken it off before, often though I've been tempted to!'

'You do, too! You don't know what you do do! How do you think I like it? I've got my pride you know! I can take emotional scenes as well as the next girl – in fact sometimes I rather think I enjoy them in a kinky sort of way. Maybe I'm the kinky kind –'

He shook a fist under her nose. 'No self-analysis, please, at least while I'm speaking! Have you any interest in me or haven't you? And who am I? Who indeed? Man's eternal quest for identity – pity I have to carry mine out with such rotten partners.'

'If you're going to be insulting, you can go, Eddie Morré! I know perfectly well what's wrong with you, and don't think I'm not sympathetic just because I don't show it. You have built up that fine little dentist's practice just so's you will have enough money to support me comfortably when we get married, and the overwork has resulted in brain fatigue. Poor Eddie! All you need is a little rest – these fantasies about Mars and the Moon are just phantoms of escape filtering across your over-heated cerebellum, reminding you of the need for rest and quiet. You know how damned quiet it is on Mars.'

Tears filled his eyes. It seemed she really was sympathetic. And perhaps her explanation was correct. He threw his arms round her in perfect forgiveness and attempted to kiss her.

'Do you mind! Your breath stinks of cornflowers!'

The two vast human figures confronted each other in the tiny artificial town-room. Sparked by sudden anger, he grasped her more closely. They struggled. Nobody was there to see a chair tipped over and they rolled on to the floor, arms round each other's necks. After some while, they were both still. Then one of the figures rose and hurried out of the apartment, slamming the door in haste.

*

Plainly, he was in need of some form of purification. When it was dark, he changed into clean garments and walked down to the burning ghats. The usual crowds of beggars stood and lay in the temple doorway; he gave to them more generously than usual.

Inside the temple, it was stuffy, although a cool breeze moved near the floor, fluttering the tiny lights of the faithful – who were not many this evening, so that they formed only a small cluster of insects in the great dim hallowed interior of the hall.

E. V. Morilal prostrated himself for a long while, his forehead to the stone, allowing his senses to go out amid the generations who had pressed foreheads and feet to this slab in the solemn contortions of devotion. He felt no devotion, only isolation, the opposite of devotion, but the sense of other human beings was some sort of balm.

At last he rose and walked through the temple on to the ghats. Here the smells that lingered in the building took on definition: wood smoke, burning unguents, the mouldy Ganges slowly trundling by, bearing its immemorial burden of holiness, disease and filth. As ever, there were a few people, men and women, bathing in their clothes off the steps, calling on their gods as they sank into the brown flood. Morilal went tentatively to the edge of the water, scooping up a handful of the stuff and pouring it on his shaven crown, letting it run pleasurably down into his clothes.

It was all very noisy. There were boats plying on the river, and children and youths shouting on the bridge, some of them with transistor radios.

'Hello! Back in the twentieth century now!' Morilal thought sharply.

Restless, he shuffled back and forth among the funeral pyres, some of which were unlit, awaiting midnight, some of which were almost burnt out, the human freight reduced to drifting ash or a bit of recalcitrant femur. Mourners crouched by most of the biers, some silent, some maintaining an arbitrary wailing. He kept looking for his mother. She had been dead three years; she should have been immolated long ago.

His old friend Professor Chundaprassi was walking slowly up and down, helping himself along with a stick. He nodded to Morilal.

'May I have the honour and pleasure of joining you, professor, if I do not interrupt a chain of meditation?'

'You interrupt nothing, my friend. In fact, I was about to ask if you would delight me by joining me, but I feared you might be about to engage in a little mourning.'

'No, no, I have only myself to mourn for. You possibly know I have been away for some while?'

'Forgive me, but I was not aware. You recall I greeted you yesterday at the railway station. Have you been away since then?'

Morilal had fallen in with Chundaprassi, walking sedately through the puddles and wet ash; now he stopped in some confusion and gazed into the wrinkled face of his companion.

'Professor – you are a professor, so you understand many things above the powers of ordinary men such as myself – though even as I say "ordinary men such as myself", I am conscious of my own extraordinariness. I am a unique being –'

'Of course, of course, and the point really cannot be too greatly emphasised. No two men are alike! There are a thousand characteristics, as I have always maintained –'

'Quite so, but I'm hardly talking about a characteristic, if you will forgive my being so disagreeable as to interrupt you when you are plainly just embarking on an interesting if somewhat long lecture on human psychology. And forgive me, also, if I seem to be talking rather like a Dostoevsky character – it's just that lately I've been obsessed –'

'Dostoevsky? Dostoevsky?' The professor scratched his head. 'Naturally I am familiar with the major writing of the Russian novelist … But I fail momentarily to recall which of his novels is set, even partially, in Benares.'

'You mistake my meaning – unintentionally, I'm sure, since a little sarcasm is positively beyond you. I happen to be in a spot, professor, and if you can't help, then to hell with you! My trouble is that my ego, or my consciousness, or something, is not fixed in time or space. Can you believe me if I tell you that no more than a couple of hours ago, I was a *Belgian dentist* at a seaside resort?'

'Allow me to wish you good night, sir!' The professor was about to turn away when Morilal grasped him by one arm.

'Professor Chundaprassi! Please tell me why you are going so suddenly!'

'You believe you are a white man! A Belgian white man! Clearly you are victim of some dreadful hallucination brought about by reading too much in the newspapers about the colour bar. You'll be a Negro, next, no doubt! Good night!'

He pulled himself free from Morilal's grip and tottered hurriedly from the burning ghat.

'I will be a Negro and be damned to you, if I so desire!' Morilal exclaimed aloud.

'Congratulations, sir! You are quite right to exercise your freedom of judgment in such matters!' It was one of the bathers who spoke, a fat man now busily oiling his large and glistening breasts; Morilal had noticed that he was avidly listening to the conversation with the professor and had already taken a dislike to the man.

'What do you know about it?' he enquired.

'More than you may think! There are many people like yourself, sir, who are able to move from character to character, like birds from flower to flower. I myself, but yesterday, was a beautiful young Japanese lady aged only twenty years with a tiny and beautifully-proportioned body, and a lover of twenty-two of amazing ardour.'

'You are inventing filth, you fat old Bengali!' So saying, he jumped at the man, who tripped him neatly but failed to stand back in time, so that Morilal took him with him as he fell, and they rolled together, hands at each other's throat, down the slimy steps into the Ganges.

He dragged himself out of the river. For a while, as he lay on the bank with his head throbbing, he thought he had experienced another epileptic fit. Something of the chequered past came back to him, and he dragged himself up.

He was lying half out of a shallow stream, under a stone bridge. As he got to his feet, he saw the stream cut through a small country town. The place seemed to be deserted: so empty and so still that it looked almost like an artificial place. Slowly, he walked forward, down the curving street, staring at the small stone houses with their gardens neat and unmoving in the thin sun.

By the time he reached the other end of the street, where the buildings stopped and the fields began again, he had seen nobody. The only movement had come from an old cat, stuffily walking down a garden path. As he looked back the way he had come, he saw that he had just passed an unpretentious building bearing the sign POLICE STATION. For several minutes, he stared at it, and then moved briskly towards it, opened the door and marched in.

A portly man with a grey moustache that drooped uncomfortably over his lips sat reading a newspaper behind a counter. He wore a green uniform. When the door opened, he looked up, nodded politely and put down his paper.

'What can I do for you, sir?'

'I want to report a murder. In fact, I want to report three murders.'

'Three murders! Are you sure?'

'Not really. I don't know whether I killed the persons concerned or not, but it must be worth checking. There was a friend of mine, a producer, and my fiancée, and a poor black man in India. I can give you their names. At least, I think I can remember. Then there's the time and place …'

His voice died. He could see it was going to be difficult. His impulse had been to enlist help; perhaps it had not been a wise impulse. And had he ever been anyone else, or had it all been the product of a fever?

The policeman slowly came round the counter, adjusting his face until it was absolutely without expression.

'You seem to have some very interesting ideas, sir, if I may say so. You wouldn't mind if I ask you a question before you go any further? Good. You say you don't know whether you killed these unknown persons or not?'

'I – I get blackouts. I am never myself. I seem to work through a lot of different people. You'd better assume I did kill them.'

'As you like, sir. Which brings me to my next question. How do you mean, one of them was a black man from India?'

'It was as I said. He was very black. No offence meant – it's just a fact. Quite an amusing man, now I come to think of it, but black.'

'His clothes were black, sir?'

'His clothes were white. He was black. His skin. Good heavens, man, you stare at me – I suppose you know that the people of India are pretty dark?'

The policeman stared at him with blank astonishment. 'Their skins are dark, you say?'

'Am I offending you in some way? I didn't invent the idea, don't forget! As sure as the good Lord took it into his head to make you and me this rather unattractive pink-white-grey tone, he made the Indians more or less brown and the Negroes more or less black. You do know that Negroes are black, I suppose?'

The policeman banged his fist on the desk. 'You are mad! By golly, you are mad! Negroes are as white as you are.'

'You mean the Negroes in Africa?'

'Negroes anywhere! Whoever heard of a black Negro?'

'The very word means black. It's from a Latin root or something.'

'From a Greek root meaning tall!'

'You liar!'

'You simpleton!' The policeman leant over and grabbed his newspaper, smoothed it out angrily with his fists. 'Here, this will show you! I'll make you admit your stupidity, coming in here and playing your pointless jokes on me! An intellectual, I can see!'

He ruffled through the paper. Moore caught a glimpse of its title *The Alabama Star* and stared up incredulously at the policeman. For the first time, he realised the man's features were distinctly negroid, though his skin was white and his hair fair and straight. He emitted a groan of fright.

'You a Negro?'

'Course I am. And you look at this news item – FIRE IN NEGRO UNIVERSITY. See that picture. See any negro there with black skin? What's got into you?'

'You may well ask, and I wish you'd stop grasping my shirt like that – it feels as if you have some chest hair with it, thanks. I'm not trying to play a joke on you. I must be in – well, I must be in some sort of an alternate universe or something. Hey, perhaps you are kidding me! Do you really mean people in Africa and India and so on have skins the same colour as us?'

'How else could they be any other colour? Ask yourself that!'

'They were where I come from.'

'Now, how could they be? Just how could they be?'

'I don't know! It's a matter of history. Some races are white, some yellow, some brown, some black.'

'Some idea! And you say this arrangement happened in history. When?'

'I didn't say that! It happened way back … well, I don't know when.'

'I suppose your men originated from different coloured apes, huh?'

'No, I think it all happened later than that … Stone Age, maybe. … Honestly, now you confront me with it, I must admit I don't exactly know when the arrangement came about or how. It does sound a bit unlikely, doesn't it?'

'Anyone who could dream up the idea of men all different colours – wow! You must be a real nut! I suppose like it's allegorical, with the good people being white and the bad black?'

'No, no, not at all – though I admit a few of the white saw it like that. Or did I invent it all, the whole colour question? Perhaps it's all another facet of my guilt, an awful phantasm I have thrown up from the depths of my mind, where I did the murders. They can't have any subjective reality, either. Wait! I remember! I'm nearly there! Fyodor Dostoevsky, I'm coming!'

Hurriedly, he punched the policeman in the chest and braced himself for the reciprocal blow. …

He was tramping through the sand, ankle deep even in the main street of this shabby town. In the side streets, the sand climbed almost to the eaves of the shoddy wooden houses. Among the houses were buildings that he identified after a moment's thought as mosques; they were no more than huts with wooden minarets added. There were Tartars here, moving slowly in their costumes of skin, some leading the two-humped camels of Bactria behind them through the street.

The man with whiskers and a stoop was just ahead of him. Morovitch drew level and looked sideways. He recognised the beetling brow and the haunted eyes, set deep in their sockets.

'Second Class Soldier of the Line Dostoevsky?' he asked.

Dostoevsky stared back at him. 'I've not seen you in Semiplatinsk before. Are you with the Seventh Siberian Battalion?'

'The correct answer to that, operatively, is no. I – well, sir, if I could talk to you for a moment … the fact is …'

'It's not a message from Marya Dmitrievna, is it?' Dostoevsky asked impatiently, his face pale.

'No, no, nothing so banal. In fact, I have come from the future to speak to you. Please, cannot we go to your room?'

Dostoevsky led the way in a sort of daze, shaking his head and muttering. He was still serving out his exile in Siberia, no longer as a convict but as a humble soldier in the army. His present home, to which he led Morovitch, was of the simplest, a poor room in one of the small wooden houses, containing little more than a bed, a table and one chair, and a round iron stove that could scarcely heat the flimsy room when the cruel winter came round again.

Humbly, Dostoevsky offered the intruder the chair, sat down on the bed himself, and produced some tobacco so that he and the visitor might roll themselves cigarettes and smoke together.

He passed a hand wearily over his face. 'Where do you say you come from? You're not – not a Decembrist?'

'I am from what to you is the future, sir. In my age, my race recognises you as one of the great novelists of the world, by virtue of your profound insight into the guilt always lingering in the human mind. You are one of the supreme artists of suffering.'

'Alas, I can write no more! The old ability has gone!'

'But even now you must be gathering together your notes on prison life for the book you will call *The House of the Dead*. Turgenev will say the bath-house scene is pure Danté. It will be read and remembered long after you are dead, and translated far beyond the bounds of your native Russia. And greater masterpieces of guilt and suffering will follow.'

Dostoevsky hid his face in his hands. 'No more! You will silence me forever if you speak thus, whether I believe it or not. You talk like the voices inside me, when another attack is coming upon me.'

'I travelled back to you from the far future through a series of epileptic hosts. Others of my kind travel back through other illnesses – it is a matter of what we specialise in. I plan to travel slowly back through the generations to Julius Caesar, and beyond that … but you are a very important landmark on my way, for you are integral to the whole philosophy of my race, honoured sir! Indeed, you might say you were one of the founders of our philosophy.'

The writer rubbed the back of his neck in discomfort and shuffled his rough boots on the floor, unable to look straight at Morovitch. 'You keep saying "our race" and "our kind", but what am I to understand by that? Are you not Morovitch?'

'I have infested Morovitch. We are parasitic – I am merely distorting his life a little, as I have distorted the lives of those I infested on my way back to you. Ah, the emotions I have stirred! How you would relish them, Fyodor Mikhaylovich! I have been in all kinds of persons and in all kinds of worlds, even in those that lie close in the probability spectrum to Earth – to some where man never formed himself into nationalities, to one where he had never divided into races with different coloured skin, to one where he never managed to gain supremacy over his fellow animals! All, all those worlds, absolutely stuffed with suffering! If you could see them you might think you yourself had created them.'

'Now you mock me! I can create nothing, unless I have created you. Forgive me if that sounds insulting, but I have a fever on me today, which induces me to doubt somewhat your reality. Perhaps you're part of my fever.'

'I'm real enough! My race – you see I use the term again, but I would find it difficult to define it to you. You see, there are more millions of years ahead than you could comprehend, and in those long periods man changes very radically. In my time, man is first dependent on a milk-meat animal he breeds – a sort of super-cow – and then entirely parasitic upon it. Over millennia, he develops an astounding freedom and can travel parasitically back through the generations, enjoying the suffering of all, like a silverfish boring back through the pages of a large and musty volume: a silverfish who can read, sir, if you follow my image. You see – I let you into the secret!'

Dostoevsky coughed and stubbed out his ragged cigarette. He sat uncomfortably on the narrow bed, crossing and recrossing his legs. 'You know I cannot believe what you say … Yet, tell me no secrets! I already know enough for one man; I'm burdened with knowledge about which I often ask myself, What good is it? And if it is true, as you say, that I have understanding of some of the dark things in the human heart, that's only because I have been forced – though often I myself was the forcer – to look into the dark things in my own heart. And I have tried to reach truth; you are admitting, aren't you, that you distort the lives you – well, if I say "infest", it is your own word, isn't it?'

'We get more fun … A couple of days ago, I caused a Belgian dentist to jilt his girl friend. Maybe he even murdered her! We live on the dark passions. The human race always had a morbid tendency that way, you know, so don't think of us as too abnormal. Most literature is just gloating over the sorrows and sins of others – of which you are one of the supreme and most honoured exponents.'

There were little flies that flipped down from the stained walls and landed persistently on the hands and faces of the two men. Dostoevsky had rolled himself another cigarette and drew heavily on it, looking less as if he enjoyed it than as if he supposed it might defeat the flies. He spoke ramblingly. 'You have the case all wrong, sir. Forgive me if I criticise by remarking that your attitude seems very perverted and vile to me. I have never revelled in suffering, I hope …' He shook his head. 'Or perhaps I have, who knows? But you must leave me, for I feel remarkably ill of a sudden, and in any case, as I say, you are wrong.'

Morovitch laughed. 'How can millions of years of evolution be "wrong" in any sense? Man is what he is, becomes what he is from what he was. Strong emotions are a permanent need.' He rose. Dostoevsky, out of politeness, rose too, so that for a moment they stood very close together, staring into each other's eyes.

'I shall come back to see you tomorrow,' Morovitch said. 'And then I shall leave this ignorant tribesman and infest – well, sir, it will be the greatest connoisseur's treat possible from our point of view – I shall infest you, and finally gain new insights into what suffering is like. It was so as to apply, as it were, the gilt to the gingerbread, that I called first, so that I may know you inside and out.'

Dostoevsky began to laugh, but it broke at once, changing into a cough. 'I see you are, as you claim, an illness.'

'Tomorrow, I will be part of *your* illness. Goodbye, sir, and thank you for your courtesy and evident disbelief – until tomorrow!'

He turned towards the door, on which the writer had hung a battered painting of a woman. As he did so, Dostoevsky bent quickly down and snatched up the poker from its resting place beside the stove. With a mighty swing, he brought it down across the man's unprotected head, much as Raskolnikov would one day be described as bringing down the hatchet on the old lady's head in *Crime and Punishment*. With scarcely a groan, Morovitch sank to the floor, one arm sprawling out across the crumpled bed.

Dostoevsky put the poker down. Then he began to tremble.

Auto-Ancestral Fracture

For Charteris fingering a domestic thing, the shadowy city Brussels was no harbour but a straight of beach along the endless litterals of his season. The towsers on the skyline lingering spelled a cast on his persistence of vision. He had no interest in privateering among those knuckled spoils. So his multi-motorcade pitched on a paved grind and tried to prefigure the variable geometry of event.

But on that stainey patch grounded among the fossil walls and brickoliths his myth grew and the story went over big what if each ear made him its own epic? The small dogs howled underground bells rang on semi-suits and song got its undertongue heating and the well-thumbed string. Though he himself was anchored deep in the rut of a two-girl problem forgetting other fervours.

Charteris they sang to many resonances and the spring's illwinds sprang it back in a real raddle of uncanned beat and a laughter not heard the year before.

Some of the crusaders' cars were burning in the camp as if it was auto-da-fé day, where the drivniks with cheerful shuck had forgotten that the golden juice they poured down the autothroats would burn. Like precognitive mass-images of the nearing future, the reek of inflammation brought its early pain and redness to the fatidical flare. Tyres smouldered, sending a black stink lurching across the waste ground where they all shacked.

You coughed and didn't care or snow was peddled in deeper gulches to the vein's distraction. The little fugitive shaggy figures were a new tribe, high after the miracle when the Master Charteris had died and risen again in a sparky way after only three minutes following the multi-man speed death up at Aalter. Tribally, they mucked in making legends. Bead groups flowered and ceded, lyrics became old history before the turning night wheeled in drawn. Some of the girls rinsed underclothes and hung them on lines between the kerouacs while others high-jinxed the boys or got autoerotic in the dicky seats. A level thousand drivniks locusted in the stony patch, mostly British, and the word spread inspired to the spired city.

There lifespendulum ticked upside down and the time was rape for legendermoan: for the hard heads and the business hearts found that their rhythms now worked only to a less punctilious clock and specula-tion had another tone. War had turned the metrognome off chime in general pixilation to a whole new countryslide upbraided.

What raised the threshold a bit was the Brussels haze. The bombing here had been heavy as the millionaire Kuwaiti pilots themselves flipped in a gone thing and the psycho-chemicals rained down. Life was newly neolithic, weird, and drab or glittering as the hypoglossal towers stag-gered. Appalling shawls of illusion draped across the people where the grey mattered. Occult lights still veiled the rooftops and aurora borealis clouded the corner of the eye. Jamming their stations signals of new bodies scarcely suspected before or different birds of intent It was a place for the news of New Saviour Charteris to nest.

Many came, some remained; many heard, some retained Food was short and disease plentiful, plague grunted in the backstreets of the mind, and cholera in the capital, but the goodfolk had thrown off the tiresome shades of Wesciv and unhoused cults of microbes and bacteria; this was the spontaneous generation and neutral Pasteur had been wrong. These circadian days, you could whistle along your own bones and the empty plate held roses. In Flanders field, the suckling poppies rose poppy-high, puppying all along in the dugged days of war's aftermyth. Gristle though the breast was all were at it. So it was gregarious and who cared.

Of these the Escalation was foremost. Among the petering cars they made their music, Bill, black Phil, Ruby Dymond with his consolations and Featherstone-Haugh, plus Army and their technicians who saw that the more sparky sounds reached tape. This day they had escalated to a new format and a new name. They now hit the note as the Tonic Traffic and had infrasound, ground from Banjo's grinder machine worked by Greta and Flo, who shacked with them and other musicniks.

Through mirror-sunglasses they peered at the oneway world, frisking it for telling dislocations in which to savour most possibility. The flat wind-smoke covered them part-coloured. They had a new number going needling into the new stations to really pierce wax called Famine Starting at the Head. Sometimes they talked round the lyric or with laughter sent it up.

On the Golden Coast cymbals start to sound some place like a magic garden I'm just a demon on the cello. Play the clarinet pretty good too man!

In his tent-cave Charteris with two women heard the noise and distant other flutes in flower-powdered falsetto, but had his own anguish to blow through the stops of strained relationship.

Stranding his pearl underseers to glaub the timeskip of Ange Old's farce its tragictory of otherwhens and all plausticities made flesh in the mating. Like Him fashioned from parental lobotomy truncated by the mainspring glories of a rain shower slanting through the coral trees where greened the glowing white of landscape. Figures moving dragging dropping enduring in her glowworm eyes the candlesphere of hallucidity she's the mouth and cheekbox of my hope's facial tissure to come back like soft evening's curtains. It's what I see in her all all the peonies the blackbirds the white-thighs all and if not her all all I see of any voyaging.

Yet Marta has her own unopened chambers of possibility the locked door calling to my quay my coast Bohemian coast my reefs that decimate steamships. On the piston of this later Drake lost in spume rankest alternating

'Do me a fervour! I try to work on this document of human destiny and you want to know whether or not I took in the slack with Marta last night Why not trip out of needling my alternatives? Get from me!' The ceiling was only canvas billowing, standing in for plaster in a ruinous convent later old people's home, which the autobahn-builders had half-nudged out of the way as they drove their wedges into the city-heart. Undemolished now almost self-demolished this wing flew the Charteris flag; here his disciples clustered elbows brick-coloured as plaster peppered down like the dust of crunched hourglasses. As starving Brussels besieged itself for a miracle domestic drama flourinched.

'Oh entropise human detestiny!' Angeline was washed and white like concentrate campallour, still calculating against the aftermaths of warcalculus, still by the chemicals not too treblinkered. 'I don't want to know if you slacked because I know if you slacked you slackered Marta tonight last night every night and I just damned won't stand it, so you just damned fuzzy-settle for her or me! None of your either-whoring here!'

'All that old anti-life stuff snuffed it with your wesciv world – from now it's a multi-vulval state and the office blocks off.'

'Your big pronounce! Hotair your views to others, stay off top of Marta, you grotnik!'

'Meat injection and the life she needs, Angel, pumped in, like the big gymnastic sergeant you sing. She has no impact with frozen actions like long disuse now quickened with the fleetsin for her. If I poke some import all's love in fair unwar and the sailor home from the seizure! Be pacific!'

'Sea my Azov! And you messiah on a shemensplash as and when is it, eh? A matlottery! Over my bedboddy! Don't you kindermarken me mate why how you can come it I don't know – look at the consolation! Prize her legs a part you'd be licky! Caspian kid! – All dribbled-rabble and emuctory!'

'I'll baltic where my thighs thew my honey, I the upand-coming!'

'You subserbiant Dalmatian! From now on you go adriantic up some mother tree – just don't profligainst me! Didn't I the one who moist you most with nakidity remembrane to mem-brainfever pudentically, or if not twot hot hand gambidexter pulping lipscrew bailing boat in prepucepeeling arbor of every obscene stance?'

She now had the big bosombeating act, buckaneering in the dusty half-room before his ambiguity, riding to master and be mastered, knowing he punched her husband in the traffic, gesturing with scatologic to the greyer girl, Marta on the master's corner couch cuckoobird unsinging. Phantom nets of mauve and maureen joined them like three captured parrot fish, web of twain, chain of time.

'Did I ever say you were not the sparkiest? Or the bell-ringing belle-blottomed? Sap out of it angelfish and don't parrot membrain there's suck a thing as polygam.'

Among the dark hair the branches of her face in tempest

'Bombastard it's to be she or me and now's your moment of incision. Cut it out or cut your rigging!'

But he broadsided advanced grasping her by the united fronter so that when she tugged away the blouse torn buttons Ming like broken teeth and one escampaigning teeter. He laughed in lust and shrouds of anger. She slapped him across his molar plex he a quick one to her companion way and they cavorted in a tanglewords the nettingroll.

For first time Marta brought her unbending mind and body to attention scudded to his rescue from the bedspace where they had seemed and tuckered and with a dexterritory he landed them both judies with squirming gust for keel-whoring and his digit rigid as he had voided mannymoon to squire their accunts and cummerbendle in their scrubberies dualigned by real and pseudoprod tongs and clappers circumjascentedly. In out in out moonlight moonlight.

They lay repanting. Marta said, 'Oh forgive me, Father, but you gnaw my need to bring me back where the circulation stammers.'

He said nothing in a fluid state. Around lay the pages and quires of the ream of his destinotionary tract Man the Driver in which he tried by shortcuttings from the sparky philosopher to prime mankindly on the better way of awareness.

Angelina said, 'To think that all your thinking comes to this and you so big in the mind can't see the world's slippered across the plimsoll line with you just some damned wandering bump swelling with the warfallout's megabreath doing two defeated dames in a dungy belgunmaden bad! What's there of metavision ask?'

Momentarily the roseplink lining parted and he saw with her eyes lavatory life going downheeled all the way as he fledabout of madness and hiveless ones begged him to be for them and be for them the big beatal and endal to some bitter end. Scrambling back, he said to spark himself, 'I am the grate I am where fools burn for greater light and from me shall come a new order beyond your comprehandling.'

Chance in that room sat also while the ceiling billowed the dark man Cass. He now managed as Charteris agent from the dark English Midlands all his life a self-punitive in a narrow way pinned behind a counterpain in drapershop where having broken out he now netted his advantages at fifty-nine eleven three a yard all right and gaudy as the smiling tout of Saviour Charteris flower-breasted plus other sidelines.

Many-monkeyed in his head he rose now saying, 'Hail the great I am! Hail chaptered Charteris! All burn for greater light from you. You fisher us a greater net of possibilities and what you photograph is multi-photographed with all possible value.' He sprawled at Charteris's pedestal for his idol to claim him; but Charteris cooled: 'You better go and fix the cascade down to the main Frankfurt route. Under my lid the sign still burns there in a precog frame.'

'Sure, we'll skim the menu of possibilities but first you have to speak in Brussels where life's real looty for us and people know you miracled death's aaltercation where the carcentinas buckled.'

Sweat dry on a skin of eagerness.

'No growth that way, Cass, believe! In every in every no line no loot on Brussels my bombardment of images dries me out. Famine starting at the head tells me we take our bellies, away from the emptiness of a Bristles brushoff.'

Still he had no confidence in the meat of his glazed tongue.

From the corner of his eyes, the females under a flapping lid swung like two monkeys. Trees grew on beaches. New animals lurked. Wall angles hinged

'You call the dance! You are the skipper of the new Ouspenski order beyond our compension and I ship with you the greatest.' Thus Cass's little horn piping.

So saying but Cass rode on the motorcade a prey to more than piety and thus in the cholera courts of the capital. The pitted music of the back streets was his quarry. These thousand rocketting disciples gathering quantity as they moved had a needle for some supply and just a cosy cosa nostra to keep them smoking along towards the profitable reefs in a parasitical pass. He came out from the ruined building gathering air and dragging in a sort of awareness before jetting off for the centre.

Waves of reality came and went, breaking over him, drenching him. Wall angles hinged. He was aware where he was going yet at moments the streets appeared a transparent rues; he imaged that this was just another mock-up of the quest he had follyed all his life, looking for some final authority perhaps: the central point of the quest never revealed itself, so that he was driving on the B route. He sang a line of Ouspenski's: Men may torture themselves but these tortures will not make them awake. Also Charteris so worked in him that he said to himself: You see how I released more potentialities in you, Cass – you carry on several lives at once!

Men may torture themselves. He could write it for the Tonic Traffic or the Genosides or the Snowbeams to sing. Their numbers had taken over the nine-to-fives. They must make themselves awake. The magician hypnotised his sheep and they turned to mutton believing they were immortal. All flocks there to be preyed on, and this new kind no exemption. Soon to be cassoulet He always drove at more than one wheel, whoever took lead car.

In the centre of the city, people whistled along their own bones though the empty bowl held roses. The European dislocation had harvested no fields and canned no fish. In hospitals, nurses with prodromic eyes dreamed islands, doctors smiled in lunar orbits whistling down syringes or snubbed their scalpels abscessmindedly on submerged patient bones. Although it's true the bakers ritually baked in massive factories, the formulas were scrambled and even what was edible did not all reach mouths, for the distributors so hot for truth drove their loads into amnesiac fields of wheat and lay there till they fecundated in the calendar of decay. The parliament still took its conclave but all the ceremony these last two months had brought were these laws passed: a law to stop the drinking of the good earth; a law to prohibit hats from becoming unseen when the sun set; a law to make Belgian hounds sing the night away like nightingales, with an amendment asking cats to try their best in that melodious direction too; a law to permit redness in traffic lights; a law to abolish the plague; a law against Arab invasion; a law to extend the hours of sunshine in cloudy winter months; and a far-sighted law to encourage all members of parliament to be more industrious by the granting of six months leave to them per annum.

Cass had the secret contacts. A drink in a bar, a ritual holding of the glass, a certain stance, a procedure of guarded phrases, and there was help for him and he smoking secretly with seven men. Who said to him at the end of an hour or so: 'Sure, it's for trade the maximum goodness that Charteris gets billed big and comes into town. Come he must. You go and see Nicholas Boreas the film director and put to him what we say.'

And Cass was given certain assurances and pay and moved along to see the mighty and highly-sung Boreas.

Under the tawning in the semi-house time buckled and they were still saddled by the sporadic barney with Him downtrodden in a multi-positional stance on a chaircase and Marta racked on the bunk-up while Angeline barn-stormed about the gesticulating room, rehorsing her old nightmares.

'Face it, Colin, you're now stuck on an escalation okay ride along but just don't forget the old human loot like what you did to my husband or maybe that's all gone overhead in your reeling skullways maybe maybe not?'

'It was the Christmas cactus there blinding as the lorry swerved and I could never make you understand. Don't go through all that again. It's the velocity, girl –'

'Verocity nothing you killed him and why should I pull down my knickers and open up my pealy gapes for you to come in beefs me oh the sheer sheer tears of every diving day and now I shape and rave at you and who knows through the encephallic centre you have shot some of that steamin' add so I'm hipping too and like to flip oh meanin' Christ Colin what and where the dung day dirt is done and you know how I itch I never dote a damned desire without my shift and all my upbringing undone!'

And Marta said, 'You're chattering your passion into threads Angel cause isn't there enough I mean he can the carnal both twomescence and I don't mound no moral membrane in a threesome and we sort of sisterly! Isn't the organ-grinding the big thing?'

So she seemed to flip and like a seafouling man embarked on culling Marta for a frigid and bustless chick while egging her on with premari-timely oaths to reveal what a poultry little shrubby hen-penned canal awaited bushwanking or the semenship of motiongoing loiner under her counterplain and how those specious sulcal locks were just the antartickled coups of man's ambit or if more trapical then merely multi-locked the vaginisthmus of panamama!

Thus spurred slim Marta unbuckled and pulled enragged away her entire and nylonvestments to kneel up flagrantly tightitted the slander ovals with an undividual stare took them like young imporktunny pigscheeks in lividinous palmystry squeezing to pot them smoothly at all rivels cried the heir erect command insprict the gawds meanwhile thirsting out her chubby plumdendumdum with its hennaed thatch of un-own feelds and throaty labyrings of kutch with cinnamons di-splayed.

The other sneered but he to her cheeky pasture lured advanced to graze and on her stirry eyepitch clove his spiced regarb as if his universion centered there his mace approaching friggerhuddle. She now as never evoluptuary bloomed in her showy exinbintion outward easily spread her cunative flower by rolling sternbawd rumpflexed to make him see the fissile smole of spicery fragiloquent of tongue almoist articulpate well-coming with spine archipelavis and her hands abreasted eagerly. He snared his bait engorged in cleft vessalage like a landlopped fissureman on the foreshawm groined.

'So that's the little spat that catches the bawdy muckerel the briney abasement where we scomber at our libertined gaol!' So far all jackular but now a saltier infection. 'I teened tined without embarkration down that slitway my jolly tarjack yearning for the fretdown of this narrow fineconment swished-for incunceration ounspeaking O where noughtical men wisely feast in silence a coop or lock-up maybe Angel but for the brightest cockalorys no lighthouse but a folderoloflesh espressionless no landmast certainly no buoy yet more than polestar to the marinader the milky wet itself the yin-and-yank by which life orients the loadstir that aweights all tonninch on the populocean incontinents awash the very auto-incestral fracturn between generoceans mother of emoceans gulf where the seacunning sextant steers and never more gladly lock we to that flocculent in carcerationen like sheep incult cumbency on the long combers O so furly I will my rompant chuck of gristle uncanvas to cell and serve as croptive to her in the shuckling socket and set soul for dungeoness!'

He launched himself to the briney swell with merry horn-poop in her focsle and cox'nd every vibrant stroke till her unfathom ablepuddle deigned and drained his saloot but her aglued mutions rollocked on.

Angeline walked impotiently outside and some of the tribe noted or did not note – caught in their own variable relationships – how her face was fleshcrumbled with folded eyes. So it was these days and no one had too much in mind of others though the mood was good – too wrapped in selfhood and even selfishness to aggress, no matter who aggrised, on alcohol or the needle. She was thrown to a sexual nadir and would not bed, not with Charteris, not with Ruby Dymond even when he folked up the blues for her, backed by infrasound and its bowelchurning effects. Even for her it was getting not for-real, as the war-showers still lingering acidly in the old alleyways, curled into her and she too dug the spectrums of thought made visible, leaping up exclaiming from a lonely blanket to see herself sometimes surrounded by the wavering igneous racks of baleful colour: or at gentle moments able to watch bushes and elms erupt in crusty outline singed by the glow of cerebral sundowns, in which climbed and chuckled a fresh unbeaten generation of mammalphibians, toads with sprightly wings and birds of lead and new animals generally that with feral stealth stayed always out of focus.

So it was also with Nicholas Boreas but more splendidly trumpets with icing oil He too had more inhabitants than reached consciousness and drank news of the motorcade miracle from Cass in his palatial bath. A mighty figure he was, bare without a hair, though with a poet's eye he had schillered his breasts and pate by dint of a bronze lacquer to laid a sort of piebald distinction. His flower was water hyacinth and in the foetid warmth of his apartment the tuberous plants multiplied and festered. Having heard Cass's spiel, he pushed his current nymph aside and slid under water, neptunelike, snorkel between crowned teeth. There submerged, he lay as in a trance, letting the feathery floating roots caress him; tickle his lax flesh, gazing up between the stiff fleshy leaves, nibbled by snails, nudged by carp and orfe bursting past his eyelids like coronary spasms.

Finally, he rose again, hyacinth-laurelled.

'I'm in full agreement with your suggestion as long as I can make it my way. Pour all my genius in! It should be a great film: Charteris Auto-Trip or some such title. Maybe High Point Y? The first panorama of post-psychedelic man with the climax the emergence of this messiah-guy after the colossal smash-up on the motorway when he was killed then risen again unscathed. Ring my casting director on this number and we'll start auditioning straight away for someone to play Charters. Also we'll want smashees.'

Whitewhale-like he rose, brushing black ramshorns from his knotted sheepshanks and the band began to play. In his veined eye gleamed the real madness; again he could explore – now on the grandest mafiabacked scale – the fissured continent of death. His best-known film was The Unaimed Deadman, in which a white man wearing suitable garments slowly killed a negro on a deserted heliport. He had been inspired to find a negro willing to volunteer to give a real death to art; now his messianic power would transfix on a large scale the problem of the vigour-mortis intersurface.

Attended by the plushy nymph, Boreas began to issue his orders.

His organisation staggered into action.

The idea was that the film should be made with all speed to take advantage of topicality. Archives could be plundered for effective passages. Except for the climax, little footage need be newly shot Episodes from The Unaimed Deadman could be used again. In particular, there was a sequence showing the Optimistic Man doing his topological topology act which seemed applicable. The Optimistic Man walked along a wide white line with hands outstretched, his hands and head and the white line filling the whole screen against the ground. The camera slowly disengaged itself from his shoulder as the line became more intricate, rising upwards like a billowing roof, revealing that more made less sense for the Man now seemed to be doing the impossible and walking on the rim of a gigantic eye; but, with increase of altitude, the eye is seen as the eye of a horse carved from the flank of an enormous mountain. Slowly the whole horse comes into view and the Man is lost in distance; but as this anomaly clarifies another obtrudes itself for we see that the great downland on which the cabbalistic horse is etched is itself astir like a flank and itself cabaline. This mystery is never clarified, there is only the nervous indecision of the whole hill's glimpsed movement – we cut back to the Man who now, in a white suit, stretches himself out wider and wider until he can saddle the horse. He has shed all humanity but bones; skeletally, he rides the charger, which is given motion by the rippling flank on which it is engraved.

There are sequences from old-fashioned wars, when the processes of corruption sometimes had a presynchronicity to moribundity, and a shot of a nuclear bomb detonated underground, with a whole sparse country rumpling upward into a gigantic ulcerated blister and rolling outwards at predatorial speed towards the fluttering camera. There are sequences in shuttered streets, where the dust lies heavy and onions rot in gutters; not a soul moves, though a kite flutters from an overhead wire; somewhere distantly, a radio utters old-fashioned dance music interspersed with static; sunshine burns down into the engraved street; finally a shutter opens, a window opens; an iguana pants out into the roadway, its golden gullet wide.

After this came the Gurdjieff Episode, taken from a coloured Ukrainian TV musical based on the life of Ouspenski and entitled Different Levels of the Centres.

A is a busy Moscow newspaper man, bustling here, bustling there, speaking publicly on this and that. A man of affairs whom people turn to; his opinion is worth having, his help worth seeking. Enter shabby old Ouspenski with an oriental smile, manages to buttonhole A, invites him along to meet the great philosopher Gurdjieff. A is interested, tells O he will certainly spare the time. G reclines on a sunny bedstead, derelict from the mundane world; he has a flowering moustache, already turning white. He holds onto one slippered foot. In his shabby room, it is not possible to lie: nonsense is talked but not lies – the very lines of the old dresser and the plaid cloth over the table and the empty bowl standing on the deep window sill declare it.

The window has double casements with a lever-fastener in the centre. The two halves of the window swing outwards. There are shutters, latched back to the wall outside. The woodwork has not been painted for many years; it rests comfortable in morning sunlight, faded but not rotten, seamed but not too sear. It wears an expression like G's.

G gives what is a grand feast for this poor time of war. Fifteen of his disciples come, and some have an almost Indian unworldliness. They sit about the room and do not speak. With lying out of the way, presumably there is less to say. One of the disciples bears a resemblance to the actor who will play Colin Charteris.

In comes O, arm-in-arm with A, and introduces him with something of a flourish to G. G is very kind and with flowing gestures invites A to sit near him. The meal begins. There are *zakuski*, pies, *shashlik, palachinke*. It is a Caucasian feast, beginning on the stroke of noon and continuing until the evening. G smiles and does not speak. None of his people speak. A politely talks. Poor O is dismayed. We see that he realises that G has set this meal up as a test of A.

Under the spell of hospitality, soothed by the warm Khagetia wine, A sets himself out to be the public and entertaining man who can enliven even the dullest company. The chorus takes the words from his moving lips and tells us what A talks about

He spoke about the war; he was not vague at all; he knew what was happening on the Western Front.

He gave us word of all our allies, those we could trust, those we couldn't, and had a bit of innocent fun about the Belgians.

He gave us word of Germany and how already there were signs of crumbling: but of course the real enemy was the Dual Monarchy.

And here he took more wine and smiled.

He communicated all the opinions of the public men in Moscow and St Petersburg upon all possible public subjects.

Then he talked about the desiccation of green vegetables for the Army: a cause with which he was involved, he said: and in particular the desiccation of onions, which did not keep as well as cabbages.

This led him on to discuss artificial manures and fertilisers, and agricultural chemistry, chemistry in general, and the great strides made by Russian industry.

And here he took more wine and smiled.

He then showed how well he was informed upon philosophy, perhaps in deference to his host

He spoke of melioration and told us all about spiritism, and went pretty thoroughly into what he called the materialisation of hands.

What else he said we don't remember, save that once he touched on cosmogony, a subject he had somewhat studied.

He was the jolliest and certainly the happiest man in the room. And then he took more wine and smiled and said he must be off.

Poor O had tried to interrupt this monologue but G had looked at him fiercely. Now O hung his head while A heartily shook hands with G and thanked him for a pleasant meal and a very interesting conversation. Glancing at the camera, G laughed slyly. His trap had worked.

Afterwards, G jumps up and sings his song, and the disciples join in. Gradually, the whole screen is choked with whirling bodies.

While the film was being pieced together, a French actor called Minstral was engaged to play Charteris. Because France had been neutral in the war, Minstral was one of the few prepsychedelic men left in Brussels. He played tough roles. When not filming, he kept himself apart, ate tinned food sent from Toulouse, meditated in a Sufic way, occasionally visited two young Greek sisters in the suburbs, and looked at volumes of beautiful photographs published by Gallimard.

Boreas's script director, Jacques de Grand, made his way out to the motorcamp on the lunatic fringes of the city with a haircut full of gentian hairoil. He wanted to get some background for the messiah's life, him and his success-drive both.

When de Grand arrived at the smokescream, the messiah was sitting on an old bedstead, picking his toes; from his two women he had only bad images; they would not yield to his healing power and he was feeling several things at once, that nothing could be done on any level unless women were involved in creative roles, that they were trapped in a history jelly, that he was a discarded I, and that the world was on the whole perched on the back of a radioactive tortoise.

'We're very fortunate to have you here at the early stages of your career, Mr Master, and witnessing the first miracles. How you like Belgium? Planning to stay long? Planning to resurrect anyone in the near future? My card!'

The card held a hand in it on a detachable body materialising in rubber smokelp.

'It was the vision I had in Metz. That's what betrayed me on my adjourney north up the web of photofailures, fleeing that Italian camp.'

'I see.' Quick application of more refreshing hairoil, head chest mouth. *Nom*, but the PCA was thick here and all hair growing whispers on it. 'You say photofailures, I gather from reports you enlarge Ouspavski's thought?'

'Well like Ouspavski I dig the west got too hairy with everyone and so the Arabian nightmare was just a justice and on the ill-painted poser the near-nordic blonde grew a moustache like a shadow across her force. ...

'And so how about some more erections in the near future? Please speak clearly into the visiting card.'

The whole mesozoic mess-up of the best west pretensions going themselves with the buns turning to gutter and silence is golden but a Diners Club card gets you anywhere. It was the whole city of a ruined version I had, he told de Grand. 'Now Europe's bracken up from a basic oil-need-greed and beggars can ride so even Gelina and Marta and me can't get along in a harness and all clapped out of the big ambushes of Westciv, eh?'

'I see. You think the bill's at last been paid?'

'Yes, the treadbill, trodden back to low point X and the city open to the noman. My friend, that was a short round we trod, less than two hundred degenerations the flintnapping cave-sleepers first opened stareyes and we break down again with twentieth sensory perception of the circuit. ...

'I see. More hairoil quick, and you think we're back where we squirted?'

'... which bust be the time for real awakening from machinality and jump off the treads into a new race that I will lead.' And the new animals falling out of new trees on the old beaches of stone.

'Yes, I see, Master. So you have no definite pains to insurrect anyone in the near future?'

'Angelina sees if she's not by now hyacinth-hipped the waters of sickness wrys and where we might have been balsam only balsa on the flord but me urgenus impatiens spends on merely the unhealing womenwound that helotrope witch tows me with its bloodstone balmy fragrance unavailing nector's womenwound me my ackilleaseheal.'

'You motion the waters of sickness, so you don't entirely rile out the possibility of insufflation in the near-flowering fuchsia?'

Taking back the visiting cod he filed his nail-dropping in a filing *gabinetto*.

'I am a fugitive from that perfumarole yet all beneath our feet the quakeline blows and vulcanows which runway lies firm aground for all this ilyushine is a flight merely from other ilyushins and not from anything called real.' The broken wind of his sail lay under the tall shrouds of offices.

'I see. I see what you're goating at. Like there's been a disulcation. Hair owl? No? Tell me couldn't you practise on a dead child if we brought you one?'

Charteris coughed his eyeblink a world gone then back in its imposture. Lies he could take, not disfigurements.

'Perfect sample of what I'm trying to gut over with the prolapse of old stricture of christchen moralcold all pisserbill it is are phornographable smirch as childermastication to be hung by the necrophage until strange phagocyte of the crowd.'

'So you deignt insufect anyone in the puncture?'

'Lonly Angina and the flowerhip-syrup girls.'

He coughed. When world came back steadied, in the big carred-up arena, tyres were still burning. The smoke crawled and capered a black nearest brown; up the side of a ruinous housewall where wallpaper hung montaged, its shadow grew like wisteria in the palid sun. Over one side, some disciples in gaudy hats and ruby beards were making a sing-in on the torture song. Another, a guy stoked an old auto with its upholstery in flames by flinging on petrol arcing from a can. The flames flowered at him and he rolled over yelling. Several people looked across him and the unbelievable patterning of it all, life's gaudy grey riches richer richness. The world of motion-in-stillness. All rested here today from the speed death but a migratory word and they would be away again, switched on to the signal the Master would unzip from his banana-brain. Right now, even as he proclaimed, all possibilities were open to them and under the crawling black tyresmog lay no menace that did not also swerve for poetry, so the tribe let all burn.

A strip of the motorway south of Brussels to Namur and Luxembourg had been closed to traffic Boreas's men worked and sweated, hundreds of them, many skilled in electronics, to fake up the big smash-in.

Some got through their work by being cowboys. Yipping and yelping, they thundered down upon the frightened cars, which stampeded like mad steers along the course, tossing their horns and snorting and backfiring in the canyon of their cavalcade. Branding irons transfixed hot red figures.

Other men from Battersea treated the steeds as underwater wrecks. In mask and flippers, down they sank through the turbid air, securing limpet cameras to cabins and bows and battered sterns which would record the moment of the mighty metal storm, rigging their mikes unfathomably, helter-scootering.

Other men with mottled cheeks worked as if they were charge nurses in an old people's home. Their patients were as smooth as they were stiff of limb, dummies with nude sexless faces, dummies without female fractures or male mizzenmasts, non-naval dummies, dummies lacking meatmuscle or temperature who pretended to be men, dummies with plaster hair and amenorrhoea who pretended to be women, dwarf dummies with a semblance to children, all staring ahead with blue eyes impevious, upholders all of the couth past wesciv world that could afford to buy its saudistruction, all terribly brave before their oncoming death, all as unspeaking O as G desired.

Rudely, the charge nurses pressed their patients into place, the backseat-drivers and the frontseat-sitters, twisted their heads to look ahead, to stare sideways out of the windows, to enjoy their speed deathride, to be mute and unhairy and non-drivnik.

It was an all-day labour, and to wire the cars. The crews revelled that night in Namur, shacking in an old hotel or sleeping in a big marquee tent pitched on the banks of the Meuse, with a beat trobbing like a temple. Boreas went belting back to Brussels and with a shivering sight stripped virgin bare, gripped tight the snorkel in his crowned teeth and sank beneath the feathery roots of his water hyacinths. The plants were spreading like a nylon nile, growing in the steamy atmosphere over the floor and up the black-tiled walls.

'Escrape from these lootless psychedelics showing their barbed crutches round the eyes,' he gruntled wallowing, 'as if I don't own all my own univorce!'

'Don't you believe in Charteris as new Christ, darling?' the nymph asked, floating pasturised cowslips on the sumper surface. She was delicious to his sight and taste, good Flemish stock.

I believe in my film,' he said and grasping her alligator-like in his jaws he looted her down into her depths.

Next day refreshed and bellyrolled, Boreas drove down towards the scene of the faked authentic speed death with his script director de Grand who gave golden speech about the Master between cranial embrocations.

'Okay, so he was kinky about children and gone on flowers and didn't seem to have plans about bringing anyone back from the deadly nightshade. Similar to thousand of people I know or don't know as the case. Did you get a glimpse of his life story?'

'You know those ruins out by Sacré Coeur, boss? They had a five gallow saturation bomb on them when the Arab air strike came down! You can't hardly see out there. I was switched on myself and it seemed to me his logic was all logograph and missing every fourth syllable of recorded time. That fabled bird, the logogrip, took wing, was really hippocrene in all his gutterance, where I way-did but could never plum.'

'Cut out that jar-jargon, de Grand! A hell of a help you are! What about his bird?' Chin belly and balls are jetting promontories.

'I tell you the logograph, the new pterospondee, roasts on his burning shoulder!'

'His bird, his judy! Did you get to speak to her?'

'He mentioned a part of her with some circumlocution.'

'*Godverdomme!* Get her and bring her to me in my pallase tonight. Ask her to dinner! She'll give me the low-down of this Master Man! Have you sot that straight in your adderplate?'

'Is registered.' And bennies quickly swigged down in oil.

'Okay. And get some more snow delivered to Cass – some of the motorcaders need a harder ticket in the arterial lane. *Comprenez?*'

They march from each other together in the web.

His unit was already setting up the crash-in. Technicians swarmed about the location with cowherd and keelhaul cries. By somebody's noon, the cars were all linked umbiliously with cables to the power control and the dummies sitting tight. They ran through the whole operation over and over, checking and rechecking acidulously to see if in their hippie state they had overlooked a technicolor time error. The four-lane motorway was transfilmed into a great racetrick where the outgoing species could stunt-in for its one and only one-way parade, a great tracerack in tombtime where sterile generations would last for many milliseconds and great progress appear to be made as at ever-accelerating speed they hurtled on, further from shiftless and forgotten origins the unknown target. This species on the vergin of extinction bore its role with detachment, waxed unsentimentality, was collected, chaste, impeccable, punctual, stiff upper lip, unwinking gaze. Remembered its offices and bungalows of iron sunset. Its lean servants, ragged even, not so; excitement raced among them; they all believed in this authentic moment of film-life, cared not for a fake-up, slaved for Boreas's belief, harboured their dimensions.

And to Boreas when all was ready came his chief prop man, Ranceville, with shoulder-gestures and slime in his mouth's corners.

'We can't just let them gadarine like this! It's sadism! They are as human as you or me, in our different way. Couldn't there be thought inside those china skulls – china thought? China feelings? China love and sincerity!'

'Out my way, Ranceville!'

'It isn't right! Spare them, Nicholas, spare them! They got china hearts like you and me! Death will only make them realer! Real china death-in!'

'*Miljardenondedjuu!* We want them to look real, be real. What's real for if you can't use it, I ask? Now, out my way!'

'What have they ever done to you?' The mouth all slaving lotion. 'What have they ever done?'

Boreas gestured, brushing away a fly or snail from his barricaves.

'I'll tell you something deep deep down, Ranceville … I've always hated dummies ever since china shop-rows of them stared in contempt at me as a poor small boy in the ruptured alleys off Place Roup. That's how I began you know! Me a dirty slum boy, son of a Flemish peasant! Weren't they the privileged, I thought, all beautifully dresden every day by lackeys, growing no baggy genitals, working or spinning clean out the question, glazed with superiority behind glass, made in god's image more than we? Dimmies I called them to belittle them, dimmies, prissy inhibitionists! Now these shop-haunting horrors shall die for the benefit of mankind.'

'Your box-official verdict, so!' Gesture of a gaudy cross. 'Okay, Nicholas, then I ask to ride with them, to belt in boldly in the red Banshee beside these innocent chinahands. They're sinless, guiltless, cool – I'll bleed to death with them, that's all I ask!'

Open mouths gathered all round turned their stained suspicious teeth to ogle gleaning Boreas, who waited only the splittest second before he bayed from his mountain top

'Get looted, Ranceville! You're hipped! You think you can't die – you're like a drunkard sleeping in the ditch, drowning for ever because he didn't realise there was a stream running over his pillow!'

'So what, if the drinking water has drunks in it, okay, that proves its proof. How can I die the death if those dimmies are not alive?'

'You'll see how real a phoney death is!'

Now on the waiting road was silence while they chewed on it. Like workers who joined a continent's coasts by forging a new railway, the unit stood frozen by their finished work, awaiting perhaps a cascade of photographs to commemorate their achievement of new possibilities: while behind them fashionably the unlined pink faces ignored them from the cars. The mouths came forward now, to see what Boreas would say, to hear out the logic, to try once again to puzzle out how death differed from sleep and sleep from waking, or how the spring sunlight felt when you weren't there to dig it and flesh and china all one to me.

Boreas again was sweating on the heliport, in his blood the hard ticket of harm as he filmed the climax of The Unaimed Deadman, had the negro, Cassius Clay Robertson, fight to start up the engine of his little glass-windowed invalid carriage. And then the longshot of the white man in his suitable garb running impossibly fast with big gloved hands from behind the far deserted sheds, the black sheds with tarred asphalt sides, running over for the kill with mirth on his mouth. Now he could have real death again, had it offered, because the occasional man was hepped enough on art to die for it.

'Okay, Ranceville, as long as you see this is the big oneway ride, we'll draw up a waiver contract.'

Ranceville drew himself up thin. 'I shan't waver! As the Master says, we have abolished the one-ways. I believe in all alternatives. If you massacre innocents, you massacre me! Long live Charteris!'

The watching mouths drew apart from him. One pair of lips patted him on the shoulder and then stared at the hand Some sighed, some whispered. Boreas stood alone, bronze of his bare head shining. The invalid car had fired at last and was slowly lurching on the move. The white man with the terrible anger had reached it and was hammering on the glass, rocking it with his blows. They'd had a hovercamera in the cab with Robertson then, with another leeched outside the misting glass, and used for the final print shots from these two cameras alternately, giving a rocking rhythm, bursting in and out of Robertson's terror-trance.

'Get yourself in focus of the cameras!' Boreas called huskily.

With a sign to show he had heard, Ranceville climbed into the old Banshee, a scrapped blue model they found in a yard by the Gare du Nord and had hurriedly repainted. Ranceville had red on clothes and hands as he squeezed in with the dummies. Their heads nodded graciously like British royalty in an arctic Wind.

'Okay, then we're ready to go!' Boreas said. 'Stations, everyone!'

He watched all his mouths like a hawk, the only one sane, whistling under his breath the theme from The Unaimed Deadman. Things would fall apart this time from the dead centre.

Marta was sprawling on the bed practically in tears and said, 'You don't understand, Angelina, I'd no wish to pot your joint out, but my loaf was nothing, not the leanest slice, and I was just a baby doldrums until the Father came along and woke all my other I's and freeked me from my awful husband and my awful prixon home and all the non-looty things I try now to put outside the windrums.'

Angelina sat on the side of the bed without touching Marta. Her head hung down. Beyond, Charteris was holding a starve-in.

'Fine, I sympathise with you when you stop whining. We've all had subsistence-living lives in rich places. But the way things are, he belongs to me you've got to get yourself another mankind. There'll be a group-grope tonight – any grotesque grot they grapple – now that's for you instead of all this ruin-haunting here!'

'And supposing I pick on your Ruby you so despise! My life's a ruin and the light dwindles on the loving couple. The Master said to me Arise –'

'Rupture all that, daisy! You just don't spark! Look, I know how you feel, the big love-feelings heart-high, but it wasn't like that so don't try to hippie out of it. All he did was walk in and make an offer as you sat single in your little house! That doesn't mean he's yours!'

'You don't understand. … It's a religious thing and mauve and maureen webworks come from him binding me! With his sweet rocket it's a sacrament.'

The ceiling simmering like a saucepan lid and Angelina hit her with a welp of rage and called her all mangey mother-suppurating things. 'You Early Christian whore! Go throw yoursylph to other loins! He's my man and stays that way!'

In anger, she drove the Marta from this ruined arena out, and then herself collapsed on to the single bed. There she still was when de Grand riled in, slipping a little packet to Case before he sought her out. She lay and let time set over her not unpleasureably, idly listening as the raucous noise of a song and plucked strings filtered in the shadow, wondering if anything mattered. That was the crux of it; they were all escaping from a state where the wrong things had mattered; but they were now in a state where nothing matters to us. At least if I can still thing this way I'm sane – but how to put it over to them and that they should be building. ... The possibility exists, and some days he does build: almost by accident like a weaver bird adding an extra room for teenage chicks to creep up at the back where it stark and on the stares a big woman all all naked bottoms and beasts. ... Bum weaver yes Colin he still has the glimpse. ... A sort of genius and might stage a build-on. ... Pull this lot together must make him listen maybe if I put it in a song for the Tonic all get the message. The table you use the table you take immense suck cess likely me running naked through loveburrow. ... Old Mumma Goostale. ...

As she dozed he entered, not uncivil with untrimmed moustache, de Grand, of secret history in plenty parishes.

'Excuse you saw me interviewing for the film the Master. Second time I'm pleasure of drivnik-visiting.'

'I'm thinking. I know it's extinct. Blow!'

'What intelligence! I'm full of aspiration. I left my own child to come on this quest to film the lootest Masterpiece.'

'Bloody typical. Go back to your child, Paddy, marry her, bear lots of lovely morechild, marry them off, live humble, avoid oil-shares, stay away from the excitements of master-peace, rumpling upwards and rolling at speed towards the fluttering artnik.'

'The director needs your professional guy dance routine to insight the Master to him. Has a dinner cooking wed local indelicacies and you tenderly invited.'

She sat up and tugged down the flower-blue shirt and bongo beads she was wearing, her modernity unfit, forgot arrested flow, with an effort focused on him.

'The director you say?'

'Nick Boreas of The Overtaker and The Unaimed Dead now moving to High Point Y to film your husband's life in compaint colour. The great Nick Boreas you must have heard.'

'He wants the truth about Charteris? Is that what you are saying? My god, these stinking runes are so high I'm almost indechypreable – Boreas wants the truth?' She fanned herself, he also, gasping like fishes in a mean lake.

'You have me defused a moment. Excuse – some pomaid! We're making a movie not a gospel we must want material like a sort of biogriffin job, right?'

'The mythic bird what else is struth! A movie you say! You my opportunity I zip on my head boy and you take me to your leader now?' With nails she tries to calm her wild dark hair.

'My fiat awaits delighted.' He with a byzantine bow.

She paused. 'You driving? You're so high, no?'

But he was in a studio car with hired driver and they yawed towards the fossil-pattern centre with moderate risk to life.

On the brittlements of the town auroras flattered in a proud mindflagging and old phantasms took trilobites at her. She was a guttered target for their technicolon pinctuated in a single frame as the assassin went home, feeling her face flatten and balloon as if centred in a whirling telescopular site. Tumultaneously, the broad Leopold II sloughed its pavements for grey sand and cliffs cascaded up where buildings were, unpocked by window or stratum. Turning her tormented head, she saw the ocean weakly flail the macadam margins of shore bearing in change, long, resounding, raw – and knew again as some tiresome visiting professor of microscopic sanity made clear to her that hear again repetitively iron mankind zinc was on the slide between two elements, beaten back to seawrack while he prepared to digest another evolutionary change and none the less stranded because motors roared for him up the hell and highwatershed.

Such sounds seemed sexplicable, nexplicable, inexplicable, plicable, lickable, ickable, able, sickable. She was able to differentiate the roar into eight different noises, all flittering towards her under the cover of each other. Things that slid and fused let out a particularly evil gargle, so that she grasped de Grand's moustached arm and cried, 'They won't allow me to be the only one left sane, they won't allow me!'

Wrapping a moist hand about her, the scar of his lips unhealing on the face pustule its genetic slide screeching, he said, 'Baby, we all swing on the same astral plane and there's a new thing now.'

And in the variable geometry of her mind, great wings retracted and the thin whine let in stratosfear.

Boreas rose black, deadly-electric, face masked and goggled, hyacinthine from his bathpool, beetling baldbright, not unmanly, a eunuch but with fullgorged appendages. A palatial meal was being prepared in the next room.

'Let me feel you first.'

'I'm in no feeling mood.' Age-old Angeline. He invited her to swim; when she refused, he reluctantly came from the green water and swaddled himself in towels, quite prepared to wreck her.

'After the meal, the rushes!'

'I don't swim, thanks.'

'You'll have a breast stroke when you see the dimmies caroom into their smash-in!' Full of tittering good humour, he led her through, a heliogabbic figure eight of a man and she bedraggled with a little brave chin, saying, 'I want to talk seriously with you about the lying-in-state of our old world.'

He paraded with her slowly round the grand room, already partly hyacinth-invaded as they foliaged intricoarsely across the wallpagan, he speaking here and there to the chattering mass of his invitees, all to Angeline maroonly macabre and flowing from the head as part of the mythology of the palapse and from their infested breath and words crawled the crystalagmites she dreamed of dreading in the coral city trees without window or stratum.

A speech was made by one of the gaudier figmies in a tapestry, beginning by praising Boreas, ascending on a brief description of the steel industry of a nearby un-named state, and working through references to Van Gogh and a woman called Marie Brashendorf or Bratzendorf who had brought forth live puppies after a nine-day confinement up the scales of madness to a high sea reference to Atlantic grails and the difficulty of making salami from same. Then the company sat or sprawled down, Boreas taking a firm hold of Angelina to guide her next to him, one great hand under her shirt grappling the life out of her left breast into multi-variable contour.

The first course of the banquet was presented, consisting only of hot water tainted by a shredded leaf, and all following courses and intercases showed similar liquididity in these hoard times, except for warm slices of *bodding*, and no silence settled like at the G mealtime he led us all a merry dance.

'All the known world,' she said sliding in, 'loses its old staples and in only a few months everything will drop apart for lack of care. People who can must save the old order for better times before we're all psychedelic salvages and you in your film can show them how to keep a grip until the bombeffect wears thin, do a preachment of the value of pre-acidity and the need to rebuild wesciv.'

'No no no, *cherie*, concoursely, my High Point Y is an improachmen of the old technological odour, which was only built up by reprunsion and maintained by everyone's anxiety, or dummied into inhabition. Okay, so it ill go and no worries. You husbind is a saviour man who lead us to a greater dustance away from old steerotypes and a new belief in the immaterial, So I picture him.'

'Okay, I agree as everyone must that there were many greedy faults but put at its lowest wesciv maimtamed in reasonable comfort a high population which now must die badly by plague and starve off to its last wither.'

'You talk to wrong guy, girlie, because I enormously like to see those ferretty technilogy people die off with all the maimtamed burrgeoisie and black in the ground slump in bulldozing massgraves in Mechelen and Manchester.'

'You shock me, Boreas. And who then will watch your epix?'

Slices of Christmas cactus succulent and inedible were placed before them. He took her with his roystering gaze she so thin and succulenten.

'I will eye my films! To the ego egofruit. For me only is they made and to enjoy! For long since the sixties have I and many lesser I's pouring clout our decompositional fluid medium preparing for this dessintegration of sorciety and now you want again the tripewaiters and oilgushers and the offices clattering?' He sipped shallowly at the long sour *gueuze-lambic* as it came round. 'Balls to the late phase we've been through.'

'Some of the old evils maybe die but worse still live on.' She would not sup. Her eyelids low.

'We live authentic now and the new way which your husbond cries!'

Under her waif-thin lids she gauzed at the continuum mumbling guests all butterflies or hot rock without rest and each in an amber clockdrill of our mechanissmus that to new born retinal grasp showed in ever moo and ghestune.

'And are these the authenticks as you mountain?' Scorning.

Grinding his heavensgravelstone teeth, resting predirty ham on her pecked muscle, 'Don't perspine for the judge's tone when you're jabbed in the witless blox woman!'

So for the first time she muddled into revelation and the silent goose grass was again in motion that Colin grasped society went in autosleep his ennemas enemy and wanever jungle he battled in it lay only a March day's march from her own plot. In even his sickmares might be more health than this fat man's articles.

'Why did you invite me here?' And vonnegutsy whines in her visceration.

'Not for the size of your bobbies mine are bigger you slim spratlady! Listen, I want the word on your man we know you have a thing or true against him and that's for revelation.'

'If I damned well don't?'

Butterflies and hot rock flowed up the hyacynth panels to the bright openings of numerous beetel mouths of the tracery.

'If you don't theres multi-ways of setting an entire squeeze-in round the motorcave and such I warn you solo voce here and never!'

'Are you threatening me?' All round her the artichokers were unheard as her head's mainline flowed more regularly in this duress and she viewed with clarity his mantled cheeks and eyes of menace.

'If you don't want your motorcod tempered with you'll peach me the laydown with all loot on how your saviourboy committed a murder in the British traffic, didn't he?'

And the whole sparse countryside unrolling to her camera, dodging – 'Who'll temper with us – you? Our little motorcade tries to ride in innosense but always an evil parashitting grip strangles it you know you know know what I mean the Mafia with their hard relief are maffiking?'

His jelly flesh was suddenly hard contracted and the mouth gash sealed and done. 'Don't say that name in here or you'll be in a sidealley lying with the lovely lubrication gone and nothing swinging babe be warn!'

Now all jungular noises cease and the dusky rook hovers.

She was standing again in the ruined garden where sweet rocket sent its sprays among the grass and thistle and her mother screamed I'll murder you if you come in again before you're told! No flowers or fruit ever on the old entangled damson trees except the dripping mildew where their leaves curdled in brown knots perhaps she had seen them among the branches the new animal the fey dog with red tie and been inoculated with the wildered beauty of despair against this future moment's recurrence.

Music now played and the vegetattles chattered on as two flower-decked seamen sang of black sheds down a runway. One last stormblown look, Boreas had dislocated and was seen away on the otherside where the mob was most like a market marakeshed with hippie hordes and de Grand in oil-welled mirth. Moving forward, this throng swept up Angeline and broke her into a adjoining private theatre. 'What's the rush?'

'You don't swing! They're coming!'

The ceiling flew away the nightbox closed and glaring careyes filled the screen with coloured rattle 5 4 3 2 One buildings surged and broke along the autobahn at troglo-daybreak in grey unconvincing weather, autostrata punctuated by windows, their boxrooms stuffed with the comic strip of family bedroomdress as all rose crying 'Master! Charteris!' in braces and curling clips. Now paper familias folds and rises from his breakfast serially lifts the kids into the roaring garage monsters gentle monsters gentile masters one by one gliding and choking carring their human scarifice out along the dangerous beaches flashing in variable geography oriented against accident of the urban switchbank.

The film is as yet unedited. Again and a second time the mechanical riptide roars along the breach discontinuity of time and space armoured armoured green and grey and blue and red a race indeed and carried helpless in them the wheel born ones from their brickhills.

The dummies register percognitive impulses of the coming crash. Scenes of the resurrection flash like traffic controls in clarkeian universe, they view themselves disjointed in the rough joinery of impact amortised in the outstretchered ambulanes and finally in the sexton's sinkingfung drowned by stink and stone in their own neutrifaction beneath the wave freeze. With unwinking blueness they view unwivering blackness and with waxen calm survey the chinalined vacuums in their dollyskulls of this annulity their last civil divorce.

Now from far above ravening like the aerosoiling arabs the eye takes in a checkerboard black-and-white of roads marked like a deserted heliport with the far black sheds of Brussels lying low plunges like a hypodetic to disgorge the main artery of shittlecock. Its plain lanes erupt into prefognotive shock as force lines fault lines seismographic lines demarcation lines lines of variable geolatry and least resistance lines of cronology besom out from the future impact point Towards this webpoint scudding come the motordollies. They still have several agelong microseconds before point of intersex and times abolution.

In the leading car from Namur rides fashionable cool Mrs Crack dressed to the nines for high point in a teetotal expatriate sun-and-fun commando suit in well-tailored casual style of almond green nylon gaberdine of a knockout simplicity deep patch pockets and ample vaginal versatility trimmed in petunia piping planned to contrast with a snazzy safari hat of saffron acrylan especially designed for crunch-occasions and scarlet patent slingback shoes in nubile moygashel. Her house is always cool and free from hairy guests of the nonconformist world because she uses new immaculate Plastic with the exciting new impeach-coloured plastic coating and a truculent egg-timer free with every canister so get in the egg-time today! Interviewed just before her death, Mrs Crack explained, 'It's fuzzy man. I so admire my lack of vitality.' Laid her head back unspeaking on surrealistic pillow, applied Sun in the new egregious shade.

The interviewer riding bareback on the bonnet thrust the mike at her superbly tailored husband Mr Servo Crack sitting exstatically back not driving in the driving seat with no facial or racial hair painted bronze head and lips to match who said, 'We both moddle many dapper uncreased outfits often in public windows of shops and such places where the elite meet to be neat this we enjoy very much on account of antiseptic lack of any form of marital relations you understand this is not my son in the back just a prefect smaller dummy and a real growing human called

Ranceville because as you know my wife Mrs Crack Mrs Historecta Crack that is actually has no capillaceous growth upon her addendum in fact frankly no addendum so of course no capillary attraction since happily I have no gentians or testaments, in the manner of pre-psychedelic mankind so we are just goodly friends and able to constipate on the old middle-class virtues like dressing properly which escalated Europe since hanseatic times of course to the glory of god and his gentleman's gentleman the pope of beloved memory.'

He was preparing to say more and the gonaddicts were chuckling and fumbling each other in the darkroom for counterevidence of non-dummiehood when the lemanster encasing Mr Crack flung itself armoured against a monster raving in the apposite direction. Mr and Mrs Crack suffered extinction. Their perfect boy also impeccably crunched. Unfortunately the camera focusing on Ranceville failed to work so that his final blood-letting gestures were not revealed to the celebrating eyes.

Now the whole cock-up took on the slobber-slob motionrhythm of orgasm sowards the climax of the film and the wetmouthed awedience watched expectorately. More terrible than humans, the dummies caroomed stiffly forward in the slow frames pressing towards point of impact in tethered flight stretching their belts as over towards the scarring windshields they bucketed eyes of blueness still and all around them gloves and maps and michelins and scattering chocolate boxes parabolaed like pigeons startled at the buckling of the sides and still the honest eggshell eyes and spumeless lips started into nanoseconds of futurity. Gravitidal waving limp arms swinging stiff shoulders unshrugging make-up staying put them swam their butterfly in the only saline solution to the deceleration problem.

All the other armoured lemmings rushed to be in on the destruction. Expressions blank of dismay the dummies had their heads cracked and chipped and knocked and shattered and ground and mashed and eggshelled and blown away with new miracle Crump aiming their last ricocheting nanocheek towards the impactpoint of speedeath the ipaccint of speeeth ipint seeth inteeth in i i i.

Time and again the cameras peeped on the unbleeding victims and on the cracking tin carcases that with rumptured wings in courtship dragging ground tupped one another beetle-bowed in the giddyup of the randabout, till the toms built up an audiction and their cheers were heard above the hubcab of metallurging grinderbiles. But Boreas wept because his film had frightened and to the mainshaft struck him.

His tears scattered. Once they had had a goose to fatten and in the long blight of summer where the damsons festered it made some company with its simple ways not unapproachable. Once her mother brought it out a bucket of water in the heat for it to duck over and over its long head and flail its pruned wings with pleasure scattering the drops across small Angeline. She heard the wings flail now as out she crept nostalgic for the gormless bird they later ate.

At last she came back wearily to where a broken Stella Art sign buzzed and burned in the desolation of their parking lot. She stood there in a wet shift breathing. Under the mauve and maureen flash her face showed like a shuttered street from which might crawl iguaneous things. But just a mental block away where she only blindly knew directions a lane stood in old summer green some place like a magic garden where a young barefoot girl might drive her would-be swans and never think of harsher either-ors.

A small rain filled the incommense thoroughfares of night but still among the guttering buggies stilled tangents of smoke and rib-roofed skeletombs a guitar string or flute fought loneliness with loneliness and a poppied light or naked carbulb gave the flowerdpeople nightpower. Oh Phil the small dogs howl don't ask me what I'm doing on the health Col. She plashes the raddlepuddles in a dim blue fermentation. A round of vestal voices plays noughts and crosses her subterranean path with a whole sparse countryside rumpling the stone-trees. Such shadows in her way she brushes off knowing the nets that await her in the shallows of a nightsunk city. She crounches and pees by old brickhaps. Oh don't be pregnant in this tupturned world!

Sickly still bedummied by the ill winds she staggered through her own grotesquely shatteredporch to find the blanket cold and stiff and Charteris not in. Groping with all menaces she unsandaled herself and beneath crawled heavily. Charteris not in not in the starve-in still? Small sound not rain not dogs reached her and immediate anxieties peopled the grotto with haggard dimmies half in flight with speed as closing in on her she propped and stared. Even hoping-fearing it might be Ruby Dymond?

In the corner Marta only sniffing on a broken chair, lumpkin in the fluttered darklight with her crushed appeal.

'Get to bed girl!'

'The toad is going to get me pushing up my thinghs.'

'Go to sleep stop worrying till tomorrow. The holed world's had enough tonight.'

'But throbbing toadspower! It's trying to force my skull up and climb into my barn my grain and then motor me away to some awful slimy pool of toadstales!'

'You're dreaming! Pack it in!'

Laying down her tawdry head she tucked her motherless eyelids on her cheeks and took herself far away from drivniks a goosegirl in an old summer lane drove her would-be-swans barefoot And cellos hit a seldom chord.

Every day Charteris like a bird of prayer spoke to new crowds finding new things to say giving outwards and never sleeping never tired sustained by his overiding fantasy. Two three days passed so at the big starve-in for Belgium's famine or Germany's bad news. He sat with a can of beans that Cass and Cass's buddy Buddy Docre had brought him half-forking them into his mouth and smilingly half-listening to some disciples who parrited back at him a loose interpretation of what they had gleaned in all enthusiasm.

When he had filled his crop enough he rose slowly and began to walk slowly so as not to disturb the ripples of the talk from which he slowly wove his own designs half-hearing of the fishernet of feeling. In these famine days they all grew gaunt he especially captain on his scoured bridge his face clawed by multi-colour beard to startling angles and all of them in their walk angular stylised as if they viewed themselves from a crow's nest distanced. Partly this walk was designed to keep their flapping shoes on their feet and to avoid the litter in the lands stirred by thin breezes breaking: for they had now camped here three unmoving days or weeks and were a circus for the citizens who brought them wine and clothes and sometimes cake.

Charteris kept his gaze steady as hair hid his eyes in the wind hover.

Cass said gently to him almost singing, 'This evening is our great triumphal entry, Master, when we break at last from this poor rookery and the lights of Brussels will welcome you and show your film and turn the prized town over to you. We have prepared the ground well and your followers flock in by hundreds. There is no need to motor farther for here we have a fine feathered Jerusalem where you will be welcome for ever.'

Sometimes he did not say all that he thought. Privately he said to himself, 'While under the lid the finger is still to Frankfurt how shall we do more than park overnight in Belgium? How can Cass be so blind he does not see that if there is no trip there is nothing? He must be eyeless with purpose.'

So he swooped down upon the field of truth that Cass and Buddy pushed and that Cass like Angeline had no habit in his dark draper suit. Behind his shutters he saw bright-lit Cro-Magnons fearful in feathers and brutally flowered hunt the ponderous Neanderthal through fleet bush and drive them off and decimate them: not for hatred or violence but because it was the natural order and he uttered, 'Predelic man must leave our caves as we reach each valley.'

'Caves! Here's a whole hogging city ours for the carve-in!' said blind Cass. But there were those present who dug the Master and soon this casually important word of His went round and new attitudes were born in the bombsites and a solitary zither taking up this hunting song was joined by other instruments. And the world sailed too amid the Master's brainwaves.

Leaving the others aside, he stylised himself back to his ruined roost where Angeline sat with her back curved to the light unspeaking.

'After the film tonight all possibilities say we flit,' he told her.

She did not look up.

'Leave the will open to all winds and the right one blows. This is the multi-valued choice that we should snarl on and no more middle here.' Echoing his words the first engine broke air as crude maintenance started for the farther trek; soon blue smoke ripped farting across the acid perimeters as more and more switched on.

Still she had no face for him.

'You're escaping, Colin, why don't you face the truth about yourself? It's not a positive decision – you're leaving because you know that what I say about Cass and the others is a whole sparky truth and you hope to shake them off, don't you?'

'After this film and the adulation we flit on a head-start. Maybe a preach-in.' He fumbled and half-lit a half-smoked cigar with an old fouled furcoat over his shoulder.

She stood up facing him more haggard than he. 'He pushes but you don't care, Col! You have the word about the Mafia but you don't care. It was through him Marta died but you don't care. Whatever happens you don't care if we all fall dead in our trips!'

He was looking through the cracked pane. Mostly now they sat around with a trance-in going even among the rolling cars. But the beer brigade could caper – one of their plump girls danced now in the steel engraving air of a Jew's harp slow but sturdy.

'This place has lost all its loot so we'll take in my film and then we'll give it a scan and we'll blow. Open up another city. Why don't you dance, Angelpants?'

'Phil, Robbins, now Marta-oh, you really have lost all loot yourself, man! You wouldn't care if you got cut dead yourself and to think I stood up for you!'

The cigar wasn't working. His hand twitched it into a corner, he moved to the door's gape.

'You use the old fleshioned terms and feelings, Angle, all extinct with no potentiality. There's a new thing you aren't with but I begin to graveL Somewhere Marta got a wrong drug, somewhere she caught hipatitis or pushed herself over. So? It's down-trip and she had a thing we'll never know in her mind, a latent death. She was destined and that's bad We did the best and can't bind too much if she freaks out.'

Lying with the lovely lubrication gone and nothing swinging.

'Well I bind, for God's sake! I could have helped her when she mewed to me about a toad levering up her skull or whatever it was and instead I sogged back like the rest of them! It was the night of the filmrush and now tonight they let the complete epic roll – I see more death tonight – right here in the toadstool I see it!' She rapped her brow as if for answer.

'Flame,' he said. 'A light to see us off by I see but I don't see you dance like that chubby girl her cheeks. Angey, you can't motorcade – I want you to stay and shack in with the golden Boreas in Bruxelles who'll care for you and is not wholly gone.'

She threw herself at him and clutched him, holding round his neck with one hand stroking his beard his hair his ears his pileum with the other. 'No, no, I can't stay a moment in this stone vortex. Besides, my place is with you. I give you loot, I need you! You know your seed is sealed in me! Have pity!'

'Woman, you won't stay silent at Ouspenski's spread!'

'I'll switch on, I will, and be like you and all the others. I'll dance!'

He side-stepped and the vague promises of a mind-closure near engine stutter.

'You don't take one pinch of loot to my sainthood!'

'Darling, we don't have to take that come-on straight!'

Half to one side he pushed her peering through his own murk and the broken-down air, muttering, 'So let's get powered!'

'Colin – you need me! You need someone near you who isn't – you know – hippie!' Her eyes were soft again the wild goose-girl.

'That was yesterday. Listen!' He pointed among the buckling roadsters. Ruby Dymond's voice – Ruby always so turned-on to a new vibration – lifted against a Tonic rhythm singing.

Fearsome in our feathers brutally flowered
We warn the predelics we're powered
We warn the predelics we're powered
We warn the predelics we're powered
Fearsome in our feathers and brutally flowered

The Word gathered loot as gears kicked in.

And another voice came in shouting 'There are strangers over the hill, wow wow, strangers over the hill.' In the background noise of backfiring and general revving and the toothaching zither sound. More plump girls dancing.

'I need only the many now,' he said.

They required little to eat, clothes mattered not much to them, in the strengthening air was the gossamer and hard tack of webwork. What they were given they traded for the precious fluid and this stored in tanks or hidden in saucepans under car seats so that when they had to go they had plenty of go – those who ran out of golden gas got left behind sans loot sans end.

By evening, a rackety carqueue moved towards the blistered dome of Sacré Coeur and citycentre where every pinnacle concealed its iguana of night. First came the Master in the new red Banshee his Brussels disciples had brought him as tribute, saluting with Angelina huddled despairing in the back seat. Then his tribe in all gay tarnation.

From one shuttered day to the next his mindpower fluctuated and now wheelborn again he, finding the images came fast, tried to order them but what truth they looted seemed to lie in their random complexity. He radiated the net or web to all ends and to cut away strands was not to differentiate the holes. Clearly as the patterns turned in slow mindsbreeze he saw among them an upturned invalid car with wheels still spinning and by it lying a crippled negro on his back lashing out with metal crutches at a strangely dressed whiteman with machine qualities. Near at hand stood in separate frame a fat bare man with painted skull shouting encouragement by megavoice.

Simultaneously this fat bare man lay floating in a lake of flame.

Simultaneously this fat bare man lay in the throes of love with a bare bald female dolly of human scale.

Simultaneously this bare bald dolly was Angeline with her suffering shoulders.

Simultaneously the face was cracked. China griefs seeped from wounds.

Startled, he turned and looked back at her on the back seat. Catching his glance, she lifted her hand and took his reassuringly, mother to child.

She said, 'This good moment is an interim in our long deline.'

He said, 'Wear this moment then with it all *baraka* as if you had it comfortable on your feet for ever in the timeflow,' and at the prompt unprompted words his whole ornate idea of reincarnation in endless cycles flooded his hindusty horizons with eternal recurrence.

Outside their moving windows faces dystered with hunger and hope.

She said, 'They acclaim you in the streets as if you did not come with downfall for them,' gazing at the action.

Cass said to him looking angrily at her, 'They salute you and would keep you here for all the evers, *bapu*, as the wheel turns.'

*

Thin-cheeked children of Brussels ran like wolves uniting in a pack packing and howling about the car – not all acclaiming, many jeering and attempting to stop the progress. Scuffles broke out Fights kindled near the slowcade and spread like a bush fire among the stone forests. Half a mile from the Grand Place, the cars piled to a stop and crowds swarmed over them. Some of the drivniks in the cars wept but there was no help for them, the police force having dissolved to rustle cattle on the ignoble German border.

At last the Tonic Traffic managed to climb free and with other helping hands set the infrasound machine with its husky rasped throat extended towards the bobbing heads. Its low vibrations sent a grey shudder across the crowd and a vision of the sick daybreak across untilled land where an old canal dragged straight over the landscape for a hundred versts. With many hands raised to steady the terrible machine, it progressed and the crowds fell back and the other autos moved forward so they grated gradually to Grand Place, with the group bellowing song and all present taking it up as far as able, detonated underground with a whole sparse country rumpling upwards and rolling at predatorial speed towards the fluttering heart with every kind of looted image.

In the Grand Place, a huge screen structured of plastic cubes had been set up on the front of some of the old Guild houses. From the Hotel de Ville oposite, a platform was built perilously out. High resplendent equinoctial on this platform sat the golden Boreas with shadowy men behind him and amid cheering the Master also ascended to sit here among the hatcheteers.

Thus met the two great men and the Bapu knew this was the fat bare ego of megavoice who could radiate powerful drama-dreams and later a song was sung telling that they exchanged views on exitsence with particular reference to what was to be considered inside and what outside or where deautomation lay: but the truth was that the huobub in the square below was so great that both were forced to play Gurdjieff at their own feast and even the offering of Angeline as a dolly substitute which the Master intended had to be forgotten she shrinking nevertheless from him.

*

Chilled wind rose, petals sweetly scattering. The square had been given rough nautical ceiling by immense canvas sails stretched over it and secured to the stone pinnacles of the guilds encrusting the titled place like stalagmites. This ceiling kept off the seasonal rain that fell as well as supporting strings of multi-coloured lights that glowed in a square way. Now it all became more sparky as the bulbs swung and fluttered where the whole sky was one big switchedonstellation with Cassiopeia dancing and ton-weights of conserved water off-loaded with grotesque effect to the Tonic Traffic dirges. Then the circuits tailed and all milling place swung unlit except by torches and one randy probing searchlight until unknown warriors funeral-pyred a bright-burning black motor-hearse.

The night was maniac over self-sold Europe,

Fighting broke out again and counter-singing, a car was overturned converted into variable geometry and set alight to predatory slogans. It was a big loot-in with action all round.

A colour slide show beginning, the crowd settled slightly to watch and smells of reefers densed the choleric air. Glaring colours such as delft blue ornamental red dead grey tabby amber persian turquoise eyeball blue cunt pink avocado green bile yellow prepuce puce donkey topaz urine primrose body lichen man cream arctic white puss copper jasmine thatch Chinese black pekinese lavender jazz tangerine moss green gangrene green spitoon green slut green horsy olive bum blue erotic silver peyote pale and a faint civilised wedgwood mushroom that got the bird were squirted direct onto the projector lens and radiated across the place where the pinnacle cliffs of buildings ran spurted and squidged amazing hues until they came like great organic things pumping out spermatorrhoeic rainbows in some last vast chthonic spectral orgamashem of brute creogulation while the small-dogging sky howled downfalls and shattered coloured lightbulbs.

The junketing eferetted into every nanosecond, not all in many sparky spirits for those who wished to leave the square for illness or emergency unable to exculpate a limb in the milling mass. Some weaker and fainter Bruxellois fell beneath beating feet to be beaujolaised under the press. Cholera had to loot its victims standing as their bursting sweats ransacked to fertilise itself all round the strinkled garmen but bulging eyes not making much extinction in exprulsion between agony and ecstasy of a stockstill stampede sparked the harm beneath the harmony and many perished gaily unaware they burst at the gland and vein and head and vent and died swinging in the choke of its choleric fellation.

Only when morning slutted at its lucid shutters the last crazed chords and colours writhed away did the paint-spattered herd gather what their rituals had wrought. From the cattle-pensioners rattled a great and terrible exclamor! Several who had in delurium clambered to the prismatic pinnacles to lick the suppurating hues now cast themselves for a final fling down to the fast-varying-geometry of the groundwave. The rest with remouraing strength dancers horsevoiced singers drugees gaunt thieves true believers boozers and paletooled lovers crept away into clogged side alleys to coven their despair.

Only then as Boreas crawled off the platform to lie again in peace under the caressing feathers of his heated pond did the Master speak to him.

'You are an artist – come with us along the multi-value mazes of our mission. Your film caught all the spirit of our cause my life my thought the unspeaking nature of spontagnous living in mystic state!'

Then Boreas turning his great bare head and naked tear-lined cheeks like udders grey with dawn: 'You stupid *godvetdomme* acidheads and junkies all the same you live inside your crazy nuts and never see a thing beyond! So you mastered my masterpiece, was it? Pah! My fool man de Grand was supposed to bring the cans of film but in his stinking state forgot – and once caught here impossible to leave again the cattlepen. And so my masterpiece my High Point Y unseen and unshown this golden importunity!'

'We saw it all! It sparked right over with total lootage!'

Sick with disgust salivating.

'God knows what you thought you saw! God knows, I swear I'll drown myself, shoot myself, harpoon myself to death, never film again! Not only is my masterpiece unshown but not one of your armada knows it or misses it. This is the nadirene anti-death of art!'

Bitter and acid, Angerme's rank morning laughter bit them.

*

Charteris took in breezy semi-grasp Boreas's coat and pointed at the emptying square of stood squampede grey in washed-out light but ambered by flames that now consumed the pinnacles recently putrescent in other taints.

'You have no faith in transmutation or my well of the miraculous! Your oldtime art has caught a light at last! Everything you Boreas tried for broke fire materially and burns into our sounding chambers! You are my second blazer henchforth, Boreas, a black wind blowing off the old alternatives and hurricaning those who cling to what was, electric, electric, see the sign! What you making here in newchanced happens! Stellar art!' He laughed and cried tired dregs leaping leaping.

Through his blandering tears stared electric Boreas, clutching at his bare brow, screaming, 'You gurglingodfool – your rainbowheaded randyears have set fire to the place! It's the last loot! My poor beloved city burning! *Bruxelles, Bruxelles!'*

The poison that powered their inner scrutinies seeped into beetling baldbright Boreas so he saw himself tumultaneously making the cripple still upon the cabbalistic asphalt making couch among a lake of flames making love to a dummivulva making Age old Ina suffer him. His face cracked its banks china thoughts depiggied. Boreas saw more of boreased self than he could dare or wish to see. He rocked with unreason on the staggered balcony of outsight.

Manifolding with discardment he cheek in hand into the dull inner chambers of shade past old banners toothed with black lions collided with the birdlike nervous drapery-deportment figure of a human cassowary to hiss shoulder lept unmoving and instantly with locking blubber arm seized him groaning and yowling for accompaniment.

'I am ill – magisterially ill!' Hollowly to his lackneed squir.

Thus the blind bleeding the blind and dankring leech to leech upon romaining leechions highways where this wesciv sinbiote first took its blindwheeling veinhold with the cohorts tormenta in hurling knowhow to the punchy vein and murk the scenariover evermorgue till savvy was a scavengers filiure of which this sciatic scattering long kuwaited just the last blood-strained curtain. After the legendary coherets among the dark-falling walls of oh my westering world the venomilk of progross gains its bright eclipse and suppurages from the drawbridge-heads of cleverknowing Charteris gold-pated Nicholas Boreas and black jack Cass.

Nothing for Cass but this supporting role uneasy-eyed or never rubicond to shuffer with the ruined borean bulk out down a lamenting grand stair and by tenuous tenebrous betelgrained deathsquared slipways to Boreas' luxconapt

There with continuing running whines for succour, Boreas almost hauled him to his pool edge. But at the sight of those bulbous hyacinths the castaway squealed like a lifted root seeking too in the convex gilt eyes twin unaimed deadmen of himself!

'Yes, die-by-drowning, Cass, you undreaming schemer of your hireoglyphed runways! Wasn't it you who brought this pyromanichee circus into city just for hope of trade, Cass, for hope of trade? You neo-Nero para-promethean primp, they've sacked our silver-breasted capital, haven't they? Haven't they? Under the gargling lilies with your scant scruballs!'

He wrenched and tugged in buttacking flapping angony but Cass was nimble and falling took the epicurer man off balance with one tricky twisting cast of leg. Together they struck and smacked among showering orfe and weed and tame piranhas glimpsing for a nanoment undersea eyes of each with sibyling hatred widely divinited beneath the parting roots. Then Cass was sourfacing and outkelping himself, evading Boreas's doctopurulent grasp to snatch from his stocking nestling a slender beak of knife.

So they confronted, Boreas half-submanged with foliaged morses dotting his sunken suit. Then he recalled his anger with flecked lungs, leaped up brandishing his arm and in megavoice again on set bellowed in long bursting vein the terrors of his repudation!

Wilting Cass turned his tail before the wind and like a deflayded animal ran away somewhere into the smoking city-hive to hide.

That cityhive and what its singeing symbolled did cosmic Charteris survey from the shaking platform.

Angeline shook the Master's arm. 'Come on, Masterpiece, let's shake this unaimed scenario before the whole action goes Vesuvius! Come on! Uncoil the Kundalini!'

He stood enwrapped staring as the centuries fevered to the edges and breathed and blew themselves to heat again and their stones ran in showers kill slate cracked down the long glacier of mansard roofs and hurtled into the extinct square below to be devoured with its old common order in the long morain of alienation.

He pushed her away.

'Colin! Colin! I'm not flame-proof if you are! It's the last loot-in else!'

Rich curtains at the windows of an old embroidery now released a noise like cheering and whistling swept the blaze and the crushed bodies in the square below burst into conflagration with amazing joy. One or two cars were still careening madly about to lie with black bellies uppermost lewdly burning tyres still rotating as their votaries dragged themselves away. The emptying bowls held ashes and a lascivious flute held court.

Angelina was having a mild hysteric fit, crying this was London burning and slapping Charteris wildly on the face. He in his eyes scribbled on the retinal wall saw the graffiti of her blazing hate and all behind her flames like Christmas cacti flowering with a lorry coming fast recalled her husband the white land as it rushes up but no impact and his blows and knew among the microseconds lay a terminal alternative to silence her and have no more inspector at his feast for she as much as any of the predelic enemies among the Neanders dream her speckled wake.

She in her turn was not too wild to see a redder shade of crimson leap up his retaining wall and with a lesser scream now our valleys fall echoing before them now in our shattered towns the smoke clings still as the ulcerated countryside rumpled outwards at predatomi speed to her fluttering chimera she did the sleight-of-hand and dodged him as he once more sprang and pushed clutching at his ancient blue coat of Inner Relief but now no Christmas innocence. Slipping he fell and at the rickety platform edge hung down to see bloodied cobbles under surflare. With instinct she on top of him flung her bony trunk loading him back and cosseted him and goosed and mewed and sat him up and like a mother made all kindliness but milk there though the sun novaed.

Half-stunned he sighed, 'You are my all-ternatives,' and she half-wept upon him at such grudged sign.

Their hair singed and Buddy Docre came in an illusory moment with Ruby who fancied her and Bill and Greta yelling murder. They together all but not in unison climbed tumbled down the foul inner chimney stair and ran among the Sailing lava of another Eurape to the battered cavalcade jarring to take off in another street with the nervewrecked bangwaggon.

'Boreas!' cast the whiteface Master. 'We must save Boreas!'

And she glowed him amazed still in his headwound he had some human part that plugged for the schillerskulled director. But she was learning now and now stayed silent at his murderous feast with inward tremor knowing she would not break a single crust if Boreas loafed or died as maybe the Master minded: a gulf of more than language lay between them.

Vanquished she tottered against Ruby his face moonstrous in the setglow and he grasped to the smouldering pompous columns gasping 'Change gear Ange your way doesn't have to be his or my car in the Chartercade you know that you know how I skid for you even since before Phil's day two rotten no good bums –'

But he gave up as through her frantic goosetears she began on tearawy note that she was not good enough for him was no good to any man deserved to die or could render to no man the true grips of loves clutchment till the others turned back calling and Charteris took her failing wrist abraptly.

For him the self was once again in its throne called back from the purged night's exile and he commanded no more as he faced the lack of his own divinity in all its anarchic alternative. His pyre grew behind him as they barged off across the ruby pavements for as Buddy passed a reefer he flipped the photograph that he had godded himself because they had to crown some earthly king then had forgotten that he was their moulding not his make so tunnelling upwards through the sparce countryside the mole-truth set up its tiny hill that all was counterfate in a counterfeit kingdoom.

He had cried for Boreas because that artifacer could help blow blazes from his parky wavering nature with the bellows of his counterfaking craft

*

Before real miracles he had to dislocate the miraculous in himself. New dogs shagged along alleyways with ties of flame. A man ran blazing down a side street. Dischorded impages of choleranis sang along the bars of his perplextives. All were infected from him and in that pandemetic lay his power to make or sicken till nature itself couched underground.

A smoke pall canopiled overhead the new angrimals swimming powerfully in it or hopping along the crestfallen buildings. Shops stood plagened open entrailed on the echoing gravements as men noised abroad and struck at each other with fansticks more than one fire was buckling up its lootage as they acidheaded out towards the oceanic piracy of their motorways.

Famine Starting At The Head

She clad herself in nylon
Walked the flagstones by my side
The feathered eagle
To the skies
No more uprises
Instead a palm of dust grows
You know that earthly tree now bears no bread
A hand outstretched is trembling
The flagstaff has an ensign
Only madmen see
With famine starting at the head

Some judy delivers a punchline
In the breadbasket today
No fond embraces
Are afoot
Death puts a boot
Where the bounce was once
In among the listening lilies a silent tread
Bite the fruit to taste the stone
Throughout the Gobi seed awaits
The rain to stalk
Famine starting at the head

He only has to say one word
Roses grow from an empty bowl
In our shuttered streets
The cars roam
Don't need a home
Or volume control
Wandering sizeless with the unaimed dead
We hear his voice cry 'Paradise!'
On the Golden Coast the cymbals
Start to sound
Salvation starting at the head

Tortures

There's no answer from the old exchange
I want to push inside you
The sensations you find in yourself
May just be within my range

Grimly sitting round a table
Fifteen men with life at stake
They may torture themselves but those tortures
Will not make them awake

The cards were somehow different
The board I had not seen before
Their iron maiden gleamed dimly cherry-red with sex
Down in the basement I reached Low Point X

Last year they stopped their playing
Phone just ceased to buzz
But if you find them there tomorrow
Better start in there praying

Reincarnation where the cobwebs
Are comes daily from your keep
We may torture ourselves but those tortures
Cannot break our sleep

Poor A!
(Gurdjieff's Mocking Song)

Poor A! Poor A! Now there's a clever man!
He only wants to talk and he is happy!
I could have pulled his trousers off
   Un-noticed, silly chappie!

Poor A! Poor A! What sort of man is it
Who only wants to talk and he's okay?
I tell you everyone's like that –
   They fill the world today.

I might say poor old A is rather better
Then some wild talkniks I have met, a
Chap who in his way knows what is what –
On military onions he knows quite a lot.
In a superficial public way he tries to find out Why:
And he'd hate to think he ever told a lie.

Poor A! Poor A! He is no longer young!
He said so much I think and was uncouth
To guard against an awful chance
To listen to the truth –
He led himself a merry dance –
He hid his head in circumstance –
To fight against the truth!

Disciples: Poor us! Poor us! We really felt his tongue!
He drank Khagetia and chattered without ruth
To guard against his only chance
To hear G give out truth –
He led us all a merry dance –
He leads himself a dreary prance –
To smite against the truth!
To fight against the truth!

The Unaimed Deadman Theme

Foreign familiar filthy fastidious forgotten forbidden
Suicide's revelation its sunnyside hidden
Death's black-and-white checker is down on the table
Fugitive fustian funeral infinite formidable

Far down the runway the black sheds are standing
My love talks to me with a delicate air
I am the victim the assassin the wounder
Her face looks no larger as I stand close than
It simultaneously does in my telescope sights
But pleasant is walking where elmtrees paint shadow
If I fire I might as well hit me

I walked with her once where her elms brought their shadows
The dogrose dies now while the invalid car
Barks vainly and I the assassin the wounder
On the runways the markings are no longer valid
Hieroglyphs of a system now long obsolete
No this button first love yes that's the idea
If I fire I might as well hit me

Foreign familiar filthy fastidious forbidden forgotten
I sprinted a dozen times over where rotten
Things grew and she cried for a sweet-flavoured minute
Fugitive fustian funebral formidable infinite

Lament Of The Representatives
Of The Old Order
(A silent dummy dirge)

We kept up our facade
The unworld showed the third world how
And prized its pretty inhibitions
 They undressed us
 And possessed us

And now that times are hard
The unworld holds its outward show
Too late for us to change positions
 They have dressed us
 And confessed us

The Shuttered Street Girl
(Love song for flutes)

Her face showed like a shuttered street
    Under the mauve and maureen flash
From which iguanas might crawl
    Golden gullets wide

She stood there in a wet shift breathing
    And just a mental block away
A lane lay in old summer green
    Behind her pregnant eyes

Where a young barefoot girl might drive
    Her would-be-swans all day
Or night for night and day are both
    They don't apply

There's always summer in the dreaming elms
    Till your last shuttered white year
And while the small rain fills
    The thoroughfares of love

So her face in blue fermentation
    When she crouches seems
Like an ever-visiting miracle
    As she pees by old brickheaps

There's whole sparse countryside
    Buckling up from far
Underground as she stoops there
    And our small rain raining

The Infrasound Song

Where the goose drinks wait the wildmen
Wait the wildmen watching their reflections
When the damson fruits the wildmen
Wild Neanders dream their speckled sleep

They have their dances ochre-limbed to a stone's tune
And their heavy hymns for the solstice dawn
Their dead go down into their offices berobed
With ceremony. Their virgins paint
Their cinnamon lips with juice of berry
They owned the world before us

Now their valleys fall echoing our footfall
In their shattered towns the smoke clings still
Down the autobahn arrows in the afternoon
As we drive them convert them or ride them

We are the strangers over the hilltop
Peace on our brows but our dreams are armoured
Fearsome in our feathers brutally flowered
Pushing the trip-time up faster and faster
Pre-psychedelic men know that extinction
Sits on their hilltops all drearily towered
As we cavalry in with the master
Cavalry in with the master
With the master

At The Starve-In

Met this girl at the starve-in
I met this girl at the starve-in
I said I met today's girl at the starve-in
Protein deficiency's good for the loins

She said there's bad news from Deutschland
Yes she said there's bad news from Deutschland
She lay there and said there's bad news from Deutschland
Can you hear those little states marching

I raised my self kingly in the stony playsquare
Ground my elbow like a sapling in dirt
Looked through the stilled plantangents of smoke
Proclaimed that even the bad news was good

We've marched under banner headlines
Closed down the stone-aged universities
See ally fall upon ally
Oh Prague don't dismember me please
It was all in the Wesciv work-out
Now we got some other disease

Met my fate in the work-out
Man, I met my fate in the work-out
No denying I met my fate in the work-out
And no one knows what's clobbered me

Rainbows at starvation corner
There's rainbows at starvation corner
I keep seeing rainbows at starvation corner
like they're the spectrums at the feast

Met this girl at the starve-in
Yeah met this girl at the starve-in
Oh yeah I met this pussy at the starve-in
Ana we dreamed that we ruled Germany
We dreamed we ruled all Germany

It's One of Those Times

It's   sim   ply
  One of those times
      when you're going to pot
  one of those crimes
      when you really should rot
one of those times you do not

It's   sim   ply
  one of those mornings
      they've all got you taped
  one of those dawnings
      you hoped you'd escaped
one of those mornings you're raped

  The cities are falling like rain from the skies
The toadthings are leaving the ground as you watch
  You're laughing and dancing with joy and surprise
It helps with that pain in your crotch

So   it's   just
  one of those rages
      that rupture and burn
  one of those ages
      you get what you earn
  one of those pages
      you wish you could turn
'Cos its none of your bloody concern
No it's none of your bloody concern
                  It knocks you sideways
            None of your bloody concern

The Poison that Powered Their Scrutinies

The poison that powered their inner scrutinies
Seeped into beetling baldbright Boreas
So he saw himself tumultaneously
  Making the cripple still
    Upon the cabbalistic asphalt
  Making couch upon a lake of flames
  Making love to a dummy vulva
  Making Age Old Ina suffer him

  His face cracked its banks
China thoughts depiggied
Boreas saw more of his borearsed self
Than he could dare or wish to see

He rocked with unreason on
The staggered balcony of insight
Manifolding in discardment
As his capital lost all loot

The Miraculous In Search Of Me

It could all have turned out differently.
Indeed, to other peeled-off I's
The difference is an eternal recurrence:
And the stone trees that erupt along
My beaches, roots washed bone-clever
By the tow and rinse of change –
They shade one instance only of me,
For circumstance is more than character.

At this bare fence I once turned left
And became another person: laughed
Where else I cried and now sit lingering
Looking at Japanese prints;
Or in a restaurant decked with pine
Cones taste in company
Silver carp and damson tart.
                        Along the walls
Other I's went, strangers in word and deed,
Alien photocopies, spooks
Closer than blood-brothers, more alarming
Than haggard face spectral in empty room,
Lonelier than stone age campfires, doppelgangers.
They are my possibilities. Their pasts were once
My past, but in the surging wheels
And cogs become distorted. So, this one –
On a far-distant spoke! – danced
All night and had splendid lovers,
Wrote love letters still kept locked
Treasured in a bureau-drawer, knew girls
The world now knows by name and voice.

But this I chose to wander down
My stony beach, my own rejection.
My past is like a fable. Truly,
Circumstance is more than character.
Whatever other peel-offs saw –
My I was on the stranded alien land,

The restlessness of broken cities,
Mute messages that only after years
Open, the crime of vulnerability,
Patched land of people never known to be
Known or knighted, wild bombed world,
World where I taste the flavour on
The tongue, knowing not if my other eyes
Would call it happiness or doom.

   I am, but what I am –
Others may know, others may care. Only
The dear light goes in her hand
Away among the childhood trees.
In the perspectives of my mind
It never dwindles. I always live
With myself; and that's too much.
I need
The overpowering circumstance
The nostalgia of
That eternal return
As if the unstructured hours
My uninstructed hours
Of day are pulped like
Newspaper
And used on us again
With the odd word
Here and there
Locked
Starting up out of context
Treasured
An old ghost
Haunting another
Discardment.
Indeed it is
Always eternally
Turning out

Different.

Confluence

The inhabitants of the planet Myrin have much to endure from Earthmen, inevitably, perhaps, since they represent the only intelligent life we have so far found in the galaxy. The Tenth Research Fleet has already left for Myrin. Meanwhile, some of the fruits of earlier expeditions are ripening.

As has already been established, the superior Myrinian culture, the so-called Confluence of Headwaters, is somewhere in the region of eleven million (Earth) years old, and its language, Confluence, has been established even longer. The etymological team of the Seventh Research Fleet was privileged to sit at the feet of two gentlemen of the Geldrid Stance Academy. They found that Confluence is a language-cum-posture, and that meanings of words can be radically modified or altered entirely by the stance assumed by the speaker. There is, therefore, no possibility of ever compiling a one-to-one dictionary of English-Confluence, Confluence-English words.

Nevertheless, the list of Confluent words which follows disregards the stances involved, which number almost nine thousand and are all named, and merely offers a few definitions, some of which must be regarded as tentative. The definitions are, at this early stage of our knowledge of Myrinian culture, valuable in themselves, not only because they reveal something of the inadequacy of our own language, but because they throw some light on to the mysteries of an alien culture. The romanised phonetic system employed is that suggested by Dr Rohan Prendernath, one of the members of the etymological team of the Seventh Research Fleet, without whose generous assistance this short list could never have been compiled.

*

AB WE TEL MIN   The sensation that one neither agrees nor disagrees with what is being said to one, but that one simply wishes to depart from the presence of the speaker

ARN TUTKHAN   Having to rise early before anyone else is about; addressing a machine

BAGI RACK   Apologising as a form of attack; a stick resembling a gun

BAG RACK   Needless and offensive apologies

BAMAN   The span of a man's consciousness

BI   The name of the mythical northern cockerel; a reverie that lasts for more than twenty (Earth) years

BI SAN   A reverie lasting more than twenty years and of a religious nature

BIT SAN   A reverie lasting more than twenty years and of a blasphemous nature

BI TOSI   A reverie lasting more than twenty years on cosmological themes

BI TVAS   A reverie lasting more than twenty years on geological themes

BIUI TOSI   A reverie lasting more than a hundred and forty-two years on cosmological themes; the sound of air in a cavern; long dark hair

BIUT TASH   A reverie lasting more than twenty years on Har Dar Ka themes (c.f.)

CANO LEE MIN   Things sensed out-of-sight that will return

CA PATA VATUZ   The taste of a maternal grandfather

CHAM ON TH ZAM   Being witty when nobody else appreciates it

DAR AYRHOH   The garments of an ancient crone; the age-old supposition that Myrin is a hypothetical place

EN IO PLAY   The deliberate dissolving of the senses into sleep

GEE KUTCH   Solar empathy

GE NU   The sorrow that overtakes a mother knowing her child will be born dead

GE NUP DIMU   The sorrow that overtakes the child in the womb when it knows it will be born dead

GOR A   Ability to live for eight hundred years

HA ATUZ SHAK EAN   Disgrace attending natural death of maternal grandfather

HAR DAR KA   The complete understanding that all the soil of Myrin passes through the bodies of its earthworms every ten years

HAR DI DI KAL   A small worm; the hypothetical creator of a hypothetical sister planet of Myrin

HE YUP   The first words the computers spoke, meaning, 'The light will not be necessary'

HOLT CHA   The feeling of delight that precedes and precipitates wakening

HOLT CHE   The autonomous marshalling of the senses which produces the feeling of delight that precedes and precipitates wakening

HOZ STAP GURT   A writer's attitude to fellow writers

INK TH O   Morality used as an offensive weapon

JILY JIP TUP   A thinking machine that develops a stammer; the action of pulling up the trousers while running uphill

JIL JIPY TUP   Any machine with something incurable about it; pleasant laughter that is nevertheless unwelcome; the action of pulling up the trousers while running downhill

KARNAD EES   The enjoyment of a day or a year by doing nothing; fasting

KARNDAL CHESS   The waste of a day or a year by doing nothing; fasting

KARNDOLI YON TOR   Mystical state attained through inaction; feasting; a learned paper on the poetry of metal

KARNDOL KI REE   The waste of a life by doing nothing; a type of fasting

KUNDULUM   To be well and in bed with two pretty sisters

LAHAH SIP   Tasting fresh air after one has worked several hours at one's desk

LA YUN UN   A struggle in which not a word is spoken; the underside of an inaccessible boulder; the part of one's life unavailable to other people

LEE KE MIN   Anything or anyone out-of-sight that one senses will never return; an apology offered for illness

LIKI INK TH KUTI   The small engine that attends to one after the act of excretion

MAL   A feeling of being watched from within

MAN NAIZ TH   Being aware of electricity in wires concealed in the walls

MUR ON TIG WON   The disagreeable experience of listening to oneself in the middle of a long speech and neither understanding what one is saying nor enjoying the manner in which it is being said; a foreign accent; a lion breaking wind after the evening repast

NAM ON A   The remembrance, in bed, of camp fires

NO LEE LE MUN   The love of a wife that becomes especially vivid when she is almost out-of-sight

NU CROW   Dying before strangers

NU DI DIMU   Dying in a low place, often of a low fever

NU HIN DER VLAK   The invisible stars; forms of death

NUN MUM   Dying before either of one's parents; ceasing to fight just because one's enemy is winning

NUT LAP ME   Dying of laughing

NUT LA POM   Dying laughing

NUT VATO   Managing to die standing up

NUTVU BAG RACK   To be born dead

NU VALK   Dying deliberately in a lonely (high) place

OBI DAKT   An obstruction; three or more machines talking together

ORAN MUDA   A change of government; an old peasant saying meaning, 'The dirt in the river is different every day'

PAN WOL LE MUDA   A certainty that tomorrow will much resemble today; a line of manufacturing machines

PAT O BANE BAN   The ten heartbeats preceding the first heartbeat of orgasm

PI KI SKAB WE   The parasite that afflicts man and Tig Gag in its various larval stages and, while burrowing in the brain of the Tig Gag, causes it to speak like a man

PI SHAK RACK CHANO   The retrogressive dreams of autumn attributed to the presence in the bloodstream of Pi Ki Skab We

PIT HOR   Pig's cheeks, or the droppings of pigs; the act of name-dropping

PLAY   The heightening of consciousness that arises when one awakens in a strange room that one cannot momentarily identify

SHAK ALE MAN   The struggle that takes place in the night between the urge to urinate and the urge to continue sleeping

SHAK LA MAN GRA   When the urge to urinate takes precedence over the urge to continue sleeping

SHAK LO MUN GRAM   When the urge to continue sleeping takes precedence over all things

SHEAN DORL   Gazing at one's reflection for reasons other than vanity

SHE EAN MIK Performing prohibited postures before a mirror

SHEM A slight cold afflicting only one nostril; the thoughts that pass when one shakes hands with a politician

SHUK TACK The shortening in life-stature a man incurs from a seemingly benevolent machine

SOBI A reverie lasting less than twenty years on cosmological themes; a nickel

SODI DORL One machine making way for another; decadence, particularly in the Cold Continents

SODI IN PIT Any epithet which does not accurately convey what it intends, such as 'Sober as a judge', 'Silly nit', 'He swims like a fish', 'He's only half-alive', and so on

STAINI RACK NUSVIODON Experiencing Staini Rack Nuul and then realising that one must continue in the same outworn fashion because the alternatives are too frightening, or because one is too weak to change; wearing a suit of clothes at which one sees strangers looking askance

STAINI RACK NUUL Introspection (sometimes prompted by birthdays) that one is not living as one determined to live when one was very young; or, on the other hand, realising that one is living in a mode decided upon when one was very young and which is now no longer applicable or appropriate

STAIN TOK I The awareness that one is helplessly living a role

STA SODON The worst feelings which do not even lead to suicide

SU SODA VALKUS A sudden realisation that one's spirit is not pure, overcoming one on Mount Rinvlak (in the Southern Continent)

TI Civilised aggression

TIG GAG The creature most like man in the Southern Continent which smiles as it sleeps

TIPY LAP KIN Laughter that one recognises though the laughter is unseen; one's own laughter in a crisis

TOK AN Suddenly divining the nature and imminence of old age in one's thirty-first year

TUAN BOLO A class of people one only meets at weddings; the pleasure of feeling rather pale

TU KI TOK Moments of genuine joy captured in a play or charade about joy; the experience of youthful delight in old age

TUZ PAT MAIN (Obs.) The determination to eat one's maternal grandfather

U (Obs.) The amount of time it takes for a lizard to turn into a bird; love

UBI A girl who lifts her skirts at the very moment you wish she would

UDI KAL The clothes of the woman one loves

UDI UKAL The body of the woman one loves

UES WE TEL DA Love between a male and female politician

UGI SLO GU The love that needs a little coaxing

UMI RIN TOSIT The sensations a woman experiences when she does not know how she feels about a man

UMY RIN RU The new dimensions that take on illusory existence when the body of the loved woman is first revealed

UNIMGAG BU Love of oneself that passes understanding; a machine's dream

UNK TAK An out-of-date guide book; the skin shed by the snake that predicts rain

UPANG PLA Consciousness that one's agonised actions undertaken for love would look rather funny to one's friends

UPANG PLAP Consciousness that while one's agonised actions undertaken for love are on the whole rather funny to oneself, they might even look heroic to one's friends; a play with a cast of three or less

U RI RHI Two lovers drunk together

USANA NUTO A novel all about love, written by a computer

USAN I NUT Dying for love

USAN I ZUN BI Living for love; a tropical hurricane arriving from over the sea, generally at dawn

UZ Two very large people marrying after the prime of life

UZ TO KARDIN The realisation in childhood that one is the issue of two very large people who married after the prime of life

WE FAAK A park or a college closed for seemingly good reasons; a city where one wishes one could live

YA GAG Too much education; a digestive upset during travel

YA GAG LEE Apologies offered by a hostess for a bad meal

YA GA TUZ Bad meat; (Obs.) dirty fingernails

YAG ORN A president

YATUZ PATI (Obs.) The ceremony of eating one's maternal grandfather

YATUZ SHAK SHAK NAPANG HOLI NUN Lying with one's maternal grandmother; when hens devour their young

YE FLIC TOT A group of men smiling and congratulating each other

YE FLU GAN Philosophical thoughts that don't amount to much; graffiti in a place of worship

YON TORN A paper tiger; two children with one toy

YON U SAN The hesitation a boy experiences before first kissing his first girl

YOR KIN BE A house; a circumlocution; a waterproof hat; the smile of a slightly imperfect wife

YUP PA A book in which everything is understandable except the author's purpose in writing it

YUPPA GA Stomach ache masquerading as eyestrain; a book in which nothing is understandable except the author's purpose in writing it

YUTH MOD The assumed bonhomie of visitors and strangers

ZO ZO CON A woman in another field

The Dead Immortal

Mickie Houston was strikingly self-centred. But with his looks, his voice and his style – and his wife – he had gone far. And meant to go further.

Rickie Houston was strikingly beautiful. She looked even more lovely than usual as she said to her husband, 'Don't take the time-travel drug, darling. I have a terrible feeling it will kill you!'

Mickie Houston kissed her and said, 'And I have a terrific feeling it may make me immortal!'

The exchange was overheard by a gossip columnist, and soon became famous. Not only was the controversy over the new time-travel drug raging (for this was in 1969), but Rickie and Mickie were the toasts of the switched-on pop world, the duo who finally knocked the groups from the charts.

The extra publicity encouraged Mickie to go ahead with his idea. He went to the famous London clinic where the drug was being administered to the few who were reckless or rich enough to pay for the injection.

The specialist shook his head and said gravely, 'The effects of LSKK, the so-called time-travel drug, are very strange, Mr Houston. It's not an experience to be undertaken lightly. We have a duty to warn any potential time-travellers that they take their life in their hands when they undergo the injection.'

'Yeah, I heard all that jazz from my wife.'

'Really? What your wife may not have told you is that the effects of the drug are subjective, just like the effects of LSD. With LSKK, you find yourself travelling through the sort of time in which you believe.

'Thus, a Hindu who took LSKK would find himself travelling through vast cycles of time, since that concept accords with his religion. A holy man who believes only in God's time would find he travelled straight into God's presence. But for the average Englishman, like yourself, who believes time and progress go on straight ahead for ever, well, he will find himself doing just that.'

'Ha, but I'm not the average Englishman! I don't believe in time-travel at all. It's just a lot of mystical nonsense and you're cashing in on the fashion for it.'

The specialist put on a ghastly genial smile.

'You're just doing this for publicity, eh?'

'All I believe in is the present. I live for the living moment, that's me!'

That's what Mickie said as the needle sank into his arm and 250ccs of LSKK coursed through his veins. Cameramen were there to record the moment, and Rickie kissed him. Truth to tell, he was a little tired of her, so that even the prospect of never seeing her again did not worry him. Strewn throughout time, he visualised an endless line of pretty girls.

Even as Rickie's lips touched his, Mickie Houston disappeared.

Powered by LSKK, he drifted into the future, the staggering future where the centuries are thicker than the cells in the bloodstream. For most time-travellers, the effect of LSKK soon wore off and they settled to rest one by one in a remote time at a certain hour of a certain day, as even the leaf that blows furthest from an autumn tree will eventually come to rest somewhere.

But because Mickie believed only in the present moment, he drifted on for ever, imprisoned in his bubble of time like a bubble in a glacier.

Fixed in the gesture of kissing Rickie, he watched the millennia float by. He never wearied, since none of his personal time passed. But outside time passed; the world wearied. The great concourse of the human race began to thin.

Generation after generation had looked on with admiration and amusement as the handsome young man in old-fashioned clothes drifted through their lives, standing always on the same spot in the same romantic attitude. Indeed, Mickie had become something of a world-myth. A small green park was created round him in the midst of the fantastic city. The thousand thousand generations came to look at him here. But the mighty stream dwindled to a trickle eventually. Fixed in his bubble, Mickie saw the trees of the park grown shaggy and old and seamed. Eventually they fell one by one, and the great building behind them. The city was dying, and the human race with it. Few people came to see the world-myth now.

Another race of beings had inherited Earth, phantasmal beings like comets, blazing in solitary beauty like comets that had grown to prefer forests to the deserts of space. The sun that shone upon their millions of centuries of peace and fruitfulness shrank to the apparent size of a grape; it emitted an intense white light like a magnesium flare. So it seemed there was always moonlight on earth.

Still an occasional human came, fur-clad, to the place where Mickie stood imprisoned on the plain. Finally, two humans came together, very small and silent, to look at him for the best part of a magnesium-white day.

They asked each other, 'He will be the last of our kind; but is he dead or is he immortal?' So they echoed the once-famous exchange that Mickie and Rickie had had, so very long ago.

No one else ever came again. Even the comet-people faded eventually. Eventually, even the sun faded. Even the stars burned dim and faded. The universe had grown old. Time itself faded and ... slowly ... came to a stop ...

There, poised on the brink of the last second of eternal time, Mickie stood transfixed in his bubble.

And with his lips still pursed in the moment of that long-gone kiss, he asked himself the final question, 'Am I dead or am I immortal?'

Down the Up Escalation

Being alone in the house, not feeling too well, I kept the television burning for company. The volume was low. Three men mouthed almost soundlessly about the Chinese rôle in the Vietnam war. Getting my head down, I turned to my aunt Laura's manuscript.

She had a new hairstyle these days. She looked very good; she was seventy-three, my aunt, and you were not intended to take her for anything less; but you could mistake her for ageless. Now she had written her first book – 'a sort of autobiography', she told me when she handed the bundle over. Terrible apprehension gripped me. I had to rest my head in my hand. Another heart attack coming.

On the screen, figures scrambling over mountain. All unclear. Either my eyesight going or a captured Chinese newsreel. Strings of animals – you couldn't see what, film slightly overexposed. Could be reindeer crossing snow, donkeys crossing sand. I could hear them now, knocking, knocking, very cold.

A helicopter crashing towards the ground? Manuscript coming very close, my legs, my lips, the noise I was making.

There was a ship embedded in the ice. You'd hardly know there was a river. Snow had piled up over the piled-up ice.

Surrounding land was flat. There was music, distorted stuff from a radio, accordions, and balalaikas. The music came from a wooden house.

From its misty windows, they saw the ship, sunk in the rotted light. A thing moved along the road, clearing away the day's load of ice, ugly in form and movement. Four people sat in the room with the unpleasant music; two of them were girls in their late teens, flat faces with sharp eyes; they were studying at the university. Their parents ate a salad, two forks, one plate. Both man and woman had been imprisoned in a nearby concentration camp in Stalin's time. The camp had gone now. Built elsewhere, for other reasons.

The ship was free of ice, sailing along in a sea of mist. It was no longer a pleasure ship but a research ship. Men were singing. They sang that they sailed on a lake as big as Australia.

'They aren't men. They are horses!' My aunt.

'There are horses aboard.'

'I certainly don't see any men.'

'Funny-looking horses.'

'Did you see a wolf then?'

'I mean, more like ponies. Shaggy. Small and shaggy. Is that gun loaded?'

'Naturally. They're forest ponies – I mean to say, not ponies but reindeer. "The curse of the devil", they call them.'

'It's the bloody rotten light! They do look like reindeer. But they must be men.'

'Ever looked one in the eye? They are *the* most frightening animals.'

My father was talking to me again, speaking over the phone. It had been so long. I had forgotten how I loved him, how I missed him. All I remembered was that I had gone with my two brothers to his funeral; but that must have been someone else's funeral, someone else's father. So many people, good people, were dying.

I poured my smiles down the telephone, heart full of delight, easy. He was embarking on one of his marvellous stories. I gulped down his sentences.

'That burial business was all a joke – a swindle. I collected two thousand pounds for that, you know, Bruce. No, I'm lying! Two and a half. It was chicken feed, of course, compared with some of the swindles I've been in. Did I ever tell you how Ginger Robbins and I got demobbed in Singapore at the end of the war, 1945? We bought a defunct trawler off a couple of Chinese business men – very nice old fatties called Pee – marvellous name! Ginger and I had both kept our uniforms, and we marched into a transit camp and got a detail of men organised – young rookies, all saluting us like mad – you'd have laughed! We got them to load a big LCT engine into a five-tonner, and we all drove out of camp without a question being asked, and – wham! – straight down to the docks and our old tub. It was boiling bloody hot, and you should have seen those squaddies sweat as they unloaded the engine and man-handled –'

'Shit, Dad, this is all very funny and all that,' I said, 'but I've got some work to do, you know. Don't think I'm not enjoying a great reminiscence, but I have to damned work, see? Okay?'

I rang off.

I put my head between my hands and – no, I could not manage weeping. I just put my head between my hands and wondered why I did what I did. Subconscious working, of course. I tried to plan out a science fiction story about a race of men who had only subconsciousnesses. Their consciousnesses had been painlessly removed by surgery.

They moved faster without their burdening consciousnesses, wearing lunatic smiles or lunatic frowns. Directly after the operation, scars still moist, they had restarted World War II, some assuming the roles of Nazis or Japanese or Jugoslav partisans or British fighter pilots in kinky boots. Many even chose to be Italians, the role of Mussolini being so keenly desired that at one time there were a dozen Duces striding about, keeping company with the droves of Hitlers.

Some of these Hitlers later volunteered to fly with the Kamikazes.

Many women volunteered to be raped by the Wehrmacht and turned nasty when the requirements were filled. When a concentration camp was set up, it was rapidly filled; people have a talent for suffering. The history of the war was rewritten a bit. They had Passchendaele and the Somme in; a certain President Johnson led the British forces.

The war petered out in a win for Germany. Few people were left alive. They voted themselves second-class citizens, mostly becoming Jewish Negroes or Vietnamese. There was birching between consenting adults. These good folk voted unanimously to have their subconsciousnesses removed, leaving only their ids.

*

I was on the floor. My study. The name of the vinolay was – it had a name, that rather odious pattern of little wooden chocks. I had it on the tip of my tongue. When I sat up, I realised how cold I was, cold and trembling, not working very well.

My body was rather destructive to society, as the Top Clergy would say. I had used it for all sorts of things; nobody knew where it had been. I had used it in an unjust war. Festival. It was called Festival. Terrible name, surely impeded sales.

I could not get up. I crawled across the floor towards the drink cupboard in the next room. Vision blurry. As I looked up, I saw my old aunt's manuscript on the table. One sheet had fluttered down on to the Festival. I crawled out into the dining-room, through the door, banging myself as I went. Neither mind nor body was the precision ballistic missile it once had been.

The bottle. I got it open before I saw it was Sweet Martini, and dropped it. It seeped into the carpet; no doubt that had a name too. Weary, I rested my head in the mess.

'If I die now, I shall never read Aunt Laura's life …'

Head on carpet, bottom in air, I reached and grasped the whisky bottle. Why did they make the stuff so hard to get at? Then I drank. It made me very ill indeed.

It was Siberia again, the dread reindeer sailing eternally their ships across the foggy ice lakes. They were munching things, fur and wood and bone, the saliva freezing into icicles as it ran from their jaws. Terrible noise, like the knocking of my heart.

I was laughing. Whoever died dreaming of reindeer – who but Lapps? Digging my fingers into the nameless carpet, I tried to sit up. It proved easier to open my eyes.

In the shady room, a woman was sitting. She had turned from the window to look at me. Gentle and reassuring lines and planes composed her face. It took a while to see it as a face; even as an arrangement against a window, I greatly liked it.

The woman came over to look closely at me. I realised I was in bed before I realised it was my wife. She touched my brow, making my nervous system set to work on discovering whether the signal was a pain or pleasure impulse, so that things in there were too busy for me to hear what she was saying. The sight of her speaking was pleasurable; it moved me to think that I should answer her.

'How's Aunt Laura?'

The messages were coming through, old old learning sorting out speech, hearing, vision, tactile sensations, and shunting them through the appropriate organs. The doctor had been; it had only been a slight one, but this time I really would have to rest up and take all the pills and do nothing foolish; she had already phoned the office and they were very understanding. One of my brothers was coming round, but she was not at all sure whether he should be allowed to see me. I felt entirely as she did about that.

'I've forgotten what it was called.'

'Your brother Bob?'

My speech was a little indistinct. I had a creepy feeling about whether I could move the limbs I knew were bundled with me in the bed. We'd tackle that challenge as and when necessary.

'Not Bob. Not Bob. The...the ...'

'Just lie there quietly, darling. Don't try to talk.'

'The...carpet ...'

She went on talking. The hand on the forehead was a good idea. Irritably, I wondered why she didn't do it to me when I was well and better able to appreciate it. What the hell was it called? Roundabout?

'Roundabout ...'

'Yes, darling. You've been here for several hours, you know. You aren't quite awake yet, are you?'

'Shampoo ...'

'Later, perhaps. Lie back now and have another little doze.'

'Variety ...'

'Try and have another little doze.'

One of the difficulties of being a publisher is that one has to fend off so many manuscripts submitted by friends of friends. Friends always have friends with obsessions about writing. Life would be simple – it was the secret of a happy life, not to have friends of friends. Supposing you were cast away on a desert island disc, Mr Hartwell, what eight friends of friends would you take with you, provided you had an inexhaustible supply of manuscripts?

I leaned across the desk and said, 'But this is worse than ever. You aren't even a friend of a friend of a friend, auntie.'

'And what am I if I'm *not* a friend of a friend?'

'Well, you're an aunt of a nephew, you see, and after all, as an old-established firm, we have to adhere to certain rules of – etiquette, shall we call it, by which –'

It was difficult to see how offended she was. The pile of manuscript hid most of her face from view. I could not remove it, partly because there was a certain awareness that this was really the sheets. Finally I got them open.

'It's your life, Bruce. I've written your life. It could be a bestseller.'

'Variety... No, Show Business ...'

'I thought of calling it "By Any Other Name" ...'

'We have to adhere to certain rules ...'

It was better when I woke again. I had the name I had been searching for: Festival. Now I could not remember what it was the name of.

The bedroom had changed. There were flowers about. The portable TV set stood on the dressing-table. The curtains were drawn back and I could see into the garden. My wife was still there, coming over, smiling. Several times she walked across to me, smiling. The light came and went, the flowers changed position, colour, the doctor got in her way. Finally she reached me.

'You've made it! You're marvellous!'

'*You've* made it! *You're* marvellous!'

No more trouble after that. We had the TV on and watched the war escalate in Vietnam and Cambodia.

Returning health made me philosophical. 'That's what made me ill. Nothing I did...under-exercise, over-eating...too much booze...too many fags...just the refugees.'

'I'll turn it off if it upsets you.'

'No. I'm adapting. They won't get me again. It's the misery the TV sets beam out from Vietnam all over the world. That's what gives people heart attacks. Look at lung cancer – think how it has been on the increase since the war started out there. They aren't real illnesses in the old sense, they're sort of prodromic illness, forecasting some bigger sickness to come. The whole world's going to escalate into a Vietnam.'

She jumped up, alarmed. 'I'll switch it off!'

'The war?'

'The set.'

The screen went blank. I could still see them. Thin women in those dark blue overalls, all their possessions slung from a frail bamboo over a frail shoulder. Father had died about the time the French were slung out. We were all bastards. Perhaps every time one of us died, one of the thin women lived. I began to dream up a new religion.

They had the angels dressed in UN uniform. They no longer looked like angels, not because of the uniform but because they were all disguised as a western diplomat – nobody in particular, but jocular, uneasy, stolid, with stony eyes that twinkled.

My angel came in hotfoot and said, 'Can you get a few friends of friends together? The refugees are waiting on the beach.' There were four of us in the hospital beds. We scrambled up immediately, dragging bandages and sputum cups and bed pans. The guy next to me came trailing a plasma bottle. We climbed into the helicopter.

We prayed en route. 'Bet the Chinese and Russian volunteers don't pray on the trip,' I insinuated to the angel.

'The Chinese and Russians don't volunteer.'

'So you make a silly insinuation, you get a silly innuendo,' the plasma man said.

God's hand powered the chopper. Faster than engines but maybe less reliable. We landed on the beach beside a foaming river. Heat pouring down and up the sideways. The refugees were forlorn and dirty. A small boy stood hatless with a babe hatless on his back. Both ageless, eyes like reindeer's, dark, moist, cursed.

'I'll die for those two,' I said, pointing.

'One for one. Which one do you choose?'

'Hell, come on now, angel, isn't my soul as good as any two god-damned Viet kid souls?'

'No discounts here, bud. Yours is shop-soiled, anyway.'

'Okay, the bigger kid.'

He was whisked instantly into the helicopter. I saw his dirty and forlorn face at the window. The baby sprawled screaming on the sand. It was naked, scabs on both knees. It yelled in slow motion, piddling, trying to burrow into the sand. I reached slowly out to it, but the exchange had been made, the angel turned the napalm on to me. As I fell, the baby went black in my shadow.

'Let me switch the fire down, if you're too hot, darling.'

'Yuh. And a drink …'

She helped me struggle into a sitting position, put her arm round my shoulders. Glass to lips, teeth, cool water in throat.

'God, I love you, Ellen, thank God you're not …'

'What? Another nightmare?'

'Not Vietnamese …'

It was better then, and she sat and talked about what had been going on, who had called, my brother, my secretary, the Roaches…'the Roaches have called'…'any Earwigs'?…the neighbours, the doctor. Then we were quiet a while.

'I'm better now, much better. The older generation's safe from all this, honey. They were born as civilians. We weren't. Get me auntie's manuscript, will you?'

'You're not starting work this week.'

'It won't hurt me. She'll be writing about her past, before the war and all that. The past's safe. It'll do me good. The prose style doesn't matter.'

I settled back as she left the room. Flowers stood before the TV, making it like a little shrine.

Full Sun

The shadows of the endless trees lengthened toward evening and then disappeared, as the sun was consumed by a great pile of cloud on the horizon. Balank was ill at ease, taking his laser rifle from the trundler and tucking it under his arm, although it meant more weight to carry uphill and he was tiring.

The trundler never tired. They had been climbing these hills most of the day, as Balank's thigh muscles informed him, and he had been bent almost double under the oak trees, with the machine always matching his pace beside him, keeping up the hunt.

During much of the wearying day, their instruments told them that the werewolf was fairly close. Balank remained alert, suspicious of every tree. In the last half hour, though, the scent had faded. When they reached the top of this hill, they would rest – or the man would. The clearing at the top was near now. Under Balank's boots, the layer of dead leaves was thinning.

He had spent too long with his head bent toward the brown-gold carpet; even his retinas were tired. Now he stopped, breathing the sharp air deeply, and stared about. The view behind them, across tumbled and almost uninhabited country, was magnificent, but Balank gave it scarcely a glance. The infrared warning on the trundler sounded, and the machine pointed a slender rod at a man-sized heat source ahead of them. Balank saw the man almost at the same moment as the machine.

The stranger was standing half-concealed behind the trunk of a tree, gazing uncertainly at the trundler and Balank. When Balank raised a hand in tentative greeting, the stranger responded hesitantly. When Balank called out his identification number, the man came cautiously into the open, replying with his own number. The trundler searched in its files, issued an okay, and they moved forward.

As they got level with the man, they saw he had a small mobile hut pitched behind him. He shook hands with Balank, exchanging personal signals, and gave his name as Cyfal.

Balank was a tall slender man, almost hairless, with the closed expression on his face that might be regarded as characteristic of his epoch. Cyfal, on the other hand, was as slender but much shorter, so that he appeared stockier; his thatch of hair covered all his skull and obtruded slightly onto his face. Something in his manner, or perhaps the expression around his eyes, spoke of the rare type of man whose existence was chiefly spent outside the city.

'I am the timber officer for this region,' he said, and indicated his wristcaster as he added, 'I was notified you might be in this area, Balank.'

'Then you'll know I'm after the werewolf.'

'*The* werewolf? There are plenty of them moving through this region, now that the human population is concentrated almost entirely in the cities.'

Something in the tone of the remark sounded like social criticism to Balank; he glanced at the trundler without replying.

'Anyhow, you've got a good night to go hunting him,' Cyfal said.

'How do you mean?'

'Full moon.'

Balank gave no answer. He knew better than Cyfal, he thought, that when the moon was at full, the werewolves reached their time of greatest power.

The trundler was ranging about nearby, an antenna slowly spinning. It made Balank uneasy. He followed it. Man and machine stood together on the edge of a little cliff behind the mobile hut. The cliff was like the curl of foam on the peak of a giant Pacific comber, for here the great wave of earth that was this hill reached its highest point. Beyond, in broken magnificence, it fell down into fresh valleys. The way down was clothed in beeches, just as the way up had been in oaks.

'That's the valley of the Pracha. You can't see the river from here.' Cyfal had come up behind them.

'Have you seen anyone who might have been the werewolf? His real name is Gondalug, identity number YB5921 stroke AS25061, City Zagrad.'

Cyfal said, 'I saw someone this way this morning. There was more than one of them, I believe.' Something in his manner made Balank look at him closely. 'I didn't speak to any of them, nor them to me.'

'You know them?'

'I've spoken to many men out here in the silent forests, and found out later they were werewolves. They never harmed me.'

Balank said, 'But you're afraid of them?'

The half-question broke down Cyfal's reserve. 'Of course I'm afraid of them. They're not human – not real men. They're enemies of men. They are, aren't they? They have powers greater than ours.'

'They can be killed. They haven't machines, as we have. They're not a serious menace.'

'You talk like a city man! How long have you been hunting after this one?'

'Eight days. I had a shot at him once with the laser, but he was gone. He's a grey man, very hairy, sharp features.'

'You'll stay and have supper with me? Please. I need someone to talk to.'

For supper, Cyfal ate part of a dead wild animal he had cooked. Privately revolted, Balank ate his own rations out of the trundler. In this and other ways, Cyfal was an anachronism. Hardly any timber was needed nowadays in the cities, or had been for millions of years. There remained some marginal uses for wood, necessitating a handful of timber officers, whose main job was to fix signals on old trees that had fallen dangerously, so that machines could fly over later and extract them like rotten teeth from the jaws of the forest. The post of timber officer was being filled more and more by machines, as fewer men were to be found each generation who would take on such a dangerous and lonely job far from the cities.

Over the eons of recorded history, mankind had raised machines that made his cities places of delight. Machines had replaced man's early inefficient machines; machines had replanned forms of transport; machines had come to replan man's life for him. The old stone jungles of man's brief adolescence were buried as deep in memory as the coal jungles of the Carboniferous.

Far away in the pile of discarded yesterdays, man and machines had found how to create life. New foods were produced, neither meat nor vegetable, and the ancient wheel of the past was broken forever, for now the link between man and the land was severed: agriculture, the task of Adam, was as dead as steamships.

Mental attitudes were moulded by physical change. As the cities became self-supporting, so mankind needed only cities and the resources of cities. Communications between city and city became so good that physical travel was no longer necessary; city was separated from city by unchecked vegetation as surely as planet is cut off from planet. Few of the hairless denizens of the cities ever thought of outside; those who went physically outside invariably had some element of the abnormal in them.

'The werewolves grow up in cities as we do,' Balank said. 'It's only in adolescence they break away and seek the wilds. You knew that, I suppose?'

Cyfal's overhead light was unsteady, flickering in an irritating way. 'Let's not talk of werewolves after sunset,' he said.

'The machines will hunt them all down in time.'

'Don't be so sure of that. They're worse at detecting a werewolf than a man is.'

'I suppose you realise that's social criticism, Cyfal?'

Cyfal pulled a long sour face and discourteously switched on his wristphone. After a moment, Balank did the same. The operator came up at once, and he asked to be switched to the news satellite.

He wanted to see something fresh on the current time exploration project, but there was nothing new on the files. He was advised to dial back in an hour. Looking over at Cyfal, he saw the timber officer had tuned to a dance show of some sort; the cavorting figures in the little projection were badly distorted from this angle. He rose and went to the door of the hut.

The trundler stood outside, ever alert, ignoring him. An untrustworthy light lay over the clearing. Deep twilight reigned, shot through by the rays of the newly risen moon; he was surprised how fast the day had drained away.

Suddenly, he was conscious of himself as an entity, living, with a limited span of life, much of which had already drained away unregarded. The moment of introspection was so uncharacteristic of him that he was frightened. He told himself it was high time he traced down the werewolf and got back to the city: too much solitude was making him morbid.

As he stood there, he heard Cyfal come up behind. The man said, 'I'm sorry if I was surly when I was so genuinely glad to see you. It's just that I'm not used to the way city people think. You mustn't take offence – I'm afraid you might even think I'm a werewolf myself.'

'That's foolish! We took a blood spec on you as soon as you were within sighting distance.' For all that, he realised that Cyfal made him uneasy. Going to where the trundler guarded the door, he took up his laser gun and slipped it under his arm. 'Just in case,' he said.

'Of course. You think he's around – Gondalug, the werewolf? Maybe following you instead of you following him?'

'As you said, it's full moon. Besides, he hasn't eaten in days. They won't touch synthfoods once the lycanthropic gene asserts itself, you know.'

'That's why they eat humans occasionally?' Cyfal stood silent for a moment, then added, 'But they are a part of the human race – that is, if you regard them as men who change into wolves rather than wolves who change into men. I mean, they're nearer relations to us than animals or machines are.'

'Not than machines!' Balank said in a shocked voice. 'How could we survive without the machines?'

Ignoring that, Cyfal said, 'To my mind, humans are turning into machines. Myself, I'd rather turn into a werewolf.'

Somewhere in the trees, a cry of pain sounded and was repeated.

'Night owl,' Cyfal said. The sound brought him back to the present, and he begged Balank to come in and shut the door. He brought out some wine, which they warmed, salted, and drank together.

'The sun's my clock,' he said, when they had been chatting for a while. 'I shall turn in soon. You'll sleep too?'

'I don't sleep – I've a fresher.'

'I never had the operation. Are you moving on? Look, are you planning to leave me here all alone, the night of the full moon?' He grabbed Balank's sleeve and then withdrew his hand.

'If Gondalug's about, I want to kill him tonight. I must get back to the city.' But he saw that Cyfal was frightened and took pity on the little man. 'But in fact I could manage an hour's freshing – I've had none for three days.'

'You'll take it here?'

'Sure, get your head down – but you're armed, aren't you?'

'It doesn't always do you any good.'

While the little man prepared his bunk, Balank switched on his phone again. The news feature was ready and came up almost at once. Again Balank was plunged into a remote and terrible future.

The machines had managed to push their time exploration some eight million years ahead, and there a deviation in the quanta of the electromagnetic spectrum had halted their advance. The reason for this was so far obscure and lay in the changing nature of the sun, which strongly influenced the time structure of its own minute corner of the galaxy.

Balank was curious to find if the machines had resolved the problem. It appeared that they had not, for the main news of the day was that. Platform One had decided that operations should now be confined to the span of time already opened up. Platform One was the name of the machine civilisation, many hundreds of centuries ahead in time, which had first pushed through the time barrier and contacted all machine-ruled civilisations before its own epoch.

What a disappointment that only the electronic senses of machines could shuttle in time! Balank would greatly have liked to visit one of the giant cities of the remote future.

The compensation was that the explorers sent back video pictures of that world to their own day. These alien landscapes produced in Balank a tremendous hunger for more; he looked in whenever he could. Even on the trail of the werewolf, which absorbed almost all his faculties, he had dialled for every possible picture of that inaccessible and terrific reality that lay distantly on the same time stratum which contained his own world.

As the first transmissions took on cubic content, Balank heard a noise outside the hut, and was instantly on his feet. Grabbing the gun, he opened the door and peered out, his left hand on the door jamb, his wristset still working.

The trundler sat outside, its senses ever-functioning, fixing him with an indicator as if in unfriendly greeting. A leaf or two drifted down from the trees; it was never absolutely silent here, as it could be in the cities at night; there was always something living or dying in the unmapped woods. As he turned his gaze through the darkness – but of course the trundler – and the werewolf, it was said – saw much more clearly in this situation than he did – his vision was obscured by the representation of the future palely gleaming at his cuff. Two phases of the same world were in juxtaposition, one standing on its side, promising an environment where different senses would be needed to survive.

Satisfied, although still wary, Balank shut the door and went to sit down and study the transmission. When it was over, he dialled a repeat. Catching his absorption, Cyfal from his bunk dialled the same programme.

Above the icy deserts of Earth a blue sun shone, too small to show a disc, and from this chip of light came all terrestrial change. Its light was bright as full-moon's light, and scarcely warmer. Only a few strange and stunted types of vegetation stretched up from the mountains toward it. All the old primitive kinds of flora had vanished long ago. Trees, for so many epochs one of the sovereign forms of Earth, had gone. Animals had gone. Birds had vanished from the skies. In the mountainous seas, very few life-forms protracted their existence.

New forces had inherited this later Earth. This was the time of the majestic auroras, of the near absolute-zero nights, of the years-long blizzards.

But there were cities still, their lights burning brighter than the chilly sun; and there were the machines.

The machines of this distant age were monstrous and complex things, slow and armoured, resembling most the dinosaurs that had filled one hour of the Earth's dawn. They foraged over the bleak landscape on their own ineluctable errands. They climbed into space, building there monstrous webbed arms that stretched far from Earth's orbit, to scoop in energy and confront the poor fish sun with a vast trawler net of magnetic force.

In the natural course of its evolution, the sun had developed into its white dwarf stage. Its phase as a yellow star, when it supported vertebrate life, was a brief one, now passed through. Now it moved toward its prime season, still far ahead, when it would enter the main period of its life and become a red dwarf star. Then it would be mature, then it would itself be invested with an awareness countless times greater than any minor consciousnesses it nourished now. As the machines clad in their horned exoskeletons climbed near it, the sun had entered a period of quiescence to be measured in billions of years, and cast over its third planet the light of a perpetual full moon.

The documentary presenting this image of postiquity carried a commentary that consisted mainly of a rundown of the technical difficulties confronting Platform One and the other machine civilisations at that time. It was too complex for Balank to understand. He looked up from his phone at last, and saw that Cyfal had dropped asleep in his bunk. By his wrist, against his tousled head, a shrunken sun still burned.

For some moments, Balank stood looking speculatively at the timber officer. The man's criticism of the machines disturbed him. Naturally, people were always criticizing the machines, but, after all, mankind depended on them more and more, and most of the criticism was superficial. Cyfal seemed to doubt the whole role of machines.

It was extremely difficult to decide just how much truth lay in anything. The werewolves, for example. They were and always had been man's enemy, and that was presumably why the machines hunted them with such ruthlessness – for man's sake. But from what he had learnt at the patrol school, the creatures were on the increase. And had they really got magic powers? – Powers, that was to say, that were beyond man's, enabled them to survive and flourish as man could not, even supported by all the forces of the cities. The Dark Brother: that was what they called the werewolf, because he was like the night side of man. But he was not man – and how exactly he differed, nobody could tell, except that he could survive when man had not.

Still frowning, Balank moved across to the door and looked out. The moon was climbing, casting a pallid and dappled light among the trees of the clearing, and across the trundler. Balank was reminded of that distant day when the sun would shine no more warmly.

The trundler was switched to transmission, and Balank wondered with whom it was in touch. With Headquarters, possibly, asking for fresh orders, sending in their report.

'I'm taking an hour with my fresher,' he said. 'Okay by you?'

'Go ahead. I shall stand guard,' the trundler's speech circuit said.

Balank went back inside, sat down at the table, and clipped the fresher across his forehead. He fell instantly into unconsciousness, an unconsciousness that force-fed him enough sleep and dream to refresh him for the next seventy-two hours. At the end of the timed hour, he awoke, annoyingly aware that there had been confusion in his skull.

Before he had lifted his head from the table, the thought came: we never saw any human beings in that chilly future.

He sat up straight. Of course, it had been an accidental omission from a brief programme. Humans were not so important as the machines, and that would apply even more in the distant time. But none of the news flashes had shown humans, not even in the immense cities. That was absurd; there would be lots of human beings. The machines had covenanted, at the time of the historic Emancipation, that they would always protect the human race.

Well, Balank told himself, he was talking nonsense. The subversive comments Cyfal had uttered had put a load of mischief into his head. Instinctively, he glanced over at the timber officer.

Cyfal was dead in his bunk. He lay contorted with his head lolling over the side of the mattress, his throat torn out. Blood still welled up from the wound, dripping very slowly from one shoulder onto the floor.

Forcing himself to do it, Balank went over to him. In one of Cyfal's hands, a piece of grey fur was gripped.

The werewolf had called! Balank gripped his throat in terror. He had evidently roused in time to save his own life, and the creature had fled.

He stood for a long time staring down in pity and horror at the dead man, before prising the piece of fur from his grasp. He examined it with distaste. It was softer than he had imagined wolf fur to be. He turned the hairs over in his palm. A piece of skin had torn away with the hair. He looked at it more closely.

A letter was printed on the skin.

It was faint, but he definitely picked out an 'S' to one edge of the skin. No, it must be a bruise, a stain, anything but a printed letter. That would mean that this was synthetic, and had been left as a fragment of evidence to mislead Balank...

He ran over to the door, grabbing up the laser gun as he went, and dashed outside. The moon was high now. He saw the trundler moving across the clearing toward him.

'Where have you been?' he called.

'Patrolling. I heard something among the trees and got a glimpse of a large grey wolf, but was not able to destroy it. Why are you frightened? I am registering surplus adrenalin in your veins.'

'Come in and look. Something killed the timber man.'

He stood aside as the machine entered the hut and extended a couple of rods above the body on the bunk. As he watched, Balank pushed the piece of fur down into his pocket.

'Cyfal is dead. His throat has been ripped out. It is the work of a large animal. Balank, if you are rested, we must now pursue the were-wolf Gondalug, identity number YB5921 stroke AS25061. He committed this crime.'

They went outside. Balank found himself trembling. He said, 'Shouldn't we bury the poor fellow?'

'If necessary, we can return by daylight.'

Argument was impossible with trundlers. This one was already off, and Balank was forced to follow.

They moved downhill toward the River Pracha. The difficulty of the descent soon drove everything else from Balank's mind. They had followed Gondalug this far, and it seemed unlikely he would go much farther. Beyond here lay gaunt bleak uplands, lacking cover. In this broken tumbling valley, Gondalug would go to earth, hoping to hide from them. But their instruments would track him down, and then he could be destroyed. With good luck, he would lead them to caves where they would find and exterminate other men and women and maybe children who bore the deadly lycanthropic gene and refused to live in cities.

It took them two hours to get down to the lower part of the valley. Great slabs of the hill had fallen away, and now stood apart from their parent body, forming cubic hills in their own right, with great sandy cliffs towering up vertically, crowned with unruly foliage. The Pracha itself frequently disappeared down narrow crevices, and the whole area was broken with caves and fissures in the rock. It was ideal country in which to hide.

'I must rest for a moment,' Balank gasped. The trundler came immediately to a halt. It moved over any terrain, putting out short legs to help itself when tracks and wheels failed.

They stood together, ill-assorted in the pale night, surrounded by the noise of the little river as it battled over its rocky bed.

'You're sending again, aren't you? Whom to?'

The machine asked, 'Why did you conceal the piece of wolf fur you found in the timber officer's hand?'

Balank was running at once, diving for cover behind the nearest slab of rock. Sprawling in the dirt, he saw a beam of heat sizzle above him and slewed himself round the corner. The Pracha ran along here in a steep-sided crevasse. With fear lending him strength, Balank took a run and cleared the crevasse in a mighty jump, and fell among the shadows on the far side of the gulf. He crawled behind a great chunk of rock, the flat top of which was several feet above his head, crowned with a sagging pine tree.

The trundler called to him from the other side of the river.

'Balank, Balank, you have gone wrong in your head!'

Staying firmly behind the rock, he shouted back, 'Go home, trundler! You'll never find me here!'

'Why did you conceal the piece of wolf fur from the timber officer's hand?'

'How did you know about the fur unless you put it there? You killed Cyfal because he knew things about machines I did not, didn't you? You wanted me to believe the werewolf did it, didn't you? The machines are gradually killing off the humans, aren't they? There are no such things as werewolves, are there?'

'You are mistaken, Balank. There are werewolves, all right. Because man would never really believe they existed, they have survived. But we believe they exist, and to us they are a greater menace than mankind can be now. So surrender and come back to me. We will continue looking for Gondalug.'

He did not answer. He crouched and listened to the machine growling on the other side of the river.

Crouching on the top of the rock above Balank's head was a sinewy man with a flat skull. He took more than human advantage of every shade of cover as he drank in the scene below, his brain running through the possibilities of the situation as efficiently as his legs could take him through wild grass. He waited without stirring, and his face was grey and grave and alert.

The machine came to a decision. Getting no reply from the man, it came gingerly round the rock and approached the edge of the crevasse through which the river ran. Experimentally, it sent a blast of heat across to the opposite cliff, followed by a brief hail of armoured pellets.

'Balank?' it called.

Balank did not reply, but the trundler was convinced it had not killed the man. It had somehow to get across the brink Balank had jumped. It considered radioing for aid, but the nearest city, Zagrad, was a great distance away.

It stretched out its legs, extending them as far as possible. Its clawed feet could just reach the other side, but there the edge crumbled slightly and would not support its full weight. It shuffled slowly along the crevasse, seeking out the ideal place.

From shelter, Balank watched it glinting with a murderous dullness in the moonlight. He clutched a great shard of rock, knowing what he had to do. He had presented to him here the best – probably the only – chance he would get to destroy the machine. When it was hanging across the ravine, he would rush forward. The trundler would be momentarily too preoccupied to burn him down. He would hurl the boulder at it, knock the vile thing down into the river.

The machine was quick and clever. He would have only a split second in which to act. Already his muscles bulged over the rock, already he gritted his teeth in effort, already his eyes glared ahead at the hated enemy. His time would come at any second now. It was him or it…

Gondalug alertly stared down at the scene, involved with it and yet detached. He saw what was in the man's mind, knew that he looked a scant second ahead to the encounter.

His own kind, man's Dark Brother, worked differently. They looked farther ahead just as they had always done, in a fashion unimaginable to homo sapiens. To Gondalug, the outcome of this particular little struggle was immaterial. He knew that his kind had already won their battle against mankind. He knew that they still had to enter into their real battle against the machines.

But that time would come. And then they would defeat the machines. In the long days when the sun shone always over the blessed Earth like a full moon – in those days, his kind would finish their age of waiting and enter into their own savage kingdom.

Just Passing Through

Colin Charteris climbed out of his red Banshee, stood for a moment stretching by it. The machine creaked and snapped, the metal cooling after its long duel across the motorways of Europe. Charteris took off his inflatable padded lifesuit, flung it into the back of the car, turned up the temperature of his one-piece to compensate for what felt like near-nudity. Hero: he had covered the twenty-two hundred kilometres from Catanzaro down on the Ionian Sea to Metoz, France, in twenty-four hours' driving, and had sustained no more than a metre-long gouge along the front outside fender.

Outside Milano, where the triple autostrada made of the Lombardy plain a geometrical diagram, he had narrowly avoided a multiple crash. They were all multiple crashes these days. The image continued to multiply itself over and over in his mind, like a series of cultures in their dishes: a wheel still madly spinning, crushed barriers, buckled metal, sunlight worn like thick make-up over the impossibly abandoned attitudes of death. Charteris had seen it happen, the fantastic speeds suddenly swallowed by car and human frames with the sloth of the super-quick, when anything too fast for retina register could spend forever spreading through the labyrinths of consciousness. By now, the bodies would all be packed neatly in hospital or mortuary, the autostrada gleaming in perfect action again, the death squads lolling at their wheels in the nearest rastplatz, reading paperbacks; but Charteris's little clicker-shutter mechanisms were still busy re-running the actual blossoming moment of impact.

He shook his head, dislodging nothing. He had parked beside Metoz cathedral. It was several centuries old, but built of a coarse yellow stone that made it, now prematurely floodlit in the early evening, look like a Victorian copy of an earlier model.

The ground fell steeply at the other end of the square. Stone steps led down to a narrow street, all wall on one side and on the other prim little drab narrow façades closing all their shutters against the overwhelming statement of the cathedral.

Across one of the façades, a sign said, 'Hotel des Invalides'.

'Krankenhaus,' Charteris said.

He pulled his suitcase out of the boot of the Banshee and dragged himself over to the hotel, walking like a warrior coming across a desert, a pilot walking over a runway after a mission. He emphasised the tragedy of it slightly, even grunting as he walked. The other cars parked in the square were a shabby bunch. Removing his gaze from his own egotistical landscapes, he saw this part of the cathedral square had been bought up as a used car lot. There were prices in francs painted to one side of each windscreen, as if denoting the worth of the driver rather than the vehicle.

The Hotel des Invalides had a brass handle to its door. Charteris dragged it down and stepped into the hall, into unmitigated shadow. A bell buzzed and burned insatiably until he closed the door behind him. He walked up the corridor, and only with that motion did the hall take on existence. There was a pot plant dying here beside an enormous piece of furniture – or it could be an over-elaborate doorway into a separate part of the establishment. On the walls, enormous pictures of blue-clad men being blown up among scattering sandbags. A small dense black square figure emerged at the end of the passage. He drew near and saw it had permed hair and was a woman, not young, not old, smiling.

'*Haben Sie eirt Zimmer? Ein persortn, eine Nacht?*'

'*Jahr, jahr. Mil eine Dusche oder ohne?*'

'*Ohne.*'

'*Zimmer Nummer Zwanzig, Monsieur.*'

German. The *lingua franca* of Europe.

The madame called for a dark-haired girl, who came hurrying and smiling with the key to room twenty. She led Charteris up three flights of stairs, the first flight marble, the second and third wooden, the third uncarpeted. Each landing was adorned with large pictures of Frenchmen dying or conquering Germans in the first world war.

'This is where it all began,' he said to the back of the girl.

She paused and looked down at him. *'Je ne comprends pas, M'sieur.'*

No windows had been opened for a long while. The air smelt of all the bottled lives that had suffered here. Constriction, miserliness, conservation over all. He saw the red limbs leaping again as if for joy within the bucketing autostrada cars. If there were only the two alternatives, he preferred the leaping death to the desiccating life. He knew how greatly he dreaded both, how his fantasy life shuttled between them. *One more deadly mission: blast Peking, or spend ten years in the hotel in Metoz.*

He was panting on the threshold of Zimmer Twenty. By opening his mouth, he did so without the girl hearing him. She was – he was getting to that age when he could no longer tell – eighteen, twenty, twenty-two? Pretty enough.

Motioning to her to stay, Charteris crossed to the first of two tall windows. He worked at the bar until it gave way and the two halves swung into the room.

Great drop on this, the back of the hotel. In the street below, two kids with a white dog on a lead. They looked up at him, becoming merely two faces with fat arms and hands. Thalidomites. He could not shut away the images of ruin and deformity.

Buildings the other side of the alley. A woman moving in a room, just discerned through curtains. A waste site, two cats stalking each other among litter. A dry canal bed, full of waste and old cans. Wasn't there also a crushed automobile? A notice scrawled large on a ruined wall: NEUTRAL FRANCE THE ONLY FRANCE. Certainly, they had managed to preserve their neutrality to the bitter end; the French experience in the two previous world wars had encouraged that. Beyond the wall, a tree-lined street far wider than necessary, and the Prefecture. One policeman visible.

Turning back, Charteris cast a perfunctory eye over the furnishings of the room. They were all horrible. The bed was specially designed for chastity and early rising.

'Combien?'

The girl told him. Two thousand six hundred and fifty francs. He had to have the figure repeated. His French was rusty and he was not used to the French government's recent devaluation.

'I'll take it. Are you from Metoz?'

'I'm Italian.'

Pleasure rose in him, a sudden feeling of gratitude that not all good things had been eroded. In this rotten stuffy room, it was as if he breathed again the air of the mountains.

'I've been living in Italy since the war, right down in Catanzaro,' he told her in Italian.

She smiled. 'I am from the south, from Calabria, from a little village in the mountains that you won't have heard of.'

'Tell me. I might have done. I was doing NUNSACS work down there. I got about.'

She told him the name of the village and he had not heard of it. They laughed.

'But I have not heard of NUNSACS,' she said. 'It is a Calabrian town? No?'

He laughed again, chiefly for the pleasure of doing it and seeing its effect on her. 'NUNSACS is a New United Nations organisation for settling and if possible rehabilitating war victims. We have several large encampments down along the Ionian Sea.'

The girl was not listening to what he said. 'You speak Italian well but you aren't Italian. Are you German?'

'I'm Montenegrin – a Jugoslav. Haven't been home since I was a boy. Now I'm driving over to England.'

As he spoke, he heard Madame calling impatiently. The girl moved towards the door, smiled at him – a sweet and shadowy smile that seemed to explain her existence – and was gone.

Charteris put his case down on the table under the window. He stood looking out for a long while at the dry canal bed, the detritus in it making it look like an archaeological dig that had uncovered remains of an earlier industrial civilisation.

Madame was working in the bar when he went down. Several of the little tables in the room were occupied. He could tell at a glance they were all local people. The room was large and dispiriting, the big dark wood bar on one side being dwarfed and somehow divorced from the functions it was supposed to serve. A television set flickered in one corner, most of those present contriving to sit and drink so that they kept an eye on it, as if it were an enemy or at least an uncertain friend. The only exceptions to this were two old men at a table set apart, who talked industriously, resting their wrists on the table but using their hands to emphasise points in the conversation. One of these men, who grew a tiny puff of beard under his lower lip, soon revealed himself as M'sieur.

Behind M'sieur's table, and set in one corner by a radiator, was a bigger table, a solemn table, spread with various articles of secretarial and other use. This was Madame's table, and to this she retired to work with some figures when she was not serving her customers. Tied to the radiator was a large and mangy young dog, who whined at intervals and flopped continually into new positions, as though the floor had been painted with anti-dog powder. Madame occasionally spoke mildly to it, but her interests were clearly elsewhere.

All this Charteris took in as he sat at a table against the wall, sipping a pernod, waiting for the girl to appear. He saw these people as victims of an unworkable capitalistic system dying on its feet. The girl came after some while from an errand in the back regions, and he motioned her over to his table.

'What's your name?'

'Angelina.'

'Mine's Charteris. That's what I call myself. It's an English name. I'd like to take you out for a meal.'

'I don't leave here till late – ten o'clock.'

'Then you don't sleep here?'

Some of the softness went out of her face as caution, even craftiness, overcame her, so that momentarily he thought, she's just another lay, but there will be endless complications to it in this set-up, you can bet! She said, 'Can you buy some cigarettes or something? I know they're watching me.'

He shrugged. She walked across to the bar. Charteris watched the movement of her legs, the action of her buttocks, trying to estimate whether her knickers would be clean or not. He was a fastidious man. Angelina fetched down a packet of cigarettes, put them on a tray, and carried them across to him. He took them and paid without a word. All the while, the M'sieur's eyes were on him.

Charteris forced himself to smoke one of the cigarettes. They were vile. Despite her neutrality in the Acid Head War, France had suffered from shortages like everyone else. Charteris was pampered, with illegal access to NUNSACS cigars, which he enjoyed.

He looked at the television. Faces swam in the green light, talking too fast for him to follow. There was some nonsense about a cycling champion, a protracted item about a military parade and inspection, shots of international film stars dining in Paris, something about a murder hunt somewhere. Not a mention of the two continents full of nut cases who no longer knew where reality began or ended. The French carried their neutrality into every facet of their lives.

When he had finished his pernod, he went over and paid Madame at her table and walked out in the square.

It was night, night in its early stages when the clouds still carried hints of daylight through the upper air. The floodlighting was gaining on the cathedral, chopping it into alternate vertical sections of void and glitter, so that it looked like a cage for some gigantic prehistoric bird. Beyond the cage, the traffic on the motorway snarled untiringly.

He went and sat in his car and smoked a cigar to remove the taste of the cigarette, although sitting in the Banshee when it was still made him oddly uneasy. He thought about Angelina and whether he wanted her, decided on the whole he did not. He wanted English girls. He had never even known one but, since his earliest days, he had longed for all things English, as another man he knew yearned for anything Chinese. He had dropped his Montenegrin name to christen himself with the surname of his favourite English writer.

About the present state of England, he imagined he had no illusions. When the Acid Head War broke out between the US and China, Russia had come in on the Communist side. Canada and Australia had aligned themselves with America, and Britain – perhaps still nourishing dreams of a grander past – had backed into the war in such a way as to offend her allies while at the same time involving most of the other European nations, Germany, Italy, and Scandinavia amongst them – and France always excluded. By an irony, Britain had been the first country to suffer the PCA Bomb – the Psycho-Chemical Aerosols that spread hallucinatory mental states across the nation. As a NUNSACS official, Charteris was being posted to work in Britain on rehabilitation work; as a NUNSACS official, he knew the terrifying disorder he would find there. He had no qualms about it.

But first there was this evening to be got through … He had said that so often to himself. Life was so short, one treasured it so intensely, and yet it was also full of desolating boredom. The acid head victims all ever the world had no problems with boredom; their madnesses precluded it; they were always well occupied with terror or joy, whichever their inner promptings led them to; that was why one envied the victims one spent one's life trying to save. The victims were never tired of themselves.

The cigar tasted good, extending its mildness all round him like a mist. Now he put it out and climbed from the car. He knew of only two ways to pass the evening before it was time to sleep; he could eat or he could find sexual companionship. Sex, he thought, the mysticism of materialism. It was true. He sometimes needed desperately the sense of a female life impinging on his with its unexplored avenues and possibilities, so stale, so explored, were his own few reactions. Back to his mind again came the riotous movements of the autostrada victims, fornicating with death.

On his way towards a lighted restaurant on the far side of the square, he saw another method by which to structure the congealing time of the French evening. The little cinema was showing a film called SEX ET BANG-BANG, forbidden to anyone under sixteen. He glanced up at the ill-painted poster, showing a near-naked blonde with an ugly shadow like a moustache across her face, and muttered, 'Starring Petula Roualt as Al Capone,' as he passed.

As he ate in the restaurant, he thought about Angelina and madness and war and neutrality; it seemed to him they were all products of different time-senses. Perhaps there were no human emotions, only a series of different synchronicity microstructures, so that one 'had time for' one thing or another. He suddenly stopped eating. He saw the world – Europe, that is, precious, hated Europe that was his stage – purely as a fabrication of time, no matter involved. Matter was an hallucinatory experience, merely a slow-motion perceptual experience of certain time/emotion nodes passing through the brain. No, that the brain seized on in turn as it moved round the perceptual web it had spun, would spin, from childhood on. Metoz, that he apparently perceived so clearly through all his senses, was there only because all his senses had reached a certain dynamic synchronicity in their obscure journey about the biochemical web. Tomorrow, responding to some obscure circadian rhythm, they would achieve another relationship, and he would appear to move on. Matter was an abstraction of the time syndrome, much as the television had enabled Charteris to deduce bicycle races and military parades which held, for him, even less substance than the flickering screen. Matter was hallucination.

Charteris sat unmoving. If it were so, then clearly he was not at this restaurant table. Clearly there was no plate of cooling veal before him. Clearly Metoz did not exist. The autostrada was a projection of temporal confluences within him, perhaps a riverine dialogue of his entire life. France? Earth? Where was he? What was he?

Terrible though the answer was, it seemed unassailable. The man he called Charteris was merely another manifestation of a time/emotion node with no more reality than the restaurant or the autostrada. Only the perceptual web itself was 'real'. 'He' was the web in which Charteris, Metoz, tortured Europe, the stricken continents of Asia and America, could have their being, their doubtful being. He was God. ...

Someone was speaking to him. Dimly, distantly, he became aware of a waiter asking if he could take his plate away. So the waiter must be the Dark One, trying to disrupt his Kingdom. He waved the man off, saying something vaguely – much later, he realised he had spoken in Serbian, his native tongue, which he never used.

The restaurant was closing. Flinging some francs down on the table, he staggered out into the night, and slowly came to himself in the open air.

He was shaking from the strength and terror of his vision. As he rested against a rotting stone wall, its texture patterning his fingers, he heard the cathedral clock begin to chime and counted automatically. It was ten o'clock by whatever time-level they used here. He had passed two hours in some sort of trance.

In the camp outside Catenzaro, NUNSACS housed ten thousand men and women. Most of them were Russian, most had been brought from one small district of the USSR. Charteris had got his job on the rehabilitation staff by virtue of his fluent Russian, which was in many respects almost identical with his native tongue.

The ten thousand caused little trouble. Almost all of them were confined within the tiny republics of their own psyches. The PCA Bombs had been ideal weapons. The psychedelic drugs used by both sides were tasteless, odourless, colourless, and hence virtually unde-tectable. They were cheaply made. They were equally effective whether inhaled, drunk, or filtered through the pores of the skin. They were enormously potent. The after-effects, dependent on size of dose, could last a lifetime.

So the ten thousand crawled about the camp, smiling, laughing, scowling, whispering, as bemused with themselves and their fellows as they had been directly after the bombing. Some recovered. Others over the months revealed depressing character changes.

The drugs passed through the human system unimpaired in strength. Human wastes had to be rigorously collected – in itself a considerable undertaking among people no longer responsible for their own actions – and subjected to rigorous processing before the complex psychochemical molecules could be broken down. Inevitably, some of the NUNSACS staff picked up the contagion.

And I, thought Charteris, I with that sad and lovely Natrina ...

I am going psychedelic. That vision must have come from the drug.

He had moved some way towards the Hotel des Invalides, dragging his fingers across the rough faces of the buildings as if to convince himself that matter was still matter. When Angelina came up to him, he scarcely recognised her.

'You were waiting for me,' she said accusingly. 'You are deliberately waylaying me. You'd better go to your room before Madame locks up.'

'I – I may be ill! You must help me.'

'Speak Italian. I told you, I don't understand German.'

'Help me, Angelina. I must be ill.'

'You were well enough before.'

'I swear ... I had a vision. I can't face my room. I don't want to be alone. Let me come back to your room!'

'Oh no! You must think I am a fool, Signor!'

He pulled himself together.

'Look, I'm ill, I think. Come and sit in my car with me for ten minutes. I need to get my strength back. If you don't trust me, I'll smoke a cigar all the time. You never knew a man kiss a pretty girl with a cigar in his mouth, did you?'

They sat in the car, she beside him looking at him rather anxiously. Charteris could see her eyes gleam in the thick orange light – the very hue of time congealed! – bouncing off the walls of the cathedral. He sucked the rich sharp smoke down into his being, trying to fumigate it against the terrible visions of his psyche.

'I'm going back to Italy soon,' she said. 'Now the war's over, I may work in Milano. My uncle writes that it's booming there again now. Is that so?'

'Booming.' A very curious word. Not blooming, not booing. Booming.

'Really, I'm not Italian. Not by ancestry. Everyone in our village is descended from Albanians. When the Turks invaded Albania five centuries ago, many Albanians fled in ships across to the south of Italy to start life anew. The old customs were preserved from generation to generation. Did you hear of such a thing in Catenzaro?'

'No.' In Catenzaro he had heard the legends and phobias of the Caucasus, chopped and distorted by the kaleidoscopes of hallucination. It was a Slav, and not a Latin, purgatory of alienation.

'As a little girl, I was bilingual. We spoke Squiptar in the home and Italian everywhere else. Now I can hardly remember one word of Squiptar! My uncles have all forgotten too. Only my old aunt, who is also called Angelina, remembers. It's sad, isn't it, not to recall the language of your childhood? Like an exile?'

'Oh, shut up! To hell with it!'

By that, she was reassured. Perhaps she believed that a man who took so little care to please could not want to rape her. Perhaps she was right. While Charteris nursed his head and tried to understand what was inside it, she chattered on a new tack.

'I'll go back to Milano in the autumn, in September when it's not so hot. They're not good Catholics here. Are you a good Catholic? The French priests – ugh, I don't like them, the way they look at you! Sometimes I hardly seem to believe any more … Do you believe in God, Signor?'

He turned and looked painfully at her orange eyes, trying to see what she was really saying. She was a terrible bore, this girl.

'If you are really interested, I believe we each have Gods within us, and we must follow those.'

'That's stupid! Those gods would just be reflections of ourselves and we should be indulging in egotism.'

He was surprised by her answer. Neither his Italian nor his theology was good enough for him to reply as he would have liked. He said briefly, 'And your god – he is just an externalisation of egotism. Better to keep it inside!'

'What terrible, wicked blasphemy for a Catholic to utter!'

'You little idiot, I'm no Catholic! I'm a Communist. I've never seen any sign of your God marching about the world.'

'Then you are indeed sick!'

Laughing angrily, he grabbed her wrist and pulled her towards him. As she struggled, he shouted, 'Let's make a little investigation!'

She brought her skull forward and struck him on the nose. His head seemed to turn cathedral-size on the instant, flood-lit with pain. He hardly realised she had broken from his grip and was running across the square, leaving the Banshee's passenger door swinging open.

After a minute or two, Charteris locked the car door, climbed out, and made his way across to the hotel. The door was locked; Madame would be in bed, dreaming dreams of locked chests. Looking through the window into the bar, he saw that M'sieur still sat at his special table, drinking wine with a crony. Madame's wretched dog sprawled by the radiator, still restlessly changing its position. Charteris tapped on the window.

After a minute or two, M'sieur unlocked the door from inside and appeared in his shirtsleeves. He stroked his tiny puff of beard and nodded to himself, as if something significant had been confirmed.

'You were fortunate I was still up, M'sieur. Madame my wife does not like to be disturbed when once she has locked up the premises. My friend and I were just fighting some of our old campaigns before bed.'

'Perhaps I have been doing the same thing.'

He went up to his room. It was filled with noise. As he walked over to the window and looked out, he saw that a lock on the dry canal had been opened. Now it was full of rushing water, coursing over the car body and other rubbish, slowly moving them downstream. All the long uncomfortable night, Charteris slept uneasily to the noise of the purging water.

In the morning, he rose early, drank Madame's first indifferent coffee of the day, and paid his bill. His head was clear, but the world seemed less substantial than it had been. Carting his bag out to the car, he dressed himself in his lifesuit, inflated it, strapped himself in, and drove round the cathedral onto the motorway, which was already roaring with traffic. He headed towards the coast, leaving Metoz behind at a gradually increasing speed.

Multi-Value Motorway

She too was obsessed with pelting images. Phil Brasher, her husband, was growing more and more violent with Charteris, as if he knew the power was passing from him to the foreigner. Charteris had the certainty Phil lacked, the *gestalt*. Certainty, youth, handsome. He was himself. Also, perhaps, a saint. Also other people. But clearly a bit hipped, a heppo. Two weeks here, and he had spoken and the drugged Loughborough crowds had listened to him in a way they never did to her husband. She could not understand his message, but then she had not been sprayed. She understood his power.

The pelting images caught him sometimes naked.

Nerves on edge. Army Burton, played lead guitar, passed through her mind, saying, 'We are going to have a crusade.' Lamp posts flickered by, long trees, a prison gate, furry organs. She could not listen to the two men. As they walked over the withdrawn meaning of the wet and broken pavement, the hurtling traffic almost tore at their elbows. That other vision, too, held her near screaming pitch; she kept hearing the squeal of lorry wheels as it crashed into her husband's body, could see it so clear she knew by its nameboards it was travelling from Glasgow down to Naples. Over and over again it hit him and he fell backwards, disintegrating, quite washing away his discussion, savage discussion of multi-value logic, with Charteris. Also, she was troubled because she thought she saw a dog scuttle by wearing a red and black tie. Bombardment of images. They stood in a web of alternatives.

121

Phil Brasher said, 'I ought to kill Charteris.' Charteris was eating up his possible future at an enormous pace. Brasher saw himself spent, like that little rat Robbins, who had stood as saint and had not been elected. This new man, whom he had at first welcomed as a disciple, was as powerful as the rising sun, blanking Brasher's mind. He no longer got the good images from the future. Sliced bread cold oven. It was dead, there was a dead area, all he saw was that damned Christmas cactus which he loathed for its meaninglessness, like flowers on a grave. So he generated hate and said powerfully and confusedly to Charteris, 'I ought to kill Charteris.'

'Wait, first wait,' said Colin Charteris, in his own English, brain cold and acid. 'Think of Ouspenski's personality photographs. There's a high gloss. You have many alternatives. We are all rich in alternatives.' He had been saying that all afternoon, during this confused walk, as he knew. Ahead a big blind wall. The damp smudged crowded city, matured to the brown nearest black, gave off this rich aura of possibilities, which Brasher clearly was not getting. Charteris had glimpsed the world-plan, the tides of the future, carried with them sailor-fashion, was not so much superior to as remote from the dogged Brasher and Brasher's pale-thighed wife, Angelina, flocking on a parallel tide-race. Many alternatives; that was what he would say when next he addressed the crowds. Power was growing in him; he stood back modest and amazed to see it and recognise its sanctity like his father had. Brasher grabbed his wet coat and waved a fist in his face, an empty violent man saying 'I ought to kill you!' Traffic roared by them, vehicles driven by drivers seeing visions, on something called Inner Relief Road.

The irrelevant fist in his face; teeth in close detail; in his head, the next oration. You people – you midland people are special, chosen. I have come from the south of Italy from the Balkans to tell you so. The roads are built, we die on them and live by them, neural paths made actual. The Midlands of England is a special region; you must rise and lead Europe. Start a new probability. Less blankly put than that, but the ripeness of the moment would provide the right words, and there would be a song, Charteris we cry! He could hear it although it lay still coiled in an inner ear. Not lead but deliver Europe. Europe is laid low by the psychedelic bombs; even neutral France cannot help, because France clings to old nationalist values. I was an empty man, a materialist, failed Communist, waiting for this time. You have the alternatives now to wake yourselves and kill the old serpent.

You can think in new multi-value logics, because that is the pattern of your environment. The fist swung at him. The entire sluggish motion of man aiming it. Angeline's face was taking in the future, traffic-framed, dark of hair, immanent, luminous, freight-ful. It seemed to me I was travelling aimlessly until I got here stone cold from hotter beds too young father I called you from that flooded damned bank.

'I was just passing through on my way to Scotland, belting up the motorway in expedition. But I stopped here because of premonitions shy as goldfish thought. Think in fuzzy sets. There is no either-or black-white dichotomy any more. Only a spectrum of partiallys. Live by this, as I do – you will win. We have to think new. Find more directions make them. It's easy in this partially country.'

But Brasher was hitting him. World of movement lymphatic bursting. He looked at the fist, saw all its highways powerlines and tensions as Brasher had never seen it, fist less human than many natural features of the man-formed landscape in this wonderful traffic-tormented area. A fist struck him on the jaw. Colliding systems shock lost all loot.

Even in this extreme situation, Charteris thought, multivalue logic is the Way. I am choosing something between being hit and not being hit; I am not being hit very much.

He heard Angeline screaming to her husband to stop. She seemed not to have been affected by the PCA Bombs, carrying her own neutrality through the brief nothing hours of the Acid Head War. But it was difficult to tell; bells rang even when classrooms looked empty or birds startled from cover. Charteris had a theory that women were less affected than men. Stridulations of low tone. He would be glad to measure Angeline's rhythm but disliked her screaming now. Bombardment of images, linked to her scream – theory of recurrence? – especially toads and the new animal in the dead trees at home.

There was a way to stop her screaming without committing oneself to asking her to cease. Charteris clutched at Brasher's ancient blue coat, just as the older wattled man was about to land another blow. The great wheeling scab of metropolis. Behind Brasher, on the other side of Inner

Relief, lay an old building made of the drab ginger stone of Leicestershire, to which a modern glass-and-steel porch had been tacked. A woman was watering a potted plant in the porch. All was distinct to Charteris while he pulled Brasher forward and then heaved him backward into Inner Relief little watering can of copper she had.

The lorry coming from the north swerved out to avoid. The old Cortina blazing along towards it spun across the narrow verge, swept away lady's glass-and-steel porch, copper can gone like that, and was itself hit by a post office van which had swerved to avoid the lorry. The lorry still bucking across the road hit another oncoming car which could not stop in time. The world's noise on granite. Another vehicle its Brakes squealing ran into the wall within feet of where Charteris and Angeline stood, and crumpled to a prearranged device too quickly, cicatrices chirping open. A series of photographs, potentialities multiplying or cancelling, machines as bulls herded.

'So many alternatives,' Charteris said wonderingly. He was interested to see that Brasher had disappeared, bits of him distributed somewhere among the wreckage. He remembered the multiple crash on the auto-strada near Milano. Or was it a true memory? Was the Milano crash merely a phantasm of a mind already on the swerge of delision or some kind of dream-play-back awry both the crashes the same crash or another his own predestination already in the furniture maybe wrong delivery wrong addrents from the dreamvelope where that stamping grind unsorted the commutations of the night's post orifices or who knew who was in serge of what when on.

At least the illusion was strong on particularity with the photograves unblurred. If it happened or not or would or did it on this internal recurrence was a jolt, sparky as all algebra, and he saw a tremendous rightness in the blossom of the implact and shapes of wreckage; it was like a marvellous – he said it to the girl, 'It is like a marvellous complex work of sculpture, where to the rigorous manformed shapes is added chance. Wider theory of numbers aids decimation. The art of the fortuitous.'

She was green and drab, swaying on her heels. He tried looking closely at the aesthetic effect of this colour-change, and recalled from somewhere in his being a sense of pity like a serpentstir. She was hurt, shocked, although he saw a better future for her. He must perform a definite action of some sort: remove her from the scene and the blood-metal steaming.

She went unprotestingly with him.

'I think Charteris is a saint. He has spoken with great success in Rugby and Leicester,' Army Burton said.

'Wide to whatever comes along,' Banjo Burton said. 'Full of loot.'

'He has spoken with great success in Rugby and Leicester,' Robbins said, thinking it over. Robbins was a faded nineteen, the field of his hair unharvested; he was the eterminal art student; his psychedelic-disposed personality had disintegrated under the efflict of being surrandied by add heads, although not personally caught by the chemicals of Arab design.

They sat in an old room dark bodies curtains drawn tight and light a blur on the papered walls.

Outside in the Loughborough streets night and day kept to the dialogue. Small dogs ran between stone seams.

Army used his uniform as barracks. Banjo had been a third-yearer, had turned agent, ran the pop group, the Escalation, operated various happenings; he had run Robbins as a saint with some reward, until Robbins had deflated one morning into the role of disciple cold cracked lips on the blue doorstep. They all lived with a couple of moronic girls in old housing in the middle of tumbletown, overlooking the square high moronic rear of F. W. Woolworth's. All round the town waited new buildings designed to cope with hypothetical fast-growing population; but conflicting eddies of society had sent people hearing echoes in each other's rooms gravitating towards the old core. The straggle of universities and technical colleges stood in marshy fields. It was February.

'Well, he spoke with great success in Leicester,' Burton said, 'made them believe in a sex-style.'

'Ay, he did that. Mind you, I was a success in Leicester,' Robbins said, 'Apathy's like bricks there to build yellow chapels on some fields you care to name.'

'Don't run down Leicester,' Greta squeaked. 'I came from there. At least, my uncle did the one with the dancing cat I told you about ate the goldfish. Did I ever tell you my Dad was a Risparian? An Early Risparian. My Mum would not join. She only likes things.'

Burton dismissed all reminiscence with a sweep of his hand. He lit a reefer and said, 'We are going to have a crusade, burn trails, make a sparky party of our Charter-flightboy, really roll. Play the noise-game.'

'Who's gone off Brasher then?'

'Stuff Brasher. You've seen our new boy. He's a song!'

He could see it. Charteris was good. He was foreign and people were ready for foreigners and exotic toted even in a tuning eyeball. Foreigners were exotic. Charteris had this whole thing he believed in some sort of intellectual thing fitted the machine-scene. People could take it in or leave it and still grab the noise of his song. Charteris was writing a book too. You couldn't tell he was real or phoney it didn't matter so he couldn't switch off.

The followers were already there. Brasher's following. Charteris beat Brasher at any meeting. You'd have to watch for Brasher. Big munch little throat. The man thought he was Jesus Christ Even if he is Jesus Christ, my money's on Charteris. He's got loot! Colin Charteris. Funny name for a Jugoslav!

'Let's make a few notes about it,' he said 'Robbins, and you, Gloria.'

'Greta.'

'Greta, then. A sense of place is what people want – something to touch among all the metaphysics, big old jumbos in the long thin grass. Charteris actually likes this bloody dump its dogshitted lanes. I suppose it's new to him. We'll take him round the houses, tape-record him. Where's the tape-recorder?' He was troubled by images and a presentiment that they would soon be driving down the autobahns of Europe. He saw a sign to Frankfurt, rubbed hands over his Yorkskull pudding eyes.

'I'll show him my paintings,' Robbins said. 'And he'll be interested about the birds all close local stuff.'

'What about the birds in all areas?

'A sense of place, you said with the jumbos in the long grapes. What they do, you know, like the city, the birds like the city.' They liked the city, the birds. Took its bricks for leaves. He had watched, down where the tractor was bogged down in the muddy plough, stood himself bogged all day in content, the landscape the brown nearest black under the thick light. It was the sparrows and starlings, mainly. There were more of them in the towns. They nested behind neon signs, over the fish and chip shops, near the Chinese restaurants, by the big stores, furniture stores, redemption shops, filling stations, for warmth, and produced more babies than the ones in the country, learning a new language. More broods annually. The seagulls covered the ploughed field. They were always inland. You could watch them, and the lines of the grid pencilled on the sky. They were evolving, giving up the sea. Woodgulls. The Greater Mole Gull. Or maybe the sea had shrivelled up and gone. Shrunk like melted plastic God knows what the birds are up to, acid-headed like everything else. Doing the pattern-thing themselves. 'City suits the birds. It has built-in pattern.'

'What are you talking about?' She loved him really, but you had to laugh. His dandy lion-yellow hair.

'We aren't the only ones with a population expulsion. The birds too. Remember that series of painting I did of birds, Banjo? Flowers and weeds, too. Like a tide. Pollination expulsion.'

'Just keep it practical, sonny. Stick to buildings, eh?' Maybe he could unzip his skull, remove the top like a wig, and pull that distracting Frankfurt sign dripping out of his brain batter.

'The Pollination Explosion,' Charteris said. 'That's a good title. I write a poem called The Pollination Explosion, about the deep pandemic of nature. The idea just came into my head. And the time will come when you try to betray me to leave me desolate between four walls.'

She said nothing.

'There could be trees in our future if the brain holds up.'

Angeline was walking resting on his arm, saying nothing. He had forgotten where he had left the Banshee; it was pleasure padding through the wet, looking for it. They strolled through a new arcade, where one or two shops functioned on dwindling supplies. A chemist's; Get Your Inner Relief Here; a handbill for the Escalation, Sensational and Smelly. Empty shells where the spec builder had not managed to sell shop frontage, all crude concrete, marked by the fossil-imprints of wooden battens. City pattern older than wood stamped by brain-print. Messages in pencil or blue crayon, YOUNG IVE SNOGGED HERE, BILL HOPKINS ONLY LOVES ME, LOVES LOST ITS LOOT, CUNT SCRUBBER. What was a cunt scrubber? Something like a loofah, or a person? Good opening for bright lad!

The Banshee waited in the rain by a portly group of dustbins exchanging hypergeometic forms, moduli of the cosmic rundown. It was not locked. They turned out an old man sheltering inside it.

'You killed my husband,' Angeline said, as the engine started. The filling station up the road gave you quintuple Green Shields on four gallons. Nothing ever changed except thought. Thought was new every generation, or they thought it was new, and she heard old wild music playing.

'The future lies fainting in the arms of the present.'

'Why don't you listen to what I'm saying Colin? You're not bloody mad, are you? You killed my husband and I want to know what you're going to do about it!'

'Take you home.' They were moving now. Although his face ached, he felt in a rare joking mood as after wine in the deep home forests.

'I don't live out this direction.'

'Take you to my home. My place. Where I build a sort of project from. I've started making a new model for thought. You came once, didn't you, with Brasher in some untidy evening? It's not town, not country. You can't say which it is; that's why I like it – it stands for all I stand for. In the mundane world and France, things like art and science have just spewed forth and swallowed up everything else. There's nothing now left that's non-art or non-science. A lot of things just gone. My place is neither urban nor non-urban. Fuzzy set, its own non categorisable catasgory. Look outwards, Angeline! Wonderful!' He gave a sort of half-laugh by a wall, his beard growing in its own silence.

'You Serbian bastard! There may have been a war, the country may be ruined, but you can't get away with murder! Justice doesn't just fuzz off! You'll die, they'll shoot you!' There was no conviction in her voice; his sainthood was drowning her old self, or whatever he had behind eyes.

'No, I shall live, be justice. I haven't fulfilled any purpose yet, a sailor but the ocean's still ahead, hey?' The car was easing on to the Inner Relief. Behind them, ambulances and a fire engine and police cars and breakdown vans were nuzzling the debris. 'I've seen reality, Angeline – Kragujevac, Metz, Frankfurt – it's lying everywhere. And I myself have materialised into the inorganic, and so am indestructible, auto-destruct!'

The words stoned him. Since he had reached England, the psychedelic effect had gained on him daily in gusts. Cities had speaking patterns, worlds, rooms. He had ceased to think what he was saying; the result was he surprised himself, and this elation fed back into the system. Every thought multiplied into a thousand. Words, roads, all fossil tracks of thinking. He pursued them into the amonight, struggling with them as they propagated in their deep burrows away from the surface. Another poem: On the Spontaneous Generation of Ideas During Conversation. Spontagions Ideal Convertagion. The Conflation of Spongation in Idations. Agenbite of Auschwitz.

'Inwit, the dimlight of my deep Loughburrows. That's how I materialised, love! Loughborough is me, my brain, here – we are in my brain, if s all me. The nomad's open to the city. I am projecting Loughborough. All its thoughts are mine, in a culmination going.' It was true. Other people, he hardly saw them, caught in bursts, crossflare, at last shared their bombardment of images.

'Don't be daft – it's raining again! Don't go daft. Talk proper.' But she sounded frightened.

They swerved past factories, long drab walls, filling stations, long ochre terraces, yards, many genera of concrete.

Ratty little shops now giving up; no more News of the World, Guinness. Grey stucco urinal. Coal yard, Esso Blue. A railway bridge, iron painted yellow, advertising Ind Coope, sinister words to him. More rows of terrace houses, dentured, time-devoured. A complete sentence yet to be written into his book; he saw his hand writing the truth is in static instants. Then the semis, suburbanal. More bridges, side roads, iron railings, the Inner Relief yielding to fast dual-carriage, out onto the motorway, endless roads crossing over it on primitive pillars. Railways, some closed, canals, some sedge-filled, a poor sod pushing a sack of potatoes on the handlebars of his bike across a drowning allotment, footpaths, cycle-paths, catwalks, nettlebeds, waste dumps, scrap-pits, shortcuts, fences.

Geology. Strata of different man-times. Tempology. Each decade of the past still preserved in some gaunt monument. Even the motorway itself yielding clues to the enormous epochs of pre-psychedelic time: bridges cruder, more massive in earliest epoch, becoming almost graceful later, less sick-orange; later still, metal; different abutment planes, different patterns of drainage in the under-flyover bank, bifurcated like enormous Jurassic fern-trees Here we distinguish by the characteristics of this medium-weight aggregate the Wimpey stratum; while, a little further along, in the shade of these cantilevers, we distinguish the beginning of the McAlpine seam. The layout of that service area, of course, belongs characteristically to the Taylor Woodrow Inter-Glacial. Further was an early electric generating station with a mock-turkish dome, desolate in a field. All art, assuaging. Pylons, endlessly, too ornate for the cumbersome land, assuaging. Multiplacation.

The skies were lumped and flaky with cloud, Loughborough skies. Squirting rain and diffused lighting. No green yet in the hedges. The brown nearest black. Beautiful. ...

'We will abolish that word beautiful. It carries implications of ugliness in an Aristotelian way. There are only gradations in between the two. They pair. No ugliness.'

'There's the word "ugliness", so there must be something to attach it to, mustn't there? And don't drive so fast.'

'Stop quoting Lewis Carroll at me!'

'I'm not!'

'You should have allowed me to give you the benefit of the doubt.'

'Well, steer properly! You lost your loot or something?'

He flicked away back onto his own side of the motorway, narrowly missing an op-art Jag, its driver screaming over the wheel. I also drive by fuzzy sets, he thought admiringly. The two cars had actually brushed; between hitting and not-hitting were many degrees. He had sampled most of them. The lookout to keep was a soft watch. It was impossible to be safe – watering your potted plant, which was really doing well, impossible. A Christmas cactus it could be, you were so proud of it. The Cortina, Consortina, buckling against – you'd not even seen it, back turned, blazing in a moment's sun, Christ, just sweeping the poor woman and her pathetic little porch right away in limbo!

'Never live on Inner Relief.' Suddenly light-hearted and joking.

'Stop getting at me! You're really rather cruel, aren't you?'

'*Jebem te sunce*! Look, Natrina – I mean, Angelina, I love you, I dream you.'

'You don't know the meaning of the word!'

'So? I'm not omniscient yet. I don't have to know what it is to do it, do I? I'm just beginning, the thing's just beginning in me, all to come.

I'll speak, preach! Burton's group, Escalation Limited, I'll write songs for them. How about Truth lies in Static Instants? Or When We're Intimate in the Taylor Woodrow Inter-Glacial. No, no – Accidents and Aerodynamics Accrete into Art. No, no! How about … Ha, I Do My Personal Thinking In Pounds Sterling? Or Ouspenski Has It All Ways Always. Or The Victim and the Wreckage Are The Same. The Lights Across the River. Good job I threw away my NUNSACS papers. Too busy. I'll fill the world till my head bursts. Look – *zbogom*, missed him! What a driver! Maybe get him tomorrow! Must forget these trivialities, which others can perform. Kuwait was the beginning! I'm just so creative at present, look, Angelina –'

'It's Angeline. Rhymes with "mean".' She couldn't tell if he was joking.

'My lean angel mean, Meangeline. I'm so creative, feel my temple! And I sense a gift in you too as you struggle out of old modes towards creams of denser feeling. What's it going to be we got to find together eh?'

'I've got no gins. My ma told me that.'

'Anyhow, see that church of green stone? We're there. Almost. Partially there. Fuzzy there. Kundalinically there. *Etwas there.*'

But this *etwas* country was neither inhabitable nor uninhabitable. It functioned chiefly as an area to move through a dimensional passage, scored, scarred, chopped by all the means the centuries had uncovered of annihilating the distance between Loughborough and the rest of Europe, rivers, roads, rails, canals, dykes, lanes, bridges, viaducts. The Banshee bumped over a hump-backed bridge, nosed along by a municipal dump, and rolled to a stop in front of a solitary skinned house.

Squadrons of diabolical lead birds sprang up to the roof of the house, from instant immobility to instant immobility on passage from wood to city. Slates were broken by wind and birds. Sheer blindness had built this worthy middle-class house here, very proper and some expense spared in the days before currency had gone decimal. It stood in its English exterior pluming as if in scaffolding. A land dispute perhaps. No one knew. The proud owner had gone, leaving the local council easy winners, to celebrate their triumph in a grand flurry of rubbish which now lapped into the front garden, eroded, rotting intricate under the creative powers of decay. Cans scuttled down paths. Caught by the fervour of it, the Snowcem had fallen off the brick, leaving a leprous dwelling, blowing like dandruff round the porch. And she looked up from the lovely cactus – he had admired it so much, bless him, a good husband – just in time to see the lorry sliding across the road towards her. And then, from behind, the glittering missile of the northbound car. ...

Charteris leant against the porch, covering his eyes to escape the repetitive image. It had been, was ever coming in the repetitive web.

'It was a conflux of alternatives in which I was trapped, all anti-flowered. I so love the British – you don't understand! I wouldn't hurt anyone. ... I'm going to show the world how –'

'You won't bring him back by being sorry.'

'Her, the woman with the cactus! Her! Her! Who was she?'

The Escalation had taken over an old Army Recruiting Office in Ashby Road. These surroundings with their old english wood and gymnast smells had influenced two of their most successful songs, 'The Intermittent Tattooed Tattered Prepuce' and 'A Platoon of One' in the Dead Sea Sound days. There were four of them, four shabby young men, sensational and smelly, called, for professional purposes, Phil, Bill, Ruby and Featherstone-Haugh; also Barnaby, who worked the background tapes to make supplementary noise or chorus. They were doing the new one. They could hear the ambulances still squealing in the distance, and improvised a number embodying the noise called 'Lost My Ring In the Ring Road'. Bill thought they should play it below, or preferably on top of, 'Sanctions, Sanctions'; they decided to keep it for a flip side if they ever made the old circuit of recording.

They began to rehearse the new one.

Bank all my money in slot machines
These new coins are strictly for spending
Old sun goes on its rounds
Now since we got the metric currency
I do my personal thinking in pounds
We haven't associated
Since twelve and a half new pence of money
Took over from the half-a-crowns
Life's supposed to be negotiable, ain't it?
But I do my personal thinking in pounds

*

Greta and Flo came in, with Robbins and the Burtons following. Army Burton had lost his lovely new tie, first one he ever had. He was arguing that Charteris should speak publicly as soon as possible – with the group at Nottingham on the following night; Robbins was arguing that there had been a girl at the art college called Hypothermia; Banjo was telling about London. Greta was saying she was going home.

'Great, boys, great, break it up! You've escalated, like I mean you are now a choir, not just a group, okay, this secular stint? At Nottingham tomorrow night, you're a choir, see? So we hitch our fortunes to Colin Charteris, tomorrow's saint, the author of Fuzzy Sets.'

Oh, he's on about sex again! I'm going home,' said Greta, and went. Her mum lived only just down the road in a little house on the Inner Relief; Greta didn't live there any more, but they had not quarrelled, just drifted gently apart on the life-death stream. Greta liked squalor and the arabesque decline. What she could not take were the rows of indoor plants with which her mother hedged herself.

> Sister, they've decimalised us
> All of the values are new
> Bet you the five-penny piece in my hip
> When I was a child on that old £.s.d.
> There was a picture of a pretty sailing ship
> Sailing on every ha-penny ...

They were used to Burton's madness. He had got them the crowds, the high voices from the front aisles. They needed the faces there, the noise, the interference, the phalanx of decibels the audience threw back at them in self-defence, needed it all, and the stink and empathy, to give right out and tear a larynx. In the last verse, The goods you buy with this new coinage, they could have talkchant as counterpoint instead of instrument between lines. May be even Saint Charteris would go for that. Saint Loughborough? Some people said he was a Communist, but he could be all the things they needed, even become fodder for song. They looked back too much. The future and its thoughts they needed. Lips close, New pose, Truth lies in static instants. Well, it had possibilities.

With Charteris tranced, labouring at his masterwork, cutting, superimposing, annotating, Angeline wandered about the house. A tramp lived upstairs in the back room, old yellow mouth like an eye-socket. She avoided him. The front room upstairs was empty because it got so damp where the rain poured in. She stood on the bare frothy boards staring out at the sullen dead sea with shores of city rubbish, poor quality rubbish, becalming flocks of gulls, beaks as cynical as the smiles of reptiles from which they had originated. Land so wet, so dark, so brown nearest black, late February and the trains all running half-cocked with the poor add head drivers forgetting their duties, chasing their private cobwebs, hot for deeper stations. Nobody was human any more. She'd be better advised to take LSD and join the psychotomimjority, forget the old guilt theories, rub of old mother-sores. Charteris gave her hope, seemed he thought the situation was good and could be improved within fuzzy limits, pull all things from wreckage back.

Wait till you read 'Man the Driver', he told Phil Brasher. You will see. No more conflicts once everyone recognises that he always was a hunter, all time. The modern hunter has become a driver. His main efforts do not go towards improving his lot, but complicating ways of travel. It's all in the big pattern of time-space-mind. In his head is a multi-value motorway. Now, after the Kuwait *coup*, he is free to drive down any lane he wants, any way. No external frictions or restrictions any more. Thus spake Charteris. She had felt compelled to listen, thus possibly accomplishing Phil's death. There had been a rival group setting up in the cellars of Loughborough, the Mellow Bellows. They had taken one title out of thin air: There's a fairy with an Areopagitica, No external frictions or restrictions, We don't need law or war or comfort or that bourgeois stuff, No external frictions or restrictions. Of course, they did say he was a communist or something. What we needed was freedom to drive along our life lines where we would, give or take the odd Brasher. More irrational fragments of the future hit her: through him, of course; a weeping girl, a – a baked bean standing like a minute scruple in the way of self-fulfilment.

She wanted him to have her, if she could square her conscience about Phil. He was okay, but – yes, a change was so so welcome. Sex, too, yes, if he didn't want too much of it. The waste always lay outside the window. He was clean-looking; good opening for bright lad – where had she overheard that? Well, it was self-defence. Wow that smash-up, still she trembled.

The gulls rose up from the mounds of rotting refuse, forming lines in the air. A dog down there, running, free, so free, companion of man, sly among the mountains. Perhaps now man was going to be as free as his companion. Trees in their future? Green? Bare?

Tears trickling down her cheek. Tears falling new from her sad speckled dreams. Even if it proved a better way of life, good things would be lost. Always the loss, the seepage. My sepia years. Sorry, Phil, I loved you all I could for six of them, but I'm going to bed with him if he wants me. The big gymnastic sergeant marching marching. It's you I'm going to betray, not him, if I can make it, because he really has something, don't know what. I don't know if he's what he says, but he is a sort of saint. And you did hit him first. You hit him first. You were always free with your fists. You were that.

She went downstairs. Either that running dog wore a tie or she was going acid head like the others.

'It's a bastard work, a mongrel,' he said. He was eating something out of a can; that was now his way, no meals, only snacks, the fuzzy feeder. Kind of impersonal.

'I'm a mongrel, aren't I? Some Gurdjieff, more Ouspenski, time-obsessed passages from here and there, no zen or that – no Englishmen, but it's going to spread from England out, we'll all take it, unite all Europe at last. A gospel. Falling like PCA. America's ready, too. The readiest place, always.'

'If you're happy.' She touched him. He had dropped a baked bean on to the masterwork. It almost covered a word that might be 'self-fulfilment'.

'See those things crawling in the bare trees out there? Elms, are they? Birds as big as turkeys crawling in the trees, and toads, and that new animal. I often see it. There is an intention moving in them, as there is in us. They seem to keep their distance.'

'Darling, you're in ruins, your mind, you should rest!'

'Yes. Happiness is a yesterday phase. Say, think, "tension-release", maintain a sliding scale, and so you do away with sorrow. Get me, you just have a relief from tension, and that's all you need. Nothing so time-consuming as happiness. Nothing personal. If you have sorrow, you are forced to seek its opposite, and vice versa, so you should try to abolish both. Wake, don't live automatic, I'll get it clear. Time ... I must speak to people, address them. You have some gift I need. Come round with me, Angelina? Take me on, share my sack.'

She put her arms about him. The big gymnastic sergeant. There was some stale bread on the table, crumbs among the books he was breaking up and crayoning. Activity all the time, her windows, wind over the turning mounds. 'When you love me, love, there'll be something personal in it?'

'It's all evolving, angel, stacked with loot.'

When the Escalation came along, the two of them were half-lying on the camp-bed, limbs entangled, not actually copulating.

Greta wept, supported by two of the group. Featherstone-Haugh touched a chord on his balalaika and sang, 'Her mother was killed by a sunlit Ford Cortina, and the road snapped shut'.

Ruby Dymond turned his cheeks into a poor grey.

'Man the Driver,' Chapter Three. Literature of the Future Affecting Feeling of the Future. Ouspenski's concept of mental photographs postulates many photographs of the personality taken at characteristic moments; viewed together, these photographs will form a record by which man sees himself to be different from his common conception of himself – and truer. So, they will suggest the route of life without themselves having motion. The truth is in static instants; it is arrived at through motion. Motion of auto-crash, copulation, kinetic self-awak-enings of any kind. There are many alternatives. Fiction to be mental photographs, motion to be supplied purely by reader. Music as harpoon to sleeping entrails, down out the howls of smaller dogs. Action a blemish as already in existence. Truth thus like a pile of photos, self-cancelling for self-fulfilment, multi-valued. Indecision multi-incisive and non-auto-matic Impurity of decision one of the drives towards such truth-piles; the Ouspenskian event of a multiple crash on a modern motorway an extreme example of such impurities.

Wish for truth involved here. Man and landscape interfuse, science presides. Machines predominate.

Charteris stood at the window listening to the noise of the group, looking out at the highly carved landscape. Hedges and trees had no hint of green, were cut from iron, their edges jagged, ungleaming with the brown nearest black, although the winds drove rain shining across the panorama. Middays reduced job-lots from Coventry. Vehicles scouring down the roads trailed spume. Roads like seas like fossilised thought, coproliths of ancestral loinage, father-frigger. The earlier nonsense about the terrors of the population explosion; one learned to live with it. But mistakes still being made. The unemployed were occupied, black midland figures of animated sacks, inplanting young trees along the grand synclines and barrows of the embankments and cuttings and underpasses, thereby destroying their geometry, mistakenly interfusing an abstract of nature back into the grand equation. Got to banish that dark pandemic nature. But the monstrous sky, squelching light out of its darkest corners, counteracted this regressive step towards out-dated reality moulds. The PCA bombs had squirted from the skies; it was their region. Science presided.

> There was a picture of a pretty sailing ship
> Sailing every ha'penny.
>
> The goods you buy with this new coinage
> Weren't made any place I heard of
> They give out the meagerest sounds
> But I don't hear a thing any longer
> Since I do my personal thinking in pounds
>
> I had a good family life and a loving girl
> But I had to trade them in for pounds

The damned birds were coming back, too, booking their saplings, grotesques from the pre-psychedelic twilife, ready to squirt eggs into the first nests at the first opportunity. They moved in squadrons, heavy as lead, settled over the mounds of rubbish, picking out the gaudy Omo packets. They had something planned, they were motion without truth, fugitive, to be hated. He had heard them calling to each other in nervous excitement, 'Omo, Omo'. Down by the shores of the dead sea, down by the iron sunset, they were learning to read, a hostile art. And the new animal was among them by the dead elms.

Angeline was comforting Greta, Ruby watching her every fingertip, Burton was turning the pages of 'Man the Driver', thinking of a black and red tie he had worn, his only tie. Words conveyed truth, he had to admit, but that damned tie had really sent him. He thought he had tied it round the neck of a black dog proceeding down Ashby Road. Spread the message.

'Greet, you didn't hear of a dog involved in this pile-up?'

'Leave her alone,' Angeline said 'Let her cry it out. It's like a tide.'

'There's been a dislocation,' Burton said.

'He did it, you know,' Greta wept. 'You can't have secrets in this city any more. Well, it's more of an urban aggregation than a city, really, I suppose. He pushed the whole chain of events into being, piled up all them lorries, killed by mum and everything.'

'I know,' Angeline said. The heart always so laden, the gulls always so malignant.

In the old kitchen among gash-cans where a single brass tap poured a thin melody out of one note, Ruby had her alone at last clasping her thin wrists by each tapering tendon her face still with youth in its whole imprint.

'Don't start anything, Ruby, get back to play your piece with the boys.'

'You know how I feel about your continued days, how you always play my piece, and now I see you lay with Charteris.'

She pulled from him and he caught her again, a slight look of ox under his eyebrushes. 'I mind mine, you mind yours, you hip me Ruby though I know you mean well!'

'Look, the rumour is he killed Phil —'

Frantic, and a churning mound of rubbish at the sill, 'Ruby, if you are trying to make me —'

'I won't kid, I never liked Phil, you know that, but to go round with the guy who did it —'

She was as thin from her lethargy as stretched teeth could make her. He has something that's all I know, and hope I need among you scene-makers, I don't have to trust him. ...'

In the next room they were calling and formationed birds dipped like sleet across her vision. 'Remember me? I was around before you met Brasher, I knew you when you were a little lanky girl I used to come and play with your brothers, gave you your first kiss –'

'It's looking back, Ruby, looking back,' despairing.

'I thought you loved me, you used to ride on my cycle.'

'It's past, Ruby.' She was afraid of her own tears the very nature of her grottoed self. Leaning back over the choked draining board, she saw the face of him move across her visage like a lantern burning impatience, mutter, turn under its hair-bush and leave her there with the one-note melody unlistened to but ever-piercing.

Creaming crowds in Nottingham to greet the Escalation, teenagers blurry in the streets, hardly whispering, the middle-aged, the old, the crippled and the halt, all those who had not starved, all those who had not died from falling into fires or ditches on roads, all those who had not wandered away after the aerosols drifted down, all those who had not fallen down dead laughing, all those who had not opened their spongy skulls with can-openers to let out the ghosts and the rats. All were hot for the Escalation under the seams of their grey clouts.

After two numbers, the boys, sensational and smelly, had the crowds throwing noise back at them. Burton stood up, announced Saint Charteris, asked if anyone had seen a stray dog wearing a red and black tie. The Escalation howled their new anthem.

Obsolescent Loughborough
With slumthing to live through
Charteris we cry
Is something to live by
Try a multi-valued slant
On the instant instant

*

He had scarcely thought out what he was going to say. The pattern was there, misty or clear. It seemed so apparent he felt it did not need uttering, except they should wake and know what they knew. The slav dreamers, Ouspenski and the rest, sent him travelling with his message through to his outpost of Europe. If the message had validity, it was shaped by journey and arrival. He couldn't always stand helpless across the river. In Metz, he had realised the world was a web of forces. Their minds, their special Midland minds had to become repositories of thinking also web-like, dear but indefinite, instant but infinite.

If they wanted exterior models, the space-time pattern of communicationways with which their landscape was riddled functioned as a master plan, monster plan of mind-pattern. All the incoherent repirations that filled their lives would then fall into place. The empty old nineteenth-century houses built by new classes which now stood rotting in ginger stone on hillsides, carriageways either approached or receded like levels of old lakes, they were not wasted; they functioned as landmarks. No more eggless waters. Nothing should be discarded; everything would re-orient, as the ginger stone mansions or the green stone churches were re-oriented by the changing landscape dynamic, and the crash-ups escalated to a love-in. He was lead of the New Thought. The Fourth World System, Man the Driver, would appear soon, all would wake.

So the words sprang up like bolted birds.

Greta stood and screamed, 'He killed Our Mum! Poor old girl with her flowers! He caused the multi-maxident on the Inner Relief. Kill him! Kill him!'

'Kill him!' also cried Ruby.

White-faced Angeline said from the platform for all to hear, 'And he killed my husband, Phil, you all knew him.' It was sin to her whether she spoke or not; she worked by old moralities, where someone was always betrayed.

Their troubled eyes all turned to his eyes, seeking meaning, like stars in the firment.

'I thought they were going to crucify you,' said Featherstone-Haugh after offering the Serb a glance through perspectives later to be of more transfixion over the desiccated lustrums of western worships, crowns of thorns, crosses of scorn, the love-kill. You couldn't tell the bits of wreckage from the bits of victims. He couldn't stop his heart beating.

'It's true! The lorry was sweeping along the great artery from Glasgow down to Naples, In Naples, they will also mourn. We are all one people now, Europeople, and although this massive region of yours is as special as the Adriatic Coast or the Dutch Lowlands, or the steppes of central Asia, the similarity is also in the differences. It's the impact, as you must feel. You know of my life, that I was Communist like my father, coming from Serbia in Jugoslavia, that I lived long in Italy, dreamed all my while of England and the wide cliffs of Dover. Now I arrive here after the dislocation and fatal events begin, spreading back along my trail. It's a sign. See how in this context even death is multi-valued, the black nearest brown. Brasher falling back into the traffic was a complex impulse-node from which effects still multiplicate along all tension lines. We shall all follow that impulse to the last fracture and serial of recorded time. The Escalation and I are now setting out on a motor-crusade down through our Europe, the autobahns; the war, dislocation, to ultimate unity. All of you come too, a moving event to seize the static instant of truth! Come too! Wake! There are many alternatives!'

They were crying and cheering, discarding I's. It would take on truth be a new legend, a new communication in the ceaseless dialogue, the ground complexes given younger significance. Even Angeline thought, Perhaps he will really give us something to live by, more than the old fun grind. It surely can't really matter, can it, whether there was a dog with a tie or not; the essential thing was that I saw it and stand by that A phenomenon's only itself eh? So it doesn't matter whether he is right or not; just stay in the Banshee with him. Pray the warmth's there, the loot.

You couldn't tell wreckage from victim in the fast-turning shade-shapes of obliquity.

He was talking again, the audience were cheering, the group were improvising a driving song about a Midland-minded girl at the wheel of a sunlit automobile. An ambiguity about whether they meant the steering or the driving wheel.

Plugging the night's orifices with solid sound.

The Intermittent Tattooed Tattered Prepuce

The moonlight of a June night
Casts shadows of crashing airliners
Onto the orthostrada of gaunt erections
Moonlight moonlight
Filling empty patios

And the big gymnastic sergeant's marching marching
And the intermittent tattooed tattered prepuce
Does bayonet practice on a sweet civilian girl

Oh love's a crash a parade-ground bash
An auto-immune disorder from which issues
A pair of bodies destroying their own tissues

Left right left right left
In out in out on guard
Lovers of the world unite
You've nothing to lose but appetite
If winter comes can the following one
Be more than a year away

Could this be loot because I feel
The flying human parts and the bits of steel
In an auto-concussion are the modern way
The military way
Of committing love

And the big gymnastic sergeant's marching marching
And the intermittent tattooed tattered prepuce
Does bayonet practice on a syphilitic civilian girl

Oh love's a smash a uniform cash
Negotiable when the moving parts peeling
Can autocade feeling anti-flowered healing speedily stealing
And the big gymnastic leather-cheeked sergeant's marching
    marching marching

And the intermittent inter-continental tattered tattooed
      prepuce prepuce
Does bayonet practice on a civilised civilian sybaritic syphilitic
Bayonet practice on a civilised civilian sybaritic syphilitic
               Civilised civilian sybaritic syphilitic
               Civilised civilian sybaritic syphilitic
                         Supergirl
Left right left right
Moonlight moonlight
Up the motorways of love

PHIL, BILL, RUBY AND FEATHERSTONE-HAUGH

Small Dogs Howling

When you sank on my knee in the buggy
You forked your loving tongue in my mouth
And you worked me and made me come

Though your hair didn't fit you properly
I still resemble the blur of your fingers
When the small dogs are howling

    Tray Blanche and Sweetheart on the hem
    Oh throw your acidhead at them

Lives deprived and broken
Bottles empty by dawn
While we were crotching together
Did you mind my shoes was torn

Some place like a magic garden
My friends all call me Rajah
And I'm a demon on the cello

Don't ask me what we're doing on the heath love
Because the estate has become divided
And we're one with the ones who won

This place well the car broke down
But the street lamps were your tall wild lilies
And I couldn't hear the small dogs howling

    Tray Blanche and Sweetheart on the hem
    Oh throw your acidhead at them

THE MELLOW BELLOW

Dreaming

Swept under sleep's terminator
We send out blindfold signals
To a listener in dim Andromeda
We send out our folded signals
To the listeners in all Andromedas
Hoping dreading response

Beyond the lighted alleyways
The multi-motorways of time
Yesterday's day regurgitates
Itself back through the limbic brain
Backwards rattling through orifices
Of ancient bugging systems

Alpha rhythms delta rhythms
Dark transmissions old as sandstone
Wild as pop
      Between communiques
Another sleep-form new-invented
Topiaries upwards outwards
         Through our
Dull planetary bodies other
Messages secreted in the pores
Are also played out backwards
On an unknown waveband

   These thin signals
Pipe from us in automated
Bursts
     To be picked up on stars
        White dwarfs
Monitored in nebulae
Identified
In other galaxies as

      'Dark

Bodies hitherto quite unsuspected'
And still between all human noises
Our figures with their own intent
Run daylight and silence backwards

When you target in to my
Perceptions
Am I reading you?
My fullness is a part
Of your thin signals
My visions
Wreckage of your orbit

From *The Threepenny Space Opera*

Another Dreaming Poem

My letters delay in their personal boxes
Uncertainty is on the whole my element
And the astrabahns bifurcate steeply

Low temperatures
Curtains drawn tight
A blur on the papered walls
And the night branches drooping
On the furred paths of grass

What you might call my pessimism
Is merely a long dedication
Of involved enquiry
Passionate and still deepening
Into the lost events of everybody's

Days those past and those to come
And those standing on end unsorted
In the night's post orifices

The great well of personal stuff
I don't know or wish to know
Floods me with messages

Is it myself
I walk with or happiness
Found in the low night street
Footsteps on the pavement
Echoing in more than one house

Pattern More Than City Mind

The city has built-in pattern
    city
    city   pattern
    city
          built-in pattern

Mind is more than city
        more than city
Mind   more
         more than
Mind   city

Roads run like fossil thought
       run
              fossil
              fossil
          like fossil

Mind   more
    city
      roads
         fossil
Built-in   thought

Cities
Cities have   patterns
      built-in
Cities
Cities have built-in patterns

       more
Minds are more
Minds
Minds
Minds are more than cities

   road   thoughts
A road   fossilised
   road runs
   road runs
A road runs like fossilised thoughts

Roads   patterns
      runs
         cities
             fossilised
Thoughts   minds

WE'RE ALL FOR THE DARK!
Or, Life's Never Been Better

If you've ever sailed on the ocean
Or cheered when a port hove in sight
There's one thing you'll know – that emotion
Is better indulged in at night!

Since the time when old Noah
Spent those nights in the Ark
With the animals pairing –
It's best after dark!

CHORUS: Life's never been better!
Each night lasts a year –
Stuffed with women and music
And piss-ups and beer!

The girls that by daylight
Would blush to be stark,
Decide that their blushes
Won't show in the dark!

CHORUS: Lift's never been better, etc.

Just yesterday breakfast,
We got lit in the park –
And the fire went on burning
Till long after dark.

CHORUS: Life's never been better, etc.

Next morning so early,
We were up with the lark.
We shot it down dead and –
Crawled back in the dark!

CHORUS: Life's never been better, etc.

If you lose your way travelling
And the small dogs do bark,
All the signposts will tell you –
'This way to the dark!'

CHORUS: Life's never been better, etc.

As Jesus remarked once
To Matthew and Mark,
'To Hell with Big Daddy –
We're all for the dark!'

CHORUS: Life's never been better!

Each night lasts a year –
Stuffed with women and music
And piss-ups and beer!
Stuffed with women and music
And piss-ups and beer!

ANONYMOUS

Through The New Arcade

My sweet sweet Phil so often brutal
My bloody Phil so sometimes gentle
The trouble was you didn't love enough
You didn't have to hit him
Those years
I'm too sentimental
You were always too bloody sodding rough
You were too much like my mother
Completely misreading universal patterns
Thinking you could always have your way
Oh Christ my sweet damned Phil
You burst apart
Bits of body wreckage
I never knew I never knew another
Human being was that frail I always hated
All that ranting made me ill
Deep in my heart
You tired me
Even before my sticky-fingered schooldays
I'd learned to sweat it out and all about
But I'm too sentimental
Hanging on to any hand that waited
Well you inspired me
You burst apart
Once and so I stuck by you
The fool I was
                    When you've been crated
You'll see you'll see I saw
The way he looked at me I liked it
And he took your blows so gentle
And he spoke as if he knew
Of universal patterns far beyond me
Perhaps he recognised I could be true

Trying to Low

Angline
Anjline
Angelea
Agelea
Aglina
Agline
Can I miss-spell your attitudes
Speech is silver silence earns no interest
Angeline think of me in your own coin
Angline
Gelina
Jellybeana
Agile Geline
In the timescapes of your countenance
My hopes stand paralysed
Paraphrased in flesh and pore
O Ingeline
Itchelino
Age Old Ina
One day I'll get it right

The Night that All Time Broke Out

The dentist bowed her smiling to the door, dialling a cab for her as he went. It alighted on the balcony as she emerged.

It was a non-automatic type, old-fashioned enough to be considered chic. Fifi Fevertrees smiled dazzlingly at the driver and climbed in.

'Extra-city service,' she said. 'The village of Rouseville, off Route Z4.'

'You live in the country, huh?' said the cab driver, sailing up into the pseudo-blue, and steering like a madman with one foot.

'The country's okay,' Fifi said defensively. She hesitated and then decided she could allow herself to boast. 'Besides, it's even better now they got the time mains out there. We're just being connected to the time main at our house – it should be finished when I get home.'

The cabby shrugged. 'Reckon it's costly out in the country.'

'Three payts a basic unit.'

He whistled significantly.

She wanted to tell him more, wanted to tell him how excited she was, how she wished daddy was alive to experience the fun of being on the time main. But it was difficult to say anything with a thumb in her mouth, as she looked into her wrist mirror and probed to see what the dentist had done to her.

He'd done a good job. The new little pearly tooth was already growing firmly in the pink gum. Fifi decided she had a very sexy mouth, just as Tracey said. And the dentist had removed the old tooth by time gas. So simple. Just a whiff of it and she was back in the day before yesterday, reliving that pleasant little interlude when she had taken coffee with

Peggy Hackenson, with not a thought of any pain. Time gas was so smart these days. She positively glowed to think they would have it themselves, on tap all the while.

The bubble cab soared up and out of one of the dilating ports of the great dome that covered the city. Fifi felt a momentary sorrow at leaving. The cities were so pleasant nowadays that nobody wished to live outside them. Everything was double as expensive outside, too, but fortunately the government paid a hardship allowance for anyone like the Fevertrees, who had to live in the country.

In a couple of minutes they were sailing down to the ground again. Fifi pinpointed their dairy farm, and the cabby set them neatly down on their landing balcony before holding out his paw for an extortionate number of kilopayts. Only when he had the cash did he lean back and unlock Fifi's door with one foot. You couldn't put a thing over these chimp drivers.

She forgot all about him as she hurried down through the house. This was the day of days! It had taken the builders two months to install the central timing – two weeks longer than they had originally anticipated – and everywhen had been in an awful muddle all that time, as the men trundled their pipes and wires through every room. Now all was orderly once more. She positively danced down the stairs to find her husband.

Tracey Fevertrees was standing in the kitchen, talking to the builder. When his wife burst in, he turned and took her hand, smiling in a way that was merely soothing to her, though it disturbed the slumbers of many a local Rouseville maiden. But his good looks could hardly match her beauty when she was excited as she was at present.

'Is it all in working order?' she asked.

'There is just one last-minute snag,' Mr Archibald Smith said grudgingly.

'Oh, there's always a last-minute snag! We've had fifteen of them in the last week, Mr Smith. What now?'

'It's nothing that should affect you here. It's just that, as you know, we had to pipe the time gas rather a long way to you from the main supply down at Rouseville works, and we seem to have a bit of trouble maintaining pressure. There's talk of a nasty leak at the main pit in the works, which they're having a job to plug. But that shouldn't worry you.'

'We've tested it all out here and it seems to work fine,' Tracey said to his wife. 'Come on and I'll show you!'

They shook hands with Mr Smith, who showed a traditional builderly reluctance to leave the site of his labours. Finally he moved off, promising to be back in the morning to pick up a last bag of tools, and Tracey and Fifi were left alone with their new toy.

Among all the other kitchen equipment, the time panel hardly stood out. It was situated next to the nuclear unit, a discreet little fixture with a dozen small dials and twice that number of toggle switches.

He pointed out to her how the time pressures had been set: low for corridors and offices, higher for bedrooms, variable for the living room. She rubbed herself against him and made an imitation purr.

'You are thrilled, aren't you, honey?' she asked.

'I keep thinking of the bills we have to pay. And the bills to come – three payts a basic unit – wow!' Then he saw her look of disappointment and added, 'But of course I love it, darling. You know I'm going to be delighted.'

Then they bustled through the house, with the controls on. In the kitchen itself, they set themselves back to a recent early midmorning. They floated in time past at the time of day Fifi favoured most for kitchen work, when the breakfast chores were over and it was long before the hour when lunch need be planned and dialled. Fifi and Tracey had selected a morning when she had been feeling particularly calm and well; the entire ambience of that period swept over them now.

'*Mar*vellous! Delicious! I can do anything, cook you anything, now!'

They kissed each other, and ran into the corridor, crying, 'Isn't science wonderful!'

They stopped abruptly. 'Oh no!' Fifi cried.

The corridor was in perfect order, the drapes in place and gleaming metallically by the two windows, controlling the amount of light that entered, storing the surplus for off-peak hours, the creep-carpet in place and resprayed, carrying them smoothly forward, the panelling all warm and soft to the touch. But they were time-controlled back to three o'clock of an afternoon a month ago, a peaceful time of day – except that a month ago the builders had been at work here.

'Honey, they'll ruin the carpet! And I just know the panelling will not go back properly! Oh, Tracey, look – they've disconnected the drapes, and Smithy promised not to!'

He clutched her shoulder. 'Honey, everything's in order, honest!'

'It's not! It's not in order! Look at these dirty old time tubes everywhere, and all these cables hanging about! They've ruined our lovely dust-absorbent ceiling – look at the way it's leaking dirt over *everything*!'

'Honey, it's the time effect!' But he had to admit that he could not credit the perfect corridor his eyes registered; he was carried away like Fifi by his emotions of a month ago when he viewed the place as it had been then, in the hands of Smithy and his terrible men.

They reached the end of the passage and jumped into the bedroom, escaping into another time zone. Peeping back through the door, Fifi said tearfully, 'Gosh, Trace, the power of time! I guess we just have to alter the controls for the corridor, eh?'

'Sure, we'll tune in to a year ago, say a nice summer's afternoon along the passage. You name it, we dial it! That's the motto of Central Time Board, isn't it? Anyhow, how do you like the time in here?'

After gazing round the bedroom, she lowered her long lashes at him. 'Mm, sort of relaxed, isn't it?'

'Two o'clock in the morning, honey, early spring, and everyone in the whole zone sleeping tight. We aren't likely to suffer from insomnia now!'

She came and stood against him, leaning on his chest and looking up at him. 'You don't think that maybe eleven at night would be a more – well, *bedroomy* time?'

'You know I prefer the sofa for that sort of thing, honey. Come and sit on it with me and see what you think about the living room.'

The living room was one flight down, with only the garage and the dairy on the two floors below between them and the ground. It was a fine large room with fine large windows looking over the landscape to the distant dome of the city, and it had a fine large sofa standing in the middle of it.

They sat down on this voluptuous sofa and, past associations being what they were, commenced to cuddle. After a while Tracey reached down to the floor and pulled up a hand-switcher that was plugged into the wall.

'We can control our own time from here, without getting up, Fifi! You name the time and we flip back to it.'

'If you're thinking of what I *think* you're thinking, then we'd better not go back more than ten months because we weren't married before that.'

'Now, come on, Mrs Fevertrees, are you getting old-fashioned or some-thing? You never let that thought bother you before we were married.'

'I did too! – Though maybe more *after* than at the time, when I was sort of carried away.'

He stroked her pretty hair gently. 'Tell you what I thought we could try sometime – dial back to when you were twelve. You must have been very sexy in your preteens, and I'd sure as hell love to find out. How about it?'

She was about to deliver some conventional female rebuke, but her imagination got the better of her. 'We could work back to when we were tots!'

'Attaboy! You know I have a touch of the Lolita complex!'

'Trace – we must be careful unless in our excitement we shoot back past the day we were born, or we'll wind up little blobs of protoplasm or something.'

'Honey, you read the brochures! When we get up enough pressure to go right past our birth dates, we simply enter the consciousness of our nearest predecessors of the same sex – you your mother, me my father, and then your grandmother and my grandfather. Farther back than that, time pressure in the Rouseville mains won't let us go.'

Conversation languished under other interests until Fifi murmured dreamily, 'What a heavenly invention time is! Know what, even when we're old and grey and impotent, we'll be able to come back and enjoy ourselves as we were when we were young. We'll dial back to this very instant, won't we?'

'Mmmm,' he said. It was a universally shared sentiment.

That evening, they dined off a huge synthetic lobster. In her excitement over being on the time mains, Fifi had somehow dialled a slightly incorrect mixture – though she swore there was a misprint in the cookbook programming she had fed the kitchputer – and the dish was not all it should be. But they dialled themselves back to the time of one of the first and finest lobsters they had ever eaten together, shortly after their meeting two years before. The remembered taste took off the disappointment of the present taste.

While they were eating, the pressure went.

There was no sound. Externally, all was the same. But inside their heads, they felt themselves whirling through the days like leaves blown over a moor. Mealtimes came and went, and the lobster was sickening in their mouths as they seemed to chew in turn turkey, or cheese, or game, or trifle or sponge pudding or ice cream or breakfast cereal. For several mind-wrenching moments they sat there at table, petrified, while hundreds of assorted tastes chased themselves over their taste buds. Tracey jumped up gasping and cut off the time flow entirely at the switch by the door.

'Something's gone wrong!' he exclaimed. 'It's that guy Smith. I'll dial him straightaway. I'll shoot him!'

But when Smith's face floated up in the vision tank, it was as bland as ever.

'The fault's not mine, Mr Fevertrees. As a matter of fact, one of my men just dialled me to say that there's trouble at the Rouseville time works, where your pipe joins the main supply. Time gas is leaking out. I told you this morning they were having some bother there. Go to bed, Mr Fevertrees – that's my suggestion. Go to bed, and in the morning all will probably be fixed again.'

'Go to bed! How dare he tell us to go to bed!' Fifi exclaimed. 'What an immoral suggestion! He's trying to hide something, that man. I'll bet this is some mistake of his and he's covering up with this story about a leak at the time works.'

'We can soon check on that. Let's drive down there and see!'

They caught the elevator down to the ground floor and climbed into their land vehicle. City folk might laugh at these little wheeled hovercraft, so quaintly reminiscent of the automobiles of bygone days, but there was no doubt that they were indispensable in the country outside the domes, where free public transport did not reach.

The doors opened and they rolled out, taking off immediately and floating forward a couple of feet above the ground. Rouseville lay over a low hill, and the time works was just on the far fringe of it. But as they sighted the first houses, something strange happened.

Though all was quiet, the land vehicle began to jerk around wildly. Fifi was flung about, and the next moment they were stuck in a hedge.

'Heck, these things are heavy! I must learn to drive one sometime!' Tracey said, climbing out.

'Aren't you going to help me down, Tracey?'

'Aw, I'm too big to play with girls!'

'You gotta help me! I lost my dolly!'

'You never had no dolly! Nuts to you!'

He ran on across the field and she had to follow him, calling as she ran. It was just so difficult trying to control the clumsy heavy body of an adult with the mind of a child.

She found her husband sitting in the middle of the Rouseville road, kicking and waving his arms. He giggled at her. 'Tace go walkey-walkey!' he said.

But in a few moments they were able to move along again on foot, though it was painful for Fifi, whose mother had been lame toward the end of her life. Together they hobbled forward, two young things in old postures. When they entered the little domeless village, it was to find most of the inhabitants about, and going through the whole spectrum of human age-characteristics, from burbling infancy to rattling senility. Obviously, something serious had happened at the time works.

Ten minutes and a few generations later, they arrived at the gates. Standing below the Central Time Board sign was Smith. They did not recognise him; he was wearing an anti-time gas mask, its exhaust spluttering as it spat out old moments.

'I thought you two might turn up!' he exclaimed. 'Didn't believe me, eh? Well, you'd better come in with me and see for yourselves. They've struck a major gusher and the cocks couldn't stand the pressure and collapsed. My guess is they'll have to evacuate the whole area before they get this one fixed.'

As he led them through the gates, Tracey said, 'I just hope this isn't Ruskie sabotage!'

'Rusty what?'

'Ruskie sabotage. The work of the Russians. I presume this plant is secret?'

Smith stared at him in amazement. 'You gone crazy, Mr Fevertrees? The Russian nation got time mains just the same as us. You were on honeymoon in Odessa last year, weren't you?'

'Last year, I was on active service in Korea, thank you!'

'Korea?!'

With mighty siren noises, a black shape bearing red flashing lights above and below its bulk settled itself down in the Time Board yard.

It was a robot-piloted fire engine from the city, but its human crew tumbled out in a weird confusion, and one young fellow lay yelling for his pants to be changed before the Time Board men could issue them with anti-time gas masks. And then there was no fire for them to extinguish, only the great gusher of invisible time that by now towered over the building and the whole village, and blew to the four corners, carrying unimagined or forgotten generations on its mothproof breath.

'Let's get forward and see what we can see,' Smith said. 'We might just as well go home and have a drink as stand here doing nothing.'

'You are a very foolish young man if you mean what I suppose you to mean,' Fifi said, in an ancient and severe voice. 'Most of the liquor currently available is bootleg and unsafe to consume – but in any case, I believe we should support the President in his worthy attempt to stamp out alcoholism, don't you, Tracey darling?'

But Tracey was lost in an abstraction of strange memory, and whistling 'La Paloma' under his breath to boot.

Stumbling after Smith, they got to the building, where two police officials stopped them. At that moment a plump man in a formal suit appeared and spoke to one of the police through his gas mask. Smith hailed him, and they greeted each other like brothers. It turned out they were brothers. Clayball Smith beckoned them all into the plant, gallantly taking Fifi's arm – which, to reveal his personal tragedy, was about as much as he ever got of any pretty girl.

'Shouldn't we have been properly introduced to this gentleman, Tracey?' Fifi whispered to her husband.

'Nonsense, my dear. Rules of etiquette have to go by the board when you enter one of the temples of industry.' As he spoke, Tracey seemed to stroke an imaginary side whisker.

Inside the time plant chaos reigned. Now the full magnitude of the disaster was clear. They were pulling the first miners out of the hole where the time explosion had occurred; one of the poor fellows was cursing weakly and blaming George III for the whole terrible matter.

The whole time industry was still in its infancy. A bare ten years had elapsed since the first of the subterrenes, foraging far below the Earth's crust, had discovered the time pockets. The whole matter was still a cause for wonder, and investigations were as yet at a comparatively early stage.

But big business had stepped in and, with its usual bigheartedness, seen that everyone got his fair share of time, at a price. Now the time industry had more capital invested than any other industry in the world. Even in a tiny village like Rouseville, the plant was worth millions. But the plant had broken down right now.

'It's terrible dangerous here – you folks better not stay long,' Clayball said. He was shouting through his gas mask. The noise here was terrible, especially since a news commentator had just started his spiel to the nation a yard away.

In answer to a shouted question from his brother, Clayball said, 'No, it's more than a crack in the main supply. That was just the cover story we put out. Our brave boys down there struck a whole new time seam and it's leaking out all over the place. Can't plug it! Half our guys were back to the Norman Conquest before we guessed what was wrong.' He pointed dramatically down through the tiles beneath their feet.

Fifi could not understand what on earth he was talking about. Ever since leaving Plymouth, she had been adrift, and that not entirely metaphorically. It was bad enough playing Pilgrim Mother to one of the Pilgrim Fathers, but she did not dig this New World at all. It was now beyond her comprehension to understand that the vast resources of modern technology were fouling up the whole time schedule of a planet.

In her present state, she could not know that already the illusions of the time gusher were spreading across the continent. Almost every communication satellite shuttling above the world was carrying more or less accurate accounts of the disaster and the events leading up to it, while their bemused audiences sank back through the generations like people plumbing bottomless snowdrifts.

From these deposits came the supply of time that was piped to the million million homes of the world. Experts had already computed that at present rates of consumption all the time deposits would be exhausted in two hundred years. Fortunately, other experts were already at work trying to develop synthetic substitutes for time. Only the previous month, the small research team of Time Pen Inc., of Ink, Penn, had announced the isolation of a molecule nine minutes slower than any other molecule known to science, and it was firmly expected that even more isolated molecules would follow.

Now an ambulance came skidding up, with another behind it. Archibald Smith tried to pull Tracey out of the way.

'Unhand me, varlet!' quoth Tracey, attempting to draw an imaginary sword. But the ambulance men were jumping out of their vehicles, and the police were cordoning off the area.

'They're going to bring up our brave terranauts!' Clayball shouted.

He could hardly be heard above the hubbub. Masked men were everywhere, with here and there the slender figure of a masked nurse. Supplies of oxygen and soup were being marshalled, searchlights swung overhead, blazing down into the square mouth of the inspection pit. The men in yellow overalls were lowering themselves into the pit, communicating to each other by wrist radio. They disappeared. For a moment a hush of awe fell over the building and seemed to spread to the crowds outside.

But the moment stretched into minutes, and the noise found its way back to its own level. More grim-faced men came forward, and the commentators were pushed out of the picture.

'It thinks me we should suffer ourselves to get gone from here, by God's breath!' Fifi whispered faintly, clutching at her homespun with a trembling hand. 'This likes me not!'

At last there was activity at the head of the pit. Sweating men in overalls hauled on ropes. The first terranaut was pulled into view, wearing the characteristic black uniform of his kind. His head lolled back, his mask had been ripped away, but he was fighting bravely to retain consciousness. Indeed, a debonair smile crossed his pale lips, and he waved a hand at the cameras. A ragged cheer went up from the onlookers.

This was the intrepid breed of men that went down into the uncharted seas of time gas below the Earth s crust, risking their lives to bring back a nugget of knowledge from the unknown, pushing back still further the boundaries of science, unsung and unhonoured by all save the constant battery of world publicity.

The ace commentator had struggled through the crowd to reach the terranaut and was trying to question him, holding a microphone to his lips while the hero's tortured face swam before the unbelieving eyes of a billion viewers.

'Hell down there. ... Dinosaurs and their young,' he managed to gasp, before he was whisked into the first ambulance. 'Right down deep in the gas. Packs of 'em, ravening. ... Few more hundred feet lower and we'd have fetched ... fetched up against the creation ... of the world. ...'

They could hear no more. Now fresh police reinforcements were clearing the building of all unauthorised persons before the other terranauts were returned to the surface, although of their earth capsule there was as yet no sign. As the armed cordon approached, Fifi and Tracey made a dash for it. They could stand no more, they could understand no more. They pelted for the door, oblivious to the cries of the two masked Smiths. As they ran out into the darkness, high above them towered the great invisible plume of the time gusher, still blowing, blowing its doom about the world.

For some while they lay gasping in the nearest hedge. Occasionally one of them would whimper like a tiny girl, or the other would groan like an old man. Between times, they breathed heavily.

Dawn was near to breaking when they pulled themselves up and made along the track toward Rouseville, keeping close to the fields.

They were not alone. The inhabitants of the village were on the move, heading away from the homes that were now alien to them and beyond their limited understanding. Staring at them from under his lowering brow, Tracey stopped and fashioned himself a crude cudgel from the hedgerow.

Together, the man and his woman trudged over the hill, heading back for the wilds like most of the rest of humanity, their bent and uncouth forms silhouetted against the first ragged banners of light in the sky.

'Ugh glumph hum herm morm glug humk,' the woman muttered.

Which means, roughly translated from the Old Stone, 'Why the heck does this always have to happen to mankind just when he's on the goddam point of getting civilised again?'

Afterword:

If ever a dangerous vision was rooted in real life, 'The Night That All Time Broke Out' is. I should explain that I am at present living in a remote corner of Oxfordshire, England, where I have purchased a marvellous old sixteenth-century house, all stone and timber and thatch, and considerably slumped in disrepair. I said to my friend Jim Ballard, the SF writer, 'It looks as if it's some strange vegetable form that has grown out of the ground,' and he replied, 'Yes, and it looks as if it's now growing back in again.'

In an effort to keep the house above ground, my wife and I decided to have it put on to main drainage and fill in the old cesspit. Our builders immediately surrounded the place with gigantic ditching systems and enormous pipes. In the thick of it all, I wondered how future generations would cope with similar problems. The result you see here.

At a rough count, this is my one hundred and tenth published story. I gave up work ten years ago and took up writing instead. It was one of the best ideas I ever had. I believe my story presented here contains one of the whackiest ideas I ever had. (Let's hope there are a few more whacky ideas in my head – I'd hate to have to go back to work. ...)

Randy's Syndrome

Gordana stood in the foyer of the Maternity Hospital, idly watching cubision as she waited for Sonia Greenslade. A university programme was showing shots of fleas of the cliff swallow climbing up a cliff swallow's legs, alternating with close-ups of a cadaverous professor delivering himself at length on the subject of parasitology. Gordana felt convinced that she could understand him if she tried, and if there were not weightier things on her mind.

When Sonia came up, her face crimson, she took Gordana's arm and tried to hustle her away.

'Just a moment,' Gordana said. A line of fleas was working its way steadily up a sheet of damp laboratory glass. 'Negative geotropism!'

'Let's get out of here, honey!' Sonia begged. She tugged Gordana towards the stride-strip entrance of the hospital, looking rather like a mouse towing a golden hamster – for she was only five months on the way against the blonde Gordana's nine-month season. 'Let's get home – you can watch GB in my place if you like. I just can't bear to stay here one moment longer. I was brought up modest. The things that doctor does to a woman without turning a hair! – Makes me want to die!'

The high colour disappeared from her cheeks as they sped homewards along the strip. This was the quietest time of day in their level, mid-morning, when most of the millions of the city's inhabitants were swallowed into offices and factories. For all that, the moving streets with their turntable intersections were spilling over with people, the monoducts hissed overhead, and beneath their feet they could feel and hear the snarl of the subwalk supply lanes. Both women were glad to get into Block 661.

'Maybe we'd better go into the canteen,' Sonia suggested, as they swept into the porch. 'John was on night duty last night, and he's bound to be writing now. He'll get all neurotic if we disturb him.'

Gordana just wanted to be by herself; but since she was wrapped in placidity at this period, she said nothing, allowing her voluble little friend to drag her into the bright-lit canteen on the second level. She sank gratefully into a chair, setting her bulk down into comfort with a sigh.

'He sure works hard,' Sonia said. 'He's nearly finished the eighteenth chapter.'

'Good.' Although the Greenslades happened to live in a flat on the same floor as Gordana and Randy, Gordana doubted whether they would ever have become friends but for the chance of their pregnancies coinciding. Randy was a simple guy who worked on an assembly line in the day and watched cubision and cuddled his wife in the evening; John was a scholar who packaged dinner cereals all night and wrote a book on the Effect of the Bible on Western Civilisation, 1611–2005, during the day. Gordana was large and content, Sonia was small and nervous. The more Sonia talked, the more Gordana retreated into her little world dominated by her loving husband and, increasingly, her unborn child.

Together, the two girls scanned the canteen menu. Rodent's meat was in fashion this week; the man at the next table was eating chinchilla con carne. Sonia ordered a beaver-berger. Gordana settled for a cup of coffeemix.

'Go on and eat if you want to; it's all the same to me.'

She looked round nervously. The voice sounded so terribly loud to her, a shout that filled her being, yet nobody else noticed a thing. 'Just coffeemix,' she sub-vocalised. Mercifully, silence then; it had gone back into its mysterious slumbers, but she knew it would soon rouse completely and wanted to be alone with it when that happened.

'... Still and all, I mustn't keep on about John,' Sonia said. 'It's just – well, you know, he works such long hours and I don't get enough sleep and he will play back what he's written so loud. Some of it is very interesting, especially the bit he's got to now about the Bible and evolution. John says that even if the Bible was wrong about evolution and society, that's no reason for it to have been banned by the government in 2005, and that it doesn't have the harmful effects that they claim. … Say, honey, what did the medics say about you back at the hospital? Didn't they say you were overdue?'

'Yep, ten days overdue. My gynaecologist wants to induce it next week, but I'm not going to let him. Men never have any faith in nature. I want my baby born when it wants to be born and not before.'

Sonia tilted her little head to one side and fluttered her eyes in admiration 'My, you're so good at sticking up for yourself, Gordana Hicks, I just wish I were that brave. But suppose they grab you next week and *force* you to go through with it?'

'I'm not going back there next week, Sonia.'

'But I'll be lonely there without you!'

'You'll get by.'

'Oh, I'll never get by. I get just so embarrassed, it isn't true. And having to sit in that hot room with all those other girls with no panties on for half an hour, and you can guess they are all placed the same way.' She glanced anxiously at the man at the next table to see if he had heard what she said. 'Well, I just think they run that place as if it was an assembly line of breeding cows.'

'They're certainly crowded –'

'Crowded! I said to one of the other girls, I said, "They run this place as if it was an assembly line of breeding cows", and do you know what she told me – big woman with straggly hair and her breath smells of garlic – she said that a million and a half babies are born every week in this city alone! So you see why –'

Gordana laughed, the mellow chime that her husband claimed would open any door. 'A million and a half babies a week! No, I don't believe it.'

'Well, perhaps it was a million and a half a year. But whatever it was, I can tell you it was a pretty high figure and this woman said the city authorities were desperate about living space and the food shortage. Wouldn't care to finish my beaver-berger, would you?'

'It's the fault of the men,' Gordana said crisply, rising to her feet. 'They got us in this condition; they should organise the world better, Instead, all they do is talk.'

'Isn't that just what I tell John,' Sonia agreed, wiping her mouth. 'He says it's the influence of the Bible still lingering on, with all its "go forth and multiply" propaganda. But men have always got excuses – the longer I live with them, really, the more I despise them. I know my mother used to say "Familiarity breeds contempt".'

'But you can't breed without it,' called the man at the next table, smiling coarsely over his plate of meat.

Offended, the two women whisked out of the canteen, though Gordana's whisk was remarkably like a lumber.

Gordana kept their flat very tidy and cleaned, or had done until the languors of this last month. Not that there was much to keep clean. She and Randy had a single room in which to live, ten feet by twelve, with a bed that swung ingeniously down from the ceiling. Their one un-opening window looked on to the hissing monoduct, so that they generally kept it opaqued.

They were six levels below ground level. Their building, a low *avant garde* one situated in the suburbs, had thirty-two stories, twenty-four of them above ground. With luck, and not too many kids, they might expect to rise, on Randy's pay-scale, to the twenty-eighth floor in successful middle age, only to sink back underground, layer by layer, year by year, like sediment, as they grew older and less able to earn. Unless something awful happened, like civilisation falling or bursting apart at the seams, as it threatened to do.

Having left Sonia at her flat door, tiptoeing in to see if John was working or sleeping, Gordana put her feet up in her own room and massaged her ankles. Listlessly, she switched on the wall taper, to listen to the daily news that had just popped through the slot.

It had nothing to offer by way of refreshment. The project for levelling the Rocky Mountains was meeting trouble; the plague of mutated fish was still climbing out of the sea near Atlantic City, covering sidewalks a foot deep; the birth rate had doubled in the last ten years, the suicide rate in the last five; Jackie 'Knees' Norris, famed CB star, was unconscious from a stroke. Abroad, there was a rash of troubles. Europe was about to blow itself up, Indonesia had done so. Gordana switched off before the catalogue was complete.

A vague claustrophobia seized her. She just wished Randy earned enough to let them live up in the daylight. She wanted her baby brought up in daylight.

'Then why doesn't Randy study for a better job?'

'Negative geotropism,' she answered aloud. 'We work our way up towards the sun like the fleas working their way up the swallow's legs.'

The foetus made no attempt to understand that, perhaps guessing that it was never likely to meet either swallows or fleas in the flesh. Instead, it repeated its question in the non-voice that roared through Gordana's being, *'Why doesn't Randy study for a better job?'*

'Do try and call him Daddy, or Pop, not Randy. It makes it sound as if I wasn't married to him for the next five years.'

'Why doesn't he try and get a better job?'

'Darling, you are about to emerge into a suffocatingly overcrowded world. There's no room for *anything* any longer, not even for success. But your dad and me are happy as things are, and I don't want him worrying. Look at that John Greenslade! He spent five years working at the CB University course, doubling up on History and Religion and Literature streams, and where'd it get him when he took his diploma? Why, nowhere – all places were filled. So he drives himself and his wife mad, working all his spare hours, trying to pump all that education back out of his system into some magnabook that nobody is going to publish. No, my boy, we're just fine as we are. You'll see as soon as you arrive!'

'I don't want to arrive!'

'So you keep saying – it was the first thing you ever said to me, three months ago. But nature must take its course.'

Ironically, his voice echoed hers: *'Nature must take its course.'*

He had heard her say it often enough, or listened to it echo round her thoughts since the time he had first made her aware that his intelligence was no longer dormant. Gordana had never been scared. The embryo was a part of her, its booming and soundless voice – produced, she suspected, as much in her own head as in his little cranium that was fed by her blood-stream – seemed as much part of her as the weight she carried before her.

Randy had been hostile when she told him about the conversations at first. She still wondered what he really thought, but was grateful that he seemed resigned to the situation; she wanted no trouble. Perhaps he still did not fully believe, just because he could not hear that monstrous tiny voice himself. However he had managed it, he seemed content with things as they were.

But when Randy returned that evening, he had a nasty surprise for her. She knew something was wrong the moment he came in, even before he kissed her.

'We're in trouble, old pet,' he said. He was pale, small, squat – The Packaged Modern Man, she thought, with nothing but affection – and tonight the genial look about his eyes was extinguished. 'I've notice to quit at the end of the week.'

'Oh, sweetie, why? They can't do this to you, you know they can't! You were so good at the job, I'm sure!'

After the usual protestations, he broke off and tried to explain.

'It's this World Reallocation of Labour Act – they're closing the factory down. Everyone's been fired.'

'They can't do that!' she wailed. 'People will always need wrist-computers!'

'Sure they will, but we manufacture for the Mid-European block. Now we've set up a factory in Prague, Czechoslovakia, that is going to turn out all parts on the spot, cut distribution costs, give employment to a million Mid-Europeans.'

'What about a million Mid-Americans!'

'Hon, you think we got over-population problems, you should see Europe!'

'But we're at *war* with Czechoslovakia!'

He sighed. You couldn't explain these things to women. 'That's just a political war,' he said, 'like our contained war with Mongolia, but a degree less hot. Don't forget that the Czechs are not only in the Comblok politically, they are now in the Eurcom economically, not to mention Natforce strategically. We have to help those goddamned Czechs or bust.'

'So you're bust,' she sighed.

Randy was annoyed. 'I could have broken this news better if you could still manage to sit on my knee. When are you going to give birth, I want to know? What are they going to do about it down at that goddamned hospital?'

'Randy Hicks, I will give birth when I am good and ready and not before.'

'It's all very well for you, but how do you think a man feels? I want you with your figure back again, sweetie pie.' He sank to his knees against her, whispering, 'I want to love you again, sugar, show you how much I love you.'

'Oh no, you don't!' she exclaimed. 'We've only been married ten months yet! I know you went against the law, Randy, I'm not a fool. We're just not going to have a whole brood of kids – I want to see daylight through my window before I die – I –'

'Daylight! All you think of is daylight!'

'Tell him I won't be born until the world is a fit place to be born into!'

The sound of that bloodstream voice recalled Gordana to realities. She laughed and said, 'Randy junior says he is not appearing on the world scene until the world scene looks rosier. We'd better try to fix you up with a job, pet, instead of quarrelling.'

The days that followed were exhausting for both Gordana and Randy. Randy left the one-room flat early every morning to go looking for a job. Since private transport had long since been forbidden inside city areas, he was forced to use the crowded urban transports, often travelling miles to chase the rumour of work. Once he took a job for three days pouring concrete, where the foundations of a new government building had pierced through the earth's crust into the Mohoroviic discontinuity below, creating a subterranean volcanic eruption; then he was on the hunt again, more exhausted than ever.

Gordana was left alone. She had Sonia Greenslade to visit with her once or twice, but Sonia was too busy worrying about John to be best company: John was under threat of dismissal at the packing plant if his work did not improve. On the next day that she was due to report to the hospital, Gordana went out instead and took a robowl up to the surface.

It was a fine sweet sunlit day with one white cloud shaped like a flea moving in a south-westerly direction over the city. This was summer as she remembered it; she had forgotten how sharply the summer breeze whistled between blocks and how chill the shadows of the giant buildings were. She had forgotten, too, that it was forbidden to walk on the surface. And she had forgotten that transport was for free only on one's own living-level. She paid out of her little stock of cash to get to the first green park.

The park was encased in glass and air-conditioned against the hazards of weather. It was tiled throughout and thronged with people at this hour of the afternoon. An old church stood in the middle of the crowded place, converted into a combined museum and fun house. She went in, past the turnstiles and swings and flashing machines and 'Test-Your-Heterosexuality' girls, into a dim side arcade where vestments were exhibited. People were pressed thick against the cases, but there was space in the middle of the aisle to stand still a minute without getting jostled. Gordana stood without getting jostled and, to her surprise, began to cry.

She did it very quietly, but was unable to stop. People began to gather round her, curious at the sight. Hooliganism one noticed in public, but never crying. Soon there was a big crowd round her. The men began to laugh uncomfortably and make remarks. Two gawky creatures with shaven heads and sidewhiskers, who could not be said to be either boys or men, began to mimic her for each other's delight. The blobby-nosed one gave a running commentary on Gordana's actions.

'New tear forming up in her left eye, folks. This one'll be a beaut, that's my guess, and I've seen tears. I'm World's Champion Tear Spotter Number One! Yeah, it's swelling up to the lid, yeah, gosh, there she tumbles, very pretty, very nice, nice delivery, she's infanticipating I should say, got no husband, just a good-time girl having a bad time, and now another tear gathering strength in her right eye – no, no, tears in both eyes! Oh, this is really some performance here, and she's trying to catch them in a handkerchief, she's making quite a noise –'

'Help me!' Gordana said to her unborn child. It was the first time she had ever addressed it without waiting to hear it speak.

'I brought you here so that you could make public the latest development.'

'You brought me here?'

'I can communicate to you on more than one conscious level, and some of your lower levels are very open to suggestion.'

'I don't want to be here – I hate these people!'

'So do I! You expect me to be born into this world among these zombies? What do you think I am? I'm not arriving till the world improves. I'll stay where I am for ever, do you hear?'

That was the point at which Gordana had hysterics.

Eventually they got her out of the old church and into an ambulance. She was shot full of sedative and shipped down to her own living-level.

When she woke, she was in her own room, in her own bed, looking mountainous under the bedclothes. Randy was sitting by her, stroking her hand, and looking remarkably downcast. She thought perhaps he was reflecting on how long he had had to sleep on the floor because the bed was too full of her, but when he saw her eyes opening, he said bitterly, 'This jaunt of yours has cost us ninety-eight smackers on the public services. How are we going to pay that?'

Then, seeing he had hurt her, he tried to make up to her. He was sorry to be snide but he thought she had run away. He could not find a job, they might have to leave the flat, and weren't things just hell? In the end, they were both crying. Arms round each other, they fell asleep.

But without knowing it, Gordana had already solved their financial problems. The ambulance crew that shipped her home had reported her case to the Maternity Hospital, and now a thin stream of experts began to arrive at the flat – and not only gynaecologists, but a sociologist from Third Level University and a reporter from *Third Level News*. They all wanted to investigate Gordana's statement that her baby would not be born till the world improved. Since they lived in a cash society, Randy had no trouble at screwing money out of them before they could get in to see his wife. In a short while, Gordana was news, and the interviews doubled. The cash flowed in and Randy bought himself a doorman's cap and smiled again.

'It's all very well for you, darling,' Gordana said one evening, as he strolled into the room and flung his hat into a corner. 'I get so tired telling them the same things over and over and posing for profile photos. When's it all going to end?'

'Cherub, I regret to say it's ending any moment now. We've had our day. You are news no longer! No longer are you a freak but one of many.'

She flung a cushion at him and stamped. 'I am not a freak and I never was a freak and you are just a miserable, horrible cheapskate little man to say I am!'

He leapt to her side and embraced as much of her as he could get his arms round.

'I didn't mean it, hon, really, not that way, you know I didn't, you know I love you, even if you are ten months gone. But look at the papers!'

He held a couple of coloureds out to her.

The story was all over the front page. Gordana was by no means the only pebble on the beach. No babies were being born all the way across the country, and there were hundreds of thousands of pregnancies of almost ten months' duration. Gordana's hysterics had triggered off the whole fantastic story. The medical world and the government were baffled or, as the headlines put it, STATE STALKS STORK STRIKE. One columnist was inclined to blame Comblok for the trouble, but that seemed hardly likely since a wave of unbirths was reported from all capitals of the world.

Gordana read every word carefully. Then she sprawled on the bed and looked her husband in the eye.

'Randy, there's no mention here of any woman being able to communicate with her unborn child the way I can.'

'Like I told you, honey, you're unique – that was the word I was looking for – unique.'

'I suspect all these mothers-to-be can talk with their babies same as I can. But you're the only person I told about that, and these women must feel as I do. It's a private thing. I want you to promise me you will not tell a soul I can talk to our baby. Promise?'

'Why, sure, hon, but what harm would it do? It wouldn't hurt you or junior.'

'It's woman's instinct, Randy, that's why, and that's reliable. People would only make capital out of it. Now, promise you'll keep the secret.'

'Sure, pet, I promise, but look, one of all these millions of expectant women is going to leak the secret, you know, and then it will not be a secret any more –'

'That's why it is essential to say nothing!'

'– But the guy – the gal who leaks it first could sure clean up a lot of dough if he leaked it to the right place!'

'Randy!'

'Why we could even move up into the upper levels, with daylight and all, the way you always wanted.'

'Randy, get out of my sight! Get out and don't come back! Haven't you made enough money already out of my misfortune without debasing us both? Get out and get yourself an honest job, and don't come back till you've got one.'

Randy sat drinking in a bar where they served a pretty strong shlivowitz, imported from Jugoslavia to save that country's economy, then in a state of crisis. The man with him was listening to what he said and buying him more shlivowitz; his name was Paddy van Dyck and he was Urban Psychology Romancer for the leading weekly *Mine;* he was saying, 'But let's get this clear, Mr Hicks, you say *you* never heard the baby speak?'

'Who's carrying it, her or me, I'd like to know? It's sort of telepathy, a telephone – I mean a telephone system, right up the bloodstream, just the two of them talking away, I'm left out of it completely, she doesn't want me any more, told me to clear out and get a job, doesn't love me any more.'

'Yes, so I believe you were saying earlier, Mr Hicks.'

Van Dyck brought a very large sum of money from his pocket. It had a sobering effect on Randy.

'This is for an immediate exclusive interview. No one else is to see your wife for purposes of interview for the next seven days. Understood?'

'Christ, yes. You have me convinced. Let me count it.'

'Let's go to your flat at once.'

But at the flats, Randy's courage failed. He recalled the promise he had made to Gordana so recently. In the hall, he caught sight of Sonia Greenslade, who nodded at him disapprovingly; she was putting on weight fast now. But van Dyck would allow no hesitation, and Randy was forced to open his door and march in.

A man was sitting on the bed beside Gordana.

'Hey! You're a fast worker, aren't you?' Randy exclaimed.

His wife gave him a dazzling smile and held out a puffy hand to him. 'Come along, darling! Where've you *been?* I thought things over and changed my mind about our little secret. This is Mr Maurice Tenberg of CB "Master-view", who is going to handle me exclusively for the next month.'

'For a considerable fee, Mr Hicks,' Tenberg said, rising and extending his hand. 'Your wife is a perspicacious business woman.'

By reflex, Randy held out his hand. It was stuffed with van Dyck's greenbacks. They were suddenly whipped away. Startled, he looked over his shoulder, in time to see van Dyck leave. The man knew when he was out-gunned.

*

The clutter of the cubision equipment in the hall was a considerable obstruction to the occupants of the flats, particularly those unfortunates like Sonia and John Greenslade on the same floor as the Hickses. As they climbed over cables or skirted trollies and monitor banks and powerpacks, they could see into the Hicks's room, which had lost the personality of its owners and was now a studio. Gordana's bed had given way to a fancy couch, and the cooking-equipment and sink were shrouded behind a wall-length curtain from the Props Department.

Gordana herself was heavily made up and dressed in a new gown. She was the star turn in an hour-long programme showing at a peak period on national networks. A panel of famous men had discussed the Baby Drought, as it was called, and now Maurice Tenberg was interviewing Gordana.

Subtly, he stressed both the human and the sensational side of the problem, the woman loving her child despite its irregularity, the novelty of a world into which no child had been born for six weeks, and now this remarkable new development where the mother could communicate subvocally with her infant. Finally, he turned to address the 3-D cameras direct.

'And now we are going to do something that has never been done before. We are going to attempt to interview a human being while it is still in the womb. I am going to ask Randy junior questions, which will be relayed to him by Gordana. She will speak out loud to him, but I would like to emphasise that that is just for her convenience not his. Randy Junior shares her bloodstream and so appears able to have access to all the thought processes going on in her brain.'

Tenberg turned to Gordana and, addressing himself to her stomach, said, 'Can you tell us what sort of a world you are living in down there?'

Gordana repeated the question in a low voice. There was a long silence, and then she said, 'He says he lives in a great universe. He says he is like a thousand fish.'

'That's not a very clear answer. Ask him to answer more precisely. Is he aware of the difference between day and night?'

She put the question to him, and was aware of her child's answer growing like a tidal wave sweeping towards the shores of her understanding. Before it reached her, she knew it would overwhelm her.

The foetus within could vocalise thoughts no better than she could. But without words, it threw up at her a pictorial and sensory summary of its universe, a scalding hotchpotch of the environment in which it lived. Dark buildings from a thousand reveries, drowning faces, trees, household articles, landscapes that swelled grandly by like escaping oceans, an old ruined church, numberless, numberless people invaded her.

This was her son's world, gleaned from her, cast back – a world for him, floating in his cell without movement, which knew no dimensions of space. Everything, even the glimpses of widest desert or tallest building, came flattened in a strange two-dimensional effect, like the image dying in a cubision box when the tube blows. But if the embryo world had no space, it had its dimensions of time.

In its reverie-life, the embryo had been free to drift in the deep reaches of its mother's mind, hanging beyond time where its mother's consciousness was unable to reach. It had no space, but it had, as it claimed, a great universe indeed!

As the flow of images smothered her, driving her into a deep faint, Gordana saw – knew – her mother, grandmother, great-grandmother – they were all there, seemingly at once, her female line, back and back, the most vividly remembered experience of a human life, faces looking down smiling, oddly similar, smiling, fading slowly as they flickered by, lowly faces at last, far back in lapsed time, their eyes still full of gentleness but at last no longer human, only small and shrewd and scared.

And over those maternal faces raced great gouts of light and shadow, as the cardinal facts of existence made themselves felt not as abstracts but as tangible things: birth and love and hunger and reproduction and warmth and cold and death. She was a mammal again, no longer a tiny unit in a grinding life-machine whose dark days were enacted before a background of plastic and brick; she was the live thing, a clever mammal, running from cold to warmth among the thronging animal kingdom, an animated pipeline from the distant past of sunlight and blood. She tried to cry at the magnificence and terror of what she felt … her mouth opened, only a faint animal sound emerged.

Of course, it made highly viewable CB. A doctor hurried on to the set and revived her, and in no time Tenberg was pressing ahead with the interview.

'He gave you a shock, didn't he, Gordana? What did your baby show you?'

With eyes closed, she said, 'The womb world. I saw the womb world. It is a universe. He is right ... he has a freedom to live we have never known. Why should he want to be born from all that into this miserable cramped flat?'

'Your husband tells me you will be able to move up above ground soon,' Tenberg said, firmly cheerful. Gordana could not be said to respond to his tone.

'He can roam ... everywhere. I'm just an ignorant woman and yet he can find in me a sort of wisdom that our brick and plastic civilisation has disqualified. ... He's – oh, God! – he's more of a whole person than anyone I've ever met. He's seen –'

Observing that Gordana was on the brink of tears, Tenberg grasped her wrist and said firmly, 'Now, Gordana, we are wandering a little, and it is time we put another question to your son. Ask him when he is going to be born?'

Dutifully, she pulled herself together and repeated the question. She knew by his reply that Randy Junior too was exhausted by the attempt to communicate. His reply came back pale and without emotional tone, and she was able to repeat it aloud as he sub-vocalised.

'He says that he and all babies like him have decided not to be born into our world. It is our world, and we have made it and must keep it. They don't want it. It is too unpleasant a place for them. ... I don't understand ... oh, yes, he wishes us to pass on this message to all other babies, that they are to control their feeding so that they grow no more and do not incapacitate their mothers further. From now on, they will remain as a parasitical subrace ...'

Her voice faltered and died as she realised what was said. And it was this crucial statement on which everyone, almost throughout the world, dwelt next morning. This was the point, as an astute commentator was to remark, at which the Baby Drought developed from an amusing stunt to a national conspiracy – for Randy Junior has succeeded in communicating with all other unborn children through their watching mothers – and to a global disaster.

In the Hicks flat, panic broke out, and the producer of the show ran forward to silence Gordana. But she had something else to convey to the world from her son. Eyes shut, she raised one hand imperiously for silence and said, 'He says that to him and his kind, the foetuses, their life is the only life, the only complete life, the only life without isolation. The birth of a human being is the death of a foetus. In human religions which spoke of an afterlife, it was only a pale memory of the fore-life of the foetus. Hitherto, the human race has only survived by foeticide. Humans are dead foetuses walking. From now on, there will be only foetuses. ...'

The crises, financial, political, national, ecumenical, educational, sociological, economic, and moral, through which the world was staggering, seemed as nothing after that. If the foetuses meant what they said, the human race was finished: there was a traitor literally within the gates.

In maternity hospitals, a series of emergency operations took place. Man could not bear to be defeated by mere unborn children. Everywhere, surgeons performed caesarean operations. Everywhere, the results were the same: the infants involved died. Frequently their mothers died with them. Within a few days, most countries had declared such operations illegal.

Gordana was immune from this wave of panic. She was too famous to be tampered with. She was made President of the Perpetually Pregnant, she was sent gifts and money and advice. Nevertheless, she remained downcast.

'Come on, hon, smile for Poppa!' Randy exclaimed, when he returned to the little flat a week after the momentous interview. Taking her in his arms, he said, 'Know what, Gordy, you and I are going topside to see your new flat! It's all fixed – well, it's not fixed, but we can take possession, and then we'll get it decorated and move in as soon as we can.'

'Darling Randy, you're so sweet to me!' she said sadly.

'Course I'm sweet to you, darling – who wouldn't be? But aren't you even going to ask me how many floors up we'll be? We're going to be fourteen floors above ground level! How do you like that? And we are going to have two rooms! How about that, hon?'

'It is wonderful, Randy.'

'Smile when you say that!'

They went to see the flat. The tenants had just died – at least the old lady had died and her husband had submitted to euthanasia – and everywhere was in a mess. But the view from the windows was fine and real sunlight came through them. All the same, Gordana remained low in spirits. It was as if life was a burden that was becoming too much for her to bear.

What with legal delays and decorators' delays, it was a month before Randy and Gordana Hicks moved into their new flat. On the last day in the old one, Gordana went and said a tearful goodbye to Sonia Greenslade, whose pregnancy was so well advanced that she and her child were communicating. She felt an unexpected reluctance to leave the old environment when the time came.

'You are happy here, Gordy?' Randy asked, when they had been installed for a week in their new home.

'Yes,' she said. She was sitting on a new couch that converted into a bed at night – no more cots that folded up into the ceiling. Randy sat on the window sill, looking down at the teeming city. He did no work now and looked for none; money was in plentiful supply for once in their lives and he was making the most of the situation by doing nothing, and eating and drinking too much.

'You don't sound very happy, I'd say.'

'Well, I am. It's just – just that I feel we have sold ourselves, and the child.'

'We got a good price, didn't we?'

She winced at his cynicism. Slowly she got up, looking steadily at him. 'I'm going back down to the third level to see Sonia,' she said. 'We've got no friends on this level.'

'Tell me if I'm boring you!'

'Randy, I only said I was going to see Sonia.'

'Go on, then, don't make a song and dance about it – though you'd be hard put to dance in your state. For gosh sakes, Gordy, how goddamned long are you going to lumber about my life in that mountainous state?'

She faced him. 'Just so long as my baby wants it this way. The matter doesn't rest with you.'

He came down off the window sill. 'You know what I think? I think you are having an immoral affair with that foetus! I reckon I could divorce you on grounds –' He stopped and grabbed her arms, hiding the pain on his face in her shoulder. 'I'm sorry, hon, I won't fly off the handle, I love you, you know, but how much longer are you damned women going to louse up the world?'

*

Sonia was delighted to see her old neighbour again. She invited Gordana in and they sat painfully at one end of the little room, close together, while John Greenslade sat at the other end of the room wrestling with the Bible and Western Civilisation. He was a small ragged man, not much taller than his wife and decidedly thinner. He sat in an old pair of slacks and a sweat-shirt, peering through his contact lenses at his phototape, occasionally uttering a sentence or two into it, but mainly scratching his head and muttering and playing back references in the mountains and alps of magnabooks piled round him. He paid no attention to the women.

'Mine's going to be a little boy – that is, I mean mine *is* a little boy, I mean to say. A little boy foetus,' Sonia confided, fluttering her eyelashes. 'I don't make him any garments and we haven't prepared a creche or anything – you do sort of save money that way, don't you think? His thoughts are coming on nicely, he talks quite well now – and he's not eight months yet, fancy! It is rather exciting, isn't it?'

'I don't know. I feel kind of depressed all the time.'

'My, that'll pass! Now you take me, I don't feel depressed at all, yet I'm much smaller than you, so I find Johnny heavy to carry. He seems to press down on my pelvis just *here.* Maybe when he's more responsive, I can get him to move round a bit. I get cramps, you know, can't sleep, get terribly restless, but no. I'm not a bit depressed. And you know what, Johnny already seems to take an interest in what John is writing. When John reads his stuff aloud, I can *feel* little Johnny drinks it all in. I don't think it's just my imagination, I can feel him drink it all in. He's going to be quite a little scholar!'

Gordana broke in on what threatened to become a monologue. 'Randy Junior doesn't talk much to me any more. I have a guilty feeling I lost his confidence when I let him be interviewed before all the world. But he's working away down there. Sometimes, I can't explain, but sometimes I feel he may be going to take me over and run me as if I were his automobile.'

'But we *are* their automobiles in a way, bless their sweet little hearts!'

'Sonia, I am not an automobile!'

'No, I didn't mean personally, naturally. But women – well, we women are used to being chattels, aren't we? Of men certainly, so why not of our babes?'

'You've been reading too much from the Bible!'

'As John always says, there was a lot of sense in that old book.'

'Will you confounded women keep your confounded voices down!' John shrieked, scattering reference books.

The days went by, and the weeks and months. No babies were born alive. The foetuses of the world had united. They preferred their vivid and safe pre-life to the hazards of human existence. The vast sums of money that the nations had hitherto devoted to defence were channelled increasingly into research on the birth problem.

Some of this money went to purchase the services of a noted psychiatrist, Mr Herbert Herbinvore, an immense pastoral man with shrewd eyes, a hairy mole on one cheek, and a manner so gentle it made him look like a somnambulist. He was appointed to get what sense he could out of Gordana, and they met for an hour every day.

In these sessions, Herbinvore coaxed Gordana into going over all her past life and into the reverie-life of her unborn child. He made copious notes, nodded wisely, closed his eyes, and went away smiling each morning at eleven-thirty.

When this had been going on for some weeks with no noticeable result, Gordana asked him, 'Are you coming to any conclusions yet, Herbert?'

He twinkled slightly at her. 'Surprisingly enough, yes. My assumptions are based on the opinion I have reached, that you are a woman.'

'You don't say!'

'But I do say, my dear. It's something that mankind has never seriously taken into account – the femaleness of women, I mean. How did your foetus and every other foetus suddenly begin to communicate to you? Because that's what foetuses have always done with their mothers; that's why the months of pregnancy are such a dreamy time for most women. It has come to be a much more outward thing now because of the crisis, but women have always been in contact with the verities of life that little Randy exposed to you. Man is cut off from that, and has to make the external world, without much aid from his womankind. It is, as they say, a man's world. More and more, these last centuries, the external world has ceased to resemble the reality that women know of subconsciously. When the conflict between the two opposites became sharp enough, the foetuses were jerked into a state of wakefulness by it – with the results we are now experiencing.'

Suddenly she was overcome with laughter. It seemed so silly, this fanciful stuff he was talking! As if he had any idea of what it was like to be a woman – yet he was telling her. 'And does – and does' – she controlled herself – 'does what you are saying now resemble most reality or the external world?'

'Mrs Hicks, you laugh like a sick woman! Man has adapted to his world, woman has failed to. Woman has stuck in the little reality-world. You take this matter too lightly. Unless you and all the other women like you pull yourselves together and deliver the goods, there isn't going to be any sort of reality to adjust to, because the human race will all be extinct.'

'How dare you call my son "goods"? He is an individual, and exists for his own self and not for any abstract like the human race. That's another man's notion if I ever heard one!'

He nodded so gently that it seemed he must rock himself to sleep. 'You more than confirm my diagnosis.'

They were both silent for a little while, and then Gordana asked, 'Herbert, have you ever read the Bible?'

'The Bible? It was long ago debunked as a work of cosmology, while as a handbook of etiquette it is entirely out of date. No, I haven't read it. Why do you ask?'

'A friend told me it says "Go forth and multiply". I wondered if maybe a woman wrote it?' And she started to laugh again. The sound of her son's voice within cut off her giggles.

'Mom, what is it like to be a man? Why is it so different?

She had forgotten, as so often she did, that every conversation she had was available to Randy Junior as soon as it registered in her mind. 'Those are silly questions, darling. Go back to sleep,' she said.

'What did he ask?' Herbinvore enquired, looking more relaxed than ever.

'Never mind,' she muttered. Randy was repeating his questions. He repeated them after Herbinvore had left and throughout the afternoon, as though he could not believe there were things his omnipresent host did not know. He was only silenced when Sonia came to visit in the afternoon.

Sonia looked tearstained and dishevelled. She clutched at Gordana and looked at her wild-eyed.

'Is your husband here?'

'No. Out as usual.'

'Listen, Gordana, my poor little babykins has gone stark staring crazy! He wanted to know a whole lot of things I couldn't answer, and so I got John to answer, and then Johnny got interested in John's work, you know how they are. I just can't satisfy him. And now this morning – what do you think? – he ordered me to work at the photo-taper when my husband was getting some sleep, and then he just took over my mind, and made me write the most utter nonsense!'

She waved a tape at Gordana. Gordana reached for it, but Sonia snatched it away.

'If you listen to it, you'll think my poor little baby has gone mad. He's digested everything from my husband's brain and scrambled it all up, and you'll think he's gone mad. As a matter of fact, *I* think he's gone mad. ...'

As she went into wails of misery, Gordana grabbed the tape and thrust it into the wall tapespeaker.

Sonia's voice filled the room – Sonia's voice, but barely recognisable as such, as it slowly pronounced its nonsense.

'Here no able, sow no able, spee no able, was the mogger of the three mogries, mescalin, feminine, and deuteronomy, and by their boots ye shall know them. And it came to pass water, and darkness was over the face of the land, so that the land hid its face and could not look itself in the I, as was prophesied even in the days of the lesser prophets, particularly those born of the linen of Bluff King Hal, Hal King Bluff, and of course Bess Queen Good. Though she had the soul of a woman, she had the body of a man, kept in her privy where none should see. Woe to women who commit deuteronomy!

'The former treatise are shorter than the ones you are wearing, O excellent Thuck; yet, yea verily and between you and me and this magadeath, the royal lineage shall not pass away nor the land of the Ambisaurs which devour the sledded Politicians on the ice, nor the sun in the morning nor the moon in June, and as long as rivers cease to run this treaty shall stand between us though dynasties pass: you, you, and your airs and assigns and all who inherit, viz., your mother, your mother-in-law, daughter, female servant, ass, cow, sister, governess, god-daughter, or any other species of deuteronomous female, hereinafter referred to as The Publishers, shall not brew Liquor on the premises or allow anything to ferment or rot except on the third Sunday after Sexagesima, Boadecia, or Cleopatra, unto the third and fourth degeneration, for ever and ever, Amen.'

The silence grew in the room until Sonia said in her tiniest voice, 'You see, it's utterly meaningless. ...'

'It seemed to me to have lots of —' Gordana broke off. The foetus within her was making a noise like laughter; it said, *'Now do you believe in Santa Claustrophobia!'*

Urgently, Gordana said, 'I'm sorry, Sonia, you must get out of here, before you infect Randy Junior with the madness too. He is starting to talk nonsense as well.'

Without ceremony, she hustled her little bulging friend out of the door and leant against it, panting.

'You're going to try and scare us, aren't you?' she said aloud.

'Do you suffer from negative geotropism? Remember the fleas, climbing ever upward? You know what they were doing.'

'Annoying the swallows! But you're not going to be a flea, you're going to be a man.'

'The fleas were climbing upwards towards the light. Let there be light, let there be light!'

Whimpering softly, she crept over to the couch, lay down on it, and began meekly to give birth.

Randy Hicks, Herbert Herbinvore, Maurice Tenberg, the Mayor of the city, the Director of the Maternity Hospital, a gynaecologist and her assistant, three nurses, and an inquisitive shoeshine boy who happened to be passing stood round Gordana's bed, admiring her and her baby as they slept the deep sleep that only sedation can bring.

'She'll be just fine,' Herbinvore murmured to Randy, standing more relaxedly than most men sit. 'Everything is working out as I predicted. Don't forget, I was consulting your friend Sonia Greenslade every morning from eleven-thirty till twelve-thirty, and I could see how these foetuses were feeling. They liked their little world, but they were getting past it. Remember what your son was supposed to have said about a foetus having to die for a human to be born?'

Randy nodded mutely.

'Then picture how a human would feel if his life were unnaturally protracted to two hundred years; he would long for death and for what our superstitious ancestors would have called the Light Beyond. Young Randy felt like that. The time came when he had to overcome the forces ranged against him and move forth to be born.'

Randy pulled himself out of his daze. He longed to kneel and embrace his sleeping wife, but was cagey about the nurses who might laugh at him. 'Wait a bit, Doc, how do you mean he had to overcome the forces ranged against him? What forces? It was his idea not to get born in the first place.'

Only an old cow asleep in a meadow deep in grass could have shaken her head as gently as Herbinvore did now in contradiction.

'No, no, no, I fear not. Things were not as they might have seemed to laymen like you. As I shall be saying to the world over the CB later tonight, the foetuses really had no option in the matter. The world was at crisis – half a dozen crises – and the women just suddenly came out with a mass neurosis. You might even say that world tension had paralysed women like Gordana, paralysed their uterine contractions so that labour could not take place. There are examples in the insect kingdom – among the flies, for instance – of creatures that can control their pregnancies until the moment is fit, so this incident is not entirely without precedent. It was the women that didn't want babies – nothing to do with what the babies felt at all.'

'But you heard what my kid – what Randy Junior said.'

'No, Mr Hicks, I did not. I never heard him utter a word. Nor did you. Nor did anyone else. We have only the word of the reluctant mothers that their babes spoke. That idea is all nonsense. Telepathy is nonsense, hogwash! The whole idea was just part and parcel of the womanly mass neurosis. Now that it looks as if the world's on the upgrade again, the girls are all giving birth. I'll guarantee that by tomorrow there's not a delayed pregnancy left!'

Randy felt himself compelled to scratch his head, but the whirling thoughts there refused to come to heel. 'Gosh!' he said.

'Precisely. I have it all diagnosed.' The grass in the meadow was well up to the cow's hocks. 'In fact, I will tell you something else –'

But Randy had already heard too much. Breaking away from the hypnotic sight of Herbinvore pontificating, he braved the nurses and flung himself down beside Gordana. Rousing gently, she wrapped an arm about him. The baby opened its blue eyes and looked at its father with a knowing and intelligent air.

Unperturbed, the psychiatrist continued to hold forth for the good of the company. 'I will tell you something else. When I had completed my diagnosis, I placed Mrs Greenslade under slight hypnosis to persuade her to write the nonsense she did. That was quite enough to scare the women into their senses again. ... I have the feeling that possibly when this whole affair is written about in times to come, it may well be known as "Herbinvore's Syndrome" ...'

The babe on the bed fixed him with a knowing eye.

'Nuts!' it said.

Still Trajectories

The juke box played a number called 'Low Point X'. It was the pub favourite the night that Speed Supervisor Jan Koninkrijk was forced to stay in the second floor back room on his way home from Cologne. He had looked out over small cluttered roofs and heard the record, heard it again in his sleep, dreaming of speed as the melancholy tug boats hooted outside the hotel where the Meuse became the Maars.

The girl in the bar, so fair, good North Dutch stock in that dull South Dutch town, hair almost milk-coloured, face so pale and sharp, interested in the sports end of the paper.

She tried to be nice to me that night, to smile with warmth, Koninkrijk, speeding into Belgium, said to himself. I'm not interested much in stray women any more, but her life has a mystery. ... The pathos, having to serve five per cent alcoholic drinks and watch night after night games of cards played always by the same men, listening to the tugs and 'Low Point X'. Was she signalling for help? I snooped on dialogues of the blood, Only silence there except for Low Point X giving its coronary thud. ... I'd better get back to Marta, no signals from her prison. Maybe this time she will be improved, so weary.

His Mercedes burned over the highway and hardly touched it, licking at one-sixty kilometres an hour along the autobahn from Cologne and Aachen through Brussels to Ostend and so across to England. Piercing his mazed thoughts, Koninkrijk kept a sharp eye for madmen: the highway's crash record was bad – his switched-on cops called it Hotpants Highway since the days of the Acid Head War. But this overcast after-noon brought little opposition, so he plunged forward, whistled to himself, joy, boy, joy.

She would be slowing, fewer admirers, maybe one faithful one, coming to the bar every evening. Her goodwill under strain. She smiled and smiled and was a victim. If he pitied, he must still love. It was the possibilities she represented that he thirsted for. Her hand as she stretched out for his guilders. A fine line, ah, that marvellous mystery of the female, something so much finer than just sex. Streamlined. With an un-Dutch gesture, he had kissed her hand; they were alone; they had looked at each other, he not much the older. Had put ten cents in the juke box for her to hear 'Low Point X' again as he walked out. Just to please her.

Had he really looked at her? Had she ever really seen herself? Had she something to reveal, hidden and sweet, to the man who went seeking properly for it? But that was his old romantic idea. No one went seeking others any more; under the psychedelic effect of the bombs, they sought only themselves – and never found.

He lived at Aalter, just off the Highway, in a thin house. 'My life is an art object,' he said jokingly. There were the alternatives; his wife's presence, that girl's presence, his job, his possible new appointment in Cologne, his office, that mad Messiah in England; all were different parts of his mind, all were different parts of the planetary surface; neither of which could be reached without the other; it was possible that one was the diagram of the other; all that was certain was that the linking medium was speed. Certainly there was speed, as the dial said, 175 kilometres, registering also in the coronary thud.

For some miles, Koninkrijk had been neglecting his thoughts as his eyes took in familiar territory. He was beyond Brussels now. Here the enlargements to the Highway were on a grand scale. Two more lanes were being laid in either direction, thus doubling the previous number. But the new lanes were all twice the width of the previous ones, to allow for the fuzzy-set driving of speedsters under the spell of PCA bombs dropped indiscriminately over Europe. Lips of senile earth had been piled back, cement towers erected; long low huts; immense credit boards with complicated foreign names; lights, searchlights for night work; immense square things on wheels and tracks, yellow-bellied cranes; scaffolding, tips, mounds, ponds, mountains of gravel; old battered cars, new ones gaudy as Kandinskys and Kettels; and between everything chunky toy figures of men in striped scarlet luminescent work-coats. Into the furrows he saw the new animal go. These men were creating the whole chaos only for speed, the new super fuzzy speed.

He slowed at the Aalter turn. It was impossible to say how much he had been affected personally by the sprays, but he recognised that his viewpoint had altered since that time, although he was working in France at the time of the war; France had remained neutral and the old lie that Tenenti TV protects the eyes. Piedboeuf. He slowed as he began the long curve off, its direction confused by the impedimenta of construction on either side. Aalter was already being eaten into under the road-widening scheme, the old Timmermans farmhouse obliterated.

The thin grim house occupied by the Koninkrijks was the only one left inhabited in the street, owing to the improvements scheme. The seismological eruptions of the European psyche had thrown up a mass of agglomerate that half buried nearby terraces. A bulldozer laboured along the top of the ridge like a dung beetle, level with the old chimneys where smoke had once risen from a neighbourly hearth. That was over now. There was no past or future, only the division between known and unknown, sweeping on. The daffodils stood stiff in the Koninkrijk drive against just such a contingency, keeping the devouring detritus at bay.

A thin rain, after moving across the North German Plain for hours, enveloped Aalter as Koninkrijk climbed from the Mercedes. The bellowing machines against my silent house so featureless and she in there, and the new animal with its wet eyes watching. He was not sure about the new animal; but he was slow now, on his feet and no longer stretched at speed, consequently vulnerable. He bowed his head to the drizzle and made for the closed opaque glass porch. She would have no such refuge of privacy; only a back room behind the bar, all too accessible to the landlord when he rose at last, stale from his final cigar and five-per-center, to try and fumble from her that missing combination of success he had failed to find in the hands of knock-out whist. Marta, as the unknown crept closer, at least had the privilege.

Marta Koninkrijk awaited this minute and all the other buried minutes a secret someone to crush her up into life; or so she hoped or feared. She sat away all the sterile hours of her husband's absence; she needed them. The bombs had blessed her half into a long-threatened madness, though she was not so insane that she did not try to conceal from her husband how far she lived away from him, or to conceal from herself how cherished was the perfection of immobility. She sat with her hands on her lap, sometimes reaching out with a finger to trace a hair-fine crack on the wall. Daring, this, for the day was nearing when the cracks would open and the forces of the earth pour in while the new machines rode triumphantly above the spouting chimney-tops.

Koninkrijk had installed omnivision in the thin house for her. She could sit and comfort her barren self by leaving the outer world switched off while the inner world was switched on. From the living room, with its frail furniture and brilliant bevelled-edge mirrors, she could watch intently the row of screens that showed the other rooms of the house; the screens extended her senses, always so etiolated, palely over the unfrequented mansion, giving her unwinking eyes in the upper corners of five other rooms. Faintly mauve, nothing moved in them all day except the stealthy play of light and shade trapped there; nothing made a sound, until the receptors picked up the buzz of an early fly, and then Marta leant forward, listening to it, puzzled to think of another life encroaching on her life. No bicycle wheel turns in the unpedalled mind. The omnivision itself made a faint noise like a fly, fainter than her breathing, conducted so tidily under her unmoving little bust. The stuffy rooms had their walls hung with gleaming mirrors of many shapes and pictures of small children in cornfields which she had brought here from her childhood; they could be viewed in the omnivision screens. Sometimes, she flicked a switch and spoke with a tremor into an empty room.

'Jan!'

'Father!'

The rooms were full of incident from her immobile bastion in a wooden-armed chair. Nothing moved, but in the very immobility was the intensest vibration of life she knew, so intense that, like a girlhood delight, it must be kept covert. The very intensity almost betrayed the secrecy for, when the key intruded downstairs into the elaborate orifice of the lock, there appeared still to be a universe of time before he would appear at the stair top and discover that long-tranced immobility of hers. Only after several millenia had passed and the radiations of unresolved thought subsided somewhat, and the rasp of the key registered in each room's audio-receptor, did she steal quickly up, dodging the slender image of herself transfixed in every looking-glass, and creep on to the landing to pull the lever in the toilet, assuring him of her activity, her normality, her earthy ordinariness. Into the lavatory bowl rattled a fall of earth. One day it would flood the house and blank out the last mauve image.

Always when he mounted the narrow stairs it was to the sound of rushing water. He put his wet one-piece neatly on its hook before he turned and embraced his wife. Dry compressed inflexible orifices tangentially met. When he moved restlessly round the room, disrupting all the eons of stillness, the furniture shook; and from without, the obscene grunts of a dirt-machine, pigging in to clay layers.

'Any news?'

'I haven't been out. The machines. I didn't really feel. …'

He crossed to the omnivision, switched over to Brussels. Some confused scenes in some sort of a stadium. The cameraman could be on a perpetual trip judging by his crazy work. Perhaps it was some sort of a beauty contest; there were girls in bikinis, but a lot of older women had turned up too – one at least in her seventies, flesh grouty and wrinkled. One of them was shouting, angry perhaps at getting no prize. A band played – not 'Low Point X'. He left it, looked at her, smiled, crossed to a narrow table and picked up the paper, neatly folded.

'You haven't opened the paper.'

'I didn't have time. Jan –'

'What?'

'Nothing. How was Aachen?'

'We've got this British saint, Charteris, coming through Aalter tomorrow.'

'Who's he?'

'I'll have to be on duty early.'

'Do you think he'll – you know –'

'He's a great man,' spoken not looking up as he searched the muddled columns. Piracy in the Adriatic. The Adriantic. New ocean, unknown to pre-psychedelic man. Many such hideous discoveries made every day. Of what degree of reality? 'A saint, at least.'

One page four he found it, a brief mention. New Crusade. Thousands rallying to support new prophet of multi-complex event. From Loughborough in the heart of England's stormy industrial Midlands may emerge new movement that will eventually embrace all of war-torn Europe, says our London correspondent. Prophet of multi-complex event, Jugoslav-born Colin Charteris is rallying take place in absolute darkness and Flemish observers agree that no thousands to his inspirational thinking. His first crusade motorcade through Europe is due at Ostend at four p.m. today and leaves tomorrow for what one commentator describes as several hundred automobiles pouring down here past Aalter at full speed. I'm bound to have more than one crash to deal with; better ring area squads now. Permanent alert from five tomorrow. Inform all hospital services too. Show eager. The tumbling bodies doing their impossible antics among ricochetting metals the dirty private things too beautifully ugly to be anything but a joke. Oh in my loins oh Lord disperse do they have the orange tip butterfly in England?

Both in their frail beds, a gulf of fifty-seven point oh nine centimetres between them. Darkness and the omnivision switched off but that connection nevertheless merely dormant: there would be another time when the currents would flow and the impulses re-establish that which ancestrally was where the glades of the forest stood like wallpaper all round in murmurous shade when the murderous mermaid pulls aside her jalousie and letting in the whispering brands of braided hair stretching to the closed clothed pillows. Koninkrijk he, suddenly rousing, felt the vibrations welling up through him. It was true, one was the diagram of the other, and nobody could decide which. Either vast machines were passing a hundred yards away on the arterial road, shaking the house minutely in its mortared darkness; or else accumulated fats and silts were building up in the arteries about his heart, stirring his whole anatomy with the premonitions of coronary thrombosis. If he woke Marta, he could presumably decide which was happening; yet even then there was the growing ambiguity about what a happening actually constituted. He could now recognise only areas in which the function-vectors of events radiated either inwards or outwards, so that the old habit of being precise was misleading where not down-right irrelevant. And he added to himself, before falling again into trembling sleep, that the Loughborough gospel of multi-complex was already spreading, ahead of its prophet.

*

Angeline was crying in the arms of Charteris on the long damp beaches of Ostend. The Escalation dirged by a dying fire: Her mother married a sunlit Ford Cortina. All the cars, most of them oparted, many stolen, clustered about the red Banshee along the promenade where Belgians loitered and sang, switched on by the rousing words of Charteris.

Take pictures of yourselves, he had said, pictures every moment of the day. That's what you should do, that's what you do do. You drop them and they lie around and other people get into them and turn them into art. Every second take a picture and so you will see that the lives we lead consist of still moments and nothing but. There are many still moments, all different. You have all these alternatives. Think that way and you will discover still more. I am here but equally I am elsewhere. I don't need so much economy – it's the pot-training of the child where the limitation starts. Forget it, live in all regions, part, split wide, be fuzzy, try all places at the same time, shower out your photographs to the benefit of all. Make yourself a thousand and so you achieve a great still trajectory, not longwise in life but sideways, a unilateral immortality. Try it, friends, try it with me, join me, join me in the great merry multicade!

All Angeline said after was, 'But you aren't indestructible any more than I really saw a dog in a red tie that time.'

He hugged her, half-hugged her, one arm round her while with the free hand he forked in beans to his mouth, at once feeding but not quite feeding as he said, 'There's more than being just organical, like translaterated with the varied images all photopiled. You'll soon begin to see how fuzzy-set-thinking abolishes the old sub-divisions which Ouspensky calls functional defects in the receiving apparatus. As I told the people, self-observation, the taking of soul photographs, brings self-change, developing the real I.'

'Oh, stop it, Colin, you aren't fun to be with any more when you talk like that! Did you or did you not kill my husband, besides, I don't see how you can get away with this multiple thing; I mean, some things are either-or, aren't they?'

With Angelina hanging crossly on his arm, he got up from the voluptuous sand and, moving to the water's edge surrounded by midnight followers, flung the bean tin into the galileean dark.

'What things?'

'Well, either I'm going to have your child or I'm not, isn't that right?'

'Are you going to have a child?'

'I'm not sure.'

'Then there's a third possibility.' Some of them had lights and ran clothed into the water to retrieve the tin, sacred floggable relic, unmindful of drowning. And the bean can moved over the face of the waters, out of reach, oiling up and down with orange teeth. Beyond it, the ambiguity of lunar decline and terrestrial rotation filtering into the distance.

A dirty boy there called Robbins, who had once been acclaimed a saint in Nottingham, ran into the water calling to Charteris, 'You are greater than me! So stop me drowning myself!'

Charteris stood by the margin of the sea ignoring Robbins as he floundered. Then he turned towards Ostend and said, 'Friends, we must defy the great either-orness of death. Among the many futures that lie about like pebbles on this beach are a certain finite number of deaths and lives. I see us speeding into a great progressional future which every blind moment is an eight-lane highway. Beside our acceleration rides death, because the bone comes where the meat is sweetest. Tomorrow, I precog that death will swallow me and throw me back to you again, and you will then see I have achieved the farther shore of either-orness.'

'A miracle!' cried the pop group. Angeline hugged him close, aware that he had to say nothing she could understand and still he was most wonderful. Behind them, clutching the holy relic of the bean tin, struggling and evacuating, Robbins went down into an unlit road beyond all terrestrial trajectory.

The promenade like a grey ridge of firn in early dawnlight. Beyond the post-glacial shelf, where lights burned between night and day, stood derelict projects of hotels, petrified by the coming of war; some half-built, some half-demolished, all blank-eyed, broken-doored, with weeds in the foundations and leprous remains of human habitation. Here from their catalepsy crawled the crusaders, scratching themselves in the ambiguous morning and blowing acid breath. Angeline wondered if her period would come today and boiled coffee for her lord and master on a fold-up stove; she was uncertain whether or not she felt sick, and, if she did feel sick, whether it was because she was pregnant or because she dreaded the prospect of another day's crazy part-automatic driving. Well, it was a fuzzy set world.

Some of them were already revving their cars or driving them over the ice-rim on to the sand as being the quickest way to extricate from the grand muddle of beached beasts. Maintenance was going on to a limited extent, mainly in the sphere of bits of rope tying on bits of machine. The sparky thing currently was to fill blown eggshells with paint and then stick them on to the bonnet with adhesive plaster; when you got moving, the paint peed out in crazy trickles or blew across the windscreen and roof of the automobile or, under sudden acceleration, the egg burst like a duff ventricle. Only Charteris's Banshee was unadorned by such whims. Like France, it was neutral. And Red.

'Where we going today, Col?'

'You know.'

'Brussels?'

'Some name like that.'

'Then where? Tomorrow? The day after, where?'

'That's it. You hit the road I mean the mood exactly. More coffee?'

'Drink the first lot, darling, then you get some more; didn't you learn any such thing when you were a boy? You know, this isn't a crusade – it's a migration!'

The coffee ran down his chin, he was only half-drinking, as he nodded his head and said, 'Sheer inspiration, yes! Crusade has only one object. Migratory is more instinctive, more options open.'

He expanded the theme as they climbed into the car, talking not only to her but to sharp-featured Burton and other people who impinged, Burton always nagging for favours. He had ceased to think what he was saying. It was the migratory converse; the result was that he astonished himself and this elation fed back into his system, rephotographed a thousand times, each time enlarged in a conflagration of spongation in idation or inundation of conflation, so that he could pursue more than one thought simultaneously down into its deep loughburrows, snooper-trooper fashion.

Burton was bellowing something at the top of his voice, but the engines drowned out what he said as they began to roll along the grey deserted front, between echoing shutters and sea. The new autorace, born and bred on motorways; on these great one-dimensional roads rolling they Möbius-stripped themselves naked to all sensation, tearing across the synthetic twen-cen lan-skip, seaming all the way across Urp, Aish, Chine, to the Archangels, godding it across the skidways in creasingack selleration bitch you'm in us all.

Great flood of tatterdemalion vehicles in multicolour flooded out on to the Hotpants Highway, rushing, swerving, grinding, bumping, south towards Aalter and the infinite, travelling up to one-fifty photographs per minute, creasing axle aeration.

He lumbered up from the vast brown inaccessible other-world of sleep and went hurriedly to shave. In the second bed, the wilting leaf of his wife still silent among her own shades.

As he looked at his motionless face, Koninkrijk thought of the good North Dutch girl back in the little hotel in Maastricht. Baby you won't get no sex off of me in low point X. The last crash, driving with the cop fast to the scene of the accident maybe the same today my form of gratification just a vampire. It was a little Renault nose deep in a cliff of lorry, as if snuggling there. The terrible anticipation as he jumped out of the still-moving car and ran towards it; in a year of life, maybe one moment of truth; in a hundred miles of speedtrack, this one node. A tractor-driver running forward, explaining in thick Flemish accident. I saw un I saw un, he swerve out to overtake me, this lorry pull up to let him by, see, this other chap don't pull up in time the first chap get clear away, ought to be a bloody law against it. There is a law against it, out my way.

There! All the luggage in the back of the car tumbled forward over the shoulders of the driver. He wears no safety belt or harness, is utterly smashed, yet he lives and groans, seems to be begging for something – in German?

The ambulance arriving almost at once, men also staring in through the now-public car windows. They ease the man out bit by bit; the lorry-driver and the tractor-driver stand by, masking their helplessness with explana-tions and repeated phrases. Koninkrijk with his dirty curiosity, recalling it again now obsessively with self-hate, mauls over the blood-gobbed contents of the car after the ambulance men have eased most of the victim clear.

His cold little distorted image of the man-run world held only this driving and crashing, nothing else; everything else led to climactic moments of driving and crashing, the insane technological fulfilment offered by the first flint arrowhead, the schizophrenic fulfilment of man's nature divided against himself since he invented good and bad – to all that, crashung und drivung were the climax. Eating and defecating and the rest were just preparatory processes, getting the body ready for the next leap out to the road. Things other people did were just substitutes for the speed death. The Chinese peasants, grovelling up to their kneecaps in paddy, longing for the day when they, too, could enjoy speed death.

He looked at his eyes in horror. His mind could not keep off the subject. There would be another call today; he must get down to the station, fearing and hoping. The Charteris crusade was invented for his particular philosophy Charteris is rallying take place in absolute darkness. He heard Marta switch the omnivision on as he dried his razor.

The immense cliff of earth loomed even higher above his neat red tiles this morning: chugging things like match boxes laboured up there, black against sky. New clay tumbling among daffodils. It was better in the station of the Speed Police – more like being in a liner, less like drowning in a sea.

'Good morning, Jan.'

'Morning, Erik.'

Koninkrijk went up to the tower, where two uniformed men lounged, chatting, smoking cheroots. He could look down through the glass roof of the duty room just below, see the current shift relaxed with their feet up, snuggled in wicker chairs, reading paperbacks and magazines. When the warning sirened, the room would be suddenly untidily empty, the paperbacks curly with open pages rubbed in the floor.

He glanced at the instrument panel, took a reading of traffic states from other stations along the Highway. Building up from Ostend.

Already, the first cars of the crusade were bursting along the Aalter stretch. From the station tower, a fine view; nobody saw it but Koninkrijk, as he read his own keynotes from the vast maimed spread; the remainder of the dutyites rested their minds among galloping tales of big-breasted women, affrays with Nazis in occupied Scandinavia, shoot-ups in Fort Knox, double-crossings in Macao, or the litter of the previous night's activities; two officers going off-duty exchanged dirty stories over a concession-price Stella Artois in the canteen; reality had a poor attendance, and I'm really the only one but even my eye's half ahead to the time when the English messiah Banshee jets past here in the Saddle of the speed death king and half back to the thought of that Maastricht girl maybe with her I would at last find that certain thing O Lord God I know I don't often, but what am I to do about Marta in schizophrenia catching.

What do you think about this government rumpus eh they say it's the food shortage but the Walloons are at the bottom of this you can bet Yeah food shortage they call it a world famine but we know who's at the bottom yeah we know who's at the bottom of it yeah Walloons.

What does she do in there all day long and I'll have to move her at the week-end or they bury the house tombs doleful voices but how will I persuade her Christ O Lord God get out there move man move leave it all behind since her confounded father interfering old.

The warning went and he was down into the front park as the men milled. He climbed into N-Car Five; the slam of his door was echoed by others. News was coming over the car-radio of a multi-vehicle pile-up on the south lane of the Highway two kilometres north of Aalter. Low Point X. Let's go and they roared under the underpass and bucketted out on the feed and from the feed on to the Highway proper, yellow barrier barrels and red-warning lights slicing by the hubs. Yacketter yacketter speedbeaches of the freeworld man-madman intersurface.

The speedometer was his thermometer, creeping up and the familiar dirty excitement creaming in him. For someone the moment of truth had come the shuttling metal death 3-Ding fast before the windscreen and still many marvellous microseconds safely before impact and the rictus of smiling fracture as the latent forces of acceleration actualised. Koninkrijk hated himself for this greedimaginative vampactof his high-flown. Already they were barking beyond the ditched town, the PILE WONDER sign, the pasty dungheat at the Voeynants house shuttered, and beyond the road-widening the crash-fences started on either side, cambered outwards and curved at the top to catch escaping metal. Fast shallow breathing.

The accident heralded itself ahead. Bloodstream flowing south faltered, slowed, dribbled. Koninkrijk's vagus nerve fluttered with empathy. Somewhere ahead was the actual thrombus, all but entirely blocking the artery. The police car swung into the nearest emergency lane. Koninkrijk was out before it stopped and unlocking the barrier between lanes, hoiking a walkie-talkie with him. Sun warm on his shoulders grass too long against the chain link got to keep nature out of this the weedicides this bloody war.

It was a typical nose-to-tail job, with ten cars involved, some pig-a-back on others like rough parody of animal embrace. Some still filtering through, all heads craned to see desperately want to know if man still stuffed with red blood.

'Koch, Schachter, Deslormes, proceed to the rear, get the barriers up and signals ten kilometres back so there's no further escalation.'

Moving forward as he spoke.

'Mittles and Araméche, you keep a northward lane free for ambulances.'

But they knew. They all needed shouting and excitement and the roar of engines.

So like last time and maybe next time. A lumbering Swiss truck with Berne number plates slewed half-off the verge. Into its rear, nose crumped, a red Banshee. Man wrapped round steering wheel, head against shattered screen, piled luggage in back spewed forwards over his body and shoulders, some broken open, passenger door broken open, oparted ancient Wolseley piled into rear of Banshee, then terrible cluster of vehicles, British registration mostly, patterned crazily. One shot free, burning steadily against outside barrier, lying on its side. People running limping crawling still in trampled grass shouting and crowding and curiosity reality loose among the psychos. The police helicopter clattering up overhead, photographing it all, fanning the smoke flat across the wreckage.

Loudspeakers barking farther along the road as Koch got to work.

Ambulances arriving, men at the double with float-stretchers, doing their instant archaeology, digging down through the thin metallic strata to where life had pulsed a few tiny eons ago, surfacing with primitive and unformed artifacts of flesh. Someone saying, 'The Banshee was Charteris's car.' Time converting entirely into activity as matter converted into energy.

Two hours' work later, Koninkrijk sitting exhausted jacket off on the muddied verge, listening in a daze to Charteris speaking to the elect.

'You know I half-foretold this would happen as we cavalcaded south. Here's a sort of semi-miracle as more-or-less predicted yesterday or whenever it was when we were at that place. The only places we really need are the in-between places that aren't places for they are trajectories of maximum possibility – you see how forced stoppage in this place here created maximum non-possibility for many of us which we call death, the low point where all avenues end. All our avenues end but we must build what extensions we can. For Burton my agent the avenue is right at a dead breakage. He, Burton, who hailed from the Midland city of Coventry where cars are born stopped me as we drove out of that place and begged to be allowed to ride my chariot. He was unable to give reasons for his desire and for that reason my wife Angelina and I took to his heap while he in triumph rode the Banshee. So it can all be explained away that he had some suicidal wish or that he as a good agent stage-managed it to look like a miracle that I was spared from death as predicted or that if I had driven no pile-up would have occurred, or that either this accident was already pre-performed in any of its guises or that it was in some way willed by me or us all corporately from some messianic drive in our hidden minds. If you all seek dutifully for the certainty of this occasion, each of you will find a different solution more satisfying than others to you, and so that will be regarded by you as the most "probable" solution, and so like renegade compasses you will each point to a different pole of truth, where on this ribbon all will indicate a personal mean. That I beg you to treasure, relish the uncertainty, shun certainty, search the fuzzy set, for when you find accepted probability, it must merely be a conspiracy not to be free between two or more of you. All this I shall say less certainly in my book Man the Driver, but never more inspiredly than now in this moment by the tyred road where this loss so belts us in.'

He pitched forward on his face as Angeline ran forward to break his fall. The uniformed police, the tatty audience, sun-specked, entropised again.

Koninkrijk saw his chance. Running forward to two police, he said lowly, 'Get him into my car and let's take him back to HQ.'

*

He was sitting up on the hard white bunk picking with a fork at police ham and beans on a hard white police plate in the hard grey migrainey room, with Angeline hard by him, and Koninkrijk respectful standing.

'Another miracle? I'm only a pawn. But I will see your wife, yes, bombardment of images, something in the Belgian aura we must incorporate to compensate for Burton and I intuit she could have a need for me. Or a sort of need for which we could substitute a fulfilment.' He half-smiled, sipping at a tumbler of water, sifting the water across his palate, seeing the plastic glass was made in France: Duraplex.

'I think she is schizophrenic, sir. She flushes the what's-it when I come in.'

'We all do, most of us. The wish to live more than one life – natural now, as the brain complexifies from generation. The world will soon tolerate only multi-livers. You too? No dream world or semi-realised thing aborting in the mental motorways?'

Slight bricky flush concealed under Koninkrijk's jowls. All the joys and sorrows really aborted into a secret drain-life none shared except for the tired willowy hand stretched over the sports page of a Maastricht paper.

'They do clash sometimes. I'll drive you to the house.'

The girl came too. So he did not live entirely inside himself, or else found there echoes from those about him. So he could be a genuine messiah – but what nonsense when he himself claimed but semi-messiahood, and after all, Europe wasn't the Levant, was it? In under a kilometre, small space to burn the gas.

'I'll speak to her alone, Supervisor.'

'Very well. You'll find her reserved.' Nervous glance at the woman Angeline. 'Not pretty. Very thin, I think the spring disagrees with her.'

And father had said that she should have a new bicycle
On her birthday at the end of May, as summer
Began; but they had been too poor when her birthday arrived
And he had given her instead a carton of crayons –
The very best Swiss crayons –
But she had never used them just to show her displeasure
Because she had wanted to rove the Ardennes countryside;
And perhaps it was since then that her father had been cold

To her and ceased to show his love. Sometimes it almost seemed
That if she kept rigid still he might appear stern
In one of the other noiseless rooms, dark
And showing his slight and characteristically lop-sided smile,
Saying, Marta, my child, come to your old Papa!
She had arranged the mirrors differently in the rooms,
Stacking them so that she could also observe the landing
Via one of the violet-tinted screens
With a side glance down along
The melancholy perspective
Of the stair-
Case.
Later, she would have to move herself
To clean the house; but she so much preferred the sight of her
Lair in abstraction through mirror and screen
That first she must be permitted
This vigil of watching and listening the morning through.
All her private rooms were unused by other
Persons; nobody was allowed
To come and go in them; their silence was the sanctity
Like even unto the sanctity
Yea of St Barnabas Church
Yea wherein she had visited, visited every Sunday
As a child with her parents every Sunday stiffly
Dressed in Sabbath clothes;
But this secret silence was of a different quality;
Each room she surveyed possessed individual silences:
One, a more rickety silence,
Another a more rumpled one;
Another a veined silence;
Another like a cross-section through calf's meat,
With a young-patterned texture;
Another with a domineering glassy silence;
These deserted quiets were more balmful and constricting
To her viscera than April's flowers.
A starker shade of silence ruled the stairwell.

Stealthily she moved her attention to it and
Came upon her father standing
There waiting amid the shade.
In his attitude of great attention she knew him. 'Marta!' 'Father, I
Am here!' 'Don't be alarmed!' 'Oh, Father,
You have come at last!' She could not understand but Delight grew high
and flowered in the stalks of her confusion,
Telling itself as always in a burst of penitence
And self-reproach, till her lips grew younger. He
Attempted no answer to her flow, advanced
Towards her through the mirrored rooms, walking
Delicate as if he saw
The ancient barbs she still cultivated sharp
About his path. She flung herself at him, all she had to give
As she gave her self-denigration, closing her eyes, clutching
Him. He half-leaned, half-stood, half-understanding
The scent of trauma in the scene, glancingly taking
In the fetishistic idols of emptiness on the bare walls, seeing
Again the clever duplication of life she had contrived
Imaged in the bottom of his French plastic tumbler: Duraplex:
She has her alternatives. 'Live
In both worlds, Marta, come with me!' 'Father, you give
Me your blessing once again?' 'I give
You my new blessing – fuzzy though you may find it, you must
Learn to live by it, you understand? My wish is this,
That you sojourn with nobody who desires to force you to live
On one plane at a time all the time: time must be divisible
And allowed gordian complexities. You must be
At once the erring child as we all are
And the reasoning adult as we all try to be
No strain placed on either
The two together tending towards
The greatly hopeful state we half-call godliness
Is that semi-understood?'
'And Jan, Papa?'
'For a while you come to live with me and Angelina

And let your man go free, for he has been more cut
By your trammels than you. You must learn to bide Outside
Where constriction binds less and one later spring you may
Come together again to find water flushing in the earth
Closet.' 'I see father.' Now she looked at him and realised
Like a trump turned up
He was not entirely her father, but the revelation had no
Poison: beneath the last moment's hand of mighty truth
Another shuffled: that in truth Marta did not want her father
And would now sprout free of him and his mirroring
Eyes that saw her only with disfavour: so her lips
Growing younger a mask cracked and fluttered
To the carpet unnoticed. 'Jan
And I will meet again, Father? After I have duped him so badly
With my hateful secret passion all these over-furnished
Years? There is no final parting?' 'Well,
There's really no final meeting.
It's one's own collusions that conspire or not towards
Another person – but you'll see directly. ... Come along
There's a daffodil or two left outside in the wet and soon
Sweet rocket will flower in your secret garden, Marta.' She
Looked at his eyes. They went down the stairs, undusted
That and every following morning, leaving the omni-vision working
Still. The cracks rioted on the walls like bindweed, flowering in peeled
distemper; and as they grew more open-lipped, the rumbling town-
destroying machines clowned over the roof-tree and clay pouted through
the fissures. The mirroring screens showed how the earth soiled in
through every whispering room, bringing familiar despoliation; but by
then the sweet rocket flowered for Marta.

Jan also, as the reformed crusade turned south, turned east, burning
his tyres and singing the song whose words he had forgotten and never
knew, towards freer arms whose meaning he had never known, where
the Meuse became the Maars.

Two Modern Myths

The first Earth ship settled down on Mars. Its round feet came down into the stony infertile sands of a crater, and there it stood. Great mysterious milestone in the history of man ...

There were four men in the ship. They had drawn lots and one man had won. Or lost. His name was Jim. He was the first one to get out of the ship and walk on the alien surface of Mars.

From their ship, the other three could clearly see the strange object, standing isolated in the twilight. They kept it covered with instruments and weapons, tensely watching as Jim approached to make an investigation.

'All quiet out here,' he said. His voice, transmitted to the ship, sounded tremulous inside his space helmet.

He moved forward, staring at that inexplicable manifestation on a world proved empty of all but the lowest forms of life. Apart from a few acres of lichen and moss, the whole planet was frigid, barren, dead ... and yet ...

The figure was coming towards him, moving steadily, involuntarily, Jim halted and stared at it. It was encased in a suit against the bitingly cold and thin air; it wore a helmet; inside the helmet, two eyes looked out, returning his glare.

'I'm frightened,' Jim said. The words came out unbidden, echoing in the ship. He had been frightened before, but never like this, never so metaphysically frightened to the roots of his being.

Chiefly the look in its eyes ... You could not tell what it intended. You could see that even it could not tell what it intended. It might become perhaps wise and benevolent; or it could spread its own forms of death and torture and misery across planet after planet, populating the galaxy with worlds of suffering where before had been only the awesome neutral silences of inorganic matter.

Jim reassured himself that this was just his own reflection facing him, but the terror remained. If it was he, then he was alien. He had a girl back on Earth; they would get married when he arrived home. They would have children, and the generations would march forward, on and on ... all changed by the historic steps he took today, as Columbus had changed the world by stepping on a foreign shore. And all – strangers to themselves.

He said, 'We're mad – we've come all this way to explore this planet, and we haven't even explored ourselves.'

They kept quiet in the ship, not jeering at what he said.

Encouraged, he added, 'We don't even know if our objectives are good or evil.'

And it was imperative they should know that. At any moment now, the Being who had set that great mile-wide mirror in his path was going to come and demand an answer.

The shifting sands moved over the face of the Earth and would soon engulf it.

For millennia now the oceans had been dry and the last tide had washed against the unending shore. The Earth was old. Its heart was cold, its skin dry and wrinkled with encroaching dust. Like a living thing, the sands multiplied, wombed in the deserts where navies once sailed.

The death of moisture meant the death of man. A human being is not watertight: his vital juices evaporate like water from an unglazed pitcher. One by one, and then tribe by tribe and nation by nation, man disappeared as magically as he had come.

His bones were powdered by the moving grit, his mineral salts dissolved into the sand.

Yet for a long time he had managed to postpone his final extinction. With every technological device at his command, he fought off the deserts in a losing battle that was not lost for centuries.

Now the battle was almost over. The old pastures, the woodlands, the hills, even the regions of ice at either pole – all were covered by the sand. All the works of man, his cities, roads and bridges, were engulfed by the dunes. Every insect, bird and animal lay sleeping under that treacherous yellow blanket. Only in one last valley, in one last house, did one last spark of life survive.

The Last Man on Earth came out of his door and stood regarding the scene. His valley was small and shallow, and completely ringed round the top with glass walls. This morning there was something new to see: the sand had arrived.

The sand pressed and surged against the glass like a living thing, tawnier and more terrible than a lion.

It rose and spread round the invisible obstacle. It could be heard whispering against the glass trying to get in.

The glass cracked. Breaking under the pressure behind it, a whole section of it fell inwards. At once a great arm of yellow sand reached into the valley and spread its fingers round the house. More followed, and more behind that, until a great wedge sliding in from the rear buried the back of the house up to its eaves.

Without revealing any great emotion, the Last Man on Earth watched this invasion from the front garden. Over the lawn at his feet spread the tide, looking golden and soft and almost inviting. It seemed harmless; it was irresistible.

So little time now remained. There was one last thing, the Last Man on Earth could do. Turning, he ran through the sand that lay ankle-deep over the porch and hurried into the house to find a bucket and spade.

A moment later he emerged triumphant.

The Last Man on Earth was only six years old. He started to build a sandcastle.

Wonder Weapon

This story takes place many centuries ago, back in the first century when the thought of Mao prevailed over the whole Earth, and an alien race arrived in a great ship to investigate us.

The Supreme Lord of Earth, Lim Chu Tsequo, bowed to the Antaresian ambassador.

'In the name of the people of this celestial globe, I welcome you and your civilisation to Earth,' he said.

Speaking through his interpreter, the massive representative of the planet of Antares answered appropriately. The two beings scrutinised each other. Their biological differences were great; the man was bisexual mammalian stock, whereas the Antaresian, being of reptilian descent, was oviparous. Equally alien were the histories, customs, and aspirations behind their different ways of thinking.

'What hidden weaknesses,' the Supreme Lord asked himself, 'lie in this monstrous race, which I can turn to the profit of my people?'

Aloud he said, 'The universe is an empty place, and you are our first contact with its peoples. That our two races live in such a desert of vacuum is alone enough to make us brothers.'

'Even brothers of the same hatch,' the Ambassador told himself, 'mistrust each other at times. What hidden strengths lie in this monstrous race which might become a danger to our people?'

Aloud he said, 'Our meeting will have its difficulties and its rewards, but no reason exists why we should not both benefit from it.'

A feast had been prepared for this first diplomatic meeting between

Earthman and alien. Before it began, however, Lim drew his distinguished and ungainly visitor aside, leading him down a corridor to a balcony which commanded a view over a pleasant and varied landscape, with soldiers marching in the foreground, carrying banners with vivid communist slogans.

'Is this not a fine spectacle?' the Supreme Lord asked. 'Here you see Earth in miniature, cities, rivers, mountains, forests, and a prospect of the sea. You look at a beautiful world – and a world entirely at peace.'

The reptilian visitor was impressed. 'Indeed, though you have no interstellar travel, the secret of such peace is something we cannot claim on Antares.'

The Supreme Lord bowed at the compliment, although his cunning would not permit him to take it at its face value.

'Our secret is an open one,' he said. 'Only one nation now lives on Earth. In earlier centuries this world held many races and ideologies. War was almost continuous.'

'What wrought such a great change?'

'We Chinese discovered a weapon with the power of life and death – a painless death, it is true, but death for all that,' said the Supreme Lord, observing the effect of his words.

'Other nations had the same weapon – some of them claimed to have invented it – but Red Chinese potentialities were greater than theirs, so it enabled us to conquer the world.'

'Are you telling me,' the Antaresian asked, 'that you turned this weapon against all the other races?'

'No,' said Lim. 'We used it on ourselves.'

A puzzled silence radiated from the ambassador. Then he said, 'You interest me, sir.'

'No doubt you would like to see this wonder weapon,' replied the Supreme Lord, gazing impassively over the landscape.

'Indeed I would, if it is not secret.'

'Secret? No, it is not secret – most men are armed with it nowadays.'

Dipping into one of the capacious pockets of his tunic, the Supreme Lord produced a small artifact, which lay lightly in the palm of his hand.

'There it is, our wonder weapon. Simplicity itself, as all great things are simple.' He spoke with veiled irony, wondering if he had already found a point of weakness in their culture. 'Do you have anything resembling this on Antares?'

The ambassador's spines rattled together, perhaps in a negative gesture. He stretched out a tentacle; the Red Chinese ruler withdrew his hand.

'I confess you awaken my curiosity,' said the alien, gracefully covering his disappointment. 'No doubt you are equally interested in the methods by which we cover the light years of space.'

The Supreme Lord nodded.

'As you say, we shall both learn from this contact. World-wide Red China has much to offer; our expansion into the galaxy could benefit all.' He again produced the little object from his pocket, balancing it in his palm.

'Perhaps in exchange for the secrets of this small gadget you may care to demonstrate to us the principles governing interstellar flight.'

'Firstly I must hear more about this thing, this wonder weapon, in your hand.'

'Certainly, Excellency. Rather like space travel, this thing is simple in theory; only its application in practice is difficult. In itself, it is nothing; its power lies in the force of the ideas behind it. The man in the street has to be educated up to using it. This my race managed to do some years after we had adopted Mao's thought. When the weapon came into general use, we were able at last to master our full resources, to raise our standard of living, to transform our technology – and, in short, to burst outwards and conquer the world, starting with Russia, reducing it to the peaceful state which you now see.'

The ambassador gazed fascinated at the harmless-looking object resting in the Supreme Lord's palm.

'You are formidable people,' he said.

'No, Excellency, not until Mao's ideas made us so,' said the Ruler of Earth, slipping the little plastic Coil back into his pocket. 'Now, let us eat before coming to terms.'

...And the Stagnation of the Heart

Under the weight of sunlight, the low hills abased themselves. To the three people sitting behind the driver of the hover, it seemed that pools of liquid – something between oil and water – formed constantly on the pitted road ahead, to disappear miraculously as they reached the spot. In all the landscape, this optical illusion was the only hint that moisture existed.

The passengers had not spoken for some while. Now the Pakistani Health Official, Firoz Ayub Khan, turned to his guests and said, 'Within an hour, we shall be into Calcutta. Let us hope and pray that the air-conditioning of this miserable machine holds out so long!'

The woman by his side gave no sign that she heard him, continuing to stare forward through her dark glasses; she left it to her husband to make an appropriate response. She was a slender woman of dark complexion, her narrow face made notable by its generous mouth. Her black hair, gathered over one shoulder, was disordered from the four-hour drive down from the hill station.

Her husband was a tall spare man, apparently in his mid-forties, who wore old-fashioned steel-rimmed spectacles. His face in repose carried an eroded look, as if he had spent many years gazing at just such countries as the one outside. He said, 'It was good of you to consent to letting us use this slow mode of transport, Dr Khan. I appreciate your impatience to get back to work.'

'Well, well, I am impatient, that is perfectly true. Calcutta needs me – and you too, now you are recovered from your illness. And Mrs Yale also, naturally.' It was difficult to determine whether Khan's voice concealed sarcasm.

'It is well worth seeing the land at first hand, in order to appreciate the magnitude of the problems against which Pakistan and India are battling.'

Clement Yale had noted before that his speeches intended to mollify the health official seemed to produce the opposite effect. Khan said, 'Mr Yale, what problems do you refer to? There is no problem anywhere, only the old satanic problem of the human condition, that is all.'

'I was referring to the evacuation of Calcutta and its attendant difficulties. You would admit they constituted a problem, surely?'

This sort of verbal jostling had broken out during the last half-hour of the ride.

'Well, well, naturally where you have a city containing some twenty-five million people, there you expect to find a few problems, wouldn't you agree, Mrs Yale? Rather satanic problems, maybe – but always stemming from and rooted in the human condition. That is why executives such as ourselves are always needed, isn't it?'

Yale gestured beyond the window, where broken carts lay by the roadside. 'This is the first occasion in modern times that a city has simply bogged itself down and had to be abandoned. I would call that a special problem.'

He hardly listened to Khan's long and complicated answer; the health official was always involving himself in contradictions from which verbiage could not rescue him. He stared instead out of the window as the irreparable world of heat slid past. The carts and cars had been fringing the road for some while – indeed, almost all the way from the hospital in the hills, where East Madras was still green. Here, nearer Calcutta, their skeletal remains lay thicker. Between the shafts of some of the carts lay bones, many of them no longer recognisable as those of bullocks; lesser skeletons toothed the wilderness beyond the road.

The hover-driver muttered constantly to himself. The dead formed no obstacle to their progress; the living and half-living had yet to be considered. Pouring out of the great ant-heap ahead were knots of human beings, solitary figures, family groups, men, women, children, the more fortunate with beasts of burden or handcarts or bicycles to support themselves or their scanty belongings. Blindly they moved forward, going they hardly knew whither, treading over those who had fallen, not raising their heads to avoid the oncoming hover-ambulance.

For centuries, the likes of these people had been pouring into Calcutta from the dying hinterland. Nine months ago, when the government of the city had fallen and the Indian Congress had announced that the city would be abandoned, the stream had reversed its direction. The refugees became refugees again.

Caterina behind her dark glasses took in the parched images. Mankind driven always drive the bare foot on the way the eternal road of earth and no real destination only the way to water and longer grass. Will we be able to get a drink there always the stone beneath the passing instep.

She said, 'I suppose one shouldn't hope for a shower when we get there.'

Ayub Khan said, 'The air-condition is not all it should be, lady. Hence the sensation of heat. There has not been proper servicing of the vehicle. I shall make some appropriate complaints when we arrive, never wonder!'

Jerking to avoid a knot of refugees, the hover rounded a shoulder of hill. The endless deltaic plain of the Ganges stretched before them, fading in the far distance, annihilating itself in its own vision of sun.

To one side of the track stood a grim building, the colour of mud, its walls rising silent and stark. Not a fortress, not a temple: the meaningless functionalism, now functionless, of some kind of factory. Beside it, one or two goats scampered and vanished.

Ayub Khan uttered a command to the driver. The hover slid to one side. The road near at hand was temporarily deserted. Their machine bumped over the ditch and drifted towards the factory, raising dust high as it went. Its engines died, it sank to the ground. Ayub Khan was reaching behind him for the holstered rifle on the rack above their heads.

'What's this place?' Yale asked, rousing himself.

'A temporary diversion, Mr Yale, that will not occupy us for more than the very moment. Maybe you and your lady will care to climb out with me for a moment and exercise? Go steadily remembering you were ill.'

'I have no wish to climb out, Dr Khan. We are urgently needed in Calcutta. What are we stopping for? What is this place?'

The Pakistani doctor smiled and took down a box of cartridges. As he loaded the rifle, he said, 'I forget you are not only recently sick but also immortal and must take the greatest care. But the desperate straits of Calcutta will wait for us for ten minutes' break, I assure you. Recall, the human condition goes on for ever.'

The human condition goes on for ever sticks stones bows and arrows shotguns nuclear weapons quescharges and the foot and face going down into the dust the perfect place for death. She stirred and said, 'The human condition goes on for ever, Dr Khan, but we are expected in Dalhousie Square today.'

As he opened the door, he smiled. 'Expectancy is a pleasing part of our life, Mrs Yale.'

The Yales looked at each other. The driver was climbing down after Ayub Khan, and gesticulating excitedly. 'His relish of power likewise,' Yale said.

'We cadged the ride.'

'The ride – not the moralising! Still, part of abrasion.'

'Feeling right, Clem?'

'Perfectly.' To show her, he climbed out of the vehicle with a display of energy. He was still angry with himself for contracting cholera in the middle of a job where every man's capacity was stretched to the utmost; the dying metropolis was a stewpot of disease.

As he helped Cat down, they felt the heat of the plains upon them. It was the heat of a box, allowing no perspective but its own. The moisture in it stifled their lungs; with each breath, they felt their shoulders prickle and their bodies weep.

Ayub Khan was striding forward, rifle ready for action, the driver chattering excitedly by him, carrying spare ammunition.

Time, suffering from a slow wound, was little past midday, so that the derelict factory was barren of shadow. Nevertheless, the two English moved instinctively towards it, following the Pakistanis, feeling as they went old heat rebuffed from the walls of the great fossil.

'Old cement factory.'

'Cementary.'

'Mortarl remaniés …'

'Yes, here's an acre stone indeed …'

The rifle went off loudly.

'Missed!' said Ayub Khan cheerfully, rubbing the top of his head with his free hand. He ran forward, the driver close behind him. Ramshackle remains of a metal outbuilding stood to one side of the factory façade; a powdered beam of it collapsed as the men trotted past and disappeared from view.

And the termites too have their own empires and occasions and never over-extend their capacities they create and destroy on a major time-scale yet they have no aspirations. Man became sick when he discovered he lived on a planet when his world became finite his aspirations grew infinite and what the hell could those idiots be doing?

Switching on his pocket fan, Yale walked up the gritty steps of the factory. The double wooden door, once barred, had long since been broken down. He paused on the threshold and looked back at his wife, standing indecisively in the heat.

'Coming in?'

She made an impatient gesture and followed. He watched her. He had watched that walk for almost four centuries now, still without tiring of it. It was *her* walk: independent, yet not entirely; self-conscious, yet, in a true sense, self-forgetting; a stride that did not hurry, that was neither old nor young; a woman's walk; Cat's walk; a cat-walk. It defined her as clearly as her voice. He realised that in the preoccupations of the last two months, in doomed Calcutta and in the hospital ward, he had often forgotten her, the living her.

As she came up the steps level with him, he took her arm.

'Feelings?'

'Specifically, irritation with Khan foremost. Secondarily, knowledge we need our Khans …'

'Yes, but how now to you?'

'Our centuries – as ever. Limit gravely areas of non-predictability in human relations among Caucasian-Christian community. Consequent accumulation of staleness abraded by unknown factors.'

'Such as Khan?'

'Sure. You similarly abraded, Clem?'

'He has chafage value. Ditto all sub-continent.'

His fingers released her arm. The brown flesh ever young left no sign of the ephemeral touch. But the Baltic virus would have quickly healed the harshest grip he could have bestowed.

They looked into the old chaos of the factory, moved in over rubble. A corpse lay in a side office, open-mouthed, hollow, without stink; something slid away from under, afraid for its own death.

From the passage beyond, noise, echoey and conflicting.

'Back to the float?'

'This old temple to India's failure –' He stopped. Two small goats, black of face and beardless, came at a smart clip from the back of the darkness ahead, eyes – in Ayub Khan's pet word – 'satanic', came forward swerving and bleating.

And from the far confusion of shadow, Ayub Khan stopped and raised his rifle. Yale lifted a hand as the shot came.

Temples and the conflicting desires to make and destroy ascetic priests and fat ones my loving husband still had his tender core unspoilt for more years.

The goats tumbling past them, Yale sagging to the ground, the noise of the shot with enormous power to extend itself far into the future, Cat transfixed, and somewhere a new ray of light searching down as if part of the roof had given way.

Rushing forward, Ayub Khan gave Cat back her ability to move; she turned to Yale, who was already getting to his feet again. The Pakistani calling, his driver behind him.

'My dear and foolish Mr Yale! Have I not rifled you, I sincerely trust! What terrible disaster if you are dead! How did I know you crept secretly into this place? My godfathers! How you did scare me! Driver! *Pani lao jhaldi!*'

He fussed anxiously about Yale until the driver returned from the ambulance with a beaker of water. Yale drank it and said, 'Thank you, I'm perfectly well, Dr Khan, and you missed me, fortunately.'

'What do you imagine you were doing?' Cat asked.

Hold your hands together so they will not shake and your thighs if he had been killed murder most dreaded of crimes even to short-livers and this idiot –

'Madam, you must surely see that I was shooting at the two goats. Though I hope thoroughly that I am a good Muslim, I was shooting at those two damned satanic goats. That action needs not any justification, surely?'

She was still shaking and trying to recover her poise. High abrasion value okay! 'Goats? In here?'

'Mrs Yale, the driver, and I have seen these goats from the road and chase after them. Because the back of this factory is broken, they escape from us into here. We follow. Little do we know that you creep secretly in from the front! What a scare! My godfathers!'

As he paused to light a mescahale, she saw his hand was shaking; the observation restored a measure of sympathy for the man. She further relaxed her pulse-count by a side-glance at Yale, for their glances by now, cryptic as their personal conversations, told them as much; certain the shot was careless, he was already more interested in the comedy of Ayub Khan's reactions than his own.

Yes many would find him a negative man not seeing that the truth is he has the ability to add to his own depths other people's. He stands there while others talk saintly later he will deliver the nub of the matter. My faith of which he would disapprove indeed I have an obligation not to be all faith must also fill my abrasion quota for him!

'You know, I really hate these little satanic goats! In Pakistan and India they cause the chief damage to territory and the land will never revive while goats are upon it. In my own province, I watch them climb the trees to eat up new tender shoots. So the latest laws to execute goats, reinforced with rewards of two new-rupees per hoof, are so much to my thinking, more than you Europeans can understand ...'

'That is certainly true, Dr Khan,' Yale said. 'I fully share your dislike of the destructive power of the goat. Unfortunately, such animals are a part and parcel of our somewhat patchy history. The hogs that ensured that the early forests, once felled by stone axes, did not grow again, and the sheep and goats that formed man's traditional food supplies, have left as indelible a mark on Europe as on Asia and elsewhere. The eroded shores of the Mediterranean and the barren lands all round that sea are their doing, in league with man.'

Does the pressure of my thought make him speak of early mankind now? Through these centuries glad and stern I have come to see man's progress as a blind attempt to escape from those hopeful buffoons so exposed to chance yet chance beats down like weather whatever you cover your back with we know who live a long while that the heart stagnates without abrasion and the great abrader is chance.

Now Ayub Khan had perked up and was smiling over the fumes of his mescahale, gesturing with one hand.

'Now, now, don't be bitter, Mr Yale – nobody denies that the Europeans have their share of minor troubles! But let's admit while we are being really frank that they also have all the luck, don't they? I mean to say, to give one example, the Baltic virus happened in their part of the world, didn't it? just like the Industrial Revolution many hundreds of years ago.'

'Your part of the world, Doctor, has enough to contend with without longevity as well!'

'Precisely so! What is an advantage to you Europeans, and to the Americans behind their long disgraceful isolationism, is a disadvantage entirely to the unlucky Asiatic nations, that is what I am saying. That is precisely why our governments have made longevity illegal – as you well know, a Pakistani suffers capital punishment if he is found to be a long-liver, just because we do not solve our satanic population problem so very easily as Europe. So we are condemned to our life-expectancy of merely forty-seven years average, against your thousands! How can that be fair, Mr Yale? We are all human beings, wherever we live on the planet of Earth, Equator or Pole, my godfathers!'

Yale shrugged. 'I don't pretend to call it fair. Nobody calls it fair. It just happens that "fairness" is not a built-in natural law. Man invented the concept of justice – it's one of his better ideas – but the rest of the universe, unfortunately, doesn't give a damn for it.'

'It's very easy for you to be smug.'

He looks so angry and hurt his skin almost purple his eyeballs yellow rather like a goat himself not a good representative of his race. But the antipathy can never be overcome the haves and the have-nots the Neanderthal and the Cro-Magnon the rich and the poor we can never give what we have. We should get back into the float and drive on. I'd like to wash my hair. The goats moved endlessly across the plain with every step they took the great enchanted ruin behind them crumbled into a material like straw and as they went and multiplied long grasses sprang out of the human corpses littering the plain and the goats capered forward and ate.

'Smugness does not enter the matter. There are the facts and –'

'Facts! Facts! Oh, your satanic British factualism! I suppose you call the many goats facts? How does it come about, ask yourself, how does it come about that these goats can live forever and I cannot, for all my superior reasoning powers?'

Yale said, 'I fear I can only answer you with more factualism. We know now, as for many years we did not, that the Baltic virus is extraterrestrial in origin, most probably arriving on this planet by tektite. To exist in a living organism, the virus needs a certain rare dynamic condition in the mitochondria of cells known as rubmission – the Red Vibrations of the popular press – and this it finds in only a handful of terrestrial types, among which are such disparate creatures as copepods, Adelie penguins, herring, man, and goats and sheep.'

'We have enough trouble with this satanic drought without immortal goats!'

'Immortality – as you call longevity – is not proof against famine. Although the goats' reproductive period is in theory infinitely extended, they are still dying for lack of nourishment.'

'Not so fast as the humans!'

'Vigilance will certainly be needed when the rains come.'

'You immortals can afford to wait that long!'

'We are *long-livers*, Dr Khan.'

'My godfathers, define for me the difference between longevity and immortality in a way that makes sense to a short-lived Pakistan man!'

'Immortality can afford to forget death and, in consequence, the obligations of life. Longevity can't.'

'Let's get on to Calcutta,' Cat said. Vultures perched on the top of the stained façade: she found herself vulnerable to their presence. She walked across to the doorway. The driver had already slipped out at the back of the factory.

On the long road the humble figures. When did that woman last have a bath to have to bear children in such conditions. This is what life is all about this is why we left the stainless towers of our cooler countries their comforts and compromises in the broken down parts of the world there is no pretence about what life is really like Clem and I and the other long-livers are merely clever western artefacts of suspended decay everyday we know that one day we shall have to tumble into slag each our own Calcutta oh for God's sake satanically can it!

The men were following her. She saw now that Ayub Khan had laid a hand on Yale's arm and was talking in more friendly fashion.

The hover's door had been left open. It would be abominably hot in there.

Two skeletal goats cross the road, ears lop, parading before two refugees. The refugees were men walking barefoot with sticks, bags of belongings slung on their backs. For them, the goats would represent not only food but the reward the government offered for hooves. Breaking from their trance, they waved their arms and wielded their sticks. One of the goats was struck across its serrated backbone. It broke into a trot. Ayub Khan raised his rifle and fired at the other goat from almost point-blank range.

He hit it in the stomach. The creature's back legs collapsed. Piddling blood, it attempted to drag itself off the road, away from Ayub Khan. The two refugees fell on it, jostling each other with scarecrow gestures. With an angry shout, Ayub Khan ran forward and prodded them out of the way with the rifle barrel. He called to the driver, who came at a trot, pulling out a knife; squatting, he chopped at the goat's legs repeatedly until the hooves were severed; by that time, the animal appeared to be dead.

The government will pay. Like all Indian legislation this bounty favours the rich and the strong at the expense of the poor and weak. Like everything else cool Delhi justice melts in the heat.

Above the factory entrance, the vultures shuffled and nodded in understanding.

Straightening, Ayub Khan gestured to the two refugees, inviting them to drag the body off. They stood stupidly, not coming forward, perhaps fearing attack. Clapping his hands once, Ayub Khan dismissed them and turned away, circling the goat's carcass.

To Caterina he said, 'Just allow me one further moment, madam, while I shoot down this second goat. It is my public duty.'

To sit in the shade of the ambulance or go and watch him carry out his public duty. No choice really he shall not think us squeamish we don't need his uncouth exhibition to tell us that even we are in the general league with death. Remember after Clem and I returned from the bullfight in Seville Philip no more than seven years old I suppose asked Who won? and cried when we laughed. We must be brave bulls *toros bravos* who live on something less prone to eclipse than hope.

Yale said, 'Follow and these can at least claim what's left.'

'Sure, and we attend caprine execution.'

'Gory caprice!'

'Goat kaputt.'

'You over-hot?'

'Just delay. Thanks.' Smiles in the general blindness.

'Delay produce of no goal within fulfilment.'

'Vice versa too, suppose.'

'Suppose. Eastern thing. Hence Industrial Rev never took here.'

'Factory example, Clem.'

'So, quite. Wrongly situated regards supply, power, consumers, distribution.'

Calcutta itself a similar example on enormous satanic scale. Situated on Hooghli, river now almost entirely silted up despite dramatic attempts. And the centuries-old division between India and Pakistan like a severed limb the refugees breaking down all attempts at organisation finally the water-table under the city hopelessly poisoned by sewage mass eruptions of disease scampering mesolithic men crouching in their cave exchanging illnesses viruses use mankind as walking cities.

'Calcutta somewhat ditto.'

'Ssh, founded by East India merchant, annoy Khan!'

They looked at each other, just perceptibly grinning, as they walked round to the back of the factory.

The surviving goat was white-bodied, marked with brown specks; its head and face were dark brown or black, its eyes yellow. It walked under a series of low *bashas*, now deserted, apparently once used as huts for the factory-owners. Their thatched walls, ruinous, gave them an air of transparency. The light speared them. Beyond them, the undistinguished lump of Calcutta lay amid the nebulous areas where land met sky.

Ravenously, the goat reached up and dragged at the palm leaves covering a *basha* roof. As a section of the roof came down in a cascade of dust, Ayub Khan fired. Kicking up its bounty-laden heels, the goat disappeared among the huts.

Ayub Khan reloaded. 'Generally, I am a satanically sound marksman. It is this confounded heat putting me off that I chiefly complain of. Why don't you have a shot, Yale, and see if you do a lot better? You English are such sportsmen!' He offered the rifle.

'No, thanks, Doctor. I'm rather anxious for us to be getting on to Calcutta.'

'Calcutta is just a tragedy – let it wait, let it wait! The hunting blood is up! First, let's have a little fun with this terrible satanic goat!'

'Fun? It was public duty a moment ago!'

Ayub Khan looked at him. What are you doing here, anyway, with your pretty wife? Isn't this all *fun* for you as well as public duty? Did you have to come to our satanic Asia, ask yourself?'

Isn't he right don't we eternally have to redeem ourselves for the privilege of living and seeing other life by sacrificing death Clement must have said the same thing often to himself by sacrificing death did we not also sacrifice the norms of normal life in this long-protracted life is not our atonement our fun helping supervise the evacuation of Calcutta our goat-shoot. In his eyes we can never redeem ourselves only in our own eyes.

'Instead of papering over the cracks at home, Doctor, we prefer to stand on the brink of your chasms. You must forgive us. Go and shoot your goat and then we will proceed to Calcutta.'

'It is very very curious that when you seem to be talking better sense, I am not able to understand you. Driver, *idhar ao!*'

Gesturing to the driver, the health official disappeared behind the threadbare huts.

On the road, the refugees still trod, losing themselves in the mists of distance and time. Individuality was forgotten: there were only organisms, moving according to certain laws, performing antique motions. In the Hooghli, water flowed, bringing down silt from source to delta, the dredgers rusting, the arteries clogging, little speckled crabs waving across grey sandbanks.

Drake-Man Route

So maybe this was the real Charteris or a personal photograph of him
wire-wheeling towards the metropolis none too sure if matter was not
hallucination, smiling and speaking with a tone of unutterable kindness
to himself to keep down the baying images. Uprooted man. Himself a
product of time, England a product of literature. It was a good period
and to dissolve into all branches – great new thing with all potentials,
prosperity and prenury.

He saw it, see-saw the new thing, scud across the scudding road
before him, an astral projection perhaps, all legs, going all ways at once.
A man could do that.

He wanted to communicate his new discoveries, pour out the profusion of his confusion to listeners, in madness never more nerved or
equilustral, all paradised by the aerosols until the unclipped hedges of
mind grew their own utopiary.

His car snouted out one single route from all the possible routes
and now growled through the iron-clod night of London's backyards:
papiermâché passing for stone, cardboard passing for brick, only in the
yellow fanning wash of French headlights; pretence all round of solidity,
permanence, roofs and walls and angles of a sly geometry, windows
infinitely opaque on seried sleepers, quick corners, snickering bayonets
at vision's angles, untrodden pavements, wide eyes reflected from blind
shops, the ever-closing air, the epic of unread signs, and under the bile
blue fermentation of illumination, roundabouts of concrete boxed by
shops and a whole vast countryside rumpling upwards into the night

under the subterranean detonation of unease. The steering wheel swung it all this way and that, great raree show-down for foot-down Serbs. Song in the wings, other voices.

Round the next corner FOR YOUR THROAT'S SAKE SMOKE a van red-eyed – a truck no *trokut*! – in the middle of the guy running out waving bloody leather – Charteris braked spilling hot words as the chasing thought came of impact and splat some clot mashed out curving against a wall of shattered brick so bright all flowering: a flowering cactus a Christmas cactus rioting in an anatomical out-of-season.

Car and images dominoed into control as the man jumped back for his life and Charteris muscled his Banshee past the van to a halt.

All along the myriad ways of Europe that sordid splendid city in the avenues Charteris had driven hard. He thought of them spinning down his window thrusting out his face as the vanman came on the trot.

'You trying to cause a crash or something?'

'You were touching some speed, lad, come round that corner like you were breaking the ruddy speed record, can you give me a lift I've broken down?'

He looked broken down like all the English now narrowly whooping up the after-effects of the Acid Head War, with old leather shoulders and elbows and a shirt of macabre towelling, no tie, eyes like phosphorescence and a big mottled face as if shrimps burrowed in his cheeks.

'Can you give me a lift, I say? Going north by any chance?'

The difficulty of the cadence of English. Not the old simple words so long since learnt by heart as the gallant saint slipped into the villainous captain's cabin pistol in hand but simply the trick of drawing; vocal from the mouth.

'I am going north yes. What part of it are you wanting to reach?'

'What part are you heading for?'

'I – I – where the Christmas cactus blooms and angelina flowers –'

'Heck, another acid nut, look, lad, are you safe to be with?'

'Forgive me I it's they you see I take you north okay, only I'm just a bit confused by anywhere you want I go why not?'

He couldn't think straight, couldn't aim straight though he sighted his intellect at the target the bullets of thought were multi-photographed and kept recurring and stray ricochets spanged back again and again like that succulent image that perhaps he thought sniped him from his future – and why not if the Metz vision was true and he no more than a manifestation on a web of time in which matter was the hallucination. Bafflement and yet suffusing delight as if a great havering haversack was lifted off his back simplifying under its perplexities such personal problems as right or wrong.

'If you feel that way. You are a foreigner? France was not affected they say played it cool stayed neuter. Friend to the Arab world. Lost all loot, I say. Okay I'll get my gear name's Banjo Burton by the way.'

'Mine's Charteris. Colin Charteris.'

'Good.'

Burly of shoulder he ran back to the van all conked and hunched fifty yards back, struggled at the rear and then returned for help. So Charteris not unloath climbed into the silent stage set of this *quartier* looking about licking the desolation – London London at last this ouspenskian eye beholds this legendary if meagre exotic scene. Lugging at the back of the van the other man Banjo Burton pulls at something and between them they drag it machinery across the indoor road: a passing speedster and for a moment they are both outdoors again.

'What you got here?'

'Infrasound equipment,' as they load it into the back of Charteris's car backs bending grunting in work lonely company under the night eyes. Then stand there half-inspecting each other in the semi-dark you do not see me I do not see you: you see your interpretation of me I see my interpretation of you. Moving to climb into the front seats heftily he swinging open the door with unrecorded muscling asks, 'So you're French then are you?'

'I am Serbian.'

Great conversation stopper slammer of doors internally quasi-silent revving of engines and away. The start and bastion of Europe oh they know not Serbia. O Kossovo the field of blackbirds where the dark red peonies blow but then on into the Turkish night of another era of the mobility soothed soon the shouldered man begins to manifest his flat voice as if speed harmonised it.

'I'll not be sorry to get out of London and home again though mind you you certainly see some funny things here make you laugh if you feel that way I mean to say people are more open than they used to be.'

Open? Minds open? You don't mean thoughts flowing from one to another like a net a web?'

'I don't mean that as far as I know. I don't get what goes on in the heads of you blokes though I don't mind telling you. And when I say laugh it's really enough to make you cry. I was up in Coventry when they dropped the bombs.'

The light and lack of it played across his cragged face as he fumbled for a cigarette and lit it very close to his face between a volcano crater of cupped hands all afire to the last wrinkle and looking askance with extinct pits said through smoke, 'I mean to say this is the end of the world take it or leave it.'

But this goblin had no hex on the charmed Charteris who sang 'In English you have a saying where there's life there's hope and so here no end – one end maybe but a straggle of new starts.'

'If you call going back to caveman level new start, look mate I've been around see I got a brother was in the army he's back home now because why because the forces all broke up – no discipline once the air is full of this cyclodelic men'll fall about with laughing rather than stand in a straight line like they don't get it, eh? So similarly where's your industry and agriculture going without discipline I tell you this country and all the other countries like Europe and America they're grinding to a standstill and only the bloody wogs fit to hold a spoon and fork.'

As they clattered up a long forlorn street built a century back archaic blind shuttered shattered in the stony desert just for the sheer delight of going Charteris thus: 'New disciplines grind from the stand only the old bind gone I can't argue it but industrial's a crutch thrown away.'

Can't argue it but one day with a tuned tongue I will my light is in this darkness as his face splashes flame so the sweet animal lark of my brain will be cauterise a flamingot of golden flumiance.

Though by the deadly nightshade sheltered figures rankled in vacant areas moving in groups with new instinct and on missing slates derisive the city's cats also tabbled in doubled file for every shadow a shadower.

'Your army brother got the aerosolvent?'

'Got some sort of religious kick like his whole brain's snarled up. Wide open to what ever comes along.'

'As we were meant to be.'

Banjo Burton laughed and coughed at the same time pouring smoke as if it were all he had to give.

'Bust open I'd say that's no way to go on like. Mark my words it's the end and cities hit real bad like London and New York and Brussels they copped it worst they're sinking with all hands and feet. Still a man does what he can so I run the group and hope like I mean not much one man can do after all if people aren't going to work proper they've got to do something so they trace for the sparky sound right?'

Tunnelling in his own exploding reverie where a whole sparse countryside under the sun rustled with the broken dreams of Slavs he signalled 'Sound?'

'I got a group. I manage them. I also launched the Nova Scotia Treadmill Orchestra. Used to be the Genosides. Remember their "Deathworld Boy"?'

'I was thinking your van should you just leave it?'

'It wasn't mine. I picked it up.'

Silence and night fading between them and between furry teeth the jaded taste of another sunrise until Burton huddled deeper and said again, 'I got this group.'

The camp had been full of eyes and there it had all started his first promptings on this solitary migration. 'What group?'

'A group like. Musicians. You know. … We used to be called the Dead Sea Sound now we changed to The Escalation now we're going to have infrasound like and the great roar tiding in over the heady audience in surges of everyone doing, his fruit-and-nutmost.' He waved his hand at the sky and said, 'There's no equation for a real thing what you think?'

'Musicians eh?'

'Aye damned right musicians.' He began to sing and the lost references added one more stratum to Charteris' tumbled psychogeology where many castled relics of experience lay. Untaught by his old politico-philosophical system to dig introspection he now nevertheless eased that jacket and shovelled down into his uncommon core to find there ore and always either/or, and on that godamnbiguity to snag his blade and whether there in the subsoil did not lie Kidd's treasure of all possibility, doubloons, pistoles for two, and gold moidores to other ways of thought.

Blinded by this gleam of previous metal he turned upon the singer huddled in his shadow and said, 'You could be another strand to the web or why not if all routes I now sail are ones of discovery and screaming up this avenue I also circumnavigate myself with as much meaning as your knighted hero Francis Drake.'

'I reckon as you've gone wrong somewhere this is the Portobello Road.'

'In my hindquarters reason's seat I see I sit sail unknowing but that Christmas cactus may be a shore and is there not a far peninsula of Brussels?' Trying to look into a possible future port.

'I don't know what you mean man look where you're going.'

'I think I look I think I see. Enchanted mariner ducks into unknown bays and me with a laurel on my brow I see. ...'

Charteris could not say what he saw and fell silent in a daze of future days; but what he had said moved Burton from his trental mood to say, 'If you're keeping on down the Harrow Road I have a friend in St John's Wood name of Brasher who would also be glad of a lift north like a sort of religious chap in many ways a prophet with strange means about him and god's knuckleduster when he's crossed.'

'He wants to go north?'

'Aye his wife and all that that. And my brother that I told you he was in the army well he acts as sort of disciple to Phil that's this bloke Brasher he's a bit of a touch nut but he's reckoned a bit of a prophet and he was in this plane crash and don't tell me it wasn't god's luck he managed to escape. ...'

The slow bonfire of unaccustomed words flickered on the tired minds consuming and confusing leaves of yesterday but for Charteris no meaning sunk low in the cockpit of his predestined dreams where the ashes of father domination were a trance-element and just said lazily, 'We can pick him up.'

'He's in St John's Wood I've got his address here on a bit of paper wait a bit like he's shacked up with some of his disciples. I tell you saints and seers are two a penny just lately, better turn off at this next traffic signals.'

Weren't these lay songs and carnal fictions a brighter fire than any burning in a regulation grate blessed by clergy or a funeral just the darker extension of forests lights illusions the frustration of material branches in leaf-fall or flooded delight where my dad went down.

The whole town had turned out to attend his father's funeral. Only he stayed at home. Finally, impulses of guilt and love sent him out, dressed as he was, to join the mourners.

Heavy rains had caused flooding, and the floods had delayed the progress of the funeral. It was growing dark. He drove along the winding valley road in the car: lately his father's car now his by inheritance. His father's old raincoat lay on the back seat. He did not like to throw it out The car held the smell of his father.

It was dark under the mountain. The swollen river glinted. Between him and the river were broken and twisted trees where people went to laze on summer afternoons; lately, parties of picnickers had taken to driving over here from Svetozarevo, leaving their beer cans under the bushes. Now the beer cans were afloat. It was not easy to see where the deeps of the river began. The water was running fast and stern.

He could see solitary people walking on the other side of the river. The bridge was down; he could not get across. He drove on, winding and twisting round the rumps of mountainside.

A few lamps marked the other bank of the river now. A small rain began to fall, smearing the lights. He could just make out knots of people. When he came to the second bridge, he saw that a large area in front of it had flooded; he could not drive across. Stopping the car on a bank, he climbed out and started to wade through the flood. Music was playing on the far bank, coming to him fitfully. He caught his foot on something submerged under the dark water and fell, landing on hands and knees. With a curse, he got up and went back to the car. He drove on.

Now he could see the cemetery across the intervening waste of waters. His father had been a good Communist; he was going to get a good funeral, with an Orthodox priest presiding, and members of the Party present, humble in their raincoats.

The light was ragged from wild clouds. An island, a mere strip crowned with elders and beeches, stood between him and a dear view of the funeral party opposite. When he stopped the engine, he could just hear the voice of the priest, and could make out the man's head under a lantern.

He drove farther down the road, then back, looking for a better vantage point. There was none. He contemplated going all the way back to the village and then starting again down the other road; but it would take too long, and by then the ceremony might be entirely over. Painfully lack of alternative. Eventually, he backed the car across the road – there would be no more traffic on it today – so that its nose faced out towards the flood.

He turned on the headlights, letting them glare across the river, and stood by the car with the door hanging open, staring across himself. Rain clung to his face. It was really impossible to distinguish what was going on. He paddled among the flooded trees, staring, staring, at the far bank.

'Daddy!' he cried.

And past the greeneyes swinging right past Stones with headlights and Leeds Permanent all bordered up a glimpsed group of girls running down a dark turn legs and ankles what the blackbirds on the bloody field or through my poppied dark autobreasted antiflowered the desired succubae come to me with their dark mandragoran flies.

Lost vision. Other avenues. The natural density of loins.

And all these drunken turnings as again they lost themselves a simplified pantographic variablegeometric seedimensional weltschmerzanschauungerstrasshole of light-dashed caverns rumpussed in the stoned night were names to beat on inner ears with something more than sense: Westbourne Bridge Bishop's Bridge Road Eastbourne Terrace Praed Street Norfolk Place South Wharf Road Praed Street again and then more confidently up the Edgware Road and Maida Vale and St John's Wood Road and past Lord's with the unread signs and now more rubbish in the streets and on the rooftops gliding unobtrusively another turning worlds day and so to where the man called Brasher lived.

Here so long had been his drive that when the man called Burton left to give a call Charteris dozed in a dover head down upon the steering wheel and let this longplanned city substantiate itself around him in dawning colour. In his shuttered sleep he saw himself drawn from the ground multi-pronged and screaming with several people standing ceremonially but their heads averted or under cowls to whom he was then able to speak so that they moved through whole sparse countrysides of rooms and chambers and compartments, always ascending or descending stairs. Though all was malleable it seemed to him he had a winged conversation with two two women but one of them was maimed and the other took wings and burst out from a window for some sort of freedom although they heard an old man cry that beyond the sprawling giant of a building the buildings began again.

When he was aroused he could not say whether it was he that woke or the serpent within him.

Banjo Burton was talking at the car window without making himself understood his face landscaping so Charteris followed him towards crumbling semi-daylight house and that appeared the correct procedure. Mention of breakfast chill cramped in the dull limbs part still down in cup of coffee at least hospitality south of Italy and my nose still smarting from that blow in Metz they're upstairs he went after along the million gravel.

Old grey steps to the old brown building tucked in iron railings curled to a dilute Italian mode and in the grey-brown hall black-and-red tiles of the same illusory epoch and everywhere on every side apart from the murmuring of voices rich dull rich dull patterning making claims delaying senses – asking always of each moment was it eternal could one walk through the hall and walk forever through the hall: become no more than an experience of the hall as stiff-legged from the car one in the hall's embrace and the murmuring these ephemeral halls eternally retaining.

Then again another sumptuous time-bracket and the millennial-ephemeral world of the worn stair-carpet asking always what can be the connection between this and that moment except deep in the neovortex of old apemen in masquerading mansions and the smell of England tea old umbrellas jam trees and maybe corsets? And the voices nestlings at the rocking lifetop.

Utters at the top of the stairs and another time-bracket somehow one comes through them with people milling and what really goes on who sees or in my father's head. Patterny people all minority men and women with hands Byzantine and kindly expressions born to ingenuflect. Pinkness below the high hair. Dove voices with one voice angry madbulling the china-shoppers about it: the bullman for the crestfallen times all head and shoulders all bitumen surface blunt as a block shaking Charteris' hand saying 'My name's Phil Brasher I'm you will have heard of me I lead the people the new Proceed making extricate from the dull weavings of mundanity –'

'Proceed what?'

'The name of the new religion you should of heard of it they know me better in Loughborough a failed saint there Robbins announced me inadvertently in the market with crowds howling like dogs in great schemuzzle of relevation I was born.'

And now they gazed at each other under a naked bulb with Charteris all a smooth man but for the starting English whiskers his tongue always in an easy niche and only sound within the eternal squeal of tyres too late and the erotic gridlestone of bodies lying lively on the highway jumped up and jerked off speedwise. Opposed to him Brasher everywhere chunky and wattled from suit or cheeks or breeks a fine managerie odour and premeating him no favourable aspect of the future. They were both betrayed as beyond the recording old records began again.

How they saw each other. Each in isolation shipwracked. Always a farther coast beneath the coastline. I now my own mariner seized from sealess Serbia crossed at last the saint rowing with muffed oars down foggy Port of London to the crimeship or Sir Francis circumaggraving the globe under my own prowess crossed the eggless waters to these shores this man this mantle.

They saw each other in a frost of violence crystallised recognised – a thousand self-photographing photographs fell about them on each a glimpse without its clue a fist a wrist a shoe a wall a word a cry Charteris we cry we hear his voice cry Paradise. What crazed triumph as Charteris foresuffers in utter puzzlement but yet did he not already do it all in menace of future hour.

In contrast Brasher he. Ashen he mounts back his anger on an unsound rampant saying, 'I'll not ride anywhere with you or where the lorries sweep. Isn't there's a limit a limbo a limit somewhere isn't there? You must know that I am the great Sayer and cannot in my mouth's teeth be dumb before these my followers.' They cheer and bring thin coffee always offstage like little paper faces. 'Now you arrive here and fatal events begin spreading forward along my trail and every premonition to an ashtip. See all how even death is multi-valved and in its colour black nearest brown. Back into the traffic no not I! No more moving no more movement only to still and take what I teach.'

And all those present said, 'Not the ashtits. Sickle ourselves on still-nesss,' like the backrow of the chorus.

But Burton drew Charteris aside and said, 'It's the PCA bombs he's not too bad will be glad to get home to his wife it's just he's psychic sees a bad image in you like and the menuts of a future hour.'

Bombardment of images. Peltocrat. White thighs with peonies curling between and the walk up narrow stair, *božur m'sieur*. All that he took and let the others burst about and drank his thin naked carcinomatous London coffee as they milled and mixed paper lips over china lip all textures communicasement.

And Brasher came near again something in a suit and narrowly said encouraged by Charteris' absence of aggression, 'You also pedal a belief, my foreign friend? From France if my infirmation is correct.'

'Now I arrive here and fatal events spread forward along the trails. I am quoting, but we are nothing to each other and I have no word yet. I was a member in my own country of the party, but enough of that, I'm dazed here maybe not fully awake the afflict of that Arabian nightmoil.'

The heavy man now pressed against him against the banisters.

'Tell me nothing you parisher this is my perish get it I had a miraculous survival from the air crash we're going to hit great wheeling scabs of metropolis mouths teeth and you keep quiet. I'm the Sayer here.' As panic stammer as if he still fell.

'I'll be getting on if you object. Objectivity of speeches. I have no feelings and the day spurs me, or Burton if he still wants to come.'

Tremor by the side of the mouth speaking independently.

'Come on Phil,' says Burton and to Charteris, 'He's coming but he's just suspicious of you because he saw you in the crashing plane, an apparition. On him rides the word like.'

'Nonsense,' said Charteris, 'That countryside rumpling upwards your distorted vision it was Brasher that interweaves my thoughts! I get it now the plane diving down to, well. I'm going thanks. I want no part of this man's dream nor did I ever fly with him in any plane.'

As if this abdication soothed Brasher he came forward again and barred Charteris' way brushing aside Burton saying, 'On that plane among the vestal virgings southwards you usurped my sodding seat and as we came –'

'Driving, driving, I have not flown, now get that through your acid head –'

'I only spared the flashing plashing, and all those cute little bits of stuff – now look here my foreign friend, I have a right to my share of any bits of crumpet as suffer conversion to Proceed and you –'

'Let him go Phil, he only offered you a lift to Lough along with me so are you coming, and this lot and your harum can come on after.' Thus Burton and in a closed sentence for Charteris, 'He's an old mate of mine or was till religion got him – now he's worse to manage than the Escalation. Everyone's the solo instrument in this scene.'

So was it that with papered-on cheers from the walk-on parts they took the legend down the dirty creaking stairs and to the floor below the tiles returning and in the darkness waited for a moment unknowing within the shelter of the judas house before the inward-gazing judas-hole: and then went forth.

Precognition is a function of two forces he told himself and already wished that he might record it in case the thought drifted from him on the aerosolar light. Precognotion. Two forces: mind of course and also time: the barriers go down and somewhere a white-thighed woman waits for me –

These are not my images. Bombardment of others' images. Autobreasted succubae again from Disflocations.

Yet my image the white-thighed, although I have not seen them already familiar like milk inside Venetian crystal all the better to suck you by. But my precognotions slipping.

It's not only that mind can leap aside from its tracks but that the tracks must be of certain property: so there are stages I have crossed to reach this point the first being the divination of time as a web without merely forward progress but all directions equally so that the essential I at any moment is like a spider sleeping at the centre of its web always capable of any turn and the white thorn thighs turning. Only that essential Gurdjieffian I aloof. And secondly the trip-taking soaked air of London tipping me off my traditional cranium so that I allow myself a multi-dimensional way.

Zbogom, what am I now if not more than man, mariner of my seven seizures.

More than pre-psychedelic man.

Me homo viator

She homo victorine

She haunts me as I hope to haunt her. Not so far north as Scotland.

In his treadmillrace he was on her thought scent moving along the web taking a first footfall consciously away from antique logic gaining gaining and losing also the attachment to things that keeps alive a thousand useless I's in a man's life seeing the primary fact the sexual assertion that she took wing whoever she was near to these two strange men.

Then he knew that he was the last trump of his former formal self to ascend from the dealings at Dover by the London lane and the other caught cards of his pack truly at discard trapped in old whists and wists.

He had a new purpose that was no more a mystery only now in this moment of revelation was the purpose yet unrevealed. Magical now he played the car scudding and leaping and bouncing from the surface of the road to the madland of the midlands. He wondered if voices cried his name or a paper face tore screaming down to living flesh.

Low hills whirled by like bonfires.

And while Charteris took his frail barque into strange seasoned seas, life on the textbook level continued in the back of the Banshee where Brasher uncomfortably crouched next to the group's equipment held forth to Burton once more of his traumatic trip when the wings failed the pilot's part of reason.

'I knew the flaming plane was going to crash before ever I got into it.' Brasher reliving the drama of his predictive urges all terror cotta at his wattles.

As his simple sentence speared a few facts on the material surface, they twisted under and swam to Charteris through the accumulating fathoms of his flooding newness, garbed in beauty and madness speckled.

Brasher's plane was one of the last to fly. It brought the members of the Stockholm Precognitive Congress back to Great Britain on flight S614 leaving Arlanda Airport from Runway 3 at 1145 hours local time or maybe it was later because the airport clock had taken to marking an imperceptible time of its own and your pilot was Captain Mats Hammarström who welcomes you a bored-looking man whose wooden face conceals a maelstrom of beauty caught from the falling aerosoused air.

Takeoff kindly fasten

And soon we're over the frosty snowy terrain astonishing

Suggestive contours showing through the ecological extract a Ben Nicholson low relief with public hair

Frosted lakes new formations tracks to abstracks spoor of industry neat containments of terrain scarred forests pattern appearing as we rise where no pattern was where no pattern was intended. Models too precise for truth marvellous

Clouds scraping ground. As clouds thicken sun lights them draws a screen over the world so on the fantastic stage-set a new world solid appears untrodden by man whiter-than-white more-than-arctic world of cloudbergs where nothing polar could survive miraculous

All this mindmoving while trim succulent young air-hostesses minister to the passengers pretending in their formal blue uniforms courtesy SAS that they know nothing of ersex. To nobody's deception. The masquerade keeps the serpent sleeping forms part of the formalised eroticism of pre-psychedelic times that these nubile and gleaming maidens should minister to men above the cloud formations incredible

Old concepts of godliness harnessed to conceits of airline schedules

What price the crack-up Brasher

The maidens are antidotes to this bleak world of freedom and their secret confined spaces stand alone against the idiot acreage of sky tremendous

Their suggestive contours show through the uniformal abstracts low reliefs in high style delicious

Delicate unpruned lips offer small torque before a tailspin

Plane begins to descend perhaps Brasher flinches at the white land as it rushes up but no impact. Is plane or cloud intangible. So swallowed by these mountains and valleys on which nobody ever built erewhonderful

Great wheeling scab of metropolis below thirty thousand streetscars cutting through the primaeval concrete crust. Silver paternal Thames threading through it a curling crack of sky and your Captain Mats Hammarström takes it into his capital notion to land upon it

All Brasher had lumbered in his bare cranian retort were an old Cortina and a lorry with Glasgow numberplate. So much for precognition. Next second. Your Captain got Tower Bridge. Slap. In. The Ouspenskian Eye.

'The plane sank in the flaming river like a stone and I was the only one who survived,' concluded Brasher.

Charteris nearly ran into a group of people he swerved they scattered and adrenalin generated cleared his brain.

'People all group,' he said. 'Changed living pattern.'

'Aye, well, it's the bombs,' said Banjo Burton. 'They're regrouping, lost all loot. Ideas of solitude and togetherness have changed. They listen to a new sound semi-entirely.'

'I was lucky to get away. I nearly drowned,' Brasher insisted.

'It's a new world,' said Charteris. 'I can begin to hear it like an earquake.'

'The group will be glad to see me back,' said Burton. 'The Escalation.'

'My exploration of it,' said Charteris with the vehicle vibrant

'Loughborough will welcome me,' said Brasher. 'And my wife of course.'

Charteris was laughing with a random note to mesh into the engine noise. The silver thread of road his narrow sea and he Sir Francis? Then where these Englishmen went might well prove his cape of good hope.

'This infrasound really breaks people up,' said Burton.

'Robbins is no more than a feeble pseudo-saint,' said Brasher. 'I must train up a new disciple, find someone to master the illogic of the times or generally clamp a baffle onto the flux.'

'Train me,' said Charteris.

The road ran north and north and always on never homesick its own experience. They saw towns and houses and sometimes people in groups but more often trees heavy with a new black wooden winter growth and everything stretched very thin over the great drum of being. Juiced the car caperilled forwards northwoods. And the three men sat in the car, dose together, also apart, with their wits about them knowing very little indeed of all the things of which they were entirely aware. Functioning. Of a function. Existing in more ways than they could possibly learn to take advantage of.

Fragment of a Much Longer Poem

Oh one day I shall walk ahead
Up certain sunken steps into a hall
Patterned with tiles in black and red
And recognise the colour and the place
As well as if I once walked back
In time up certain sunken steps
And came into a hall with black
And red tiles in a certain coded
Pattern that makes me think I tread
Up sunken steps into a hallway and
Confront a tiled floor patterned red
And black which makes me think I stand

Circadian Rhythm

I've got circadian rhythm
You've got circadian rhythm
We've got circadian rhythm –
   So the town-clock's stopped for good

In the night-time I see daylight
And my white nights outshine daytime –
It beats the living daylight
Out of one-time lifetime

Spill my living daylights down my shirt-front
Chase my living nightmares round my shirt-tail
All my trite cares
They're just rag and bob-tail

So I've got circadian rhythm
You've got circadian rhythm
We've got circadian rhythm –
   So we ain't going home no more

THE DEAD SEA SOUND

The First and Future Paradise

We all know it –
There was primordial epoch
In which everything was decided
An exemplar for future ages.

Let's say it again –
You glimpse it sometimes behind bedroom
Curtains – a paradise and then
Catastrophe! They constitute the present.
Meaning what we do now is an end trajectory
Trajectory.
When I love you love
There's nothing personal in it.

The decisive deed took place before us
Essential preceeding actual.
We must confront mythic ancestors
Unless we wish for ever
To be driven by our whirlwinds
To live in their old nostalgias.

Paradise is lingering legend in our day
The world's smiles are few and wintry.
And the mountains no longer shore the sky.
But one may be a mountain even now –
It's not too late! – if you pursue your self
If you can make cosmic journeys
Be a shaman not a sham man.

Dangers lie in the self, serpents
Lurk but there are new animals
And auxiliaries and tongues
To help psychopomps and singers
(Listen to birds and the throat of the cockatoo!)

Friendship with the animals who are
Beyond broken time, and schizophrenics:
Bliss of other bodies: the paradisiac
Journeys beyond life and
Death: pushing of utterance into

Mystery of myth: these are the four known ways

To the seat of the Free

The Free who live in the Tree

The Cosmic Tree

Above the Sea

Of Being

Death is the sin

And on the many motor-roads

Until we attain incombustibility

We fly in its qualifying fact

Man the driver close

To the ultimate tick

We all know it

All we have to do is

Wake and know it.

And abolition of that curtain time

Which killed

The primordial epoch.

Fall About Laughing

When we tell them that we're in love
Men'll fall about laughing
When the lion gets around to lying down with the dove
Men'll fall about laughing

When they try to work the machines
Men'll fall about laughing
Ride a bike or open a can of sardines
Men'll fall about laughing

What happened to the old straight line
Is no affair of yours or mine
Or the guys who run the place
It's such an awful disaster
When the mind's not the master
You can't even keep a straight face

When we say that the wild days are back
Men'll fall about laughing
When they find out that we're sharing a sack
Men'll fall about laughing
Men'll fall about laughing

THE DEAD SEA SOUND

Formal Topolatry of Aspiring Forms

```
                              L
                        B L I S S
                              F
                        A N G E L
                        U       I   O
                        T       V   U
                        O       E   G
                        B I R T H
                        R           B
                        E           O
                        A F T E R
                        S           O
                        T           U
A N T I F L O W E R E D     G
  N         I       A   D E A T H
  V I G I L         V       A
  I         T       E       T
  L O U G H B O R O U G H
```

Love's Nocturnal Entry into Bombed Coventry

```
                              C
      L M                     C A S H
      L O S E                 C H A R T E R S
   C O V E N T R Y            R E V E A L   H
T U N E R   R                 C A P E R I L   A
A N D   B Y E                 N O R   N O R D
T O       A                   I       N       E
N I G H T                     A S S U A G E S
                              C
                              L
                              O
                              U
      S I L E N C E D
```

Topography of an Unrealised Affair

```
              C
        H E L L O
        E   O   O
        A   V   L
        S T R E S S
```

An Anagrammatical Small Square

War was:
Sin ran:
S saw a rani
In a raw ass.
W A R
A   A
S I N

D A C I D A C
D A C I D A C I D
A C I D A C I D A
A C I D   A C I
        H E A D
C I   I D   D A
I D   D A   C A C
    A C I D A C I D A C
    I D A C I D A C
    D A C I D A C I
        C I D A C I
        D A C I
        A C I D

A I I I I I I I I I
I I I I I I I I I I   I
I I I I I I I I I I I I
I I I I I I I I I I I I
I I I I I I c I I I I I I
I I I I I I I I I I I I
I I I I I I I I I I I I
I I I I I I I I I I I I
    I I I I I I I I I I
    I   I I I I I I I I
        I I I I I I I I
        I I I I I I I D

250

Dreamer, Schemer

Come into my dream! Let's live in the life we dreamed of – and see its unhappy endings!

Ego City sprawled and sprawled. In two decades, what had once been merely a modest new entertainment centre had grown to the size of a big city. Already, as many lines of communication homed on it as on the capital.

The residents of Ego City were mainly concerned in one way or another with the making of play-outs. Play-outs were the art form of the century. Play-outs dominated the entertainment world. Play-outs marked the revolutionary point where show business and medical therapy mingled. Everyone needed play-outs.

In two decades of existence, Ego City had seen a number of real dramas, as well as its countless myriad staged ones. Many fortunes had been made and lost there, many companies swallowed, many corporations run out of business. Behind the vast and smooth-working facades of Ego City ran a private history of boardroom battles, orgies, sumptuous dinners, suicides, courage and compromise every bit as startling as the play-outs.

Current king of the play-out empire was Lee Roger Irnstein, billed in the tabloids as Mr Dream King. Lee Roger Irnstein was a millionaire many times over. His personal income, it was estimated, rivalled that of any one of the smaller European nations. He had climbed to where he was by being an insomniac, working continuously for fifteen years when all his opponents had had to snatch an occasional nap, and by keeping an unsleeping watch for the weaknesses of his opponents. Lee Roger Irnstein was not a crook. Nor was he honest; he was simply a single-minded man who never missed any opportunity for advancement through such weaknesses as indecision, compassion or indifference.

Lee Roger Irnstein was tall, wrinkled, totally grey. His age was forty-four. His expression was pleasant enough. But his eyes never blinked, and once their gaze had found an opponent's face it never left it, so that eventually the opponent was almost glad to yield to defeat and sink away out of sight. Despite this characteristic, there was nothing that visibly marked Lee Roger Irnstein off from the rest of his fellow men. The factor that did that was hidden in secrecy from almost everyone but his current wife, Famagusta Martitia, and his downtrodden twelve-year-old son, Lee Roger.

Those two knew that Lee Roger Irnstein had never taken part in a single play-out.

That vast kingdom over which Lee Roger Irnstein ruled presented a glittering facade to the world. Great triumphal arches, high towers, sky balloons, greeted the millions who poured into town from all over the world for their taste of that shaped reality that was so much better, so much sweeter, so much more vivid than the ordinary reality of everyday.

But at one point, the huge industrial complex had broken down into a chaos of rubbish. The massive functional shapes of play-out technology slumped into an avalanche of waste. This was at Southside, along Gulch Road. Here were the extraordinary dumps of Ego City, a landscape of hills and valleys consisting entirely of all the expensive castoffs of the city, from the largest and glossiest of indestructible packing cases down to once-used dancing slippers, from saloon cars that had been discarded at a drunken whim down to unopened packs of cigarettes thrown away because the cellophane had proved a touch resistant, from private planes that had suddenly ceased to please down to nail-clippers that were too blunt to clip, from monstrous slabs of rusty switch-gear down to still-bright contact lenses.

In this wilderness lived Bernie Burr.

Except for the fact that he never shaved, Bernie Burr looked rather like Lee Roger Irnstein. He too was tall, wrinkled and totally grey. He also was forty-four. His expression was pleasant enough but his gaze – whatever it had once done – now never managed to meet the gaze of another human being. It kept wandering off, as if his eyes were too weak to meet the eyesight of anyone else. This was very unlike the behaviour of the eyes of Lee Roger Irnstein, the man who had defeated Bernie Burr.

Bernie lived with a tattered lady of his own age called Barley in a battered blue packing case that had once housed a Patterson's Piorgium Model 'Dandy.' His days were spent scrounging through the enchanted detritus of the Gulch Road dump, his nights telling Barley the story of the great days when he owned half of Ego City. In consequence, Barley spent most of her nights drinking and most of her days asleep with her mouth open on the seat they had pulled out of an old Pullman coach.

It was a curious thing that Bernie Burr should have only that one obsessive topic of conversation. A couple of miles away, in surroundings as luxurious as Bernie's were dreadful, Roger Lee Irnstein similarly had only one topic of conversation to inflict on Famagusta Martitia and Lee Roger Junior. It was the same topic.

'It was a confrontation,' he told them. 'A classical confrontation. This Bernie Burr wanted to take us over, and we wanted to take him over. It seemed he had all the power, and he slapped this ultimatum on me. I had to accept his corporation's terms by the next morning or else. Then he made one false move.'

'I know, he came to see you that evening,' Lee Roger Junior said.

'Who's telling this? Go away and play if you can't keep quiet! As I got home that evening, Bernie Burr was waiting in the drive. He caught hold of my jacket and begged me to accept the ultimatum. Said he was having trouble with his directors and he would be thrown out if this deal didn't go through. I told him he was crazy, but he said if I accepted the terms of the ultimatum, he'd see I was okay. It would solve both our troubles, he said. Now what makes a man be that weak?'

Famagusta Martitia said, 'He must have been under a terrible strain, honey!'

'Ker-rist, honey, we all were. But why is it that at such a moment of truth one man shows weak and another strong? I mean, it's all wrapped up in the enigma of personality, isn't it? Anyhow, he'd given me his head on a plate. Next morning, I rejected the ultimatum, Bernie Burr got the push just as he said he would, and in the confusion I bought up all his backers piecemeal. Ever since then, nobody's ever heard of Bernie again and I've been boss of Ego City.'

His wife caressed one of his earlobes. 'You deserve it, honey, you've been real lucky!'

Lee Roger Irnstein pulled away as if she had tweaked his ear. 'Lucky, honey! Lucky nothing! That was the most unlucky day of my life. At heart I'm just a dreamer, only I never get time to dream. I could have been a great musician instead of a captain of industry. I've been so busy running Ego City, I've never had time to fulfill my personal destiny.'

'Then, honey, why did you knock down Bernie Burr like you did?'

'Because I'm the man I am, and I seize chances. I just never had a chance to be a great musician.'

'Then the man you are isn't a great musician, honey.'

Lee Roger Irnstein got up and began to pace up and down.

'Nobody knows the man I am except me, honey.'

Famagusta Martitia went over to the drink machine and had it pour them both another drink. 'I don't think that you know the sort of man you are, honey. You ought to go to a play-out. You know, enter one anonymously. It would sort you out tremendously and show you exactly the sort of man you really are.'

'Now you're talking nonsense, honey! You know I own those things. I don't have to indulge in them.'

'I think you're scared, honey.'

And that's how it happened that, a few drinks later, Lee Roger Irnstein was persuaded to enter one of his own play-outs.

Meanwhile, back at the old blue packing case, Bernie Burr was telling Barley of the crisis that had ruined his life.

'I played it clever. I drove down to this guy Irnstein's fancy mansion and collared him when he arrived home. I offered him a perfectly foolproof deal to get these guys off my neck who were riding me, with a big cut for him. Next day, us two could have run Ego City between us.'

'Ah, you couldn't run a hot dog stall!' Barley said.

'In those days I could. I had genius then. But that creep Irnstein loused it all up. He double-crossed me next morning, and from then on I was finished.'

Barley hiccupped. 'You played into his hands, sounds to me. You got chicken!'

'I was meant to be a big boss, not a bum! It was just I played my hand wrong. All I need is another chance to prove it. Just one more chance.'

'Don't give me that again! Every day I hear the same tune! Look, Bernie, if you had the same chance again, you'd louse it up in the same way, see? Because it's your destiny to be a bum!'

He rose to his feet, clutching the bottle as he did so.

'Don't you call me a bum, you old bat! At heart I'm a very responsible man, a captain of industry, a millionaire, a –'

'A bum!' Barley finished. 'You're kidding yourself! If you want to find out the sort of jerk you really are, why don't you go into a play-out and see for yourself, instead of boring me with your load of hogwash?'

He poured her another drink. 'I love you, Barley,' he said brokenly, ''cause you always know what's best for me.'

What happened when you entered one of the play-out theatres was not simple, but it was fast. Pleasant machines put you under light hypnosis to remove any surface inhibitions. You then stated roughly what your problem was, or what situation you wanted to amuse yourself with that evening. These reports were flashed to a group of human and computer analysts and coordinated with the reports of everyone else entering the play-outs at the same time. People with similar ends in view were grouped together. Cast lists were formed, and immense script-writing machines assembled a plot to fit the personalities involved.

While this was going on, and it took only a minute, you were being given the drugs that would most easily enable you to behave as the personality you wished to be. Then the plot came on, was played to you subliminally, and the costuming and make-up departments saw to it that you looked the part. By the time that was done, you had your role effortlessly memorised – though there was always room left for adlibbing.

All over Ego City stood the play-out theatres, many of them of tremendous size – the sexual theatres being the smallest because those who wanted that sort of play-out needed little action in their scripts. After the makeup department had finished with you, you would be conveyed by tube to the appropriate theatre, if you were not already there. Many of the theatres specialised in period plays, because it had been found that people could express their basic needs more freely when out of their own time. No one troubled about historical accuracy. It was the spirit that counted. In the theatres were no audiences, only participants – actors working with other actors, but each isolated in his or her own little ego.

In Theatre Fifty-Five, it was a blustery spring day in the sixth or seventh century. Dramatically lit by the only sunbeam to penetrate the cloud overhead, King Petrovich stood with his arms akimbo, looking south towards the mountains, while his wife, Branka, waited behind him at a respectful distance.

Petrovich was tall, wrinkled, totally grey. His age was forty-four, his expression was not unpleasant. But as he looked toward the valley down which his army must pass on the morrow, a frown creased his forehead.

Behind him, a temple was being built. Behind that stretched his army, resting, cooking their lean rations. Women and children mingled with the men of Petrovich's army. And behind them were the other followers, the rabble who had followed his triumphant progress for five years across the wildernesses of Eastern Europe.

'You must rest and eat now, O my king, in preparation for the morrow's march into Illyria,' Branka said, taking his arm timidly.

'Cease, woman! Petrovich cannot rest while the fate of his peoples is at stake.'

'It is a heavy burden you bear, my lord.'

She was beautiful, tall, pale, red of lip, her hair black and skilfully dressed, hanging down to her waist. Petrovich seized her by the waist and kissed her till her mouth was bruised.

'Aye, the burden of my fate is heavy, woman, as you say. Therefore I go to pray.'

Branka fell back as the king strode forward into the temple. The rude palisade of the temple was decorated in a crude manner with the figures of soldiers and naked maidens. Inside, the roof was red and the walls hung with tapestries. Although the carpenters were still at work on the temple, their mallet-strokes echoing through the interior, the priests were already busy, and the smoke from a burnt offering drew tears in the king's eyes.

He prostrated himself before his god, a great wooden idol twice his size. It had two bodies and four heads, all of them fearsome. Against one of its massive thighs lay its saddle, bridle and mighty silver sword, which Petrovich alone of all his people was strong enough to wield in battle.

His prostrations were brief. He rose, scattering the priests, and strode into the open towards his great tent of hide which took twenty men to pitch. A scout ran up to him, panting, and bowed.

'Well, varlet?'

'My lord, the King of the Illyrians is in the camp. He desires word with you.'

'King Donikpus? How comes he here?'

'My lord, he comes in peace and even now awaits your gracious permission to speak with you.'

'Have him brought to my tent.'

Striding in through the heavy damask curtain, Petrovich scattered his serving women.

'But you must sustain yourself, O my King!' Branka cried.

'No time for that – get these women from my sight! Bring me good Transylvanian wine. Donikpus, King of Illyria, is here to see me.'

The queen gasped. 'But my lord, he is your sworn enemy! Has he not vowed to slay you tomorrow when you march into his lands?'

'There's villainy afoot. I'll see that I question him closely.'

'O my King, whispers are abroad that your general Yovan thinks to spread mutiny among your subjects.'

Petrovich stroked his great iron grey beard and raised an eyebrow. 'I have no time to waste on the sub-plot now, woman. Stick to the main scripts. Where's the wine?'

A great oxhorn bound in silver and splashing over with the dark red liquor of Transylvania was brought to him. As he quaffed it back, trumpets sounded without and General Yovan entered with the King of the Illyrians and attendant lords, etc.

Donikpus and Petrovich stared each other in the eye. Donikpus, for all his outlandish garb and armour that aped the Roman, was not unlike his rival though he wore no beard. He was tall, wrinkled and would probably have been fair were he not totally grey. He was forty-four years of age; his expression would have been pleasant were he not scowling now. Branka thrust an oxhorn of wine into his hand, and the tension in the tent somewhat relaxed.

'You realise your head is in jeopardy every moment you remain in my camp?' Petrovich said.

'You do not imagine I enter this pagan place for pleasure?'

'State your business and be gone!'

'Mind I do not go without stating it! Or your corpse, Petrovich, will lie reeking in the dust by tomorrow's sunset.'

'You dare to threaten me, Donikpus? I'll ride into battle with your body rolling behind my horse!'

'I'll have you driven back to the wilds from which you came!'

'I'll have your entrails strewn through every field between here and Kief!'

General Yovan coughed. 'My lords, the script, I pray! Should not the King of the Illyrians state his business?'

'You're right,' Donikpus said, quaffing his wine. 'Petrovich, we are both in mortal danger. I come to offer an alliance.'

'An alliance with you!' boomed Petrovich. 'What means this?'

'Ride with me two leagues to the hills, and I will show you proof of the danger. Unless you are afraid. ...'

Petrovich looked about him, at the anxious face of his wife, the stolid face of Yovan, the stem faces of the attendant lords, etc. He took another great drag at his wine. 'I'll ride with you,' he said. As his wife ran with him weeping to his horse he said to her, 'And keep an eagle eye on the dastardly designs of General Yovan.'

'Sure, honey,' she said. 'So will I, by my troth.'

Entirely unaccompanied, the two kings rode together out of camp. It was sunset now, and all the western sky was a ragged mass of red and gold cloud. The ground beneath them was dark as they spurred their steeds up the side of the hill.

At last they reined at the summit. The camp lay behind, fires twinkling here and there, an occasional burst of hoarse song rising even to this eminence. South lay the mountains and the sombre valley of the Siva River.

'That way you and your host must go tomorrow,' Donikpus said, pointing down the valley. 'You will be wiped out from behind. You see that old stone Mithraic temple over there, at the beginning of the valley?'

'It is deserted. My scouts examined it thoroughly this afternoon.'

'Empty it is, Petrovich. But under it are great caves. All this barren mountain is a maze of caves. Those caves are filled with half the Illyrian host. When you have passed, they will burst out and attack you from the rear, while the other half will attack from the front. You will be slaughtered to a man.'

Petrovich turned his scowling regard to the other, searching that wrinkled face lit by the light of the dying sun.

'You are the Illyrian king, yet you tell me this! How so?'

And Donikpus explained. He was in trouble, particularly with his upstart son, Prince Gorgues, who would lead the ambush. Donikpus wanted to do a deal with Petrovich. He would fix things so that they would have an alliance together, and in the morning, they could unite forces and wipe out Gorgues. 'We can probably mop up your General Yovan too,' he suggested.

Silence fell, and a moon rose in the sky while Petrovich considered these things. A night bird was singing. At last Petrovich spoke.

'You have delivered your whole nation into my hands,' he said. 'I shall be prepared for the ambush tomorrow, I shall capture Gorgues and tell him of your deceit, and he will wipe you out. I can then wipe him out in my own good time. You have no courage, and so you are defeated before you start! This is the moment of truth, Donikpus, is it not?'

The Illyrian king's teeth flashed in a sneer. 'You opportunist, Petrovich! Uneasy lies the head that wears the crown, I say! Those that live by the sword shall die by the sword! Farewell, false king! I'll match you yet!'

Setting spur to his palfrey, he galloped down the long slopes towards the forbidding valley that marked the marches of his kingdom, leaving Petrovich to sit and brood on the hill.

A torrent of confused emotion ran through Petrovich. He recalled all he had said to Branka – and all he had not said; he recalled all he had ever done – and all he had not done; he recalled all he hoped to be – and all he hoped not to be.

The sky was free of cloud now. All the stars shone down, and a comet or two appeared.

Suddenly, Petrovich spurred his horse and galloped down into the valley along the path that the Illyrian king had taken. He had come to a decision.

To his surprise, he saw that Donikpus had stopped, turned about and was riding back. Both men, alarmed by the other's change of plans, drew swords. They charged towards each other at a gallop and met by the rushing Siva River with a clash of metal.

'Halt, then!' cried Donikpus. 'It's too late to change your mind, you braggart king! I want my crown no more. I'm a dreamer at heart, not a ruler, I'm off into the mountains among the simple people. I shall grow a beard and become a wandering musician, singing the ballads of my people.'

'You can't do that!' Petrovich exclaimed. 'I'm tired of kingship, too. Besides, I have a better voice than you!'

'You lie! My voice is the finest in all the coastlands of Illyria!'

'Pah, that pipsqueak voice! Donikpus, you couldn't keep a baby awake with your singing, and you must die –'

But even as he lunged forward with his silver sword, the king of Illyria lunged forward with his gold one. For a moment, the light of the comets flashed along their deadly blades. Both men grunted almost in unison. Silence fell. Then, very slowly, one king toppled off his horse towards the left stirrup and the other towards the right stirrup. Since they were facing each other, they fell on top of each other and rolled together into the rapid stream, where the wavelets, chill from the heights of the mountain, washed over their sightless eyes.

All this time, Gorgues was carousing in a stimulating fashion inside the limestone mountain, while exciting things were happening to General Yovan in the queen's tent. …

Precautions were taken so that participants in play-outs, when leaving the theatres after their roles were done, did not meet any fellow actors. But since these precautions had been arranged by Bernie Burr in the days when he owned half of Ego City, he had small trouble in circumventing them.

So when Lee Rogers Irnstein came to climb into his self-driven limousine, he found a ragged figure waiting for him in the shadows.

'Lee?' Bernie asked huskily. 'Say, Lee, I recognised you in there!'

Without thinking, Lee Rogers Irnstein clutched Bernie's hand. 'Bernie! I recognised you – after all these years!'

'Several centuries, hasn't it been?' Bernie said dryly.

'Say, I really learnt something about myself in there,' Lee Rogers Irnstein said. 'Should have gone long ago, like Famagusta said.'

'You made a swell Illyrian king,' Bernie said. 'And you know what I learnt about myself? That I am really happier as I am than as a king or a captain of industry or in any post with responsibility. I could have double-crossed you, but at the last moment I ratted out!'

They both lit Irnstein cigars, and that magnate said, emotion in his voice, 'You were a great warrior king, Bernie. I kind of admired that beard of yours. And I liked your Branka, too. Showed good taste.'

He was in an uncharacteristically sentimental mood. His death as Donikpus – stabbed by a prop sword made of a wonderful alloy that disintegrated immediately on touching human flesh – had momentarily softened him. Gazing at Bernie, he said, 'Know what I learnt about myself? I'm just not destined to be a wandering minstrel or a great musician or any of that stuff. I may think I want to be, but that way spells death for me. In the future, I shall be content with the humbler role of king of the Illyrians. I mean, of course, of Ego City.'

A long silence fell, while they leaned against the car.

'We really got ourselves sorted out in there,' Bernie said. 'Wonderful form of entertainment we invented between us.'

'Say, Bernie, I'm not just saying this, but it really has been swell meeting you again. Like the good old days.'

Bernie nodded. Looking cautiously about to see that nobody could overhear them, he said, 'Look, Lee, why don't I come and see you in the morning? I've got a little proposition to put to you that could make all the difference to both of us. ...'

Dream of Distance

You are watching this film, eager to taste its first scenes. All you have been treated to as yet, as the flimsy curtains draw back and reveal a monstrous silent sea, is a great panorama of waves and sunlight. Islands sail in the distance like ships.

No titles, no credits, fly at you over the water. There is no music. Yes, there is sound – the noise of unease, a noise that does not belong here. Someone standing outside your bedroom door, footsteps on the roof, a furry thing following you underground.

All the time, you travel over the water.

The islands show green. That and a certain quality in the atmosphere – as indefinable as the dry and melancholy-sweet flavour of life – tell you it is April. Spring is beginning again, is surely coming again, just as fools and wise men had every reason to expect it would.

And April is sacred to Venus.

Boats scatter on the water. The men with their dark faces are at home in them; they fit the boats as the boats fit the waves. In one boat, a man sings a song to himself as he looks down into the water. Nothing is still here except his regard, and even that cannot anchor the boat; it glides evasively and some feet below on the dappled bottom of the sea a clouded doppelganger moves with it. All things have counterparts.

While you are growing into a straight true lad, learning your lessons, while you decided what you would do and be in life, while the red fuses burned you into bud, you also had a counterpart, a white silent thing – perhaps a car crash, say. It lay with all the other stills on some future desk, to be glanced at sideways, not recognised. One day you would have to sit at that desk and pick it up. Stop and listen in the woods of April, as you do homage to Venus, listen to that furry thing moving underground as you move, listen to the noise of unease.

So the viewpoint moves over the water to no sound of lapping.

Caesar traced his descent from Aeneas who sprang, it is said, from the union of Mars and Venus. So great Caesar promoted the worship of Venus Victrix. This is true Mediterranean water, where vessels sailed bearing news of her verdant name. This sea too has its counterparts.

On this planet, in this place, the sea at the middle of the Earth, men worship Venus in the fourth month.

Do you see the foam on the small waves? The breeze blows sharp. And those flat breastless isles? Could they be the islands of the Cyclades, where Greek Aphrodite was born? That furred sound of unease is hushed. You never heard it go, but in its place, sweetly, sounds a honeyed voice. Ah, young lovers, lie close together tonight; breathe each other's breath, taste each other's juices, be uncurbed. Although the moon may rise here evermore, although the seas lap for ever at Naxos' shore, your loving limbs will sink below next moment's wave! All those bright carmines of your secret places, their spring is also autumn; no singer's lip can give you melody tomorrow!

You see it all on the forward-rushing screen. You take it for real. No other animal knows your happiness, no other animal can plumb your sorrows. No animal but you could carve an Aphrodite or build himself a lead grave.

Now there is another thing coming on the waves. You cannot distinguish what it is.

Those Romans of the classic age – they fruitfully confused Aphrodite with Venus. The common sea-faring men kissed her marble mons veneris to secure themselves from storm and shipwreck. So the goddess girls merge, so legends merge. Mistakes are made, never intentionally, but with a higher intent, creating all art, fructifying.

I too have pressed my lips there, sucked and kissed. Nothing I cared for shipwreck then! Behind that gaping body, mediterranean, garden-flowering fertile, Cytherean, furred, sourceful and resourceful, the worshipped girls, and duskier hags, Ishtar and Astarte.

It is a gate beyond the prow. A massive double gate, arched perhaps of wood, mossed, and made of dull iron or some leaden prehistoric timber, scarred, furred with lichen, spurred with seawrack.

Forward more slowly. The great gates are closed. Sea all about, silent, waiting. The sparrow the dove the swan the swallow wait there. You are crying. In the fourth month on Venus, maybe they worship some phantom Earth that in a Cytherean mind accumulated legends. The beautiful light goes underground before these prehistoric doors.

Ships wait to go in. Slowly they open, unexpectedly, great lock gates grating in a sombre gait. Beyond another world of counterparts. You go in and all you inherit is now a saga – bearded or beardless they sing it in your pristine kingdom; but because this is my story the great gates close again and the mediterranean light shines. Venus and Mars have never been so close.

Now says the audience, how characteristic that he should tell his story twice removed. But perhaps if I had gone I would not be here now. Aren't these voyages mine still? Do not verdant islands still sail like ships? What if I weep? Moisture is elemental, and silently the curtains draw together and draw together while the sea is still moon-blue. My bitch love this is your display.

You and I lie in the auditorium as the curtains draw together, hissing with the sound of waves and serpents.

Send Her Victorious, or, The War Against the Victorians, 2000 AD

The news hit New York in time to feature in the afternoon editions. No editor splashed it very large, but there it was, clear enough on the front pages:

MANY DEATHS IN CASTLE CATASTROPHE
and
QUEEN'S HOME GONE
and
BRITAIN'S ENEMIES STRIKE?

Douglas Tredeager Utrect bought two papers as he fought his way to the Lexington Advanced Alienation Hospital, where he was currently engaged as Chief Advisor. The news did not tell him as much as he wished to know, which he found was generally the way with news. In particular, it did not mention his English friend, Bob Hoggart.

All that was said was that, during the early afternoon, a tremendous explosion which might be the work of hostile foreign powers had obliterated the grounds of the royal park of Windsor, Berkshire, England, and carried away most of Windsor Castle at the same time. Fortunately, the Queen was not in residence. Fifty-seven people were missing, believed killed, and the death roll was mounting. The Army was mobilising and the British Cabinet was meeting to discuss the situation.

Utrect had no time to worry over the matter, deeply though it concerned him. As soon as he entered his office in the Advanced Alienation Hospital, he was buttonholed by Dr Froding.

'Ah, Utrect, there you are! Your severe dissociation case, Burton. He attacked the nurse! Quite inexplicable in such a quiet patient – rather, only explicable as anima-hostility, which hardly fits with his other behaviour. Will you come to see him?'

Utrect was always reluctant to see Burton. It alarmed him to discover how attracted he was by the patient's psychotic fantasy world. But Froding was not only a specialist on the anima; he was a forceful man. Nodding, Utrect followed him along the corridor, thrusting his moody reindeer's face forward as if scenting guilt and danger.

Burton sat huddled in one corner of his room – a characteristic pose. He was a pale slight man with a beard. This appeared to be one of the days when his attention was directed to the real world; his gestures toward it were courtly, and included the weariness which is so often a part of courtliness, although here it seemed more, Utrect thought, as if the man were beckoning distantly, and part of him issuing fading calls for help. Don't we all? he thought.

'We are pleased to receive your majesty,' Burton said, indicating the chair, secured to the floor, on which Utrect might sit. 'And how is the Empress today?'

'She is away at present,' Utrect said. He nodded toward Froding, who nodded back and disappeared.

'Ah, absent, is she? Absent at present. Travelling again, I suppose. A beautiful woman, the Empress, your majesty, but we must recognise that all her travelling is in the nature of a compulsion.'

'Surely, Herr Freud; but, if we may, I would much rather discuss your own case. In particular, I would like to know why you attacked your nurse.'

Burton looked conspiratorial. 'This Vienna of ours, your majesty, is full of revolutionaries these days. You must know that. Croats, Magyars, Bohemians – there is no end to them. This nurse girl was hoping to get at your majesty through me. She was in the pay of Serbian assassins.'

He was convinced that he was Sigmund Freud, although, with his small stature and little copper-coloured beard, he looked more like Algernon Charles Swinburne, the Victorian poet. He was convinced that Utrect was the Emperor Franz Josef of Austria. This confused mental state alternated with periods of almost complete catatonia. Year by year, the world's mental illnesses were growing more complex, spiralling toward ultimate uterine mindlessness, as the ever-expanding population radiated high dosages of psychic interference on all sides.

Although Burton's case was only one among many, its fascination-repulsion for Utrect was unique, and connected, directly but at a sub-rational level, with the commission on which he had sent Bob Hoggart to London, England. Many were the nights he had sat with Burton, humouring the man in his role, listening to his account of life in Vienna in the nineteenth century.

As a result, Utrect knew Vienna well. Without effort, he could hear the clatter of coaches in the streets, could visit the opera or the little coffee houses, could feel the cross-currents that drifted through the capital of the Hapsburgs from all corners of Europe. In particular, he could enter the houses, the homes. There was one home he loved, where he had seen a beautiful girl with a peacock feather; there, the walls were clear-coloured and plain, and the rooms light with dark-polished pieces of furniture. But he knew also the crowded homes of Freud's acquaint-ances, had made his way toward overstuffed horsehair sofas, knocking a Turkish rug from an occasional table, brushed past potted palms and ferns. He had sat and stared at dim volumes, too heavy to hold, which contained steel engravings of customs in the Bavarian Alps or scenes from the Khedive's Egypt. He had seen Johannes Brahms at a reception, listened to recitals of the Abbé Liszt and the waltzes of Johann Strauss. He knew – seemed to know – Elizabeth of Austria, Franz Josef's beau-tiful but unhappy wife, and occasionally found himself identifying her with his own doomed wife, Karen. He felt himself entirely at home in that distant Victorian world – far more at home than an alienist with an international reputation in the year 2000 should be.

This afternoon, as Burton rambled on about treason and conspira-cies at court, Franz Josef's attention wandered. He had an illusion much greater than one man's madness to diagnose. He knew that he, his companions, his ailing wife, the great bustling world, faced imminent disaster. But he continued to dispense automatic reassurance, while sustaining the role of the Emperor.

As he left Burton at last, Froding happened to be passing along the corridor. 'Does he seem disturbed?'

'I cannot make sense of the fellow,' Utrect said. Then he recalled himself. He was not the Emperor, and must not talk like him. 'Er – he is quiet at present, probably moving toward withdrawal. Pulse rate normal. See that he is monitored on "A" Alert tonight.'

Dismissing Froding rather curtly, he hurried to his office. He could catch a news bulletin in four minutes. He flicked on the desk 3V and opened up his wrisputer, feeding it the nugatory data contained in the paper report on Windsor Castle. He added to the little computer, 'More details when the newscast comes up. Meanwhile, Burton. He attacked his nurse, Phyllis. In his Freud persona, he claims that she was a revolutionary. Revolution seems to be dominating his thinking these days. He also claims an anti-Semitic conspiracy against him at the university. Multi-psychotic complex of persecution-theme. Indications his mental condition is deteriorating.'

Switching off for a moment, Utrect swallowed a pacifier. Everyone's mental condition was deteriorating as the environment deteriorated. Burton had simply been cheated out of the presidency of a little tin-pot society he had founded; that had been enough to topple him over the brink. Utrect dismissed the man from his mind.

He ignored the adverts scampering across the 3V screen and glanced over the routine daily bulletins of the hospital piled on his desk. Under the new Dimpsey Brain Pressure ratings, the figures in all wards were up at least .05 over the previous day. They had been increasing steadily, unnervingly, for a couple of years, but this was the biggest jump yet. The World Normality Norm had been exceeded once more; it would have to be bumped up officially again before alarm spread. By the standards of the early nineties, the whole world was crazy; by the standards of the seventies, it was one big madhouse. There were guys now running banking houses, armies, even major industries, who were proven around the bend in one or more (generally many more) of three thousand two hundred and six Dimpsey ways. Society was doing its best to come to terms with its own madness: more than one type of paranoia was held to be an inescapable qualification for promotion in many business organisations.

The oily voice seeping from the 3V screen asked, 'Ever feel this busy world is too much for you? Ever want to scream in the middle of a crowd? Ever want to murder everyone else in your apartment building? Just jab a Draculin. ... Suddenly, you're all alone... ! Just jab a Draculin. ... Remember, when you're feeling overpopulated, just jab a Draculin. ... Suddenly, you're all alone!' Drug-induced catatonia was worth its weight in gold these days.

Struggling under all his responsibilities, acknowledged or secret, Utrect could admit to the fascination of that oily siren voice. He was burdened with too many roles. Part of his morbid attraction to the Burton case lay in the fact that he liked being Franz Josef, married to the beautiful Elizabeth. It was the most restful part of his existence!

The oily voice died, the news flared. Utrect switched on his wrisputer to record. A picture of Windsor Castle as it had been intumesced from the 3V confronted Utrect. He stared tensely, omitting to blink, as shots of the disaster came up. There was very little left of the residence of the anachronistic British sovereigns, except for one round tower. The demolition was amazing and complete. No rubble was left, no dust: level ground where the building and part of the lawn had been.

The commentator said, 'The historic castle was only on the fringe of a wide area of destruction. Never before has one blow destroyed so much of the precious British heritage. Historic Eton College, for centuries the breeding ground of future aristocrats, has been decimated. Shrine of world-famous historic nineteenth century Queen Victoria, at Frog-more, situated one mile south-east of the castle, was wiped out completely.'

Bob Hoggart! I sent you to your death! Utrect told himself. He switched off, unwilling to listen to the fruitless discussion about which enemy nation might have knocked off the castle; *he* knew what had wrought the terrible destruction.

'Hoggart,' he said to the wrisputer. 'You have a record of his probable movements at the time when disaster struck Windsor. What are your findings?'

The little machine said, 'Hoggart was scheduled to spend day working at Royal Mausoleum and – to cover his main activity – investigating nearby cemetery adjoining mausoleum, in which lesser royalties are buried. At time destruction happened, Hoggart may have been actually at Royal Mausoleum. Prediction of probability of death, based on partial data: fifty-six point nine percent.'

Burying his face in his hands, Utrect said, 'Bob's dead, then. ... My fault. ... My guilt, my eternal damned guilt ... A murderer – worse than a murderer! Hoggart was just a simple but courageous little shrine-restorer, no more. Yet subconsciously I manoeuvred him into a position where he was certain to meet his death. Why? Why? Why do I actually hate a man I thought I really liked? Some unconscious homosexual tendencies maybe, which had to be killed?' He sat up. 'Pull yourself together, Douglas! You are slumping into algolagnic depression, accentuated by that recurrent guilt syndrome of yours. Hoggart was a brave man, yes; you ordered him to go to Windsor, yes; but you in turn had your orders from the PINCS. There is no blame. These are desperate times. Hoggart died for the world – as the rest of us will probably do. Besides, he may not be dead after all. I must inform PINCS. Immediately.'

One thing at least was clear, one thing at least stood out in fearful and uncompromising hues: the universe lay nearer to the brink of disaster than ever before. The dreaded Queen Victoria had struck and might be about to strike again.

The United States, in the year 2000, was riddled with small and semi-secret societies. All of its four hundred million inhabitants belonged to at least one such society; big societies like the Anti-Procreation League; small ones, like the Sons of Alfred Bester Incarnate; crazy ones, like the Ypslanti Horse-Hooves-and-All-Eating Enclave; dedicated ones, like the Get Staft; religious ones, like the Man's Dignity and Mulattodom Shouting Church; sinister ones, like the Impossible Smile; semi-scholarly ones, like the Freud in His Madness Believers, which the insane Burton had founded; save-the-world ones, like All's Done In Oh One Brotherhood.

It was in the last category that the Philadelphia Institute for Nineteenth Century Studies belonged. Behind the calm and donnish front of PINCS, a secret committee worked, a committee comprising only a dozen men drawn from the highest and most influential ranks of cosmopolitan society. Douglas Tredeager Utrect was the humblest member of this committee; the humblest, and yet his aim was theirs, his desire burned as fiercely as theirs: to unmask and if possible annihilate the real Queen Victoria.

Committee members had their own means of communication. Utrect left the Advanced Alienation Hospital and headed for the nearest call booth, plunging through the crowded streets, blindly pushing forward. He was wearing his elbow guards but, even so, the sidewalk was almost unendurable. The numbers of unemployed in New York City were so great, and the space in their overcrowded flats and rooms so pronounced, that half the family at any one time found life more tolerable just padding around the streets.

To Utrect's disgust, a married couple, the woman with an eighteen-month-old child still being breast-fed, had moved into the call booth; they were employees of the phone company and had evidence of legal residence. However, since Utrect could show that this was an hour when he could legitimately make a call, they had to turn out while he dialled.

He got three wrong numbers before Disraeli spoke on the other end. The visiscreen remained blank; it was in any case obscured by a urine-soaked child's nightshirt. Disraeli was a PINCS' code name; Utrect did not know the man's real one. Sometimes, he suspected it was none other than the President of the United States himself.

'Florence Nightingale here,' Utrect said, identifying himself, and said no more. He had already primed his wristputer. It uttered a scream lasting point six of a second.

A moment's silence. A scream came back from Disraeli's end. Utrect hung up and fled, leaving the family to take possession again.

To get himself home fast, he called a rickshaw. Automobiles had been banned from the city centre for a decade now; rickshaws provided more work for more people. Of course, you had to be Caucasian Protestant to qualify for one of the coveted rickshaw-puller's licences.

He was lucky to qualify for a luxury flat. He and his wife, Karen, had three rooms on the twenty-fifth floor of the Hiram Bucklefeather Building – high enough to evade some of the stink and noise of the streets. The elevator generally functioned, too. Only the central heating had failed; and that would have been no bother in mild fall weather had not Karen been cyanosis-prone.

She was sitting reading, huddled in an old fur coat, as Utrect entered the flat.

'Darling, I love you!' she said dimly, glancing up, but marking her place on the page with a bluish fingertip. 'I've missed you so.'

'And me you.' He went to wash his hands at the basin, but the water was off.

'Have a busy day, darling?' At least she pretended to be interested.

'Sure.' She was already deep back in – he saw the title because she, as undeviatingly intellectual now as the day he married her, held it so that he might see – *Symbolic Vectors in Neurasthenic Emotional Stimuli*. He made a gesture toward kissing the limp hair on her skull.

'Good book?'

'Mm. Absorbing.' Invalidism had sapped her ability to tell genuine from false. Maybe the only real thing about us is our pretences, Utrect thought. He patted Karen's shoulder; she smiled without looking up.

Cathie was in the service-room-cum-bedroom, sluggishly preparing an anaemic-looking piece of meat for their supper. She was no more substantial than Karen, but there was a toughness, a masculine core, about her, emphasised by her dark skin and slight downy moustache. Occasionally, she showed a sense of humour. Utrect patted her backside; it was routine.

She smiled. 'Meat stinks of stilbestrol these days.'

'I didn't think stilbestrol had any odour.'

'Maybe it's the stilbestrol stinks of meat.'

They'd done OK, he thought as he locked himself in the bathroom-toilet. They'd done OK. With his two sons, Caspar and Nero, they were a household of five, minimum number in relation to floor space enforced by the housing regulations. Karen and Cathie had enjoyed a Lesbian relationship since graduate days, so it was natural to have Cathie move in with them. Give her her due, she integrated well. She was an asset. Nor was she averse to letting Utrect explore her hard little body now and then.

He dismissed such sympathetic thoughts and turned his attention to the wrisputer, which slowed Disraeli's phoned scream and retransmitted it as a comprehensible message.

'Whetther or not Robert Hoggart managed to fulfil his mission at the Windsor mausoleum is immaterial. Its sudden destruction is conclusive proof that he, and we, were on the right track with our Victoria hypothesis. We now operate under Highest Emergency conditions. Secret PINCS messengers are already informing Pentagon in Washington and our allies in the Kremlin in Moscow. Now that the entity known as Queen Victoria has revealed her hand like this, she will not hesitate to distort the natural order again. The fact that she has not struck until this minute seems to indicate that she is not omniscient, so we stand a chance. But clearly PINCS is doomed if she has discovered our secret. You will stand by for action, pending word from Washington and Moscow. Stay at home and await orders. Out.'

As he switched off, Utrect was trembling. He switched on again, getting the wrisputer to launch into a further episode of the interminable pornographic story it had been spinning Utrect for years; it was a great balance-restorer; but at that moment there was a banging at the toilet door, and he was forced to retreat.

He was a man alone. The Draculin situation, he thought wryly. Alone, and hunted. He looked up at the seamed ceiling apprehensively. That terrible entity they called Queen Victoria could strike through there, at any time.

The sons came home from work, Caspar first, thin, strawy, colourless save for the acne rotting his cheeks. Even his teeth looked grey. He was silent and nervous. Nero came in, two years the younger, as pallid as his brother, blackheads and adolescent pimples rising like old burial mounds from the landscape of his face. He was as talkative as Caspar was silent. Grimly, Utrect ignored them. He had some thinking to do. Eventually, he retreated into the shower, sitting on the old tiles. Queen Victoria might not see him there.

The evening dragged by. He was waiting for something and did not know what, although he fancied it was the end of the world.

The doomed life of the place slithered past. Utrect wondered why most of the tenants of the Hiram Bucklefeather Building had harsh voices. He could hear them through the walls, calling, swearing, suffering. Cathie and Karen were paying cards. At least the Utrect apartment preserved reasonable quiet.

Utrect's sons, heads together, indulged in their new hobby. They had joined the Shakespeare-Spelling Society. Their subscription entitled them to a kit. They had built the kit into an elaborate rat-educator. Two rats lived in the educator; they had been caught in the corridor. The rats had electrodes implanted in the pleasure centres of their brains. They were desperate for this pleasure and switched on the current themselves;

when it was on, the happy creatures fed themselves up to seven shocks a second, their pink paws working the switches in a frenzy of delight.

But the current was available only when the rats spelled the name SHAKESPEARE correctly. For each of the eleven letters the rats had a choice of six letters on a faceted drum. The letters they chose were flashed onto a little screen outside the educator. The rats knew what they were doing, but, in their haste to get the coveted shock, they generally misspelled, particularly toward the end of the word. Caspar and Nero tittered together as the mistakes flashed up.

THAMEZPEGPE

SHAKESPUNKY

SRAKISDOARI

The Utrect tribe ate their stilbestrol steak. Since the water supply was on, Karen washed up, wearing her coat still. Utrect had thought he might take a walk when the pedestrians thinned a little, despite PINCS' orders, but it was too late now. The hoods were out there, making the night unsafe even for each other. Every eight days, New York City needed one new hospital, just to cope with night injuries, said the statistics.

MHAKERPEGRE

SHAKESPEAVL

Utrect could have screamed. The rats played on his latent claustrophobia. Yet he was diverted despite himself, abandoning thought, watching the crazy words stumble across the screen. He thought as he had often thought: supposing man did not run the goddamned rats? Supposing the goddamned rats ran men? There were reckoned to be between three and four million people already in the Shakespeare-Spelling Society. Supposing the rats were secretly working away down there to make men mad, beaming these crazy messages at men which men were forced to read and try to make some sort of meaning of? When everyone was mad, the rats would take over. They were taking over already, enjoying their own population explosion, disease-transmitting but disease-resistant. As it was, the rats had fewer illusions than the boys. Caspar and Nero had a rat-educator; therefore they believed they were educating rats.

SIMKYSPMNVE

SHAKESPEARE

The Bard's name stayed up in lights when the rodents hit the current-jackpot and went on a pleasure binge, squealing with pleasure, rolling on their backs, showing little white thighs as the current struck home. Utrect refused to deflect his thoughts as Cathie and the boys crowded around to watch. Even if these rats were under man's surveillance, they were not interfered with by man once the experiment was set up. The food that appeared in their hoppers must seem to do so by natural law to them, just as the food thrusting out of the ground came by a natural law to mankind. Supposing man's relationship to Queen Victoria was analogous to the rats' relationship to man? Could they possibly devise some system to drive *her* crazy, until she lost control of her experiment?

CLUKYZPEGPY

Pleasure was brief, sorrow long, in this vale of rodential tears. Now the creatures had to pick up the pieces and begin again. They had always forgotten after the pleasure-bout.

DRALBUCEEVE

The family all slept in the same room since Utrect had caught the boys indulging in forbidden activity together. Their two hammocks now swung high over the bed in which the women slept. Utrect had his folding bunk by the door, against the cooker. Often, he did not sleep well, and could escape into the living room. Tonight, he knew, he would not sleep.

He dreamed he was in the Advanced Alienation Hospital. He was going to see Burton, pushing through the potted palms to get to the patient. An elderly man was sitting with Burton; Burton introduced him as his superior, Professor Krafft-Ebing of Vienna University.

'Delighted,' Utrect murmured.

'Clukyzpegpy,' said the professor. 'And dralbuceeve.'

What a thing to say to an Emperor!

Groaning, Utrect awoke. These crazy dreams! Maybe he was going mad; he knew his Dimpseys were already pushing the normality norm. Suddenly it occurred to him that the whole idea of Queen Victoria's being a hostile entity in a different dimension was possibly an extended delusion, in which the other members of PINCS conspired. A mother-fear orgy. A multiple mother-fear orgy – induced by the maternal guilt aspects of overpopulation. He lay there, trying to sort fantasy from reality, although convinced that no man had ever managed the task to date. Well, Jesus, maybe; but if the Queen Victoria hypothesis was correct, then Jesus never existed. All was uncertain. One thing was clear, the inevitable chain of events. If the hypothesis was correct, then it could never have been guessed earlier in the century, when normality norms were lower. Overpopulation had brought universal neurosis; only under such conditions could men reasonably work on so untenable a theory.

The Cheyne-Stokes breathing of his wife came to him, now labouring heavily and noisily, now dying away altogether. Poor dear woman, he thought; she had never been entirely well; even now, she was not entirely ill. In somewhat the same way, he had never loved her wholeheartedly; but even now, he had not ceased to love her entirely.

Tired though he was, her frightening variations of breathing would not let him rest. He got up, wrapped a blanket around himself, and padded into the next room. The rats were still at work. He looked down at them.

SLALEUPEAKE

SLAKBUDDDVS

Sometimes, he tried to fathom how their sick little brains were working. The Shakespeare-Spelling Society issued a monthly journal, full of columns of misspellings of the Bard's name sent in by readers; Utrect pored over them, looking for secret messages directed at him. Sometimes the rodents in their educator seemed to work relaxedly, as if they knew the desired word was bound to come up after a certain time. On other occasions, they threw up a bit of wild nonsense, as if they were not trying, or were trying to cure themselves of the pleasure habit.

DOAKERUGAPE

FISMERAMNIS

Yes, like that, you little wretches, he thought.

The success of the Shakespeare-Spelling Society had led to imitations, the All-American-Spelling, the Rat-Thesaurus-Race, the Anal-Oriented-Spelling, and even the Disestablishmentarianism-Spelling Society. Rats were at work everywhere, ineffectually trying to communicate with man. The deluxe kits had chimps instead of rats.

SHAPESCUNRI

SISEYSPEGRE

Tiredly, Utrect wondered if Disraeli might signal to him through the tiny screen.

DISPRUPEARS

The exotic words flickered above his head. He slept, skull resting on folded arms, folded arms resting on table.

Burton was back as Freud, no longer disconsolate as the sacked president of the Freud in His Madness Believers but arrogant as the arch-diagnoser of private weaknesses. Utrect sat with him, smoking in a smoking jacket on a scarlet plush sofa. It was uncertain whether or not he was Franz Josef. There were velvet curtains everywhere, and the closed sweet atmosphere of a high-class brothel. A trio played sugary music; a woman with an immense bust came and sang a poem of Grillparzer's. It was Vienna again, in the fictitious nineteenth century.

Burton/Freud said, 'You are sick, Doctor Utrect, or else why should you visit this church?'

'It's not a church.' He got up to prove his point, and commenced to peer behind the thick curtains. Behind each one, naked couples were copulating, though the act seemed curiously indistinct and not as Utrect had visualised it. Each act diminished him; he grew smaller and smaller. 'You're shrinking because you think they are your parents,' Burton/Freud said superciliously.

'Nonsense,' Utrect said loudly, now only a foot high. 'That could only be so if your famous theory of psychoanalysis were true.'

'If it isn't true, then why are you secretly in love with Elizabeth of Austria?'

'She's dead, stabbed in Geneva by a mad assassin. You'll be saying next I wish I'd stabbed my mother, or similar nonsense.'

'You said it – I didn't!'

'Your theories only confuse matters.'

An argument developed. He was no higher than Freud's toecap now. He wanted to pop behind a pillar and check to see if he was not also changing sex.

'There is no such thing as the subconscious,' he declared. Freud was regarding him now through pink reflecting glasses, just like the ones Utrect's father had worn. Indeed, it came as no surprise to see that Freud, now sitting astride a gigantic smiling sow, *was* his father. Far from being nonplussed, the manikin pressed his argument even more vigorously.

'We have no subconscious. The nineteenth century is our subconscious, and you stand as our guardian to it. The nineteenth century ended in 1901 with the death of Queen Victoria. And of course it did not really exist, or all the past ages in which we have been made to believe. They are memories grafted on, supported by fake evidence. The world was invented by the Queen in 1901 – as she has us call that moment of time.'

Since he had managed to tell the truth in his dream, he began to grow again. But the hairy creature before him said, 'If the nineteenth century is your subconscious, what acts as the subconscious of the Victorians?'

Utrect looked about among the potted palms, and whispered. 'As *we* had to invent mental science, *you* had to invent the prehistoric past – that's your subconscious, with its great bumping monsters!'

And Burton was nodding and saying, 'He's quite right, you know. It's all a rather clumsy pack of lies.'

But Utrect had seen that the potted palms were in fact growing out of the thick carpets, and that behind the curtains stalked great unmentionable things. The velvet drapes bulged ominously. A great stegosaurus, lumbering, and rounder than he could have imagined, plodded out from behind the sofa. He ran for his life, hearing its breathing rasp behind him. Everything faded, leaving only the breathing, that painful symptom of anemia, the Cheyne-Stokes exhalations of his wife in the next room. Utrect sprawled in his chair, tranquil after the truth-bringing nightmare, thinking that they (Queen Victoria) had not worked skilfully enough. The mental theories of 2000 were organised around making sense of the mad straggle of contradiction in the human brain. In fact, only the Queen Victoria hypothesis accounted for the contradictions. They were the scars left when the entirely artificial set-up of the world was commenced at the moment they perforce called 1901. Mankind was not what it seemed; it was a brood of rats with faked memories, working in some gigantic educator experiment.

SHAKESPEGRL

SHAKERPEAVE

Like the rats, he felt himself near to the correct solution. Yes! Yes, by God! He stood up, almost guilty, smiling, clutching the blanket to his chest. Obviously, analytic theory, following the clues in the scarred mind, could lead to the correct solution, once one had detected the 1901 barrier. And he saw! He knew! They were all cavemen, stone age men, primitive creatures, trying to learn – what? – for the terrible woman in charge of this particular experiment. Didn't all mental theory stress the primitive side of the mind? Well, they *were* primitive! As primitive and out of place as a stegosaurus in a smoking room.

SHAKESPEARL

Shakespearls before swine, he thought. He must cast his findings before PINCS before *She* erased him from the experiment. Now that he *knew*, the Queen would try to kill him as she had Hoggart.

There it was again. ... He went to the outer door. He had detected a slight sound. Someone was outside the flat, listening, waiting. Utrect's mind pictured many horrible things. The stegosaurus was lying in wait, maybe.

'Douglas?' Dinosaurs didn't talk.

'Who is it?' They were whispering through the hinge.

'Me. Bob, Bob Hoggart!'

Shaking, Utrect opened up. Momentary glimpse of dim-lit corridor with homeless people snoozing in corners, then Hoggart was in. He looked tired and dirty. He staggered over to the table and sat down, his shoulders slumping. The polished restorations expert looked like a fugitive from justice.

SHAMIND

Utrect cut off the rats' source of light.

'You shouldn't have come here!' he said. 'She'll destroy this building – maybe the whole of New York!'

Hoggart read the hostility and fear in Utrect's expression.

'I had to come, Florence Nightingale! I jumped a jumbojet from London. I had to bring the news home personally.'

'We thought you were dead. PINCS thinks you're dead.'

'I very nearly am dead. What I saw ... give me a drink, for God's sake! What's that noise?'

'Quiet! It's *my* wife breathing. Don't rouse her. She suffers from haemoglobin-deficiency with some other factors that haven't yet been diagnosed. One of these new diseases they can't pin down –'

'I didn't ask for a case history. Where's that drink?' Hoggart had lost his English calm. He looked every inch a man that death had marked.

'What have you found?'

'Never mind that now! Give me a drink.'

As he drank the alcohol-and-water that Utrect brought him, Hoggart said, 'You heard she blasted the mausoleum and half Windsor out of existence? That was a panic move on her part – proves she's human, in her emotions at least. She was after me, of course.'

'The tomb, man – what did you find?'

'By luck, one of the guards happened to recognise me from an occasion when I was restoring another bit of architecture where he had worked before. So he left me in peace, on my own. I managed to open Queen Victoria's tomb, as we planned.'

'Yes! And?'

'As we thought!'

'Empty?'

'Empty! Nothing. So we have our proof that the Queen, as history knows her – our fake history – does not exist.'

'Another of her botches, eh? Like the Piltdown Man and the Doppler Shift and the tangle of nonsense we call Relativity. Obvious frauds! So she's clever, but not all that clever. Look, Bob, I want to get you out of here. I'm afraid this place will be struck out like Windsor at any minute. I must think of my wife.'

'OK. You know where we must go, don't you?' He stood up, straightening his shoulders.

'I shall phone Disraeli and await instructions. One thing – how come you escaped the Windsor blast?'

'That I can't really understand. Different time scales possibly, between her world and ours? Directly I saw the evidence of the tomb, I ran for it, got into my car, drove like hell. The blast struck almost exactly an hour after I opened the tomb. I was well clear of the area by then. Funny she was so unpunctual. I've been expecting another blast ever since.'

Utrect was prey to terrible anxiety. His fingers trembled convulsively as he switched off his wrisputer, in which this conversation was now recorded. Before this building was destroyed, with Karen and all the innocent people in it, he had to get Hoggart and himself away. Grabbing his clothes, he dressed silently, nodding a silent good-bye to his wife. She slept with her mouth open, respiration now very faint. Soon, he was propelling Hoggart into the stinking corridor and down into the night. It was two-thirty in the morning, the time when human resistance was lowest. He instinctively searched the sky for a monstrous regal figure.

Strange night cries and calls sounded in the canyons of the streets. Every shadow seemed to contain movement. Poverty and the moral illness of poverty settled over everything, could almost be felt; the city was an analogue of a sick subconscious. Whatever her big experiment was, Utrect thought, it sure as hell failed. The cavemen were trying to make this noble city as much like home territory as they could. Their sickness (could be it was just homesickness?) hung in the soiled air.

By walking shoulder-to-shoulder, flick-knives at the alert, Utrect and Hoggart reached the nearby call booth without incident.

'Night emergency!' Utrect said, flinging open the door. The little family were sleeping in papoose hammocks, hooked up behind their shoulder blades, arms to their sides, like three great chrysalids. They turned out, sleepy and protesting. The child began to howl as its parents dragged it onto the chilly sidewalk.

Hoggart prepared a wrisputer report as Utrect dialled Disraeli. When his superior's throaty voice came up – again no vision – Hoggart let him have the scream. After a pause for encoding, another scream came from the other end. The wrisputer decoded it. They had to state present situation. When they had done this, a further scream came back. The matter was highest priority. They would be picked up outside the booth in a couple of minutes.

'Can we come back in, mister? The kid's sick!'

Utrect knew how the man felt.

As they bundled in, Utrect asked, 'When are you getting a real place?'

'Any year now, they say. But the company's agreed to heat the booth this winter, so it won't be so bad.'

We all have blessings to count, Utrect thought. Until the experiment is called off. …

He and Hoggart stood outside, back to back. A dark shape loomed overhead. A package was lowered. It contained two face masks. Quickly, they put them on. Gas flooded down, blanketing the street. A whirler lowered itself and they hurried aboard, immune from attacks by hoods, to whom a whirler would be a valuable prize. They lifted without delay.

Dr Randolph Froding's lips were a thin pale scarlet. As he laughed, little bubbles formed on them, and a thin spray settled on the glass of the television screen.

'This next part of my experiment will be very interesting, you'll see, Controller,' he said, glancing up, twinkling, at Prestige Normandi, Controller of the Advanced Alienation Hospital, a bald, plump man currently trying to look rather gaunt. Normandi did not like Dr Froding, who constantly schemed for the controllership. He watched with a jaundiced eye as, on Froding's spy screen, the whirler carried Hoggart and Chief Adviser Utrect over the seamy artery of the Hudson.

'I can hardly watch any longer, Froding,' he said, peering at his wrisputer. 'I have other appointments. Besides, I do not see you have proved your point.'

Froding tugged his sleeve in an irritating way.

'Just wait and watch this next part, Controller. This is where you'll see how Dimpsey Utrect really is.' He mopped the screen with a Kleenex, gesturing lordly with it as if to say, 'Be my guest, look your fill!'

Normandi fidgeted and looked; Froding was a forceful man.

They both stared as, in the 3V, the whirler could be seen to land on a bleak wharf, where guards met Utrect and Hoggart and escorted them into a warehouse. The screen blanked for a moment and then Froding's spy flipped on again, showing Utrect and Hoggart climbing out of an elevator and into a heavily-guarded room, where a bulky man sat at a desk.

'I'm Disraeli,' the bulky man said.

Froding nudged the Controller. 'This is the interesting part, Controller! See this new character? Notice anything funny about him? Watch this next bit and you'll see what I'm getting at.'

On the screen, Disraeli was shaking hands with Hoggart and Utrect. He wore the uniform and insignia of a general. He led the two newcomers into an adjoining room, where ten men stood stiffly around a table.

Bowing, Disraeli said, 'These are the other members of our secret committee. May I introduce Dickens, Thackeray, Gordon, Palmerston, Gladstone, Livingstone, Landseer, Ruskin, Raglan, and Prince Albert, from whom we all take our orders.'

As Utrect and Hoggart moved solidly around the group, shaking hands and making the secret sign, distant Machiavellian Dr Froding chuckled and sprayed the screen again.

'At last I'm proving to you, Controller, what I've been saying around the Lexington for years – Utrect is clean Dimpsey.'

'He looks normal enough to me.' Dirty little Froding; so clearly after Utrect's job as well as Normandi's own.

'But observe the others, Prince Albert, Disraeli and the rest! They aren't real people, you know, Controller. You didn't think they were real people, did you? Utrect thinks they are real people, but in fact they are dummies, mechanical dummies, and Utrect is talking to them as if they were real people. That proves his insanity, I think?'

Taken aback, Normandi said, '… Uh … I really have to go now, Froding.' Horrified by this glimpse into Froding's mentality, Normandi excused himself and almost ran from the room.

Froding shook his head as the Controller hurried away. 'He too, poor schmuck, he too is near his upper limit. He will not last long. It's all this overcrowding, of course, general deterioration of the environment. The mentality also deteriorates.'

He had his own method of safeguarding his own sanity. That was why he had become a member of the Knights of the Magnificent Microcosm. Although, as a bachelor, he was allowed only this one small room with shared conveniences with the specialist next door, he had rigged up internal 3V circuits in it so as to enlarge his vistas enormously. Leaning back, Froding could look at a bank of three unblinking screens, each showing various parts of the room in which he sat. One showed a high view of the room from above the autogrill, looking down on Froding from the front and depicting also the worn carpet and part of the rear wall where there hung a grey picture executed by a victim of anima-hostility. One showed a view across the length of the room from behind the door, with the carpet, part of the table, part of the folding bed, and the corner in which Froding's small personal library, together with his voluminous intimate personal dream diary, was housed in stacked tangerine crates. One showed a view from a corner, with the carpet, the more comfortable armchair, and the back of Froding's head as he sat in the chair, plus the three screens on which he was watching the three views of his room which included a view of him watching the three screens in his room on which he was watching this magnificent microcosm.

Meanwhile, at the subterranean PINCS HQ, Utrect had recognised Prince Albert; it was the Governor of New York City.

'We have a brief report of your activities in England, Hoggart,' Albert said. 'One question. How come you took so long to get here? You knew how vital it was to alert us.'

Hoggart nodded. 'I got away from Victoria's mausoleum before the destruction, as I told Nightingale and Disraeli. The information I thought I ought to reserve until I could talk to a top authority like yourself, sir, was this. Once Windsor and the Royal Mausoleum were destroyed, I believed I might be safe for an hour or two. So I went back.'

'You went back to the devastated area?'

The Englishman inclined his head. 'I went back to the devastated area. You see, I was curious to find out whether the Queen – as I suppose we must continue to call her – had been trying to obliterate me or the evidence. It was easy to get through the police and military cordon; it was only just going up, and the devastation covers several square miles. Finally, I got to the spot where I judged the mausoleum had stood. Sure enough, the hole under the vault was still there.'

'What is so odd about this hole?' Dickens asked, leaning forward.

'It's no ordinary hole. I didn't really have time to look into it properly, but it – well, it baffles the sight. It's as if one were looking into a space – well, a space with more dimensions than ours; and that's just what I suspect it is. It's the way – a way, into Queen Victoria's world.'

There was a general nodding of heads. Palmerston said in a crisp English voice, 'We'll take your word for it. Each of us bears a navel to indicate our insignificant origins. This hole you speak of may be Earth's navel. It is a not unreasonable place to expect to find it, in the circumstances, given the woman's mentality. We'd better inspect it as soon as possible. It will be guarded by now, of course.'

'You can fix the guards?' Disraeli asked.

'Of course,' Palmerston said.

'How about shooting a bit of hardware through the hole?'

They all consulted. The general feeling was that since they and possibly the whole world were doomed anyway, they might as well try a few H-bombs.

'No!' Utrect said. 'Listen, think out the situation, gentlemen! We all have to accept the truth now. At last it is in the open. Our world, as we believed we knew it, is a fake, a fake almost from top to bottom. Everything we accept as a natural factor is a deception, mocked-up by someone – or some civilisation – of almost unbelievable technological ability. Can you imagine the sheer complexity of a mind that invented human history alone? Pilgrim Fathers? Ice Age? Thirty Years' War? Charlemagne? Ancient Greece? The Albigensians? Imperial Rome? Abe Lincoln? The Civil War? All a tissue of lies – woven, maybe, by poly-progged computers.

'OK. Then we have to ask: *why?* What did they go to all the trouble for? Not just for fun! For an experiment of some kind. In some way, we must be a benefit to them. If we could see what that benefit was, then we might be in a bargaining position with – Queen Victoria.'

There was a moment of silence.

'He has a point,' Dickens said.

'We've no time,' Disraeli said. 'We want action. I'll settle for bombs.'

'No, Disraeli,' Albert said. 'Florence Nightingale is right. We have everything to lose by hasty action. Victoria – or the Victorians – could wipe us out if they wanted. We must bargain if possible, as Nightingale says. The question is, what have we got that they need?'

Everyone started talking at once. Finally, Ruskin, who had the face of a well-known Russian statesman, said, 'We know the answer to that. We have the anti-gravitational shield that is the latest Russo-American technological development. Next month, we activate it with full publicity, and shield the Earth from the moon's harmful tidal action. The shield is the greatest flowering of our Terrestrial technology. It would be invaluable even to these Victorians.'

This brought a general buzz of agreement.

Utrect alone seemed unconvinced. Surely anyone who had set up a planet as an experimental environment would already have full command of gravitational effects. He said, doubtfully, 'I think that psychoanalysts like myself can produce evidence to show that the Victorians' experiment is in any case nearly over. After all, experiments are generally run or financed only for a limited time. Our time's almost up.'

'Very well, then,' said Ruskin. 'Then our anti-gravitational screen is the climax of the experiment. We hold onto it and we parley with the Victorians.'

It seemed that the PINCS committee members would adopt this plan. Disraeli, Utrect, and Hoggart were to fly to Britain, meet Palmerston there, and put it into action. The three of them snatched a quick meal while the rest of the committee continued its discussion. Hoggart took a shower and a Draculin.

'Guess you were right to adopt a more gentle approach to Victoria,' Disraeli told Utrect. 'I'm just a dog-rough Army man myself, but I can take a hint. We can't expect to kill her. She's safe in her own dimension.'

'I feel no animosity toward Victoria,' Utrect said. 'We still survive, don't we? Perhaps it is not her intention to kill us.'

'You're changing your mind, aren't you?' Hoggart said.

'Could be. You and I are still alive, Bob! Maybe the object of the experiment was to see if we could work out the truth for ourselves. If we are actually of a primitive cave-dwelling race, maybe we've now proved ourselves worthy of Victoria's assistance. She just could be kind and gentle.'

The other two laughed, but Utrect said, 'I'd like to meet her. And I have an idea how we can get in contact with her – an idea I got from some rats. Let me draw you a sketch, Disraeli, and then your engineers can rig it for us in a couple of hours.'

Disraeli looked strangely at him. 'Rats? You get ideas off rats?'

'Plenty.' And then he started trembling again. Could Victoria really be kind when she had them all in a vast rat-educator, or did he just *hope* she was, for his own and Karen's sake?

When Disraeli was studying the sketch Utrect made, Hoggart said confidentially in the latter's ear, 'This Disraeli and all the other committee members – you don't see anything funny about them?'

'Funny? In what way?'

'They are real people, aren't they, I suppose? I mean, they couldn't be dummies, animated dummies, could they?' He looked at Utrect very chill and frightened.

Utrect threw back his head and laughed. 'Come on, Bob! You're suggesting that Queen Victoria could have some sort of power over our minds to deceive us utterly – so that, for instance, when we get to England we shall not really have left the States at all! So that these people are just dummies and this is all some sort of paranoid episode without objective reality! Absolute nonsense!'

'It didn't happen. It was a phantasm of my tired over-crowded brain, without objective reality. Senior members of my staff do not spy on each other.'

Thus spake Prestige Normandi, Controller of the Advanced Alienation Hospital to himself, as he strode away from Froding's room down the crowded corridor toward his office. He was trying not to believe that Froding really had a bug ray on Utrect; it was against all ethics.

Yet what were ethics? It was only by slowly jettisoning them and other principles that people could live in such densities as Central New York; something had to give; their rather stuffy fathers back in the sixties would have found this city uninhabitable. Under the sheer psychic pressure of population, what was an odd hallucination now and again?

A case in point. The woman coming toward him along the corridor, that regal air, those grand old-fashioned clothes … Normandi had a distinct impression that this was some old-time sovereign, Queen Victoria or the Empress Elizabeth of Austria. He wasn't well up in history. She sailed by, seemed to shoot him a significant glance, and was gone.

Impressed, he thought, she really might have been there. Maybe it was a nurse going off duty, member of some odd society or other. Normandi disapproved of all these societies, believing they tended to encourage fantasies and neuroses, and was himself President of the Society for the Suppression of Societies. All the same, he was impressed enough by the regal apparition to pause at Burton's cell; Burton would know what to think, it was in his line.

But he was too tired for the Freud act. With his hand on the door knob, he paused, then he turned away and pushed through the mob Which always jostled along the corridor, toward his own little haven.

Safely there, he sat at his desk and rested his eyes for a minute. Froding was scheming against Utrect. Of course Utrect was probably spying against someone else. It was really deplorable, the state they had come to. Sadly, he slid open a secret drawer in his deck, switched on the power, and clicked switches. Then he sat forward, shading his eyes, to watch the disgusting Froding spying on Utrect.

Utrect and Hoggart were half comatose, eyes shaded against the bilious light inside the plane as it hurtled eastward across the Atlantic, England-bound.

The communications equipment Utrect had specified had been built and was stowed in the cargo hatch. Not until they were landing at

Londonport in a rainy early afternoon did the news come through. Gripping Utrect's shoulder, Disraeli handed him a message from the PINCS undersea headquarters.

It read: 'Regret to report that the Hiram Bucklefeather Building on Three Hundredth at Fifteenth was obliterated at seven-thirty this morning. All the occupants, estimated at upward of five thousand, were immediately annihilated. It is certain this was the work of the entity known as Queen Victoria.'

'Your place?' Disraeli asked.

'Yes.' He thought of Karen with her cyanosis and her tragic breathing. He thought of the two unhappy lads, dying a few feet apart. He thought of Cathie, a patient woman. He even recalled the two rats, slaving over their spelling. But above all, he thought of Karen, so keen to seem intellectual, so hopeless at being anything, her very psyche sapped by the pulsating life about her. He had always done too little for her. He closed his eyes, too late to trap a tear. His wife, his girl.

Lovely Elizabeth of Austria, murdered needlessly on a deserted quay beside her lady-in-waiting – an irrelevant tableau slipping in to perplex his grief. All sweet things dying.

As they hurried across the wet runway, Hoggart said shakily, 'Victoria was after *me*, the bitch! She's a bitch! A bloody cow of a bitch, Douglas! Think of it – think of the way she built herself into the experiment as a sort of mother figure! Queen of England – sixty glorious years. Empress of India. She even named the age after herself. The Victorian Age. God Almighty! Began the experiment with her own supposed funeral, just for a laugh! What a cosmic bitch! By God ...' He choked on his own anger.

Palmerston was there to meet them in a military car. He shook Utrect's hand. He had heard the news. 'You have my deepest sympathy.'

'Why did she – what I can't understand – why did she destroy the building five hours after we had left?' Utrect asked painfully, as they whizzed from the airport, their apparatus stowed in the back of the car.

'I've worked that out,' Hoggart said. 'She missed me by an hour at Windsor, didn't she? It's British Summer Time here – the clocks go forward an hour. In New York, she missed us by five hours. She can't be all-knowing! She's going by Greenwich Mean Time. If she'd gone by local time, she'd have nailed us dead on both occasions.'

'Ingenious,' Disraeli admitted. 'But if she can see us, then how could she make such a mistake?'

'I told you I thought there might be different dimensions down this hole we are going to investigate. Obviously, *time* is a little scrambled as well as the space between her world and ours, and it doesn't help her to be as effective as otherwise she might be. That could work to our advantage again.'

'God knows, we need every advantage we can get,' Palmerston said.

Alone in his little office, Controller Prestige Normandi sat shading his eyes and suffering the crowded woes of the world, but always watching his tiny secret screen, on which Dr Froding, in his room, sat scanning the exploits of Utrect on his tiny screen. Psychic overcrowding with a vengeance, the Controller thought; and all the events that Utrect was now undergoing: were they real or, as Froding claimed, a paranoid episode without objective reality, enacted by dummies? Froding crouched motionless watching in his chair; Normandi did the same.

A knock at the door.

Quickly sliding the spy screen away in the secret door of his desk, Normandi rapped out an official order to enter.

Froding stepped in, closing the door behind him.

Suddenly atremble, Normandi clutched his throat. 'Good Dimpsey! You're not really there. Froding, you're just a paranoid delusion! I must get away for a few days' rest! I know you're really down in your room, watching Utrect, sitting comfortably in your chair.'

Swelling two inches all around, Froding stamped his foot. 'I will not be referred to as a paranoid delusion, Controller! That is a dummy sitting in my chair; it has taken over and will not leave when asked. So I have wrung from you a confession that you spy on your staff! You have not heard the end of this, by any means, nor even the beginning.'

'Let's be reasonable, Froding. Have a calmer with me.' Hurriedly, Normandi went to a secret cupboard and brought out pills and a jug of chlorinated water. 'We are reasonable men; let us discuss the situation reasonably. It boils down to the old question of what is reality, does it not? As I see it, improved means of communication have paradoxically taken mankind further from reality. We are all so near to each other that we seek to keep apart by interposing electronic circuits between us. Only psychic messages get through, but those we still prefer not to recognise officially. Can I believe anything I see Utrect doing when he is removed from me by so many scientifico-artistic systems? The trouble is, our minds identify television, even at its best, with the phantasms of inner vision – wait! I must write a paper on the subject!' He picked up a laserpen and scrawled a note on his writing screen. 'So, contemporary history, which we experience through all these scientifico-artistic media, becomes as much a vehicle for fantasy as does past history, which comes filtered through the medium of past-time. What's real, Froding, tell me that, what is real?'

'Which reminds me,' Froding said coldly. 'I came in to tell you that Burton/Freud has escaped within the last few minutes.'

'We can't let him get away! He's our star patient, nets us a fortune on the weekly "Find the Mind" show!'

'I feel he is better free. We cannot help him at Lexington.'

'He's *safer* confined here.'

Froding raised an eyebrow loaded with irony. 'You think so?'

'How did he get away?'

'His nurse Phyllis again, poor Phyllis. He attacked her, tied her up, and left his cell disguised as a woman, some say as Queen Victoria.'

Effortlessly, Normandi made anti-life noises with his throat. 'I saw her – him. She – he – passed me in the corridor. He – she – shot me a significant glance, as the writer says. ... What are we to do?'

'You're the Controller. ...' But not for so much longer, Froding thought Events were rolling triumphantly in his direction. Utrect was as good as defeated; now Normandi also was on his way out. All he had to do now was get rid of that damned dummy sitting in his armchair.

Undisturbed by the gale of psychic distortion blowing about him, the dummy sat uncomfortably in Dr Froding's chair and stared at the 3V screen.

In it, he could see Palmerston's large military car slowing as it reached the outskirts of Windsor. The pale face of Utrect looked out at the military barriers and machine gun posts.

Inwardly, Utrect fermented with anger at the thought of what had happened to his wife. All the hate in his unsettled nature seemed to boil to the surface. He had claimed that Victoria might be kind! He had spoken up against throwing bombs at her! Now he wished he could throw one himself.

Gradually, his emotionalism turned into something more chilly. He recalled the way poor insane Burton was lapsing back into nineteenth-century dreams. He knew thousands of cases in New York alone. And all the little secret societies that covered America – they could be interpreted as a regression toward primitivism, as if a long hypnosis were wearing off. He recalled what they had said earlier: the big experiment was coming to an end. The various illusions were breaking up, becoming thin, transparent. Hence the widespread madness – to which, he realised bitterly, he was far from immune. He had enjoyed too deeply pretending to be the Emperor Franz Josef; now his real life Elizabeth had also been randomly assassinated.

So what was the aim of it all? Timed to run just a hundred years, only a few more weeks to go, this ghastly experiment of Victoria's had been aimed to prove *what?*

He could not believe that all mankind was set down on this temporary Earth merely to develop the Russo-American anti-gravitational shield. Victoria could have got away with a simpler, cheaper environmental cage than this, had she just required the development of the shield. No, the point of it all had to be something that would explain the great complexity of the teeming Terrestrial races, with all their varying degrees of accomplishment and different psychologies.

They were slogging across the wet and blasted ground of Windsor now, with two assistants dragging the communications equipment. Utrect stopped short. He had the answer!

It went through him like a toothache. He pictured the rats again. Man had carried out simple population-density experiments with rats as long ago as the nineteen-fifties. Those rats had been given food, water, sunlight, building material, and an environment which, initially at least, had been ideal. Then they had been left without external interference to breed and suffer the maladies resulting from subsequent over-population.

Now the experiment was being repeated – on a human scale!

It was the human population explosion – the explosion that mankind, try as it might, had never been able to control – which was being studied.

Now it was breaking up because Victoria had all the data she needed. He figured that lethal interstellar gas would enfold Earth on New Year's Day 2001, a few weeks from now. Project X terminated successfully.

Unless ...

The assistants were fixing up the communicator so that it shone down the hole. Soldiers were running up with a generator. A respectful distance away, tanks formed a perimeter, their snouts pointing inward. Each tank had a military figure standing on it, binoculars focused on the central group. A whirler hovered just above them, 3V cameras going. The rain fell sharply, bubbling into the pulverised ground.

Utrect knew what happened to rats at the end of an experiment. They never lived to a ripe old age. They were gassed or poisoned. He knew, too, where the rats came from. He had a vision of the true mankind – primitive people, on a primitive planet, scuttling like rats for shelter in their caves while the – the Victorians, the super-race, the giants, the merciless ones, the gods and goddesses, hunted them, picked them up squealing, conditioned them, dropped them into the big educator. To breed and suffer. As Karen had suffered.

Now, Disraeli and Palmerston gave the signal. Lights blazed along the facets of the communicator. Their message flashed down into the hole, one sentence changed into another and back, over and over, as the letter drums rolled.

IRECOGNISEYOU

QUEENVICTORIA

OFFERIDENTITY

CONSIDERPEACE

The rats were trying to parley!

For the first time, Utrect stared down into the hole that had once been hidden by the mausoleum – Earth's navel, as Palmerston had put it. The light coming from it was confusing. Not exactly too bright. Not exactly too dim. Just – wrong. Nastily and disturbingly wrong. And – yes, he swore it, something was moving down there. Where there had been emptiness, a confused shadow moved. The bitch goddess was coming to investigate!

Utrect still had his flick-knife. He did not decide what to do; he simply started doing it. The others were too late to hold him back. He was deaf to Hoggart's shout of warning. Avoiding the signalling device, he ran forward and dived head-first into the dimension hole.

It was a colour he had not met before. A scent in his nostrils unknown. An air fresher, sharper, than any he had ever breathed. All reality had gone, except the precious reality of the blade in his hand. He seemed to be falling upward.

His conditioning dropped away, was ripped from his brain. He recalled then the simple and frightened peoples of the caves, living in community with some other animals, dependent mainly on the reindeer for their simple needs. There had not been many of them, comparatively speaking.

And the terrible lords of the starry mountains! Yes, he recalled them too, recalled them as being enemies whispered of in childhood before they were ever seen, striding, raying forth terrible beams of compulsion ... lords of stars and mountains. ...

The vision cut off as he hit dirt. He was wearing a simple skin. Grit rasped between his toes as he stood upright. He still had his knife. Scrubby bushes roundabout, a freshness like a chill. Strange cloud formations in a strange sky. *And a presence.*

She was so gigantic that momentarily he had not realised she was there. Of course I'm mad, he told himself. That guy in Vienna – he would say this was the ultimate in mother fixations! Sure enough, she was too big to fight, too horribly horribly big!

She grabbed him up between two immense pudgy fingers. She was imperious, regal, she was Queen Victoria. And she was not amused.

The dummy viewing the scene from Dr Froding's armchair stirred uncomfortably. Some of the things one saw on 3V nowadays were really too alarming to bear.

Dr Froding entered and pointed an accusing finger at the dummy.

'I accuse you of being the real Dr Froding!'

'If I am the real Dr Froding, who are you?'

'I am the real dummy.'

'Let's not argue about such minor matters at a time like this! Something I have just witnessed on the box convinces me that the world, the galaxy, the whole universe as we know it – not to mention New York City – is about to be destroyed by lethal interstellar gas.'

Froding jerked his head. 'That's why I want to be the dummy!'

The Serpent of Kundalini

At the French port, they were sceptical, smiling, nodding, looking wizened, walking behind their barriers in a clockwork way. He stood there waving his nunsacs papers which later, on the ferry going across to England, he consigned to the furtive waters.

They let him through at the last, making it clear he would find it harder to get back once he was out.

As yet he had nothing to declare.

Once the French coast and customs were left behind, he fell asleep.

When Charteris woke, the ship had already moored in Dover harbour and was absolutely deserted except for him. Even the sailors had gone ashore. Grey cliffs loomed above the boat. The quays and the sea were empty. The void was made more vacant by its transparent skin of flawless early spring sunshine.

The unwieldy shapes of quays and sheds did nothing to make the appearance of things more likely.

Just inside one of the customs sheds on the quay, a man in a blue sweater stood with his arms folded. Charteris saw him as he was about to descend the gangplank, and paused with his hand on the rail. The man would hardly have been noticeable; after all, he was perhaps thirty yards away; but, owing to a curious trick of acoustics played by the empty shed and the great slope of cliff, the man's every sound was carried magnified to Charteris.

The latter halted between ship and land, hearing the rasp of the waiting man's wrists as he re-folded his arms, hearing the tidal flow of his breath in his lungs, hearing the infinitesimal movement of his feet in his boots, hearing his watch tick through the loaded seconds of the day.

Very slowly, Charteris descended to the quay and began to walk towards the distant barriers, marching over large yellow painted arrows and letters meaningless to him, reducing him to a cipher in a diagram. Still water lay pallidly on his left. His course would take him close to the waiting man.

The noise of the waiting man grew.

The new vision of the universe which Charteris had been granted in Metz was still with him. All other human beings were symbols, nodes in an enormous pattern. This waiting man symbol could be death. He had come to England to find other things, a dream, white-thighed girls, faith. England, the million manarchies of ruined minds oerthrown.

'This deadness that I feel will pass,' he said aloud. The waiting man breathed by way of reply: a cunning and lying answer, thought Charteris. The motordeath images were gone from his crucible. Unstained porcelain. Bare. A flock of seagulls, white with black heads that swivelled like ball-bearings, sailed down from the cliff top, scudding in front of Charteris, and landed on the sea. They sank like stones. A cloud slid over the sun and the water was immediately the brown nearest black.

He reached the barrier. As he swung it wide and passed through, the noises of the waiting man died. To stand here was the ambition of years. Freedom from father and fatherland. Charteris knelt to kiss the ground; as his knees buckled, he glanced back and saw, crumpling over one of the yellow arrows, his own body. He jerked upright and went on. He recalled what Gurdjieff had said: attachment to things keeps alive a thousand useless I's in a man; these I's must die so that the big I can be born. The dead images were peeling from him. Soon he himself would be born.

He was trembling. Nobody wants to change.

The town was large and grand. The windows and the paintwork, Charteris thought, were very English. The spaces formed between buildings were also alien to him. He heard himself say that architecture was a kinetic thing essentially: and that photography had killed its true spirit because people had grown used to studying buildings on pages rather than by walking through them and round than and seeing them in relationship to other urban objects. In the same way, the true human spirit had been killed. It could only be seen in and by movement. Movement. At home in his father's town, Kragujevac, he had fled from stagnation, its lack of alternatives and movement.

Conscious of the drama of the moment, he paused, clutching his chest, whispering to himself, *Zbogom!* For the thought was revelation. A philosophy of movement. ... Sciences like photography must be used to a different purpose, and motion must be an expression of stillness. Seagulls rise from a flat sea.

A stony continental city in the grey prodigal European tradition, with wide avenues and little crooked alleys – a German city perhaps, perhaps Geneva, perhaps Brussels. He was arriving in a motor cavalcade, leading it, talking an incomprehensible language, letting them worship him. Movement. And a sullen English chick parting her white thighs, hair like clematis over white-washed wall, applause of multitudinous starlings, beaches, night groaning with weight-lifter strength.

Then the vision was gone.

Simultaneously, all the people in the Dover street began to move. Till now, they had been stationary, frozen, one dimensional. Now, motion gave them life and they went about their chances.

As he walked through their trajectories, he saw how miscellaneous they were. He had imagined the English as essentially a fair northern race with the dark-haired among them as startling contrast. But these were people less sharp than that, parti-coloured, piebald, their features blunted by long intermarriage, many stunted with blurred gestures, and many Jews and dark people among them. Their dress also presented a more tremendous and ragged variety than he had encountered in other countries, even his own Serbia.

Although these people were doing nothing out of the ordinary, Charteris knew that the insane breath of war was exhaled here too. The home-made bombs had splashed down from England's grey clouds; and the liquid eyes that turned towards him held a drop of madness. He thought he could still hear the breathing of the waiting man; but as he listened to it more closely, he realised that the people near him were whispering his name – and more than that.

'Charteris! Colin Charteris – funny name for a Jug!'

'Didn't he go and live in Metz?'

'Charteris is pretending that he swam the Channel to get here.'

'What's Charteris doing here? I thought he was going to Scotland!'

'Did you see Charteris kiss the ground, cheeky devil!'

'Why didn't you stay in France, Charteris – don't you know it's neutral?'

A woman took her small girl by the hand and led her hurriedly into a butcher's shop saying, 'Come away, darling. Charteris raped a girl in France!' The butcher leant across the counter with a huge crimson leg in his hands and brought it down savagely on the little girl's head – Charteris looked round hastily and saw that the butcher was merely hanging a red boloney sausage on a hook. His eyes were betraying him. His hearing was probably not to be trusted, either. The arrows still worried him.

Anxious to get away from the whispering, whether real or imaginary, he walked along a shopping street that climbed uphill. Three young girls went before him in very short skirts. By slowing his pace, he could study their legs, all of which were extremely shapely. The girl on the outside of the pavement, in particular, had beautiful limbs. He admired the ankles, the calves, the dimpling popliteal hinges, the thighs, following the logic of them in imagination up to the sensuously jolting buttocks, the little swelling buds of fruit. Motion, again, he thought: without that élan vital, they would be no more interesting than the butcher's meat An overpowering urge to exhibit himself to the girls rose within him. He could fight it only by turning aside into a shop; it was another butcher's shop; he himself hung naked and stiff on a hook, white, and pink-trottered. He looked directly and saw it was a pig's carcass.

But as he left the shop, he saw another of his discarded I's was peeling off and crumpling over the counter, lifeless.

A bright notice on a wall advertised the Nova Scotia Treadmill Orchestra.

He hurried on to the top of the hill. The girls had gone. Like a moth, the state of the world fluttered in his left ear, and he wept for it The West had delivered itself to the butchers. France Old Folks Home.

A view of the sea offered itself at the top of the hill. Breathing as hard as the waiting man, Charteris grasped some railings and looked over the cliff. One of those hateful phantom voices down in the town had suggested he was going to Scotland; he saw now that he was indeed about to do that; at least, he would head north. He hoped his new-found mental state would enable him to see the future with increasing clarity;

but, when he made the effort, as if it might be, his eyesight misted over at any attempt to read small print, the endeavour seemed bafflingly self-defeating: the small print of the future bled and ran – indeed, all he could distinguish was a notice reading something like LOVE BURROW which would not resolve into GLASGOW, some sort of plant with crimson blooms and ... a road accident? – until, trying to grapple with the muddled images, he finally even lost the *direction* in which his mind was trying to peer. The breathing was in his head and chest.

Cinging to the railings, he tried to sort out his random images, LOVE BURROW was no doubt some sort of Freudian nonsense; he dismissed the crimson Christmas blooms; his anxiety clustered round the accident – all he could see was a great perspective of clashing and clanging cars, aligned down the beaches of triple-carriageways like a tournament. The images could be past or future. Or merely fears. Always the prospect of crashing and tumbling climaxes.

He had left his car on the ship. What was ahead was unknown, even to him with the budding powers – in a breathless moment like a ducking – and the sea was grey. Clutching the railings, Charteris felt the ground rock slightly. The deck. The deck rocked. The sea narrowed like a Chinese eye. The ship bumped the quay. A call to muster stations amid starling laughter.

He stood at the rail, trying to adjust, as the passengers left the ship and their cars were driven away from the underdeck. He looked up at the cliffs; gulls swooped down from them: and floated on the oily sea. He listened and heard only his own breathing, the rasp of his own body in his clothes. In or out of trance he stood: and the quay emptied of people.

'Is the red car yours, sir?'

'You are Mr Charteris, sir?'

Slowly he turned towards the English voice. He extended a hand and touched the fabric of the man's tunic. Nodding without speaking, he made his way slowly below deck. Slowly, he walked down the echoing belly-perspective of the car deck to where his Banshee stood. He climbed in, searched in his pocket for the ignition key, slowly realised it was already in the ignition, started up, and drove slowly over the ramp onto English concrete, English yellow arrows.

He looked across to the customs shed. A man stood there half in shadow, in a blue sweater, arms folded. He beckoned. Charteris drove forward and found it was a customs man. A small rain began to fall as the man looked laconically through Charteris's grip.

'This is England, but my dream was more true,' he said.

'That's as may be,' said the man, in surly fashion. 'We had a war here, you know, sir, not like you lot in France. You'd expect a bit of dislocation, sort of, wouldn't you?'

'Dislocation, my God, yes!'

'Well, then. ...'

As he rolled forward, the man called out, 'There's a new generation!'

'And I'm part of it!'

He drove away, enormously slow, and the slimy yellow arrows licked their way under his bonnet, TENEZ LA GAUCHE. LINKS FAHREN. DRIVE ON THE LEFT. WATNEY'S BEER. The enormous gate swung open and he felt only love. He waved at the man who opened the gate; the man stared back suspiciously. England! Brother we are treading where the Saint has trod!

The great white lumpish buildings along the front seemed to settle. He turned and looked back in fear at the ship – where – what was he? In the wet road, crumpled over one of the arrows, lay one of his I's, just as in the vision, discarded.

Only now did he clearly recall the details of the vision.

To what extent was a vision an illusion, to what extent a clearer sort of truth?

He recollected the England of his imagination, culled from dozens of Saint books. A sleazy place of cockneys, nursemaids, policemen, slums, misty wharves, large houses full of the vulnerable jewellery of beautiful women. That place was not this. Well, like the man said, there had been a war, a dislocation. He looked at these people in these streets. The few women who were about moved fast and furtive, poorly and shabbily dressed, keeping close to walls. Not a nursemaid among them. The men did not stir. A curse of alternate inertia had been visited upon the English sexes. Men stood waiting and smoking in little groups, unspeaking; women scurried lonely. In their eyes, he saw the dewy glints of madness. Their pupils flashed towards him like animal headlights, feral with guanin, the women's green, the men's red like wolfhounds or a new animal

A little fear clung to Charteris.

'I'll drive up to Scotland,' he said. Bombardment of images. He was confusing his destiny: he would never get there. Something happened to him ... would happen. Had happened – and he here and now was but a past image of himself, perhaps a dead image, perhaps one of the cast-off I's that Gurdjieff said must be cast off before a man could awaken to true consciousness.

He came to the junction where, in his vision, he had turned and walked up the steep shopping street. With determination, Charteris wrenched the wheel and accelerated up the hill. Under sudden prompting, he glanced over his shoulder. A red Banshee with himself driving had split away and was taking the other turning. Did that way lead to Scotland or to .... Love Burrow? His other I caught his gaze just momentarily, pupils flashing blank guanin red, teeth bright in a wolf snarl.

That's one I I'm happy to lose ...

As he climbed up the hill, he looked for three girls in miniskirts, for a butcher's shop. But the people were the shabby post-catastrophe crowd, and most of the shops were shuttered: all infinitely sadder than the vision, however frightening it had been. Had he been frightened? He knew he embraced the new strangeness. Materialism had a silver psychedelic bullet through its heart; the incalculable took vampire-flight. The times were his.

Already, he felt a cooler knowledge of himself. Down in the south of Italy, that was where this new phase of life had festered for him, in the rehabilitation camp for the slav victims, away from his paternal roof. In the camp, he had been forced to wander in derangements and had learnt that sanity had many alternatives, a fix for individual taste.

From his personal revolt, definition was growing. He could believe that his forte was action directed by philosophy. He was not the intro-spective; on the other hand, he was not the simple doer. The other I's would be leaves from the same tree.

And where did these thoughts lead? Something impelled him: perhaps only the demon chemicals increasing their hold on him; but he needed to know where he was going. It would help if he could examine one of his cast-off I's. As he reached the top of the hill, he saw that he still stood gripping the railings and staring out to sea. He stopped the car.

As he walked towards the figure, monstrous things wheeled in the firmament.

His hearing became preternaturally acute. Although his own footsteps sounded distant, very near at hand were the tidal flow of his breathing, the tick of his watch, the stealthy rustle of his body inside its clothing. Like the man said, there had been a war, a dislocation.

As his hand came up to touch the shoulder of the Gurdjieffian I, it was arrested in mid-air; for his glance caught the sight of something moving on the sea. For a moment, he mistook it for some sort of a new machine or animal, until it resolved itself under his startled focus into a ship, a car ferry, moving dose in to the harbour. On the promenade deck, he saw himself standing remote and still.

The figure before him turned.

It had broken teeth set in an indefinite mouth, and dark brown pupils of eyes gripped between baggy lids. Its nose was brief and snouty, its skin puffed and discoloured, its hair as short and tufted as fur. It was the waiting man. It smiled.

'I was waiting for you, Charteris!'

'So they were hinting down in the town.'

'You don't have any children, do you?'

'Hell, no, but my ancestry goes right back to Early Man.'

'You'll tell me if you aren't at ease with me? Your answer reveals, I think, that you are a follower of Gurdjieff?'

'Clever guess! Ouspenski, really. The two are one – but Gurdjieff talks such nonsense.'

'You read him in the original, I suppose?'

'The original what?'

'Then you will realise that the very times we live in are somewhat Gurdjieffian, eh? The times themselves, I mean, talk nonsense – but the sort of nonsense that makes us simultaneously very sceptical about the old rules of sanity.'

'There were no rules for that sort of thing. There never were. You make them up as you go.'

'You are not much more than a kid! You wouldn't understand. There are rules for everything once you learn them.'

Charteris was feeling almost no apprehension now, although his pulse beat rapidly. Far below on the quay, he could see himself climbing into the Banshee and driving towards the customs shed.

'I must be getting along,' he said formally. 'As the Saint would say, I have a date with destiny. I'm looking for a place called …' He had forgotten the name; that image had been self-cancelling.

'My house is hard by here.'

'I prefer a softer kind.'

'It is softer inside, and my daughter would like to meet you. Do come and rest a moment and feel yourself welcome in Britain.'

He hesitated. The time would come, might even be close, when all the gates of the farmyard would be closed to him; he would fall dead and be forgotten; and continue to stare for ever out through the window at the blackness of the garden. With a simple gesture of assent – how simple it yet remained to turn the wrist in the lubricated body – he helped the waiting man into the car and allowed him to direct the way to his house.

This was a middle-class area, and unlike anywhere he had visited before. Roads of small neat houses and bungalows stretched away on all sides, crescents curved off and later rejoined the road, rebellion over. All were neatly labelled with sylvan names: Sherwood Forest Road, Dingley Dell Road, Herbivore Drive, Woodbine Walk, Placenta Place, Honeysuckle Avenue, Cowpat Avenue, Geranium Gardens, Clematis Close, Creosote Crescent, Laurustinus Lane. Each dwelling had a neat little piece of garden, often with rustic work and gnomes on the front lawn. Even the smallest bungalows had grand names, linking them with a mythical green nature once supposed to have existed: Tall Trees, Rolling Stones, Pan's Pantiles, Ocean View, Neptune Tiles, The Bushes, Shaggy Shutters, Jasmine Cottage, My Wilderness, Solitude, The Laurustinuses, Our Oleanders, Florabunda.

Charteris grew angry and said, 'What sort of a fantasy are these people living in?'

'If you're asking seriously, I'd say, security masquerading as a little danger.'

'We aren't allowed this sort of private property in Jugoslavia. It's an offence against the state.'

'Don't worry! This way of life is dead – the war has killed it. The values on which this mini-civilisation has been built have been swept away – not that most of the inhabitants realise it yet. I keep up the pretence because of my daughter.'

The waiting man began to breathe in a certain way. Charteris regarded him curiously out of the corner of his eye, because he fancied that the man was accomplishing rather an accurate parody of his daughter's breathing. So good was it that the girl was virtually conjured up between them; she proved to be, to Charteris's delight, the one of the three girls in a mini-skirt he had most admired while walking up the hill, perhaps a year younger than himself. The illusion lasted only a split second, and then the waiting man was breathing naturally again.

'All pretence must be broken! Maybe that is the quest on which I came to this country. Although we are strangers and should perhaps talk formally together, I must declare to you that I believe very deeply that there is a strange force latent in man which can be awakened.'

'Kundalini! Turn left here, down Petunia Park Road.'

'What?'

'Turn left.'

'What else did you say? You were swearing at me, I believe?'

'Kundalini. You don't know your Gurdjieff as well as you pretend, my friend. So-called occult literature speaks of Kundalini, or the serpent of Kundalini. A strange force in man which can be awakened.'

'That's it, then, yes! I want to awaken it. What are all these people doing in the rain?'

As they drove down Petunia Park Road, Charteris realised that the English middle-classes were standing neatly and attentively in their gardens; some were performing characteristic actions such as adjusting ties and reading big newspapers, but most were simply staring into the road.

'Left here, into Brontosaurus Broadway. Listen, my boy, Kundalini, that serpent, should be left sleeping. *It's nothing desirable!* Repulsive though you may find these people here, their lives have at least been dedicated – and successfully, on the whole – to mechanical thought and action, which keep the serpent sleeping. I mean, security masquerading as a little danger is only a small aberration, whereas Kundalini –'

He went into some long rigmarole which Charteris was unable to follow; he had just seen a red Banshee, driven by another Gurdjieffian I, slide past the top of the road, and was disturbed by it. Although there was much he wanted to learn from the waiting man, he must not be deflected from his main north-bound intention, or he might find himself in the position of a discarded I. On the other hand, it was possible that going north might bring him into discardment. For the first time in his life, he was aware of all life's rich or desiccating alternatives; and an urge within him – but that might be Kundalini – prompted him to go and talk to people, preach to them, about cultivating the multi-valued.

'Here's the house,' said the waiting man. 'Pear Tree Palace. Come in and have a cup of tea. You must meet my daughter. She's your age, no more.'

At the neat little front gate, barred with a wrought-iron sunset, Charteris hesitated. 'You are hospitable, but I hope you won't mind my asking – I seem myself to be slightly affected by the PCA bombs – hallucinations, you know – I wondered – aren't you also a bit – touched –'

The waiting man laughed, making his ugly face look a lot uglier. 'Everyone's touched! Don't be taken in by appearances here. Believe me, the old world has gone, but its shell remains in place. One day soon, there will come a breath of wind, a new messiah, the shell will crumple, and the kids will run streaming, screaming, barefoot in the head, through lush new imaginary meadows. What a time to be young! Come on, I'll put the kettle on! Wipe your shoes!'

'It's as bad as that? –'

The waiting man had opened the front door and gone inside. Uneasy, Charteris paused and looked about the garden suburb. Kinetic architecture here had spiked the viewpoint with a crazy barricade of pergolas, patios, bay windows, arches, extensions, all manner of dinky garages and outhouses, set among fancy trees, clipped hedges, and painted trellis. Watertight world. All hushed under the fine mist of rain. Neighbourhood of evil for him, small squares of anaemic fancy, wrought-iron propriety.

He found himself at the porch, where the gaunt rambler canes already bore little snouts of spring growth. There'd be a fine show of New Dawn in four more months. An enchantment waited here. He went in, leaving the door open. He wanted to hear more about Kundalini.

At the back of the house, the waiting man pottered in a small kitchen, all painted green and cream, every surface covered with patterned stuff and, on a calendar, a picture of two people tarrying in a field. Behind the frozen gestures of the couple, sheep broke from their enclosure and surged among the harvest wheat to trample it with delight.

'My daughter'll be back soon.' The waiting man switched on a small green-and-cream dumpy streamlined radio from which the dumpy voice of a disc-joker said, 'And now for those who enjoy the sweet things of life, relax right back for the great all-time sound of one of the great bands of all time and we're spinning this one just especially for Auntie Flora and all the boys at "Nostalja Vista", 5 The Crossings, The Tip, Scrawley, in Bedfordshire – the great immortal sound of you guessed it the Glenn Miller Orchestra playing "Moonlight Serenade".'

Out in the garden winter birds plunged.

'"All-time sound" – you are for music?' asked the waiting man as he beat time and watched the treacly music as it rose from the kettle spout and steamed across the withered ceiling.

'My daughter isn't in. I expect she'll be back soon. Why don't you settle down here with us for a bit? There's a nice little spare room upstairs – a bit small but cosy. You never know – you might fall in love with her.'

He remembered his first fear of the waiting man: that he would detain Charteris in the customs shed. Now, more subtly, the attempt at detention was again being made.

'And you're a follower of Gurdjieff, are you?' Charteris asked.

'He was rather an unpleasant customer, wasn't he? But a magician, a good guide through these hallucinatory times.'

'I want to waken a strange force that I feel inside me, but you say that is Kundalini, and Gurdjieff warns against waking it?'

'Very definitely! Most definitely! G says *man* must awake but the snake, the serpent, must be left sleeping.' He made the tea meticulously, using milk from a tube which was lettered Ideal. 'We've all got serpents in us, you know!' He laughed.

'So you say. We also have motives that make our behaviour rational, that have nothing to do with any snakes!'

The waiting man laughed again in an offensive way.

'Don't laugh like that! Shall I tell you the story of my life?'

Amusement. 'You're too young to have a life!' He dropped saccharine pills into the tea.

'On the contrary! I've already shed many illusions. My father was a stone-mason. Everyone respected him. He was big and powerful and harsh and sad. Everyone said he was a good man. He was an Old Communist, a power in the Party.

'When I was a small boy, there was a revolt by the younger generation. They wanted to expel the Old Communists. Students everywhere rose up and said, "Stop this antique propaganda! Let us live our lives!" And in the schools they said, "Stop teaching us propaganda! Tell us facts!" You know what my father did?'

'Have your tea and be quiet!'

'I'm talking to you! My father went boldy out to meet the students. They jeered him but he spoke up. "Comrades," he said, "You are right to protest – youth must always protest. I'm glad you have the courage to speak up because for a long while I have secretly felt as you do. Now I have your backing, I will change things. Leave it to me!" I heard him say it and was proud.'

And he heard now the all-time orchestra never dead.

'I became fervent then myself. Sure enough, father made changes. Everyone said that the young idealists had won and in the schools they taught how the Old Communism had been okay but the new non-propagandist kind was better. The young ringleaders of the revolt were even given good jobs. It was wonderful.'

'Politics don't interest me,' said the waiting man, stirring his tea. 'Do you care for music?'

'Five years later, I had my first girl. She said she would let me in on a secret. She was part of a revolutionary group of young men and girls. They wanted to change things so that they could live their lives freely, and they wanted the schools and newspapers to stop all the propaganda. They determined to expel the Young Communists.

'For me, it was a movement of terrible crisis! I realised that Communism was a just system for hanging on to what you had, no better than Capitalism. And I realised that my father was just a big fraud – an opportunist, not an idealist. From then on, I knew I had to get away, to live my own life.'

The waiting man showed his furry teeth and said, 'That's hardly as interesting to me as what I was telling you about the serpent, I think you must admit. There's no such thing as an "own life".'

'What is this serpent of Kundalini then? Come on, out with it, or I could pretty easily brain you with this kettle!'

'It's an electric kettle!'

'I don't care!'

At this proof of Charteris's recklessness, the waiting man backed away, helped himself to a saccharine pill, and said, 'Enjoy your tea while it's hot! Forget your father – it's something we all have to do!'

'Yes siree, one of the great ones in the Miller style. And now for a welcome change of pace –'

Charteris was conscious of a mounting pressure inside him. Something was breathing close to his left ear and stealing away.

'Answer my question!' he said.

'Well, according to G, the serpent is the power of the imagination – the power of fantasy – which takes the place of a real function. You get my meaning? When a man dreams instead of acting, when he imagines himself to be a great eagle or a great magician ... that's the force of Kundalini acting in him ...'

'Cannot one act and dream?'

The waiting man appeared to double up, sniggering in repulsive fashion with his fists to his mouth. Love Burrow – that was the sign, and a pale-thighed wife beside him. ... His place was there, wherever that was. This Pear Tree Palace was a trap, a dead end, the waiting man himself an ambiguous either/or/both/and sign, deluding yet warning him: perhaps a manifestation of Kundalini itself. He had got his tasks in the wrong order; clearly, this was a dead end with no alternative, a corner of extinction. What he wanted was a new tribe!

Now the waiting man's sniggers were choking him. Above their bubbling din, he heard the sound of a car engine outside, and dropped his teacup. The tea sent a dozen fingers across the cubist lino. Over his fists, the little doubled figure glared blankly red at him. Charteris turned and ran.

Through the open door. Birds leaped from the lawn to the eaves of the bungalow, leaden, from motionlessness to instant motionlessness.

His heart's beat dragged in its time-snare like a worn serenade.

Down the path. The rain had lured out a huge black slug which crawled like a torn watch-strap before him. The green-and-cream radio still dialled yesterday.

Through the gate. The sun, set for ever with its last rays caught in mottled iron.

To the road. But he was a discarded alternative. A red Banshee was pulling away, with one of his glittering I's at the wheel, puissant, full of potential, multi-valued, saviour-shaped.

He ran after it, calling from the asphalt heart of Brontosaurus Broadway, leaping over the gigantic yellow arrows. They were becoming more difficult to negotiate. His own powers, he knew, were failing. He had chosen wrongly, become a useless I, dallying with an old order instead of seeking new patterns.

Now the arrows were almost vertical, LINKS FAHREN. The red car was far away, just a blur moving through the barrier, speeding unimpeded for. ...

He still heard breathing, movements of clothes, the writhing of toes inside shoe-caps. But these were not his. They belonged to the Charteris in the car, the undiscarded I. He no longer breathed.

As he huddled over the arrow, gulls tumbled from the cliff and sank into the water. Over the sea, the ship came. Up the hill, motors sounded. In the head, barefoot, a new age.

There had been a war, a dislocation.

Time Never Goes By

You must remember this
That beds get crumpled skirts get rumpled
And hedges grow up into trees
Cinemas close and the parking lot
Loses its last late Ford
Everything goes by the board
But Time Never Goes By

And when true lovers screw
Novelty wears off the affair's off
Perfume fades from the air
The bright spinning coin will tarnish and
The miser forget his hoard
Everything goes by the board
But Time Never Goes By

The watch keeps ticking true enough
But time's glued down to something stronger
It's a fixture   Do enough
But every second's a second longer
Try your best you'll be impressed
Every minute has centuries in it

It's still the same old story
Characters change events rearrange
Plot seems to wear real thin
Coffins call for running men
Hated or adored
Everything goes by the board
But Time Never Goes By

NOVA SCOTIA TREADMILL ORCHESTRA

Rosemary Left Me

Beyond the buildings the buildings
Begin again
Beyond recording the old records
Spin again

It's sort of sad it's kind of safe
It seems so sour
The things that are past will fortify
The menace of the coming hour

My Rosemary left me outside The Fox
Said I smelt said I didn't care
Then why do I keep her pubic hair
Tied up in ribbon in a sandalwood box

Now I've found Jeanie cute as you please
Tight little skirt and leather jerkin
Soon I'll get the scissors working
History comes bobbing on back like knees

So I go ahead tho I know ahead
Winds blow ahead
Two steps forward one step back
Trodden in another tread

Beyond recording the old records
Spin again
Beyond the buildings the buildings
Begin again

THE GENOSIDES

Little Paper Faces

He goes through the land
His tomorrow in his pocket
He seeks a land
Where the faces fit the heads

Little paper faces
Little paper faces
Little paper faces
Yeh, with hand-drawn expressions

He crosses over the sea
Pilgrim of the Pilgrim Age
He hopes to see
A different mask beneath the skull

Little paper faces
Little paper faces
Little paper faces
Yeh, with crayoned experience

Little paper faces
Little paper faces
Little paper faces
Yeh, papered on the paper bone

THE ESCALATION

The Tell-Tale Heart-Machine

I had to charter a private plane to fly down to my country place on the island. All the way, even more insistent than the knowledge that I was ruined, I was haunted by the knowledge that, because I could no longer afford to be flown home, I would have to sell the island. It was that last bit of bad news that I most dreaded breaking to Jane.

She met me with the ancient Bentley at the airstrip.

'You look tired, Daddy. You are going to be fed and put to bed.' Thus her first words.

'You really know how to sap a man's confidence! It's all nonsense and, anyway, you always say that.'

'It's always true.'

'And I always refuse to go to bed.'

She was – well, it was five years since Viv was killed – yes, Jane was twenty-two. The plane crash, the death of her mother, my long spell as an invalid ... they had distorted her life pattern. She was just slightly too bossy; she scared away the boys, although she was pretty enough. She drove well. Just like her mother.

It was good to see the house again. Mrs Singer, the housekeeper, came and said Hello. I sat in a chair and relaxed while drinks were brought. I raised the glass, Jane raised hers. We drank.

God, I thought, what happiness I have survived, and what misery!

'So you and Jerry Keynes are thrown out of Lawrence Life-Forms, Daddy.'

'Have you been watching the battle on TV?'

She nodded. 'You were right to stand up for your point of view.'

'The shareholders thought otherwise.'

'Will it help you to talk about it?' There again was the note I dread to hear in Jane. Life was passing her by. She was living out of her depth. Nobody really says: 'Will it help you to talk about it?' She had picked up the phrase from a telly-play.

'I really am tired,' I said. 'I'll take your advice, go to bed, sleep off the worries of the last week, wake like new in the morning.'

'How's your heart, Daddy?'

'Best bit of me. You know that!' We smiled – as we had smiled before, over those same words.

As she left me at the top of the stairs, she said, 'Tomorrow, you must come and see the dinosaurs. They like their new pens.'

'Good!' But of course the dinosaurs would have to go, like everything else ...

Deciding to take a shower, I undressed slowly in the bathroom. In these rooms now, there were few reminders of my wife. The bedside lamp had been hers. She had chosen the carpet. She smiled from a photograph, a distant Viv, not enjoying the photographic studio.

What would she have said if she were alive to see her father, the great Sir Frank Lawrence, turn his son-in-law and the other junior partner out of the firm? She had always known he was a ruthless man; Lawrence Chemicals had been his father's creation; but the startling synthetic life-form developments of the nineteen-nineties had been all Frank's doing, as had the establishment of Lawrence Life-Forms. I had helped substantially; but I had remained a contract man.

As I slid out of my vest and started the shower running, I told myself as he had started me in the business, he had now pushed me out of it. That counted as fair play, by worldly standards. And he brought his daughter into the world, the old bastard!

I caught sight of myself in the long mirror as I climbed into the shower. Thin stringy body. Forty-five years old, looking more like fifty-five. Nothing to what I looked like after the plane crash, of course.

I hadn't touched another woman since Viv died. One of the reasons was plain to see. The surgeons had made a good job of the operation, but the flesh across my left breast was puckered and distorted by scar tissue. It filled me with distaste still; I never wanted to see anyone else flinch away from it.

After breakfast, Jane took me to see the steggies and brontos. It was a typical island day, with more cloud than you need scudding by, but the sun frequently beaming forth.

'We're going to have to sell all this, Jane.'

I suppose I had thought she would have realised it. But she caught her breath and stopped.

'You'll – be able to get another directorship, Daddy?'

'Not at Frank's salary.'

'But you can start up in opposition now, making synthetic life of your own.'

'I'm finished with synthetic life, Jane. I really believe that this is the classic case where Man has overstepped his powers. Now that Frank has announced his intention of synthesising human beings, I'm more sure than ever that I'm right. We really are pre-empting powers that do not belong to us.'

Her jaw set. I saw it for the first time. She had something of her maternal grandfather in her. She too disagreed with me.

'I've never heard you talk religion before now, father! What has been discovered is something slowly led up to, capping the scientific work of many centuries. You're afraid of it.'

'Yes.'

Her face coloured. She burst out, 'I don't wonder Grandfather threw you out!' With that, she turned and hurried away.

The dinosaurs were a solace, as always. They strutted in their new cages, before a romantic diorama, munching on the lush grass. Jane certainly took good care of them.

These were the first animals to be synthesised. It had been my idea to start on dinosaurs, building from fragments of bone presented from a museum. We had four stegosaurs, two brontosauri wallowing in a little pond, and a brace of iguanadon. They stood about six inches high and were, of course, sterile. Nowadays, we – Lawrence Life-Forms, I mean – do considerably better. In a separate cage was a super little tyrannosaur, eight inches high, prowling about with cat movements, glaring at me.

I stood for a long time, wondering what we had started. Synthetic life ... When we had not solved one tithe of the problems of natural life ... And Frank was promising his newly constituted board to have a synthetic serving-man on the market within five years ...

In the end, rather than think about it, I wandered back to the house.

Frank was there, standing against the empty fireplace. Jane stood near him. Mrs Singer had brought them sherry. As I took in the scene, I realised I had heard a helicopter fly over, but had taken no notice.

'You shouldn't have come,' I said harshly. I thought that at sixty-five he looked as if he had more years to go than I; but he was never involved in a plane crash.

'The board room battle was one thing,' he said. 'You and Jerry Keynes were just two individuals who stood in my way, in the way of what I see as right. Privately it is a different matter, Robert. Keynes means nothing to me, but you are one of the family. I feel about you –'

'You can't divorce the two sides, Frank,' I said. 'I tried to go along with them too long; now that you've chucked me out, I don't have to try.'

'I didn't chuck you out, man! You got outvoted!'

'Outsmarted!'

'Daddy,' Jane said. 'Try to listen to what Grandfather is going to say.'

My anger was rising; I liked the feeling. 'Don't tell me – he's going to make an offer!'

'Wrong, Robert! I have made an offer to Jane, and she has accepted. I've offered her a very large sum for this estate.' He named the price; it was about three times as much as I'd have got on the open market.

'You are forgetting. This is my estate, and I sell when I wish to whom I wish.'

'Give it to Jane. She will sell it to me. I will give it to her.'

'I've done my last deal with you, Frank.'

He came up close and said, gently, 'Let me help you privately, Robert. As a favour to me. You know why.'

'I don't know why.'

His gaze dropped. He said, 'After the plane crash ... you and Viv lingered near death for several days. I realised then how I loved my daughter, how little I had ever done for her.'

'Don't make me weep, Frank. I prefer you in your hard-hitting role.'

'Maybe. I had plenty of time to think. You were lying there on a heart-machine; Viv was unconscious with irreversible brain damage. Both your lives seemed to be suspended while I made up my mind.'

'Egotism, Frank!'

'Those days were years. Remember, my own wife had died only two months before, and I had been told she would never have died if I had turned up that last day as I had promised.'

'You stayed at the office.'

'Never mind that. That's my business. I'm talking about you. On the tenth day, the surgeons decided Viv was dying. That was when they flew in the heart-op specialist from South Africa – at my expense. You know what happened. There was nothing wrong with Viv's heart; her damage was to brain and kidneys. They operated. They gave you her heart. So you survived.'

I was shaking. Jane came to me. 'Why do you bring all this up again? Don't I know it? Don't I live with it every day? What are you trying to do, Frank – get your daughter's heart back from me? For God's sake, you've done enough – go away!'

He went to the other end of the room, sat down, lit a cigar. His hand trembled.

'Robert, I am not reproaching you. In you, a part of my daughter lives. I only want to tell you what you did not know. The problems with the heart-op come afterwards – in particular the body's fight to reject its new heart, the auto-immune reaction. You know what the surgeons said in your case? They said you hardly manifested that reaction.'

He stopped to let it sink in. I said nothing.

'Well, it was a question of love, wasn't it? Your mind controlling physical reaction, wasn't it? You really loved Viv. You didn't blame her even subconsciously for the crash, or the usual immune reaction would have established itself. You lay there unconscious and proved your love was perfect.'

'Would you leave, please, Frank? You are a hard man, as you aspire to be. You also have a disgusting sentimental streak, as do most hard men. This whole notion that love can overcome antibodies is sheer sentimental fantasy. I was simply a surgical case that worked out well – the operation is not the hazardous thing it was ten years ago.'

I got up and walked out into the garden again. The sun was momentarily shining. I went and stood in the shrubbery. Jane eventually found me there.

'Father, I cannot, cannot understand you! I know how much you loved mother, and how hard her death hit you. Why should you make yourself out to be so callous in front of Grandfather?'

I decided to touch her, and then thought better of it.

'I can't accept or attempt emotional blackmail, Jane!'

'You mean you won't do a deal with Grandfather!'

'Of course I won't do a deal, just to salve his conscience!'

The helicopter whirled overhead, turned, made for the mainland.

I could see Jane was very angry. 'Why the devil should you withhold the salving of his conscience? What special right have you to administer a moral law? It was precisely because you tried to do that that you were kicked out of Lawrence Life-Forms! Now what future have you? What future have *I* got, either? You've let me spend five years looking after you – oh, I have no complaints! – but you're quite ready to see our home go down the drain just to spite someone who wanted to help us!'

'It was not spite, Jane! It—'

'Oh, don't tell me! Ethical principles! You and your ethical principles! But really, it's spite, isn't it? You want to hurt Grandfather – it's just as simple as that! You have mother's heart, and you have now taken it from him!'

'This heart – it's an organ, an anonymous machine! Don't try and build some symbolic thing about it! You're angry and upset, Jane, Don't say something you will regret, don't spoil the relationship between us!'

'I'm not sure I *want* any relationship with you!' And with that she turned and left me.

So went our family quarrel. Nothing was resolved.

It was four and a half months before I saw my daughter again. I was living in my town flat then, with most of the rooms empty of furniture.

When Jane appeared, I was so glad to see her that at first I did not realise how ill she looked.

She took my hand and asked, 'Have you heard the news?'

'The house was auctioned yesterday,' I said. 'It fetched its reserve price. You shouldn't have walked out on me, Jane. At least give me the credit of meaning well with regard to your grandfather! And our quarrel – yours and mine – it must not be final. In life, only death is final. Emotional entanglements, financial entanglements – they're never final.'

'I'm going to live my own life, Father, from now on.'

'Good! Do it for good reasons, though, not to defy me. Who's right in all this, who's wrong? I behaved – as I thought best. My morality is clear, to me at least. But I don't understand Frank's. Lawrence Life-Forms go from strength to strength. Our pocket-sized dinosaurs are nothing now. The world's zoos will soon be stocked with life-size dinosaurs. Synthetic human beings are just a few years away.'

'Father, you could never have stopped that development!'

'They'll have trouble. I know! Am I not myself synthetic?'

As I said this, I felt my heart beating strongly within its scarred cage. I forced myself to say, 'Jane, I want your respect and – and your love. You must love me for myself, not just because I keep a part of your mother alive, as Frank does.'

'I came to tell you, Father. That was my news. Frank shot himself yesterday. It's in all the papers.'

Reaction would come later. 'I don't look at newspapers any more,' I said automatically; then: 'Why?'

'You've always been the one finding clever reasons,' she said. As she looked down challengingly at me, I realised how she would be keeping something of her grandfather alive, down through the years.

Total Environment

I

'What's that poem about "caverns measureless to man"?' Thomas Dixit asked. His voice echoed away among the caverns, the question unanswered. Peter Crawley, walking a pace or two behind him, said nothing, lost in a reverie of his own.

It was over a year since Dixit had been imprisoned here. He had taken time off from the resettlement area to come and have a last look round before everything was finally demolished. In these great concrete workings, men still moved − Indian technicians mostly, carrying instruments, often with their own headlights. Cables trailed everywhere; but the desolation was mainly an effect of the constant abrasion all surfaces had undergone. People had flowed here like water in a subterranean cave; and their corporate life had flowed similarly, hidden, forgotten.

Dixit was powerfully moved by the thought of all that life. He, almost alone, was the man who had plunged into it and survived.

Old angers stirring in him, he turned and spoke directly to his companion. 'What a monument to human suffering! They should leave this place standing as an everlasting memorial to what happened.'

The white man said, 'The Delhi government refuses to entertain any such suggestion. I see their point of view, but I also see that it would make a great tourist attraction!'

'Tourist attraction, man! Is that all it means to you?'

Crawley laughed. 'As ever, you're too touchy, Thomas. I take this whole matter much less lightly than you suppose. Tourism just happens to attract me more than human suffering.'

They walked on side by side. They were never able to agree.

The battered faces of flats and houses – now empty, once choked with humanity – stood on either side, doors gaping open like old men's mouths in sleep. The spaces seemed enormous; the shadows and echoes that belonged to those spaces seemed to continue indefinitely. Yet before ... there had scarcely been room to breathe here.

'I remember what your buddy, Senator Byrnes, said,' Crawley remarked. 'He showed how both East and West have learned from this experiment. Of course, the social scientists are still working over their findings; some startling formulae for social groups are emerging already. But the people who lived and died here were fighting their way towards control of the universe of the ultra-small, and that's where the biggest advances have come. They were already developing power over their own genetic material. Another generation, and they might have produced the ultimate in automatic human population control: anoestrus, where too close proximity to other members of the species leads to reabsorption of the embryonic material in the female. Our scientists have been able to help them there, and geneticists predict that in another decade –'

'Yes, yes, all that I grant you. Progress is wonderful.' He knew he was being impolite. These things were important, of revolutionary importance to a crowded Earth. But he wished he walked these eroded passageways alone.

Undeniably, India had learned too, just as Peter Crawley claimed. For Hinduism had been put to the test here and had shown its terrifying strengths and weaknesses. In these mazes, people had not broken under deadly conditions – nor had they thought to break away from their destiny. *Dharma* – duty – had been stronger than humanity. And this revelation was already changing the thought and fate of one-sixth of the human race.

He said, 'Progress is wonderful. But what took place here was essentially a religious experience.'

Crawley's brief laugh drifted away into the shadows of a great gaunt stairwell. 'I'll bet you didn't feel that way when we sent you in here a year ago!'

What had he felt then? He stopped and gazed up at the gloom of the stairs. All that came to him was the memory of that appalling flood of life and of the people who had been a part of it, whose brief years had evaporated in these caverns, whose feet had endlessly trodden these warren-ways, these lugubrious decks, these crumbling flights....

II

The concrete steps, climbed up into darkness. The steps were wide, and countless children sat on them, listless, resting against each other. This was an hour when activity was low and even small children hushed their cries for a while. Yet there was no silence on the steps; silence was never complete there. Always, in the background, the noise of voices. Voices and more voices. Never silence.

Shamim was aged, so she preferred to run her errands at this time of day, when the crowds thronging Total Environment were less. She dawdled by a sleepy seller of life-objects at the bottom of the stairs, picking over the little artifacts and exclaiming now and again. The hawker knew her, knew she was too poor to buy, did not even press her to buy. Shamim's oldest daughter, Malti, waited for her mother by the bottom step.

Malti and her mother were watched from the top of the steps.

A light burned at the top of the steps. It had burned there for twenty-five years, safe from breakage behind a strong mesh. But dung and mud had recently been thrown at it, covering it almost entirely and so making the top of the stairway dark. A furtive man called Narayan Farhad crouched there and watched, a shadow in the shadows.

A month ago, Shamim had had an illegal operation in one of the pokey rooms off Grand Balcony on her deck. The effects of the operation were still with her; under her plain cotton sari, her thin dark old body was bent. Her share of life stood lower than it had been.

Malti was her second oldest daughter, a meek girl who had not been conceived when the Total Environment experiment began. Even meekness had its limits. Seeing her mother dawdle so needlessly, Malti muttered impatiently and went on ahead, climbing the infested steps, anxious to be home.

*

Extracts from Thomas Dixit's report to Senator Jacob Byrnes, back in America: *To lend variety to the habitat, the Environment has been divided into ten decks, each deck five stories high, which allows for an occasional pocket-sized open space. The architecture has been varied somewhat on each deck. On one deck, a sort of blown-up Indian village is presented; on another, the houses are large and appear separate, although sandwiched between decks – I need not add they are hopelessly overcrowded now. On most decks, the available space is packed solid with flats. Despite this attempt at variety, a general bowdlerisation of both Eastern and Western architectural styles, and the fact that everything has been constructed out of concrete or a parastyrene for economy's sake, has led to a dreadful sameness. I cannot imagine anywhere more hostile to the spiritual values of life.*

The shadow in the shadows moved. He glanced anxiously up at the light, which also housed a spy-eye; there would be a warning out, and sprays would soon squirt away the muck he had thrown at the fitting; but, for the moment, he could work unobserved.

Narayan bared his old teeth as Malti came up the steps towards him, treading among the sprawling children. She was too old to fetch a really good price on the slave market, but she was still strong; there would be no trouble in getting rid of her at once. Of course he knew something of her history, even though she lived on a different deck from him. Malti! He called her name at the last moment as he jumped out on her. Old though he was, Narayan was quick. He wore only his dhoti, arms flashing, interlocking round hers, one good powerful wrench to get her off her feet – now running fast, fearful, up the rest of the steps, moving even as he clamped one hand over her mouth to cut off her cry of fear. Clever old Narayan!

The stairs mount up and up in the four corners of the Total Environment, linking deck with deck. They are now crude things of concrete and metal, since the plastic covers have long been stripped from them.

These stairways are the weak points of the tiny empires, transient and brutal, that form on every deck. They are always guarded, though guards can be bribed. Sometimes gangs or 'unions' take over a stairway, either by agreement or bloodshed.

*

Shamim screamed, responding to her daughter's cry. She began to hobble up the stairs as fast as she could, tripping over infant feet, drawing a dagger out from under her sari. It was a plastic dagger, shaped out of a piece of the Environment.

She called Malti, called for help as she went. When she reached the landing, she was on the top floor of her deck, the Ninth, where she lived. Many people were here, standing, squatting, thronging together. They looked away from Shamim, people with blind faces. She had so often acted similarly herself when others were in trouble.

Gasping, she stopped and stared up at the roof of the deck, blue-dyed to simulate sky, cracks running irregularly across it. The steps went on up there, up to the Top Deck. She saw legs, yellow soles of feet disappearing, faces staring down at her, hostile. As she ran toward the bottom of the stairs, the watchers above threw things at her. A shard hit Shamim's cheek and cut it open. With blood running down her face, she began to wail. Then she turned and ran through the crowds to her family room.

I've been a month just reading through the microfiles. Sometimes a whole deck becomes unified under a strong leader. On Deck Nine, for instance, unification was achieved under a man called Ullhas. He was a strong man, and a great show-off. That was a while ago, when conditions were not as desperate as they are now. Ullhas could never last the course today. Leaders become more despotic as Environment decays.

The dynamics of unity are such that it is always insufficient for a deck simply to stay unified; the young men always need to have their aggressions directed outwards. So the leader of a strong deck always sets out to tyrannise the deck below or above, whichever seems to be the weaker. It is a miserable state of affairs. The time generally comes when, in the midst of a raid, a counter-raid is launched by one of the other decks. Then the raiders return to carnage and defeat. And another paltry empire tumbles.

It is up to me to stop this continual degradation of human life.

As usual, the family room was crowded. Although none of Shamim's own children were here, there were grandchildren – including the lame granddaughter, Shirin – and six great-grandchildren, none of them more than three years old, Shamim's third husband, Gita, was not in. Safe in the homely squalor of the room, Shamim burst into tears, while Shirin comforted her and endeavoured to keep the little ones off.

'Gita is getting food. I will go and fetch him,' Shirin said.

When UHDRE – Ultra-High Density Research Establishment – became operative, twenty-five years ago, all the couples selected for living in the Total Environment had to be under twenty years of age. Before being sealed, in, they were inoculated against all diseases. There was plenty of room for each couple then; they had whole suites to themselves, and the best of food; plus no means of birth control. That's always been the main pivot of the UHDRE experiment. Now that first generation has aged, severely. They are old people pushing forty-five. The whole life cycle has speeded, up – early puberty, early senescence. The second and third generations have shown remarkable powers of adaptation; a fourth generation is already toddling. Those toddlers will be reproducing before their years attain double figures, if present trends continue. Are allowed, to continue.

Gita was younger than Shamim, a small wiry man who knew his way around. No hero, he nevertheless had a certain style about him. His life-object hung boldly round his neck on a chain, instead of being hidden, as were most people's life objects. He stood in the line for food, chattering with friends. Gita was good at making alliances. With a bunch of his friends, he had formed a little union to see that they got their food hack safely to their homes; so they generally met with no incident in the crowded walkways of Deck Nine.

The balance of power on the deck was very complex at the moment. As a result, comparative peace reigned, and might continue for several weeks if the strong man on Top Deck did not interfere.

Food delivery grills are fixed in the walls of every floor of every deck. Two gongs sound before each delivery. After the second one, hatches open and steaming food pours from the grills. Hills of rice tumble forward, flavoured with meat and spices. Chappattis fall from a separate slot. As the men run forward with their containers, holy men are generally there to sanctify the food.

Great supply elevators roar up and down in the heart of the vast tower, tumbling out rations at all levels. Alcohol also was supplied in the early years. It was discontinued when it led to trouble; which is not to say that it is not secretly brewed, inside the Environment. The UHDRE food ration has been generous from the start and has always been maintained at the same level per head of population although, as you know, the food is now ninety-five percent factory-made. Nobody would ever have starved, had it been shared out equally inside the tower. On some of the decks, some of the time, it is still shared, out fairly.

One of Gita's sons, Jamsu, had seen the kidnapper Narayan making off to Top Deck with the struggling Malti. His eyes gleaming with excitement, he sidled his way into the queue where Gita stood and clasped his lather's arm. Jamsu had something of his father in him, always lurked where numbers made him safe, rather than run off as his brothers and sisters had run off, to marry and struggle for a room or a space of their own.

He was telling his father what had happened when Shirin limped up and delivered her news.

Nodding grimly, Gita said, 'Stay with us, Shirin, while I get the food.'

He scooped his share into the family pail. Jamsu grabbed a handful of rice for himself.

'It was a dirty wizened man from Top Deck called Narayan Farhad,' Jamsu said, gobbling. 'He is one of the crooks who hangs about the shirt tails of ...' He let his voice die.

'You did not go to Malti's rescue, shame on you!' Shirin said.

'Jamsu might have been killed,' Gita said, as they pushed through the crowd and moved towards the family room.

'They're getting so strong on Top Deck,' Jamsu said. 'I hear all about it! We mustn't provoke them or they may attack. They say a regular army is forming round ...'

Shirin snorted impatiently. 'You great babe! Go ahead and name the man! It's Prahlad Patel whose very name you dare not mention, isn't it? Is he a god or something, for Siva's sake? You're afraid of him even from this distance, eh, aren't you?'

'Don't bully the lad,' Gita said. Keeping the peace in his huge mixed family was a great responsibility, almost more than he could manage.

As he turned into the family room, he said quietly to Jamsu and Shirin, 'Malti was a favourite daughter of Shamim's, and now is gone from her. We will get our revenge against this Narayan Farhad. You and I will go this evening, Jamsu, to the holy man Vazifdar. He will even up matters for us, and then perhaps the great Patel will also be warned.'

He looked thoughtfully down at his life-object. Tonight, he told himself, I must venture forth alone, and put my life in jeopardy for Shamim's sake.

Prahlad Patel's union has flourished, and grown until now he rules all the Top Deck. His name is known and dreaded, we believe, three or four decks down. He is the strongest – yet in some ways curiously the most moderate – ruler in Total Environment at present.

Although he can be brutal, Patel seems inclined for peace. Of course, the bugging does not reveal everything; he may have plans which he keeps secret, since he is fully aware that the bugging exists. But we believe his interests lie in other directions than conquest. He is only about nineteen, as we reckon years, but already grey-haired, and the sight of him is said to freeze the muscles to silence in the lips of his followers. I have watched him over the bugging for many hours since I agreed to undertake this task.

Patel has one great advantage in Total Environment. He lives on the Tenth Deck, at the top of the building. He can therefore be invaded only from below and the Ninth Deck offers no strong threats at present, being mainly oriented round an influential body of holy men, of whom the most illustrious is one Vazifdar.

The staircases between decks are always trouble spots. No deck-ruler was ever strong enough to withstand attack from above and, below. The staircases are also used by single troublemakers, thieves, political fugitives, prostitutes, escaping slaves, hostages. Guards can always be bribed, or favor their multitudinous relations, or join the enemy for one reason or another. Patel, being on the Top Deck, has only four weak points to watch for, rather than eight.

Vazifdar was amazingly holy and amazingly influential. It was whispered that his life-object was the most intricate in all Environment but there was nobody who would lay claim to having set eyes upon it. Because of his reputation, many people on Gita's deck – yes, and from farther away – sought Vazifdar's help. A stream of men and women moved always through his room, even when he was locked in private meditation and far away from this world.

The holy man had a flat with a balcony that looked out onto mid-deck. Many relations and disciples lived there with him, so that the rooms had been elaborately and flimsily divided by screens. All day, the youngest disciples twittered like birds upon the balconies as Vazifdar held court, discussing among themselves the immense wisdom of his sayings.

All the disciples, all the relations, loved Vazifdar. There had been relations who did not love Vazifdar, but they had passed away in their sleep. Gita himself was a distant relation of Vazifdar's and came into the holy man's presence now with gifts of fresh water and a long piece of synthetic cloth, enough to make a robe.

Vazifdar's brow and cheeks were painted with white to denote his high caste. He received the gifts of cloth and water graciously, smiling at Gita in such a way that Gita – and, behind him, Jamsu – took heart.

Vazifdar was thirteen years old as the outside measured years. He was sleekly fat, from eating much and moving little. His brown body shone with oils; every morning, young women massaged and manipulated him.

He spoke very softly, husbanding his voice, so that he could scarcely be heard for the noise in the room.

'It is a sorrow to me that this woe has befallen your stepchild Malti,' he said. 'She was a good woman, although infertile.'

'She was raped at a very early age, disrupting her womb, dear Vazifdar. You will know of the event. Her parents feared she would die. She could never bear issue. The evil shadowed her life. Now this second woe befalls her.'

'I perceive that Malti's role in the world was merely to be a companion to her mother. Not all can afford to purchase who visit the bazaar.'

There are bazaars on every floor, crowding down the corridors and balconies, and a chief one on every deck. The menfolk choose such places to meet and chatter even when they have nothing to trade. Like everywhere else, the bazaars are crowded with humanity, down to the smallest who can walk – and sometimes even those carry naked smaller brothers clamped tight to their backs.

The bazaars are great centres for scandal. Here also are our largest screens. They glow behind their safety grills, beaming in special programmes from outside; our outside world that must seem to have but faint reality as it dashes against the thick securing walls of Environment and percolates through to the screens. Below the screens, uncheckable and fecund life goes teeming on, with all its injury.

Humbly, Gita on his knees said, 'If you could restore Malti to her mother Shamim, who mourns her, you would reap all our gratitude, dear Vazifdar. Malti is too old for a man's bed, and on Top Deck all sorts of humiliations must await her.'

Vazifdar shook his head with great dignity. 'You know I cannot restore Malti, my kinsman. How many deeds can be ever undone? As long as we have slavery, so long must we bear to have the ones we love enslaved. You must cultivate a mystical and resigned view of life and beseech Shamim always to do the same.'

'Shamim is more mystical in her ways than I, never asking much, always working, working, praying, praying. That is why she deserves better than this misery.'

Nodding in approval of Shamim's behaviour as thus revealed, Vazifdar said, 'That is well. I know she is a good woman. In the future lie other events which may recompense her for this sad event.'

Jamsu, who had managed to keep quiet behind his father until now, suddenly burst out, 'Uncle Vazifdar, can you not punish Narayan Farhad for his sin in stealing poor Malti on the steps? Is he to be allowed to escape to Patel's deck, there to live with Malti and enjoy?'

'Sssh, son!' Gita looked in agitation to see if Jamsu's outburst had annoyed Vazifdar; but Vazifdar was smiling blandly.

'You must know, Jamsu, that we are all creatures of the Lord Siva, and without power. No, no, do not pout! I also am without power in his hands. To own one room is not to possess the whole mansion. But ...'

It was a long, and heavy *but*. When Vazifdar's thick eyelids closed over his eyes, Gita trembled, for he recalled how, on previous occasions when he had visited his powerful kinsman, Vazifdar's eyelids had descended in this fashion while he deigned to think on a problem, as if he shut out all the external world with his own potent flesh.

'Narayan Farhad shall be troubled by more than his conscience.' As he spoke, the pupils of his eyes appeared again, violet and black. They were looking beyond Gita, beyond the confines of his immediate surroundings. 'Tonight he shall be troubled by evil dreams.'

'The night-visions!' Gita and Jamsu exclaimed, in fear and excitement.

Now Vazifdar swivelled his magnificent head and looked directly at Gita, looked deep into his eyes. Gita was a small man; he saw himself as a small man within. He shrank still further under that irresistible scrutiny.

'Yes, the night-visions,' the holy man said. 'You know what that entails, Gita. You must go up to Top Deck and procure Narayan's life-object. Bring it back to me, and I promise Narayan shall suffer the night-visions tonight. Though he is sick, he shall be cured.'

III

The women never cease their chatter as the lines of supplicants come and go before the holy men. Their marvellous resignation in that hateful prison! If they ever complain about more than the small circumstances of their lives, if they ever complain about the monstrous evil that has overtaken them all, I never heard of it. There is always the harmless talk, talk that relieves petty nervous anxieties, talk that relieves the almost noticed pressures on the brain. The women's talk practically drowns the noise of their children. But most of the time it is clear that Total Environment consists mainly of children. That's why I want to see the experiment closed down; the children would adapt to our world.

It is mainly on this fourth generation that the effects of the population glut show. Whoever rules the decks, it is the babes, the endless babes, tottering, laughing, staring, piddling, tumbling, running, the endless babes to whom the Environment really belongs. And their mothers, for the most part, are women who – at the same age and in a more favoured part of the globe – would still be virginally at school, many only just entering their teens.

Narayan Farhad wrapped a blanket round himself and huddled in his corner of the crowded room. Since it was almost time to sleep, he had to take up his hired space before one of the loathed Dasguptas stole it. Narayan hated the Dasgupta family, its lickspittle men, its shrill women, its turbulent children – the endless babes who crawled, the bigger ones with nervous diseases who thieved and ran and jeered at him. It was the vilest family on Top Deck, according to Narayan's oft-repeated claims; he tolerated it only because he felt himself to be vile.

He succeeded at nothing to which he turned his hand. Only an hour ago, pushing through the crowds, he had lost his life-object from his pocket – or else it had been stolen; but he dared not even consider that possibility!

Even his desultory kidnapping business was a failure. This bitch he had caught this morning – Malti. He had intended to rape her before selling her, but had become too nervous once he had dragged her in here, with a pair of young Dasguptas laughing at him. Nor had he sold the woman well. Patel had beaten down his price, and Narayan had not the guts to argue. Maybe he should leave this deck and move down to one of the more chaotic ones. The middle decks were always more chaotic. Six was having a slow three-sided war even now, which should make Five a fruitful place, with hordes of refugees to batten on.

... And what a fool to snatch so old a girl – practically an old woman!

Through narrowed eyes, Narayan squatted in his corner, acid flavours burning his mouth. Even if his mind would rest and allow him to sleep, the Dasgupta mob was still too lively for any real relaxation. That old Dasgupta, now – he was like a rat, totally without self-restraint, not a proper Hindu at all, doing the act openly with his own daughters. There were many men like that in Total Environment, men who had nothing else in life. Dirty swine! Lucky dogs! Narayan's daughters had thrown him out many months ago when he tried it!

Over and over, his mind ran on his grievances. But he sat collectedly, prodding off with one bare foot the nasty little brats who crawled at him, and staring at the screen flickering on the wall behind its protective mesh.

He liked the screens, enjoyed viewing the madness of outside. What a world it was out there! All that heat, and the necessity for work, and the complication of life! The sheer bigness of the world – he couldn't stand that, would not want it under any circumstances.

He did not understand half he saw. After all, he was born here. His father might have been born outside, whoever his father was; but no legends from outside had come down to him: only the distortions in the general gossip, and the stuff on the screens. Now that he came to reflect, people didn't pay much attention to the screens any more. Even he didn't.

But he could not sleep. Blearily, he looked at images of cattle ploughing fields, fields cut into dice by the dirty grills before the screens. He had already gathered vaguely that this feature was about changes in the world today.

'… are giving way to this …' said the commentator above the rumpus in the Dasgupta room. The children lived here like birds. Racks were stacked against the walls, and on these rickety contraptions the many little Dasguptas roosted.

'… food factories automated against danger of infection …' Yak yak yak, then.

'Beef-tissue culture growing straight into plastic distribution packs …' Shots of some great interior place somewhere, with meat growing out of pipes, extruding itself into square packs, dripping with liquid, looking rather ugly. Was that the shape of cows now or something? Outside must be a hell of a scaring place, then! '… as new factory food at last spells hope for India's future in the …' Yak yak yak from the kids. Once, their sleep racks had been built across the screen; but one night the whole shaky edifice collapsed, and three children were injured. None killed, worse luck!

Patel should have paid more for that girl. Nothing was as good as it had been. Why, once on a time, they used to show sex films on the screens – really filthy stuff that got even Narayan excited. He was younger then. Really filthy stuff, he remembered, and pretty girls doing it. But it must be – oh, a long time since that was stopped. The screens were dull now. People gave up watching. Uneasily, Narayan slept, propped in the corner under his scruffy blanket. Eventually, the whole scruffy room slept.

The documentaries and other features piped into Environment are no longer specially made by UHDRE teams for internal consumption. When the UN made a major cut in UHDRE's annual subsidy, eight years ago, the private TV studio was one of the frills that had to be axed. Now we pipe in old programmes bought off major networks. The hope is that they will keep the wretched prisoners in Environment in touch with the outside world, but this is clearly not happening. The degree of comprehension between inside and outside grows markedly less on both sides, on an exponential curve. As I see

*it, a great gulf of isolation is widening between the two environments, just as
if they were sailing away from each other into different space-time continua.
I wish I could think that the people in charge here – Crawley especially – not
only grasped this fact but understood that it should be rectified immediately.*

Shamim could not sleep for grief.

Gita could not sleep for apprehension.

Jamsu could not sleep for excitement.

Vazifdar did not sleep.

Vazifdar shut his sacred self away in a cupboard, brought his lids
down over his eyes and began to construct, within the vast spaces of
his mind, a thought pattern corresponding to the matrix represented by
Narayan Farhad's stolen life-object. When it was fully conceived, Vazifdar
began gently to inset a little evil into one edge of the thought-pattern....

Narayan slept. What roused him was the silence. It was the first time
total silence had ever come to Total Environment.

At first, he thought he would enjoy total silence. But it took on such
weight and substance....

Clutching his blanket, he sat up. The room was empty, the screen
dark. Neither thing had ever happened before, could not happen! And
the silence! Dear Siva, some terrible monkey god had hammered that
silence out in darkness and thrown it out like a shield into the world,
rolling over all things! There was a ringing quality in the silence – a
gong! No, no, not a gong! Footsteps!

It was footsteps, O Lord Siva, do not let it be footsteps!

Total Environment was empty. The legend was fulfilled that said Total
Environment would empty one day. All had departed except for poor
Narayan. And this thing of the footsteps was coming to visit him in his
defenceless corner....

It was climbing up through the cellars of his existence. Soon it
would emerge.

Trembling convulsively, Narayan stood up, clutching the corner of
the blanket to his throat. He did not wish to face the thing. Wildly, he
thought, could he bear it best if it looked like a man or if it looked
nothing like a man? It was Death for sure – but how would it look?
Only Death – his heart fluttered! – only Death could arrive this way....

His helplessness…. Nowhere to hide! He opened his mouth, could not scream, clutched the blanket, felt that he was wetting himself as if he were a child again. Swiftly came the image – the infantile, round-bellied, cringing, puny, his mother black with fury, her great white teeth gritting as she smacked his face with all her might, spitting…. It was gone, and he faced the gong – like death again, alone in the great dark tower. In the arid air, vibrations of its presence.

He was shouting to it, demanding that it did not come.

But it came. It came with majestic sloth, like the heartbeats of a foetid slumber, came in the door, pushing darkness before it. It was like a human, but too big to be human.

And it wore Malti's face, that sickeningly innocent smile with which she had run up the steps. No! No, that was not it – oh, he fell down onto the wet floor: it was nothing like that woman, nothing at all. Cease, impossibilities! It was a man, his ebony skull shining, terrible; and magnificent, stretching out, grasping, confident. Narayan struck out of his extremity and fell forward. Death was another indelible smack in the face.

One of the roosting Dasguptas blubbered and moaned as the man kicked him, woke for a moment, saw the screen still flickering meaninglessly and reassuringly, saw Narayan tremble under his blanket, tumbled back into sleep.

It was not till morning that they found it had been Narayan's last tremble.

I know I am supposed to be a detached observer. No emotions, no feelings. But scientific detachment is the attitude that has led to much of the inhumanity inherent in Environment. How do we, for all the bugging devices, hope to know what ghastly secret nightmares they undergo in there? Anyhow, I am relieved to hear you are flying over.

It is tomorrow I am due to go into Environment myself.

IV

The central offices of UHDRE were large and repulsive. At the time when they and the Total Environment tower had been built, the Indian Government would not have stood for anything else. Poured cement and rough edges was what they wanted to see and what they got.

From a window in the office building, Thomas Dixit could see the indeterminate land in one direction, and the gigantic TE tower in the other, together with the shantytown that had grown between the foot of the tower and the other UHDRE buildings.

For a moment, he chose to ignore the Project Organiser behind him and gaze out at what he could see of the table-flat lands of the great Ganges delta.

He thought, It's as good a place as any for man to project his power fantasies. But you are a fool to get mixed up in all this, Thomas!

Even to himself, he was never just Tom.

I am being paid, well paid to do a specific job. Now I am letting woolly humanitarian ideas get in the way of action. Essentially, I am a very empty man. No centre. Father Bengali, mother English, and live all my life in the States. I have excuses ... Other people accept them; why can't I?

Sighing, he dwelt on his own unsatisfactoriness. He did not really belong to the West, despite his long years there, and he certainly did not belong to India; in fact, he thought he rather disliked India. Maybe the best place for him was indeed the inside of the Environment tower.

He turned impatiently and said, 'I'm ready to get going now, Peter.'

Peter Crawley, the Special Project Organiser of UHDRE, was a rather austere Bostonian. He removed the horn-rimmed glasses from his nose and said, 'Right! Although we have been through the drill many times, Thomas, I have to tell you this once again before we move. The entire –'

'Yes, yes, I know, Peter! You don't have to cover yourself. This entire organisation might be closed down if I make a wrong move. Please take it as read.'

Without indignation, Crawley said, 'I was going to say that we are all rooting for you. We appreciate the risks you are taking. We shall be checking you everywhere you go in there through the bugging system.'

'And whatever you see, you can't do a thing.'

'Be fair; we have made arrangements to help!'

'I'm sorry, Peter.' He liked Crawley and Crawley's decent reserve.

Crawley folded his spectacles with a snap, inserted them in a leather slipcase and stood up.

'The UN, not to mention subsidiary organisations like the WHO and the Indian government, have their knife into us, Thomas. They want to close us down and empty Environment. They will do so unless you can provide evidence that forms of extra-sensory perception are developing inside the Environment. Don't get yourself killed in there. The previous men we sent in behaved foolishly and never came out again.' He raised an eyebrow and added dryly, 'That sort of thing gets us a bad name, you know.'

'Just as the blue movies did a while ago.'

Crawley put his hands behind his back. 'My predecessor here decided that immoral movies piped into Environment would help boost the birth rate there. Whether he was right or wrong, world opinion has changed since then as the spectre of world famine has faded. We stopped the movies eight years ago, but they have long memories at the UN, I fear. They allow emotionalism to impede scientific research.'

'Do you never feel any sympathy for the thousands of people doomed to live out their brief lives in the tower?'

They looked speculatively at each other.

'You aren't on our side any more, Thomas, are you? You'd like your findings to be negative, wouldn't you, and have the UN close us down?'

Dixit uttered a laugh. 'I'm not on anyone's *side*, Peter. I'm neutral. I'm going into Environment to look for the evidence of ESP that only direct contact may turn up. What else direct contact will turn up, neither of us can say as yet.'

'But you think it will be misery. And you will emphasise that at the inquiry after your return.'

'Peter – let's get on with it, shall we?' Momentarily, Dixit was granted a clear picture of the two of them standing in this room; he saw how their bodily attitudes contrasted. His attitudes were rather slovenly; he held himself rather slump-shouldered, he gesticulated to some extent (too much?); he was dressed in threadbare tunic and shorts, ready to pass muster as an inhabitant of Environment. Crawley, on the other hand, was very upright, stiff and smart in his movements, hardly ever gestured as he spoke; his dress was faultless.

And there was no need to be awed by or envious of Crawley. Crawley was encased in inhibition, afraid to feel signalling his aridity to anyone who cared to look out from their own self-preoccupation. Crawley, moreover, feared for his job.

'Let's get on with it, as you say.' He came from behind his desk. 'But I'd be grateful if you would remember, Thomas, that the people in the tower are volunteers, or the descendants of volunteers.

'When UHDRE began, a quarter-century ago, back in the mid-nine-teen-seventies, only volunteers were admitted, plus whatever children they had. The tower was a refuge then, free from famine, immune from all disease. They were glad, heartily glad, to get in, glad of all that Environment provided and still provides. Those who didn't qualify rioted. We have to remember that.

'India was a different place in 1975. It had lost hope. One crisis after another, one famine after another, crops dying, people starving, and yet the population spiralling up by a million every month.

'But today, thank God, that picture has largely changed. Synthetic foods have licked the problem; we don't need the grudging land any more. And at last the Hindus and Muslims have got the birth control idea into their heads. It's only *now*, when a little humanity is seeping back into this death-bowl of a subcontinent, that the UN dares complain about the inhumanity of UHDRE.'

Dixit said nothing. He felt that this potted history was simply angled towards Crawley's self-justification; the ideas it represented were real enough, heaven knew, but they had meaning for Crawley only in terms of his own existence. Dixit felt pity and impatience as Crawley went on with his narration.

'Our aim here must be unswervingly the same as it was from the start. We have evidence that nervous disorders of a special kind produce extra-sensory perception – telepathy and the rest, and maybe kinds of ESP we do not yet recognise. High-density populations with reasonable nutritional standards develop particular nervous instabilities which may be akin to ESP spectra.

'The Ultra-High Density Research Establishment was set up to inten-sify the likelihood of ESP developing. Don't forget that. The people in Environment are supposed to have some ESP; that's the whole point of the operation, right? Sure, it is not humanitarian. We know that. But that is not your concern. You have to go in and find evidence of ESP, something that doesn't show over the bugging. Then UHDRE will be able to continue.'

Dixit prepared to leave. 'If it hasn't shown up in quarter of a century –'

'It's in there! I know it's in there! The failure's in the bugging system. I feel it coming through the screens at me – some mystery we need to get our hands on! If only I could prove it! If only I could get in there myself!'

Interesting, Dixit thought. You'd have to be some sort of a voyeur to hold Crawley's job, forever spying on the wretched people.

'Too bad you have a white skin, eh?' he said lightly. He walked towards the door. It swung open, and he passed into the corridor.

Crawley ran after him and thrust out a hand. 'I know how you feel, Thomas. I'm not just a stuffed shirt, you know, not entirely void of sympathy. Sorry if I was needling you. I didn't intend to do so.'

Dixit dropped his gaze. 'I should be the one to apologise, Peter. If there's anything unusual going on in the tower, I'll find it, never worry!'

They shook hands, without wholly being able to meet each other's eyes.

V

Leaving the office block, Dixit walked alone through the sunshine toward the looming tower that housed Total Environment. The concrete walk was hot and dusty underfoot. The sun was the one good thing that India had, he thought: that burning beautiful sun, the real ruler of India, whatever petty tyrants came and went.

The sun blazed down on the tower; only inside did it not shine.

The uncompromising outlines of the tower were blurred by pipes, ducts and shafts that ran up and down its exterior. It was a building built for looking into, not out of. Some time ago, in the bad years, the welter of visual records gleaned from Environment used to be edited and beamed out on global networks every evening; but all that had been stopped as conditions inside Environment deteriorated, and public opinion in the democracies, who were subsidising the grandiose experiment, turned against the exploitation of human material.

A monitoring station stood by the tower walls. From here, a constant survey on the interior was kept. Facing the station where the jumbles of merchants' stalls, springing up to cater for tourists, who persisted even now that the tourist trade was discouraged. Two security guards stepped forward and escorted Dixit to the base of the tower. With ceremony, he entered the shade of the entry elevator. As he closed the door, germicides sprayed him, ensuring that he entered Environment without harbouring dangerous micro-organisms.

The elevator carried him up to the top deck; this plan had been settled some while ago. The elevator was equipped with double steel doors. As it came to rest, a circuit opened, and a screen showed him what was happening on the other side of the doors. He emerged from a dummy air-conditioning unit, behind a wide pillar. He was in Patel's domain.

The awful weight of human overcrowding hit Dixit with its full stink and noise. He sat down at the base of the pillar and let his senses adjust. And he thought, I was the wrong one to send; I've always had this inner core of pity for the sufferings of humanity; I could never be impartial; I've got to see that this terrible experiment is stopped.

He was at one end of a long balcony onto which many doors opened; a ramp led down at the other end. All the doorways gaped, although some were covered by rugs. Most of the doors had been taken off their hinges to serve as partitions along the balcony itself, partitioning off overspill families. Children ran everywhere, their tinkling voices and cries the dominant note in the hubbub. Glancing over the balcony, Dixit took in a dreadful scene of swarming multitudes, the anonymity of congestion; to sorrow for humanity was not to love its prodigality. Dixit had seen this panorama many times over the bugging system; he knew all the staggering figures – 1500 people in here to begin with, and by now some 75,000 people, a large proportion of them under four years of age. But pictures and figures were pale abstracts beside the reality they were intended to represent.

The kids drove him into action at last by playfully hurling dirt at him. Dixit moved slowly along, carrying himself tight and cringing in the manner of the crowd about him, features rigid, elbows tucked in to the ribs. *Mutatis mutandis*, it was Crawley's inhibited attitude. Even the children ran between the legs of their elders in that guarded way. As soon as he had left the shelter of his pillar, he was caught in a stream of chattering people, all jostling between the rooms and the stalls of the balcony. They moved very slowly.

Among the crowd were hawkers, and salesmen pressed their wares from the pitiful balcony hovels. Dixit tried to conceal his curiosity. Over the bugging he had had only distant views of the merchandise offered for sale. Here were the strange models that had caught his attention when he was first appointed to the UHDRE project. A man with orange goateyes, in fact probably no more than thirteen years of age, but here a hardened veteran, was at Dixit's elbow. As Dixit stared at him, momentarily suspicious he was being watched, the goat-eyed man merged into the crowd; and, to hide his face, Dixit turned to the nearest salesman.

In only a moment, he was eagerly examining the wares, forgetting how vulnerable was his situation.

All the strange models were extremely small. This Dixit attributed to shortage of materials – wrongly, as it later transpired. The biggest model the salesman possessed stood no more than two inches high. It was made, nevertheless, of a diversity of materials, in which many sorts of plastics featured. Some models were simple and appeared to be a little more than elaborate *tughra* or *monogram* which might have been intended for an elaborate piece of costume jewellery; others, as one peered among their interstices, seemed to afford a glimpse of another dimension; all possessed eye-teasing properties.

The merchant was pressing Dixit to buy. He referred to the elaborate models as 'life-objects.' Noticing that one in particular attracted his potential customer, he lifted it delicately and held it up a miracle of craftsmanship, perplexing, *outré*, giving Dixit somehow as much pain as pleasure. He named the price.

Although Dixit was primed with money, he automatically shook his head. 'Too expensive.'

'See, master, I show you how this life-object works!' The man fished beneath his scrap of loincloth and produced a small perforated silver box. Flipping it open, he produced a live wood-louse and slipped it under a hinged part of the model. The insect, in its struggles, activated a tiny wheel; the interior of the model began to rotate, some sets of minute planes turning in counterpoint to others.

'This life-object belonged to a very religious man, master.'

In his fascination, Dixit said, 'Are they all powered?'

'No, master, only special ones. This was perfect model from Dalcush Bancholi, last generation master all the way from Third Deck, very very fine and masterful workmanship of first quality. I have also still better one worked by a body louse, if you care to see.'

By reflex, Dixit said, 'Your prices are too high.'

He absolved himself from the argument that brewed, slipping away through the crowd with the merchant calling after him. Other merchants shouted to him, sensing his interest in their wares. He saw some beautiful work, all on the tiniest scale and not only life-objects but amazing little watches with millisecond hands as well as second hands; in some cases, the millisecond was the largest hand; in some, the hour hand was missing or was supplemented by a day hand; and the watches took many extraordinary shapes, tetrakishexahedrons and other elaborate forms, until their format merged with that of the life-objects.

Dixit thought approvingly: the clock and watch industry fulfills a human need for exercising elaborate skill and accuracy, while at the same time requiring a minimum of materials. These people of Total Environment are the world's greatest craftsmen. Bent over one curious watch that involved a colour change, he became suddenly aware of danger. Glancing over his shoulder, he saw the man with the unpleasant orange eyes about to strike him. Dixit dodged without being able to avoid the below. As it caught him on the side of his neck, he stumbled and fell under the milling feet.

VI

Afterwards, Dixit could hardly say that he had been totally unconscious. He was aware of hands dragging him, of being partly carried, of the sound of many voices, of the name 'Patel' repeated.... And when he came fully to his senses, he was lying in a cramped room, with a guard in a scruffy turban standing by the door. His first hazy thought was that the room was no more than a small ship's cabin; then he realised that, by indigenous standards, this was a large room for only one person.

He was a prisoner in Total Environment.

A kind of self-mocking fear entered him; he had almost expected the blow, he realised; and he looked eagerly about for the bug-eye that would reassure him his UHDRE friends outside were aware of his predicament. There was no sign of the bug-eye. He was not long in working out why; this room had been partitioned out of a larger one, and the bugging system was evidently shut in the other half – whether deliberately or accidentally, he had no way of knowing.

The guard had bobbed out of sight. Sounds of whispering came from beyond the doorway. Dixit felt the pressure of many people there. Then a woman came in and closed the door. She walked cringingly and carried a brass cup of water.

Although her face was lined, it was possible to see that she had once been beautiful and perhaps proud. Now her whole attitude expressed the defeat of her life. And this woman might be no more than eighteen! One of the terrifying features of Environment was the way, right from the start, confinement had speeded life-processes and abridged life.

Involuntarily, Dixit flinched away from the woman.

She almost smiled. 'Do not fear me, sir. I am almost as much a prisoner as you are. Equally, do not think that by knocking me down you can escape. I promise you, there are fifty people outside the door, all eager to impress Prahlad Patel by catching you, should you try to get away.'

So I'm in Patel's clutches, he thought. Aloud he said, 'I will offer you no harm. I want to see Patel. If you are captive, tell me your name, and perhaps I can help you.'

As she offered him the cup and he drank, she said, shyly, 'I do not complain, for my fate might have been much worse than it is. Please do not agitate Patel about me, or he may throw me out of his household. My name is Malti.'

'Perhaps I may be able to help you, and all your tribe, soon. You are all in a form of captivity here, the great Patel included, and it is from that I hope to deliver you.'

Then he saw fear in her eyes.

'You really are a spy from outside!' she breathed. 'But we do not want our poor little world invaded! You have so much – leave us our little!' She shrank away and slipped through the door, leaving Dixit with a melancholy impression of her eyes, so burdened in their shrunken gaze.

The babel continued outside the door. Although he still felt sick, he propped himself up and let his thoughts run on. 'You have so much – leave us our little….' All their values had been perverted. Poor things, they could know neither the smallness of their own world nor the magnitude of the world outside. This – this dungheap had become to them all there was of beauty and value.

Two guards came for him, mere boys. He could have knocked their heads together, but compassion moved him. They led him through a room full of excited people; beyond their glaring faces, the screen flickered pallidly behind its mesh; Dixit saw how faint the image of outside was.

He was taken into another partitioned room. Two men were talking. The scene struck Dixit with peculiar force, and not merely because he was at a disadvantage.

It was an alien scene. The impoverishment of even the richest furnishings, the clipped and bastardised variety of Hindi that was being talked, reinforced the impression of strangeness. And the charge of Patel's character filled the room.

There could be no doubt who was Patel. The plump cringing fellow, wringing his hands and protesting, was not Patel. Patel was the stocky white-haired man with the heavy lower lip and high forehead. Dixit had seen him in this very room over the bugging system. But to stand captive awaiting his attention was an experience of an entirely different order. Dixit tried to analyse the first fresh impact Patel had on him, but it was elusive.

It was difficult to realise that, as the outside measured years, Patel could not be much more than nineteen or twenty years of age. Time was impacted here, jellified under the psychic pressures of Total Environment. Like the hieroglyphics of that new relativity, detailed plans of the Environment hung large on one wall of this room, while figures and names were chalked over the others. The room was the nerve centre of Top Deck.

He knew something about Patel from the UHDRE records. Patel had come up here from the Seventh Deck. By guile as well as force, he had become ruler of Top Deck at an early age. He had surprised UHDRE observers by abstaining from the usual forays of conquest into other floors.

Patel was saying to the cringing man, 'Be silent! You try to obscure the truth with argument. You have heard the witnesses against you. During your period of watch on the stairs, you were bribed by a man from Ninth Deck and you let him through here.'

'Only for a mere seventeen minutes, Sir Patel!'

'I am aware that such things happen every day, wretched Raital. But this fellow you let through stole the life-object belonging to Narayan

Farhad and, in consequence, Narayan Farhad died in his sleep last night. Narayan was no more important than you are, but he was useful to me, and it is in order that he be revenged.'

'Anything that you say, Sir Patel!'

'Be silent, wretched Raital!' Patel watched Raital with interest as he spoke. And he spoke in a firm reflective voice that impressed Dixit more than shouting would have done.

'You shall revenge Narayan, Raital, because you caused his death. You will leave here now. You will not be punished. You will go, and you will steal the life-object belonging to that fellow from whom you accepted the bribe. You will bring that life-object to me. You have one day to do so. Otherwise, my assassins will find you wherever you hide, be it even down on Deck One.'

'Oh, yes, indeed, Sir Patel, all men know –' Raital was bent almost double as he uttered some face-saving formula. He turned and scurried away as Patel dismissed him.

Strength, thought Dixit. Strength, and also cunning. That is what Patel radiates. An elaborate and cutting subtlety. The phrase pleased him, seeming to represent something actual that he had detected in Patel's makeup. An elaborate and cutting subtlety.

Clearly, it was part of Patel's design that Dixit should witness this demonstration of his methods.

Patel turned away, folded his arms, and contemplated a blank piece of wall at close range. He stood motionless. The guards held Dixit still, but not so still as Patel held himself.

This tableau was maintained for several minutes. Dixit found himself losing track of the normal passage of time. Patel's habit of turning to stare at the wall – and it did not belong to Patel alone – was an uncanny one that Dixit had watched several times over the bugging system. It was that habit, he thought, which might have given Crawley the notion that ESP was rampant in the tower.

It was curious to think of Crawley here. Although Crawley might at this moment be surveying Dixit's face on a monitor, Crawley was now no more than an hypothesis.

Malti broke the tableau. She entered the room with a damp cloth on a tray, to stand waiting patiently for Patel to notice her. He broke away at last from his motionless survey of the wall, gesturing abruptly to the guards to leave. He took no notice of Dixit, sitting in a chair, letting Malti drape the damp cloth round his neck; the cloth had a fragrant smell to it.

'The towel is not cool enough, Malti, or damp enough. You will attend me properly at my morning session, or you will lose this easy job.'

He swung his gaze, which was suddenly black and searching, onto Dixit to say, 'Well, spy, you know I am Lord here. Do you wonder why I tolerate old women like this about me when I could have girls young and lovely to fawn on me?'

Dixit said nothing, and the self-styled Lord continued, 'Young girls would merely remind me by contrast of my advanced years. But this old bag – whom I bought only yesterday – this old bag is only just my junior and makes me look good in contrast. You see, we are masters of philosophy in here, in this prison-universe; we cannot be masters of material wealth like you people outside!'

Again Dixit said nothing, disgusted by the man's implied attitude to women.

A swinging blow caught him unprepared in the stomach. He cried and dropped suddenly to the floor.

'Get up, spy!' Patel said. He had moved extraordinarily fast. He sat back again in his chair, letting Malti massage his neck muscles.

VII

As Dixit staggered to his feet, Patel said, 'You don't deny you are from outside?'

'I did not attempt to deny it. I came from outside to speak to you.'

'You say nothing here until you are ordered to speak. Your people – you outsiders – you have sent in several spies to us in the last few months. Why?'

Still feeling sick from the blow, Dixit said, 'You should realise that we are your friends rather than your enemies, and our men emissaries rather than spies.'

'Pah! You are a breed of spies! Don't you sit and spy on us from every room? You live in a funny little dull world out there, don't you? So interested in us that you can think of nothing else! Keep working, Malti! Little spy, you know what happened to all the other spies your spying people sent in?'

'They died,' Dixit said.

'Exactly. They died. But you are the first to be sent to Patel's deck. What different thing to death do you expect here?'

'Another death will make my superiors very tired, Patel. You may have the power of life and death over me; they have the same over you, and over all in this world of yours. Do you want a demonstration?'

Rising, flinging the towel off, Patel said, 'Give me your demonstration!'

Must do, Dixit thought. Staring in Patel's eyes, he raised his right hand above his head and gestured with his thumb. Pray they are watching – and thank God this bit of partitioned room is the bit with the bugging system!

Tensely, Patel stared, balanced on his toes. Behind his shoulder, Malti also stared. Nothing happened.

Then a sort of shudder ran through Environment. It became slowly audible as a mixture of groan and cry. Its cause became apparent in this less crowded room when the air began to grow hot and foul. So Dixit's signal had got through; Crawley had him under survey, and the air-conditioning plant was pumping in hot carbon dioxide through the respiratory system.

'You see? We control the very air you breathe!' Dixit said. He dropped his arm, and slowly the air returned to normal, although it was at least an hour before the fright died down in the passages.

Whatever the demonstration had done to Patel, he showed nothing. Instead, he said, 'You control the air. Very well. But you do not control the will to turn it off permanently – and so you do not control the air. Your threat is an empty one, spy! For some reason, you need us to live. We have a mystery, don't we?'

'There is no reason why I should be anything but honest with you, Patel. Your special environment must have bred special talents in you. We are interested in those talents; but no more than interested.'

Patel came closer and inspected Dixit's face minutely, rather as he had recently inspected the blank wall. Strange angers churned inside him; his neck and throat turned a dark mottled colour. Finally he spoke.

'We are the centre of your outside world, aren't we? We know that you watch us all the time. We know that you are much more than "interested"! For you, we here are somehow a matter of life and death, aren't we?'

This was more than Dixit had expected.

'Four generations, Patel, four generations have been incarcerated in Environment.' His voice trembled. 'Four generations, and, despite our best intentions, you are losing touch with reality. You live in one relatively small building on a sizeable planet. Clearly, you can only be of limited interest to the world at large.'

'Malti!' Patel turned to the slave girl. 'Which is the greater, the outer world or ours?'

She looked confused, hesitated by the door as if longing to escape. 'The outside world was great, master, but then it gave birth to us, and we have grown and are growing and are gaining strength. The child now is almost the size of the father. So my step-father's son Jamsu says, and he is a clever one.'

Patel turned to stare at Dixit, a haughty expression on his face. He made no comment, as if the words of an ignorant girl were sufficient to prove his point.

'All that you and the girl say only emphasises to me how much you need help, Patel. The world outside is a great and thriving place; you must allow it to give you assistance through me. We are not your enemies.'

Again the choleric anger was there, powering Patel's every word.

'What else are you, spy? Your life is so vile and pointless out there, is it not? You envy us because we are superseding you! Our people – we may be poor, you may think of us as in your power, but we rule our own universe. And that universe is expanding and falling under our control more every day. Why, our explorers have gone into the world of the ultra-small. We discover new environments, new ways of living. By your terms, we are scientific peasants, perhaps, but I fancy we have ways of knowing the trade routes of the blood and the eternities of cell-change that you cannot comprehend. You think of us all as captives, eh? Yet you are captive to the necessity of supplying our air and our food and water; we are free. We are poor, yet you covet our riches. We are spied on all the time, yet we are secret. You need to understand us, yet we have no need to understand you. You are in *our* power, spy!'

'Certainly not in one vital respect, Patel. Both you and we are ruled by historical necessity. This Environment was set up twenty-five of our years ago. Changes have taken place not only in here but outside as well. The nations of the world are no longer prepared to finance this project. It is going to be closed down entirely, and you are going to have to live

352

outside. Or, if you don't want that, you'd better cooperate with us and persuade the leaders of the other decks to cooperate.'

Would threats work with Patel? His hooded and oblique gaze bit into Dixit like a hook.

After a deadly pause, he clapped his hands once. Two guards immediately appeared.

'Take the spy away,' said Patel. Then he turned his back.

A clever man, Dixit thought. He sat alone in the cell and meditated.

It seemed as if a battle of wits might develop between him and Patel. Well, he was prepared. He trusted to his first impression, that Patel was a man of cutting subtlety. He could not be taken to mean all that he said.

Dixit's mind worked back over their conversation. The mystery of the life-objects had been dangled before him. And Patel had taken care to belittle the outside world: 'funny dull little world,' he had called it. He had made Malti advance her primitive view that Environment was growing, and that had fitted in very well with his brand of boasting. Which led to the deduction that he had known her views beforehand; yet he had bought her only yesterday. Why should a busy man, a leader, bother to question an ignorant slave about her views of the outside world unless he were starved for information of that world, obsessed with it?

Yes, Dixit nodded to himself. Patel was obsessed with outside and tried to hide that obsession; but several small contradictions in his talk had revealed it.

Of course, it might be that Malti was so generally representative of the thousands in Environment that her misinformed ideas could be taken for granted. It was as well, as yet, not to be too certain that he was beginning to understand Patel.

Part of Patel's speech made sense even superficially. These poor devils were exploring the world of the ultra-small. It was the only landscape left for them to map. They were human, and still burning inside them was that unquenchable human urge to open frontiers.

So they knew some inward things. Quite possibly, as Crawley anticipated, they possessed a system of ESP upon which some reliance might be placed, unlike the wildly fluctuating telepathic radiations which circulated in the outside world.

He felt confident, fully engaged. There was much to understand here. The bugging system, elaborate and over-used, was shown to be a complete failure; the watchers had stayed external to their problem; it remained their problem, not their life. What was needed was a whole team to come and live here, perhaps a team on every deck, anthropologists and so on. Since that was impossible, then clearly the people of Environment must be released from their captivity; those that were unwilling to go far afield should be settled in new villages on the Ganges plain, under the wide sky. And there, as they adapted to the real world, observers could live among them, learning with humility of the gifts that had been acquired at such cost within the thick walls of the Total Environment tower.

As Dixit sat in meditation, a guard brought a meal in to him.

He ate thankfully and renewed his thinking.

From the little he had already experienced – the ghastly pressures on living space, the slavery, the aberrant modes of thought into which the people were being forced, the harshness of the petty rulers – he was confirmed in his view that this experiment in anything like its present form must be closed down at once. The UN needed the excuse of his adverse report before they moved; they should have it when he got out. And if he worded the report carefully, stressing that these people had many talents to offer, then he might also satisfy Crawley and his like. He had it in his power to satisfy all parties, when he got out. All he had to do was get out.

The guard came back to collect his empty bowl.

'When is Patel going to speak with me again?'

The guard said, 'When he sends for you to have you silenced for ever.'

Dixit stopped composing his report and thought about that instead.

VIII

Much time elapsed before Dixit was visited again, and then it was only the self-effacing Malti who appeared, bringing him a cup of water.

'I want to talk to you,' Dixit said urgently.

'No, no, I cannot talk! He will beat me. It is the time when we sleep, when the old die. You should sleep now, and Patel will see you in the morning.'

He tried to touch her hand, but she withdrew.

'You are a kind girl, Malti. You suffer in Patel's household.'

'He has many women, many servants. I am not alone.'

'Can you not escape back to your family?'

She looked at the floor evasively. 'It would bring trouble to my family. Slavery is the lot of many women. It is the way of the world.'

'It is not the way of the world I come from!'

Her eyes flashed. 'Your world is of no interest to us!'

Dixit thought after she had gone, She is afraid of our world. Rightly.

He slept little during the night. Even barricaded inside Patel's fortress, he could still hear the noises of Environment: not only the voices, almost never silent, but the gurgle and sob of pipes in the walls. In the morning, he was taken into a larger room where Patel was issuing commands for the day to a succession of subordinates.

Confined to a corner, Dixit followed everything with interest. His interest grew when the unfortunate guard Raital appeared. He bounded in and waited for Patel to strike him. Instead, Patel kicked him.

'You have performed as I ordered yesterday?'

Raital began at once to cry and wring his hands. 'Sir Patel, I have performed as well as and better than you demanded, incurring great suffering and having myself beaten downstairs where the people of Ninth Deck discovered me marauding. You must invade them, Sir, and teach them a lesson that in their insolence they so dare to mock your faithful guards who only do those things –'

'Silence, you dog-devourer! Do you bring back that item which I demanded of you yesterday?'

The wretched guard brought from the pocket of his tattered tunic a small object, which he held out to Patel.

'Of course I obey, Sir Patel. To keep this object safe when the people caught me, I swallow it whole, sir, into the stomach for safe keeping, so that they would not know what I am about. Then my wife gives me sharp medicine so that I vomit it safely again to deliver to you.'

'Put the filthy thing down on that shelf there! You think I wish to touch it when it has been in your worm-infested belly, slave?'

The guard did as he was bid and abased himself.

'You are sure it is the life-object of the man who stole Narayan Farhad's life-object, and nobody else's?'

'Oh, indeed, Sir Patel! It belongs to a man called Gita, the very very same who stole Narayan's life object, and tonight you will see he will die of night-visions!'

'Get out!' Patel managed to catch Raital's buttocks with a swift kick as the guard scampered from the room.

A queue of people stood waiting to speak with him, to supplicate and advise. Patel sat and interviewed them, in the main showing a better humour than he had shown his luckless guard. For Dixit, this scene had a curious interest; he had watched Patel's morning audience more than once, standing by Crawley's side in the UHDRE monitoring station; now he was a prisoner waiting uncomfortably in the corner of the room, and the whole atmosphere was changed. He felt the extraordinary intensity of these people's lives, the emotions compressed, everything vivid. Patel himself wept several times as some tale of hardship was unfolded to him. There was no privacy. Everyone stood round him, listening to everything. Short the lives might be; but those annihilating spaces that stretch through ordinary lives, the spaces through which one glimpses uncomfortable glooms and larger poverties, if not presences more sour and sinister, seemed here to have been eradicated. The Total Environment had brought its peoples total involvement. Whatever befell them, they were united, as were bees in a hive.

Finally, a break was called. The unfortunates who had not gained Patel's ear were turned away; Malti was summoned and administered the damp-towel treatment to Patel. Later, he sent her off and ate a frugal meal. Only when he had finished it and sat momentarily in meditation, did he turn his brooding attention to Dixit.

He indicated that Dixit was to fetch down the object Raital had placed on a shelf. Dixit did so and put the object before Patel. Staring at it with interest, he saw it was an elaborate little model, similar to the ones for sale on the balcony.

'Observe it well,' Patel said. 'It is the life-object of a man. You have these' – he gestured vaguely –'outside?'

'No.'

'You know what they are?'

'No.'

'In this world of ours, Mr Dixit, we have many holy men. I have a holy man here under my protection. On the deck below is one very famous holy man, Vazifdariji. These men have many powers. Tonight, I shall give my holy man this life-object, and with it he will be able to enter the being of the man to whom it belongs, for good or ill, and in this case for ill, to revenge a death with a death.'

Dixit stared at the little object, a three-dimensional maze constructed of silver and plastic strands, trying to comprehend what Patel was saying.

'This is a sort of key to its owner's mind?'

'No, no, not a key, and not to his mind. It is a – well, we do not have a scientific word for it, and our word would mean nothing to you, so I cannot say what. It is, let us say, a replica, a substitute for the man's being. Not his mind, his being. In this case, a man called Gita. You are very interested, aren't you?'

'Everyone here has one of these?'

'Down to the very poorest and even the older children. A sage works in conjunction with a smith to produce each individual life-object.'

'But they can be stolen and then an ill-intentioned holy man can use them to kill the owner. So why make them? I don't understand.'

Smiling, Patel made a small movement of impatience. 'What you discover of yourself, you record. That is how these things are made. They are not trinkets; they are a man's record of his discovery of himself.'

Dixit shook his head. 'If they are so personal, why are so many sold by street traders as trinkets?'

'Men die. Then their life-objects have no value, except as trinkets. They are also popularly believed to bestow ... well, personality-value. There also exist large numbers of forgeries, which people buy because they like to have them, simply as decorations.'

After a moment, Dixit said, 'So they are innocent things, but you take them and use them for evil ends.'

'I use them to keep a power balance. A man of mine called Narayan was silenced by Gita of Ninth Deck. Never mind why. So tonight I silence Gita to keep the balance.'

He stopped and looked closely at Dixit, so that the latter received a blast of that enigmatic personality. He opened his hand and said, still observing Dixit, 'Death sits in my palm, Mr Dixit. Tonight I shall have you silenced also, by what you may consider more ordinary methods.'

Clenching his hands tightly together, Dixit said, 'You tell me about the life-objects, and yet you claim you are going to kill me.'

Patel pointed up to one corner of his room. 'There are eyes and ears there, while your ever-hungry spying friends suck up the facts of this world. You see, I can tell them I can tell them so much and they can never comprehend our life. All the important things can never be said, so they can never learn. But they can see you die tonight, and that they will comprehend. Perhaps then they will cease to send spies in here.'

He clapped his hands once for the guards. They came forward and led Dixit away. As he went back to his cell, he heard Patel shouting for Malti.

IX

The hours passed in steady gloom. The UN, the UHDRE, would not rescue him; the Environment charter permitted intervention by only one outsider at a time. Dixit could hear, feel, the vast throbbing life of the place going on about him and was shaken by it.

He tried to think about the life-objects. Presumably Crawley had overheard the last conversation, and would know that the holy men, as Patel called them, had the power to kill at a distance. There was the ESP evidence Crawley sought: telecide, or whatever you called it. And the knowledge helped nobody, as Patel himself observed. It had long been known that African witch doctors possessed similar talents, to lay a spell on a man and kill him at a distance; but how they did it had never been established; nor, indeed, had the fact ever been properly assimilated by the West, eager though the West was for new methods of killing. There were things one civilisation could not learn from another; the whole business of life-objects, Dixit perceived, was going to be such a matter: endlessly fascinating, entirely insoluble....

He thought, returning to his cell, and told himself: Patel still puzzles me. But it is no use hanging about here being puzzled. Here I sit, waiting for a knife in the guts. It must be night now. I've got to get out of here.

There was no way out of the room. He paced restlessly up and down. They brought him no meal, which was ominous.

A long while later, the door was unlocked and opened.

It was Malti. She lifted one finger as a caution to silence, and closed the door behind her.

'It's time for me … ?' Dixit asked.

She came quickly over to him, not touching him, staring at him.

Though she was an ugly despondent woman, beauty lay in her time-haunted eyes.

'I can help you escape, Dixit. Patel sleeps now, and I have an understanding with the guards here. Understandings have been reached to smuggle you down to my own deck, where perhaps you can get back to the outside where you belong. This place is full of arrangements. But you must be quick. Are you ready?'

'He'll kill you when he finds out!'

She shrugged. 'He may not. I think perhaps he likes me. Prahlad Patel is not inhuman, whatever you think of him.'

'No? But he plans to murder someone else tonight. He has acquired some poor fellow's life-object and plans to have his holy man kill him with night-visions, whatever they are.'

She said, 'People have to die. You are going to be lucky. You will not die, not this night.'

'If you take that fatalistic view, why help me?'

He saw a flash of defiance in her eyes. 'Because you must take a message outside for me.'

'Outside? To whom?'

To everyone there, everyone who greedily spies on us here and would spoil this world. Tell them to go away and leave us and let us make our own world. Forget us! That is my message! Take it! Deliver it with all the strength you have! This is our world – not yours!'

Her vehemence, her ignorance, silenced him. She led him from the room. There were guards on the outer door. They stood rigid with their eyes closed, seeing no evil, and she slid between them, leading Dixit, and opening the door. They hurried outside, onto the balcony, which was still as crowded as ever, people sprawling everywhere in the disconsolate gestures of public sleep. With the noise and chaos and animation of daytime fled, Total Environment stood fully revealed for the echoing prison it was.

As Malti turned to go, Dixit grasped her wrist.

'I must return,' she said. 'Get quickly to the steps down to Ninth Deck, the near steps. That's three flights to go down, the inter-deck flight guarded. They will let you through; they expect you.'

'Malti, I must try to help this other man who is to die. Do you happen to know someone called Gita?'

She gasped and clung to him. 'Gita?'

'Gita of the Ninth Deck. Patel has Gita's life-object, and he is to die tonight.'

'Gita is my step-father, my mother's third husband. A good man! Oh, he must not die, for my mother's sake!

'He's to die tonight. Malti, I can help you and Gita. I appreciate how you feel about outside, but you are mistaken. You would be free in a way you cannot understand! Take me to Gita, and we'll all three get out together.'

Conflicting emotions chased all over her face. 'You are sure Gita is to die?'

'Come and check with him to see if his life-object has gone!'

Without waiting for her to make a decision – in fact she looked as if she were just about to bolt back into Patel's quarters – Dixit took hold of her and forced her along the balcony, picking his way through the piles of sleepers.

Ramps ran down from balcony to balcony in long zigzags. For all its multitudes of people – even the ramps had been taken up as dosses by whole swarms of urchins – Total Environment seemed much larger than it had when one looked in from the monitoring room. He kept peering back to see if they were being followed; it seemed to him unlikely that he would be able to get away.

But they had now reached the stairs leading down to Deck Nine. Oh, well, he thought, corruption he could believe in; it was the universal oriental system whereby the small man contrived to live under oppression. As soon as the guards saw him and Malti, they all stood and closed their eyes. Among them was the wretched Raital, who hurriedly clapped palms over eyes as they approached.

'I must go back to Patel,' Malti gasped.

'Why? You know he will kill you,' Dixit said. He kept tight hold of her thin wrist. 'All these witnesses to the way you led me to safety – you can't believe he will not discover what you are doing. Let's get to Gita quickly.'

He hustled her down the stairs. There were Deck Nine guards at the bottom. They smiled and saluted Malti and let her by. As if resigned now to doing what Dixit wished, she led him forward, and they picked their way down a ramp to a lower floor. The squalor and confusion were greater here than they had been above, the slumbers more broken. This was a deck without a strong leader, and it showed.

He must have seen just such a picture as this over the bugging, in the air-conditioned comfort of the UHDRE offices, and remained comparatively unmoved. You had to be among it to feel it. Then you caught also the aroma of Environment. It was pungent in the extreme.

As they moved slowly down among the huddled figures abased by fatigue, he saw that a corpse burned slowly on a wood pile. It was the corpse of a child. Smoke rose from it in a leisurely coil until it was sucked into a wall vent. A mother squatted by the body, her face shielded by one skeletal hand. 'It is the time when the old die,' Malti had said of the previous night; and the young had to answer that same call.

This was the Indian way of facing the inhumanity of Environment: with their age-old acceptance of suffering. Had one of the white races been shut in here to breed to intolerable numbers, they would have met the situation with a general massacre. Dixit, a half-caste, would not permit himself to judge which response he most respected.

Malti kept her gaze fixed on the worn concrete underfoot as they moved down the ramp past the corpse. At the bottom, she led him forward again without a word.

They pushed through the sleazy ways, arriving at last at a battered doorway. With a glance at Dixit, Malti slipped in and rejoined her family. Her mother, not sleeping, crouched over a wash bowl, gave a cry and fell into Malti's arms. Brothers and sisters and half-brothers and half-sisters and cousins and nephews woke up, squealing. Dixit was utterly brushed aside. He stood nervously, waiting, hoping, in the corridor.

It was many minutes before Malti came out and led him to the crowded little cabin. She introduced him to Shamim, her mother, who curtsied and rapidly disappeared, and to her step-father, Gita.

The little wiry man shooed everyone out of one corner of the room and moved Dixit into it. A cup of wine was produced and offered politely to the visitor. As he sipped it, he said, 'If your stepdaughter has explained the situation, Gita, I'd like to get you and Malti out of here, because otherwise your lives are worth very little. I can guarantee you will be extremely kindly treated outside.'

With dignity, Gita said, 'Sir, all this very unpleasant business has been explained to me by my step-daughter. You are most good to take this trouble, but we cannot help you.'

'You, or rather Malti, have helped me. Now it is my turn to help you. I want to take you out of here to a safe place. You realise you are both under the threat of death? You hardly need telling that Prahlad Patel is a ruthless man.'

'He is very very ruthless, sir,' Gita said unhappily. 'But we cannot leave here. I cannot leave here – look at all these little people who are dependent on me! Who would look after them if I left?'

'But if your hours are numbered?'

'If I have only one minute to go before I die, still I cannot desert those who depend on me.'

Dixit turned to Malti. 'You, Malti – you have less responsibility. Patel will have his revenge on you. Come with me and be safe!'

She shook her head. 'If I came, I would sicken with worry for what was happening here and so I would die that way.'

He looked about him hopelessly. The blind interdependence bred by this crowded environment had beaten him – almost. He still had one card to play.

'When I go out of here, as go I must, I have to report to my superiors. They are the people who – the people who really order everything that happens here. They supply your light, your food, your air. They are like gods to you, with the power of death over every one on every deck – which perhaps is why you can hardly believe in them. They already feel that Total Environment is wrong, a crime against your humanity. I have to take my verdict to them. My verdict, I can tell you now, is that the lives of all you people are as precious as lives outside these walls. The experiment must be stopped; you all must go free.

'You may not understand entirely what I mean, but perhaps the wall screens have helped you grasp something. You will all be looked after and rehabilitated. Everyone will be released from the decks very soon. So, you can both come with me and save your lives; and then, in perhaps only a week, you will be reunited with your family. Patel will have no power then. Now, think over your decision again, for the good of your dependants, and come with me to life and freedom.'

Malti and Gita looked anxiously at each other and went into a huddle. Shamim joined in, and Jamsu, and lame Shirin, and more and more of the tribe, and a great jangle of excited talk swelled up. Dixit fretted nervously.

Finally, silence fell. Gita said, 'Sir, your intentions are plainly kind. But you have forgotten that Malti charged you to take a message to outside. Her message was to tell the people there to go away and let us make our own world. Perhaps you do not understand such a message and so cannot deliver it. Then I will give you my message, and you can take it to your superiors.'

Dixit bowed his head.

'Tell them, your superiors and everyone outside who insists on watching us and meddling in our affairs, tell them that we are shaping our own lives. We know what is to come, and the many problems of having such a plenty of young people. But we have faith in our next generation. We believe they will have many new talents we do not possess, as we have talents our fathers did not possess.

'We know you will continue to send in food and air, because that is something you cannot escape from. We also know that in your hidden minds you wish to see us all fail and die. You wish to see us break, to see what will happen when we do. You do not have love for us. You have fear and puzzlement and hate. We shall not break. We are building a new sort of world, we are getting clever. We would die if you took us out of here. Go and tell that to your superiors and to everyone who spies on us. Please leave us to our own lives, over which we have our own commands.'

There seemed nothing Dixit could say in answer. He looked at Malti, but could see she was unyielding, frail and pale and unyielding. This was what UHDRE had bred: complete lack of understanding. He turned and went.

He had his key. He knew the secret place on each deck where he could slip away into one of the escape elevators. As he pushed through the grimy crowds, he could hardly see his way for tears.

*

X

It was all very informal. Dixit made his report to a board of six members of the UHDRE administration, including the Special Project Organiser, Peter Crawley. Two observers were allowed to sit in, a grand lady who represented the Indian Government, and Dixit's old friend, Senator Jacob Byrnes, representing the United Nations.

Dixit delivered his report on what he had found and added a recommendation that a rehabilitation village be set up immediately and the Environment wound down.

Crawley rose to his feet and stood rigid as he said, 'By your own words, you admit that these people of Environment cling desperately to what little they have. However terrible, however miserable that little may seem to you. They are acclimatised to what they have. They have turned their backs to the outside world and don't *want* to come out.'

Dixit said, 'We shall rehabilitate them, re-educate them find them local homes where the intricate family patterns to which they are used can still be maintained, where they can be helped back to normality.'

'But by what you say they would receive a paralysing shock if confronted with the outside world and its gigantic scale.'

'Not if Patel still led them.'

A mutter ran along the board; its members clearly thought this an absurd statement. Crawley gestured despairingly, as if his case were made, and sat down saying, 'He's the sort of tyrant who causes the misery in Environment.'

'The one thing they need when they emerge to freedom is a strong leader they know. Gentlemen, Patel is our good hope. His great asset is that he is oriented towards outside already.'

'Just what does that mean?' one of the board asked.

'It means this. Patel is a clever man. My belief is that he arranged that Malti should help me escape from his cell. He never had any intention of killing me; that was a bluff to get me on my way. Little, oppressed Malti was just not the woman to take any initiative. What Patel probably did not bargain for was that I should mention Gita by name to her, or that Gita should be closely related to her. But because of their fatalism, his plan was in no way upset.'

'Why should Patel want you to escape?'

'Implicit in much that he did and said, though he tried to hide it, was a burning curiosity about outside. He exhibited facets of his culture to me to ascertain my reactions – testing for approval or disapproval, I'd guess, like a child. Nor does he attempt to attack other decks – the time-honoured sport of Environment tyrants; his attention is directed inwardly on us.

'Patel is intelligent enough to know that we have real power. He has never lost the true picture of reality, unlike his minions. So *he wants to get out.*

'He calculated that if I got back to you, seemingly having escaped death, I would report strongly enough to persuade you to start demolishing Total Environment immediately.'

'Which you are doing,' Crawley said.

'Which I am doing. Not for Patel's reasons, but for human reasons. And for utilitarian reasons also – which will perhaps appeal more to Mr Crawley. Gentlemen, you were right. There are mental disciplines in Environment the world could use, of which perhaps the least attractive is telecide. UHDRE has cost the public millions on millions of dollars. We have to recoup by these new advances. We can only use these new advances by studying them in an atmosphere not laden with hatred and envy of us – in other words, by opening that black tower.'

The meeting broke up. Of course, he could not expect anything more decisive than that for a day or two.

Senator Byrnes came over.

'Not only did you make out a good case, Thomas; history is with you. The world's emerging from a bad period and that dark tower, as you call it, is a symbol of the bad times, and so it has to go.'

Inwardly, Dixit had his qualifications to that remark. But they walked together to the window of the boardroom and looked across at the great rough bulk of the Environment building.

'It's more than a symbol. It's as full of suffering and hope as our own world. But it's a manmade monster – it must go.'

Byrnes nodded. 'Don't worry. It'll go. I feel sure that the historical process, that blind evolutionary thing, has already decided that UHDRE's day is done. Stick around. In a few weeks, you'll be able to help Malti's family rehabilitate. And now I'm off to put in my two cents' worth with the chairman of that board.'

He clapped Dixit on the back and walked off. Inside he knew lights would be burning and those thronging feet padding across the only world they knew. Inside there, babies would be born this night and men die of old age and night-visions....

Outside, monsoon rain began to fall on the wide Indian land.

The Village Swindler

The great diesel train hauled out of Naipur Road, heading grandly south. Jane Pentecouth caught a last glimpse of it over bobbing heads as she followed the stretcher into the station waiting-room.

She pushed her way through the excited crowd, managing to get to her father's side and rejoin the formidable Dr Chandhari, who had taken charge of the operation.

'My car will come in only a few moments, Miss Pentecouth,' he said, waving away the people who were leaning over the stretcher and curiously touching the sick man. 'It will whisk us to my home immediately, not a mile distant. It was extremely fortunate that I happened to be travelling on the very same express with you.'

'But my father would have been—'

'Do not thank me, dear lady, do not thank me! The pleasure is mine, and your father is saved. I shall do my level best for him.'

She had not been about to thank this beaming and terrifying Hindu. She trembled on the verge of hysterical protest. It was many years since she had felt so helpless. Her father's frightening attack on the train had been bad enough. All those terrible people had flocked round, all offering advice. Then Dr Chandhari had appeared, taken command, and made the conductor stop the train at Naipur Road, this small station apparently situated in the middle of nowhere, claiming that his home was near by. Irresistibly, Jane had been carried along on the steamy side of solicitude and eloquence.

But she did believe that her father's life had been saved by Dr Chandhari. Robert Pentecouth was breathing almost normally. She hardly

367

recognised him as she took his hand; he was in a coma. But at least he was still alive, and, in the express, as he bellowed and fought with the coronary attack, she had imagined him about to die.

The crowd surged into the waiting-room, all fighting to lend a hand with the stretcher. It was oppressively hot in the small room; the fan on the ceiling merely caused the heat to circulate. As more and more men surged into the room, Jane stood up and said loudly, 'Will you all please get out, except for Dr Chandhari and his secretary!'

The doctor was very pleased by this, seeing that it implied her acceptance of him. He set his secretary to clearing the room, or at least arguing with the crowd that still flocked in. Bending a yet more perfect smile upon her, he said, 'My young intelligent daughter Amma is fortunately at home at this present moment, dear Miss Pentecouth, so you will have some pleasant company just while your father is recovering his health with us.'

She smiled back, thinking to herself that the very next day, when her father had rested, they would return to Calcutta and proper medical care. On that she was determined.

She was impressed by the Chandhari household despite herself.

It was an ugly modernistic building, all cracked concrete outside – bought off a film star who had committed suicide, Amma cheerfully told her. All rooms, including the garage under the house, were air-conditioned. There was a heart-shaped swimming pool at the back, although it was empty of water and the sides were cracked. High white walls guarded the property. From her bedroom, Jane looked over the top of the wall at a dusty road sheltered by palm trees and the picturesque squalor of a dozen hovels, where the small children stood naked in doorways and dogs rooted and snarled in piles of rubbish.

'There is such contrast between rich and poor here,' Jane said, surveying the scene. It was the morning after her arrival here.

'What a very European remark!' said Amma. 'The poor people expect that the doctor should live to a proper standard, or he has no reputation.'

Amma was only twenty, perhaps half Jane's age. An attractive girl, with delicate gestures that made Jane feel clumsy. As she herself explained, she was modern and enlightened, and did not intend to marry until she was older.

'What do you do all day, Amma?' Jane asked.

'I am in the government, of course, but now I am taking a holiday. It is rather boring here, but still I don't mind it for a change. Next week, I will go away from here. What do you do all day, Jane?'

'My father is one of the directors of the new EGNP Trust. I just look after him. He is making a brief tour of India, Pakistan, and Ceylon, to see how the Trust will be administered. I'm afraid the heat and travel have over-taxed him. His breathing has been bad for several days.'

'He is old. They should have sent a younger man.' Seeing the look on Jane's face, she said, 'Please do not take offence! I am meaning only that it is unfair to send a man of his age to our hot climate. What is this trust you are speaking of?'

'The European Gross National Product Trust. Eleven leading European nations contribute 1 per cent of their gross national product to assist development in this part of the world.'

'I see. More help for the poor over-populated Indians, is that so?' The two women looked at each other. Finally, Amma said, 'I will take you out with me this afternoon, and you shall see the sort of people to whom this money of yours will be going, if they live sufficiently long enough.'

'I shall be taking my father back to Calcutta this afternoon.'

'You know my father will not allow that, and he is the doctor. Your father will die if you are foolish enough to move him. You must remain and enjoy our simple hospitality and try not to be too bored.'

'Thank you, I am not bored!' Her life was such that she had had ample training in not being bored. More even than not being in command of the situation, she hated failing to understand the attitude of these people. With what grace she could muster, she told the younger woman, 'If Dr Chandhari advises that my father should not be moved, then I will be pleased to accompany you this afternoon.'

After the light midday meal, Jane was ready for the outing at two o'clock. But Amma and the car were not ready until almost five o'clock, when the sun was moving towards the west.

Robert Pentecouth lay breathing heavily, large in a small white bed. He was recognisable again, looked younger. Jane did not love him; but she would do anything to preserve his life. That was her considered verdict as she looked down on him. He had gulped down a lot of life in his time.

Something in the room smelt unpleasant. Perhaps it was her father. By his bedside squatted an old woman, in a dull red-and-maroon sari, wrinkled of face, with a jewel like a dried scab screwed in one nostril. She spoke no English. Jane was uneasy with her, not certain whether she was not Chandhari's wife. You heard funny things about Indian wives.

The ceiling was a maze of cracks. It would be the first thing he would see when he opened his eyes. She touched his head and left the room.

Amma drove. A big new car that took the rutted tracks uneasily. There was little to Naipur Road. The ornate and crumbling houses of the main street turned slightly uphill, became mere shacks. The sunlight buzzed. Over the brow of the slope, the village lost heart entirely and died by a huge banyan tree, beneath which an old man sat on a bicycle.

Beyond, cauterised land, a coastal plain lying rumpled, scarred by man's long and weary occupation.

'Only ten miles,' Amma said. 'It gets more pretty later. It's not so far from the ocean, you know. We are going to see an old nurse of mine who is sick.'

'Is there plague in these parts?'

'Orissa has escaped so far. A few cases down in Cuttack. And of course in Calcutta. Calcutta is the home town of the plague. But we are quite safe – my nurse is dying only of a malnutritional disease.'

Jane said nothing.

They had to drive slowly as the track deteriorated. Everything had slowed. People by the tattered roadside stood silently, silently were encompassed by the car's cloud of dust. A battered truck slowly approached, slowly passed. Under the annealing sun, even time had a wound.

Among low hills, little more than undulations of the ground, they crossed a bridge over a dying river and Amma stopped the car in the shade of some deodars. As the women climbed out, a beggar sitting at the base of a tree called out to them for baksheesh, but Amma ignored him. Gesturing courteously to Jane, she said, 'Let us walk under the trees to where the old nurse's family lives. It perhaps would be better if you did not enter the house with me, but I shall not be long. You can look round the village. There is a pleasant temple to see.'

Only a few yards farther on, nodding and smiling, she turned aside and, ducking her head, entered a small house with mud walls.

It was a long blank village, ruled by the sun. Jane felt her isolation as soon as Amma disappeared.

A group of small children with big eyes was following Jane. They whispered to each other but did not approach too closely. A peasant farmer, passing with a thin-ribbed cow, called out to the children. Jane walked slowly, fanning the flies from her face.

She knew this was one of the more favoured regions of India. For all that, the poverty – the stone age poverty – afflicted her. She was glad her father was not with her, in case he felt as she did, that this land could soak up EGNP money as easily, as tracelessly, as it did the monsoon.

Walking under the trees, she saw a band of monkeys sitting or pacing by some more distant huts, and moved nearer to look at them. The huts stood alone, surrounded by attempts at agriculture. A dog nosed by the rubbish heaps, keeping an eye on the monkeys.

Stones were set beneath the big tree where the monkeys paced. Some were painted or stained, and branches of the tree had been painted white. Offerings of flowers lay in a tiny shrine attached to the main trunk; a garland withered on a low branch above a monkey's head. The monkey, Jane saw, suckled a baby at its narrow dugs.

A man stepped from behind the tree and approached Jane.

He made a sign of greeting and said, 'Lady, you want buy somet'ing?'

She looked at him. Something unpleasant was happening to one of his eyes, and flies surrounded it. But he was a well-built man, thin, of course, but not as old as she had at first thought. His head was shaven; he wore only a white dhoti. He appeared to have nothing to sell.

'No, thank you,' she said.

He came closer.

'Lady, you are English lady? You buy small souvenir, some one very nice thing of value for to take with you back to England! Look, I show – you are please to wait here one minute.'

He turned and ducked into the most dilapidated of the huts. She looked about, wondering whether to stay. In a moment, the man emerged again into the sun, carrying a vase. The children gathered and stared silently; only the monkeys were restless.

'This is very lovely Indian vase, lady, bought in Jamshedpur, very fine hand manufacture. Perceive beautiful artistry work, lady!'

She hesitated before taking the poor brass vase in her hands. He turned and called sharply into the hut, and then redoubled his sales talk. He had been a worker in a shoe factory in Jamshedpur, he told her, but the factory had burned down and he could find no other work. He had brought his wife and children here, to live with his brother.

'I'm afraid I'm not interested in buying the vase,' she said.

'Lady, please, you give only ten rupees! Ten rupees only!' He broke off.

His wife had emerged from the hut, to stand without motion by his side. In her arms, she carried a child.

The child looked solemnly at Jane from its giant dark eyes. It was naked except for a piece of rag, over which a great belly sagged. Its body, and especially the face and skull, were covered in pustules, from some of which a liquid seeped. Its head had been smeared with ash. The baby did not move or cry; what its age was, Jane could not estimate.

Its father had fallen silent for a moment. Now he said, 'My child is having to die, lady, look see! You give me ten rupees.'

Now she shrank from the proffered vase. Inside the hut, there were other children stirring in the shadows. The sick child looked outwards with an expression of great wisdom and beauty – or so Jane interpreted it – as if it understood and forgave all things. Its very silence frightened her, and the stillness of the mother. She backed away, feeling chilled.

'No, no, I don't want the vase! I must go–'

Muttering her excuses, she turned away and hurried, almost ran, back towards the car. She could hear the man calling to her.

She climbed into the car. The man came and stood outside, not touching the car, apologetic, explaining, offering the vase for only eight rupees, talking, talking. Seven-and-a-half rupees. Jane hid her face.

When Amma emerged, the man backed away, said something meekly; Amma replied sharply. He turned, clutching the vase, and the children watched. She climbed into the driving seat and started the car.

'He tried to sell me something. A vase. It was the only thing he had to sell, I suppose,' Jane said. 'He wasn't rude.' She felt the silent gears of their relationship change; she could no longer pretend to superiority, since she had been virtually rescued. After a moment, she asked, 'What was the matter with his child? Did he tell you?'

'He is a man of the scheduled classes. His child is dying of the smallpox. There is always smallpox in the villages.'

'I imagined it was the plague ...'

'I told you, we do not have the plague in Orissa yet.'

The drive home was a silent one, voiceless in the corroded land. The people moving slowly home had long shadows now. When they arrived at the gates of the Chandhari house, a porter was ready to open the gate, and a distracted servant stood there; she ran fluttering beside the car, calling to Amma.

Amma turned and said, 'Jane, I am sorry to tell you that your father has had another heart attack just now.'

The attack was already over. Robert Pentecouth lay unconscious on the bed, breathing raspingly. Doctor Chandhari stood looking down at him and sipping an iced lime-juice. He nodded tenderly at Jane as she moved to the bedside.

'I have of course administered an anti-coagulant, but your father is very ill, Miss Pentecouth,' he said. 'There is severe cardiac infarction, together with weakness in the mitral valve, which is situated at the entrance of the left ventricle. This has caused congestion of the lungs, which means the trouble of breathlessness, very much accentuated by the hot atmosphere of the Indian sub-continent. I have done my level best for him.'

'I must get him home, doctor.'

Chandhari shook his head. 'The air journey will be severely taxing on him. I tell you frankly I do not imagine for a single moment that he will survive it.'

'What should I do, doctor? I'm so frightened!'

'Your father's heart is badly scarred and damaged, dear lady. He needs a new heart, or he will give up the ghost.'

Jane sat down on the chair by the bedside and said, 'We are in your hands.'

He was delighted to hear it. 'There are no safer hands, dear Miss Pentecouth.' He gazed at them with some awe as he said, 'Let me outline a little plan of campaign for you. Tomorrow we put your father on the express to Calcutta. I can phone to Naipur Road station to have it stop. Do not be alarmed! I will accompany you on the express. At the Radakhrishna General Hospital in Howrah in Calcutta is that excellent man, K. V. Menon, who comes from Trivandrum, as does my own family – a very civilised and clever man of the Nair caste. K. V. Menon. His name is widely renowned and he will perform the operation.'

'Operation, doctor?'

'Certainly, certainly! He will give a new heart. K. V. Menon has performed many many successful heart-transplants. The operation is as commonplace in Calcutta as in California. Do not worry! And I will personally stand by you all the while. Perhaps Amma shall come too because I see you are firm friends already. Good, good, don't worry!'

In his excitement, he took her by the arm and made her rise to her feet. She stood there, solid but undecided, staring at him.

'Come!' he said. 'Let us go and telephone all the arrangements! We will make some commotion around these parts, eh? Your father is okay here with the old nurse-woman to watch. In a few days, he will wake up with a new heart and be well again.'

Jane sent a cable explaining the situation to the Indian headquarters of EGNP in Delhi (the city which ancient colonialist promptings had perhaps encouraged the authorities to choose). Then she stood back while the commotion spread.

It spread first to the household. More people were living in the Chandhari house than Jane had imagined. She met the doctor's wife, an elegant sari-clad woman who spoke good English and who apparently lived in her own set of rooms, together with her servants. The latter came and went, enlivened by the excitement. Messengers were despatched to the bazaar for various little extra requirements.

The commotion rapidly spread farther afield. People came to inquire the health of the white sahib, to learn the worst for themselves. The representative of the local newspaper called. Another doctor arrived, and was taken by Dr Chandhari, a little proudly, to inspect the patient.

If anything, the commotion grew after darkness fell.

Jane went to sit by her father. He was still unconscious. Once, he spoke coherently, evidently imagining himself back in England; although she answered him, he gave no sign that he heard. Amma came in to say good night on her way to bed.

'We shall be leaving early in the morning,' Jane said. 'My father and I have brought you only trouble. Please don't come to Calcutta with us. It isn't necessary.'

'Of course not. I will come only to Naipur Road station. I'm glad if we could help at all. And with a new heart, your father will be really hale and hearty again. Menon is a great expert in heart-transplantation.'

'Yes. I have heard his name, I think. You never told me, Amma – how did you find your old nurse this afternoon?'

'You did not ask me. Unhappily, she died during last night.'

'Oh! I'm so sorry!'

'Yes, it is hard for her family. Already they are much in debt to the moneylender.'

She left the room; shortly after, Jane also retired. But she could not sleep. After an hour or two of fitful sleep, she got dressed again and went downstairs, obsesssed with a mental picture of the glass of fresh lime-juice she had seen the doctor drinking. She could hear unseen people moving about in rooms she had never entered. In the garden, too, flickering tongues of light moved. A heart-transplant was still a strange event in Naipur Road, as it had once been in Europe and America; perhaps it would have even more superstition attached to it here than it had there.

When a servant appeared, she made her request. After long delay, he brought the glass on a tray, gripping it so that it would not slip, and lured her out on to the veranda with it. She sat in a wicker chair and sipped it. A face appeared in the garden, a hand reached in supplication up to her.

'Please! Miss Lady!'

Startled, she recognised the man with the dying child to whom she had spoken the previous afternoon.

The next morning, Jane was roused by one of the doctor's servants. Dazed after too little sleep, she dressed and went down to drink tea. She could find nothing to say; her brain had not woken yet. Amma and her father talked continuously in English to each other.

The big family car was waiting outside. Pentecouth was gently loaded in, and the luggage piled round him. It was still little more than dawn; as Jane,

Amma, and Chandhari climbed in and the car rolled forward, wraithlike figures were moving already. A cheerful little fire burned here and there inside a house. A tractor rumbled towards the fields. People stood at the sides of the road, numb, to let the car pass. The air was chilly; but, in the eastern sky, the banners of the day's warmth were already violently flying.

They were almost at the railway station when Jane turned to Amma. 'That man with the child dying of smallpox walked all the way to the house to speak to me. He said he came as soon as he heard of my father's illness.'

'The servants had no business to let him through the gate. That is how diseases spread,' Amma said.

'He had something else to sell me last night. Not a vase. He wanted to sell his heart!'

Amma laughed. 'The vase would be a better bargain, Jane!'

'How can you laugh? He was so desperate to help his wife and family. He wanted fifty rupees. He would take the money back to his wife and then he would come with us to the Calcutta Hospital to have his heart cut out!'

Putting her hand politely to her mouth, Amma laughed again.

'Why is it funny?' Jane asked desperately. 'He meant what he said. Everything was so black for him that his life was worth only fifty rupees!'

'But his life is not worth so much, by far!' Amma said. 'He is just a village swindler. And the money would not cure the child, in any case. The type of smallpox going about here is generally fatal, isn't it, Pappa?'

Dr Chandhari, who sat with a hand on his patient's forehead, said, 'This man's idea is of course not scientific. He is one of the scheduled classes – an Untouchable, as we used to say. He has never eaten very much all during his life and so he will have only a little weak heart. It would never be a good heart in your father's body, to circulate all his blood properly.' With a proud gesture, he thumped Robert Pentecouth's chest. 'This is the body of the well-nourished man. In Calcutta, we shall find him a proper big heart that will do the work effectively.'

They arrived at the railway station. The sun was above the horizon and climbing rapidly. Rays of gold poured through the branches of the trees by the station on to the faces of people arriving to watch the great event, the stopping of the great Madras-Calcutta express, and the loading aboard of a white man going for a heart-transplant.

Furtively, Jane looked about the crowd, searching to see if her man happened to be there. But, of course, he would be back in his village by now, with his wife and the children.

Intercepting the look, Amma said, 'Jane, you did not give that man baksheesh, did you?'

Jane dropped her gaze, not wishing to betray herself.

'He would have robbed you,' Amma insisted. 'His heart would be valueless. These people are never free from hookworms, you know – in the heart and the stomach. You should have bought the vase if you wanted a souvenir of Naipur Road – not a heart, for goodness sake!'

The train was coming. The crowd stirred. Jane took Amma's hand. 'Say no more. I will always have memories of Naipur Road.'

She busied herself about her father's stretcher as the great sleek train growled into the station.

When I Was Very Jung

'I dreamed I was Jung last night,' said Saul Betatrom heavily over breakfast, showing his long lashes to his current mistress, as he poured cream over his jam puff.

'My, what fun!' Paidie exclaimed boredly. She wanted to go shopping in the bazaar, not sit or lie with Saul all the time; this Indian holiday was a real freak-out.

'Yeah, I was old Carl Jung, beard and all,' said Saul, whipping up the mixture on his plate, and spooning it toward his ample lips. 'Boy, there I was in some damned church or something in Switzerland, and this trapdoor opened at my feet—'

'Was I there?'

'No, you weren't there. I was alone, wearing this black robe, see, and I'd just formulated the concepts of psycho-analytic theory, and then this hole opened at my feet ...'

Her interest ceased when she learned that she was excluded from the dream. Hazy memories of other lovers and sexual gymnasts floated into her mind; she couldn't recall a one of them that had ever dreamed of her. She looked over the balcony at the bone-white beach, the line of canted palms, and the ocean. Paidie told herself how much this was all costing Saul and tried to feel enjoyment.

'... and there at the bottom of the lowest cellar were a couple of skulls, sort of mouldering and indistinct ...' Saul was saying. He was head of the New York branch of Zadar Smith World; suddenly recollecting the fact, he piled on more cream and added sugar to the puff.

The turbaned waiter appeared, silent at his elbow, and refilled his cup from a silver coffee pot.

'... Although I'd climbed down so far, somehow I couldn't bend down to reach those skulls. Now wasn't that a funny thing?'

'Yeah, crazy. Say, are we going down to the bazaar today, Saul?'

Licking his spoon, he gave her a heavy stare. 'They got riots in Kerala, you know that? The manager says it ain't safe outside the holiday strip.'

'Oh, Saul, let's go see the bazaar! We can take a car.'

'We'll see.' Women never listened to you, he thought. They were okay, but they didn't listen. You could pay men to listen to you, but you couldn't pay women to listen to you. Might be an idea worth developing there ... He switched on one of the rings on his finger and said into it, 'You can pay men to listen to what you say but you can't pay women to listen to what you say.' Must be a way of cashing in on a thought like that.

'*I* listen to what you say, Saulie,' Paidie said.

They collected their gear, put on dark glasses and refrigerator hats and drifted through the foyer of the hotel. On the way, Saul tossed down a few dollars – this hotel had no nonsense with rupees – and picked up a wing of chicken from a spit to chew.

He was lean, with a flat stomach – a fine hunk of masculine body, she had to admit. 'I don't know how you keep your figure, Saul. Why, you eat just about all the time and you hardly have any tummy at all to speak of. Me, I just diet and diet, yet look at the size of my thighs.' She knew they were worth looking at.

Chewing, he slouched out into the sun and stood gazing across the immense spread of the Arabian Ocean. He meditated on whether to bother answering, slewing his eyes round as he did so, taking in the scene.

The great hotel sprang up out of the sand like a fortress, its array of bulging balconies forming gun-turrets that ceaselessly watched the sea. Coloured umbrellas on the balconies, gay as death, waited to gun down the sun when it set.

The hotel was inviolate, an implacable holiday-annihilator. Round it clustered low shoddy buildings, the ramshackle bulk of an electric generator with auxiliary solar-power traps, the staff living-quarters, piles of old crates, a small sewage plant, old cars and old bicycles, a goat, an Indian charpoy with a man lying on it, rubbish in pompous containers and builders' materials.

'You want to get a Crosswell's Tape, honey. That's my secret.'

'What's a Crosswell's Tape, for God's sake?'

He winced. Zadar Smith World had handled Crosswell's promotion for six-seven years now, and this fluff had never heard of their Tape.

'It's a worm. A laboratory-mutated version of a beef tapeworm. Thoroughly safe. Only needs replacing once every decade. Lodges in the small intestine, causes no discomfort. Enables you to eat up to fifty per cent more *and* keep your figure.'

Behind the hotel was the twenty-foot-high wire barrier. It ran parallel to the sea for a long distance, as far as the eye could be bothered to see, in one direction; in the other, it angled off behind the hotel and ran down into the sea. Behind the wire barrier stood or sat solitary figures; or sometimes there was a little family group. Although there were possibly several hundreds of figures waiting behind the wire, they were motionless and well spaced, except round the gate, and so the effect was one of solitude, rather than overcrowding.

'Do you think one of those tapes would help my thighs?'

She got her camera ready to photograph the Indians behind the barrier. There was a cute little girl just standing there, not a stitch on, about four years old – you couldn't tell, really – with a cute little fat pot on her. Make a nice picture.

Their car slid up with a Sikh driver, luxuriant behind beard and green turban. Paidie took a photograph of him. The Sikh smiled and opened the car door for her. He was hairy, wow! Saul didn't have any hair at all, not anywhere on his body.

Saul caught and diagnosed her glance at the driver. 'These guys have lousy org-ratings, honey, you know that? This guy has probably never done better than seven in his life.'

In perfect English, the Sikh said, 'Excuse me, sir, but there are famine riots in the bazaar every day this week. It may be dangerous to go there.'

'The hotel must protect us. Are we supposed to stay behind that lousy chicken wire all week?'

'You are in front of it, sir. It is there for your protection.'

'Well, you protect us in the bazaar. I take it you have a revolver, man?'

'Yes sir. I have one here.'

'You shoot well?'

'I am a very good shot, sir, or I do not get this job.'

'Let's get going, then. Bazaar, and step on it!'

As the big black car slid through the gates, Saul tossed his gnawed chicken bone out of the window. The ragged crowd scrabbling in the dust for it reminded him of his dream.

'Wonder whose skulls they were? Guess it must have meant I was exploring the unconscious of mankind. You know, honey, I *am* a kind of genius. I invented the orgasm-rating system.'

'What a rotten road they have here! Say, Saul, I'd hate to *live* in India, wouldn't you? They're so dirty and poor.'

The poor and dirty were pressing close to the car, shouting or waving hands. The Sikh put his sandalled foot down and they bucked along the road.

'They're very under-developed, that's why. Yeah, the org-rating system was my big contribution to advertising. Made my name, sold a thousand products. Then the psychoanalytical guys came along and discovered my concept had real bedrock psychological truth behind it! How you like that?'

'Saul, darling, do you really think it is safe here? Suppose your dream was a warning about venturing among primitive people or something?'

The car drew up under an avenue of tattered deodar trees, where dogs scuttled and people squatted. There were a few stalls here and shrill music playing. Saul continued his lecture.

'... Since then research has proved that there are different levels of sexual enjoyment, just like different levels of sleep. Fert-Asia estimates that eighty-five per cent of the population in this area, male and female, never do any better than a grade seven orgasm. How'd you like that? And in India alone ...'

Boredom drove her out of the car. She stood under the trees, a chubby blonde in high-heeled sandals, wearing almost nothing. The scarecrows round about her had eyes of coal. They all ran to sell her anything they Had, melons, brass statues, photos of little girls embracing goats, jewels, clay figurines, dried fish. Paidie fell into a panic.

'Saul, those dream skulls! Suppose they were ours, yours and mine!'

The crowd pressed closer. She hit out with her handbag. One of the beggars touched her. Then they fell on her. Paidie was screaming.

Saul was shaking the Sikh's shoulders. 'Shoot, shoot, you lunatic! Or give me the gun!' He was vividly aware of the noise and the heat and the stink.

The Sikh started up the car, backed it swiftly away, turned, raced back for the hotel. 'Better not to shoot, sir, or we all get very much trouble.'

Saul sank back into his seat, chewing his lips. 'Maybe you're right. The hotel can send out a rescue party. She wasn't in my dream. There was just me, dressed up as Jung ... I hate dreaming about death or all that.'

Inside the hotel, it was wonderfully cool and quiet. Saul ordered a martini to soothe his nerves.

The Worm that Flies

The traveller was too absorbed in his reveries to notice when the snow began to fall. He walked slowly, his stiff and elaborate garments, fold over fold, ornament over ornament, standing out from his body like a wizard's tent.

The road along which he travelled had been falling into a great valley, and was increasingly hemmed in by walls of mountain. On several occasions, it had seemed that a way out of these huge accumulations of earth matter could not be found, that the geological puzzle was insoluble, the chthonian arrangement of discord irresolvable: and then vale and drumlin created between them a new direction, a surprise, an escape, and the way took fresh heart and plunged recklessly still deeper into the encompassing upheaval.

The traveller, whose name to his wife was Tapmar and to the rest of the world Argustal, followed this natural harmony in complete paraesthesia, so close was he in spirit to the atmosphere prevailing here. So strong was this bond, that the freak snowfall merely heightened his rapport.

Though the hour was only midday, the sky became the intense blue-grey of dusk. The Forces were nesting in the sun again, obscuring its light. Consequently, Argustal was scarcely able to detect when the layered and fractured bulwark of rock on his left side, the top of which stood unseen perhaps a mile above his head, became patched by artificial means, and he entered the domain of the human company of Or.

As the way made another turn, he saw a wayfarer before him, heading in his direction. It was a great pine, immobile until warmth entered the world again and sap stirred enough in its wooden sinews for it to progress slowly forward once more. He brushed by its green skirts, apologetic but not speaking.

This encounter was sufficient to raise his consciousness above its trance level. His extended mind, which had reached out to embrace the splendid terrestrial discord hereabouts, now shrank to concentrate again on the particularities of his situation, and he saw that he had arrived at Or.

The way bisected itself, unable to choose between two equally unprom- ising ravines, and Argustal saw a group of humans standing statuesque in the left-hand fork. He went towards them, and stood there silent until they should recognise his presence. Behind him, the wet snow crept into his footprints.

These humans were well advanced into the New Form, even as Argustal had been warned they would be. There were five of them standing here, their great brachial extensions bearing some tender brownish foliage, and one of them attenuated to a height of almost twenty feet. The snow lodged in their branches and in their hair.

Argustal waited for a long span of time, until he judged the afternoon to be well advanced, before growing impatient. Putting his hands to his mouth, he shouted fiercely at them, 'Ho then, Tree-men of Or, wake you from your arboreal sleep and converse with me. My name is Argustal to the world, and I travel to my home in far Talembil, where the seas run pink with the spring plankton. I need from you a component for my parapatterner, so rustle yourselves and speak, I beg!'

Now the snow had gone, and a scorching rain driven away its traces. The sun shone again, but its disfigured eye never looked down into the bottom of this ravine. One of the humans shook a branch, scattering water drops all round, and made preparation for speech.

This was a small human, no more than ten feet high, and the old primate form which it had begun to abandon perhaps a couple of million years ago was still in evidence. Among the gnarls and whorls of its naked flesh, its mouth was discernible; this it opened and said, 'We speak to you, Argustal- to-the-world. You are the first ape-human to fare this way in a great time. Thus you are welcome, although you interrupt our search for new ideas.'

'Have you found any new ideas?' Argustal asked, with his customary boldness.

'Indeed. But it is better for our senior to tell you of it, if he so judges good.'

It was by no means dear to Argustal whether he wished to hear what the new idea was, for the Tree-men were known for their deviations into incomprehensibility. But there was a minor furore among the five, as if private winds stirred in their branches, and he settled himself on a boulder, preparing to wait. His own quest was so important that all impediments to its fulfilment seemed negligible.

Hunger overtook him before the senior spoke. He hunted about and caught slow-galloping grubs under logs, and snatched a brace of tiny fish from the stream, and a handful of nuts from a bush that grew by the stream.

Night fell before the senior spoke. Tall and knotty, his vocal cords were clamped within his gnarled body, and he spoke by curving his branches until his finest twigs, set against his mouth, could be blown through, to give a slender and whispering version of language. The gesture made him seem curiously like a maiden who spoke with her finger cautiously to her lips.

'Indeed we have a new idea, O Argustal-to-the-world, though it may be beyond your grasping or our expressing. We have perceived that there is a dimension called time, and from this we have drawn a deduction.

'We will explain dimensional time simply to you like this. We know that all things have lived so long on Earth that their origins are forgotten. What we can remember carries from that lost-in-the-mist thing up to this present moment; it is the time we inhabit, and we are used to think of it as all the time there is. But we men of Or have reasoned that this is not so.'

'There must be other past times in the lost distances of time,' said Argustal, 'but they are nothing to us because we cannot touch them as we can our own pasts.'

As if this remark had never been, the silvery whisper continued, 'As one mountain looks small when viewed from another, so the things in our past that we remember look small from the present. But suppose we moved back to that past to look at this present! We could not see it – yet we know it exists. And from this we reason that there is still more time in the future, although we cannot see it.'

For a long while, the night was allowed to exist in silence, and then Argustal said, 'Well, I don't see that as being very wonderful reasoning. We know that, if the Forces permit, the sun will shine again tomorrow, don't we?'

The small tree-man who had first spoken, said, 'But "tomorrow" is expressional time. *We* have discovered that tomorrow exists in dimensional time also. It is real already, as real as yesterday.'

'Holy spirits!' thought Argustal to himself, 'why did I get involved in philosophy?' Aloud he said, 'Tell me of the deduction you have drawn from this.'

Again the silence, until the senior drew together his branches and whispered from a bower of twiggy fingers, 'We have proved that tomorrow is no surprise. It is as unaltered as today or yesterday, merely another yard of the path of time. But we comprehend that things change, don't we? You comprehend that, don't you?'

'Of course. You yourselves are changing, are you not?'

'It is as you say, although we no longer recall what we were before, for that thing is become too small back in time. So: if time is all of the same quality, then it has no change, and thus cannot force change. So: there is another unknown element in the world that forces change!'

Thus in their fragmentary whispers they reintroduced sin into the world.

Because of the darkness, a need for sleep was induced in Argustal. With the senior tree-man's permission, he climbed up into his branches and remained fast asleep until dawn returned to the fragment of sky above the mountains and filtered down to their retreat. Argustal swung to the ground, removed his outer garments, and performed his customary exercises. Then he spoke to the five beings again, telling them of his parapatterner, and asking for certain stones.

Although it was doubtful whether they understood what he was doing, they gave him permission, and he moved round about the area, searching for a necessary stone, his senses blowing into nooks and crannies for it like a breeze.

The ravine was blocked at its far end by a rock fall, but the stream managed to pour through the interstices of the detritus into a yet lower defile. Climbing painfully, Argustal scrambled over the mass of broken rock to find himself in a cold and moist passage, a mere cavity between two great thighs of mountain. Here the light was dim, and the sky could hardly be seen, so far did the rocks overhang on the many shelves of strata overhead. But Argustal scarcely looked up. He followed the stream where it flowed into the rock itself, to vanish forever from human view.

He had been so long at his business, trained himself over so many millennia, that the stones almost spoke to him, and he became more certain than ever that he would find a stone to fit in with his grand design.

It was there. It lay just above the water, the upper part of it polished. When he had prised it out from the surrounding pebbles and gravel, he lifted it and could see that underneath it was slightly jagged, as if a smooth gum grew black teeth. He was surprised, but as he squatted to examine it, he began to see what was necessary to the design of his parapatterner was precisely some such roughness. At once, the next step of the design revealed itself, and he saw for the first time the whole thing as it would be in its entirety. The vision disturbed and excited him.

He sat where he was, his blunt fingers round the rough-smooth stone, and for some reason he began to think about his wife Pamitar. Warm feelings of love ran through him, so that he smiled to himself and twitched his brows.

By the time he stood up and climbed out of the defile, he knew much about the new stone. His nose-for-stones sniffed it back to times when it was a much larger affair, when it occupied a grand position on a mountain, when it was engulfed in the bowels of the mountain, when it had been cast up and shattered down, when it had been a component of a bed of rock, when that rock had been ooze, when it had been a gentle rain of volcanic sediment, showering through an unbreathable atmosphere and filtering down through warm seas in an early and unknown place.

With tender respect, he tucked the stone away in a large pocket and scrambled back along the way he had come. He made no farewell to the five of Or. They stood mute together, branch-limbs interlocked, dreaming of the dark sin of change.

Now he made haste for home, travelling first through the borderlands of Old Crotheria and then through the region of Tamia, where there was only mud. Legends had it that Tamia had once known fertility, and that speckled fish had swam in streams between forests; but now mud conquered everything, and the few villages were of baked mud, while the roads were dried mud, the sky was the colour of mud, and the few mud-coloured humans who chose for their own mud-stained reasons to live here had scarcely any antlers growing from their shoulders and seemed about to deliquesce into mud. There wasn't a decent stone anywhere about the place. Argustal met a tree called David-by-the-moat-that-dries which was moving into his own home region. Depressed by the everlasting brownness of Tamia, he begged a ride from it, and climbed into its branches. It was old and gnarled, its branches and roots equally hunched, and it spoke in grating syllables of its few ambitions.

As he listened, taking pains to recall each syllable while he waited long for the next, Argustal saw that David spoke by much the same means as the people of Or had done, stuffing whistling twigs to an orifice in its trunk; but whereas it seemed that the tree-men were losing the use of their vocal chords, it seemed that the man-tree was developing some from the stringy integuments of its fibres, so that it became a nice problem as to which was inspired by which, which copied which, or whether for both sides seemed so self-absorbed that this also was a possibility – they had come on a mirror-image of perversity independently.

'Motion is the prime beauty,' said David-by-the-moat-that-dries, and took many degrees of the sun across the muddy sky to say it. 'Motion is in me. There is no motion in the ground. In the ground there is not motion. All that the ground contains is without motion. The ground lies in quiet and to lie in the ground is not to be. Beauty is not in the ground. Beyond the ground is the air. Air and ground make all there is and I would be of the ground and air. I was of the ground and of the air but I will be of the air alone. If there is ground, there is another ground. The leaves fly in the air and my longing goes with them but they are only part of me because I am of wood. O, Argustal, you know not the pains of wood!'

Argustal did not indeed, for long before this gnarled speech was spent, the moon had risen and the silent muddy night had fallen, and he was curled asleep in David's distorted branches, the stone in his deep pockets.

Twice more he slept, twice more watched their painful progress along the unswept tracks, twice more joined converse with the melancholy tree – and when he woke again, all the heavens were stacked with fleecy cloud that showed blue between, and low hills lay ahead. He jumped down. Grass grew here. Pebbles littered the track. He howled and shouted with pleasure.

Crying his thanks, he set off across the heath.

'…growth …' said David-by-the-moat-that-dries.

The heath collapsed and gave way to sand, fringed by sharp grass that scythed at Argustal's skirts as he went by. He ploughed across the sand. This was his own country, and he rejoiced, taking his beating from the occasional cairn that pointed a finger of shade across the sand. Once, one of the Forces flew over, so that for a moment of terror the world was plunged in night, thunder growled, and a paltry hundred drops of rain spattered down; then it was already on the far confines of the sun's domain, plunging away – no matter where!

Few animals, fewer birds, still survived. In the sweet deserts of Outer Talembil, they were especially rare. Yet Argustal passed a bird sitting on a cairn, its hooded eye bleared with a million years of danger. It fluttered one wing at sight of him, in tribute to old reflexes, but he respected the hunger in his belly too much to try to dine on sinews and feathers, and the bird appeared to recognise the fact.

He was nearing home. The memory of Pamitar was sharp before him, so that he could follow it like a scent. He passed another of his kind, an old ape wearing a red mask hanging almost to the ground; they barely gave each other a nod of recognition. Soon on the idle skyline he saw the blocks that marked Gornilo, the first town of Talembil.

The ulcerated sun travelled across the sky. Stoically, Argustal travelled across the intervening dunes, and arrived in the shadow of the white blocks of Gornilo.

No one could recollect now – recollection was one of the lost things that many felt privileged to lose – what factors had determined certain features of Gornilo's architecture. This was an ape-human town, and perhaps in order to construct a memorial to yet more distant and dreadful things, the first inhabitants of the town had made slaves of themselves and of the other creatures that now were no more, and erected these great cubes that now showed signs of weathering, as if they tired at last of swinging their shadows every day about their bases. The ape-humans who lived here were the same ape-humans who had always lived here; they sat as untiringly under their mighty memorial blocks as they had always done – calling now to Argustal as he passed as languidly as one flicks stones across the surface of a lake – but they could recollect no longer if or how they had shifted the blocks across the desert; it might be that that forgetfulness formed an integral part of being as permanent as the granite of the blocks.

Beyond the blocks stood the town. Some of the trees here were visitors, bent on becoming as David-by-the-moat-that-dries was, but most grew in the old way, content with ground and indifferent to motion. They knotted their branches this way and slatted their twigs that way, and humped their trunks the other way, and thus schemed up ingenious and ever-changing homes for the tree-going inhabitants of Gornilo.

At last Argustal came to his home, on the far side of the town.

The name of his home was Cormok. He pawed and patted and licked it first before running lightly up its trunk to the living-room.

Pamitar was not there.

He was not surprised at this, hardly even disappointed, so serene was his mood. He walked slowly about the room, sometimes swinging up to the ceiling in order to view it better, licking and sniffing as he went, chasing the after-images of his wife's presence. Finally, he laughed and fell into the middle of the floor.

'Settle down, boy!' he said.

Sitting where he had dropped, he unloaded his pockets, taking out the five stones he had acquired in his travels and laying them aside from his other possessions. Still sitting, he disrobed, enjoying doing it inefficiently. Then he climbed into the sand bath.

While Argustal lay there, a great howling wind sprang up, and in a moment the room was plunged into sickly greyness. A prayer went up outside, a prayer flung by the people at the unheeding Forces not to destroy the sun. His lower lip moved in a gesture at once of content and contempt; he had forgotten the prayers of Talembil. This was a religious city. Many of the Unclassified congregated here from the waste miles, people or animals whose minds had dragged them aslant from what they were, into rococo forms that more exactly defined their inherent qualities, until they resembled forgotten or extinct forms, or forms that had no being till now, and acknowledged no common cause with any other living thing – except in this desire to preserve the festering sunlight from further ruin.

Under the fragrant grains of the bath, submerged all but for head and a knee and hand, Argustal opened wide his perceptions to all that might come: and finally thought only what he had often thought while lying there – for the armouries of cerebration had long since been emptied of all new ammunition, whatever the tree-men of Or might claim – that in such baths, under such an unpredictable wind, the major life forms of Earth, men and trees, had probably first come at their impetus to change. But change itself…had there been a much older thing blowing about the world that everyone had forgotten?

For some reason, that question aroused discomfort in him. He felt dimly that there was another side of life than content and happiness; all beings felt content and happiness; but were those qualities a unity, or were they not perhaps one side only of a – of a shield?

He growled. Start thinking gibberish like that and you ended up human with antlers on your shoulders!

Brushing off the sand, he climbed from the bath, moving more swiftly than he had done in countless time, sliding out of his home, down to the ground without bothering to put on his clothes.

He knew where to find Pamitar. She would be beyond the town, guarding the parapatterner from the tattered angry beggars of Talembil.

The cold wind blew, with an occasional slushy thing in it that made a being blink and wonder about going on. As he strode through the green and swishing heart of Gornilo, treading among the howlers who knelt casually everywhere in rude prayer, Argustal looked up at the sun. It was visible by fragments, torn through tree and cloud. Its face was blotched and pimpled, sometimes obscured altogether for an instant at a time, then blazing forth again. It sparked like a blazing blind eye. A wind seemed to blow from it that blistered the skin and chilled the blood.

So Argustal came to his own patch of land, clear of the green town, out in the stirring desert, and to his wife, Pamitar, to the rest of the world called Miram. She squatted with her back to the wind, the sharply flying grains of sand cutting about her hairy ankles. A few paces away, one of the beggars pranced among Argustal's stones.

Pamitar stood up slowly, removing the head shawl from her head.

'Tapmar!' she said.

Into his arms he wrapped her, burying his face in her shoulder. They chirped and clucked at each other, so engrossed that they made no note of when the breeze died and the desert lost its motion and the sun's light improved.

When she felt him tense, she held him more loosely. At a hidden signal, he jumped away from her, jumping almost over her shoulder, springing ragingly forth, bowling over the lurking beggar into the sand.

The creature sprawled, two-sided and misshapen, extra arms growing from arms, head like a wolf, back legs bowed like a gorilla, clothed in a hundred textures, yet not unlovely. It laughed as it rolled and called in a high clucking voice, 'Three men sprawling under a lilac tree and none to hear the first one say, "Ere the crops crawl, blows fall", and the second abed at night with mooncalves, answer me what's the name of the third, feller?'

'Be off with you, you mad old crow!'

And as the old crow ran away, it called out its answer, laughing, 'Why Tapmar, for he talks to nowhere!', confusing the words as it tumbled over the dunes and made its escape.

Argustal and Pamitar turned back to each other, vying with the strong sunlight to search out each other's faces, for both had forgotten when they were last together, so long was time, so dim was memory. But there were memories, and as he searched they came back. The flatness of her nose, the softness of her nostrils, the roundness of her eyes and their brownness, the curve of the rim of her lips: all these, because they were dear, became remembered, thus taking on more than beauty.

They talked gently to each other, all the while looking. And slowly something of that other thing he suspected on the dark side of the shield entered him – for her beloved countenance was not as it had been. Round her eyes, particularly under them, were shadows, and faint lines creased from the sides of her mouth. In her stance too, did not the lines flow more downward than heretofore?

The discomfort growing too great, he was forced to speak to Pamitar of these things, but there was no proper way to express them, and she seemed not to understand, unless she understood and did not know it, for her manner grew agitated, so that he soon forwent questioning, and turned to the parapatterner to hide his unease.

It stretched over a mile of sand, and rose several feet into the air. From each of his long expeditions, he brought back no more than five stones, yet there were assembled here many hundreds of thousands of stones, perhaps millions, all painstakingly arranged, so that no being could take in the arrangement from any one position, not even Argustal. Many were supported in the air at various heights by stakes or poles, more lay on the ground, where Pamitar always kept the dust and the wild men from encroaching them, and of these on the ground, some stood isolated, while others lay in profusion, but all in a pattern that was ever apparent only to Argustal – and he feared that it would take him until the next sunset to have that pattern clear in his head again. Yet already it started to come clearer, and he recalled with wonder the devious and fugal course he had taken, walking down to the ravine of the tree-men of Or, and knew that he still contained the skill to place the new stones he had brought within the general pattern with reference to that natural harmony – completing the parapatterner.

And the lines on his wife's face: would they too have a place within the pattern?

Was there sense in what the crow beggar had cried, that he talked to nowhere? And…and…the terrible and, would nowhere answer him?

Bowed, he took his wife's arm, and scurried back with her to their home, high in the leafless tree.

'My Tapmar,' she said that evening, as they ate a dish of fruit, 'it is good that you come back to Gornilo, for the town sedges up with dreams like an old river bed, and I am afraid.'

At this he was secretly alarmed, for the figure of speech she used seemed to him an apt one for the newly-observed lines on her face, so that he asked her what the dreams were in a voice more timid than he meant to use.

Looking at him strangely, she said, 'The dreams are as thick as fur, so thick that they congeal my throat to tell you of them. Last night, I dreamed I walked in a landscape that seemed to be clad in fur all round the distant horizons, fur that branched and sprouted and had sombre tones of russet and dun and black and a lustrous black-blue. I tried to resolve this strange material into the more familiar shapes of hedges and old distorted trees, but it stayed as it was, and I became…well, I had the word in my dream that I became a *child*.'

Argustal looked aslant over the crowded vegetation of the town and said, 'These dreams may not be of Gornilo but of you only, Pamitar. What is *child*?'

'There's no such thing in reality, to my knowledge, but in the dream the child that was I was small and fresh and in its actions at once nimble and clumsy. It was alien from me, its motions and ideas never mine – and yet it was all familiar to me, I was it, Tapmar, I was that child. And now that I wake, I become sure that I once was such a thing as a *child*.'

He tapped his fingers on his knees, shaking his head and blinking in a sudden anger. 'This is your bad secret, Pamitar! I knew you had one the moment I saw you! I read it in your face which has changed in an evil way! You know you were never anything but Pamitar in all the millions of years of your life, and that *child* must be an evil phantom that possesses you. Perhaps you will now be turned into *child*!'

She cried out and hurled a green fruit into which she had bitten. Deftly, he caught it before it struck him.

They made a provisional peace before settling for sleep. That night, Argustal dreamed that he also was small and vulnerable and hardly able to manage the language; his intentions were like an arrow and his direction clear.

Waking, he sweated and trembled, for he knew that as he had been *child* in his dream, so he had been *child* once in life. And this went deeper than sickness. When his pained looks directed themselves outside, he saw the night was like shot silk, with a dappled effect of light and shadow in the dark blue dome of the sky, which signified that the Forces were making merry with the sun while it journeyed through the Earth; and Argustal thought of his journeys across the Earth, and of his visit to Or, when the tree-men had whispered of an unknown clement that forces change.

'They prepared me for this dream!' he muttered. He knew now that change had worked in his very foundations; once, he had been this thin tiny alien thing called *child*, and his wife too, and possibly others. He thought of that little apparition again, with its spindly legs and piping voice; the horror of it chilled his heart; he broke into prolonged groans that all Pamitar's comforting took a long part of the dark to silence.

He left her sad and pale. He carried with him the stones he had gathered on his journey, the odd-shaped one from the ravine at Or and the ones he had acquired before that. Holding them tightly to him, Argustal made his way through the town to his spatial arrangement. For so long, it had been his chief preoccupation; today, the long project would come to completion; yet because he could not even say why it had so preoccupied him, his feelings inside lay flat and wretched. Something had got to him and killed content.

Inside the prospects of the parapatterner, the old beggarly man lay, resting his shaggy head on a blue stone. Argustal was too low in spirit to chase him away.

'As your frame of stones will frame words, the words will come forth stones,' cried the creature.

'I'll break your bones, old crow!' growled Argustal, but inwardly he wondered at this vile crow's saying and at what he had said the previous day about Argustal's talking to nowhere, for Argustal had discussed the purpose of his structure with nobody, not even Pamitar. Indeed, he had not recognised the purpose of the structure himself until two journeys back – or had it been three or four? The pattern had started simply as a pattern (hadn't it?) and only much later had the obsession become a purpose.

To place the new stones correctly took time. Wherever Argustal walked in his great framework, the old crow followed, sometimes on two legs, sometimes on four. Other personages from the town collected to stare, but none dared step inside the perimeter of the structure, so that they remained far off, like little stalks growing on the margins of Argustal's mind.

Some stones had to touch, others had to be just apart. He walked and stooped and walked, responding to the great pattern that he now knew contained a universal law. The task wrapped him round in an aesthetic daze similar to the one he had experienced travelling the labyrinthine way down to Or, but with greater intensity.

The spell was broken only when the old crow spoke from a few paces away in a voice level and unlike his usual sing-song. And the old crow said, 'I remember you planting the very first of these stones here when you were a child.'

Argustal straightened.

Cold took him, though the bilious sun shone bright. He could not find his voice. As he searched for it, his gaze went across to the eyes of the beggar-man, festering in his black forehead.

'You know I was once such a phantom – a child?' he asked.

'We are all phantoms. We were all childs. As there is gravy in our bodies, our hours were once few.'

'Old crow...you describe a different world – not ours!'

'Very true, very true. Yet that other world once was ours.'

'Oh, not! Not so!'

'Speak to your machine about it! Its tongue is of rock and cannot lie like mine.'

He picked up a stone and flung it. 'That will I do! Now get away from me!'

The stone hit the old man in his ribs. He groaned painfully and danced backwards, tripped, was up again, and made off in haste, limbs whirling in a way that took from him all resemblance to human kind. He pushed through the line of watchers and was gone.

For a while, Argustal squatted where he was, groping through matters that dissolved as they took shape, only to grow large when he dismissed them. The storm blew through him and distorted him, like the trouble on the face of the sun. When he decided there was nothing for it but to complete the parapatterner, still he trembled with the new knowledge: without being able to understand why, he knew that the new knowledge would destroy the old world.

All now was in position, save for the odd-shaped stone from Or, which he carried firm on one shoulder, tucked between ear and hand. For the first time, he realised what a gigantic structure he had wrought. It was a business-like stroke of insight, no sentiment involved. Argustal was now no more than a bead rolling through the vast interstices around him.

Each stone held its own temporal record as well as its spacial position; each represented different stresses, different epochs, different temperatures, materials, chemicals, moulds, intensities. Every stone together represented an anagram of Earth, its whole composition and continuity. The last stone was merely a focal point for an entire dynamic and, as Argustal slowly walked between the vibrant arcades, that dynamic rose to pitch.

He heard it grow. He paused. He shuffled now this way, now that. As he did so, he recognised that there was no one focal position but a myriad, depending on position and direction of the key stone.

Very softly, he said '...That my fears might be verified ...'

And all about him – but softly – came a voice in stone, stuttering before it grew clearer, as if it had long known of words but never practised them.

'Thou ...' Silence, then a flood of sentence.

'Thou thou art, O thou art worm thou art sick, rose invisible rose. In the howling storm thou art in the storm. Worm thou art found out O rose thou art sick and found out flies in the night they bed they thy crimson life destroy. O – O rose, thou art sick! The invisible worm, the invisible worm that flies in the night, in the howling storm, has found out – has found out thy bed of crimson joy...and his dark dark secret love, his dark secret love does thy life destroy.'

Argustal was already running from that place.

In Pamitar's arms he could find no comfort now. Though he huddled there, up in the encaging branches, the worm that flies worked in him. Finally, he rolled away from her and said, 'Who ever heard so terrible a voice? I cannot speak again with the universe.'

'You do not know it was the universe.' She tried to tease him. 'Why should the universe speak to little Tapmar?'

'The old crow said I spoke to nowhere. Nowhere is the universe – where the sun hides at night – where our memories hide, where our thoughts evaporate. I cannot talk with it. I must hunt out the old crow and talk to him.'

'Talk no more, ask no more questions! All you discover brings you misery! Look – you will no longer regard me, your poor wife! You turn your eyes away!'

'If I stare at nothing for all succeeding eons, yet I must find out what torments us!'

In the centre of Gornilo, where many of the Unclassified lived, bare wood twisted up from the ground like fossilised sack, creating caves and shelters and strange limbs on which and in which old pilgrims, otherwise without a home, might perch. Here at nightfall Argustal sought out the beggar.

The old fellow was stretched painfully beside a broken pot, clasping a woven garment across his body. He turned in his small cell, trying for escape, but Argustal had him by the throat and held him still.

'I want your knowledge, old crow!'

'Get it from the religious men – they know more than I!'

It made Argustal pause, but he slackened his grip on the other by only the smallest margin.

'Because I have you, you must speak to me. I know that knowledge is pain, but so is ignorance once one has sensed its presence. Tell me more about childs and what they did!'

As if in a fever, the old crow rolled about under Argustal's grip. He brought himself to say, 'What I know is so little, so little, like a blade of grass in a field. And like blades of grass are the distant bygone times. Through all those times come the bundles of bodies now on this Earth. Then as now, no new bodies. But once...even before those bygone times...you cannot understand ...'

'I understand well enough.'

'You are Scientist! Before bygone times was another time, and then... then was childs and different things that are not any longer, many animals and birds and smaller things with frail wings unable to carry them over long time ...'

'What happened? Why was there change, old crow?'

'Men...scientists...make understanding of the gravy of bodies and turn every person and thing and tree to eternal life. We now continue from that time, a long time long – so long we forgotten what was then done.'

The smell of him was like an old pie. Argustal asked him, 'And why now are no childs?'

'Childs are just small adults. We are adults, having become from child. But in that great former time, before scientists were on Earth, adults produced childs. Animals and trees likewise. But with eternal life, this cannot be – those child-making parts of the body have less life than stone.'

'Don't talk of stone! So we live forever... You old ragbag, you remember – ah, you remember me as child?'

But the old ragbag was working himself into a kind of fit, pummelling the ground, slobbering at the mouth.

'Seven shades of lilac, even worse I remember myself a child, running like an arrow, air, everywhere fresh rosy air. So I am mad, for I remember!' He began to scream and cry, and the outcasts round about took up the wail in chorus. 'We remember, we remember!' – whether they did or not.

Their dreadful howling worked like spears in Argustal's flank. He had pictures afterwards of his panic run through the town, of wall and trunk and ditch and road, but it was all as insubstantial at the time as the pictures afterwards. When he finally fell to the ground panting, he was unaware of where he lay, and everything was nothing to him until the religious howling had died into silence.

Then he saw he lay in the middle of his great structure, his cheek against the Or stone where he had dropped it. And as his attention came to it, the great structure round him answered without his having to speak.

He was at a new focal point. The voice that sounded was new, as cool as the previous one had been choked. It blew over him in a cool wind.

'There is no amaranth on this side of the grave, O Argustal, no name with whatsoever emphasis of passionate love repeated that is not mute at last. Experiment X gave life for eternity to every living thing on Earth, but even eternity is punctuated by release and suffers period. The old life had its childhood and its end, the new had no such logic. It found its own after many millennia, and took its cue from individual minds. What a man was, he became; what a tree, it became.'

Argustal lifted his tired head from its pillow of stone. Again the voice changed pitch and trend, as if in response to his minute gesture.

'The present is a note in music. That note can no longer be sustained. You find what questions you have found, O Argustal, because the chord, in dropping to a lower key, rouses you from the long dream of crimson joy that was immortality. What you are finding, others also find, and you can none of you be any longer insensible to change. Even immortality must have an end.'

He stood up then, and hurled the Or stone. It flew, fell, rolled... and before it stopped he had awoken a great chorus of universal voice.

The whole Earth roused, and a wind blew from the west. As he started again to move, he saw the religious men of the town were on the march, and the great sun-nesting Forces on their midnight wing, and the stars wheeling, and every majestic object alert as it had never been.

But Argustal walked slowly on his flat simian feet, plodding back to Pamitar. No longer would he be impatient in her arms. There, time would be all too brief.

He knew now the worm that flew and nestled in her cheek, in his cheek, in all things, even in the tree-men of Or, even in the great impersonal Forces that despoiled the sun, even in the sacred bowels of the universe to which he had lent a temporary tongue. He knew now that back had come that Majesty that previously gave to Life its reason, the Majesty that had been away from the world for so long and yet so brief a respite, the Majesty called DEATH.

The Firmament Theorem

INTERVENTION OF FRAME BARS
Recent research has developed a camera capable of producing continuous tone film. This allows the designer a greater range of expression, such as black-and-white illustrations on a black, white or grey background, or any combination of these shades.

Patty Heyworth: *Anti-Institutional Institutions*

The sky was bluer than even art of picture postcard could depict. Vultures mucked about in it.

Captain von Tubb smiled into the camera and said, 'Yes, it takes a real man to smoke Mexican Saddle, the new nicotine-impacted cigarette with a half-life of ten days. Such a Man, Number Twenty-Nine, is Jerry Cornelius, agent extraordinary and world famous collector of English Eighteenth Century Fan-Topped Round Funnel drinking glasses.'

'*Pan*-topped,' Jerry corrected.

The director signalled to them to break off, lit a mescahale and sat down on a boulder, shielded from the intense Uruguayan sun by his gigantic brolly. Von Tubb lit a Marlboro. Jerry jerked a shoulder ambiguously at his aide, Carleton Greene. They had come all the way from Haiti just to indulge this whim – even if it was a cover for their forthcoming visit to the opera; neither would blench at a touch of pedantry now.

He took the opportunity to drop a card to Headquarters: THE SKY IS BLUER THAN EVEN THIS PICTURE POSTCARD CAN DEPICT. ROBERT GRAVES.

They would soon decode it in Ladbroke Grove.

EDVARD MUNCH: THE ROOM OF THE DEAD

Grinding his ice cream cornet underfoot, Carleton Greene strolled over to talk to Bulmer-Lytton, von Tubb's dwarfish henchman, who was busily stirring up a bath full of piranhas for the next sequence. Greene and Bulmer-Lytton had established a bizarre kind of rapport, based chiefly on a mutual love of the intoxicating batista-and-lime.

Fragments of Bulmer-Lytton's fragmentary English drifted over to Jerry. 'Orange, yes. Very strong. Like Elizabeth Taylor. Strong, very strong. You wife? Uruguay no good. Very good, very strong. Oh, thanks!'

Behind them lay the ceaseless jungles beloved by Ché.

Cornelius scanned the skies, looking beyond the circling kitehawks for Mardersbacher's Boeing 707. It would soon be time for him to assume the role of extrovert and Populist again. In his breast pocket, the fragmented Munch engraving sent out its secret call.

EVEN TODAY THE CATASTROPHE IS NOT ABSOLUTE BY DAVID JESSEL

'Don't, please don't say I never mentioned flowers,' José Caoneiro sang to himself. His song was not forbidden here in Uruguay. He had hopped over the border while all Rio was mad with carnival.

The seedy waterfront bar was almost empty. The girl Yvonne sat boredly by him, sipping her wine, smoking incessantly, watching him piece together the critical engraving, match the sunken eyes, the shoulders, the unnerving expanses of black and white. He worked with a kind of weary panache, aware of the eye of the barman, hoping the barman thought, 'So that's what an exiled song-writer looks like'.

The message telling him to get out had been in code: ZIVA SHECKLEY SILVER IS THE COLOUR WE CALL WINGS ZIVA SHECKLEY. He had not stayed to finish his Brahma Chopp.

As the last piece of the puzzle clicked into place, a shadow fell across the table. Caoneiro stood up, white-lipped, to confront the newcomer.

'Robert Graves!' he accused.

*

NATIONAL FLAGS IN INTERNATIONAL BREEZE

As the 707 roared in over darkening Montevideo, George Ancestor said, 'I have another very amusing blasphemous joke to tell you after we fasten our safety belts.'

'Gee, thanks,' said Ann Ayn Rand. Secretly she longed to get free of this bore and seek out Jerry. 'But don't you think that only people who believe in God one way or another enjoy blasphemous jokes?'

'This next one is a very amusing blasphemous joke – also not without some ordinary innuendo.'

'Yes, but I'm an agnostic, Mr Ancestor.'

Somehow it was impossible to get through to him. She retreated into her magazine. CERVIX HOLDS SECRET OF IDENTITY. COPULATORY RHYTHMS LINK WITH LUNAR ORIGIN. It had to come, she thought; now even fucking was balled up with the space race.

Beside her, relaxed and hirsute, the leader of Croatia's Populist movement told his very amusing blasphemous joke. It relied, as Ann Ayn Rand had predicted, on a thorough knowledge of the Ten Commandments.

MARVELLOUS ACTION SHOT OF HUMAN SUFFERING

As the Tory came at him again with the machete, Mardersbacher ducked, caught the man's blazer and swung him hard against the door of the elevator.

'That'll teach you to sully the name of England, you bastard!' he shouted.

Before the Tory could slump to the floor, Mardersbacher grabbed him, kneed him in the crutch, and kissed him violently on the lips.

'Excellent ambiguity!' Oliphant said, sitting on his own opponent, whom he had floored the moment before. He got up, lit a Marlboro and came over to look at the black man. 'As I thought – the Mare Imbrium playing up again!'

Mardersbacher glanced at his wrist computer.

'Four days to full moon and reversion to Puritanism unless Cornelius and his boys come through.'

'Don't be bitter. Have a Marlboro. The secret's in the blending.'

'I only use Mexican Saddle. It takes a man to smoke one. We'd better contact Lunar Module before Demansky Island is blown sky-high.'

They synchronised their self-incinerators and headed towards Ladbroke Grove, where Lunar Module was decoding a picture postcard of a decadent Munch madonna.

REPUBLICA DOS ESTADOS UNIDOS DO BRASIL

All these various links are usually achieved by coming back to one particular recognisable symbol which acts as a sort of 'home-base', before proceeding with the next step of the programming. Not only does it inform the viewer which station he is receiving, but it provides codes with natural breaks through which agents can be alerted. USE THE CAST-OFF EPIDERMIS AS BOOKENDS – *South Wales Argus*.

The hovercraft made slow time up the Amazon. Bored by the misty expanses of water, Cornelius continued to write abstracts of his Burma trip on picture postcards of the Mato Grosso. Bulmer-Lytton fiddled uneasily with his batista on the other side of the table.

'Eh, Mista Yerry! Strong, yes. What? On, you know.' He rapped the table for Jerry's attention and pointed out through the bright glaze of mist to an amorphous shape floating amid the dazzle. 'You see look, island, very strong! Orange, no? Is more bigger than Switzerlands, okay? Elizabeth, what you say? No bullshit?'

'Good,' said Jerry. 'And as natural, I hope …'

'What my friend intimates is that that freshwater fluvial island passing us on the starboard bow is of an area equivalent to Schweitz. You must pardon me if our English is not too readily comprehensible.'

Cornelius raised an eyebrow at von Tubb's flashing teeth.

'Understand very strong. The Swiss must be furious.'

Two hours later, they passed the Pan-Am Concorde that had crashed in Amazonia on its way from Miami the previous month. Already the jungle was growing over its toy hull. By then, Jerry was in the pad with Yvonne. She was having trouble with her frigidity, and made him work hard.

Romeo and Juliet (SAL 3695/6) is the first fruit of a Berlioz cycle that Phillips has embarked on. In general the performance has a fine sense of rhythm. But interior detail does not always emerge as clearly as one might wish and sometimes this prevents a phrase as crucial as the *crescendo molto* in the closing bars of the fete from making its proper point.

'We'll soon be at Manaus,' she said, as she sponged herself down afterwards. 'Do you like to be away from home so much?'

'Even Lincoln had a Gettysburg address.'

CO-OPERATIVE AVOIDANCE OF CONDITIONING IN MONKEYS' AVERSIVELY CONTROLLED BEHAVIOUR

The six lactating chimpanzees drooped over their scaffolding. Only slight movements of their dugs, dripping into calibrated gauges, revealed that they were still living. Overhead, in the domed room, the lunar simulacrum rose in majesty.

Watching over the monitors, Fred Bahai said, 'You see, Countess – we remove the conspecific and the results are still the same. Sir Frederick Hoyle is right. Every hour takes us closer to the origins of the solar system.'

Her old raddled body shuddered. 'With advancing age, the component parts tend towards congruity. My mouth is no longer watertight, the tides climacterise. Every hour takes us closer to the origins of the solar system. My osteo-arthritic hips mark the syncline of cosmological pressure as surely as an ape tit. What time is it now?'

He glanced at the chronometer. 'Long past the Devonian. By tomorrow, we'll be leaving phanerogamic time entirely.'

Entranced, they stared at the thin dribble of ape milk, and then said in chorus:

'Every hour takes us closer to the origins of the solar system.'

The first ape on the left started to giggle. It was possible to be bored, even while taking part in a big adventure. Above her pen, someone had scrawled SILVER IS THE COLOUR WE CALL WINGS on the damp white tiling.

SECRET CEREMONY, BOOM, ACCIDENT

Slow contemplative tracking shot reveals Navarro clasping body at end of sparsely-furnished room. Through windows, long boring negative vistas of North Holland are glimpsed before N. clumsily drags curtain across window pane, bringing near-dark to room.

As camera surveys rich awareness of mellow light and shadow, sound track carries N's inmost thoughts (spoken into echo chamber).

Sleep my boy my darling boy your Mummy be back soon …

So tired my little boy have a cuddle from your Daddy while he's here before the big war starts and he is gone …

Hand-held camera jolts with him up and down the room, looking over his shoulder at an infant of less than two years, as fair-haired as his father, falling asleep in his arms. ('These shots have all the almost cannibalistic hunger of filial love about them' – Philip Strick, *Sight and Sound*).

His drowsy head so near mine. A different place in there. Jesus, a different universe! … How many different universes! … Can I really lead people, know what they want? … Can he really lead people and divine what they want, like a God? For a moment, he felt real fear …

N's skull and ear come up and fill the screen.

And perhaps in the same moment his son fell asleep. Now I need a goddamned charge.

The viewpoint sinks slowly to floor level as he places the boy on a couch and covers him with a rug, so that the small figure is eclipsed by the immense dark lip of couch before N. begins to move away.

WE DON'T STAND IN LOCO PARENTIS, NOR SHOULD PARENTS

THEY HAD ARRIVED.

THEY HAD MADE IT.

Manaus, cap. of state of Amazonas, US of Brazil, sit. on the Rio Negro about 10m. from its junction with the Amazon R. (q.v.). Trading and commercial centre of the state, and chief port after newly developed Belem (q.v.). 1000m. from the ocean but only 80 ft. above sea level; temp. rarely budges below 80 F., humidity corresp. high. Pop. quarter mill. Town once centre of fabulous rubber boom at turn of cent – trade stolen by Malaya, due to crafty British (q.v.). Patti sang and Pavlova danced in huge opera house, now closed. Later visited by J. Cornelius (q.v.).

101 Things for a Clean-Minded Boy to Do Annual, 3rd Ed.

'It was here or Maracaibo,' said Jerry as they disembarked.

'What was so bad about Maracaibo?' Grotti Cruziero asked, sweating.

'You get used to it. I was here before,' Yvonne said.

Von Tubb and Bulmer-Lytton were arguing about deformation of anatomy as an aid to perspective in the paintings of Caravaggio – a typical Populist preoccupation. Cornelius let the small talk flow over him, warily casing the go-downs as they climbed the ramp. There were a few steamers here, surrounded by frailer craft. Palms thrust up their tousled armour among the sawn-off skyscrapers. It was hot. A large advert nearby cried TAKE A RISK! *SMOKE MEXICAN SADDLE. Free Insurance in Every Pack!* Neda Arneric's face smiled from a film poster, free of guile or fever.

His eye caught an intermittent beam of light flashing from an upper window. Instinctively, he grasped Yvonne's arm. She glanced where he did.

'We should make love like that, bodilessly, in sun rays.'

'It's a heliograph.'

'Semaphornication. New sensuistry. Mount me with your beam.'

But he was reading. Z-I-V-A – S-H-E-

'They're on to us. Let's take this side alley!'

As they hurried into the disgraceful little side-cut, a mere slice between rotting houses, he glanced up at its name. Avinda de Cornelius. When they name a street after you one day and chase you down it the next, that's the very marrow of life.

THE WORLD OF THE DO-IT-YOURSELF WAR

In his secret headquarters under the old Zagreb Palace of Culture, Ancestor gave curt orders that would result in a series of demotions all over Middle-Europe, the defeat of a *putsch* in Vienna, and the execution of two cherished assassins in Athens: and then returned to a moody contemplation of his forged air tickets.

'You have a photo of this Ann Ayn Rand I'm travelling with?' he asked Podovnik.

Podovnik said impassively, 'She is mid-thirties, looks like Dorothy la Paz with specs. Born Florida, USA, of native stock. She's quite a nice person – if you go for nice people. It's essential to the Populist movement that you make friendly to her.'

The Man Whose Little Finger was Stronger Than a Frontier looked moodily down at his big fingers. He lived in the world of the massive police search, the amber alert, the do-it-yourself war. Now he was faced with a personal problem. To communicate socially – away from the protocol of interrogation and command – he had to think himself back thirty-five years to a Zagreb suburb that now lay pulverised under a stretch of the InterEuropa Highway.

Maybe the damned plane would crash.

'STOP THE TWENTIETH CENTURY – IT'S THE NINETEENTH TRAVELLING IN REVERSE!'

As his cell door swung open, Jose Caoneiro raised his bruised and broken face. He had been resting his split right eye against the stone wall, just below an enigmatic poster of the Countess Anna-Maria Speranza Histaga de la Guista Perquista. To quiet his heart, he was trying to compose a new revolutionary song.

The inquisitor came in very silently, carrying a leather truncheon which Caoneiro recognised.

'Isn't that sort of thing a little old-fashioned?'

The inquisitor laughed without making a sound. 'The twentieth century is a very old-fashioned century, don't you think? Like the nineteenth run backwards.' His shoulders were bent under the prodromic weight of the building above them. His skin had the pallor of prison soup. From his pocket, he produced a Portuguese-language newspaper and waved it before his prisoner.

Sluggishly, Caoneiro's left eye picked out the headlines. RETROGRESSIVE SPERM COUNTS SPELL MICROCOSM CONCERTINA. Hoyle Postulates Devolution. He could not comprehend; was the Sperm Count some relation of the aristocratic strumpet above his head?

'I suppose you'll pretend you don't know anything about this theory, or about how your mistress Yvonne Conifern went to ground?'

'I don't know what it means.'

'Unbridled innocence is one of the major social problems of our times, compared with which the inarticulate yodellings of pop-song-composers are no more than Pavlov is to Pavlova. I suppose you will deny that all round us our continent lies vulnerable to immediate invasion by the united armed forces of lust-mad North American and Russian Soviets, simply because scab-devouring dogs like you refuse to yield to the natural national dreams of the majority, as embodied in the aspirations of our Great Leader?'

Not feeling up to philosophy, Caoneiro rested his broken teeth gently against the immense pad of his swollen lower lip.

'So we'll talk about plane-crashes,' whispered the inquisitor. 'Now – who is the *real* fake Robert Graves?'

HOUSE ABOLITION PROTEST MARCH STRIKE

Miss Brunner was being interviewed for *The World at One* at the Ladbroke Grove HQ, and giving very little away. Her difference of opinion with the BBC was of long standing.

'What was your reaction to yesterday's nuclear destruction of Demansky Island?' asked David Jessel. 'When did you last see Eric Mardersbacher? How does a field of white, blue, and red flowers figure in the Populist mythology? Why did you and Dr Evans cancel your seats in the Pan-Am Concorde just before it crashed? How do you evaluate the recent shift in world power?'

Tightly controlled, she said, 'Today's adventure doesn't lie in the impotence of action. It's a still-life in which passivity has acquired strike force. We make fossilised gestures. Everything we do comes out of a small box labelled "Made in the 1830s." It's all in Lenin's early works, before he was – ah, misinterpreted.' She fanned herself with a picture postcard of the Mato Grosso.

'And for those of us who haven't read our Lenin lately?'

'For those few, there are popular writers who have prefigured all. Simenon, Dennis Wheatley, Robert Service, Leslie Charteris, Svevo, Murray Roberts, E. Phillips Oppenheim, Rudyard Kipling, Ethel Mannin … I could go on.'

'Not all of them very popular names …'

'Greatness and popularity are not always synonymous, young man!' Her eyes were as chilly as her tone.

'Your public reading of *Portnoy's Complaint* in Zagreb last month …'

'A diversion,' she said For the first time, she allowed herself to smile. A rather artificial smile. Almost as if she were pretending to be natural on TV.

EVERYTHING OR NOTHING IS WORTH TELEVISING

They crowded into a small bar for a breather. The few deadbeats there stared at them. They acted normally to throw off suspicion. Von Tubb bought a packet of Mexican Saddle. Grotti Cruziero drank a cachaca. Bulmer-Lytton ventured into the urinal and scrawled SILVER IS THE COLOUR WE GENERALLY CALL WINGS on the wall. In his own peculiar dialect, it was a vivid insult. Carleton Greene read a paperback called *Buggering Gutenberg Museum (Mainz) Sport Glitter*. Yvonne ran her hand over Jerry's chest.

'Let's go back – death alarms me almost as much as life!'

'Shall I give you a Life Message?'

'Which one's that?'

'There's really only one: Be superb!' He ran his fingers through her hair. It was stiff with lacquer. He had forgotten she was three-quarters Negro.

Bulmer-Lytton emerged, zipping his corrupt flies.

RELATIVITY – THE WAY VAN VOGT USED TO TELL IT

His high had disintegrated, leaving him cold and mean. The taxi bounced endlessly on out of Montevideo, northwards. Nothing but road and beach, unwholesome in sunlight. Even the child-prostitutes had gone. He tried to think of the forthcoming meeting of Populist world-leaders in Manaus, but all that came was a slow clockwork orange and the smell of duryan fruit dropping from the duryan tree. He wanted to get back to Burma. The Munch aura was less strong there. Very.

'How long does this beach go on?' he asked Oliphant, irritably.

'Hundreds of miles of beach. Right the way from Montevideo to the border. And the tide never goes out.' He yelled to the driver to stop.

The engine died. The tedium of planetary waves, slogging it across from Africa, where everything had begun and would end, according to the oldest and the latest prognostications.

Oliphant pointed ahead.

The beach was broken by a field of blue, red and white flowers as far as the eye could see. The flowers made startling contrast to the blotting paper hues of ocean and forest.

'That's the power of the Populist movement. One day, the people are going to inherit!'

'Come on, that's an old Jesus joke! You didn't drag me all the way out here to crack that one.' He groped for the bottle of local whisky. After pot, what? 'The people have always been going to inherit.'

'Yeah. But now they're going to inherit next year – with your assistance. The Populist leaders will trust you, if you can find it in you to trust them. How do you like the field of flowers?'

Grudgingly, 'Aesthetics is an Old Wave Thing, isn't it? But okay, it's beautiful. Pretty fucking beautiful.'

'Let's walk then.'

They trudged over the blue, red, and white field, up to the ankles in old newsprint. Montez followed behind, cuddling the machine gun.

'Don't tell me,' he said. But Oliphant told him.

'This all was Navarro's idea – the Dutch leader. Elementary lesson in transmutation, he calls it, for cynics with no trust in people-in-the-mass.' He scooped up a torn page. In primary colours, Dagwood made a giant sandwich and was biffed by his wife for including her purgatives in it. 'See all this field of flowers, so-called – it took you in from the road? You really believed it was flowers? It's all old Yank comicbooks, *Superman*, *Astounding*, *Flash Gordon*, and dozens of others, all torn up here. The literature of the people. Becomes the most beautiful thing you ever saw. Miles of beautiful thing.'

Montez had grabbed up a page, fell to his knees dropping the gun, hot to find what happened to Steve Canyon.

'That representative of the people would rather have the flowers reconstituted,' he said, jerking a thumb at Montez.

Back at the car again, taking a slug from the Old Lord bottle, he stared back at the amazing beach. It looked like blue, white, and red flowers again. Only now he didn't care for the sight.

Switching his mind from the immediate confrontation, he began to consider Navarro's character in the light of this new revelation. The man was far from being a plodding literal-minded quasi-intellectual like Oliphant (real name Olbai Gulbai Phant) and some of the other nationals. Maybe that was because he was – as his many enemies claimed – raving mad.

He was wiping the sweat from his brow and taking another slug when Montez loomed up. In his lapel was a Jan Palach badge.

'So, Meester, 'ow you like Souse America, eh?'

'Just great. Makes me realise I really am European, and there are such things as those mythical animals, Europeans!'

413

As if in confirmation of his words, the thought came to him that it was time to return to the advertising jag. Oh Death where is thy sting with a Mexican Saddle.

'Okay, no bullshit. Orange very strong. Yes, no, daylight, Elizabeth. The fingers of the hand, good, yes. Very good, very strong.'

'He intimates he had a good piss,' interpreted von Tubb.

'Let's go,' Jerry said. He slipped on his Robert Graves mask. The others did likewise.

They crossed a main thoroughfare, alarmingly full of Volkswagens, and dived down another alley. At the far end of it, the opera house loomed.

They emerged under trees, walked cautiously round one side of the great square in which the building stood. It still looked splendid, worthy of a Patti, a Pavlova, its golden dome shining in the muzzy equatorial sun. Under a tree, mules crapped and crepuscular dogs fainted; Jerry was glad about that – he had been thinking of Graham Greene.

He stepped boldly into the open. There were cops about, big black truculent men with high boots and long truncheons. They paid attention only to the girls who passed, tawny and leonine in speckled shade.

Before the opera house was an ornamental promenade with a double flight of semi-circular stone steps leading up to it. As the party walked towards the steps, a figure darted out from under them and fired twice before running towards the shelter of the trees.

Bulmer-Lytton staggered and fell. From round his body, the Populist flag unfurled, a representation of Dali's 'Six Apparitions of Lenin on a Piano'. Blood suppurated from a hole above his left eye. As he passed the dying man, Jerry snatched the flag from the ground and they ran up the steps into the shelter of the baroque portico.

MARY MARY LIVE FOR ME

In and out of the smiling crowd
The cryptozoic spreads its coils
Like Spanish moss in international trees
Like national flags in international breeze

The rapid eye movements of my love
Sleeping near me tell their tale

Of local flowers in international dreams
Sweet local fish in international streams

A local habitation and a world-wide name
Mary Mary live for me!
Private places in the Public-Faces Game
Mary Mary live for me!
Don't die for your country
Live for me! Live for me!

A Popular Populist Song, by A. Caoneiro (in prison)

THE SICK CITIES OF HISTORY

'World supermen of the Underground: #73, Ady-Lagrand, Charles. Scarcely less fluent as an author than as artist, populist genius Ady-Lagrand has lamentably not written as copiously for publication as might have been hoped in the light of his flair for narrative and composition, as evinced in the BINARY DIVINE SAUCE SHOW ads. In his superb recital of the folk-fantasy JUST JERRY, he broke to vivid life a tale which cannot fail to bemuse readers. Again, the articles.'

At last the Countess tore herself away from the chimpanzees and allowed Fred Bahai to lead her to a coffee stall on the Embankment. Over in Lambeth, they were letting off coruscations of fireworks to celebrate the hundredth birthday of the Archbishop of Canterbury. Legends flared across the sky.

HIS NAME BE PRAISED BLESSED ARE THE LONGLIVED
YOU ASKED FOR IT ROME

As her raddled face turned chartreuse, Fred said, almost apologetically, 'Mention of religion reminds me – there was something I wanted to say to you about sex, Countess.'

She looked at her watch. 'Six tomorrow?'

'No, sex tonight. Countess, it has been a great privilege discovering the secrets of the universe with you, and over recent weeks I've found myself falling –'

'We're all falling! London's falling!' She sketched a gesture that included the coffee stall along with the Thames and the alphabetical galaxies above.

HAPPY BIRTHDAY TO YOU KNOW WHO
LET THIS BE A LESSON

'There are certain sick cities of history,' she said. 'You know them as well as I do, Fred – Bogota, Dublin, Zagreb, Calcutta, Trieste –'

'That's your subtle flattery – you know I've never been outside England.'

'Charming boy! London is also such a city. Its end inherent in its beginning, just as every baby's chromosomes carry its demise. Thus doom –'

'Er, before we get too gloomy, Countess, I must tell you I love you. I know that we're as different as the arts of Pavlov and Pavlova, but I love you!'

She dropped her coffee cup and placed her dry old lips raspingly against his. His arms went round her. She tugged one of his earlobes. He waggled his pelvis. She opened her thighs. He began to investigate the intricacies of her corset. She bit his neck. They both turned shock pink.

GOD BLESS GOD

SIX MANIFESTATIONS OF JOSEPH LOSEY BEFORE BREAKFAST

On the high ceiling of the rubber-boom building, gods and goddesses disported themselves amid clouds, cherubs, and chariots with a display of ardour and perspective that would have done credit to a dozen Tiepolos.

Some of the Populist leaders were already there, standing in an embarrassed group in the stalls, usheretteless, perhaps feeling unable to talk and smile naturally unless the Press was exploding round them. Taking Yvonne's arm, Jerry walked to meet them, muttering the password as he shook hands with Oliphant, Portnoy, Mardersbacher, Ancestor, Navarro, Munch.

'Ziva Sheckley … Ziva Sheckley … Liked your flower-power, Navarro.'

From the shadows, Ancestor said, 'Can we begin with the discussions before the others have come? Let's start in! You all know Sir Frederick

Hoyle's hypothesis, the Firmament Theorem, that every hour takes us closer to the origins of the solar system. There's no time to lose.'

'You forget that's why we met in Amazonia in the first place, Ancestor,' said Ann Ayn Rand. 'The haul along the para-evolutionary cycle is longest in these primitive parts. Here we have most time.'

She was getting back at him for all those bad jokes on the plane.

'Which is all the more reason to use that time wisely,' he said. 'I call the congress to order. So First let's take a vote. Those in favour that people remain human raise their right hands.'

The First International Congress of the Interplanetary Populist Party had begun ...

'It is a meeting that will live in history,' Miss Brunner said, when she had read the report – adding cynically to David Jessel, 'Always supposing that history is what we think it is, and has enough staying power.'

Cornelius twirled his pan-topped round funnel drinking glass and smiled. 'The title of my next film: "History – Event or Interpretation".'

'Then we'll all need staying power!' Miss Brunner said. Cornelius nodded, 'Like a pearl needs oysters.'

Greeks Bringing Knee-High Gifts

The directors' meeting was over, and the men who really counted at Crosswell's fast fled from Old Man Crosswell's sombre presence and were preparing to jet home to various parts of Europe.

Milo Priedor said to Hans Gustoffen as they moved down the corridor, 'Thanks for the support in there, Hans.'

'It got tricky for a moment, eh? It's not just that we don't need Zadar Smith World to handle our publicity any more,' Hans said, 'but we got that creep Hicks fixed into the bargain.'

'I rejoice! Not that I don't admire Hicks, in a way.'

'Oh, I *like* the man well enough ...'

They realised Carshalton Hicks was just behind and talked about the new live synthetic flowers both were growing in their offices.

Hicks took the scuttle to London, husbanding his wrath until he was in the presence of his third wife, Suomi, in their Kensington flat.

'They're crowding me again, scum like Priedor and Cox and Gustoffsen! They know I'll make managing director in two years and they throw all the dirt they can.'

Suomi was very black and very voluptuous. The inside of her mouth was an attractive pink when she laughed.

'Turn the tables on them, as you have done before, my love-pie!'

'Know what they did? They got me to propose we shift our publicity account. They all wanted it! So I did it. Then they left me out on a limb. Then Priedor moved that they accept my suggestion and left it to me to break the news to Saul Betatrom.'

She had been born in a kraal. Every item of her husband's manic world fascinated her. 'Who's Saul Betatrom?'

'The Zadar Smith World guy handles all our advertising. I have to find him a parting present to soften the blow.'

'Is that so hard?'

'What the devil do you give a guy like Betatrom? He already owns everything worth having.'

Glimpse of pink again. 'Give him something not worth having.'

'Just what I want to do, darling – just so long as it *looks* like it was well meant! This is a ticklish consignment. It has to be something people will think he would go for but which he will hate like hell …'

'Leave it to me, love-pie. Your little Suomi will think of something. Meantime, how do you like my gown?'

She started the phasing process, pressing the button at her waist. Slowly, the glittering material of her dress began to turn transparent. Beneath the dress, she wore only one other garment. It also began to turn transparent.

'Yeah,' said Saul Betatrom. Some days, like today, he didn't think so fast. So he said 'yeah' again to fill the vacuum. That free-fall orgy at Danny's place last night had about finished him.

The poisoned voice of Cox asked, 'You get my meaning, Saul?'

Betatrom fiddled with the dial on his phone, trying to get Cox's face in better focus.

'You calling from Crosswell's, Sid?'

'Of course I damned ain't,' Cox said. 'I'll spell it out for you again, Saul. You're all sluiced out with the Crosswell account, but good. Priedor and young Hicks have worked a deal with Gum Inc.'

'Gum couldn't advertise soap,' Saul said, the name of the rival agency rousing him slightly.

'Gum just took over the publicity for Lawrence's Life-Forms,' Cox reminded him. 'Now there's an account that's going to escalate for decades. These new synthetic-life animals they got …'

'Look, Sid, to hell with the natural history! Why didn't you speak up for Zadar Smith World at the meeting?'

'I was the only one who spoke for you, Saul, honest. I told the Old Man I was for you. I jeopardised my position.'

Saul could see that happening.

'So they plan to hand me the golden armchair, eh?'

'Actual choice of gift is left to Carshalton Hicks, Saul. It may not be an armchair –'

Saul had switched off.

Mrs Hicks – Suomi, the third and blackest Mrs Hicks – leaned voluptuously across at Meconin and said, 'You must enjoy handing big accounts.'

Meconin scanned the sentence for double-meanings and said, 'We are delighted to handle the Crosswell account.' Meconin was the 'm' of Gum, the surviving, the triumphal initial; both 'u' and 'G' were back in the smalltime where they belonged, whereas Meconin retired to his lunar estate every month, racing mechanical horses round the floodlit craters. He was a white, fusible, neutral-looking man and wore, this evening, a tinkling inertia suit.

Hicks said to Meconin's mistress, Merita, 'It's really cute, isn't it?'

She giggled. 'Cute isn't the word!' She didn't attempt to say what was.

Hearing that the best way to please Meconin was to delight his mistress, Hicks had brought her one of the firm's tapeworms in an environment jar. The cestode, anchored in a transparent gut, had had its metabolism speeded up. It went through its life cycle every two minutes, ovoid segments falling from it like snowflakes, dissolving in suitable nutrients into eggs, which changed into embryos as a current wafted them into another section of the jar. The embryos became active crawly creatures, and finally emerged into larval phases. These little bladder-worms, suckled in more swishing juices, turned miraculously into small tapeworms, and the whole process began again. Merita could not take her pretty eyes off it.

'It's like an allegory of all life,' Meconin said sententiously, patting Merita's hand and then turning back to moist little Mrs Hicks. 'You know, we also operate for Lawrence Life-Forms. There's a revolution in our midst! One of the great success stories of our times. They could probably make a synthetic tapeworm that would be even safer in the human gut than Crosswell's are. Why, they are now through perfecting a miniature tyrannosaurus – that's a sort of savage little prehistoric dinosaur – the world's worst mammal ever – which we are going to launch in a month's time with a big multi-million dollar campaign.'

'They sound dangerous,' Suomi said, looking at him with her mouth prettily open.

'They only come knee-high, but they're dangerous right enough. I wouldn't want one.'

'Well, guess we better get down to business. Mr Meconin, since your time is valuable,' Hicks said. He was too busy worrying about the way Meconin looked at his wife to notice the abstracted way his wife was looking into space.

It was two days later that Carshalton Hicks jetted over to New York to present Saul Betatrom with Crosswell Tapes' farewell gift to Zadar Smith World. Suomi stayed home, elegant in her new diamond chastity belt. Hicks wore a mask – the plague was bad in the poor parts of New York again and, although everything was said to be under control, he wanted to take no risks.

A couple of guys wheeled the large crate into Betatrom's office. Betatrom was big this morning, dressed for the event, high-boots and larynx-amplifier and everything. He shook Hicks' hand with a reinforced grip.

The youngest member of the Crosswell board of directors said, without removing his mask, 'Mr Betatrom, although no words can express the admiration my firm – and, I may add, myself – feels for the capable and inspired way in which you, throughout the past decade or more, have promoted –'

'Yeah, well, shag all that, Hicks,' Saul said. 'What you got in that crate?'

'This farewell gift comes from all of us – in which category I hasten to include myself – as a small –'

'Yeah, yeah, sure.' His voice filled the room. Not that he believed current superstitions that hundred-decibel voices warded off the micro-organisms responsible for the plague, but it never hurt to play safe.

He crossed to the crate, grabbed the opener key, and wrenched.

'– very small, knee-high token – of how deeply we all feel ...'

Hicks had taken the precaution of coming dressed in armoured pants.

Scaly, ugly as a man in a mask, the tyrannosaur reared up on its hind legs, swished its tail, and jerked forward.

Saul Betatrom jetted behind his desk, yelling.

Old Man Crosswell was laughing. The seemingly endless tears poured down his face. Across his desk from him sat Carshalton Hicks, face wreathed in smiles, at ease. Cox, Priedor, Gustoffen, stood by, puckering their faces into imitations of smirks.

'Goddamnit, Betatrom can't complain if the tyrannosaur *eats* him!' Crosswell wheezed. 'It's a real status symbol – the first tyrannosaur Life-Forms released, and by the end of the year everyone will want one. So from Zadar's angle his present looks real good – even if their New York boy loses a limb! Hicks, you done a good job! Thank God someone has a sense of humour round here.'

He glared at the contorted faces of Cox and Co.

'Well, you boys! Old Saul won't be too too happy to receive this little something from another of Gum's big clients, will he? Specially if it eats him! What you say, Sid?'

Cox said, 'It's not safe. I don't see it's so funny.'

Sobering, the Old Man said dangerously, 'Better ring him and tell him so, then, like you tell him everything going on here, eh?'

Priedor said hastily, 'We all think Hicks did marvellously well, Mr Crosswell. Betatrom had gotten to be a menace, and it's good to see his leg pulled – or maybe even eaten, like you say.'

Just to infuriate Cox and Priedor, the Old Man got up, put his withered arm around Hick's shoulders, and began to laugh again.

And even if it wasn't so damned funny … he'd show his confounded doctor that a good laugh now and again never hurt anyone …

The lackey at the front door of Betatrom's Adirondack mansion stood respectfully aside as Betatrom paced through the hall – well aside. Betatrom wore lead levis.

He had his pet on a goad-leash which kept it away from his ankles.

The animal had just been fed with its morning Labrador puppy – a big Labrador kennel had been established on the estate just to keep the dinosaur in meat. It was docile enough in the mornings.

'This way, Suomi,' Betatrom growled, dragging the creature down the north drive. Cowed, it did as it was told. Already, the truth had penetrated its peasized brain that Master was nasty when crossed.

Master was nasty right now. Crosswell! They were at the root of all his troubles! Sure, he'd laughed off this pet easy enough, switched the tables on Hicks, turned the jibe into kudos for himself, got the press boys to phototape him with the critter on his lap, made himself the swinging fashion-leader, killed Gum's campaign dead (Gum had planned mink-collared tyrannos as ladies, adjuncts, and now Saully Boy; had given them a reeking masculine image straight off!) ... Then Morgan Zadar had shown.

Zadar was the kingpin of Zadar Smith World, perish his guts. Lean, ascetic ... What the hell did ascetic mean, anyway? What he said went.

'I'll have to go to the funeral, Suomi,' Betatrom muttered. 'If Morgan says so.' He sat down on a bench, dragged the dinosaur to him, pulled it up beside him. Suomi sat there, showing fangs and panting lightly.

It was Humiliation. Sure, Zadar realised that. But, like Zadar said, they couldn't show how much they hated Crosswell's guts, or they would lose face. Old Man Crosswell had died laughing in his office – so Betatrom had to attend the funeral on behalf of Zadar.

He'd even have to shake the hand of the new managing director, and the hand of his scheming black wife.

Saul brightened.

'And I'll take you with me to the cremation, Suomi,' he said. 'You can scare the pants off your namesake. Maybe I'll starve you and let you run amok there.'

But he would never dare do that.

He slumped again, lonely in his own vast estate. He patted the tyrannosaur's head, kissed her scales, slid a hand round her muscular neck.

'You're the only one who loves me,' he whispered to her.

The Humming Heads

As a young man, I was eager to experience all emotions, all sensations, even the so-called forbidden ones, forbidden by society. Since I was very strong and enjoyed a violent temper, this was fairly easy to achieve.

The first man I murdered was a musician – not that I murdered him for that reason, although I had a mild dislike of music, it's true. I murdered him for two reasons: because he made a convenient victim, and because there was no other reason. Thus, I argued – and correctly – the police would have no cause to suspect me.

At that time I rented a small room on the ground floor of a house that stood in a side street. It was a simple matter to stand in the doorway after dark and wait for someone to come along when the street was deserted.

This man was slightly built and fairly old – in his forties, so it wasn't as if he had much to live for. I just went up to him and coshed him. Then I dragged him indoors and tied him to my chair and gagged him. I could have killed him in the street, but I wanted a little fun with him first.

When he came back to consciousness, I introduced myself to him under the name of Henry Bunglethrush and explained what I was going to do, He shat himself on the spot, and peed himself – I could see it spread in his trousers. Perhaps it was that which made me realise that I ought to have chosen a girl, so as to get in some real mischief before finishing her off.

I told the man that I was not quite such a cruel bastard as he might imagine from first impressions, and that I was fully prepared to grant any last request he might have. He nodded. I took the gag off carefully, with the blade of my axe against his throat.

He was weeping almost as much as I was laughing. I had a fit of the giggles. He begged me to spare his life for the sake of his wife and child. At that, I sobered up and asked him what his wife looked like.

'She's just an ordinary woman, sir,' he said.

I promised that I would spare his life as he requested if he would give me the address of his home. As I spoke, I assumed an expression of sly and incredible madness. Madness and wickedness.

This placed him in a dilemma. He obviously believed that, if he told me his address, I would kill him and then go round and kill of his wife and child too. But fear for his own life got the better of him and he blurted out his address. So I gagged him again and executed him.

Hacking his head off proved to be more difficult than I had expected. The axe was sharp enough, but I did not possess a proper chopping-block. However, the head rolled free at last. I wrapped it in a towel and shut it in a suitcase, and then get rid of the body in the river.

After a day or two, I went round to see his wife. I broke into the house at midnight and crept upstairs. Far from giggling then, I even felt somewhat scared. The woman was asleep in one room, the child in the room adjoining. I jumped on her, gagged her, and tied her up. For several hours, I practised sexual indignities on her before executing her over the edge of the bed. Neither of us said a word all this while; we were very quiet and the kid never woke up.

I carried the head away with me wrapped in a face towel, leaving the body in the bedclothes. What a shock the kid must have had in the morning when it found that!

Later, when I went to live in the country, I got the two heads out of hiding and nailed them up on my wall, side by side.

By now, I had of course ungagged them. They used to talk to each other – not about death or anything unpleasant like that, but about music. Always music. They would hum tunes to each other, her to him, him to her, or in duet. Mainly they hummed vapid things, light classics or popular music of past days. 'La Paloma' and 'Jealousy' were their favourites. We rarely got through a day without 'La Paloma' and 'Jealousy'.

At first, it was all a novelty, like cuckoo clocks and musical boxes; after a few weeks, however, it began to get on my nerves. I bellowed at them to be quiet. They were always deferential, that must be allowed, and they stopped when I told them to. Yet after a few minutes the chatter and the humming always started up again. 'The Syncopated Clock'. 'Stranger on the Shore'. 'As Time Goes By'. 'Rhapsody in Blue'. 'The Barcarolle' from *Tales of Hoffmann*. 'Easter Bonnet'. 'Danse Macabre'. 'Limehouse Blues'. 'Anything Goes'. 'Thanks for the Memory'. 'My Darling Clementine'. La Paloma'. 'Jealousy'.

Finally I had to warn them, Never hum 'La Paloma' or 'Jealousy' again, or they would go out onto the rubbish heap. Besides, they were attracting flies into the house.

For a day or two after that, they remained silent, just looking at each other. Then the chatter started again, all the nonsense about what a good year such-and-such a year had been for popular music, how they adored Offenbach and Gershwin. Inevitably, the humming began. When I came down to breakfast the next morning, they were already on 'La Paloma' and 'Jealousy'.

I took them into the garden, one in each hand. They were squealing for mercy then, with maggots falling out of their eyes like contaminated tears. With a heave, I threw them both onto the back of the rubbish heap, and that was the end of that!

It was only later I realised that I had actually come to enjoy 'La Paloma' and 'Jealousy'. Which tune I prefer is difficult to say. One day one, one day the other.

Of course, it's a crazy world, but sometimes it seems odd to me that a young man who begins life anxious to taste all emotions, all sensations, should end by humming 'La Paloma' and 'Jealousy' to himself all day.

The Moment of Eclipse

Beautiful women with corrupt natures – they have always been my life's target. There must be bleakness as well as loveliness in their gaze: only then can I expect the mingled moment.

The mingled moment – it holds both terror and beauty. Those two qualities, I am aware, lie for most people poles apart. For me, they are, or can become, one! When they do, they coincide, ah…then joy takes me! And in Christiania I saw many such instants promised.

But the one special instant of which I have to tell, when pain and rapture intertwined like two hermaphrodites, overwhelmed me not when I was embracing any lascivious darling but when after long pursuit! – I paused on the very threshold of the room where she awaited me: paused and saw…that spectre…

You might say that a worm had entered into me. You might say that there I spoke metaphorically, and that the worm perversing my sight and taste had crept into my viscera in childhood, had infected all my adult life. So it may be. But who escapes the maggot? Who is not infected? Who dares call himself healthy? Who knows happiness except by assuaging his illness or submitting to his fever?

This woman's name was Christiania. That she was to provoke in me years of pain and pursuit was not her wish. Her wish, indeed, was at all times the very opposite.

We met for the first time at a dull party being held at the Danish Embassy in one of the minor East European capitals. My face was known to her and, at her request, a mutual friend brought her over to meet me.

She was introduced as a poet – her second volume of poetry was just published in Vienna. My taste for poetry exhibiting attitudes of romantic agony was what attracted her to me in the first place; of course she was familiar with my work.

Although we began by addressing each other in German, I soon discovered what I had suspected from something in her looks and mannerisms, that Christiania was also Danish. We started to talk of our native land.

Should I attempt to describe what she looked like? Christiania was a tall woman with a slightly full figure; her face was perhaps a little too flat for great beauty, giving her, from certain angles, a look of stupidity denied by her conversation. At that time, she had more gleaming dark hair than the fashion of the season approved. It was her aura that attracted me, a sort of desolation in her smile which is, I fancy, a Scandinavian inherit-ance. The Norwegian painter Edvard Munch painted a naked Madonna once, haunted, suffering, erotic, pallid, generous of flesh, with death about her mouth; in Christiania, that madonna opened her eyes and breathed!

We found ourselves talking eagerly of a certain *camera obscura* that still exists in the Aalborghus, in Jutland. We discovered that we had both been taken there as children, had both been fascinated to see a panorama of the town of Aalborg laid out flat on a table through the medium of a small hole in the roof. She told me that that optical toy had inspired her to write her first poem; I told her that it had directed my interest to cameras, and thus to filming.

But we were scarcely allowed time to talk before we were separated by her husband. Which is not to say that with look and gesture we had not already inadvertently signalled to each other, delicately but unmistakably.

Inquiring about her after the party, I was told that she was an infanti-cide currently undergoing a course of mental treatment which combined elements of Eastern and Western thought. Later, much of this information proved to be false; but, at the time, it served to heighten the desires that our brief meeting had woken in me.

Something fatally intuitive inside me knew that at her hands, though I might find suffering, I would touch the two-faced ecstasy I sought.

At this period, I was in a position to pursue Christiania further; my latest film, *Magnitudes*, was completed, although I had still some editing to do before it was shown at a certain film festival.

It chanced also that I was then free of my second wife, that *svelte*-mannered Parsi lady, ill-omened star alike of my first film and my life, whose vast promised array of talents was too quickly revealed as little more than a glib tongue and an over-sufficient knowledge of tropical medicine. In that very month, our case had been settled and Sushila had retreated to Bombay, leaving me to my natural pursuits.

So I planned to cultivate my erotic garden again: and Christiania should be the first to flower in those well-tended beds.

Specialised longings crystallise the perceptions along the axes concerned: I had needed only a moment in Christiania's presence to understand that she would not scruple to be unfaithful to her husband under certain circumstances, and that I myself might provide such a circumstance; for those veiled grey eyes told me that she also had an almost intuitive grasp of her own and men's desires, and that involvement with me was far from being beyond her contemplation.

So it was without hesitation that I wrote to her and described how, for my next film, I intended to pursue the train of thought begun in *Magnitudes* and hoped to produce a drama of a rather revolutionary kind to be based on a sonnet of the English poet Thomas Hardy entitled 'At a Lunar Eclipse'. I added that I hoped her poetic abilities might be of assistance in assembling a script, and asked if she would honour me with a meeting.

There were other currents in my life just then. In particular, I was in negotiation through my agents with the Prime Minister of a West African republic who wished to entice me out to make a film of his country. Although I nourished an inclination to visit this strange part of the world where, it always seemed to me, there lurked in the very atmosphere a menace compounded of grandeur and sordidness which might be much to my taste, I was attempting to evade the Prime Minister's offer, generous though it was, because I suspected that he needed a conservative documentary director rather than an innovator, and was more concerned with the clamour of my reputation than its nature. However, he would not be shaken off, and I was avoiding a cultural attaché of his as eagerly as I was trying to ensnare – or be ensnared by – Christiania.

In eluding this gigantic and genial black man, I was thrown into the company of an acquaintance of mine at the university, a professor of

Byzantine Art, whom I had known for many years. It was in his study, in the low quiet university buildings with windows gazing from the walls like deep-set eyes, that I was introduced to a young scholar called Petar. He stood at one of the deep windows in the study, looking intently into the cobbled street, an untidy young man in unorthodox clothes.

I asked him what he watched. He indicated an old newspaper-seller moving slowly along the gutter outside, dragging and being dragged by a dog on a lead.

'We are surrounded by history, monsieur! This building was erected by the Hapsburgs; and that old man whom you see in the gutter believes himself to be a Hapsburg.'

'Perhaps the belief makes the gutter easier to walk.'

'I'd say harder!' For the first time he looked at me. In those pale eyes I saw an aged thing, although at the start I had been impressed by his extreme youth. 'My mother believes – well, that doesn't matter. In this gloomy city, we are all surrounded by the shadows of the past. There are shutters at all our windows.'

I had heard such rhetoric from students before. You find later they are reading Schiller for the first time.

My host and I fell into a discussion concerning the Hardy sonnet; in the middle of it, the youth had to take his leave of us; to visit his tutor, he said.

'A frail spirit, that, and a tormented one,' commented my host. 'Whether he will survive his course here without losing his mental stability, who can say. Personally, I shall be thankful when his mother, that odious woman, leaves the city; her effect on him is merely malevolent.'

'Malevolent in what respect?'

'It is whispered that when Petar was thirteen years old – of course, I don't say there's any truth in the vile rumour – when he was slightly injured in a road accident, his mother lay beside him; nothing unnatural in that – but the tale goes that unnatural things followed between them. Probably all nonsense, but certainly he ran away from home. His poor father, who is a public figure – these nasty tales always centre round public figures –'

Feeling my pulse rate beginning to mount, I inquired the family name, which I believe I had not been given till then. Yes! The pallid youth who felt himself surrounded by the shadows of the past was her son, Christiania's son! Naturally, this evil legend made her only the more attractive in my eyes.

At that time I said nothing, and we continued the discussion of the English sonnet which I was increasingly inspired to film. I had read it several years before in an Hungarian translation and it had immediately impressed me.

To synopsise a poem is absurd; but the content of this sonnet was to me as profound as its grave and dignified style. Briefly, the poet watches the curved shadow of Earth steal over the moon's surface; he sees that mild profile and is at a loss to link it with the continents full of trouble which he knows the shadow represents; he wonders how the whole vast scene of human affairs can come to throw so small a shade; and he asks himself if this is not the true gauge, by any outside standard of measurement, of all man's hopes and desires? So truly did this correspond with my own life-long self-questionings, so nobly was it cast, that the sonnet had come to represent one of the most precious things I knew; for this reason I wished to destroy it and reassemble it into a series of visual images that would convey precisely the same shade of beauty and terror allied as did the poem.

My host, however, claimed that the sequence of visual images I had sketched to him as being capable of conveying this mysterious sense fell too easily into the category of science-fiction, and that what I required was a more conservative approach – conservative and yet more penetrating, something more inward than outward; perhaps a more classical form for my romantic despair. His assertions angered me. They angered me, and this I realised even at the time, because there was the force of truth in what he said; the trappings should not be a distraction from but an illumination of the meaning. So we talked for a long time, mainly of the philosophical problems involved in representing one set of objects by another – which is the task of all art, the displacement without which we have no placement. When I left the university, it was wearily. I felt a sense of despair at the sight of dark falling and another day completed with my life incomplete.

Halfway down the hill, where a shrine to the virgin stands within the street wall, Petar's old news-vendor loitered, his shabby dog at his feet. I bought a paper from him, experiencing a tremor at the thought of how his image, glimpsed from the deep-set eye of the university, had been intertwined in my cogitations with the image of that perverted madonna whose greeds, so hesitatingly whispered behind her long back, reached out even to colour the imaginings of dry pedants like my friend in his learned cell!

And, as if random sequences of events were narrative in the mind of some super-being, as if we were no more than parasites in the head of a power to which Thomas Hardy himself might have yielded credulity, when I reached my hotel, the vendor's newspaper folded unopened under my arm, it was to find, in the rack of the ill-lit foyer, luminous, forbidding, crying aloud, silent, a letter from Christiania awaiting me. I knew it was from her! We had our connection!

Dropping my newspaper into a nearby waste bin, I walked upstairs carrying the letter. My feet sank into the thick fur of the carpet, slowing my ascent, my heart beat unmuffled. Was not this – so I demanded of myself afterwards! – one of those supreme moments of life, of pain and solace inseparable? For whatever was in the letter, it was such that, when revealed, like a fast-acting poison inserted into the bloodstream, would convulse me into a new mode of feeling and behaving.

I knew I would have to have Christiania, knew it even by the violence of my perturbation, greater than I had expected; and knew also that I was prey as well as predator. Wasn't that the meaning of life, the ultimate displacement? Isn't – as in the English sonnet – the great also the infinitely small, and the small also the infinitely great.

Well, once in my room, I locked the door, laid the envelope on a table and set myself down before it. I slit the envelope with a paper knife and withdrew her – her! – letter.

What she said was brief. She was much interested in my offer and the potential she read in it. Unfortunately, she was leaving Europe at the end of the week, the day after the morrow, since her husband was taking up an official post in Africa on behalf of his government. She regretted that our acquaintance would not deepen.

I folded the letter and put it down. Only then did I appreciate the writhe in the serpent's tail. Snatching up the letter again, I re-read it. She and her husband – yes! – were taking up residence in the capital city of that same republic with whose Prime Minister I had been long in negotiation. Only that morning had I written to his cultural attaché to announce finally that the making of such a film as he proposed was beyond my abilities and interests!

That night, I slept little. In the morning, when friends called upon me, I had my man tell them I was indisposed; and indisposed I was; indisposed to act; yet indisposed to let slip this opportunity. It was perversity, of course, to think of following this woman, this perverted madonna, to another continent; there were other women with whom the darker understandings would flow if I merely lifted the somewhat antique phone by my bedside. And it was perhaps perversity that allowed me to keep myself in indecision for so long.

But by afternoon I had decided. From a lunar distance, Europe and Africa were within the single glance of an eye; my fate was equally a small thing; I would follow her by the means so easily awaiting me.

Accordingly, I composed a letter to the genial black attaché, saying that I regretted my decision of yesterday, explaining how it had been instrumental in moving my mind in entirely the opposite direction, and announcing that I now wished to make the proposed film. I said I would be willing to leave for his native country with camera team and secretaries as soon as possible. I requested him to favour me with an early appointment. And I had this letter delivered by hand there and then.

There followed a delay which I weathered as best I could. The next two days I spent shut in the offices I had hired in a quiet part of the city, editing *Magnitudes*. It would be a satisfactory enough film, but already I saw it merely – as is the way with creative artists – as pointing towards the next work. Images of Africa already began to steal upon my brain.

At the end of the second day, I broke my solitude and sought out a friend. I confided to him my anger that the attaché had not condescended to give me a reply when I was so keen to get away. He laughed.

'But your famous attaché has returned home in disgrace! He was found robbing the funds. A lot of them are like that, I'm afraid! Not used to authority! It was all over the evening papers a couple of days ago – quite a scandal! You'll have to write to your Prime Minister.'

Now I saw that this was no ordinary affair. There were lines of magnetism directed towards the central attraction, just as Remy de

Gourmont claims that the markings on the fur of certain luxurious female cats run inescapably towards their sexual quarters. Clearly, I must launch myself into this forceful pattern. This I did by writing hastily – hastily excusing myself from my friend's presence – to the distant statesman in the distant African city, towards which, on that very evening, my maligned lady was making her way.

Of the awful delays that followed, I shall not speak. The disgrace of the cultural attaché (and it was not he alone who had been disgraced) had had its repercussions in the far capital, and my name, becoming involved, was not sweetened thereby. Finally, however, I received the letter I awaited, inviting me to make the film in my own terms, and offering me full facilities. It was a letter that would have made a less perverse man extremely happy!

To make my arrangements to leave Europe, to brief my secretary, and settle certain business matters took me a week. In that time, the distinguished film festival was held, and *Magnitudes* enjoyed from the critics just such a reception as I had anticipated; that is to say, the fawners fawned and the sneerers sneered, and both parties read into it many qualities that were not there, ignoring those that were – one even saw it as a retelling of the myth of the wanderings of Adam and Eve after their expulsion from Eden! Truly, the eyes of critics, those prideful optics, see only what they wish to see!

All irritations were finally at an end. With an entourage of five, I climbed aboard a jet liner scheduled for Lagos.

It seemed then that the climactic moment of which I was in search could not be far distant, either in time or space. But the unforeseen interposed.

When I arrived at my destination, it was to discover the African capital in an unsettled state, with demonstrations and riots every day and curfews every night. My party was virtually confined to its hotel, and the politicians were far too involved to bother about a mere film-maker!

In such a city, none of the pursuits of man are capable of adequate fulfilment: except one. I well recall being in Trieste when that city was in a similar state of turmoil. I was then undergoing a painful and exquisite love affair with a woman almost twice my age – but my age then was half what it now is! – and the disruptions and dislocations of public life, the mysterious stoppages and equally mysterious pandemoniums that blew in like the *bora*, gave a delectable contrapuntal quality to the rhythms of private life, and to those unnerving caesuras which are inescapable in matters involving a beautiful married woman. So I made discreet inquiries through my own country's embassy for the whereabouts of Christiania.

The republic was in process of breaking in half, into Christian South and Muslim North. Christiania's husband had been posted to the North and his wife had accompanied him. Because of the unrest, and the demolition of a strategic bridge, there was no chance of my following them for some while.

It may appear as anti-climax if I admit that I now forgot about Christiania, the whole reason for my being in that place and on that continent. Nevertheless, I did forget her; our desires, particularly the desires of creative artists, are peripatetic: they submerge themselves sometimes unexpectedly and we never know where they may appear again. My imp of the perverse descended. For me the demolished bridge was never rebuilt.

Once the Army decided to support the government (which it did as soon as two of its colonels were shot), the riots were quelled. Although the temper of the people was still fractious, some sort of order was restored. I was then escorted about the locality. And the full beauty and horror of the city – and of its desolated hinterland – were rapidly conveyed to me.

I had imagined nothing from West Africa. Nobody had told me of it. And this was precisely what attracted me now, as a director. I saw that here was fresh territory from which a raid on the inarticulate might well be made. The images of beauty-in-despair for which I thirsted were present, if in a foreign idiom. My task was one of translation, of displacement.

So immersed was I in my work, that all the affairs of my own country, and of Europe, and of the western world where my films were acclaimed or jeered, and of the whole globe but this little troubled patch (where, in truth, the preoccupations of all the rest were echoed) were entirely set aside. My sonnet was here; here, I would be able to provide more than a dead gloss on Hardy's sonnet. The relativity of importance was here brought to new parameters!

As the political situation began to improve, so I began to work further afield, as if the relationship between the two events was direct. A reliable Ibo hunter was placed at my disposal.

Although man was my subject and I imagined myself not to be interested in wild life, the bush strangely moved me. I would rise at dawn, ignoring the torment of early-stirring flies, and watch the tremendous light flood back into the world, exulting to feel myself simultaneously the most and least important of creatures. And I would observe – and later film – how the inundating light launched not only flics but whole villages into action.

There was a vibrance in those dawns and those days! I still go cold to think of it.

Suppose – how shall we say it? – suppose that while I was in Africa making *Some Eclipses*, one side of me was so fully engaged (a side never before exercised in open air and sunlight) that another aspect of myself slumbered? Having never met with any theory of character which satisfied me, I cannot couch the matter in any fashionable jargon. So let me say brutally: the black girls who laid their beauty open to me stored in their dark skins and unusual shapes and amazing tastes enough of the unknown to hold the need for deeper torments at bay. In those transitory alliances, I exorcized also the sari-clad ghost of my second wife.

I became temporarily almost a different person, an explorer of the psyche in a region where before me others of my kind had merely shot animals; and I was able to make a film that was free from my usual flights of perversity.

I know that I created a masterpiece. By the time *Some Eclipses* was a finished masterpiece, and I was back in Copenhagen arranging details of premiers, the regime that had given me so much assistance had collapsed; the Prime Minister had fled to Great Britain; and Muslim North had cut itself off from Christian South. And I was involved with another woman again, and back in my European self, a little older, a little more tired.

Not until two more years had spent themselves did I again cross the trail of my perverted madonna, Christiania. By then, the lines of the magnet seemed to have disappeared altogether: and, in truth, I was never to lie with her as I so deeply schemed to do: but magnetism goes underground and surfaces in strange places; the invisible suddenly becomes flesh before our eyes; and terror can chill us with more power than beauty knows.

My fortunes had now much improved – a fact not unconnected with the decline of my artistic powers. Conscious that I had for a while said what I needed to say, I was now filming coloured narratives, employing some of my old tricks in simpler form, and, in consequence, was regarded by a wide public as a daring master of effrontery. I lived my part, and was spending the summer sailing in my yacht, *The Fantastic Venus*, in the Mediterranean.

Drinking in a small French restaurant on a quayside, my party was diverted by the behaviour of a couple at the next table, a youth quarrelling with a woman, fairly obviously his paramour, and very much his senior. Nothing about this youth revived memories in me; but suddenly he grew tired of baiting his companion and marched over to me, introducing himself as Petar and reminding me of our one brief meeting, more than three years ago. He was drunk, and not charming. I saw he secretly disliked me.

We were more diverted when Petar's companion came over and introduced herself. She was an international film personality, a star, one might say, whose performances of recent years had been confined more to the bed than the screen. But she was piquant company, and provided a flow of scandal almost unseemly enough to be indistinguishable from wit.

She set her drunken boy firmly in the background. From him, I was able to elicit that his mother was staying near by, at a noted hotel. In that corrupt town, it was easy to follow one's inclinations. I slipped away from the group, called a taxi, and was soon in the presence of an unchanged Christiania, breathing the air that she breathed. Heavy lids shielded my madonna's eyes. She looked at me with a fateful gaze that seemed to have shone on me through many years. She was an echo undoubtedly of something buried, something to resurrect and view as closely as possible.

'If you chased me to Africa, it seems somewhat banal to catch up with me in Cannes,' she said.

'It is Cannes that is banal, not the event. The town is here for our convenience, but we have had to wait on the event.'

She frowned down at the carpet, and then said, 'I am not sure what event you have in mind. I have no events in mind. I am simply here with a friend for a few days before we drive on to somewhere quieter. I find living without events suits me particularly well.'

'Does your husband–'

'I have no husband. I was divorced some while ago – over two years ago. It was scandalous enough: I am surprised you did not hear.'

'No, I didn't know. I must still have been in Africa. Africa is practically soundproof.'

'Your devotion to that continent is very touching. I saw your film about it. I have seen it more than once, I may confess. It is an interesting piece of work – of art, perhaps one should say only–'

'What are your reservations?'

She said, 'For me it was incomplete.'

'I also am incomplete. I need you for completion, Christiania – you who have formed a spectral part of me for so long!' I spoke then, burningly, and not at all as obliquely as I had intended.

She was before me, and again the whole pattern of life seemed to direct me towards her mysteries. But she was there with a friend, she protested. Well, he had just had to leave Cannes on a piece of vital business (I gathered he was a minister in a certain government, a man of importance), but he would be back on the morning plane.

So we came gradually round – now my hands were clasping hers – to the idea that she might be entertained to dinner on *The Fantastic Venus*; and I was careful to mention that next to my cabin was an empty cabin, easily prepared for any female guest who might care to spend the night aboard before returning home well before any morning planes circled above the bay.

And so on, and so on.

There can be few men – women either – who have not experienced that particular mood of controlled ecstasy awakened by the promise of sexual fulfilment, before which obstacles are nothing and the logical objections to which we normally fall victim less than nothing. Our movements at such times are scarcely our own; we are, as we say, possessed: that we may later possess.

A curious feature of this possessed state is that afterwards we recall little of what happened in it. I recollect only driving fast through the crowded town and noticing that a small art theatre was showing *Some Eclipses*. That fragile affair of light and shadow had lasted longer, held more vitality, than the republic about which it centred! I remember thinking how I would like to humble the arrogant young Petar by making him view it – 'one in the eye for him', I thought, amused by the English phrase, envious of what else his eyes might have beheld.

Before my obsessional state, all impediments dissolved. My party was easily persuaded to savour the pleasures of an evening ashore; the crew, of course, was happy enough to escape. I sat at last alone in the centre of the yacht, my expectations spreading through it, listening appreciatively to every quiet movement. Music from other vessels in the harbour reached me, seeming to confirm my impregnable isolation.

I was watching as the sun melted across the sea, its vision hazed by cloud before it finally blinked out and the arts of evening commenced. That sun was flinging, like a negative of itself, our shadow far out into space: an eternal blackness trailing after the globe, never vanquished, a blackness parasitic, claiming half of man's nature!

Even while these and other impressions of a not unpleasant kind filtered through my mind, sudden trembling overcame me. Curious unease seized my senses, an indescribable *frisson*. Clutching the arms of my chair, I had to fight to retain consciousness. The macabre sensation that undermined my being was – this phrase occurred to me at the time – that I *was being silently inhabited*, just as I at that moment silently inhabited the empty ship.

What a moment for ghosts! When my assignation was for the flesh!

Slightly recovering from the first wave of fear, I sat up. Distant music screeched across the slaty water to me. As I passed a hand over my bleared vision, I sat that my palm bore imprinted on it the pattern of the rattan chair arm. This reinforced my sense of being at once the host to a spectral presence and myself insubstantial, a creature of infinite and dislocated space rather than flesh.

That terrible and cursed malaise, so at variance with my mood preceding it! And even as I struggled to free myself from it, my predatorial quarry stepped aboard. The whole yacht subtly yielded to her step, and I heard her call my name.

With great effort, I shook off my eerie mood and moved to greet her. Although my hand was chill as I clutched her warm one, Christiania's imperious power beamed out at me. The heavy lids of Munch's volup-tuous madonna opened to me and I saw in that glance that this impres-sive and notorious woman was also unfolded to my will.

'There is something Venetian about this meeting,' she said, smiling. 'I should have come in a domino!'

The trivial pleasantry attached itself to my extended sensibilities with great force. I imagined that it could be interpreted as meaning that she acted out a role; and all my hopes and fears leaped out to conjure just what sort of a role, whether of ultimate triumph or humiliation, I was destined to play in her fantasy!

We talked fervently, even gaily, as we went below and sat in the dim-lit bar in the stem to toast each other in a shallow drink. That she was anxious I could see, and aware that she had taken a fateful step in so compromising herself: but this anxiety seemed part of a deeper delight. By her leaning towards me, I could interpret where her inclinations lay; and so, by an easy gradation, I escorted her to the cabin next to mine.

But now, again, came that awful sense of being occupied by an alien force! This time there was pain in it and, as I switched on the wall-lights, a blinding spasm in my right eye, almost as though I had gazed on some forbidden scene.

I clutched at the wall. Christiania was making some sort of absurd condition upon fulfilment of which her favours would be bestowed; perhaps it was some nonsense about her son, Petar; at the same time, she was gesturing for me to come to her. I made some excuse – I was now certain that I was about to disintegrate – I stammered a word about preparing myself in the next cabin – begged her to make herself comfortable for a moment, staggered away, shaking like an autumn leaf.

In my cabin – rather, in the bathroom, jetty lights reflected from the surface of the harbour waters projected a confused imprint of a porthole on the top of the door. Wishing for no other illumination, I crossed to the mirror to stare at myself and greet my haggard face with questioning.

What ailed me? What sudden illness, what haunting, had taken me – overtaken me – at such a joyful moment?

My face stared back at me. And then: *my sight was eclipsed from within...*

Nothing can convey the terror of that experience! Something that moved, that moved across my vision as steadily and as irretrievably as the curved shadow in Hardy's sonnet. And, as I managed still to stare at my gold-haloed face in the mirror, I *saw* the shadow move in my eye, traverse my eyeball, glide slowly – so eternally slowly! – across the iris from north to south.

Exquisite physical and psychological pain were mine. Worse, I was pierced through by the dread of death – by what I imagined a new death: and I saw vividly, with an equally pain-laden inner eye, all my vivid pleasures, carnal and spiritual alike, and all my gifts, brought tumbling into that ultimate chill shadow of the grave.

There at that mirror, as if all my life I had been rooted there, I suffered alone and in terror, spasms coursing through my frame, so far from my normal senses that I could not hear even my own screams. And the terrible thing moved over my eyeball and conquered me!

For some while, I lay on the floor in a sort of swoon, unable either to faint or to move.

When at last I managed to rise, I found I had dragged myself into my cabin. Night was about me. Only phantoms of light, reflections of light, chased themselves across the ceiling and disappeared. Faintly, feebly, I switched on the electric light and once more examined the trespassed area of my sight. The terrible thing was transitory. There was only soreness where it had been, but no pain.

Equally, Christiania had left – fled; I learned later, at my first screams, imagining in guilty dread perhaps that her husband had hired an assassin to watch over her spoiled virtue!

So I too had to leave! The yacht I could not tolerate for a day more! But nothing was tolerable to me, not even my own body; for the sense of being inhabited was still in me. I felt myself a man outside society. Driven by an absolute desperation of soul, I went to a priest of that religion I had left many years ago; he could only offer me platitudes about bowing to God's will. I went to a man in Vienna whose profession was to cure sick minds; he could talk only of guilt-states.

Nothing was tolerable to me in all the places I knew. In a spasm of restlessness, I chartered a plane and flew to that African country where I had once been happy. Though the republic had broken up, existing now only in my film, the land still remained unaltered.

My old Ibo hunter was still living; I sought him out, offered him good pay, and we disappeared into the bush as we had previously done.

The thing that possessed me went too. Now we were becoming familiar, it and I. I had an occasional glimpse of it, though never again so terrifyingly as when it eclipsed my right eye. It was peripatetic, going for long submerged excursions through my body, suddenly to emerge just under the skin, dark, shadowy, in my arm, or breast or leg, or once – and there again were terror and pain interlocked – in my penis.

I developed also strange tumours, which swelled up very rapidly to the size of a hen's egg, only to disappear in a couple of days. Sometimes these loathsome swellings brought fever, always pain. I was wasted, useless – and used.

These horrible manifestations I tried my best to keep hidden from everyone. But, in a bout of fever, I revealed the swellings to my faithful hunter. He took me – I scarcely knowing where I went – to an American doctor who practised in a village near by.

'No doubt about it!' said the doctor, after an almost cursory examination. 'You have a loiasis infestation. It's a parasitic worm with a long incubation period – three or more years. But you weren't in Africa that long were you?'

I explained that I had visited these parts before.

'It's an open-and-shut case, then! That's when you picked up the infection.'

I could only stare at him. He belonged in a universe far from mine, where every fact has one and only one explanation.

'The loiasis vector is a blood-sucking fly,' he said. 'There are billions of them in this locality. They hit maximum activity at dawn and late afternoon. The larval loiasis enters the bloodstream when the fly bites you. Then there is a three-four year incubation period before the adult stage emerges. It's what you might call a tricky little system!'

'So I'm tenanted by a worm, you say!'

'You're acting as unwilling host to a now adult parasitic worm of peripatetic habit and a known preference for subcutaneous tissue. It's the cause of these tumours. They're a sort of allergic reaction.'

'So I don't have what you might call a psychosomatic disorder?'

He laughed. 'The worm is real right enough. What's more, it can live in your system up to fifteen years.'

'Fifteen years! I'm to be haunted by this dreadful succubus for fifteen years!'

'Not a bit of it! We'll treat you with a drug called diethyl-carbamazine and you'll soon be okay again.'

That marvellous optimism – 'soon be okay again!' – well, it was justified in his sense, although his marvellous drug had some unpleasant side effects. Of that I would never complain; all of life has unpleasant side effects. It may be – and this is a supposition I examine in the film I am at present making – that consciousness itself is just a side effect, a trick of the light, as it were, as we humans, in our ceaseless burrowings, accidentally surface now and again into a position and a moment where our presence can influence a wider network of sensations.

In my dark subterranean wanderings, I never again met the fatal Christiania (to whom my growing aversion was not strong enough to attract me further!); but her son, Petar, sports in the wealthier patches of Mediterranean sunshine still, surfacing to public consciousness now and again in magazine gossip columns.

Ouspenski's Astrabahn

Sparkily flinging up stones from the tired wheels the gravelcade towed darkness. Headlights beams of granite bars battering the eternal nowhere signposting the dark. The cuspidaughters of darkness somebody sang play toe with the spittoons of noon the cuspidaughters of darkness play toe with the spittoons of noon the cuspidaughters of darkness play toe with the spittoons of noon. Only some of the blind white eyes of joyride was yellow or others but altirely because the bashing the cars the jostling in the autocayed. And hob with the gobs of season.

In these primitive jalopsides herding their way like shampeding cattletrap across the last ranges of Frankreich that square squeezing country sang the drivniks. Cluttering through stick-it-up-your-assberg its nasal neutral squares its window-bankage to where the Rhine oiled its gunmottal under the northstar-barrels and a wide bridge warned zoll. Break lights a flutter red I'd ride the rifled engines ricochetting off the tracered flow below.

Cryogenetic winds bourning another spring croaking forth on the tundrugged land doing it all over and bloodcounts low at a small hour with the weep of dream-pressure in the cyclic rebirth-redeath calling for a fast doss all round or heads will roll beyond the tidal rave. RECHTS FAHREN big yellow arrows splitting the roadcrown. Writhing bellies upward large painted arrows letters meaningless distant burners seducing him to a sighfer in a diaphragm.

Clobwebbed Charteris stopped the Banshee. He and Angeline climb out and he wonders if he sees himself lie there annulled, looks up into the blind white cliffs of night cloud to smell the clap of spring break its alternature. About him grind all the autodisciples flipping from their pillions and all shout and yawn make jacketed gestures through their fogstacks.

They all talk and Gloria comes over says to Angeline, 'Feels to me I have bound the hound across this country before.'

'It's the flickering of an unextinguished loveplay starting odour at this stale standpoint Glor.'

'So you say? It lies here under night yet? Like some other place! You should say we wanted to come here or was that some place else?'

Hearing distonished by the hour.

'Anyhow, I can cool inspection while we get the kettle on this groggy mote.'

And other yattering earvoices crying to him through the labyrinths set in a concrete head of nightsloth he Charteris Shaman with the painful yellow arrows almost vertical more difficult to negotiate and maybe transfixed his own powers watercoarsed. More than the voices, breathing, ominous movements of bodies inside clothes, writhing of toes inside shoes and sly growth of the corkscrewing curls inside a million pants locutions and dislocations.

Breathing deep to force out his voice drown the sense of drowning he said, 'We hit the present aimed alternative friends. So let's doss down and tear off a new chain tomorrow rate where we stunned.'

Wraithlike in the dying beams, they pulled out sacks or piled together on backseats or a few took pains to boil up coffee or tea with pale flames dazed upon their chained eyelids or fleeting countrysides pillowed on their greasy locks of sleep. So was Angeline's belly mountained with the Drake-Man's seed but she nestled alone under blankets. He harboured to the girl who had joined the motorcad at Luxembourg Elsbeth with her fine young Jewish warmth.

Humbly they all had to narrow to the enemy breath of night flood with their closing rhythms lowered body temperature slatted Venetian thoughtpulses that all blankets and small fires and pillows could not dam or defer for more than

*

Deeper limbos other deaths crueller sleeps exist in which the fuzzed alternative Is stand watching peeling off from the spool of probability like negatives that never reach the developer haunting the slumberer click of shutter snicker of rapid eye movement old self-photographs number the data-reducer

Aged amokanisms of comprension guttering

Mending morn he takes delight knowing her juiciness in feeling the tousled dryness of crutch and turning that unseen smile to mossture Whereon she wrickles and strokes his semierect griston with a thigh giving him mandate pulling plump arms compulsively about his neck constrictly harsh add breath of morn mingled and the high old stinkle of feet and bum and body in the bag mantling them as he mounts smelsbeth all here and now be physical like all stubble on the rolling summer mountains where the skies steam upward over the incredible brow and motion everywhere in the sapient earth multi-limbed freedom of the heat –

Breaking in the harsh cries of uniform throats and yells of drivniks together with some rumpling and footmaching where the pace is fractured. This Rhine-bridge and engines roaring all hell out there and my juices seeping unpropelled sort of semi-ohgasm shit it's just a slimeoff this time Elsbeth honeypit.

Big boots by his nose passing and Charteris emerges to dianoise the seem. Oh boy the metal camp or mobile scrap-dump wheeled junkade raddling the end of bridge nose to nose or tail like they just beetled out the Rhine and disciples heads among them flowering in cool dazes like they stargazed an astrobahn.

Bucketing about bigbooted the Deutscher polizei falling around the bumpers and crying for order.

Charteris laughing and feeling for his jeans propped on one elbow.

'Hey, dig the inspired popular image of worldorder in this pure pink faces of authority shining and lovely smarched uniforms spruce like pressed plants running!' But gathering his mind to take a closer fix on them he snuffed that the Schwabe fell apart uniform-wise many without belts or buttons or boots or Klimpenflashengewurstklumpen to their name and even the jackets hung upon a bygone hook elsewhere. Still for effect they scraped traffink jam noises from their throats.

One crusader broke from the autodump with his bedroll yelping and the big lorries had him down and up and a one-two round the shaggy side-chops left right left right moonlight moonlight to the fuzzwagon.

'You try the uncivil disobendiate! God help you!' they yelled.

'Get this goddamned mobile scrap mobile!' they yelled.

'This is a nice tidy police state not a drosshouse!' they yelled.

'We'll have you Schrott-makers shot!' they yelled.

'Clear the way for the traffic!' they yelled, though the road flowed as silent as the river straight back to Switzerland like cut cloth and Army jumped up with his flute and piped and others sang, 'Clear the way for the traffic Nice clean autobahns we want to see Leave no human litter lay Clear the traffic for the way' as the cops schwarmereid in among their vehicles.

One looked down at all Elsbeth showed as she sat up, yelled, 'Ach ein Zwolfpersonenausschnitt!' and she snatched her vest about her vocal bubes, crying back abuse at him with a vingor jangled decibels adding to the general racket where one or two cars started up and backed or bucked smokily on the region great dizzy din.

Angeline came hurrying as he bent up and with attention in another part pulled at his jeans saying, 'Colin you see they're going to take our kids off to the nick if you don't do something quick we defied law and odur by settling right down here in the traffic route forgetting it was going to be sunrise soon or something mad or else just tired I don't know but you better do something quick.' On Elsbeth she could not look the dark hair round her shoulders and all entrances slack.

'Only we're traffic the only traffic apart from us there's no another car in sight it don't make a hold-up holed up here.'

'Better go and tell that to the Fuehrer here he comes!'

Pointing to a big white police car like a spaceship a yacht a heinleiner beyond reach of storms opening all ways and spilling most noticeably a mighty man in a white uniform big patched with a thousand medals like over-stamped bundle of laundry and boots and a cap with bright peak while rammed in his bathysphere a monster cigar approaching and two minions round him crying the Kommandant.

Then all the Schwabe crying 'Who in charge here?'
Sawn trees on parade streetside.
Time like a never-rolling steam.
Bridge of nerve-defying metalangles.

Slowly the cries silence the scene and all stock-still except a little morning breeze through which the drivniks are thin and pale with hair that made them in England part of nature growing right down sweet and unswept from hair and head and lips and cheeks and shoulder part of the pubic earth itself but here on this barren not so damned good and analogous. 'Who in charm hair?'

All get a charge or no one. Petrifaction of inner posture though Army pipes.

Heaving still his unzipped hipjeans Charteris he moves among the carmaze towards the white man Angeline at his side small but big seeing the eternal pattern as the object arrangement makes a readymade more beautiful than planned an emblem of eternity capable of slowing time something he had known before this marvellous he inside the ducks-and-drake man skimming over a deeper ocean of truth in which he wished to dive deeper and deeper away from the times too grave for mere communication on an average plane or old grey steps misleading to old brown building rucked in railings curled to dilate Italian-made and now up he's in a grey-brown room black-and-red tiles of a transcendental patterning oh rest me again for ever in the minds murmuring mysteries where I belong and could walk through and walk through forever the hall the long within withit for ever the pattern where time stalks sideways birds flying backwards reemerge as lizards before the days never-ending.

'You are in charge of this rabble?' The brilliant laundry bundle before his unzipped eyes and what was that place where I was I was there for a minute? eternity? Metzronome tick? In some late time-bracket feasting beyond this schwabian illusion of the present tell them why not.

Did they hand me over old betrayal?

Raising his voice, 'I am in all command and to me time swings back off its hinge mersing the tiny present – no, no, I tell you – I am Charteris. Paradise is in me I feel it I know it!' Now he waved his arms saw them above him making off in the sky this way that seeking the new dimensions or old dimensions seen as fresh alternatives as the birds cryrated into lizards and the new anima instantly back to stone. 'What we have seen is worth all collapse and the old Christianity world so rightly in ruins if you forsake all and live where there is most life in the world I offer. There the alternatives flick flock thickly by and again with his hands and hair he conveyed to there the great intellectual system that Man the Driver synthesised relating all phenomena and postulating a new map – a map he said wandering in and out of speech as dropping his jeans entirely he climbed hair-legged onto the heinleiner car and rallied them all – a man deminiating the topography related belaying a sparky relationship between this Europlexion and the explexion of conventual time the time by which predecydic man imposed himself against nature by armed marching cross-wise to conceal body-mind apart hide dissillusion.

Cheering and singing only the cops stamped around and offered dials of non-radiance. He still upbraidcast.

'And to these levels also another pirate transmitter with emissions on the self-life-mitter band for you got to mash your own consciousness into the introwaving road routage and the general timeweb only achieve by the discipation of my thought the discipation of proper erectitude like a discipation of any distinct order and to achieve finally well you need what Ouspenski calls certain luggage and then the true sidereal time can faze with your arcadian rhythms of living.'

'Get off my automobile!' said the big pink white laundry-bundle chief of police.

Two policement hupped Charteris down as he called, 'For all of you also timeflow can hold the orbital radiance of a spyers web if you will follow me. Let your circharacters centrifuse in the spinrads of centri-course! Follow me or you will drown in the flowing timeflow!'

So he comes away kicking as they assimob and fling his pants at him wrapping round the timeflapperture. You are not asleep at this moment. Many things were like sleep many things had no relationship to reality. Truer: reality had no relationship to the true things. They just built these wooden walls with wooden windows to sail on regardless. Many things that I said at that time must have surprised my companions in this strange adventure very much. I was surprised by much myself. I stopped and turned towards G. He was smiling. His old friendly fallible familiar smile. 'Afterwards it was very strange for me to remember the things I had said.' I was walking along the Troitsky street and everyone was asleep.

The Schwabe officers conferred with rapid eye movements and a thin cracked music started from the escampade. Many things that I said at that time. The brilliant laundry bundle made clockwork gestures parabola starting and ending at low point X and two polizei grabbed Ouspenkian I.

Set a speech to clash a speech.

Orated the laundrobund in machine-style 'Fine leadership I have appreciape and the exhaustation but even god almighty must here be circumstrict according to the authority of law and not park his car contrary to stated regalations. Else there's distrumblanches and the crumble-off of state and diction but right here is still my desportment and you hippies are all contraveined. So it's a rest this hairshirted male-fracture do his freakout in a cell! Move!'

'Hey, they're going to take away our saviour!' warcried Ruby Dymond running to Angelside. He flung a reality-object or unvariable geometry and metallic origin in semi-lethal parabol and the other sleep-runners started to mill marvellously unstewing from their rancid and auto-breasted pluckered in to the uniform defeat Hit a Kraut for Easter. Then leaped the bold gendarmes also acid-hipped but swinging in the name of Ordentlichkeit to let battle commensurate with duty the PCA bombs when dissembling produced according to each character in its own intensification.

By the perspective transfixed was the police point with its flags and signs and from here gorged more polizei slowly inflating themselves with self-pumping steps as they evolved themselves from the middle distance becoming part of the foregrind where the mass milled and Herr Polizeikommissar Laundrei clasped enchanted Charteris to his postage stamps.

Ordentlichkeit having boots and truncheons won.

So a march began slowly and with bloody eyes and ripgear and straggling struggle to the lock-up all baretoed hepos while by the cobbles a few wooden pudestrials started at the delinquents Herr and Frau Krach and little Zeitgeist Krack who when pushed bobbed up again and soberly registered gut show nodding as the procession hobnobbed to the great slapup HQ with many drivniks still plunching.

Now the harsh bones of that great creature were stone and its flesh mortar and plaster painted democrappic yellow lying in feigned fossil sleep and all its viscerca dark and cool with powerfailure or the awful processes of parquet flooring turning corridors reflected dim outside light entrailing from all surfaces constantly interrupted returning interrupted broken continuous of a special manufacture greylight patent You are no longer awake many things that I said.

The blundering polizei themselves bemused. Pattern of bars no more italianate where the reverie bursts into the old brown building but industrial north dull parallels to close the mind unblown. Clash of bars and swinging blatterplang with no regard ringing unanswerable. The sittlichkeitsvergehen of German standingrheumonly.

Blundering they grey big honey cops with striding arms dull in the confinement space swing swinging to the repetitive doors themselves trapping on the wrong side and commense hammer-cry which the disciples stand dumbfloundered like a whole new range of unfeeling in a brown nearest black till one judy shrieks that they are merely stacked in the corridor. All begin panicake panicake round the shattered vision down or up stone steps or mindless groins digested seeking exit. Bars bars false leads dead ends long vistas dim greylight like a broken circuit entrailing from all sourplaces in the harsh bones time's loot-out rings unanswerable. More cops flushtuate in the hide-and-seek. Now bellies the whole building rangorously. Mindfallen new race rapidly cell-dwells and all anti-flowered. Garish alarms zibbernaut into cavities the grot graves. Life down to the low point of textbook level. Lungs hammer limbs scissor feet clatter in the machineage moment.

Clever guards slamslamslam outer doorment. In the maze long vistas slowly the charterisers clobbered and clapped into parallel cells. The harsh bones cease their crunk but from the lesser interstine sounds an invisible flute.

Entranced by Herr Laundrei's door stood his buddyguard Hirst Wechsel who opened to let in the Herr and Charteris followed to pour them both thin schnapps but Charteris stood amazed to find almost tangible reality transformed into this particular figment with a bare rich squareness of hard black forest wood in even the softer things while the Laundrei cordially explained how the State now malfunctioned owing to the temporary emergency following psycho-chemical spraying on which the scientists of the nation were feverishly working to produce an infallible errorproof arabproof antidope that would guarantee to the race that took it a thousand years of sanitary sanity without deviations in any direction such as weakness brought on among even the most favoured of peoples though of course any old racist theories were long discredited.

'I don't need to tell you as an Englishman that.' Laughing and even Hirst Wechsel operating musculature of a broad grin.

However with the joking aside it must be privately confessed that the malfunctioning of government already touched upon causes certain complications of a legislative nature away and beyond the mere dying of six or seven million fellowcountrymen from famine brought on from lack of organisation at the headquarters perhaps stemming from the lack of discipline at the hindquarters any leadership vital to a dynamic nation and one of these legislative failures was that he here ran his little police force as an independent army you might say.

'What do you mean what you going to do with all my friends in the cells we're no invading army only tourists tourists spreading the light?'

Spreading the light was a happy expression was it not of course one knows that light like all basic things such as shall we say sex is made of hydrogen but one can well imagine this sort of hydrogen-compound-condiment to be spread on ones bread like butter you excuse of I joke and the musculature again mindblowing.

'My friends in the cells?'

All dependent upon Saint Charteris himself. We two would talk it was necessary to establish if you were a genuine leader but if so well here was this modest little army maybe a little barebooted in the shall we say head but knowing well on which side of the condiment their light shone put it together with the crying need for a proper leadership to the country after all you could not be content with genuine messiah to remain head only of those hairy things with people inside a ragged flock of feathered friends like a new animals hopping from instant immobility to instant immobility leaping from the lawn close-clipped to the eaves of the bungalow where the sunset for ever in its ironed mottling how different oh my dear British decline from this a

comic white-uniformed A busy Moscow newspaper man so its necessary to test you if you pass of course all pardons all round but when a
traffic regulation is violated it is after all violated I mean that is basic
philosophy old man eh nicht war.

So comes forth Hirst Wechsel with forms laden for Charteris to fill
while Laundrei quits the room. Sitting at a table in unkindly light he
stares through the lines and dots and little boxes anweisungen defences
against the light take multi-forms of all the forms of dreaming activity
is perhaps the deepest passivity is true guise activity lies and this is the
landt where the truly eat the lotus suffering is permanent obscure and
dark and shares the nature of infinity they even invent the concept of
antisuffering a clever form to conceal real angst and infectious disease
if any suppose I pretended to fall in with his idea might the multi-word
not be spread his clouted clowns all accidentally aid me oh zbogom
the old serpent but my rotten thoughts far from the driving have no
wing-ding next of kin my fruitful angeline something still gets through
perhaps for your stake.

There he wrestled locked mute in the hard Rhenish light till Wechsel
brought him a warm sausage.

'How you love my boss?'

'For me he is just a uniform.'

'Isn't it engorgeous uniform?'

'That's incompatible.'

'I don't think so, I think it suits him a treat White just sets off his
complexion.'

'Off-white.'

'He doesn't exercise enough.' He bent lower so that his labroses were
almost in contact with the folded labyrinths of statement. 'He's more of
a thinker you see. He's a great thinker he has his own laboratory here
I'll show you while he's out come on.'

'This sausage is enough adventure my adversary.'

'Glad you like it but look you see his place here.' It rocked over to
another door flinging wide and beyond again the stark geometry and
pohlar parade of apparatus old Boreas with his realitoys. He shook his
head and commenced resuming the patterplexity of the intraformity
Wechsel hovered.

'He wouldn't mind you seeing it not if I let you I don't quite know how he strikes you but he's really a very kind man indeed a thinker and keeps himself very clean insists that I keep myself clean too finds you lot very unhygienic you're not a real prophet are you you don't somehow look the part I reckon my boss will come up with the solution to the world's troubles I do I sincerely do he works all night sometimes goes without sleep I never saw such a saintly man.'

State blood group and whether you have ever been donor or donator of blood or practised acupuncture.

'He's trying to synthesise Hydrogen 12 that's what he's doing in there synthesis says the Rhine river is the main artery of the body corporate analogous to an actual organism which with a chain contraction would convey Hydogen 12 from source to mouth and thus infect the total statement and spread from Germany out into the oceans until the druplets fructify the mondial globule in profit from his inversion and never no more by any deviation from the correctum orderly way of life you ought to concourse him about it oh it's a real privilege to work for such a splendid man and for such a splendid man and for such a splendid uniformed official man he's marching marching marching of which the human race is capable is caperble is capeer-bull!' All this vocal accompaniment to a sort of sweeping jig about the black-forested room with a lightly pointed jacktoe fluttering and the odd coy pirouette to saint's unheeding back.

Down behind the parallel bars they took some semiphysical jerks at guitars and howled an improvised stave in memory of odour and the wild-headed moment. To the bargemen this music dumped by me over the liquid hydrogen 12 with a fine echoing prison flow as if the great stone creature finally foundered its voice in its tailpiece.

Above all that Meinherr Laundrei revealed himself from under the white parcel and took on oblation in a blackforest-scented bath gristoning with Wechsel to perform the mastaging dry him compulsively and clad him in a flowing white towelling bathrobe with white matching leather-boots erminelined. So came he glowing forth murkless unto his feathery captive now socketted by the deep-eyed window watching natural France gobble off the golden phallus of the sun.

'Before I go to labour all night in my what I jokingly call my private den of stinks – cracklehund Hirst makes with the musculature – you and I Herr Charteris will have a discussion on philosophy and the sexual dynamic for in this little beleagured miniskirt of empire where we repel the frontiers with jockstrips against such penny barbarous tribes as the cascaders penisenvy sagacity as whores hardon to come by.' Coughing clearing throttle wattle and daubed crimson uncontrollable freudian slipway fazing him.

Groping in drawer of desk sitting down heavily letting robe flap bringing out in fist mighty cigars. 'Pardon, we must be good buddies and talk with proper form and usury, nict war. Have a nice big Lungentorpedo.'

'Don't use tobacco.'

'Well, you should. Smoke always smoke keeps me calm in this duration of stress yes yes very good for the nerve scenters and concentrates the mind on the objection – here take one!'

'I don't use the stuff!'

'We will see who uses it and who doesn't. Hirst get the Schnapps!'

'Immediately master.'

'Hurry you fool!' He stood glowering in towelling the boy came and trembling poured two measures from the bottle then adroitly downed the measure through an open throat calling simultaneously for more and shouting for one for Charteris.

'It's just prison poison.' Tipping it on the wood floor.

'Insulting dog!' He swinging a ham in clever textbook demonstration of anatomical leverage connecting with physiognomy of seated opponent with consequential impact subsequential entropyloss carrying victim off chair continuity of energy in previously steady state universe. 'That will teach you when your betters try to show you courtesy men in dirty rags have to be polite and look after their manners in good order now get up!'

He rises against gravity and the giantkiller smokes himself back into better humour behind grey self-made curtain haze finally saying, 'Now we will discuss privately my sex problems in absolute confidence. Hirst kindly make yourself scared. You see for a man like me in the very power of my prime and pink used to violent exercise and and shall we say such constant hobbies as swordplay and horseriding even since extreme infancy for my grandfather and father harsh men and great believers in mortification and also if I say so with all modesty both genitalmen were profound thinkers and unrecognised scientific genius who may yet save the world beginning with our own blessed soil – come I show you about my stinks den as I talk – and these rare gifts also going gland in glove with great administrative qualities and strong gift of leadership – Hirst!'

'Sir!' Anxious nose only round door executing own cute disarming bow and the musculate animate.

'Have I not strong gifts for leadership?'

'The strongest and for what it's worth a really kind man indeed a thinker –'

'Go! You're discharged!' Marching into the laboratory waving his torpedo like a wand at the alchemaic impedimenta lowering voice to his own reverence, 'All these rare qualities Charteris rare qualities and yet how shall I say. Though I am so bushy with all these schemes I am tornamented by the synthesis of the flesh the sins of the flesh and in this as in all things I am outrageous and priapic it is a torment to me for how can I be holy its the one aspect of leadership I perceive imme-diately that you have and I have not for its the sex centre perpetually overheating and my degenerative organ perpetually tumessing. Naturally once I have mangled to synthesise my Hydrogen 12 and release it in the Rhineflow then all such tortures can be extirpanted and we stump out sex altogether it rolls us with a rod of iron stump it out you hear' – he tripped over a snaking cable and grasped the workbench. 'In a properly functioning world this random element will not be introduced but till then in my torment I ask you what sort of help you are a seer and prophet can give me that is an order I give for the positive assistance of mankind and in exchange my assistance on future.'

'Would the truth awaken you or your serpent?'

'I am a depraved man though a hero and savant and great leader. You see I confess without jurisprudence! Save me from that snake-in-my-grass I need your truth.'

'It is import to know if you have the Kundalini –'

'Yes yes I admit I have practised that vile sin and fallen into many fellacious ways so how am I to lead if I am led by my unruly part.'

Gurdjieff also that sly old city shaman in his worn slippers smiled under his moustache at similar questions always coming back – eternal recurrence and the nostalgia of constantly repeated for people of lost possibilities who had drawn away into a deeper dust. His truth could be told to Laundrei in such a way as to defeat him and keep him in G & O powerlessness.

'Sex is a normal and natural way to horness energy and create further possibilities in the organisms. Being alpervasive like hydrogen it forms one of the main springs of the multivalued and self-creating fuzziness so we find philosophicantly that everything people do connected with sex-politincs reliction art theatre music is all sex. People go to the theatre or church or sport event not for its own sake but simply because there in the crowds of men and women is the centre of gravity of sex. That's why people go to any meeting or occasion or rally. You are merged each more than you note in a general empathy. So you see sex is the principal motive force of all mechanicalness. Hypnosis depends upon it. So you must ledgerdemise more room for this extralactivity among your other rattributes so become more mechanical.'

'So!' Dragging in a fever on the torpedo sucking down the smoky poison of the GO-warning. 'So! Mechanicalness yes the great modern force all working with the beneficiency of the machination. That is how it will be under hydrogen eration! We'll strop this nonsense of astral bodies then and the whispering anoise of spirituality – only physical bodies aloud hen. You are right. I will be glad and make myself machinelike.' He strode up and down. 'Hirst!' Hirst. 'Hirst be a good boy take this saint and lock him up in a singlecell then first thing tomorrow we will make one last little testicle and see how the godhead manages miracles.'

As they paced through the dim stonebone maze Wechsel said, 'I don't know what you did to him but I can tell he's going to be a devil tonight I'm half scared to go back there his rod of iron!' Leaving Charteris in a dark locked place returning to his manchine.

Charteris lying back recalled as best he could the immortal conversation and foxy old G saying to his disciples that mechanicalness was the destroyer as he well knew and sex was not mechanicalness when itself and not masquerading – pure when pure evil when self-deceiving – and here he had helped in the disintegration of Laundrei in real G style by getting him on a sterile trackway.

*

Once recurrent more experience of night in which a planet rounds its imagrained edges and sky blancks like an eyelid or the minds downcast clearing hevens daze echoes playback the dischard progrimm in drems highspield Discofete

But steamputteed kommandant made brief apparition at his bunk-side to announce to Charteris half-awaken yar the saints worms of advice will be utilised to tranceform the polizei more mechanical he must also himself become roboterotic marshalling already phallis-callthenics for daily parage. Drill square all pressure and corrupt piston pulling pushing with electonic force jackoff-booted polizei will present forearms per zent fore ARMS perfect eunision now massturbashing on the march commense updown updown keep the tumessence there you in the rear wank that man links links links reckt links moonlight moonlight stick out your chesticles there prick up the undressing in front no shooting before I give the command shoot or there will be someone up on a dishcharge

So the penal square shakes to footdrilling objection of personelity like the sparse wilderness pillowing forth and all the prairie under plough cracking thorowing up fooldrilling objects anjy

old coffins craking ramshack doors grimd open where look grabbling mummies of skeletall desire the nocterning dead hold to themselves weathered wallflowers in sepia phornogravure with my lurching steps forced farce-to-farce grim-croaking incumberland heavies waddled I barely foot it down into trumpery old decade church protestine that the sign mislaid my tread shell of smellarage

furflying estumnal dust all all round all excrusimation of the impalid rose out ostone damp damp sump turannean roomour me my arms outstranked shaden light shaden light makes motet anthemist clearing reviles three of the gravure mumbos jumble fearwards at me futhorks in their scrulls two intently loading on me trumperished rainment with schoden goods hairglooms one whose armoured hanks all sack-wristed one a serafemale in the old embroidered light and third fligger blackly small in fumireal drapery transponting water before him flauting to transfuse me from this fissure I at his viscage of necromerey cream I with object tennor openjewl before the three am earn rem ream cream scream screaming

He startled up at shaking shoulderhand and there was his penumbral cell and Herr Laundrei amoured in white no colour anywhere from dreams. The oiled daze echoes pluckback of shady freudulence.

'You – creaking out holy man all down the passage don't toll me your nightmars!'

'They were three here –'

'I I have watched and parayed all nightlong now morning climes again and I must make a last taste of you.'

'What do you know of disintegrayment and the night's boil down'

'Dawn and the test-down for you holy howling man!'

Charteris pushed aside the rancid blanket and stiffly stood at the end of his spare of implements. Nobody spoke or thought of food mindgruel was concentrated on leverage of limb and closed probability.

So clammy-early it was in the great stone creature that men lay bedburied in the gravy of yesterday only the kommandant and Charteris burned two sallow candles of constriction. Starextinguishing light here laid its loot aside and stood mourning on stony vigil. As they descended greyshot down stonesteps from the cells no waking sounds splashed. Although my snuffering bids me stay. Out by a small rear door stabbed by foggy chill with brainwitchingday sulking the cobbled stains end gutter round the yellow corner to confront the bleak new year of morning with a wide submersed expanse flat wash of water chimera on which adrift a phlotasm of opalque edifices.

Black maimed thing rising from the closed front steps bulging towards them gestures and some tone returns.

'Angelune! In disembroidered night you waiting for a skiff on this translucid tide to the far world-weather.'

She ransacked and clung to him her stark touch finding him substantial. 'Colin, darling. Oh Colin, you did come for me I knew you would! They said there was a state law against women having babies in prison – "No women allowed to have babies in state prison" as if it was okay for men – so they locked me out – I've been in some state –'

'It's the crossroads they nail us just this marlarky day.'

'Colin I've been so frightened –'

'Malady love we're all nervended the least of worries in this imposition.'

Herr Laundrei spoke firmly, 'We are busy, lady. Stand back, enjoy your compulsory freedom while it has you or there will be worse trouble we can always eject you back across the rational frontier. Stand back.'

'Wait I'll be retiding.' He turned towards the misty Rhine of low points to avoid her gravied eyes. 'On such a morning like water flowing from everyone's head the old hopeless human thing that made misery humantic.'

'Stand back from him, woman!'

He a thing seen with no direct looking always looming trailing scented metallic dust seizing of joints and the nervending christendoom of the epoch.

'Colin, leave this crimped luniform let's get away – Colin you hear me? What speedy offence are we supposed to?'

'Ploughed up mummies grappling in the density of this nether atmosphere demanding me if I own the upper tributes.' Or with full-bellying sail becalms my prowed course into the lumonstricity.

Kommandant with slicing motion fends her off uttering low counter-revolutionary cyclic sounds designatory of machinery and with his grasp quick leftrightleft motorvates his figurehead forwards through the pall across with every step the verge the lined lanes of astrobahn the marchens of the wide crewcut embanks the ruhig waters of dark-thighed Rhine all veiled by low uncertain mornlight

Here the phull-dicked imaginings of galaxies lie raped to ashes.

Now I embark with each step on a new voyage these patterned halls know that entranced exits lie cell-to-cell and on these horning ghats ripples ever spreading outwards to the banks of death my personality strikes to every second of time's encompassment with the ouspenskian eye drowsing in light of this multipacity infinite riches of a god one human tread.

Quailed from their male abrogation she as always fell back into her second reposition stood in the vast vacancy of space and her long submission drowned unknowing. To amend her carped deforces she preened the cressfallen hair glaring in a shard of mirror I had this in Phil's day his days my fizzog without the equality of Elsbeth well that's what Mum always used to say I'd never be what my brothers were he doesn't think enough of me I wonder why I hang around like I do honest I did try to break in to prison to reach you Col do my best I'm not a bloody saint you know. ...

On dark grey muscles Loreldrei mechs to the edge of the shrouded flood and beckons stands ramrigid in the rigmilrole and utters 'I do believe you are a divine leader come again to lead and you shall find me pillar of discipline rather than discussion greater the force the more obedience demanded test myself to the utmost as we gather in intensity and momentum with all inner conflicts canalised and final unification I will be the new man of steel in your crusade but to you saint John beloved disciplin bare to beat about and a whipping boy to all else steelsteel your right hand man march and convert and "Hydrogen 12 molecularising the regiments of converts and no sex but autosex the machineries" again restore correct government superstricture everywhere under one leader for united world realisation of paradise.'

Thus grandiloquently gesturing he might himself have advanced buoyantly upon the flood so ravelwrapped in the heavy swaddle of futurity or peering into more than mist. But checked himself on the bank and elevated both hands for the pelissed shore.

'Give the last proof I need walk across to neutral Frank shore and back again on the waters! Show me a miracle!'

He Charteris peered into the mist of all precarious passages one perhaps no more than others or bird's flight unmarked through solvent air the golden hind through antipodean mazes seeing self-photographs peel off in fluttering disarray disgorging by hair's gesture from the previous one with he the unknown triggering agantdealer. Which way was forwarmths? In this multi-perceptual cosweb was there still again as in the old maths world a unirection? Or he autostarring across a fresh infirmament? How many discarded duplicants of time how many sparky charges switched their currents turned awry or this big chance mist and he here in obscurity and discard with the sun set for ever its last rays caught in mottled iron further he for ever here in obscurity and discard with the vacant headlights fixed across that flood with something dear going down to cross to cross!

But wet feet? Webbing?

Walking.

And bursting out of the old limits.

Disintegrating and redissembling beyond the old disloccasion.

The assumed world had its own appuisances. From the dodgy vapours buaterknifed one blunted braid of sun among the clipped bank trees.

Lit the couched vampours. Lit the nightflushed Rhinebow. Lit a figure striding on the far bank Charteris in a black mack sly and dry spectral!

Staring double glaze of Laundrei tottering on the brink.

The figure looking back and signalling.

Charteris transfixed in terror, *Jebem te pas mater!* the horrors still my damned slavonik addled acid head of schizogod!

Optic skull thought pertifozzing up through eystrils and morifices crapulolsar welkanschauung

end in beginning's mouth serpent tail in serpent's mouth

my cerebelly mindwind blowing it

fling yourself in and drown this false baptistry of self this tripped pretence.

But Laundrei screaming with a forged belief cried Paradise closed his eyes

fell two paces to the left

revelation

vision triumphing over event

Gibbering sprawling he fell to the ground spotted the master's feet clutched his ankles splurged his pedestrian kisses there crying as if all contractions were miracles and madness an escape from self. Then reeling up he took to his own heels and plodded automadly back to Polizei HQ.

Angeline with feathers in her lair moved thinly through the washout bearing her female burden and kneeling by him on the cobbles gazing down on man's first disobedience and the fall-out of our mortal minds lifted his head from the rhinestone and cradled it.

'Oh my exile darling how the splashes flecked me from the down and you too on the very verge my love my lover love.'

'Angela listen what alternatives. ... Either I walked across the water or else we are finally ruinous of the mind and gluttony starting at the head fleshes out my phantasms.'

'There there my love we all must fight our way in and out the misticuffs remember it's the PSA bombs isn't it we're only human.'

'Are we any more? Is Serbia sunk? What effects who knows for sure any more than when the first brain blossomed who was there to cry for Kossovo. If that effect gives new alternatives I may have walked across the water and be mad the same time.'

'We'll get away we'll go away I'll be good to you. South it's Switzerland and the cooler air less loony-lunged.'

'But perhaps I must counter terms with what I am or else stand starving at my own feast. This polizei man with his sagging wrists and lungentorpedos will escalcade me to the flowerpitching streets of capital cheering and I in blessing raised above the motorcade my hand over all more multivalued in their addleation crying Charteris Paradise and liberating them all their eyelids autolipped with my celestine kiss and my driving words echoed at every diestamped intake.'

'Colin it's not for you just temptation of a family form. You remember how they godded you.'

'My hand in the altobreasted egocade raised in motivalue over every man's addle.'

'Not you not you my love. You still distinguish truth at heart!'

'And spreading my parts foreverywhere Charteris – the only but is but can I go where they have godded me when the green sparkling fuse of belief burns in their mansions not mine! That's my question not yours no one loots me. What happens when the contagion comes from them to me and not from me to them will I tire of its simplicity their cheers merely a form of invalid silence?'

On the old backterial bed his wise big toe wagged to the moultitude.

He sat up bedraggled and round their human shoulders the shawls of mist drew away in sepia although underground the new animals in rotted lead rodded and rutted in obscurity.

'Stay with me privately away from chariots my lovebird keep on our autocade into the cool bewildernesses of the Alps.' I too have my presentiments to express and he could have been stark to the fanaticides of marching menchen a word of leadership the old ambitions gleam its better a ruined mind than the old agonisms they still wait by the reeded bank and that flat white sluggy bastart. 'Colin you take that escalading way into the capital with clouds of cheering fantiks and they'll *crucify* you.'

'I creamed openjewlled at his vision over the water but the chance is just variable. Stop riding me. Woman be more multi!'

'Don't jeer at me who's in the family way by you you'll go the way of all saviours and they'll crucify you. They always need another crucifixion. There's never enough for them!' Tears bursting now.

He turned his twilight into her pregnant eyes at the disturbulence there transfixtured by her word. 'Is it another eternal recurrence then? Series of fake christs on series of faked crosses? How's the multiplicity figure?'

Her head shook the ragged locks of it like dishabitation. 'Don't ask me Colin my old dad was a methodist. He used to spout like Christ had a new idea of individual salve instead of massalve so they killed him because my old dad said we weren't really individual yet – that sort of spiritual crap.'

'The capitualism of God's son with his loser takes all and blessed are the earth-grabbing meek. Gogetting what you have you hold like the world's big dealers but that's all done now. Wesciv's chunks fall off. The individual's chunks fall off. Nothing holds.' He looked to the sunken ground in wan contemplay with cheeks shagged to pick at his appearing toe.

She touched him. 'Even for a faked christ it's real death's real isn't it so? You didn't want to die – didn't in Brussels.'

The blackmacked figure dry and inspectral in the mindwind.

He glared swift murder at her like a dowsed headlight.

Standing he found which side of the river he stood and surely never on that neutral shore a trick of light still puzzling his mindfit miracle. Under the sawn plane trees he coldly said to her 'Go and sprout by stone dam of dross I want to think.'

You pulverise the mere shadow of cerebral shade she cried at him but then less bitterly with an clouded smile not to torture himself or believe she would not wait. Why did she never give her animal feelings full rein? More and more what it was he wanted seemed denied or she herself likewise with no refuge in full psychotomimicry.

The parallel bars still had a whichsidedness and that morning at wurst-time the mix-up again occurred so that captor and captive could not determine their roles except by elaborate reference beyond their bother. They fed well and in the pale pulped meat anyone could spit out the odd punctueating fingermail helped on by pepper seasoning and nature's which-sideness of eater-eaten question.

On the dull air any bruised noses healed and oiled calm of illusion deadened buttons that otherwise shone spite. The big heavies had hepos inside which slowly rolled to fuzzier beats as they warmed to acid freakuency one polizei sang moonjune songs four hours at a standing.

It was anything time to undergo the elemental rituals of friendship that mystical state where reservations stand their sharp points in the corner and fires blurr in a common grate.

Some of them unbuttoning their tunics revealed amazing feats of tatotemism etched in tomato pink and inkblink blue where one glimpsed disembedded legs pierced hearts tangles of thorns weeping faces famous negroes dripping daggers mercedes battleships obscene inscriptions and butterflutes gothickly growing round breast or gristle so Gloria screamed from underneath 'Ooh this bloke's body's his mindmap!'

All untold the fey atmosfuddle of selforiented libidoting wooze trix-fixed the constabulary into poets longhaired boxers instrumentalists vocalists meditationers on a semisyllable card trick-exponents voyeurs of the worlds box word-munchering fellowsophere semi-lovers of course with the greatest pretensions wrackonteurs charmers butchboys frenchmen twokissing mystics like-feathered nestlings vanvogtian auto-biographers laughers chucklers starers stargazers villagers and simple heart-burglars all seeing themselves shining in their hip-packet mirrors.

Often they spoke of Charteris he had their licences. The wind blew from his direction but Ruby and the group had their baffles up. Music took on a shield of all blows.

At the same time a dead leaf whisked through the circle of vision over the step and was gone into the darkness that always surrounded the circle of vision. But none of the watchers any longer cared for the old movements.

To these unguarded guards now came packed and stamped Laundrei with his Hirst Wechsel perched on an epaulette squealing he 'Heraus heraus' and Paulette 'Up you tumbling bitches' all over the brothel-mongering assheadquarters to sprinkle them across the parryground.

Soon the ribble-rabble were hearing the glad news of stentorian tone glandruffling immensity Charteris was son of god and would groove a hand in the march on Frankfurt and Bonn and Berlin estabellish a new odour and cheers from the unbelieving believers saving on to Moscow what about Moscow assisted of course by his pop those present and the secret weapong Hydrogenous 12 and and new ornamated selfrepelled Supersex mascodistic marchers but whatever the band played each had his own tune.

'These hyenas no longer have any respect for the state,' angrily crying Laundrei.

'Nor the individual either' – Wechsel turning into a cockatoo and brightly fluttering into the tropical foliage underhead.

Under the sawn-off planes he passed with a certain tread certain tread certain tread patterning their well-drawn branches spick span spick span how long to pass this one memorise its meaning shape how long to pass this one memorise its meaning shape how long to pass or its internal shape the banal is grotesque

    these trees automated in their neat dressing

    roots ploughing through eternal metal and asphalt cracking

    three old figures cryptic

    robing me robbing me

    the lights of other daze

    grotesque is trees with their winter crewcut

    into each second the eternal nanoccurrences of isness and these trees is there just one tree I keep perceiving as I permeate more of the metzian webtime or all particles of myself springing from me on random time trajectories

all the words I have said or spoken were minced of my blood my semen my moan-barrow of weeping tissue in disinegation

what is I in truth is in their locality not here

trees ruin me too particular

and the specified woman

anonymous

all anonymous that felty well in the lanquid dark against thighs of unknown speech and every faculty distended to some farther shore like aface with nothing personal in it just the big chemical loot-in of eternal burn-down in the nerved networks and elastic roadways of me is the traffic passing for thought but this eternal recurrence of trees signals me that no decision is possible that decision is impossible for everything will come again back to the same centre

alternatives must be more multi-valued than that I either go with Kommandant on his hosanno dominotion or speed with Angel south but if one crossed martyranny if the other another series of eitherors with death always the first choice

somewhere find a new word new animal

transgress

in their heads they have only old words

insisting that history repeats itself

the stale hydrogenes of a previous combustion rolling in an old river and elder landscape footprinted to the last tree gnarled landscape of I stamped flat by the limbous brain

its their behaviour and its geared experience is lessening and cuts me down to sighs morality nostalgia sentiment closure falsight all I have to drive through their old faded photograph of life

how that crumbling nightdream thunderclouds round my orizons

He looked up hand on the trunk of the last tree before the square opened heavy swaddled and spring held jacknifed in the winds.

Growing in the Rhine perspective was fumirealdrapery sly and dry figurative –

the confruction? the momentum of truth?

It grew and in the daggered sublight clearly personed the familiar was the merely familiar Crass the once-agent exdrapist pusher scamp-follower lost or fled when Brussels blurned showing his teeth now in a smile of grating.

'The eternal returns' said Charteris. Up and down the bare bole spring's first flies crawled across the corse of winter. Over the supplicatory amputree they hastened towards infinite points of intersexion and in the top cropped branches thudded his great blackmacked bird leashing its vulturine feathers claws beaks calling through its raw red wurst of neck.

'Master forgive me you must have thought my feet were in the eternal flying dust and the impaled rose from my sumpturanean stool.'

'I don't want to talk of decay.'

The fustian feathers held a small vibration. 'Who knows what will talk or decay when all people your paradise of multivalour. I have kept under my wigspan and my grations led me here to you. Your servant still.'

'I don't want to talk Cass so come down from that Judas tree the looming decision of all direction and to make something new devise from under that old moustache while the wescivilians of lost possibilities drawn into deeper dusk where the parallel bars have no in or out.'

So Cass took his arm and said, 'I know of your systemstrain. You're hung up on a curve. Earlier when the mists were shipping to the tugladen mouth I saw and signalled you across the flux but you had other directions. I am too poorly without potension to flutter up into your tree of notice but you are as rich as a new Christ in populous and you must not park here by the rivenstribe but autocass on to domination and the world your word.'

'Cass off! Back into the bare branches!'

'No I tell you winging the way to my master your humble serpent boarded with an old widowed impoverished official who in his long-rowed rooms above the Alzette ravines lodges two coachdrivers and a filling station owner he tells me how the continent fills into small strifes for lack of leadership –'

'Cass –'

'Speak at the world's megaphone Master. These small strifes are your larger battlefield or the states your pulpit. Pay the big taxi fare to a Rome address! Talk out the lungs cancer. Rocket right up the lordly astralbahn. Flush the worlds motions into your own bowl and I'll back you.'

The door of the big square refrigerator burst open as Angeline came in upon her metatarsals her chicken bones and plum eyes and the whole different meaning of sunlit succour sumpt.

'Hello Cass I thought we'd lost you doing the suttee act in sparky Brussels.'

Lips bone-infested – 'You still campfollowing you widowed mite!'

'Colin the fat commander is letting the boys unlocked in a sort of panjandramonica and what are we going to do?'

Flighting off the carrion cross he took her and half-kissed her murmuring nonnegotiably relishing the bold bare bones in her like branches.

'Oh Angeline I see you're among the favoured yet I wish you'd tell the master to unpack his oysterand smash the saviour-part into a real cruscade.'

'That's all nonsense. We're trying to turn into human beings first Cass and don't need your snow-job for aid.'

Beady he preened among his black scales. 'Body's so womanish and nothing beyond. You want him all to yourself don't you you selfish bitch but times change and he's got nothing to lose it's not like I mean the Germany's not the Holy Land in any sense –'

But blank. World of total silence. Box off. A last mind-bowing disloca-tion. He had his fix with the elemental and the deep dischian roots under the eternal subsurface where they sleepwalked and the elegant connec-tions between love and death. He saw through. Dropped. Turned human.

To them he grew bearded beaded and feathered. Primal. Behind them the old grey square and fineformed town hall of an earlier clockage rich in history sauce now served in bright plumage as it flowered to his wisdom.

'Listen the multi-valued answer. All resolved. I had it in my dream aiming down the old clothes.' Thai mute in his wonderment so she asked him darling?

'Whatever you all think you think you all think in the old stale repeating masadistrick Judeo-Christian rhythm because its in your bloodshed. Your heritage taken or rejected dominant Be rich as Christ indeed. But Croesus Christ is to me pauperised an old figment and just another capitalist lackey whose had our heads isn't it? It's the histiric recess over and over a western eternal recurrence of hope and word and blood and sword and Croesus vitimises your thinkstreams.' Continued in this blastheme of Christ Plutocrat schekelgrabbing bled-white chris-tendamn till Cass fluttered.

'I don't believe in him either Master you know that.'

'No difference. History jellied and you can't drip out. You're hooked in his circuit and the current circulates.' Bigger than the first tiny Metz web so it grew in his mind another layer yet of Europlexion and walking along Troitsky Street he saw the old dimensions all shagged out and Christ on the clockwork cross with in his sly brown eyes that frantic glimpse of progress on the astralplane and from our deathbeds that vanvogtian upward surge into heaven's arms. The cult of the third day the White House open to any mother-loving son. All transdacted in the following lanes to metaphysical materials of the insurance steam shovelling society and the space race.

Heaven is money in the bank. Your cash helps our cathedral. Jesus saves his flesh negotiable anywhere.

'Colin love the world doesn't just begin anew my baby will have to have the past to build on and rebuild.'

'Breathing the old west dust and breathing out the old west dust. No. That old ethic-ethnic LSD has automated us two thousand years and now the fracture there's been a mislocation so let's jump it from the steamcross and say for ever farewell to that crazy nailedup propheteer. Look girl I don't refuse to go your way or refuse to go Laundrei's way or refuse to go Cass's way or refuse to go any way. I refuse to hit the worn-out Creased or anti-creased way. For me new tracks and stuff the old ding-dong the belfry-belt.'

Cass laughing poorly, 'No no if there's an opportunity you get in first that's nature!'

She was shaking her head running her toe in the dust as if tracing out a hieroglimpse of some secret there.

'You're mad Colin. Honey it not just Christ and all that it's a bit different for you cos you're a Serb there are mountains in between but the West thing we're still on a Greek trajectory of ordering knowledge Phil told me that.'

'The Greek thing was okay but it would have got nowhere without the sufferinfusion of our nazerining friend embodying the rags to riches poorman's son outalk outsmart white-house-in-the-sky trouble-stirring miracle-working superman and then pow-wow-kersplat-but-oh-boy-on-the-third-day punchline echoed ever since by every comicstirup.'

'Master Master you can't change all that.' Trembling out a little reefer and suckling on a long light in viperbeak. 'Only through leading. You can't change history. We're what we are.'

'We're also what we're not. See Cass I can't change the churn of history but it changed itself when the sprinkler-bombs came now we live in a wornout mode and the old Glenn Miller musicrap still canting us out of a new canticle in the old worn wesciv groove.'

'Maybe you're right. Lead us only away Master we'll follow in blind belief!'

'Leading is out makes blindness and the old swingdom of heaven is just slopporific. Opium of the pupil.'

She saw him new on a fought decision. She saw him. She saw he saw himself. He saw himself new. Still lying but deeper lies? Mirror distortions embedded? Every moment its equivocation like a tile pattern she saw him new. In the omniparacusis she heard him defrock Christ. A womb-shelled thing broke and bled. She stood outside herself her scars her incompletion. Her first vision of the current time explosure.

From Cass's ears smoke poured and the tiny chambers even the metatarsals in a big big scald like the church of England burning up its bullion of belief and he craftily slipping out of the transvestory vanishing into the haze as if exorcised.

She had been conjured. Limply by one arm taking him she moved up to a nearby passing mountain and there cried solemn anger that he ploughed up every midnight corpse that ever fell to make them die again for his psychosis. Charteris laughed knowing she had never seen inside a church. She swore. The oaths in banners marched the mountainside. She owned her aggression at last. She had born him long enough his womanising his slobishness his selfhood and the godding. Now he must cut his act to play a human off-stage role.

He pushed her. 'Tour act comes from the same cass pageant the cult of individuals but it's a mass life and death get it? Phases not people! Drop out that's all, Angelbird. Dig that everything else has already dropped. Play to a new music right and dance to another measure down your long within. Cass off and shack with Ruby or take me on my own road but I cant stand halfway up this mutterhorn.'

Scratching her head covering up sad for all losses she alone locatered for. 'Its Cass Colin Cass I'm afraid of you're so helpless he just a paracide to any order he might do for you you know he emanates the old iscarrot role. If the present's already past like you say Cass'll have you nailed.'

People were coming he heard and was glad to distract her.

He gestured to the band as they materialised into the plass. 'I've the job for Cass.'

Jailgates gaped wide and the tumblebellies on the bangle-drums were all in advance with brashing autos percussed cymballically all heads on the anonymass.

So now he warmed on the ticking of another prayer wheel turning in his stream and all the faces blowing to him were with their petals and the bloom of youthair cheeking them. So now was he no crusoed a toottall further in this islanded desertion and some would carry onto his farshore. So now though his carriage had never taken him beyond the stony trees he sent his mark scudding across the printless beaches. So now he grew her elbowing arm as the force pressed at the instress of his radiance.

Hurryburlying Laundrei came on the surge with the autociples but Charteris stopped them. Climbed onto a bench under a sign that told the miles to Frankfurt old cosy sign made metal from the long attic store in thought. Waved his arms caught cheers. People scuddling like leaves under his farsight the whole seas surge of them.

Told them: I was in another vision. I broke free and discarded myself my former selves my sleep chained L.

Here through me the world tumbled to a new terminator.

Here we begin a new age the postpsychotomimetic age free from anshirt shittoleths and the grey grimmages stripped off.

Here the old programming of Godspain got its long last playback in the searoots of our occulture.

Here the nails scattered from my hands and fingers.

In the square they milled and sledded letting their origins down with mood music thrombic. The body hair buttressed and limbs rebuddied Metamorphin slipper waker-slip. What they heard they herded and sluice-juices ran underfoot As he luted their animinds. Ages went down into oceanic undertow. Civilians poured in and the old grey and biscuit buildings titaniced down into a glacial cobblesea. Inunvation of hands, plattening feet of limbic brand. Churning flowermotion with eddying scruffles sob-streperous among the onebacked beats.

To one side apart Ruby with an own thing to peddle. Also Elsbeth sailing all in selfmassage grown apart her two stout legs foliaging flesh belonging to the fused moment under the strain of canvas her salience gybes to generationing point her wild delicacy a sapiutan as she fixes on him rattling from his orificial platform.

Now from his purgent words the mucous remembranes of the sinking swimmers distend to farcy forms and the saprophagous outpour transfluxes the time's ergot so that while it floats into her labyrinthine passages she feels the smooth buddoming trunks and timber shafts wheel and wheedle into grander growth in her skeleton the sapling stalked stuff supplanting bone nodes of branch staring under skin at hip and pelvis shin breast and elbow her obnubil features suddenly the whole unatomy its soft syruped holes its husks hairs and horned teeth beats

into greenamelled leaf!

Laundrei always more antiflowered broke his spate asked 'What's the vision on when we move to conquer?'

'The broken off gods chumble over into obscrudity –'

'Okay, very satisfactory to know but there's still the Berlin question.'

His old sly smile. 'Now its your blastoff down the astrabahn to the straits of power while the wind blows favourable on your high traject. All go who will and nobody constrained in any form. I stay here. Our photographs peel separate here.'

'No' – ship without figurehind and he launched into the long machineries of a vocal gripe while others also had their temperature and again mazed denizens pander to the labyrinths until finally Charteris barks again.

'It was my vision Laundrei you astracade it while it just sustains me while you image yourself into your machine-dream-role.'

'*Scheisskopf!* You haven't the face to back your prognosis!' Hirst fluttering and swatching behind with birdlife gestures of ascent.

'You take with you my second-in-commandant the Cass here as my man in your camp.'

'Wechsel is my aide-de-camp.' Peaching his plumage.

'Cass makes liaison. Cass your new commander keeps him in a mind of miracles the claws pruned and darkness at the ninth hour.'

Dark brown pantry eyes glistering up the mottled cliff of medalled white seeking lodgement, 'Meinherr glad to be of service and tote the –'

'Action man and the junkered footfill all autobreasted with all joints in my pistongrip right? Right. It's a decision then. Herr Charteris we go to escalade in the name of glory and unity. We shall meet again. Men! Men! Follow men! Action! Scramble! Form paltroons! Clap to ventricles! Astrabahn and utopia!' Cass and Wechsel astraddlediddle as the revvrevv-revving struts and pattern merges from the millrace.

'Hydrogen 12 be with you' pronounced.

Saluters.

Now espousing their autos the deutschlanded gentry marry boot to rod hand to bar knee to rod bum to seat helter to skelter in a barrackroar of infective warcalls. The autocaders also spark their plugged enzymes and batter backwards into the crass planes curling bumpers and blue monoxide wolves through the pack like feral all everyone legs or wheels like tight little humans under hair astride. But Army Burton comes to Charteris. 'Hey you want your little master race girl any longer?'

'The name?'

'Your little master race girl Elsbeth?'

'She Jewish'

They used to call that the master race.

No that was the Germans.

I forgot. Another world. You want her.

You want her you take her you going on with Laundrei?

Also Ruby Dymond in human shape to Angeline grasping her hand in oldworld form moving her behind a treebole.

'Is this straight Charteris is hiving off on his own do I read the thing right?'

'Ruby he's straightening out past the world. Who knows this chemifect may all wear off in a few days and old time start up again so I stick with him and see he doesn't get himself killed in the general curfuffle.'

His furtive shrugs of pain the hurt deep under a moist pelt. 'But he tried to kill you honey – look leave him he's got nothing for you the disintegration man himself and you with me so cosy.'

'Sometimes he's kind to me maybe all I deserve.' Now from the long brackets of her inherited eyes spark the first tear.

'You all screwed up, Angey, honest I hate to see you be done down and come off with us!'

His secret words fended her. Drawing up, wiping off her wet nose on a handback, she says in bitter tone, 'Don't mix me up Ruby if he needs me I can't help it!'

'So you said about Phil and now this same mistake all over! Honey I beg I got to go the others are rolling now come on and this last time break your unlucky cycle!'

Stilly with a crumpled face, 'Ruby – Ruby – he needs me!'

'I need you, he tried to kill you!'

'Well he's desperate!'

Of a sullen the wild ox sprouted under his eyebushes, 'Oh fuck you you silly stubble bitch!' and with that he was bending his giant back among the common melée with all commotion. All were multi-backed to fusilage along dead reckoning; Army only faced the demasted master.

Looking around at the hoofers and the revvobiles with the groups starting up the Famineers and Deutchofiles and a quick brainscan. We got to orient with the action dont let grass go under our teeth eh its a lawn of asia.

Briefly they made palmhistry. High road. Low road. Scotland afore ye. Never meet again. There we all parted. Franfurt sign. Poxeaten poxibilities. Army farewell.

So the acceleration of mechanical joybox and the old foot-down thirst of essolution. Jerk of cerebral juices destiny carvorting down the long within and the crazy internal Kilometrage a brown near black instressed masteracing. On the bumpers nestled the new animal plural in solidity and near life as the pinballing progress meshed from the plass. Lopped tree lopped tree lopped tree lopped tree lopp tree stood ruinously neat the clibbered rectungstone cobbles tie red rodentures of the town hall biting sky the buildings semisubmerged on their shoals and all else on a low primevil light as wheels bore tribe dust smoke noise away dying sullen. In the lime embedded lost lingerers sank to the fossil mouth under drab oolite.

The natives of the tableau mooched across the tattlefield or on fours dragged off the injured. Small dogs were there tearing at fingers and jugulars as life slumped back to textbook level. Two figures stood anonymously round the Frankfurt sign. Buildings burned with the cool air-burling flames of time.

Beneath this conbastion in shelfence sank the bronto-structures the rathaus and gaunt grandosaurs down under the cobblesea without windowed strata still chronsuming themselves and on the tide big stone forests bursting green and all verdure trumpling brack out the Rhine to what was in uttered mindchaos downwards.

The saint with Angelina executing the bipedal homosap walk on the way to the banshee all yellowspeckle as of toads bellyupwoods squeeping to right themselves and chunks falling off the western wold where the alternatives feralled. The car lumbering and she mutely asking where drained from her own sacrifice.

'Where?'

'He'll swing to destruct with self-inflected Cass and all.'

'I asked you where you think we going.'

'And all the music-muckers with them to the endless ends they clave all dreaming they aren't dreaming in Kundalini-coils,' under the sediment of long custom embedded Looking ahead at the rockwalls, tyres tweeting on curbstones.

'You don't care a bit what happens to them Col do you!'

'A new continuum has to alp itself from the screenery and potentiality is low from old corpses so mulch the old trodisues out of the worldbody.'

Her young face shrunk back to its ultimate socket. 'You hate everything!'

'Schweitz doesn't line my inscape baby we'll push east ... Anyhow Anj I love everything that really has a shape.'

The rocking days closed over them, nights and afternoons with random weather, her womb rounding against the cracked april dayflight, the whole gestation-infestation opera yelling out on the revolutionary stage with mumps of pelting birds peeling larvae popping buds paregoric eggs in the drain downwards to emptying order-tors bared to the basalt. Until all his cogitations produced only To live with people Anj be with people love them hate their userpenting sleep, in a monosigh.

So you still breathe jesuspirations!

Get disenstrangled of this loot-in with Christ eh for gods ache its not for me that or you or anyone else ever agame that deathorglory boy with his nailed-up mystery and mining pain with promise has all foiled up virtue against crudelty and permanan revel oution of our clockwatch west so now we break the square old charmed cycle. Be not do Anj be not do.

Amid the sprockets of his coinage he trod again the uncertain footage of his film seeing how it all fell in eternal recurrents and eddies of beening and borning with the ever-etrancing of steps slideways in tombtime to the opening price of verture where the goahead geton-or-getout of caputulist christ was turd to ambivled materialschism and every grass and brute caught for an exploit.

So as the Pleonastocene Age curtled to a closure the banshee crumbled under the chundering glearbox to grow up into deeply scarlet peony by the sacred roadslide where they finely went on foot with Anjie meandering through the twilicker her golden grey goose beside her it in its beak holding gently to her smallest twigged finger with Charteris choked in his throat's silence.

Beneath them turned a greenfused planet where foliage unscrewed itself from the earthworld and they afflected by its field down to the last gaussroot of being. The wayfarers on their way youngbuds straplings or grey elders were of that earth-world impacted and she by this soothed Angey lifted from her lost garden and said to saint in a recurrent phrase

All the known noon world loses its old staples and everything drops apart You should show us how to keep a grip until the bomfact wears thin and fight the growing forest.

When there was no forest were mock-ups of forest. When no PCAs organised religions as mock-ups of the personal paradise. Learn it angel not too hardly that the ferrocities of white officegoers had to crackup and tuck your city inside the only building is. Even in old concretions there pattered those our starcasters who went barefoot to the real experience hold their faith.

Expurience of drugged disorient

Disorient we want and the nonwestered sun of soma.

In the dark under piping bushes the talk was all bodies they became interchanged statement to threnody stamen to peony ransacked of all loved lute.

He had grown out of too many lifetimes but this span bridged all there was valued. For her too no longer the grey-lagging little girl but that also. Some easement in the general break.

To the evereast they talked and walked among the littling humlets with stopped steeples while to meet them avrilanched from there even from Serbia itself curled hunters forest away but a day now readings in its roots small black ringletting pigs and its boles whisperfaced littlemen and its trunks the glowing eyes and razorbones of subsisterly glowing eyes and razorbones and its branches the quick lead thing still scunnered with eyes and bones enterbal and in the leaves scabrerattle of birdsong and in the earth beneath a whole sparce tempscape ciscum-stantialing the grotted world

She broke with elmed summer into twain and he glazed through the furry wires of his conch to see his baby girl with Anjys lip of beads touch still between them the poor wages of pain words how everstretched never pinioned truth flying feathers of lovenests sprawling at heroic dusks sumptuary in feeling midfeeling deepernal but the white always winning as light flapped and varicosed in rustickled veins it cried at night barehead in all garrots where he spoke or harped silence as the concrete towers regressed.

The girl needled her small tranjecstory by his side or sprang after the rumpattering piglets in golden time so Anjy offered again seamly thewd thighs in splicing gesture. In him inarticulate patterns fuzzed and fazed stridulant through leafmoulded enterospection daytripping beyond his old throught records fobsilled deep only sometimes distirred by menacimages someone always drowning in beanstained waters beyond shingles behind a line of noctous epijean figures where shilluettes the sherd.

Living barefate in sheughs or hams where travellers now could share salaami and bread in humbled rooms they lodged craking ramshack many citizens lined to speak many he felt he could reckonise their plane shapes crossing and recrossing between him and the recessed light all asked him What you make of christs tearching or even Are you anti-Christ

So he Friends think fuzzed in diseither-organised for midpaths neither for nor anti what he said its Those whore not for me are agrainst me just a bit more punchy phallacy in westrun style there's a newtrality to cultivate to be more receptive look for shades patterns where this goodevil stuff cant rise he startled too many hares for Man the Drover

The shins of the flesh mere alimbic fantasy

Don't be for or against anyone only the waking thing that lies in sleep

Hold firm to dreamament

Its the pattern of percertivity

Awakes the greater sleep

Don't think we're too well made or permanent

You are more merged each than you believe

Better sensuous than sensible

All you must have within is outside among verdance Christ and the westering thing supposited the inside out

Never imagined where all the roads would lead

Here

The eternal position

You have to have been there first
Many theres
For the here no multernatives
His thought chewed deeper and deeper into the ruralities as the herding greentides lipped them
Other thought impacted two thousand years
Driver man became pedestrian. Be not do

At times he trod in every belief beneath a broken art sign or died again the thousand psychic deaths of croesus christs last autobile age
Barked the shins of the flesh under dogroses till senescence
Saw and herded many nakedassed children to become holy men and whoremongers and homebodies
Talked less wondered more thought of crafty old G only a span along the net leaning on an old rope bed picking his toes as christs millerimage hitler came and went
Never knew anger allowed himself to be laughed at by strangers
She knew they who knew did not laugh who laughed did not know
Yawned as the plumpricked autumn grilled her hearsole
Tried not to teach but learn from his disciples
Peeled off the long long sepiage of photographs
Watched aeroplanes in another sky
News from the statedepartmented north not reaching
Scratched himself
Taught the disciples to sit and weigh dust
All alternatives and possibilities exist through old mottled gums under a spreading square tree where some tiles still lodged but ultimately of course
Ultimately they asked listening
Poignantly shall I tell them
No way of telling anyone only through silence
Ultimately of course
They let the vast blackdrop curtain their waiting

In the hours of morning he said I will answer your ultimate question thinking that glowing eyes and razorbones burned unattended

So under the sparky starcover he let her old arms hill him but the brain still burned towards its wisdom he crept away from her guzzling sleep amid the multibrood climbed out through the stiffly hole in their thatched roof lay flat there under pulverised galaxies

Put his arm over the curved spine of roof rough and warm breathing

Gigantic beast patient

My ultimate wisdom my nonsense

Suddenly wildly flightening the hateful faces of his discarded selves when a man dreams instead of acting falling by the wayside the slow bonfire of unaccustomed words had he had a bad dream the archetypal figures or was he still lying arrowed on a hyperborean shore.

Feeling himself half-slipping from the roof he roused ultimately of course

Keeping an fuzzed open mind

That wasnt enough the forests are back

Brains just an early model half unwaked shaped for the forests

You want it both ways

Did I have it both ways

Made and destroyed lived and tomorrow maybe

Both means two more than two many ways many many ways my chief word to the world Ive been thought as well as body spirit and prick soul and stomach both

Slipping back into old astotelian ways of thought slipping off this damned roof cold

Was aristoddle also christ the proudwalker too old too damned old to think clearly back to nearderthal times

Climbed slowly down off the roof woke one of his grandaughters who went with care to blow on the embers and brew him a mug of redcurrant tea the warmth back to basics

Pinhole camera my sight of shapes all fluffed

Either too old or too young to think but who knows old angeline where was it I met her I loved her loved her in my way loved her being in many women

Thought about waking her till dawn came then she stirred bent nearly double came patted his gnarled hand and said something he had forgotten his bit I had a little speech for you

Heard too many of your speeches in my time you have to make your ultimate speech today do you know what you are going to say do you ever know

Perceived that this old place is really a great beast cantering us over the nightplane

Give me your animist patter again waking us all up in the small hours

Once they were everlasting hours

Do you know what youre going to say theyll all be under the meetree expectoring you

Meant to tell you something personal angel something about a flower or a cactus or something

Tyrannical really he still had not come to the end of words

What year was it where were they she forgot finally he went out shuffling must be ninety who knows if its still this century even

I wonder if he was jealous of christ

A doityourself christkit no nails needed

They were under the tree had his old bed there where them flies flicked about in the peeving shade he smiled his crafty old G smile and sat on the bed scratched his toes maybe he really would tell them

They waited in droves

No knowing the calendar

On this special day saint you were to speak about the ultimate

Yes

Well you patterny people with hands Byzantine born to genureflect below the low hair weigh dust well let it drip an hour or two we may not have beaten time but it no longer drives us desperate before it nothing like a catastrophe to lengthen lifespan pledge my last liquors to humbug the humbuggers and the ones who never made it

If they knew the flip old thoughts I blaspheme against my own holiness

Green and tawny under the tree the patterns they mean

We learnt to sit under trees again stop looking for better trees concentrate yourself under an inferior tree

One of his grandsons sneaking away he had news of an organised state north somewhere what was his name that man dead now a white sort of gown or uniform Boreas no matter

Concentrated on his big toes the long within
We learnt to sit under trees again the longer without
In the old days
Now the empty bowl
But I can remember sitting in a car and driving all through the night
Remember the old autostrada del sole the red lights paired tinily
capable ceaseless countless swarming pintabling under the hills and over
the bridges viaducts mighty mountains headlines slicing nature in two
not a thing ever like it never no greater thrill we were all little christs
then own death or salvation right there in your steering hands.

Autocrashes fall of orgone-content like copulation bayonet-practicide
war nothing personal in it only all things inferfused and the exhaust-
throat snarling

The sparks died into the earth finally
My capital crime nostalgia
Fault of early brain model flickering
During the long silence a small boy trotted round with fruit to eat
and a disciple deferentially handed the saint an apple cut by his pocket
knife the saint mumbled a segment

When they were all silent he sat up toes in the dirt
They waited
He waited
Their dull conformist minds he would have to give them holy law
okay but spiced with heresy let them grit it right up their nostrils

Ultimately he said
At least they would always hold him immobile in their eyes not exactly
the posture he had once aimed for but only fair he had tried genuinely tried
To hold them all in his eyes
It must embody what he had always thought must enshrine him at
the same time contain the seeds of his liberation in another generation
must be as old as the hills as old as the hills must gleam like headlights
were holy law and heresy he started again and they listened

All possibilities and alternatives exist but ultimately
Ultimately you want it both ways

*

Later much later when his old bed had been devoured they propped up the branches with long poles and stuck a sign on the tree and later still they had to build a railing round the tree and later still tourists came metalboxed driving down from the north to stare and forget whatever was on their minds

Bridging Hour In Wesciv

Cryogenetic wings
  bourning another spring
   croaking forth on
the tundragged wrathland
  scything it allover
   and the bloodcurrencies down
stunted figures anneal in the blasts
  inner postures unrelented
   to known corporeal gestures
stubble growing on man mire cloud
  all linked by nanoseconds
   loud with the permafogs
of marching equinox
  the paradox of kernels blackly
   sprouting sour green wicks

in the small northern hour
  reptile hearts crawl slackly
   lymphatic tensions twist
necks of old lithite parrots
  chuckling through engrammatic
   viscions
    the braincage
under the screw of dreamneed
  rejects lost alltermatives
   anagrits of maters stream
in cyclic slumberth crawling
  for a far stossal round
   orrey edswill rold
be yon tigal rave

The Miraculous By Numbers

Singing Jail Blues

Something's familiar about singing in a jail
It's one of those situations you
Hit racial memories of
Singing in a jail
When freedom is compulsory sitting on a hill
You'll sometimes find you're wishing you
Could smell the can again
Singing in a jail
You sing your heart out
Or let a fart out
Everything's a cock-up
The only time you're
Free from crime you're
Sitting in the lock-up
Don't want remission or justice or bail
Down at the bottom it's just like
The top when you're
Singing in a jail

Angeline Disconsolate

Somewhere along the unwinding road of chance
My feline lover slunk into another bed
Somewhere along the unbending read of hand
He palmed himself off on another breach
With life-lines double-crossed in semi-trance
He took maiden voyage to another beach
And I am left disconsolate

Somewhere an unsubtle effleurage of cat
In the uncertain jungledom of If
Seduced him Auto-breasted fur-lined she
Somehow all anti-flowered stole him
For his massage means more than meaning
More than buts poor purr-loined lover he
And I am left disconsolate

Where was the will involved in this affray
Somewhere along the all-winding road of chance
Where the decisions unlocked from careful chests
Somewhere And if the minor keys of guilt
Are played no more then how is happiness
More than an organ-peeling dance
And I am left disconsolate

Always in the bad old world guilt-lines
Somewhere would trip us along the road of chance
But unlined now we spring-healed harm
Ourselves response without responsibility
The fountain only plays
A tinkering simple that effects no balm
And I am left disconsolate

Living: Being: Having
An epic in Haiku

I

On the Rhine's chill banks
  Somebody in a raincoat
   Nobody walking

    Or a river bird
      Trying hard to memorise
       The brown nearest black

This is a tidy
  Nation even its madnesses
   Go uniformed

    We place our faith in
      Bigger and better messiahs
      Or Hydrogen 12

      Richer than God his
        Son. No wonder we nailed on
        The Cross Croesus Christ

I spat in the ditch
  It's time we got the taste of
  Nails out of our mouths

II

Every day smoulders
In the ashes of burnt-out
Possibilities

Not thinking of death
And well-combed I came across
A blank sheet of paper

The leaden birds hope
That time's pulses flow past them
And we conversely

In their plush armchair
Of blood our lusts sit waiting
For dawn or lights-out

Irrelevance
In the darkness toothache while
Digging the happenings

Bad experiences
And the deaths of old countries
Make a raree-show

III

Let's get personal
   Or is the thigh on my thigh
      Just its own meaning

         Together we dreamed
            Freedom was compulsory
               And both woke screaming

One raised fingertip
   Her red lips moving smiling
      Cells multiplying

         Stroking your slim breasts
            And slender flutes flattering
               A jumped-up penis

Tired dreams of action
   Flowers in an empty bowl
      A wooden rain falls

World and mind two or
   One? Funny how the simplest
      Question blows your mind!

His Prowed Course

Galaxy-crushing light alight on the pane
Flatters into velvet
Stands stockstill while the early motes dance
And gloom nestles deeper down a flight
Of steps. Beyond the flowering window
The scene of all disaster is awash
Would you believe a crucifixion?
The icebaus eddy on a washed-out sound
Music of the luted galaxies
All the cold vigils of the nightshift
Have robed me for my dilemma
Beyond the flowering windowpains
That input-output lends my daynight flights

The Data-Reduced Loaf

Put it this way The multidimensional stimuli
Suggest that the body lying on the eurobed
Is in some way 'mine' The body that in some way's
'Hers' enters bearing a wooden famine bowl
Empty of all but sunlight which she sets

I go too fast Five lines are not
By any means n photographs The bowl
Her skirt the lines the changing light
The retina that's self-abused with sight
Shuffles the negatives into
The million-year-old data-reducer
Behind It's a time exposure really
The changing light her legs the legs the lines
Caught in my ancient processor
Why should I trust it?
Supposing I am a chimera?

Put it this way Perhaps a multitude
Of interconnecting cells were so arranged
About a wooden bowl
In self-interest of course
That some progression could be made
Dimensionally The bowl the table
Its legs her legs my legs the light
Swarming between her and the deep-set panes
                    All without meaning
Until the heartbreaking isinglass
Of time seeps in to give to stimuli
Relationship and passage
                    And permanence
Did some of the fluid jelly-up
The data-reducer? Light
That holds universes spellbound

With its speed Instant light
Inexorable star-extinguishing light
Towering dark-proof light
Kindly light velvet on my knuckles
Beyond anachronism spaceshipping
Light light recordbreaking speedier
Than computer-thought
                Light do you fall
And grovel and crawl with million year sloth
Up the sludgy both-canal between retina
And data-reducer?
Does the old optic nerve
Slow you to child's pace?
                Should these archaic forms
Of calf and floor and leg and bowl assume
Uptodate angles and distortions

Should a new geometry inter
Their degrees inside my skull Should
In my presbyopia
There have been a new circuitry
To sort out time's passages and sight's

Should I still be a victim of
Old neolithic close-work that
Excludes me now from possibilities?

Put it this way Suppose that what I take
For 'me' is lying on this mattress
When what I take for 'her' arrives
Bowl in hand appears to arrive
Achieves in time and dimension
A presence verifiable
In my old time-machining eye
The greatest novelist
Of our space/time wrote his novel

Five million words about an unnamed girl
Arising one morning from her bed
Going across the room to open
Her casement window Of course he had
The tactical sense to leave it all unfinished
But he oversimplified
Has anyone ever opened
Or finished opening

The multidimensional stimuli
But time is a multitude and to
'My' mattress what we chose to think
Is 'her'
The repetitive event of sex
              Comes in eternal recurrence

Only the old data-reducers cut
The exposures down reducing all
To unity Put it this way
That 'she' is multitudinously among
The motes and lines and famine bowls and beds
Which punctuate that single node of time
For me and say that single node
Replicates
Endlessly to the last progressions
Of a universal web

If there were roses or daylight in the bowl
If there was someone in the middle-distance
If the faint sounds that came to 'me'
If I was there prepared to love
If we see anything but photographs
Torn from a neolithic eye
Put it this way
Time is a multitude
And 'she' far more than one

Tophet

('Tophet: an ancient place of human sacrifice near Jerusalem; later a place of refuse disposal.' Dict.)

I was prepared to sacrifice
Myself-or all else but myself.
Too harsh. I almost sacrificed
Myself. I would have done. One has
To be much surer time allows
Such liberty of gesture or
That the gesture is not just
In essence someone else's. I
Saved myself to do some further good
I say some further good. The tide of faith
Dawdled. What did I do unto myself?
Acidhead mind and flesh corrode. Too harsh.
I am the refuse tip of all I was.

Boot of Revelations

Letting their origins down
    with mooed music
The cattle milled and sledded
    in the clapped out square
Boddihair buttressed
    limbs rebuddied
Metamorphic sleep-awake-asleep
    perception flickers

As he disintegrates
    himself
      into their programmed
Brainclumps with unbuckled words
Bending the ticked time-factory
Each circadian partment stuffed
    with old writs

As words begin disimigrate
    upripe postures fold
        into a sea of herdivores
under the diss o' loot ness
    words began

What they heard they herded
  churned through mass orifices
    fossils mouth-vented

Eighty

Under the scoured thatch
Locked beams bar our disorder
Once maybe I had religion
   Suffering had a future

Now I need only a shawl
I'm a crab's claw
A broken wing blunted instrument
   Won't work or play

His veins are dried string
Not even knotted
His thoughts keep kicking
   Every day further to the well

This place will never be home
Problems keep their old address
Now I'm just an old householder
   And the house holds me.

Twenty

The days burn like a hairdryer Rattle
Out loud as Friday's money
Suddenly see problems like opening twots
   Needing my thrust

Events make tyres strike concrete
Slicing me forward every direction
Negotiable Nights are jackpots
   Giving back and front

Style does it all style
The city's open to the nomad
Everywhere's home and clear eyes
   Never questioned

Friends wink like traffic lights
I can do more than yesterday
Motorcameleon-like
   I'm change itself

Death Of A Philosopher

Oh, no, he went well at last – more his old self,
And yet as if *sure* at last . . . . Perhaps the Way smoothes
For the Gooduns . . . . Cryptic as ever his last words were –
Surprised – 'So
      Soon
      Sooth
      Soothes . . . .'

Charteris

He was a self-imagined man
Old when still young
But there's always
Time and everywhere
Recurrently eternally
A hive of selves

He left in the air
Skeleton structures
Of thought
And thoughtlessness

To some of us
They are unfinished
Palaces to some
Slums of nothingness

An ambiguity
Haunted him haunts
All men clarity
Has animal traits

The bombs were only
In his head
On his memorial tree
A joker wrote
KEEP VIOLENCE IN THE MIND
WHERE IT BELONGS

Since the Assassination

She had no sensation of falling.

In perfection, she rode the thin air down, her body in a rigidly exultant attitude as she plunged towards the blue American earth, controlling her rate of fall by the slightest movements of neck and head.

In these tranced moments, she almost lost the sense of her own identity. She was pleased to strip off her character, always feeling it inadequate. Because of that, sky-diving had become a consolation then an obsession; she was too remote from herself to be other than remote from her husband, Russell Crompton, Secretary of State. And since the assassination of the President, a month ago, the vast new burdens he had had to shoulder – burdens foreshadowing the future – had driven them even farther apart.

So every day she flung herself from his private plane, snatching seconds of a rapture immeasurable on terrestrial time scales. I feel now the future in the instant.

Those seconds were compressed with luminous comprehensions, hard to grasp when the sky-dive was over, when she was confined to earth. In the city one knows not the great hinterland. She understood that a new epoch was about to emerge – on the ground, little men without wisdom sought to deliver it, just as they sought to find the assassin, rating one task no higher than the other. Her husband also hoped to be strong and great on these points but, in her reading of his character, she denied him the ultimate power. She knew a man who had that kind of power: Jacob Byrnes, Jake, hero, victim, clown, seer: and spoke his name secretly into her breathing mask. His thought reaches me.

Her great swoop through the upper air had brought her to 2,250 feet. Now her relationship with the ground was an imminent one, and she pulled at her ripcord to release the first parachute; her equipment was of the simplest, as if she liked to keep this miracle natural.

Below her grew the drop zone, recently created in one corner of the Russell estate. Crompton was richer than Jake Byrnes, the craftier politician too, which was why he had survived where Jake had gone under. Why compare the two? She had Jake on her mind, had a sudden image of him – no, that did not make sense; these images of the future could not always be regarded as precognitive since perhaps more than one kind of time prevailed undetected in the universe: but the image clearly showed her welcoming Jake into his own house. He had been injured in some way but was smiling at her. Curious; in their rare meetings, he seemed not to like her greatly.

Before she landed, square in the target area, she saw Russell was waiting for her, a lonely figure leaning against his black roadster, wearing the simple mack he affected when he was experiencing isolation and wanted to feel like one of the people.

He came towards her frowning, so that she was careful to avoid tumbles and to land on her feet. A last-moment spill of wind took her running towards him; Crompton had to put out a hand to stop her, steadying her by the shoulder.

'Rhoda! I thought I'd find you playing this game. I want you to come on a drive with me.'

He was stern because he disliked this obsession of hers. A Freudian was Crompton, who liked in his relaxed moments to talk the straight jargon and explain grandly to Rhoda that she suffered from the death wish and was 'really' trying to kill herself by this sky-diving. With more oblique views on what was reality, she kept her own counsel; a reserved woman.

She took off her goggles and unzipped her leather suit. He could not but observe her red lips and the fine fair hair suddenly blowing free. A marvellous unreachable woman who irritated him at this moment because she would not ask where he wanted her to go.

'Get a shower and change, will you? I'm going to drive down to Gondwana Hills and consult Jacob Byrnes. I want you to come along.'

Again he waited for her to sneer and ask, 'So that I can defend you from your old flame Miriam Byrnes?' But she never sneered, never said the obvious. Maybe that was what he enjoyed about Miriam and her like; when politics had grown so complex, women should remain simple. Did this one read his thoughts? He looked away, frightened about his own transparency; nervous illness simmered inside him, manifesting itself in disquieting intuitions that others knew evil things about him; he felt himself trapped in a gothic entanglement of questioning. The robust wisdom of Byrnes would act like a salve.

'Is Jacob Byrnes back in favour?' she asked, as he walked with her towards the changing-room.

'They're calling him in this present trouble. If only we could find the killer, get the reporters off our necks, get behind shelter, stop this glare of public scrutiny. ... I figure it might pay to see him. I want him to meet ... Never mind that. My office tell me even Vice-President Strawn rang him day before yesterday.'

President Strawn, she thought; the demotion must be meaningful. She shucked off her suit and strode naked into the shower; let him look.

Whatever happened, she too wished to see Byrnes. The image was healthful.

The little dictation machine stood silent for five minutes before ex-Secretary of State Jacob Byrnes completed his sentence. In that while, Byrnes' heavy and capable mind had hunted over a wide range of topics past and present, docketing them, methodically cataloguing and compressing them into the inadequacy of words. At last, setting down the cigar, he said '... conclude – *have* to conclude that the present is an epoch in which the new relationship between man and the universe remains, for the reasons above outlined, merely incipient. This is the central factor ...'

His central factor, at least. This vast memoir, designed in the first place to vindicate his forced retirement from the government and clear away the old scandals of ten years ago, had turned into a philosophical search; personal aspects had been lost, sunk in oceanic thinking. The pauses between sentences, the bouts of research, grew longer, Grigson's fingers above the dictation machine more idle, as Byrnes pressed hotly on, growing nearer to the truth. He knew he was getting nearer; the secret something that prevented a brave new universal relationship forming pressed down on him and on his whole estate here at Gondwana Hills, bringing him churning images, random snatches of possibility.

'What was that, Grigson?'

'"The central factor", sir.' The secretary masterfully obliterated his own personality, crushed by the Byrnes dollars, unable to crystallise into his own potential. Byrnes, who lived by empathy, derived only a blank from the man, and often longed to hit him. He had done so once, when plagued by something Miriam had done. Grigson had taken it well, of course.

'Central factor operating on the collective conscious. A break-through into a higher consciousness has been aborted by the unfavourable cross-currents of mid-twentieth century, resulting in the waking nightmare of inappropriate politico-economic systems imposing themselves all over the globe. The Cold War and the Vietnamese War must be regarded as faulty psychic frameworks through which favourable developments are eclipsed by unfavourable ones.'

Still dictating, he rose and went on to the wide balcony. There was a microphone here; no chance of Grigson not hearing. He liked to stand here and dictate, with the hills in the distance, the private landing-ground and, nearer, the ornamental lake. Nearer still, were the essential adjuncts to the house, such as the gymnasium, his son Marlo's squash court, the stables, and the swimming-pool, which lay against the broad terrace with its statuary. They were laid out in an arrangement that did not please Byrnes, although he had been meticulous with the architect about the matter; but the spatial relationship remained in some way meagre. He lifted up his eyes unto the hills. That at least was okay. Even the line of the toll-road was being erased year by year as the trees grew up. Not that he has so many more years. ...

Miriam was swimming in the pool. 'Hi!' she called, and he signalled back. There was still communication on the non-resonant level, which maybe counted for something after ten years. She swam in the nude now, her depilated body gold-brown under the water; somehow, he had ceased to worry about the staff looking on. He had even caught Grigson peeping. The tough guys on the guard fence were the most nuisance, but Byrnes had long since conceded to himself that, in view of his wife's feeble mental equilibrium, her need to exhibit herself was better not repressed. Poor little Miriam: however much she stressed the invitation, what she had to offer was pitifully ordinary.

There was more mess around the area than usual. Marlo had some contractors in, an interior décor firm, messing around with something there, some new project. His schizoid son's projects were always a sort of art-therapy; as the search for a self-cure grew more desperate, the projects seemed to grow more elaborate. Byrnes hesitated to intrude on his son's sufferings and saw very little of him nowadays. Bad empathy there. He caught a flickering feeling – one of his images – for a sort of lunar environment, hurriedly repressed an image of his cold first wife, Marlo's *mother*, Alice. Just as well Miriam saw more of Marlo than he did, although he could not imagine what they said to each other.

Grigson was on the phone. He came out on to the balcony and said, 'Private car at lodge, sir. Russell Crompton, the Secretary of State, wants to speak with you.'

'Let him drive up. Inform Captain Harris in the guard room.'

'Yes, sir.'

The only sort of affirmative statement Grigson ever made. So Russell Crompton was calling. Ever since the President's assassination, his scared successors had been phoning and radioing Byrnes. He was back in favour. It gave him some kind of guarded satisfaction, he realised. But they were all too nervous of bugging and spying to speak out. Now here was Russell Crompton, once a close friend, rolling up at his front gate! There was a nationwide search for a scapegoat, if not the killer; maybe he'd hear more about that. His particular philosophical beliefs led him to believe that the President's assassin must be a fellow-countryman; the aborted universe-relationship would not allow anything less specific. His stomach churned a little. The more one knew, the less it became!

'No more dictation, Grigson.'

Grigson smiled and nodded, picked up his briefcase, and left the room. For a moment, Byrnes lingered on the balcony, surveying the scene which was so shortly to be disturbed. Some things were of such immense value, like the peace of Gondwana Hills and the streams of thought that passed through his own mind; those were of value to him, nourished him, maintained his interest in life, and he hoped that when they were transfixed on to paper they would nourish some other people.

But personal relations also still occupied him. It was a multi-value system in which he enjoyed manoeuvring, in winning and losing points; nor was his enjoyment entirely intellectual. He liked people as he still liked life.

Nor was he too old to feel that he wanted to be seen again at best advantage by Russell Crompton when the latter arrived. Not as an ageing semi-scholar, a learned buffoon, but a jolly old political man still able to live it up as a bit of a playboy. He'd go down to the gym.

And why – he asked himself this as he crossed the room, taking a last glance at the previous muddle of his creation – why did he want to act a role with Russell? Russell, for all his faults and weaknesses, was always direct, never pretended, though he schemed; Byrnes never schemed – well, there had been occasions – but loved to pretend. But his playboy role with Russell was almost intended to be seen through; perhaps the real defence was against Russell's wife, the rather enigmatic Rhoda.

He wondered what his strong empathic sense would make of her this sunny day. That sky-diving woman ... funny habit for a woman to take up. Beautiful hair. Something told him she would be accompanying Crompton, unlikely though that seemed.

But he was going to have to talk affairs of state.

Moving in his solid way, making himself more heavy than he in fact was, Byrnes crossed the corridor, took the elevator down to ground floor, moved out into the blazing sun, stripping off his linen jacket as he went. He had a gun strapped round his waist, being a little afraid of assassination: or, alternatively, of not being able to kill himself, should he want to.

'Miriam!' he yelled, crossing by the pool.

'Hi! Coming in, Big Daddy?' She waved a brown arm languidly to him.

Screw that stupid name! 'Get out and get dressed. Secretary of State Crompton is on his way up.'

'Oh boy, Fancy Pants! Does he think we're hiding the Prexy-killer here? Will he want you to run for President? Is Rhoda coming with him?'

He passed stolidly on, through the ornate stone screens, imported from Italy and now covered with Russian vine, and made for the gym, flinging his jacket over a hook, and working away at press-ups, his face purple. He was a solidly built man on the summer side of fifty-nine and he wasn't going to let Crompton think he was past it. He meditated about his stomach as it touched the floor at regular and straining intervals. The viscera. That was where he felt things. Not a great intellectual man, but a great feeling man. That's what he had been, and almost nobody had guessed – except that bitch Alice, his first wife, who had taken full advantage of it. Even in office, he had to protect himself from the anger of others: it communicated their sickness to him; he was a stable man, wrecked by the storms about him.

You're an oddball, he thought. Few men he could really talk to. But his own company was not disagreeable. Crompton, too, was still by way of being a friend, wasn't he? Strawn too, come to that.

Nose to the ground, he thought of Rhoda again, vexed at himself for doing so. Oh no, Russell would not bring that strange silent creature, surely? But the image told him she was near.

The image took on life. She was standing among bushes; he was very frightened. She was saying, 'We have to cease to rely. ...' On what? The image was gone as soon as there. '... on logical systems'; or had he supplied that himself? After all these years, he still did not know how to deal with these moments of insight; which could only mean that his life-pattern had set wrongly long ago; maybe in childhood; he could not take full advantage of the benefits offered by these extra-sensory glimpses.

He stood up, morose. Living was so wonderful, his own faulty faculties were so wonderful; what he needed was a wise man or woman who could discuss such high matters with him. Still in his vest, he moved to the gym door. Crompton's big black Chrysler was just rolling up to the front of the house, Russell himself driving. Rhoda was in the back.

On their way to the bar room, the two men ran through a few preliminary sparring platitudes. The barman mixed them two tumblers of martini and was dismissed.

'I don't know why you want to see me, Russell, but did you have to bring your wife along?'

'Same old grumpy Jacob! You have good nags here and she can go for a gallop. She thought she'd like to see Miriam.'

'Rhoda and Miriam have nothing in common, and you know it. You afraid you've got to keep an eye on her all the while?' He was talking in this vein, he realised, because he was grumpy and had no strong urge to hear Crompton's confidences; the assassination, the troubles of the country, were things over which he had no jurisdiction and which no longer took precedence over his meditative life.

'Why don't you like Rhoda? She likes you.'

He had wanted someone to talk to and here someone was, the Secretary of State, no less. Why not say it straight out, and see what happened, forgetting the fact that Russell was plainly burdened with responsibilities and guilts and worries, and therefore a bad nuisance? 'I am an empath, Russell; I pick up other people's emotions as easily as if I had an antenna on my head. Your wife's eyes always disconcert me. They tell me things I don't want to know, about her and about myself. Look, the future is aborting before our eyes, all the big promises not getting realised; it is creating a barrier of universal mental sickness. Empaths are more sensitive to what's in the air than others. I'm telling you, all our values are false, Russell, false! If —'

'That's what I came to talk to you about,' Crompton said. 'A time louse-up. I agree the priorities are wrong, but I'm in a position to know what the priorities are. A lot of very nasty things have come up this week, things that only the President and one or two men under him knew of.' He took a hefty drink of his martini.

'Things? You mean projects?'

'Sort of. Two in particular. God, Jake, I shouldn't be talking to you about them. They're so secret – well, they are so terrible, that either one of them alters man's relationship to his environment for good and all.'

This came too alarmingly near to the subject of this morning's chapter in the masterwork. Brushing that reflection aside, Byrnes asked, 'Why *are* you talking to me about them, then?'

'I happen to believe that there is a lot of sense in all the philosophical nonsense you talk. I feel I need to hear some of it today. Plus the fact that your barman is one of the world's great artists.'

They stared at each other. It was a hard, tricky world. You had to seek your allies where you could. Although there was some residual evil tinging Crompton's aura, Byrnes said, 'If I can help, I will.'

'We could be bugged here. Let's walk outside.' He swallowed the rest of his drink.

'Bugged? Me, in my own place? The hell with that!'

'I'd feel better outside. I'm claustrophobia-inclined – too many years in Washington.'

Leaving the glasses, they walked through into the sunlight again, through the wide glass doors over which internal steel shutters could close at the touch of a flip-switch. The decorators over in the squash court were making a noise with their machines; otherwise all was silent. The guards lounged in their glass boxes; no birds flew. As the two men walked along the terrace, they caught sight of Miriam and Rhoda riding on ponies towards the hills, Miriam in a turquoise bathing-suit. Why had Miriam been so quick to get Rhoda (or herself) out of the way?

'We'll walk round the lake – if it isn't too far for you.'

'Of course it isn't too far for me,' Byrnes said. 'The years pass more healthily here than in Washington.' He felt his gun uneasily. There was always something about to materialise, sweeping down from the concealed headwaters of the past, deeds already committed in men's minds that manifested themselves like projections from the future; the present was a shock-wave between past and future.

When they seemed to him far enough from the house, Crompton started talking. The Administration had been taken by surprise by the death, as if death were an amazing thing. There had not been a strong Vice-President to take over effectively, as Truman and Johnson had done on previous occasions of crisis. Strawn was already proving ineffectual as President. And there had been the secret projects. Some were already almost an open secret among the top men, the usual routinely sinister affairs of the overkill philosophy, such as new missiles and new strains of virus that could incapacitate whole populations. There was a top-secret anti-gravity research station on the moon, a fleet of interstellar probes a-building in California. But the really burdensome things were none of these. They were two other projects; one had some connection with the anti-gravity moon station, Crompton said. The other was called Project Gunwhale.

'Gunwhale? Gunwhale? What's that?'

'I can't tell you, Jake. I can only say –'

'If you can't tell me, why come here and bring up the subject?'

'The questions it raises are so enormous. Metaphysical questions. Mankind is not ready to face such questions yet. I remember you said something to me once, somehow I remembered the phrase, about "the eternal dichotomy of life". The phrase stuck with me, and it just describes this Gunwhale Project. It seems on the surface to be one of the greatest blessings ever, yet it could easily prove the greatest curse. Its potentiality is so great – no, it can hardly be faced! We shouldn't have to face Gunwhale for at least two more generations.'

'It's something like the A-bomb was in its time?'

'Oh no, nothing like that, nothing.'

Byrnes exploded. 'I don't plan to waste a whole precious day playing guessing games with you, Russell! Either you tell me or you don't tell me! Look, I'm as much a patriot as the next man, but since I was turned out of office, I'm doing my duty by thinking – thinking, goddam it, the hardest job of work there is, thinking for all the guys who never think from one year to the next. Let me get back to my work or else tell me what you've got on your mind and let me help you.'

Crompton was looking back, squinting in the sunlight and staring towards the two figures on horseback, who were cantering now. Casually, he said, 'I back you still, Jake, when your name comes up, so it's only to you I'd say that your temper is the chief of your disqualifications from holding high office. And I wouldn't value the amateur thinking too high if I were you.' He gripped Byrnes' arm. 'You're a good guy, Jake, but you see we are all powerless. ...'

'Never think it, never say it. Look at this view – man-touched everywhere. God-touched too, maybe, but shaped by man.'

'I can't say anything about Gunwhale, though I'd like to do so. I'll tell you about the other chief headache we're landed with. One or two doctors and psychiatrists know about this, but they are under a security blanket, right under wraps. It's something that happened on the moon. Something that reveals that man's whole conception of the physical world – roughly what we call science – is, going to have to be taken to pieces and rebuilt.'

'It's to do with the anti-gravity research you mentioned?'

'Yes, but not in the way you would imagine. It's an effect the moon has on the research staff. Lunar gravity. Christ. ... Look, I'll give it you straight. For the first time ever, eight men have just spent an appreciable time – six months – on the lunar surface, away from Earth. They were relieved and brought back here last month, four or five days before the President was killed.'

They were hidden from the house now. To afford shelter from the sun, a grove of bamboos had been planted, growing down to the lake, but Crompton walked to avoid these, maybe thinking that they could be bugged. Byrnes stopped by the fishing-pier, wanting to be still and listen as the Secretary of State went on.

'Those eight men are none of them normal any more. The moon has done something to their metabolism; physiologically and psychologically, they are something other than human.'

'I don't get you. You can communicate with them?'

'With the utmost difficulty. To put the whole matter in layman's language – which is all I can understand in this matter – these moonmen are operating slightly ahead of Earth time.'

'Operating ahead. ... Living ahead of time?'

'Ahead of Earth time. Earth time is different from lunar time. They figure that each planetary body may have a different time.'

Byrnes gave a laugh of disbelief. 'You should tell that to Einstein.'

'Never mind Einstein! Look, time is in some direct way related to gravity; that's what we've learnt from our eight moonmen. Once you hear it, you shouldn't be too surprised. We've grown accustomed to thinking of Earth as being down a great gravity well; perhaps it's also down a temporal well.'

'So a time-energy equation is possible.'

Crompton looked startled. 'Nobody told me that. What do you mean, a time-energy equation?'

'Einstein's general theory has been suspect for some while; now his special theory will also have to be re-examined. But if his methods still hold good, then it may be possible to formulate a time-matter-energy relationship. Off the cuff, I'd say this paves the way for the H. G. Wells idea of a time-machine. With computers to help us, a prototype could probably be constructed in a few months. What a vista!'

He stared at the younger man, saw that Crompton was lost, his mind involved in the nebulous machinery of government, not free to speculate, reluctant to make a step that seemed obvious to Byrnes. To get him back into his stride, Byrnes asked, 'How did this temporal effect strike the men involved?' As he put the question, he felt a chill like premonition coming over him, and glanced round, wondering what psychopathic patterns must whirl like furies above the heads of any men so involved with facing the impossible.

'The main effect might not have been noticed for years, but there is a side-effect. Apparently, every living thing including man has built-in cellular clocks which keep pace with the daily revolution of the earth.'

'Circadian rhythms.'

'That's correct. You are better up in it than I am. I get no time for general reading. A long stay on the moon disrupts the cellular clocks. The clocks of this eight-man research team attempted to adjust to the period of a lunar day, which of course was impossible. They clicked over instead into Lunar Automatic, as I've heard it called. They are living .833 recurring seconds ahead of Earth Automatic. The effect now wears off at intervals, as customary gravity brings them back that .833 recurring seconds to terrestrial time. In those intervals, we can communicate with the men. Otherwise, they are schizoid or else seem not to be there at all.'

The orchestra of the inner life ground forth its disharmonies. So the break-through into higher consciousness – the very phrase he had given Grigson that morning – the break-through was now on its way, the possibility of health was again offered, presenting itself paradoxically as sickness! Certain he was being watched, Byrnes swung round, pulling his gun from its holster. Someone was in the bamboo grove, crashing forward. He fired, a reflex of self-preservation. The charging image was a phantom of himself, its mouth open, panting, its heavy old limbs jerking.

As soon as it was glimpsed, it was gone. As soon as Byrnes' shot was fired, the guard car started to roar forward; it sat continually on the landing-field, engine ticking over. In fifteen seconds, the gunmen were piling out by Byrnes' side. Controlling his fury, Byrnes reassured them and set them to searching the bamboo grove. He marched off with Crompton, knowing he would get no more out of the nervous fellow now, ignoring his questioning glance.

'Let me know if there is anything I can do on the moon question.' His voice, he thought, had never sounded so helpless. What warning was that phantasm of the living trying to convey?

'It's essential to know what leading scientists will make of this time division,' Crompton said. He was trembling from the surprise of his friend's shot; the spectre of assassination, hiding still deeper fears, was always by him. 'It's always a question of keeping off the damned reporters. Fetesti has just published a paper on the biochemistries of time; I want to get him in on this. Maybe we could have a top-level meeting with the scientists down here at Gondwana, without drawing too much attention to ourselves.'

'Do that. I'll be glad to help.' He knew it would be dangerous without knowing why. The horrid sensational web of search, treason, and brutality, which always trailed off along its edges into drugs, perversion, lies, and suicide, was spreading once more across the continent; the endemic oppression pattern that sprang from the will-to-power in man's psyche and was always breaking out in new directions; it was the greatest disrupter of a healthful emergent future and could wreck this continent as it had Africa; Byrnes had been caught in its web ten years back; he wished to keep it from Gondwana Hills. 'This whole place is at your disposal. My guard force would be glad of a real job to do.'

'An Interim Committee has been set up. I'll put it to them.' Plainly, that was all Crompton intended to say. Over his averted face fell opaque shadows, as his availability switched to shallower channels, away from the main streams of ego-anxiety.

As they walked back towards the buildings, Marlo came out of the squash court. He was a stringy youth of sixteen, wearing dirty green Scandinavian sweater and old jeans. He looked pale and ill. It was the first time Byrnes had seen him for several days. Miriam saw more of him than he did; what they had in common was beyond speculation, but at least she did not shun the child as once she had. But often he disappeared. He had taken to making long journeys, either on horseback or in his own sports car, since he was not certified; and those journeys were as unknown to his father as the fevered excursions of his spirit.

'Marlo any better these days?' Crompton asked and then, as if guessing the answer to that, 'Do you have in a resident psycho-analyst for him presently?'

'It doesn't work for Marlo. The last one tried to cure him with some new drug, and that didn't work either.'

'The boy needs Steicher, a very good man I know in Washington. Steicher would release his repressed ego-aggression.' Crompton believed in all that, but chose not to press the matter, to Byrnes' relief. He had had too much trouble from all the alienists he had engaged to help Marlo; the one before last, a guy from New York, had turned up with two mistresses, sisters.

Marlo hesitated, almost seemed not to notice them, then moved slowly in their direction.

'The death of the President appears to have upset him. On a personal level, he seems to feel little, yet, on the public level, he seems to suffer a good deal. Could be the personality pattern for the future, I guess, unless we solve a few problems. When things get too strong for him, he's completely in retreat.'

'Steicher could help.'

The weight of people in the world, the result of the population explosion, particularly oppressed the boy. Even the square miles of Gondwana seemed not to help things.

'We have to want external aid before it can help us.' He was growing slightly afraid of his son.

Crompton said, 'Rhoda said she dreamed about Marlo last night.'

'Yes?' He hardly knew whether it was true.

Making himself smile as Marlo came up, he reached out his hand to the boy, but Marlo slid away, setting his head on one side, with a gesture that seemed faintly derisory.

'They are shooting whales with guns on the lake again, Jacob,' he said. His voice was without animation; his gaze ran through his father. 'Our dear relations, sad to relate. The blue whale is now extinct, except in the cerebral seas of the soul, and our lake.'

'What are you having done in the squash court, Marlo?'

As the boy turned on his heel, his eyes just flickered slightly; his father seized on it as a gesture of invitation. Taking a hold of Crompton's arm, to show no malice was borne, he steered him after the boy, who was heading towards the court; the court had been a present for Marlo's fourteenth birthday; Marlo had played only one game of squash there, but had spent many periods living almost entirely in the court, decorating it in various bizarre styles – each of which his psychiatrists had heralded as an advance towards normality.

Byrnes thought of that phrase, 'advance towards normality', now, as he stood with Crompton and gazed at the cluttered interior of the court. The professional decorators had knocked off for lunch, and were eating beer and sandwiches in the upper gallery. Below them, only half completed, was part of a lunar crater, with the star-blotched black of space behind.

Advance towards normality. ... Just as well he had sacked the psychiatrists, operating like all psychiatrists on false premises; premises such as the notion of a received normality. As Crompton had just revealed, there was a new normality on the moon, where alien time trajectories could taint the human metabolism. And now Marlo was working towards that – like all artists, ahead of his time. But the moon mock-up was like the sterile territory of death.

He had ceased to ask himself what it meant. But Crompton asked the questions, looking decidedly uneasy.

'Just a coincidence,' Byrnes said. 'The lad's been reading space-comics.' But he had taken a whiff of illness off his son; or had he? Was he not getting whiffs of illness wherever he turned? An hour of crisis was approaching; the higher conscious was about to be born and he stood in the way of its midwives. The boy had disappeared among the builders' junk. He wanted a cigar and another drink.

The two men muttered and walked about and examined the foamed plastic that so closely resembled the seared earth of Earth's satellite, uneasy in the presence of something they could not grasp. As they finally turned to the door, it was to discover their two women framed in the doorway.

'Gosh, are you both okay?' Miriam asked. 'We thought we heard shots, and so we came back to see if anything was wrong. The guards say you saw someone in the grove, Jacob. Is that right? Are there spies around?'

She was almost a head shorter than Rhoda. She kissed Byrnes and gave Crompton a peck as well, as usual meaning nothing she said or did, Byrnes reflected. It could not be said of the alarm she expressed so prettily that it was either real or feigned. 'So long since we saw you, Russ, and I keep telling Rhoda I know you have a great big state secret to tell Jacob, but that's just an excuse and really you came down to see me.'

'You look good in your swim-suit, Miriam,' Crompton said.

'You like it? It cost a packet! Isn't it pretty material?'

Rhoda said nothing. She was terrific in her silence, Byrnes thought; good waves came from her. She was slightly larger than he cared for a woman to be, but her skin and her small, well-shaped breasts ... well, that was a line of country he no longer found it profitable to pursue; philosophy was at least partly designed to keep that sort of stuff at bay. He went towards her, conscious of how objectional he always behaved towards her. A masked attitude. He suspected she really knew how he felt about her; but if she had that amount of sensibility and perception, then why did he need to put on a performance, like an adolescent? Why did adolescents need to put on performances, come to that? Sometimes whole civilisations became involved in attitudes. The Japanese *haragei*, using attitudes as veils which were only occasionally intended to be impenetrable, saying things that were not meant. The inescapable and gigantic paradox of human behaviour: gigantic, yet so pretty. He wanted to make a note, wanted that more than the cigar or the drink.

He was standing staring at Rhoda. She stared back, entirely without defence or offence.

'Still doing the sky-diving?' Her obsessive hobby was leaping from planes; *Life* had carried an article on her.

'Uh-huh. Still doing the memoir?'

He was still inwardly bothered about the moon thing. Without smiling, he said, 'Maybe I get the same kicks out of philosophy you get out of free fall.'

'You two should compare kicks some time,' Miriam said, shrilly. 'Jacob, take Rhoda in for a cocktail while I show this crazy set-up to Russ.'

'He's seen it.' But he was glad of the excuse. On the whole, he felt women remained private even amid public affairs; it was a vanishing talent. As he led the silent woman away, he sought for ways to shed the *haragei* mask, but she seemed as remote as ever. Almost as if she had more in common with Marlo than with him. It roused his curiosity to visualise her poised in some kind of hallucinatory dream, ten miles above Earth's surface; something of that transfixed state lingered round her still.

'He hates me, you know,' Miriam told Crompton, directly Byrnes and Rhoda had disappeared. 'I cut him off from public affairs in his prime and he can't forget it.'

'He's better away from the in-fighting.'

'Oh, Russ, don't be stodgy with me, please. It's months since I saw you! I know you've got awful troubles with this assassination and all that, but I'm so lonely here. Even Marlo keeps vanishing.'

'Where is the boy?' He was following her over the lunar mock-up.

'He hides behind here. Marlo! Come out, darling! Really, he's getting nuttier than ever.'

Marlo stuck his head out from behind a pillar and said, 'You need to wear a time-suit here. You walk with death. I create my own time and I defy death!'

Miriam looked at Crompton. The words seemed to have struck him a physical blow. 'The boy knows!' he breathed. He turned and walked hurriedly away, out of the court, his hands spread in case he tripped over the equipment lying everywhere.

She followed, calling.

She hung on his arm. 'The Secretary of State scared by a nut-case! He's fun, Marlo's fun! I quite like him.'

'Fun! He's talking about death. ... And he seems to know about Lunar Automatic.'

She chattered anxiously; he continued to look as if he had seen a ghost, indifferent when she led him in through the side entrance of the house, bustled the maids out of the kitchen, and brought him a beer out of the icebox. He drank with his head down, sighing between draughts.

'You are in a load of trouble or you wouldn't be down here at this time,' Miriam said. 'Tell me about it, Russ. Maybe a silly woman's insight would help.'

'This place is bugged, I'll bet.'

She laughed. 'That's what I'm always saying.' She put her hand over his hairy wrist, but he would not look at her. She slapped him.

'You men are so awful these days, so damned important! Look at me, Russ, am I so ugly now, so old? You used to fancy me. Have you no time for private affairs any longer?'

He switched on the transistor radio set in the counter and, under cover of the music, said, 'Everything is in chaos back in Washington. Something's happened on the moon – well, it's technical and you wouldn't be interested. And another thing. Oh my God! Just before he was shot, the President was going to activate a major project, Project Gunwhale. We've got to decide – more than ordinary guys should have to decide.'

She giggled uncomfortably. 'You don't think you are an ordinary guy. Don't fool with me. You know Jacob treats me with contempt – maybe rightly. Don't you cut me out entirely. ... One more claim on you, you see! How was Europe, Russ?' He had been out of the country when the President was killed.

'Getting back to New York ... New York seems so old and incredibly burdened after those young capitals like London and Bonn and Copenhagen. Look, do something for me, Miriam. I don't really go along with these theories of Jake's but he is turning into a wise old man. He's mad, of course, shooting at phantoms, but maybe he has the greatest idea since the cavemen invented fire. Maybe it will now be possible to invent a time-machine. He said something so valuable just now, threw it out. I shall give it equal priority with my other most pressing problems when I get back to Washington.'

'Building a time-machine? I thought that was just a comic book idea!' She laughed. 'Isn't the world complicated enough without going into the future, or whatever you plan to do?'

'Maybe I was already thinking that. Look, all are agreed that right now world affairs have never been more snarled up. Ever since Hitler, nothing but terrible crises: the extermination of European Jewry, Stalin's purges, the H-bomb, the Cold War, Korea, the population explosion, famines everywhere, Communist China. The pressure is not only from the past but from the future, from mouths unborn. Somehow, we have to make a breakthrough before we bog down into universal psychosis. A time-machine could be a way – a marker-buoy sent into future time, to get help or something – I don't know, I'm talking wild.'

'Don't ask me to go into the future!'

For the first time, Crompton smiled at her with real warmth and took her hand. 'That's not what I want you to do for me. I begin to get a sort of superstition. I want you to keep a friendly eye on your step-son, Marlo. Suppose he says anything significant about the moon or time differences, or ... or people living for hundreds of years, will you note it down precisely and let me know?'

'Doesn't sound the sort of thing I'm good at.' She made eyes at him.

'I don't want your note intercepted. Could you bring it to me in Washington personally?'

She looked soberly at him. 'You do still love me a little, Russ. Of course, I'll do what you ask.'

He stood up. 'Thanks for the beer, Miriam. I'd better collect Rhoda. I have to be back for a conference at twenty hundred hours tonight.'

The newscaster was saying, 'Although the search for the late President's assassin or assassins has recently been stepped up to new levels, official circles in the capital are now admitting that hopes of an arrest are fading. Looks like this is destined to become one of the classic locked-room mysteries of all time. What did happen in the President's study, that evening of 18th August, just before dinner, while the President sat alone, studying – so it's said – an important document which is now rumoured missing? Two of his personal guard sat in the corridor outside, within earshot, yet heard nothing. Here, for a latest opinion on the White House Mystery, is this station's special political correspondent –'

Jacob Byrnes got up and walked out of the room, leaving Miriam sitting on the white velvet sofa, gazing at the screen. Like an invisible presence, Marlo hovered in the shadowed corner of the room. Turning, she called him over sharply and he came, standing a few feet away.

'I have something for you, Marlo. You know what it is, don't you? Your weekly treat. Come nearer.'

He hovered like a bird beyond the patch of lamplight, waiting to be enticed into the hand of its captor. She opened her purse and brought out a screw of paper, opening it so that he could see the cube of sugar it contained.

She gestured towards the TV set. 'For all your funny ways, you dig quite a bit about what goes on in the world, don't you? Washington and Europe, I mean. How's life on the moon?'

He reached out a hand.

'How is life on the moon, Marlo?'

'I am not alone on the moon. Earth is my piece of desolation. Many people live where I live. My mother sent me there, long ago.'

'It's cold on the moon.'

'Cold and hot. More cold, more hot than here.'

'Oh, cut the riddles, Marlo. Do you want this LSD or don't you? What do you mean, many people live on the moon?'

'... mounting pressures which were driving the late President into a position of isolation ...' said the commentator.

'There had to be a place for unwanted people, or they die of famine or in concentration camps or hospital beds. No room in beds.'

'And the President?' she asked, with sudden intuition.

Marlo shook his head. 'He would have made it all worse. There are too many people already. When the moon is crowded, where do we all go then?'

She gave him the cube of sugar and he retreated with it into the shadows. 'It will do you no good! You're mad already, I suppose you know that?'

'Just ahead of my time,' he said. 'Otherwise there would be nothing. You are nothing. Even when you have all your clothes off, you are nothing.' He put the white cube gently on to his tongue and closed his mouth; and then he stole quietly away.

Leaving the TV set to flicker in the empty room, Miriam also got up, and walked down the wide silent corridor, lugubriously lit. Fortunate she believed in reincarnation; this life sure had its dull moments. At the foot of the stairs, she paused, and then mounted slowly, until she came to her husband's work room. She rapped on the door and entered.

Byrnes was smoking his cigar. He nodded and said, 'Grigson is just sorting some old movies I want to look through. Care to come down to the theatre and see them?'

'Funnies?'

'Not funnies. Sobies. Documentaries or, in your language, dockies.'

'Must you take the piss out of me all the time, Jacob? I came up here for a bit of company.'

He did not answer. He was making notes on a pad while Grigson scuffed in the background.

'You're so busy, Jacob, so dull, shut yourself up here, never even go fishing any more.'

'I went fishing not many weeks ago.'

'That was last summer.'

'So it was last summer, my darling.'

He caught something in her face and said, 'I'm sorry we don't talk more. I must try to produce this old think-piece of mine. I want to finish it by year's end – just the philosophy bit. To hell with the personal stuff; that's forgotten. No time for it.'

'Everyone's obsessed with time.'

'Ask yourself why.'

'Oh, I know all that. Big crisis, big deal! Even Marlo's at it.'

Now he was gathering up the day's notes that Grigson had typed out, absently fumbling a pen to alter and correct and add. '"Battle between a higher plane of consciousness and a waking nightmare that …" pretentious, but it will stand. … Grigson, have you located that footage on the 1934 assassination of King Alexander of Yugoslavia yet?'

'No, sir.'

'Hurry up!'

She stood in front of her husband and said, 'Why are things worse than before? Are they objectively worse? Aren't you just getting old, Jacob?'

'Of course I am getting old! The personal memoir led me into this same question of things getting worse. It's a good question. Do you want a serious answer?'

'No, I just asked for a joke. Me, I'm never serious, am I?'

He caught her wrist as she was about to turn away. 'I'm sorry to tease. I want you, Miriam. I must have some contact with the old world, and you must be it. Listen, I will give you your answer. It's not that things are getting permanently worse; it's just that this is crisis time, what in my book I call "Clock-and-Gun Time". Such crises have occurred before. There was one towards the end of the thirteenth century in Europe, when the towns were growing rapidly, creating new densities. New densities always imply new awareness. Guns and mechanical clocks were then invented, both originating from metalsmiths. Those two inventions brought deliverance from a philosophical impasse and paved the way to renaissance. Guns brought new spatial adventure about the world. Mechanical clocks, incorporating one of the world-changing inventions, the verge-escapement with foliot, were our first precision instrument and directed our inner landscapes towards more precise thinking.

'Those clocks sprang from western society and moulded it. They were no good to the civilised Chinese, whose society had so developed that to them mechanical clocks were little more than toys.

'The same thing may be happening today. Two radical new inventions or discoveries; Russell Crompton mentioned them. They might deliver us. Or they might strike us as no more than toys, marvels. Our imagination could fail before them. We need courage and imagination.'

'That's what your book is going to give people?'

'You see the funny side of me, Miriam. Other people don't, so maybe I can help them.'

She tickled him under the chin. 'Don't do your pathos thing with me. It may have hooked me, but it won't keep me hooked. How is this gun-and-clock talk going to help anyone right now?'

'Isn't it still typical, of the dichotomy running right through life? Guns are all externality and violence; clocks are all silence and inwardness. There you epitomise western modes of thought, the ascendant mode on this planet now for several centuries. However bent we are on material things, we never entirely forget our hearts and minds. Okay, now we try at last to join them and reach a new conscious level. Damn it, woman, if the west doesn't do it, who else will?'

'Maybe you have a point there, honey. You are a wise old guy, I do know. Even Russ said so when he was here last week. By the way, I want to drive up to Washington tomorrow, do some shopping.'

'That's why you're being nice to me! Grigson, where the hell is that newsreel?'

Grigson straightened, his face flushed, clutching a plastic spool. 'I have it right here, sir.'

'You're a paragon, Grigson. Miriam – give my love to Russell Crompton if you just happen to run into him, eh?'

Rhoda threw herself from the plane.

Her brain cleared at once. All the irresolutions and obscurities – the poverty of discussion on central things – lifted at once from her mind. At over 20,000 feet, Washington could be seen for the tiny thing it was in both the real and the subterranean affairs of man. And the earth itself;

she saw the relationship now, one of magnificent cunning, as a problem that man had posed himself and was about to solve.

She spread herself, arms and legs bent backwards, fixing the world with her mons veneris, adjusting her speed by the subtlest flexion of the spine. From the fifth vertebra spouted ganglia, power, beauty, that charmed the knife-wind. It was the universal nerve centre, counter-pointed only by the blue American earth below.

She wore suit, mask, oxygen cylinder, packed two parachutes. This was her element. Rhoda was high.

There was no sensation of fall, no sensation of fear. Only the beatific equipoise of flight, the collusion with gravity and the forces of the universe, the eternity offered by two minutes of free-fall. She had been on drugs, she had recently tried one of the luxury free-fall holiday schools set up between Earth and Luna, where the very rich experienced psychedelic rapture between planets; but for Rhoda, the true kick came in riding the stratospheric layer just beyond the realm of her fellow beings.

In this tranced state, she could catch some of the stronger thoughts floating up to her. It always encouraged her to find that only pure or creative thoughts rose this high; the bad ones, of which there were plenty, stayed at around 2,500 feet, just before she pulled the rip-cord. Which was as if the mediaevals had caught a glimpse of that curious scientific fact in their vision of a heaven above and a hell below. Good thoughts breathed hydrogen, the basic substance of the universe. Up here, the all-state manhunt had no being, having no purpose.

She encountered the thoughts of retired Secretary of State Jacob Byrnes; they were rich in hydrogen these days. They penetrated her body. He was troubled. She had no lover. Her husband's thought never touched her here. She had her raptures. She was, she thought, of the future, and so had an interest in seeing it healthily born. Jake was of the past, a dinosaur with love, absurd, heroic. He would die seeing the future enter the world.

This last thought Rhoda examined carefully and languidly as she volplaned down with the world between her thighs. Jake was troubled; he had discovered a sheet of paper. Without understanding what the paper was, she saw its tendrils spread all over the world. She would have to go to help him.

The sky-diving was finishing. She had been aloft immeasurable times, but now a confident circadian clock inside informed her that she was down to 2,250 feet. She needed no altimeter. As she reached inside her leather jacket for the rip-cord, sick thoughts hit her. She caught a whiff of Marlo and knew many things. The parachute was opening; so was her whole area of perception, her mind painfully ripped open to an entirely new level of being, where all was revealed, flaming, frightening. ...

Her old life on Earth had ended. The plane that dropped her was not her husband's usual sports plane. A parascientific transference had been made; this plane had been – yes, they could not operate tied to Earth, as Wells and the others had supposed – this had been a time-vehicle, winging down out of space on the Byrnes-Fetesti time-energy equation, skimming through the stratosphere, coming as near as it dare to past-Earth, depositing her for this one vital mission to ensure that future was born unaborted.

Yes, from Russell's plane – they had wisely put her under artificial amnesia, but now it cleared – she had been captured from Russell's plane so long ago, carried into the future, trained for this moment, brought back to the point in time from which she had been taken. And the impetus that made it possible for her to come back was the perception by old Jacob Byrnes that the discovery of time-wells along with gravity-wells made time-travel practicable. ... She admired the symmetry of the design, even as she saw the terror that was to come in the next few hours. Spilling air, the sin-laden air of past-Earth, she sank towards the Drop Zone.

'I wish to resign from my job, sir,' said Grigson. 'It has become anathema to me.'

Byrnes was taken aback. 'You don't like it here?'

'It is simply that you do not like me, sir, and I cannot tolerate it any longer.' He stood rigid in a soldier's posture and had turned very pale.

Byrnes felt an immense shame. He could not face Grigson (what was his first name?); he had to go away, wander like an exile around his own estate. He had treated the man very badly, used his wealth, power, and charisma to purely ill ends, to defeat what little personality Grigson possessed. He had enjoyed doing it. He was an old, bitter, twice-defeated man; even at this moment, his wife, whose life he had blighted, was probably in the bed of one of his successors. No old bull of a herd had ever been so thoroughly routed.

And his son. ... Had he ever cared that Marlo was isolated, out of touch? With some miserable and ill-defined intent of having a reconciliation with the boy (or at least humiliating himself again?), Byrnes made his way eventually to Marlo's quarters.

It must have been at least two years since he was last in this wing of the building. That told of his neglect! But Marlo was by no means stagnating, whatever else he was doing. He had decorated this whole place, transformed the walls, with some sort of bright plastic stuff, some new material that created an illusory sense of projection, so that it seemed dangerous to walk along the corridor. There were montages too, and meaningless phrases scrawled over the walls and ceilings, WHO KNOWS SPEAKS NOT. NATURAL DENSITY OF LIONS. LIFE REQUIRES MORE LIFE.

Life requires more life. It could be a warm or a cold thought. The appearance of warmth in the new décor might overlie a colder thing: a very frigid horror; such was the image Byrnes derived, although he could admit that the outward semblance was far more cheerful than he had expected. But he paused with his hand on the boy's study door, fearful of opening it, aware only of chill pouring forth at his viscera. Strange images of death. Of course, he was only an old man, failed politician, failed memoirist, failed philosopher ... but this was not personal death he felt radiating from the room; this was a general death, which included death for the unborn as well as the living. Sick to the stomach, Byrnes opened the door and walked in.

Russell Crompton had his face buried in the warm depilation of her flesh; nevertheless, he could not avoid hearing Miriam say, 'But the guards who were outside the room – the guards must be involved in the murder.'

It was the last thing Crompton wanted to discuss. He said wearily, 'The FBI have virtually taken those two poor guys apart, and they didn't do it, period.'

'Well, what was on this paper that got stolen off the President's desk? Is there a clue there? Was the assassin a foreign spy?'

'Look, honey, if you are fishing for a detective job, forget it. The missing paper is about something called Project Gunwhale – all very hush-hush. It's a top secret memorandum concerning a certain pharmaceutical firm that has discovered a new drug which could change the whole social structure of mankind. If it turns up in the wrong place, wow!'

'Oh, another drug!' She sounded disappointed. This was, she reflected, the third Secretary of State she had lain with; how many girls could claim the same? She answered her own inward question: many more than you'd think, sweetie!

'Christ, I feel flaked out today. That conference on international affairs last night. ... Many more weeks of this and we won't be able to stand the pace. It's not the work, it's the decision-making that kills you. Man is not a deciding animal.'

'Philosophy I can get at home. Come and lie this way, here. That's better! Tell me about these moonmen. I told you Marlo reckons he lives on the moon. Are your eight moonmen getting any better, because Marlo isn't?'

'You shouldn't feed him LSD, baby.'

'I didn't mean to tell you that, Russ – you'd better forget it Anyhow, Marlo likes LSD. It brightens him up. How are your moonmen? Tell me something sensational.'

'Their condition is improving. They still flicker into invisibility occasionally, but that aberration grows less as their circadian rhythms adjust back to Earth Automatic.'

She sat up. 'Invisible? You mean you can't see them?'

'Not the ordinary sort of invisibility. It's just that when they are in the Lunar Automatic phase, they are actually .833 recurring seconds ahead of our time continuum, and consequently cannot be experienced by our senses. Nothing to be scared about, and they'll soon be entirely back to normal, thank God.'

She said, 'I'm not scared; it's just – wait!' But her incoherence did not stop him; after all, men's elaborate affairs, so wonderful if punctuated by the simplicities of bed; he liked the full life, the intrigues within the Administration, liked everything, even the withdrawals of his wife, which gave him moral excuse to diversions like Miriam. He would rise refreshed and encouraged from the seamy bed as from the foam! Already, he was more anxious to talk than to listen, and scheming for possible political advantage from this newly discovered temporal disturbance. He was ready to get up and get back in there pitching, but out of politeness to an old flame he could chat and fondle another ten minutes. Eight, maybe.

'Jake had the inspiration, saw at once that this implies entirely new possibilities for time-harnessing. I phoned Fetesti, who is a head man in the field, apparently, and he's coming to a conference in Washington this evening. A brilliant scientist, they say, Hungarian by origin. I don't want Jake to know I'm meeting Fetesti yet. ... I really ought to get dressed, pet. If the States could invent a time-machine or a time-projectile ahead of the rest of the world, that would solve most of our problems, huh?' He paused in the act of inserting his right foot in a sock and stared at her pale face. 'You okay?'

'My God, Russ. ... I told you Marlo was carrying on about living on the moon, and that it was a place for unwanted people to go.'

'Useless, honey. You don't remember exactly what Marlo said. I told you to write it all down. Something half remembered is useless.'

'Okay, okay! But he was talking metaphorically. He didn't mean really on the moon. He meant lunar time.' Suddenly she clung to Crompton, and they nearly fell off the bed together. 'You see – that's why Marlo never seems to be around. He is living in lunar time. He must have been in thought contact with the moonmen when they were carried back to Earth, sick. Their sickness must have corresponded with his. He learnt how to flip that little bit ahead. That's why he hardly ever seems to be around.'

'Marlo time-travelling? Impossible! What was that he said about the President? Try to remember!'

'Something about ... the President was going to make things worse and there were too many people in the world already. ... Russ, you don't think it was *Marlo* did it? Not *Marlo*?'

Crompton pulled his pants on, keeping his face blank. 'This is all in your head. It's just ego-aggression on your part, triggered by your guilt feelings because you get that little guy high on lysergic acid. If you could pin the assassination on him, why, you wouldn't have to feel bad at all. I know a good alienist here, guy called Steicher, specialises in repressed ego-aggression. He could help you. Why don't you go and see him?'

She sat very still, staring ahead, not listening, and he noticed with some irritation that she was trembling. 'The locked room – it would present no problem to Marlo if he could move that fraction ahead of time, emerging when he wanted to behind the President. He's acted odd ever since the moonmen came back. … He's always away, you can't find him, he goes off in his car, nobody checks where he's been.'

Putting a heavy hand on her shoulder, he said, 'Look, Miriam, granted all that, why would he want to kill the President? What's the motivation?'

Then he remembered: Rhoda had dreamed about Marlo. He was frightened of Rhoda's dreams; they belonged to some super-reality which even Steicher could not satisfactorily explain away. Rhoda had dreamed that Marlo was playing the name part in a performance, of *Macbeth,* which was held in the grounds of Gondwana. The boy had made a great Thane of Cawdor, and had also played the part of the witches, which had much amused his father, Jake Byrnes. Byrnes enjoyed having his house cast as Macbeth's castle, but grew angry when his son insisted on ending the play on the lake, saying that the bamboo grove was moving in to destroy him.

Troubled by the dream, Crompton outlined it to Miriam. To his annoyance, she brushed it aside. 'A dream means nothing; it's the facts that count. Besides, Rhoda's dream has no end.'

'It did end! I remember. She said that Macbeth refused to be killed by Macduff – and the President was playing the part of Macduff!'

'Very cute! And Macbeth killed him instead of him killing Macbeth?'

He shook his head. 'Funny, I remember I asked Rhoda that same question at the time. She did not know. These strange dreams of hers have their blanks. But it ended with Jake running out of the bamboo grove and killing Marlo.'

They stared at each other. Miriam swallowed and said, 'You do think Marlo was the President's assassin, then?'

'There's the motive – he wanted to defeat Project Gunwhale, represented in the dream by Macduff's lineage. Its existence was a threat to his life.'

'He had been to the White House as a boy, when his father was in the Administration. Maybe he could recall his way around. But a dream is just a dream.'

'No more, no less. And when I spoke to the boy last week, he said something about shooting whales on the lake. His life is a dream. With the ability to move ahead of time, our precognition becomes for him pre-action.' As he spoke, Crompton felt some of the intense fear Marlo must have done, when looking at the thickening complexity of the future.

It communicated itself to Miriam. She said, 'Russ, is Jake really going to kill Marlo? I'll have to stay here. I'm – I'm scared to go back to Gondwana.'

Mentally disturbed or not, he was again the Secretary of State. Getting into his jacket, he said, 'You believe in the actuality of symbolic levels too, don't you, Miriam? Stay here! But I'm getting down there with some police, fast. The whole nation wants that assassin *alive*.'

She seemed incapable of leaving the bed, was now cuddled down among the sheets, peering at him as he strode across the room as if she no longer recognised him. 'Russ, you don't think that the drugs I've been giving him helped upset him in any way, do you? I really only did it to spite Jake a bit? I never meant ...'

As he picked up the telephone and began to dial, he said, 'I forgot to tell you, honey. In the dream, you played Lady Macbeth.'

The room was empty. At least, Marlo was not there. It took some while to verify the fact, because the room was so crowded with strange clutter that it baffled Byrnes' sight. He was still fighting the ill-feelings in his stomach.

The boy's sickness, it is anti-life, he told himself. Just because such sickness is prevalent, we must not accept it as normal. It is a rejection. Sickness not the reverse of health but of moral responsibility. ... People must be warned. Put it in the next chapter. Add that we have to come to terms with the way mental illness functions. After all, it has its own creativity. Illness is a mystery to us. As is health. The nightmares of sleep intrude into waking, and the horrors we face by day walk masked through the night. It's gun-and-clock time, when the orchestration of the inner life falters and the conductor absconds. ...

The bad images led him to one wall which was covered with recent newspaper clippings, a whole host, secured only along their top edges – the better to rustle and live, maybe – so recent they had not yet had time to yellow. All concerned the murder of the President. Several clips of the famous shot of him slumped over his desk. He had worked till the last, all very touching. You could see the flag behind his chair.

In the middle of the assemblage of fluttering columns was a white sheet of governmental memo paper. Byrnes recognised it at once and read it. He re-read it. On the third reading, it made sense; and its place here also made sense. He clutched his belly.

It was a, top secret memorandum addressed to the late President by his advisers, subject Project Gunwhale. It advised that a comparatively obscure pharmaceutical combine, Statechem Inc., had run a three-year test on a new type of gerontotherapeutic drug, patent name Surviva, with conspicuous success on seven species of laboratory animals. No animal showed signs of ageing. Tests had also been carried out on human volunteers in the laboratory staff; although the test period was too brief for any positive results to be expected, all indications were hopeful – no signs of cellular deterioration – grey hair turning black – no deleterious side-effects. Surviva seemed to promise extreme longevity and was inexpensive to produce. Permission was requested for Statechem to ask publicly for volunteers, and for the security blanket on its findings to be lifted. Statechem directors saw no reason why injections for immortality should not be available to all in ten months from the cessation of successful testing.

At the bottom of the memo, one of the President's advisers had written in longhand, 'To go ahead with this in view of present world famines and over-population would shatter all social structures and wreck the planet in one generation.'

Pinned to the memo was another sheet, an answer in what Byrnes recognised as the President's fluid italic script: 'This is an old argument, Ted. If Statechem have it now, someone else will have it soon. We have to okay it and face the problems arising. Besides, we need the additional brain-power: imagine even an extra decade working life from every US scientist. Besides, I'm irrevocably on the side of life.' And his initials, slightly smudged. Must have been the last thing he ever wrote before the killer took him.

I'm irrevocably on the side of life. So am I, Byrnes told himself; can't help it. And immortal life? Well, you'd give it a swing. ... The resultant problems didn't bear thinking about; and the advisers, perhaps rightly, came out against the idea on that score. But the President, even more rightly, cut them down. ... Well, was going to cut them down when he was killed. By the initials of the advisers, Byrnes saw that Crompton and Strawn and two other men were involved. They would be no-sayers; and they were the ones now with the power.

And another thing. The killer. This was why he had killed. He would be a no-sayer. Saying no to life, no to the future, no to that terrible tide called progress; you had to say yes and then *do* yes. ... The killer had killed and come away with this memo.

'Marlo? Where are you?' Marlo would be a no-sayer. His insanity was one of his generation's major ways of saying no. So he had given shelter to the killer, housed the killer here, here in Gondwana Hills. The painful irony of it! The old man felt his eyes burn with tears. His own son sheltering the President's assassin!

He dashed the tears quickly away and pulled out his gun. Maybe the killer was still here. He crammed the incriminating document into his pocket and backed to the door. Wonderfully, the sick feeling had left him. All he felt now was a blind anger, against his son, against the killer, against the circumstances, which he saw were reaching out again to involve him in another disgrace; this one he could not withstand; it would encompass his book, too, overwhelm its frail merits and vital message. The future was dying, the promise of the past collapsing into chaos.

'Come out, you bastards!' he bellowed. The gaudy tatty room, thugs' hideout, nest of sickness, plotter's parlour, den for a murderer, absorbed all sound. It was full of the dull stained light as associated with sin, a stain he had seen once in a university production of *Macbeth*. Light thickens and the crow makes wing to the rooky wood. It frightened him a little. He backed into the corridor again, roared his son's name, loud as he could to bring his courage back.

Marlo appeared before him. One moment he was not there, the next he was. Although his face was the usual withdrawn blank, his eyes flared with purpose. He moved towards his father, ignoring the revolver. Byrnes was shouting at him, but it was as though neither of them heard the noise. He got his arm round his father's throat with a sudden movement and pulled him back, violently, with an unexpected hard strength. Stars swam in a red haze before Byrnes' eyes, and his voice croaked off. He fought, not understanding, the gun still in his hand, afraid even to hit Marlo with it.

Through the haze, he saw – or dreamed, it felt – Grigson run up, striking out with, of all futile Grigsonish articles, a leather briefcase. The briefcase caught Marlo hard under the eye. He at once let go of Byrnes, whimpering. Grigson, looking rather stupid, steadied himself for another blow; Byrnes sank to the floor, staring pitifully up. Marlo disappeared: flickered, vanished as if he had never been.

His senses came back. The idiot Grigson was pouring a little clear water on his face. Two servants were bending stupidly over him; there was a third man standing in the background. Byrnes roared and tried to get up. They assisted him.

'I heard your call for help, sir –'

'You did a great job, Grigson!'

'But your son disappeared, sir, vanished like a ghost!'

'The hell he did! Call the guard! Did you call the guard?'

'No, sir!'

'You're fired, Grigson!'

'If you remember, sir –'

'Go to hell!'

He staggered out, trying to orient. They had carried him to one of the bathrooms. Used to be Alice's bathroom. ... And that boy, Alice's boy, for him to attack his father, he must be hypnotised, in the power of a killer, an assassin, the assassin, hiding out in his place!

He hit the nearest alarm button, was comforted as the unholy babel broke out from the clock tower. He took the elevator down to ground level, was met at the gates by Captain Harris, head of the security team.

'Didn't you see I was being attacked over the bugging, Captain?'

'No, sir! Where were you?'

'In the west wing, could have been killed! What were your men doing?'

'Your son removed all the bugging in that part of the house.'

'Of course, he would have done. ... Listen, Captain, get hold of my son. Don't hurt him, but hold him. Lock him up safe down here. He is sheltering the President's assassin. Yes, you heard me! Get that assassin if you have to burn the place down. No, no, don't do that! Have a man go straight and guard my study, in case anyone tries to get in there and wreck my work.'

Harris nodded curtly. He lived for crisis. He issued orders all round, despatched men efficiently, told Byrnes, 'All shuttering is down, sir, and all doors are on autolock. Nobody can get out without our say so.'

'Okay.' He was mollified at last, thanking God inwardly for Harris; little Harris cared about the future, but he was great for emergencies. 'Then let me out of here, will you? I need fresh air.'

Harris deputed a younger man, who opened up the armourplated front door and let Byrnes through. He staggered out and sat on his top step as the door closed behind him. He shielded his eyes and tried to calm his heartbeat, afraid of a stroke. His throat ached. The boy had hurt him.

It was growing dark. A dreary evening, the whole landscape. Macbeth-coloured, over the hills anger and unholiness. Good things of day began to droop and drowse. A searchlight came on over the lake on the landing-field, picking him out. He stood up, feeling guilty and vulnerable, signalling to them to turn it off. The great eye did not waver. Byrnes fought an urge to hammer at the door behind him for readmittance.

His little English sports car stood by the house. Muttering angrily, he climbed in, started up, and drove across to the field, the beam following him all the way. They must have identified him, for a figure ran from the guard-tower to meet him. It was Captain MacGregor, to whom Byrnes addressed a blistering stream of abuse.

'I'm sorry about that, sir,' said MacGregor, without sounding very penitent. 'Captain Harris explained the situation to me over the phone. We have an alert on out here. But Secretary of State Crompton just radioed, sir.'

It was going to be bad. From men in office, full of ambition, only the worst could be expected. Death in their mouth and in their eyes dust. 'Well?'

'He said your son is charged with murder, sir, and you are charged with complicity, sir.'

'Washington madness! Madness!'

'He didn't radio from Washington, sir. He is flying over here, should be landing in eight minutes. Has strong police escort. Two planes. He ordered me personally to place you and your son under arrest, sir.'

'MacGregor!'

'Sir?'

'I order you to shoot those planes down.'

'Shoot ... I can't, sir!'

'The future, man! The future demands it! Shoot them down!'

'I can't do that, sir. But equally I can't arrest you, sir. You're free till they land here, sir. It gives you seven or eight minutes to get away.'

So MacGregor already judged him guilty. There was nothing he could do.

'Thanks, MacGregor.'

He walked away, past the sports car, the engine of which still ran quietly, heading blindly towards the bamboo grove. So much for philosophy. That fool, Russell. ... So he and Marlo were to be made national scapegoats. A clever idea, certainly; much better than nabbing a complete unknown; they could fake it to look as if he had been after the Presidential seat himself, maybe – any madness they cared to dream up.

Miriam must have found out that Marlo was sheltering the assassin and had gone and told Russell Crompton. He would make political capital out of it.

Rhoda took his hand and said, 'I'm here, Jake. Don't be alarmed.'

'You, Rhoda? You here? What are you doing at Gondwana?' The balm was still pouring from her, a lovely womanly emanation. She was standing on the spot where he had earlier fired at his own image; perhaps just a coincidence.

'I am on your side entirely, Jake. The future's side. I believe as you do that the world can only solve its problems by throwing them open and facing them, not by suppressing them. I also believe that it needs all the forces it can muster to do that, and that among those forces you personally are important – *and* that you will be lost, and your book with you, if you do not ride out this next ten minutes. I'll help on that. I know what is going to happen.'

'Maybe you do.'

'"Here upon this bank and shoal of time, we'll jump the life to come". But perhaps it invites ill-luck to quote Lady Macbeth!'

'Rhoda ... is the *haragei* gone? Can we speak and move freely together at last?'

'We can. I was not myself. Now I am.'

'Well, I'm beside myself! I get only chill feelings from all but you. Maybe we should cease to believe in logical systems at the expense of all others. After all, machines are now freeing us from the necessity of either – or thought; that's their job; we should deal with the nuances, where real life lives. I intuit that Russell is going to make me a scapegoat on the national scale.'

She nodded and said coolly, 'You realise that you are on the brink of madness. You must draw back. Russell has little against you save the guilt he feels for lying with your wife; but he has great ambition. To capture you and Marlo tonight and brand you with conspiring to kill the President would make him a national hero.'

In the darkening sky, the sound of engines. The new jet-copters. Yes, their lights visible overhead. The birds of vengeance settling on the tender plains of peace.

'I must go to Marlo. He's mad! They must not hurt him!'

'Think. You are rejecting the evidence of your senses, preferring to embrace sickness rather than face truth. You saw Marlo vanish. You must admit that to yourself; and then you just admit another thing ...'

The darkness seemed to torment him. Angrily he shook his great grey head about, scattering tears. Trembling, he forced himself to say, '... That he is the assassin.'

For a moment he could not see. The bamboos boiled like a midnight ocean and her words could scarcely reach him.

'Though the forces ranged against life are many, the thoughts of good always rise higher. Listen, my dear old battered Jake, you might clear yourself of complicity, but the disgrace would wreck you, break your life, disrupt the whole future course of events.'

The copters were crawling down in their own winds now. She was shouting to make him hear. 'I waited here for you because here you will see Marlo at any minute. He cannot maintain himself in the Lunar Automatic for long. He will run to shoot Russell, who – with Miriam's aid – has pieced together most of the information he needs for an arrest. Marlo has immense powers, but he is not supernatural. You do not need a silver bullet, Jake, to bring a better future into being.'

He stared into her face. 'You know I can't kill him, my son!'

She kissed him on the lips. 'You will.'

As the wind whipped round them and the two black shapes of flight began to straddle the field, she pointed. 'Your Captain Harris was too late with his lock-in! Marlo was already outside!'

Forgetting her, he hurried towards his son, a dark figure running at a crouch, using the dead ground behind the sports car to approach the machines now landing. He shouted, but Marlo did not hear. He grabbed him from behind.

To his sudden fear, he saw the knife in Marlo's hand and the blank stare in his eyes. A man like a machine, not so much sick as unable to feel human or feel for humanity. As the knife came round, Byrnes saw that Rhoda, calling aloud his own creed, was right: it was kill or be killed. Even so, he could not kill his own son: even survival had a relative value. He fired the gun down into the ground, three times, as fast as he could pull the trigger. It diverted Marlo only slightly. As the knife cut his side, Byrnes jumped on the boy's instep and punched him hard and wildly under the jaw. They tumbled to the wind-lashed ground together.

Jacob Byrnes refused to stay in the local hospital for more than a day. Bandaged tight, he got himself driven back to Gondwana Hills as soon as possible. A benevolent – a highly-charged and erotic – image told him that Rhoda Crompton would be there.

As his driver helped him out of the car, Byrnes glared loweringly round. Work on the squash court had ceased, so there were no décor men about. But an Army plane on the landing-field, five big limousines, two police vans, and a mobile forensic laboratory told him that he had visitors. They would be taking poor Marlo's quarters apart, gathering every shred of evidence for the trial – in which, judging by yesterday's news reports, his father was going to be a sort of national hero as well as one of the chief witnesses. The wretched business would involve a colossal interruption of work; he thought he could face that if Rhoda were around. His main efforts must be devoted to trying to help Marlo. Miriam could be helped through solicitors. Feeding drugs to the boy, feeding him drugs! – that took some forgiving!

At the top of the steps, Grigson met him.

'Mrs Russell Crompton is inside, sir.'

'Didn't expect to see you still here, Grigson.'

'No, sir. But I thought you might have special need of me over the next few months, in view of which I feel I should postpone my resignation a while.'

He clapped his secretary on the shoulder. 'We need you, Grigson. Help keep the cops out of my hair. We may need your dangerous briefcase again for all I know. Come along!'

But Grigson faded away in the hall, muttering excuses, as Rhoda appeared. She had parachuted in, and was carrying a pair of goggles in one hand, although she had changed into a corduroy dress. Her long ash hair was pulled into a single braid, which hung over one shoulder. Cutting through any reserve Byrnes might be feeling, she put her hands on his upper arm.

'You won't be surprised to see me, but I hope you're pleased. I figured you needed help here for a while.'

'Everyone seems to think I need help. How intuitive everyone has suddenly become! Come on upstairs, Rhoda, before I go and talk to the cops. You can make me a drink; that damned hospital was on a temperance kick.'

'How's the side?'

'It was a love bite.' He looked at her, smiled, hoping he did not look too tired and old; she seemed to find a question in his gaze.

'I've finished with Russell,' she said. 'He, of course, has finished with Miriam, having got what use he can from her, so I suppose the situation is symmetrical.'

'I ruined Miriam's life. I was too much for her. She's my responsibility; there is still help I can give – particularly now Marlo is off my hands. ... Rhoda, do they ... they don't make too much of a godamned psychodrama of his trial, do they, purgation of national guilt and all that?'

She laughed. 'I cannot foretell the future now. You defeated the predicted future the day before yesterday by not killing Marlo. So the laws of temporal causation must be reformulated – clearly *have* been reformulated in the time ahead of mine, as is shown by the way nobody travels back to a non-time-travelling age, for fear of altering temporal causation.'

They took the elevator up to Byrnes' suite of rooms where he lived and worked. He still felt shy with her, had not entirely shed the feeling of *haragei*; he was inhibited from asking her directly what role she was going to play in his life. Knowing he was now, however undeservedly, a national hero for having tackled and disarmed his assassin son, he felt his freedom curtailed. At least he could use the popularity while it lasted to promulgate the ideas he stood for. First, he must confer with Fetesti; Rhoda should sit in on that.

'You are going to be so necessary, Rhoda. ... Not just personally. You don't have to ... return to whenever it is? You can stay?'

Colouring, she said, 'Don't count on me too much, Jake. I love you, but I'm a sky-diver and that's my first love – a sort of celestial junkie, you see. But I'll live here if you'll have me. Your drop-zone is second to none.'

She looked tenderly at the emotional warmth that crept into his face, then turned to get him a stiff drink as he sank into a chair, saying as she did so, 'I have no place ahead. I was born thirty-eight years ago; the future that kidnapped me during one of my sky-dives was only twenty years ahead.'

'It must be very different.'

'Tremendously. And yet *you* would recognise it, if only because a small part lies already in your brain.' Should she go on and tell him? There were reservations in people private even from themselves; she feared that what she was going to say might shock and startle him; but while it was his personal gun-and-clock time, so late in his life, he should have it straight. 'Jake, while they were training me for this – adventure, they gave me the Surviva inoculations, a variety of the Surviva inoculations mentioned in that fatal memorandum to the late President. I'm not ... not subject to the usual three score years and ten any more.'

There was a long silence in the room.

Finally, he scratched the top of his head and said, 'People like you should always have the chance of a long, long life. I suppose that – twenty years ahead – I wasn't still lumbering around, doing good, holding forth, pontificating, was I?'

'... No. Your book was still holding forth, though, and doing good.'

'Give us that drink! Then I don't have to decide; the decision has been taken. I don't want the inoculations. The trajectory of my life is something I refuse to wrench out of its pattern for anything.' Then suddenly he was frightened at what he had said. He had done too much, suffered too much, and more of that to be got through yet, of course. The pain of Marlo's trial ...

She kissed him as she handed him the glass. Suddenly he grabbed her with all his strength, only to release her, groaning.

'My side! I'll have at you, woman, when I'm healed.'

'I hope so. Here's looking at you!'

'And you!' There was so much he wanted to ask. ... That inestimable privilege, never before granted to any mortal, of being able to look coolly ahead to the evolving future. He must not abuse it, must take it in digestible portions. One of the first questions will have to be – maybe he should make a list – how they managed to square the population explosion with having people around for longer, if the world was not going to be unbearably clogged with living bodies. But, of course, if they adopted the only possible system and gave Surviva free to everyone proved capable of benefiting from extra years (and what sort of test would that be, O Lord!), then it needed only another serum mixed with the inoculations to guarantee that the immortals did not procreate, or only to a controlled degree. The technical problems were not so great; it was the social problems that loomed so very large. Even a better politico-economic system would change so much, the wars of aggression, the famines in one state while there were gluts in another. Since world decisions were now going to be made, and the future was once more out of the log-pile, then clearly human consciousness was again on the dynamic upgrade towards a higher level of being. Longevity fitted naturally into the pattern. The pattern! Of course, that was what must be grasped – and could be grasped once the basic principle was taken; and the basic principle was so simple that the most backward African tribe embraced it whole-heartedly: life is good. And the clamour that would wake any day when Crompton announced the Surviva findings would show the west what the west had forgotten: that even sickness was precious, but life was better. Proof and proposition were all one; or to put it another way ...

'Darling, you aren't drinking your drink!'

'I just want to make a note of something,' he said.

So Far From Prague

The chauffeur stopped the car and walked smartly round to open the door for Slansky. Slansky climbed out into the ruinous street. A crowd of children gathered to watch him as he walked up the hotel steps. Its double doors were closed; abstractedly, he took in the elaborate fret of the woodwork. As he pushed, one of the doors creaked open. As he walked into the dark hall, his driver came up behind him, deposited his suitcase, and saluted, one hand to his turban, the other cupped before him.

Hardly thinking, Slansky gave him a rupee note. The man disappeared, the door closed, Slansky was left standing in the sweet dusk of the hall. I must get back home.

His despair and anger were such that he stood alone for a minute completely lost to his surroundings, mentally back in Prague. Then the sweat trickling down his collar reminded him of his physical presence.

In the gloom of the hall, flies buzzed. From a hidden radio somewhere came the hum of a *veena*. The smells too were Indian: the prickle of woodsmoke, a faulty drain somewhere, a musky perfume, the aroma of spiced food.

'Anyone here?' he asked in English.

It's a curious sort of hotel. Was there even a sign over the door? I didn't look. But Bihari Das gave me the address – he would know it was all right. No matter. Nothing here's important.

Now that he was alone, away from Sadal Bihari Das and his multi-tudinous friends, Slansky was reluctant to feel anything but anger and despair. It was curious how those emotions could be eclipsed by a much

543

slighter irritation. True, he had broken rudely away from Sadal's party, given in his honour, but surely Sadal would not have played a mean trick on him by sending him to some impossible place? Would he have to get a taxi back to Delhi?

There was a cubbyhole for reception. A dim light burned there, but all looked absolutely dead. Closed doors all round. The very air unmoving.

And growing in my wife, the world of the future – a little curled up thing with little nails and gills, hair already forming, rudimentary dreams in its head, going to live in a happier world, didn't we hope, oh Gordana, my dearest precious darling!

A glass-bead curtain hung to one side of the reception desk. Slansky pushed through it into a dim side-hall that had three doors opening from it. The smell of food lay more heavily here. Horizontal sunlight lay here at disconcerting angles, as if reflected from tarnished mirrors. Stepping forward, Slansky pushed open the nearest door and walked in.

He found himself in a living-room full of furniture, encumbered by sofas, chairs, small tables, potted plants, bureaux, bookcases, and a massive upright piano. Large photographs – faded and brown-stained, showing posed scenes or family groups, it appeared – hung in heavy frames from the walls. Detail did not present itself to Slansky, since the only illumination came from windows at the far end of the tangled room and an open door looking out across a veranda onto bright gardens beyond; the horizontal evening light insinuated itself into the room, reflecting off table-tops and the front of the piano, creating shadows that stood like solid obstacles in Slansky's way.

This much, he took in at a glance, and the fact that a second door, open in the right-hand wall, revealed a bedroom beyond, in which he glimpsed a bed veiled in mosquito netting. Then a movement caught his eye, and he saw, outlines made indistinct by the confusion of light and shadow, a man standing against the post of the door leading to the veranda. He gazed across the length of the room at Slansky.

The man was young and appeared to be wearing a uniform. He was well-built and fair; his face looked square and honest. Evidently he was a European. The expression on his face was friendly and the movement by which he revealed himself was evidently intended to be one of welcome.

Overcome by a form of embarrassment which sometimes attacked him, Slansky withdrew himself from the room before the stranger could complete his gesture. He had intruded, and was angry with himself. This evidently was a private room.

Fearing that the stranger might follow him, he walked quickly through the side-hall into a rear passage, and thus into an inner courtyard.

This was where the music came from. An Indian family was lunching here, sitting on stone flags in the shade of a further wall. They saw Slansky as soon as he stepped into the sunlight.

A grey-haired lady in a sari stood up and came to him, shooing back a pair of small boys who dared to follow her. She greeted Slansky courteously and asked if he were Slansky Sahib.

'Antonin Slansky, madam. You were expecting me?'

'Yes, sahib, we are expecting you. My son has had to go to the bazaar or he would welcome you more properly. Nevertheless, may I allow to show you your rooms?'

As he followed her back into the building, with the two boys struggling to take his luggage, he asked her if this was a hotel.

'This is the hotel for friends of Sadal Bihari Das only, sahib. He own this hotel and keeps it closed except for his personal guests. In his Delhi flat is not many room for comfort.'

'I see. And are there many guests here now beside me?'

'In the hot season is not many guests, sir. Later they come.'

She showed him into an upstairs room. It was a lounge; a bedroom and a modern bathroom led off it. Smiling and bowing, she left him, ushering the boys along with her, and at once he was left with his anger and despair, isolated in another foreign room.

My dear Czech land, your peace and beauty – what are the Russians doing to you at this hour! Their heavy armour grinding down the hopes we had this spring. My comrades – I can't stay here, I must go and join them and die, let the blood of my fingers rust the tank tracks! That our socialist allies, our brother Slavs should so betray us, and after Bratislava and Cierna – Honour is dead! I can't stay! I must fly back to Prague! To hell with the damned film project!

A radio stood on a side table, decorously covered by a linen drape decorated with beads. He swept the cover aside and switched on the set.

Music came, to his impatience a wailing and barbarous noise. He looked at his watch. Six minutes to the hour.

He passed the six minutes impatiently, striding up and down the room or gazing from his balcony at the pattern below of courtyard, tiles, and garden, with fields beyond fringed with palms. At the hour, a radio announcer began to read the news in Hindi. At five past, he read the news in English.

'Units of the Russian army are now moving into Czechoslovakia unopposed. Polish, East German, Hungarian, and Bulgarian units are also involved. Firing has been reported from Prague and other large cities such as Brno and Bratislava; in the capital itself, twenty people are reported killed, but in the main the occupation is proceeding without opposition –'

Gordana, I beg you still to be enjoying your holiday down on the Dalmatian coast and not back in Prague, don't be back in Prague, don't be back in Prague, please don't be back in Prague, stay out of Prague, stay out of our beloved country! Stay down in Yugoslavia! Now that you're pregnant, you shouldn't drive so fast. Because I know you secretly hope it will be a girl, I also hope it will be a girl.

Opening his suitcase, he stared down at its contents, seeing only the creases in the crushed clothes, trying to decipher them.

'There is still no news of the whereabouts of Mr Dubcek, key figure in the liberalisation programme implemented in the spring ...'

It is only two months since we talked together, Alexander Dubcek! You wanted me to continue to experiment in the cinema. Now where are you? I really wouldn't put it past them to shoot you. And Svoboda. They'll want a puppet government. Could they really have shot him? Is it all true? My madness, an Indian madness? Am I dreaming? It's true enough – and the Warsaw Pact ... Communism is betrayed. It's worse than a dream!

He paced about the room, walked into the bedroom, strode onto the balcony, looked aimlessly about. Below was the veranda. On it stood the stocky fair-haired man from the suite below. He turned and went in as Slansky glimpsed him. 'Friend of Bihari Das'. English perhaps. American? Will the Americans do anything? Oh, Gordana, and we have plans we haven't even planned yet. Next month you are twenty-nine and the liberalisation was proceeding. It's been so good to be alive.

The sun had almost finished its tyrannous day's business with the Ganges plain. In nearby trees, thousands of birds gathered, screaming, struggling, and excreting. People walked in the shadowed streets. He could not stay where he was, could not stay.

Pacing downstairs, he passed an old man now sitting at the reception desk and strode out into the rear courtyard. The music was playing, laden with discord. He ignored the people and the children, marching through the rear archway into the garden he had noted from his balcony.

The garden was small; imprisoned within its walls lay the heat of the day. It had a well, the swivelling arm of which, perched awkwardly on two legs, dipped down into the well like a wooden beak. There was a rear gate set in the white wall, closed and barred with a cross-beam. A battered charpoy stood by the door under a crude shelter. A lantern burned, hanging from one of the poles supporting the shelter's thatched roof. On the bed sat an old man, reading to a child. The child was almost naked; it sprawled elegantly against the side of the bed, listening abstractedly as the old man read, his ancient face pressed close to the page.

It's a real deep betrayal, destroying everything! Not the anaesthesia of a mere political betrayal, like the Anglo-French betrayal of 1938. No, this is a personal betrayal, almost brother against brother. It's only a few days since they signed the Bratislava agreement, the dogs! It's us they assassinate, each one of us, not just the liberalisation, us, us, us. In Eastern Europe, the personal life is done to death, the way the capitalist countries do it to death with financial manipulation. I'll have to go back to find Gordana. Oh my darling, stay safe!

As Slansky stood in the gathering gloom, the old man became aware of his presence. He ceased his reading and looked up. His broad old face was deformed by age, the cheeks puckered almost like blisters over the cheekbones, the white beard fibrous and clinging like cat-scratches far down the throat. Gravely marking his place in the book, he set it down and raised his hands, fingertips together, in salute. The boy copied the gesture.

'Hello. I had no intention of interrupting.'

A stick of agarbatti, held firm in a crack of the bed, smouldered into the greying air. The old man said something interrogatively.

'I don't speak any Indian languages,' Slansky said sharply. Even exchanging a salute implied more involvement than he could manage just now. Behind his thick glasses, the old man's eyes floated, large, apparently detached. Then he said something to the small boy and resumed his reading, holding the book high to catch the feeble light of his lantern.

Slansky resumed his pacing, slapping occasionally at a mosquito.

Bihari Das should have called the celebration off when he heard the news from Prague. He was always insensitive in some ways. Garrulous people are always insensitive. I must speak to him before I leave. Everything's in ruins. The Dark Ages. Fascism. Machine-people crushing individuals down until machines take over the job. Gordana. Talking in the yard to old General Rambousek, filling the yard with her pleasantness. The cobbles, her neat ankles, legs, the vine on the wall. Coming to the studios, working on those first documentaries together. Helping to improvise equipment. Her idea for the cartoon. Haven't we suffered enough ... The economy being deliberately run down, and now where is she? What would that old Indian man say if he knew? Poor old fellow ... But being dull and stupid – maybe he isn't – he would never know our anguish.

There was no peace for him in the garden.

With one last slap at the mosquitoes, he walked back into the hotel and approached the desk clerk.

'Do you speak English? I wish to talk to Mr Bihari Das on the phone. Will you please ring him at his Delhi flat for me?'

'Certainly, sir. I will get him immediately, although there is possibly an hour's delay on the Delhi line.'

'Will you try at once? I will wait here.'

He turned impatiently in the narrow hall. Bihari Das entered at the front door. He ran and embraced his friend.

'Antonin, my dear man, you see I escaped away from the awful party! Let them fiddle while Rome burns, what do I care for it if my guest of honour cannot be there?'

'I was just trying to phone you, Sadal!'

'Yes, yes, well, that will no longer be necessary! Here I am! I shall be in hot water, you mark my words, for leaving those people, but it positively does not matter to me. Let's go upstairs to your room, if we may, eh, and have a chat?' He signalled to the desk clerk to attend them.

*

In the room upstairs, darkness was plunging down. Looking from the balcony, Slansky could see the little glow-worm light at the far corner of the garden, where the old man read to the child. From the street came people's voices and music. Lightning flickered round the serrated edges of the horizon.

As he took a drink from Bihari Das, he said, 'To concentrate on film-making is beyond me. I'll have to get the first flight back to Prague tomorrow.'

Bihari Das was still in his twenties, small, dapper, full of energy, with a great crop of blue-black hair. His light blue suit and silk shirt were immaculate. He shone Slansky a smile that had ravished many a screen in the days before he took to directing instead of starring.

'I know what you are thinking, my dear man. You think I have been terribly insensitive to your predicament. Well, it is not so, though I admit I don't understand this private row between two allied Communist states. I hate politics, hate it absolutely, with the true loathing of an artist. I have phoned the airport and made a reservation for you already on the Air India flight at 10.05 hours tomorrow back to Prague. Does that make you feel better towards me?'

'I always thought well of you, Sadal. That is most thoughtful of you. Again I owe you my gratitude.'

'Say no more. Thank my secretary – it was he who executed all the painful details. He will produce the tickets tomorrow. And now – now your mind is more at ease, let us talk cinema and forget all the boredom and horror of politics. Once the Russians have helped your government stamp out all the subversive elements in the country, conditions will be back to normal and we can resume planning our joint film about the petrification of time.'

Reluctantly, Slansky said, 'It's not like that, Sadal! The subversive elements in our country are all imposed there by the Soviet Union. We have had years of rule by Moscow stooges, running down the economy, limiting our freedom of speech. They are being weeded out by Dubcek and Svoboda, and the nation is behind them. We must be our own bosses. Now the Soviet Union is trying to reimpose her rule, and we must resist in every way possible, short of taking up arms. Passive resistance – Mahatma Gandhi would have approved, for sure.'

'Gandhi's a long time ago! Let's discuss our film, Antonin, my dear man, since our time is so cut short.' He sat on a sofa and lounged back, cocking his legs up till his ankles rested on the sofa-arm. Looking dreamily at the ceiling, he said, 'Czechoslovakia after all gets economic aid and military protection from Russia all the while. She is not a strictly neutral country, like India. How can you complain?'

'Complain! When that so-called military protection means tanks sitting in the central square of every town, when the hoodlums in the Kremlin kidnap our Dubcek like Chicago hoodlums. Can you not understand what a blow has fallen, even this far from Prague?'

Bihari Das waved a hand. 'So far from Prague, we perhaps understand better. This is just a European power-brawl, isn't it, not to be rated in importance with the concerns of art.'

'Sadal – I beg you! Don't try to anger me! Even if it were just a power-brawl, it concerns *people*, it concerns *truth*, it concerns *art*. The Soviet rulers don't care for people, they don't know what truth is, they hate and fear art. They will stamp out art and truth in our country if they get the chance!'

He pressed his fingertips to his forehead. Don't tell me art and truth can never be stamped out! They have been! We have seen them stamped out twice in my country in my lifetime, by Hitler and by Stalin, and now that fearful spectre rises again. It taints all our lives. It is never dormant. It lurks here too, Bihari Das, lurks in your decadent attitude – you're never so far from Prague that you can escape the forces of evil and night. Gordana, let everything else die but you and the future you carry in your sweet belly – let truth and the rest die! They're all meaningless without their dear embodiment in you, wherever you now are, wherever you are at this very minute. Oh, I should have made you come with me and laughed at your fear of air travel, my dearest – your first presence when we were working together on that iron-ore documentary, only five years ago. That terrible hotel in Brno. 'You must try to understand that I'm going back to fight for things you take here for granted.'

Bihari Das waved a hand in disdain.

'Nonsense, my dear man, we chucked the British out, you know – oh, sure, it was almost before I was pupped! But we are no better since they have been gone and, frankly, my sympathy is rather with the British. We gave them a lot of trouble, you know. They are very simple and orderly people, much like the Russians.'

'The Soviets are imperialists, just as the British were. They have just committed a naked act of imperialist aggression against my country. Who has made you believe otherwise?'

Bihari Das sat up. 'Come on, dear man, don't give me propaganda after you are speaking so highly of art. I sympathise with you as a husband, but your country has surely got what it asked for as a troublesome satellite, and the Russians will merely restore order. Order is important, even if a few people get hurt. You must forgive me if I see the Russian point of view. Now, let's get off this boring subject and speak of what lies more closely to our hearts, for heaven's sake!'

Once, there were private places. They've gone – even here, they've gone, so far from Prague! Art has got to wear a sword. I can't talk to him. Someone has fed him lying propaganda. I can't ... 'Sadal, I can't – I don't feel well enough to talk. I'm upset.'

He sat on a chair opposite Bihari Das and the two men stared at one another.

At last, Bihari Das broke into his disarming smile. 'You should have some exercise before dinner, Antonin. You know what? At the back of this building and its garden lies my *bagh* – well, it's quite a scientific little farm really, forty acres where we grow the latest wheat varieties and hybrid millets. I have installed a tubewell and a tractor. I hoped to drive you round it.'

'Your latest craze, Sadal?'

'More than a craze! Gentlemen farmers are springing everywhere. We help the government and get rich ourselves. It's a very big development everywhere. Nowadays, it's as easy to become a millionaire in agriculture as it once was in film-making.'

'So you're going to make a second fortune!'

The winning smile again. 'I am forced to, my dear man, to pay off the tax I owe on the first. Come, we will go down, and I'll give you a fresh sniff of air, since you aren't up to talking.'

She came back from the seaside directly she heard that the Russian tanks were rolling in, while her Yugoslav friends, preparing to defend their own frontiers, talked of 'the most monstrous event in history'. She drove overnight, ignoring tiredness, and reached Prague early in the morning. She stopped in Wenceslas Square, in order to go to my office.

Already there were people in the square, mainly youngsters, surrounding the Russian tanks. Already each Russian tank had its neat little stinking pile of rubbish and excrement at the back. The Russian troops had to keep to their posts. Their nerves were on edge. Swastikas had been chalked on their vehicles. Close-up.

One tank crew could stand the tension no more. Its commander gave the order to fire. Students scattered wildly as the guns opened up. A figure in the background, uninvolved. Startled, taken by surprise. Zoom in as she falls. Blood running from some hidden place.

Oh no, my darling, no, no, not you, not my Gordana!

Beyond the torment of the stairs, the ordinary mysterious evening, still hardly advanced since last time he was here. But dark now, and everywhere the sounds of happiness of people – happiness perhaps a little hard to believe in face of that hysterical note in the *veena* music. We had it ourselves, it was ours, and above all the hope of more, if we pushed for it.

Lightning still burnished the night's darkness. Smell of fires, the family cooking in the courtyard, several vague figures squatting, talking, smoking. In the garden, the rear wooden gate propped open and a lightbulb burning among the frangipani branches, haloed with dancing insects.

'You see, we have done away with the old historic plough even in India, Antonin,' Bihari Das said. 'I am not only a very avant-garde director but a progressive in other ways!'

As he spoke, laughing relaxedly and gesticulating with an open hand, a tractor came through the gates from fields beyond and stopped beneath the shelter inside. The driver jumped down and saluted Bihari Das.

The ugly old man, evidently the watchman, still sat on his bed. As the tractor arrived, he rose slowly and shuffled over to close the gate, while the boy to whom he had been reading sped round the yard making driving noises. Bihari Das called to the old man to wait; as he and Slansky walked through into the farm, the old man bowed low to them.

Bihari Das was voluble and expert on the workings of his farm. He summoned a foreman who walked with them, a keen young man; scarcely more than a student, who had to keep silent while Bihari Das rattled off facts and figures. They showed Slansky a small vineyard with especial pride.

'The profits on grapes amount to fifteen thousand rupees per acre,' said the foreman proudly.

'That's not all profit by any means,' said Bihari Das quickly.

Why should I care how much money you make? What's going to happen to us if the Russians do stay? The old bleak censorship again, truth stifled, unable to know if your colleague is your friend or your enemy. That old creaking system of corruption that was the only possible system for obtaining necessary equipment. And you, darling, with our future growing lips inside you – we had hoped to see Communism freed from its old Stalinist straitjacket of paranoia ...

They walked back at last, silent, through into the garden. Before closing the gate for them, the old watchman picked up his little friend, pressing his shining cheek so lovingly to his blistered lips in a goodnight kiss that his spectacles were pushed against his eyes. When the boy was set down again, he ran along the path, calling to his mother, 'Mother, Mother, now I'm ready for bed at long last.'

And the tractor was a Russian model, a Belarus, made in Minsk, such as I have seen many a time slowly ploughing the clayey fields of Bohemia or the alluvial lands of Moravia, not as good as our Czech tractors, either ...

'Antonin, you know what a busy man I am – a partygoer this afternoon, a farmer this evening, and tomorrow again an artist, when I fly to Agra for a day's shooting, on which I once hoped you would join me. So we must say farewell now. My secretary will get the air tickets to you first thing. I am of course terribly sorry for all the upsets in your country, and I hope you will be able to come back here again when matters have sorted themselves out.'

'I hope so, Sadal, and next time I shall bring Gordana with me. Then I hope I shall make a more receptive guest. Thank you for your hospitality, and tell me one thing before you leave—'

'Yes, yes, of course.'

'Who is the other guest in the suite below mine?'

The famous smile slowly emerged again, expressing itself in crinkling eyes and perfect teeth. You said he was the most handsome man in the world when I introduced you in Prague, but I believe his smile would not capture you quite so much today, my love!

'He won't interfere with you, Antonin. He turns in early after dinner and will be away before the dawn.'

'Another of your guests who wasn't at your party!'

'That's because he was not invited exactly, you see, my dear man, since he is more of a business acquaintance. A mere travelling salesman, let's say, doing a lucrative business among gentlemen farmers in the Delhi region.'

'He's a Russian, isn't he?'

The smile went out and came on again.

'He's just a businessman, I am telling you. He is tired, like you, and does not speak English, only Hindi, so you could not converse. You should take a leaf out of his book and turn in early, get a good night's kip. After all, you have to be moving pretty smartly in the morning.'

'So he is Russian.'

'Just a Moscow businessman.'

They shook hands at the door of the private hotel. Waving, smiling, Bihari Das walked down the steps to his car, where a chauffeur patiently waited. Slansky closed the hotel door and stood in the hall a minute, trembling. The man sitting in the reception desk watched him politely and openly.

'Good evening,' said Slansky, and started to walk upstairs, up the drab marble steps, watching his feet tread on the carpet.

He moved swiftly over to the balcony and looked down. The Russian's veranda was not far below. He lowered himself over, hung for a second, then dropped. From inside his cluttered room, the Russian asked, 'Who's there?' An ancient standard lamp threw light and shadow over his face. He sat in his shirt sleeves writing at a table. I pulled my gun out and walked into the room. 'So you're the guy who's been stuffing Bihari Das with lying propaganda!'

At the top of the stairs, he paused. From the street came a mixture of noises; people noises, not traffic noises. In the hotel itself, silence. He went into his room and locked the door. Stood with the light off, still trembling. The enemy. Fellow Communist. When the shot rang out, he fell against the table and then slipped down, while his order books – so many pumps, so many tractors – No!

Slansky switched on the lamp and poured himself a glass of fresh lime juice and a strong tot of gin from the drinks cabinet. There were books on a shelf running right along one wall. Bihari Das's personal books – cast-outs probably, but at least they made it seem more like home.

Dostoevsky, Kafka, Koestler, dated theories of aesthetics, Reik's *The Unknown Murderer*. He was sleeping heavily and drunkenly. As I crept up to his bedside, I could see a grey pulse beating in his throat. Hurling myself on him, I sank my clawed fingers into his neck. 'This for Bohemia and truth!' I cried.

The poor old untouchable kissing the kid goodnight. What love in the gesture, the whole of everything there, his old deformed hands supporting the boy. 'Tata', the boy called him. 'Grandfather'. Maybe just an honorary position. That harmless old man, all his life opening and shutting gates. Does Bihari Das even know his name?

And if I killed Ivan down below, would it open Bihari's eyes? Famous Czech director on murder charge. As I opened his door, a creaking board gave me away. He fired from his bed, through the mosquito net, through the open bedroom doorway. I fell in agony –

There's no principle involved. I just can't kill him. He's a private person.

Suppose I captured him, held him hostage here in exchange for the safety of Alexander Dubcek? He isn't important enough. He counts for no more than the old watchman. We fell onto the floor together, grappling. I reached out for a heavy wooden ornament standing on the table. Even as she ran across the square, the tank crew opened fire again.

'No!'

I'll go down, properly dressed, and speak to him in Russian. Argue with him. Just convince one of them. That is what a civilised man should do. Behave here as if I were in Prague facing the enemy. Always correct.

He drank the gin quickly and then sipped at the cold lime.

He would hear no more. 'You Czechs by your revisionism have betrayed the Warsaw Pact,' he said. 'On the contrary,' he said coldly, 'it is you Russians who have betrayed it, as well as betraying many unspoken pacts of friendship. We knew you were old-fashioned and inclined to be heavy. We didn't know you were liars and swindlers and killers –' 'I don't wish to be offensive, sir, or spoil your visit to India, in any way, but some friends of yours who were visiting Prague as uninvited guests raped and killed my wife.'

Setting the glass down, he went to the door. As he went to the door, it was opened from the other side. The young Russian stood there. 'I came to apologise for the actions of my government,' he said. As he was opening the door – the Russian stood there with two armed men behind him. 'You are Czech?' he asked coldly. A figure stood on the landing. 'Come with me.'

It was the old lady. 'We will be serving dinner in ten minutes, sir. Will you like to come down for it or eat in your room?'

They confronted each other across the table. No, it would have to be a cool dialectical argument. 'How do you justify an armed act of aggression against a friendly fellow-country that has at no time offended against socialist morality or made overtures to imperialist powers?'

'Will any other guests be eating downstairs, madam?'

'Only the other guest, Mr Dabrynin, the Russian gentleman.' No melodramatics. It was simple. Gordana, take care of yourself; I will come for you.

'Then I will eat downstairs with Mr Dabrynin. Perhaps you will be kind enough to inform him that I shall be present.'

'No, Mr Dabrynin, there was no threat from any West German federal intelligence agents – no infiltration in any way from the anti-Communist powers. We would have welcomed them then as little as we now welcome the Soviet Occupation.'

He went back into his room, closing the door firmly behind him. The man's only some minor engineer. No threat to anyone. All the more reason to talk to him.

Gordana, I swear I would kill him if I thought anything had happened to you.

Death is not my weapon. Being an artist, I must fight with life. I must remain true to my vision. There is a commitment greater than any one situation.

My head's clear of those foul images. Read something, anything, before the dinner gong goes!

He scanned the bookshelf, put on his reading glasses, looked again, picked out almost at random a collection of the writings of the painter Giorgio de Chirico, opened it almost at random, began to read.

'Yet our minds are haunted by visions; they are anchored to everlasting foundations. In public squares shadows lengthen their mathematical enigmas. Over the walls rise nonsensical towers, decked with little multi-coloured flags; infinitude is everywhere, and everywhere is mystery. One thing remains immutable, as if its roots were frozen in the entrails of eternity: our will as creative artists ...

'Inside a ruined temple the broken statue of a god spoke a mysterious language. For me, this vision is always accompanied by a feeling of cold, as if I had been touched by a winter wind from a distant unknown country.'

The Soft Predicament

I. JUPITER. With increasing familiarity, he saw that the slow writhings were not inconsequential movement but ponderous and deliberate gesture.

Ian Ezard was no longer aware of himself. The panorama entirely absorbed him.

What had been at first a meaningless blur had resolved into an array of lights, gently drifting. The lights now took on pattern, became luminous wings or phosphorescent backbones or incandescent limbs. As they passed, the laboured working of those pinions ceased to look random and assumed every appearance of deliberation – of plan – of consciousness! Nor was the stew in which the patterns moved a chaos any longer; as Ezard's senses adjusted to the scene, he became aware of an environment as much governed by its own laws as the environment into which he had been born.

With the decline of his first terror and horror, he could observe more acutely. He saw that the organisms of light moved over and among – what would you call them? Bulwarks? Fortifications? Cloud formations? They were no more clearly defined than sandbanks shrouded in fog; but he was haunted by a feeling of intricate detail slightly beyond his retinal powers of resolution, as if he were gazing at flotillas of baroque cathedrals, sunk just too deep below translucent seas.

He thought with unexpected kinship of Lowell, the astronomer, catching imaginary glimpses of Martian canals – but his own vantage point was much the more privileged.

The scale of the grand gay solemn procession parading before his vision gave him trouble. He caught himself trying to interpret the unknown in terms of the known. These organisms reminded him of the starry skeletons of Terrestrial cities by night, glimpsed from the stratosphere, or of clusters of diatoms floating in a drop of water. It was hard to remember that the living geometries he was scanning were each the size of a large island – perhaps a couple of hundred miles across.

Terror still lurked. Ezard knew he had only to adjust the Infrared scanners to look miles deeper down into Jupiter's atmosphere and find – life? – images? – of a different kind. To date, the Jupiter Expedition had resolved six levels of life-images, each level separated from the others almost as markedly as sea was separated from air, by pressure gradients that entailed different chemical compositions.

Layer on layer, down they went, stirring slowly, right down far beyond detection into the sludgy heart of the protosun! Were all layers full of at least the traces and chimeras of life?

'It's like peering down into the human mind!' Ian Ezard exclaimed; perhaps he thought of the mind of Jerry Wharton, his mixed-up brother-in-law. Vast pressures, vast darknesses, terrible wisdoms, age-long electric storms – the parallel between Jupiter's atmospheric depths and the mind was too disconcerting. He sat up and pushed the viewing helmet back on its swivel.

The observation room closed in on him again, unchanging, wearily familiar.

'My god!' he said, feebly wiping his face. 'My god!' And after a moment, 'By Jove!' in honour of the monstrous protosun riding like a whale beneath their ship. Sweat ran from him.

'It's a spectacle right enough,' Captain Dudintsev said, handing him a towel. 'And each of the six layers we have surveyed is over one hundred times the area of Earth. We are recording most of it on tape. Some of the findings are being relayed back to Earth now.'

'They'll flip!'

'Life on Jupiter – what else can you call it but life? This is going to hit Russia and America and the whole of Westciv harder than any scientific discovery since reproduction!'

Looking at his wristputer, Ezard noted that he had been under the viewer for eighty-six minutes. 'Oh, it's consciousness there right enough. It stands all our thinking upside down. Not only does Jupiter contain most of the inorganic material of the system, the sun apart – it contains almost all the life as well. Swarming, superabundant life.... Not an amoeba smaller than Long Island. ... It makes Earth just a rocky outpost on a far shore. That's a big idea to adjust to!'

'The White World will adjust, as we adjusted to Darwinism. We always do adjust.'

'And who cares about the Black World. ...'

Dudintsev laughed. 'What about your sister's husband that you're always complaining about? He'd care!'

'Oh, yes, he'd care. Jerry'd like to see the other half of the globe wiped out entirely.'

'Well, he's surely not the only one.'

With his head still full of baffling luminescent gestures, Ezard went forward to shower.

II. LUNA. Near the deep midnight in Rainbow Bay City. Standing under Main Dome at the top of one of the view-towers. The universe out there before us, close to the panes; stars like flaming fat, distorted by the dome's curvature, Earth like a chilled fingernail clipping. Chief Dream-Technician Wace and I talking sporadically, killing time until we went back on duty to what my daughter Ri calls 'the big old black thing' over in Plato.

'Specialisation – it's a wonderful thing, Jerry!' Wace said. 'Here we are, part-way to Jupiter and I don't even know where in the sky to look for it! The exterior world has never been my province.'

He was a neat little dry man, in his mid-thirties and already wizened. His province was the infinitely complex state of being of sleep. I had gained a lot of my interest in psychology from Johnnie Wace. Like him, I would not have been standing where I was were it not for the CUFL project, on which we were both working. And that big old black thing would not have been established inconveniently on the Moon had not the elusive hypnoid states between waking and sleeping which we were investigating been most easily sustained in the light-gravity condition of Luna.

I gave up the search for Jupiter. I knew where it was no more than Wace did. Besides, slight condensation was hatching drops off the aluminium bars overhead; the draughts of the dome brought the drops down slantingly at us. Tension was returning to me as the time to go on shift drew near – tension we were not allowed to blunt with drink. Soon I would be plugged in between life and death, letting CUFL suck up my psyche. As we turned away, I looked outside at an auxiliary dome under which cactus grew in the fertile Lunar soil, sheltered only slightly from external rigours.

'That's the way we keep pushing on, Johnnie,' I said, indicating the cacti. 'We're always extending the margins of experience – now the Trans-Jupiter Expedition has discovered that life exists out there. Where does the West get its dynamism from, while the rest of the world – the Third World – still sits on its haunches?'

Wace gave me an odd look.

'I know, I'm on my old hobbyhorse! You tell me, Johnnie, you're a clever man, how is it that in an age of progress half the globe won't progress?'

'Jerry, I don't feel about the Blacks as you do. You're such an essential part of CUFL because your basic symbols are confused.'

He noticed that the remark angered me. Yet I saw the truth as I stated it. Westciv, comprising most of the Northern Hemisphere and little else bar Australia, was a big armed camp, guarding enormously long frontiers with the stagnating Black or Third World, and occasionally making a quick raid into South America or Africa to quell threatening power build-ups. All the time that we were trying to move forward, the rest of the overcrowded world was dragging us back.

'You know my views, Johnnie – they may be unpopular but I've never tried to hide them.' I told him, letting my expression grow dark. 'I'd wipe the slate of the useless Third World clean and begin over, if I had my way. What have we got to lose? No confusion in my symbols there, is there?'

'Once a soldier, always a soldier....' He said no more until we were entering the elevator. Then he added, in his quiet way, 'We can all of us be mistaken, Jerry. We now know that the freshly-charted ypsilon-areas of the brain make no distinction between waking reality and dream. They deal only with altering time-scales, and form the gateway to the unconscious. My personal theory is that Western man, with his haste for progress, may have somehow closed that gate and lost touch with something that is basic to his psychic well-being.'

'Meaning the Blacks are still in touch?'

'Don't sneer! The history of the West is nothing to be particularly proud of. You know that our CUFL project is in trouble and may be closed down. Sure, we progress astonishingly on the material plane, we have stations orbiting the Sun and inner planets and Jupiter – yet we remain at odds with ourselves. CUFL is intended to be to the psyche what the computer is to knowledge, yet it consistently rejects our data. The fault is not in the machine. Draw your own conclusions.'

I shrugged. 'Let's get on shift!'

We reached the surface and climbed out, walking in the direction of the tube where a shuttle for Plato would be ready. The big old black thing would be sitting waiting by the crater terminus and, under the care of Johnnie Wace's team, I and the other feeds would be plugged in. Sometimes I felt lost in the whole tenuous world that Wace found so congenial, and in all the clever talk about what was dream, what was reality – though I used it myself sometimes, in self-defence.

As we made for the subway, the curve of the dome distorted the cacti beyond. Frail though they were, great arms of prickly pear grew and extended and seemed to wrap themselves around the dome, before being washed out by floods of reflected electroluminescence. Until the problem of cutting down glare at night was beaten, tempers in Main Dome would stay edgy.

In the subway, still partly unfinished, Wace and I moved past the parade of fire-fighting equipment and emergency suits and climbed into the train. The rest of the team were already in their seats, chattering eagerly about the ambiguous states of mind that CUFL encouraged; they greeted Johnnie eagerly, and he joined in their conversation. I longed to be back with my family – such as it was – or playing a quiet game of chess with Ted Greaves, simple old soldier Ted Greaves. Maybe I should have stayed a simple old soldier myself, helping to quell riots in the overcrowded lanes of Eastern Seaboard, or cutting a quick swathe through Brazil.

'I didn't mean to rub you up the wrong way, Jerry,' Wace said as the doors closed. His little face wrinkled with concern.

'Forget it. I jumped at you. These days, life's too complex.'

'That from you, the apostle of progress!'

'It's no good talking.... Look, we've found life on Jupiter. That's great. I'm really glad, glad for Ezard out there, glad for everyone. But what are we going to do about it? Where does it get us? We haven't even licked the problem of life on Earth yet!'

'We will,' he said.

We began to roll into the dark tunnel.

III. RI. One of the many complications of life on Earth was the dreams of my daughter. They beguiled me greatly: so much that I believe they often became entangled with my fantasies as I lay relaxed on Wace's couch under the encephalometers and the rest of the CUFL gear. But they worried me even as they enchanted me. The child is so persistently friendly that I don't always have time for her; but her dreams are a different matter.

In the way that Ri told them, the dreams had a peculiar lucidity. Perhaps they were scenes from a world I wanted to be in, a toy world – a simplified world that hardly seemed to contain other people.

Ri was the fruit of my third-decade marriage. My fourth-decade wife, Natalie, also liked to hear Ri's prattle; but Natalie is a patient woman, both with Ri and me; more with Ri, maybe, since she likes to show me her temper.

A certain quality to Ri's dreams made Natalie and me keep them private to ourselves. We never mentioned them to our friends, almost as if they were little shared guilty secrets. Nor did I ever speak of them to my buddies sweating on the CUFL project, or to Wace or the mind-wizards in the Lunar Psyche Lab. For that matter, Natalie and I avoided discussing them between ourselves, partly because we sensed Ri's own reverence for her nocturnal images.

Then my whole pleasure at the child's dreams was turned into disquiet by a casual remark that Ted Greaves dropped.

This is how it came about.

I had returned from Luna on the leave-shuttle only the previous day, more exhausted than usual. The hops between Kennedy and Eastern and Eastern and Eurocen were becoming more crowded than ever, despite the extra jumbos operating; the news of the discovery of life on Jupiter – even the enormous telecasts of my brother-in-law's face burning over every Westciv city – seemed to have stirred up the ants' heap considerably. What people thought they could do about it was beyond computation, but Wall Street was registering a tidal wave of optimism.

So with one thing and another, I arrived home exhausted. Ri was asleep. Yes, still wetting her bed, Natalie admitted. I took a sauna and fell asleep in my wife's arms. The world turned. Next thing I knew, it was morning and I was roused by Ri's approach to our bedside.

Small girls of three have a ponderous tread; they weigh as much as baby elephants. I can walk across our bedroom floor without making a sound, but this tot sets up vibrations.

'I thought you were still on the Moon feeding the Clective Unctious, Daddy,' she said. The 'Clective Unctious' is her inspired mispronunciation of the Collective Unconscious; wisely, she makes no attempt at all at the Free-Living tail of CUFL.

'The Unctious has given me a week's leave, Ri. Now let me sleep! Go and read your book!'

I watched her through one half open eye. She put her head on one side and smiled at me, scratching her behind.

'Then that big old black thing is a lot clevererer and kinder than I thought it was.'

From her side of the bed, Natalie laughed. 'Why, that's the whole idea of the Clective Unctious, Ri – to be kinder and wiser than one person can imagine.'

'I can imagine *lots* of kindness,' she said. She was not to be weaned of her picture of the Unctious as a big black thing.

Climbing onto the bed, she began to heave herself between Natalie and me. She had brought along a big plastic talkie-picture-book of traditional design tucked under one arm. As she rolled over me, she swung the book and a corner of it caught me painfully on the cheek. I yelled.

'You clumsy little horror! Get off me!'

'Daddy, I didn't mean to do it, really! It was an acciment!'

'I don't care what it was! Get out! Go on! Move! Go back to your own bed!'

I tugged at her arm and dragged her across me. She burst into tears.

Natalie sat up angrily. 'For god's sake, leave the kid alone! You're always bullying her!'

'You keep quiet – she didn't catch you in the eye! And she's peed her bed again, the dirty little tyke!'

That was how that row started. I'm ashamed to relate how it went on. There were the tears from the child and tears from Natalie. Only after breakfast did everyone simmer down. Oh, I can be fairly objective now in this confession, and record my failings and what other people thought of me. Believe me, if it isn't art, it's therapy!

It's strange to recall now how often we used to quarrel over breakfast.... Yet that was one of the calmest rooms, with the crimson carpet spread over the floor-tiles, and the white walls and dark Italian furniture. We had old-fashioned two-dimensional oil painting, nonmobile, on the walls, and no holoscreen. In one corner, half-hidden behind a vase of flowers from the courtyard, stood Jannick, our robot housemaid; but Natalie, preferring not to use her, kept her switched off. Jannick was off on this occasion. Peace reigned. Yet we quarrelled.

As Natalie and I were drinking a last cup of coffee, Ri trotted around to me and said, 'Would you like to hear my dream now, Daddy, if you're really not savage anymore?'

I pulled her onto my knee. 'Let's hear it then, if we must. Was it the one about warm pools of water again?'

She shook her head in a dignified manner.

'This dream came around three in the morning,' she said. 'I know what the time was because a huge black bird like a starving crow came and pecked at my window as if it wanted to get in and wake us all up.'

'That was all a part of the dream, then. There aren't any crows in this stretch of Italy.'

'Perhaps you're right, because the house was sort of dirtier than it really is. ... So I sat up and immediately I began dreaming I was fat and heavy and carrying a big fat heavy talkie-book up the hill. It was a much bigger book than any I got here. I could hardly breathe because there was hardly any air up the hillside. It was a very *plain* sort of dream.'

'And what happened in it?'

'Nothing.'

'Nothing at all?'

'Nothing except just one thing. Do you know what? I saw there was one of those new Japanese cars rushing down the hill toward me – you know, the kind where the body's inside the wheel and the big wheel goes all around the body.'

'She must mean the Toyota Monocar,' Natalie said.

'Yes, that's right, Natalie, the Toyta Moggacar. It was like a big flaming wheel and it rolled right past me and went out.'

'Out where?'

'I don't know. Where do things go out to? I didn't even know where it came from! In my dream I was puzzled about that, so I looked all around and by the roadside there was a big drop. It just went down and down! And it was guarded by eight posts protecting it, little round white posts like teeth, and the Moggacar must have come from there.'

Natalie and I sat over the table thinking about the dream after Ri had slipped out into the courtyard to play; she had some flame and apricot-coloured finches in cages which she loved.

I was on her small imaginary hillside, where the air was thin and the colours pale, and the isolated figure of the child stood clutching its volume and watched the car go past like a flame. A sun-symbol, the wheel on which Ixion was crucified, image of our civilisation maybe, Tantric sign of sympathetic fires. ... All those things, and the first unmanned stations now orbiting the sun – one of the great achievements of Westciv, and itself a symbol awakening great smouldering responses in man. Was that response reverberating through the psyches of all small children, changing them, charging them further along the trajectory the White World follows? What would the news from Jupiter bring on? What sort of role would Uncle Ian, the life-finder, play in the primitive theatres of Ri's mind?

I asked the question of myself only idly. I enjoyed popping the big questions, on the principle that if they were big enough they were sufficient in themselves and did not require answers. Answers never worried me in those days. I was no thinker. My job in Plato concerned feelings, and for that they paid me. Answers were for Johnnie Wace and his cronies.

'We'd better be moving,' Natalie said, collecting my coffee cup. 'Since you've got a free day, make the most of it. You're on frontier duty with Greaves again tomorrow.'

'I know that without being reminded, thanks.'

'I wasn't really reminding you – just stating a fact.'

As she passed me to go into the kitchen, I said, 'I know this house is archaic – just a peasant's home. But if I hadn't volunteered for irregular frontier service during my off-duty spells, we wouldn't be here. We'd be stuck in Eastern or some other enormous city-complex, such as the one you spent your miserable childhood in. Then you'd complain even more!'

She continued into the kitchen with the cups and plates. It was true the house had been built for and by peasants, or little better; its stone walls, a metre thick, kept out the heat of summer; and the brief chill of winter when it rolled around. Natalie was silent and then she said, so quietly that I could scarcely hear her where I sat in the living room, 'I was not complaining, Jerry, not daring to complain....'

I marched in to her. She was standing by the sink, more or less as I imagined her, her dark wings of hair drawn into place by a rubber band at the nape of her neck. I loved her, but she could make me mad!

'What's that meant to mean – "not daring to complain"?'

'Please don't quarrel with me, Jerry. I can't take much more.'

'Was I quarrelling? I thought I was simply asking you what you meant by what you said!'

'Please don't get worked up!' She came and stood against me, putting her arms around my waist and looking up at me. I stiffened myself and would not return her gaze. 'I mean no harm, Jerry. It's terrible the way we row just like everyone else – I know you're upset!'

'Of course I'm upset! Who wouldn't be upset at the state of the world? Your marvellous brother and his buddies have discovered life on Jupiter! Does that affect us? *My* project, CUFL, that will have to close down unless we start getting results. Then there's all the disturbance in the universities – I don't know what the younger generation thinks it's doing! Unless we're strong, the Thirdies are going to invade and take over –'

She was growing annoyed herself now. 'Oh yes, that's really why we came to live down here in the back of beyond, isn't it? – Just so that you could get an occasional crack at the enemy. It wasn't for any care about where I might want to live.'

'Unlike some people, I care about doing my duty by my country!'

She broke away from me. 'It's no part of your duty to be incessantly beastly to Ri and me, is it? Is it? You don't care about us one bit!'

It was an old tune she played.

'Don't start bringing that up again, woman! If I didn't care, why did I buy you that robot standing idle in the next room? You never use it, you prefer to hire a fat old woman to come in instead! I should have saved my money! And you have the brass nerve to talk about not caring!'

Her eyes were wild now. She looked glorious standing there.

'You don't care! You don't care! You hurt your poor little daughter, you neglect me! You're always off to the Moon, or at the frontier, or else here bullying us. Even your stupid friend Ted Greaves has more sense than you! You hate us! You hate everyone!'

Running forward, I grabbed her arm and shook her.

'You're always making a noise. Not much longer till the end of the decade and then I'm rid of you! I can't wait!'

I strode through the house and slammed out of the door into the street. Thank the stars it was frontier duty the next day! People greeted me but I ignored them. The sun was already high in the South Italian sky; I sweated as I walked, and rejoiced in the discomfort.

It was not true that I bullied them. Natalie might have suffered as a child, but so had I! There had been a war in progress then, the first of the Westciv-Third wars, although we had not thought of it in quite those terms at the time, before the Cap-Com treaty. I had been drafted, at an age when others were cutting a figure in universities. I had been scared, I had suffered, been hungry, been wounded, been lost in the jungle for a couple of days before the chopper patrol picked me up. And I'd killed off a few Thirdies. Even Natalie would not claim I had *enjoyed* doing that. It was all over long ago. Yet it was still with me. In my mind, it never grew fainter. The Earth revolved; the lights on that old stage never went dim.

Now I was among the hills above our village. I sat under the shade of an olive tree and looked back. It's strange how you find yourself thinking things that have nothing to do with your daily life.

It was no use getting upset over a husband-wife quarrel, Natalie was OK; just a little hasty-tempered. My watch said close to ten o'clock. Ted Greaves would be turning up at the house for a game of chess before long. I would sit where I was for a moment, breathe deep, and then stroll back. Act naturally. There was nothing to be afraid of.

IV. GREAVES. Ted Greaves arrived at the house at about ten-fifty. He was a tall fair-haired man, dogged by ill-luck most of his military career and somewhat soured toward society. He enjoyed playing the role of bluff soldier. After many years in the service, he was now Exile Officer commanding our sector of the southern frontier between Westciv and the Blacks. As such, he would be my superior tomorrow, when I went on duty. Today, we were just buddies and I got the chess board out.

'I feel too much like a pawn myself to play well today,' he said, as we settled down by the window. 'Spent all the last twenty-four hours in the office filling in photoforms. We're sinking under forms! The famine situation in North Africa is now reinforced by a cholera epidemic.'

'The Third's problems are nothing to do with us!'

'Unfortunately we're more connected than appears on the surface. The authorities are afraid that the cholera won't respect frontiers. We've got to let some refugees through tomorrow, and they could be carriers. An emergency isolation ward is being set up. It's Westciv's fault – we should have given aid to Africa from the start.'

On the Rainbow-Kennedy flight, I had bought a can of bourbon at a duty-free price. Greaves and I broached it now. But he was in a dark mood, and was soon launched on an old topic of his, the responsibility of the States for the White-Black confrontation. I did not accept his diagnosis for one minute, and he knew I didn't; but that did not stop him rambling on about the evils of our consumer society, and how it was all based on jealousy, and the shame of the Negro Solution – though how we could have avoided the Solution, he did not say. Since we had been mere children at the time of the Solution, I could not see why he needed to feel guilt about it. In any case, I believed that the coloured races of Third were undeveloped because they lacked the intellect and moral fibre of Westciv, their hated Pinkyland.

So I let Greaves give vent to his feelings over the iced bourbon while I gazed out through the window to our inner courtyard.

The central stone path, flanked by a colonnade on which bougain-villea rioted, led to a little statue of Diana, executed in Carrara marble, standing against the far wall. All the walls of the courtyard were plastered in yellow. On the left-hand side, Ri's collection of finches chirped and flitted in their cages. In the beds, orange and lemon trees grew. Above the far wall, the mountains of Calabria rose.

I never tired of the peace of that view. But what chiefly drew my eyes was the sight of Natalie in her simple green dress. I had loved her in many forms, I thought, and at the end of the decade it would not come too hard to exchange her for another – better anyhow than being stuck with one woman a life long, as under the old system – but either I was growing older or there was something particular about Natalie. She was playing with Ri and talking to the Calabrian servant. I couldn't hear a word they said, though the windows were open to let in warmth and fragrance; only the murmur of their voices reached me.

Yes, she had to be exchanged. You had to let things go. That was what kept the world revolving. Planned obsolescence as a social dynamic, in human relationships as in consumer goods. When Ri was ten, she would have to go to the appropriate Integration Centre, to learn to become a functioning member of society – just as my other daughter, Melisande, had left the year before, on her tenth birthday.

Melisande, who wept so much at the parting ... a sad indication of how much she needed integration. We were all required to make sacrifices; otherwise the standard of living would go down. Partings one grew hardened to. I scarcely thought of Melisande nowadays.

And when I'd first known Natalie. Natalie Ezard. That was before the integration laws. 'Space travel nourishes our deepest and most bizarre wishes.' Against mental states of maximum alertness float extravagant hypnoid states which colour the outer darkness crimson and jade, and make unshapely things march to the very margins of the eye. Maybe it is because at the very heart of the richness of metal-bound space travel lies sensory deprivation. For all its promise of renaissance, vacuum-flight is life's death, and only the completely schizoid are immune to its terrors. I was never happy, even on the Kennedy-Rainbow trip.

Between planets, our most outré desires become fecund. Space travel nourishes our deepest and most bizarre wishes. 'Awful things can happen!' Natalie had cried, in our early days, flinging herself into my returning arms. And while I was away, Westciv passed its integration laws, separating parents from children, bestowing on ten-year-olds the honourable orphanage of the state, to be trained as citizens.

It all took place again before the backdrop of our sunlit courtyard, where Natalie Wharton now stood. She was thinner and sharper than she had been once, her hair less black. Some day, we would have to take the offensive and wipe out every single Black in the Black-and-White World. To my mind, only the fear of what neutral China might do had prevented us taking such a necessary step already.

'You see how old it is out there!' Ted Greaves said, misreading my gaze as he gestured into the courtyard. 'Look at that damned vine, that statue! Apart from lovely little Natalie and your daughter, there's not a thing that hasn't been in place for a couple of hundred years. Over in the States, it's all new, new, everything has to be the latest. As soon as roots begin forming, we tear them up and start over. The result – no touchstones! How long's this house been standing? Three centuries? In the States, it would have been swept away long ago. Here, loving care keeps it going, so that it's as good as new. Good as new! See how I'm victim of my own clichés! It's better than fucking new, it's as good as old!'

'You're a sentimentalist, Ted. It isn't things but other people that matter. People are old, worlds are old. The Russo-American ships now forging around the System are bringing home to us just how old we are, how familiar we are to ourselves. Our roots are in ourselves.'

We enjoyed philosophising, that's true.

He grunted and lit a flash-cigar. 'That comes well from you, when you're building this Free-Living Collective Unconscious. Isn't that just another American project to externalise evil and prune our roots?'

'Certainly not! CUFL will be an emotions-bank, a computer if you like, which will store – not the fruits of the human intellect – but the fruits of the psyche. Now that there are too many people around and our lives have to be regimented, CUFL will restore us to the freedom of our imaginations.'

'If it works!'

'Sure, if it works,' I agreed. 'As yet, we can get nothing out of our big old black thing but primitive archetypal patterns. It's a question of keeping on feeding it.' I always spoke more cheerfully than I felt with Greaves: to counteract his vein of pessimism, I suppose.

He stood up and stared out of the window. 'Well, I'm just a glorified soldier – and without much glory. I don't understand emotion banks. But maybe you overfed your big black thing and it is dying of overnourishment, just like Westciv itself. Certain archetypal dreams – the human young get them, so why not your newborn machine? The young get them especially when they are going to die young.'

Death was one of his grand themes: 'The peace that passeth all standing,' he called it once.

'What sort of dreams?' I asked, unthinking.

'To the nervous system, dream imagery is received just like sensory stimuli. There are prodromic dreams, dreams that foretell of death. We don't know what wakefulness is, do we, until we know what dreams are. Maybe the whole Black-White struggle is a super-dream, like a blackbird rapping on a windowpane.'

Conversation springs hidden thoughts. I'd been listening, but more actively I'd wondered at the way he didn't answer questions quite directly, just as most people fail to. Someone told me that it was the effect of holovision, split attention. All this I was going through when he came up with the remark about blackbirds tapping on windows, and it brought to mind the start of Ri's latest dream, when she was unsure whether she woke or slept.

'What's that to do with dying?'

'Let's take a walk in the sun before it gets too stinking hot. Some children are too ethereal for life. Christ, Jerry, a kid's close to the primal state, to the original psychological world; they're the ones to come through with uncanny prognoses. If they aren't going to make it to maturity, their psyches know about it and have no drive to gear themselves onto the next stage of being.'

'Let's go out in the sun,' I said. I felt ill. The poinsettias were in flower, spreading their scarlet tongues. A lizard lay along a carob branch. That sun disappearing down Ri's hill – death? And the eight teeth or posts or what the hell they were, on the edge of nothing – her years? The finches hopped from perch to perch, restless in their captivity.

V. SICILY. Almost before daybreak next morning, I was flying over Calabria and the toe of Italy. Military installations glittered below. This was one of the southern points of Europe which marked the frontier between the two worlds. It was manned by task forces of Americans,

Europeans, and Russians. I had left before Ri woke. Natalie, with her wings of dark hair, had risen to wave me good-bye. Good-bye, it was always good-bye. And what was the meaning of the big black book Ri had been carrying in her dream? It couldn't be true.

The Straits of Messina flashed below our wingless fuselage. Air, water, earth, fire, the original elements. The fifth, space, had been waiting. God alone knew what it did in the hearts and minds of man, what aboriginal reaction was in process. Maybe once we finished off the Thirdies, the Clective Unctious would give us time to sort things out. There was never time to sort things out. Even the finches in their long imprisonment never had enough time. And the bird at her window? Which side of the window was in, which out?

We were coming down toward Sicily, toward its tan mountains. I could see Greaves's head and shoulders in the driver's seat.

Sicily was semi-neutral ground. White and Black World met in its eroded valleys. My breakfast had been half a grapefruit culled fresh from the garden, and a cup of bitter black coffee. Voluntary regulation of intake. The other side of the looming frontier, starvation would have made my snack seem a fine repast.

Somewhere south, a last glimpse of sea and the smudged distant smoke of Malta, still burning after ten years. Then up came Etna and the stunned interior, and we settled for a landing.

This barren land looked like machine-land itself. Sicily – the northern, Westciv half – had as big a payload of robots on it as the Moon itself. All worked in mindless unison in case the lesser breeds in the southern half did anything desperate. I grabbed up my gas-cannon and climbed out into the heat as a flight of steps snapped itself into position.

Side by side, Greaves and I jumped into proffered pogo-armour and bounded off across the field in thirty-foot kangaroo-steps.

The White boundary was marked by saucers standing on poles at ten-metre intervals; between saucers, the force barrier shimmered, carrying its flair for hallucination right up into the sky.

The Black World had its boundary too. It stood beyond our force field – stood, I say! It lurched across Sicily, a ragged wall of stone. Much of the stone came from dismembered towns and villages and churches. Every now and again, a native would steal some of the stone back, in order to build his family a hovel to live in. Indignant Black officials would demolish the hovel and restore the stone. They should have worried! I could have pogoed over their wall with ease!

And a wall of eight posts....

We strode across the crowded field to the forward gate. Sunlight and gravity. We were massive men, nine feet high or more; boots two feet high; over our heads, umbrella-helmets over a foot high. Our megavoices could carry over a land-mile. We might have been evil machine-men from the ragged dreams of Blacks. At the forward gate, we entered in and shed the armour in magnetised recesses.

Up in the tower, Greaves took over from the auto-controls and opened his link with Palermo and the comsats high overhead. I checked with Immigration and Isolation to see that they were functioning.

From here, we could look well into the hated enemy territory, over the tops of their wooden towers, into the miserable stone villages, from which hordes of people were already emerging, although fifty minutes had yet to elapse before we lowered the force-screens to let any of them through. Beyond the crowds, the mountains crumbling into their thwarted valleys, fly-specked with bushes. No fit habitation. If we took over the island – as I always held we should – we would raise desalination-plants on the coast, import topsoil and fertiliser and the new plus-crops, and make the whole place flow with riches in five years. With the present status quo, the next five would bring nothing but starvation and religion; that was all they had there. A massive cholera epidemic, with deaths counted in hundreds of thousands, was raging through Africa already, after moving westward from Calcutta, its traditional capital.

'The bastards!' I said. 'One day, there will be a law all over the world forbidding people to live like vermin!'

'And a law forbidding people to make capital out of it,' Greaves said. His remark meant nothing to me. I guessed it had something to do with his cranky theory that Westciv profitted by the poor world's poverty by raising import tariffs against it. Greaves did not explain, nor did I ask him to.

At the auxiliary control panel, I sent out an invisible scanner to watch one of the enemy villages. Although it might register on the antiquated radar screens of the Blacks, they could only rave at the breach of international regulations without ever being able to intercept it.

The eye hovered over a group of shacks and adjusted its focus. Three-dimensionally, the holograph of hatred travelled toward me in the cube.

Against doorways, up on balconies decked with ragged flowers, along alleys, stood groups of Blacks. They would be Arabs, refugee Maltese, branded Sicilians, renegades from the White camp; ethnic groups were indistinguishable beneath dirt and tan and old nonsynthetic clothes. I centred on a swarthy young woman standing in a tavern doorway with one hand on a small boy's shoulder. As Natalie stood in the courtyard under the poinsettias, what had I thought to myself? That once we might have propagated love between ourselves?

Before the world had grown too difficult, there had been a sure way of multiplying and sharing love. We would have bred and raised children for the sensuous reward of having them, of helping them grow up sane and strong. From their bowels also, health would have radiated.

But the Thirdies coveted Westciv's riches without accepting its disciplines. They bred. Indiscriminately and prodigally. The world was too full of children and people, just as the emptiness of space was stuffed with lurid dreams. Only the weak and helpless and starved could cast children onto the world unregulated. Their weak and helpless and starved progeny clogged the graves and wombs of the world. That laughing dark girl on my screen deserved only the bursting seed of cannonfire.

'Call that scanner back, Jerry!' Greaves said, coming toward me.

'What's that?'

'Call your scanner back.'

'I'm giving the Wogs the once-over.'

'Call it back in, I told you. As long as no emergency's in force, you are contravening regulations.'

'Who cares!'

'I care,' he said. He looked very nasty. 'I care, and I'm Exile Officer.'

As I guided the eye back in, I said, 'You were rough all yesterday too. You played a bum game of chess. What's got into you?'

But as soon as I had asked the question, I could answer it myself. He was a bag of nerves because, he must have had word that his son was coming back from the wastes of the Third World.

'You're on the hook about your anarchist son Pete, aren't you?'

It was then he flung himself at me.

*

In the dark tavern, Pete Greaves was buying his friends one last round of drinks. He had been almost three weeks in the seedy little town, waiting for the day the frontier opened; in that time, he had got to know just about everyone in the place. All of them – not just Max Spineri who had travelled all the way from Alexandria with him – swore eternal friendship on this parting day.

'And a plague on King Cholera!' Pete said, lifting his glass.

'Better get back to the West before King Cholera visits Sicily!' a mule-driver said.

The drink was strong. Pete felt moved to make a short speech.

'I came here a stupid prig, full of all the propaganda of the West,' he said. 'I'm going back with open eyes. I've become a man in my year in Africa and Sicily, and back home I shall apply what I've learned.'

'Here's your home now, Pete,' Antonio the Barman said. 'Don't go back to Pinkyland or you'll become a machine like the others there. We're your friends – stay with your friends!' But Pete noticed the crafty old devil shortchanged him.

'I've got to go back, Antonio – Max will tell you. I want to stir people up, make them listen to the truth. There's got to be change, got to be, even if we wreck the whole present setup to get it. All over Pinkyland, take my word, there are thousands – millions – of men and girls my age who hate the way things are run.'

'It's the same as here!' a peasant laughed.

'Sure, but in the West, it's different. The young are tired of the pretence that we have some say in government, tired of bureaucracy, tired of a technocracy that simply reinforces the powers of the politicians. Who cares about finding life on Jupiter when life here just gets lousier!'

He saw – it had never ceased to amaze him all his time in Blackyland – that they were cool to such talk. He was on their side, as he kept telling them. Yet at best their attitude to the Whites was ambivalent: a mixture of envy and contempt for nations that they saw as slaves to consumer goods and machines.

He tried again, telling them about Student Power and the Underground, but Max interrupted him. 'You have to go soon, Pete. We know how you feel. Take it easy – your people find it so hard to take it easy. Look, I've got a parting gift for you. …'

Drawing Pete back into a corner, he produced a gun and thrust it into his friend's hand. Examining it, Pete saw it was an ancient British Enfield revolver, well-maintained. 'I can't accept this, Max!'

'Yes, you can! It's not from me but from the Organisation. To help you in your revolution. It's loaded with six bullets! You'll have to hide it, because they will search you when you cross the frontier.'

He clasped Max's hand. 'Every bullet will count, Max!'

He trembled. Perhaps it was mainly fear of himself.

When he was far from the heat and flies and dust and his ragged unwashed friends, he would hold this present brave image of himself, and draw courage from it.

He moved out into the sun, to where Roberta Arneri stood watching the convoy assembling for the short drive to the frontier gate. He took her hand.

'You know why I have to go, Roberta?'

'You go for lots of reasons.'

It was true enough. He stared into the harsh sunlight and tried to remember. Though hatred stood between the two worlds, there were areas of weakness where they relied on each other. Beneath the hatred were ambiguities almost like love. Though a state of war existed, some trade continued. And the young could not be pent in. Every year, young Whites – 'anarchists' to their seniors – slipped over the frontier with ambulances and medical supplies. And the supplies were paid for by their seniors. It was conscience money. Or hate money. A token, a symbol – nobody knew for what, though it was felt to be important, as a dream is felt to be important even when it is not comprehended.

Now he was going back. Antonio could be right. He would probably never return to the Third World; his own world would most likely make him into a machine.

But he had to bear witness. He was sixteen years old.

'Life without plumbing, life with a half full belly,' he had to go home and say. 'It has a savour to it. It's a positive quality. It doesn't make you less a human being. There's no particular virtue in being white of skin and fat of gut and crapping into a nice china bowl every time the laxatives take hold.'

He wondered how convincing he could make it sound, back in the immense hygienic warrens of Westciv – particularly when he still longed in his inner heart for all the conveniences and privileges, and a shower every morning before a sit-down breakfast. It had all been fun, but enough was enough. More than enough, when you remembered what the plague was doing.

'You go to see again your father,' Roberta diagnosed.

'Maybe. In America, we are trying to sever the ties of family. After you get through with religion you destroy the sacredness of the family. It encourages people to move to other planets, to go where they're told.'

He was ashamed of saying it – and yet half proud.

'That's why you all are so nervous and want to go to war all the time. You don't get enough kisses as little kids, eh?'

'Oh, we're all one-man isolation units! Life isn't as bad as you think, up there among the wheels of progress, Roberta,' he said bitterly. He kissed her, and her lips tasted of garlic.

Max slapped him on his shoulder.

'Cut all that out, fellow – you're going home! Get aboard!'

Pete climbed onto the donkey cart with another anarchist White who had recently sailed across to the island from Tunisia. Pete had arrived in the mysterious Third World driving a track full of supplies. The track had been stolen in Nubia, when he was down with malaria and dysentery. He was going back empty-handed. But the palms of those hands were soft no longer.

He shook Max's hand now. They looked at each other wordlessly as the cart driver goaded his animal into movement. There was affection there, yes – undying in its way, for Max was also a would-be extremist; but there was also the implacable two-way enmity that sprang up willy-nilly between Haves and Have-nots. An enmity stronger than men, incurable by men. They both dropped their gaze.

Hiding his embarrassment, Pete looked about him. In his days of waiting, the village had become absolutely familiar, from the church at one end of the broken-down bursts of cactus in between. He had savoured too the pace of life here, geared to the slowest and most stupid, so that the slowest and most stupid could survive. Over the frontier, time passed in overdrive.

Across the drab stones, the hooves of the donkey made little noise. Other carts were moving forward, with dogs following, keeping close to the walls. There was a feeling – desperate and exhilarating – that they were leaving the shelter of history, and heading toward where the powerhouse of the world began.

Pete waved to Max and Roberta and the others, and squinted toward the fortifications of his own sector. The frontier stood distant but clear in the pale air. As he looked, he saw a giant comic-terror figure, twice as high as a grown man, man-plus-machine, bound across the plain toward him. Bellowing with an obscene anger as it charged, the monster appeared to burn in the sun.

It came toward him like a flaming wheel rushing down a steep hill, all-devouring.

VI. EGO. Ted Greaves was my friend of long standing. I don't know why he flung himself on me in hatred just because I taunted him about his son. For that matter, I don't know why anger suddenly blazed up in me as it did.

My last spell on CUFL had left me in relatively poor shape, but fury lent me strength. I ducked away from his first blow and chopped him hard below the heart. As he doubled forward, grunting with pain, I struck him again, this time on the jaw. He brought his right fist up and grazed my chin, but by then I was hitting him again and again. He went down.

These fits had come over me before, but not for many years. When I was aware of myself again, I was jumping into the pogo-armour, with only the vaguest recollections of what I had done to Greaves. I could recall I had let the force barrier down.

I went leaping forward toward the hated land. I could hear the gyros straining, hear my voice bellowing before me like a spinnaker.

'You killed my daughter! You killed my daughter! You shan't get in! You shan't even look in!'

I didn't know what I was about.

There were animals scattering. I overturned a cart. I was almost at the first village.

It felt as if I were running at a hundred miles an hour. Yet when the shot rang out, I stopped at once. How beautiful the hills were if one's eyes never opened and closed again. Pigeons wheeling white above tawdry roofs. People immobile. One day they would be ours, and we would take over the whole world. The whole world shook with the noise of my falling armament, and dust spinning like the fury of galaxies.

Better pain than our eternal soft predicament. ...

I was looking at a pale-faced boy on a cart, he was staggering off the cart, the cart was going from him. People were shouting and fluttering everywhere like rags. My gaze was fixed only on him. His eyes were only on me. He had a smoking revolver in his hand.

Wonderingly, I wondered how I knew he was an American. An American who had seized Ted Greaves's face and tugged it from inside until all the wrinkles were gone from it and it looked obscenely young again. My executioner wore a mask.

A gyro laboured by my head as if choked with blood. I could only look up at that mask. Something had to be said to it as it came nearer.

'It's like a Western. ...' Trying to laugh?

Death came down from the Black hills till only his stolen eyes were left, like wounds in the universe.

They disappeared.

When the drugs revived me from my hypnoid trance, I was still plugged to CUFL, along with the eleven other members of my shift, the other slaves of the Clective Unctious.

To the medicos bending over me, I said, 'I died again.'

They nodded. They had been watching the monitor screens.

'Take it easy,' one of them said. As my eyes pulled into focus, I saw it was Wace.

I was used to instructions. I worked at taking it easy. I was still in the front line, where individuality fought with the old nameless tribal consciousness. 'I died again,' I groaned.

'Relax, Jerry,' Wace said. 'It was just a hypnoid dream like you always get.'

'But I died again. Why do I always have to die?'

Tommy Wace. His first name was Tommy. Data got mislaid.

Distantly, he tried to administer comfort and express compassion on his dried-up face. 'Dreams are mythologies, part-individual, part-universal. Both de-programming dreams and prognostic-type dreams are natural functions of the self-regulating psychic system. There's nothing unnatural about dreaming of dying.'

'But I died again. ... And I was split into two people. ...'

'The perfect defence in a split world. A form of adaptation.'

You could never convey personal agony to these people, although they had watched it all on the monitors. Wearily, I passed a hand over my face. My chin felt like cactus.

'So much self-hatred, Tommy. ... Where does it all come from?'

'Johnnie. At least you're working it out of your system. Now, here's something to drink.'

I sat up. 'CUFL will have to close down, Johnnie,' I said. I hardly knew what I said. I was back in the real world, in the abrasive lunar laboratory under Plato – and suddenly I saw that I could distinguish true from false.

For years and years – *I'd been mistaken!*

I had been externalising my self-hatred. The dream showed me that I feared to become whole again in case becoming whole destroyed me.

Gasping, I pushed Wace's drink aside. I was seeing visions. The White World had shed religion. Shed religion, you shed other hope-structures; family life disintegrates. You are launched to the greater structure of science. That was the Westciv way. We had made an ugly start but we were going ahead. There was no going back. The rest of the world had to follow. No – had to be led. Not shunned, but bullied. Led. Revelation!

Part of our soft predicament is that we can never entirely grasp what the predicament is.

'Johnnie, I don't always have to die,' I said. 'It's my mistake, our mistake!' I found I was weeping and couldn't stop. Something was dissolving. 'The Black-and-White are one, not two! We are fighting ourselves. I was fighting myself. Plug me back in again!'

'End of shift,' Wace said, advancing the drink again. 'You've done more than your stint. Let's get you into Psych Lab for a checkup and then you're due for leave back on Earth.'

'But do you see –' I gave up and accepted his beastly drink.

Natalie, Ri ... I too have my troubled dreams, little darling. ...

My bed is wetted and my mattress soaked with blood.

John Wace got one of the nurses to help me to my feet. Once I was moving, I could get to Psych Lab under my own power.

'You're doing fine, Jerry!' Wace called. 'Next time you're back on Luna, I'll have Jupiter pinpointed for you!'

Doing fine! – I'd only just had all my strongest and most emotionally-held opinions switched through one hundred and eighty degrees!

In the Psych Lab, I was so full of tension that I couldn't let them talk. 'You know what it's like, moving indistinguishably from hypnoid to dream state – like sinking down through layers of cloud. I began by reliving my last rest period with Natalie and Ri. It all came back true and sweet without distortion, from the reservoirs of memory! Distortion only set in when I recollected landing in Sicily. What happened in reality was that Ted Greaves and I let his son back through the frontier with the other White anarchists. I found the revolver he was trying to smuggle in – he had tucked it into his boot-top.

'That revolver was the symbol that triggered my nightmare. Our lives revolve through different aspects like the phases of the Moon. I identified entirely with Pete. And at his age, I too was a revolutionary, I too wanted to change the world, I too would have wished to kill my present self!'

'At Pete Greaves's age, you were fighting *for* Westciv, not against it, Wharton,' one of the psychiatrists reminded me.

'Yes,' I said. 'I was in Asia, and handy with a gun. I carved up a whole gang of Thirdies. That was about the time when the Russians threw in their lot with us.' I didn't want to go on. I could see it all clearly. They didn't need a true confession.

'The guilt you felt in Asia was natural enough,' the psychiatrist said. 'To suppress it was equally natural – suppressed guilt causes most of the mental and physical sickness in the country. Since then, it has gone stale and turned to hate.'

'I'll try to be a good boy in the future,' I said, smiling and mock-meek. At the time, the ramifications of my remark were not apparent to me, as they were to the psychiatrist.

'You've graduated, Wharton,' he said. 'You're due a vacation on Earth right now.'

VII. CLECTIVE. The globe, in its endless revolution, was carrying us into shade. In the courtyard, the line of the sun was high up our wall. Natalie had set a mosquito-coil burning; its fragrance came to us where we sat at the table with our beers. We bought the mosquito-coils in the local village store; they were smuggled in from the Third World, and had 'Made in Cairo' stamped on the packet.

Ri was busy at one end of the courtyard with a couple of earthenware pots. She played quietly, aware that it was after her bedtime. Ted Greaves and Pete sat with us, drinking beer and smoking. Pete had not spoken a word since they arrived. At that time I could make no contact with him. Did not care to. The ice floes were still melting and smashing.

As Natalie brought out another jar and set it on the rough wood table, Greaves told her, 'We're going to have a hero on our hands if your brother flies over to see you when he gets back from Jupiter. Do you think he'll show up here?'

'Sure to! Ian hates Eastern Seaboard as much as most people.'

'Sounds like he found Jupiter as crowded as Eastern Seaboard!'

'We'll have the Clective Unctious working by the time he arrives,' I said.

'I thought you were predicting it would close down?' Greaves said.

'That was when it was choked with hate.'

'You're joking! How do you choke a machine with hate?'

'Input equals output. CUFL is a reactive store – you feed in hate, so you get out hate.'

'Same applies to human beings and human groups,' Pete Greaves broke in, rubbing his thumbnail along the grain of the table.

I looked at him. I couldn't feel sweet about him. He was right in what he said but I couldn't agree with him. He had killed me – though it was me masquerading as him – though it had been a hypnoid illusion.

I forced myself to say, 'It's a paradox how a man can hate people he doesn't know and hasn't even seen. You can easily hate people you know – people like yourself.'

Pete made no answer and wouldn't look up.

'It would be a tragedy if we started hating these creatures on Jupiter just because they are there.'

I said it challengingly, but he merely shrugged. Natalie sipped her beer and watched me.

I asked him, 'Do you think some of your wild friends from over the frontier would come along and feed their archetypes into CUFL? Think they could stand the pace and the journey?'

Both he and his father stared at me as if they had been struck.

Before the kid spoke, I knew I had got through to him. He would not have to go quietly schizoid. He would talk to Natalie and me eventually, and we would hear of his travels at firsthand. Just a few defensive layers had to come down first. Mine and his.

'You have to be joking!' he said.

Suddenly, I laughed. Everyone thought I was joking. Depending on your definition of a joke, I felt I had at last ceased joking after many a year. I turned suddenly from the table, to hide a burning of my eyes.

Taking Natalie by the arm, I said, 'Come on, we must get Ri to bed. She thinks we've forgotten about her.'

As we walked down the path, Natalie said, 'Was your suggestion serious?'

'I think I can work it. I'll speak to Wace. Things have to change. CUFL is imbalanced.' The finches fluttered in their cages. The line of sun was over the wall now. All was shadow among our orange trees, and the first bat was flying. I loomed over Ri before she noticed me. Startled, she stared up at me and burst into tears. Many things had to change.

I picked her up in my arms and kissed her cheeks.

Many things had to change. The human condition remained enduringly the same, but many things had to change.

Even the long nights on Earth were only local manifestations of the sun's eternal daylight. Even the different generations of man had archetypes in common, their slow writhings not merely inconsequential movement but ponderous and deliberate gesture.

So I carried her into the dim house to sleep.

Supertoys Last All Summer Long

In Mrs Swinton's garden, it was always summer. The lovely almond trees stood about it in perpetual leaf. Monica Swinton plucked a saffron-coloured rose and showed it to David.

'Isn't it lovely?' she said.

David looked up at her and grinned without replying. Seizing the flower, he ran with it across the lawn and disappeared behind the kennel where the mowervator crouched, ready to cut or sweep or roll when the moment dictated. She stood alone on her impeccable plastic gravel path.

She had tried to love him.

When she made up her mind to follow the boy, she found him in the courtyard floating the rose in his paddling pool. He stood in the pool engrossed, still wearing his sandals.

'David, darling, do you have to be so awful? Come in at once and change your shoes and socks.'

He went with her without protest, his dark head bobbing at the level of her waist. At the age of five, he showed no fear of the ultra-sonic dryer in the kitchen. But before his mother could reach for a pair of slippers, he wriggled away and was gone into the silence of the house.

He would probably be looking for Teddy.

Monica Swinton, twenty-nine, of graceful shape and lambent eye, went and sat in her living-room arranging her limbs with taste. She began by sitting and thinking; soon she was just sitting. Time waited on her shoulder with the manic sloth it reserves for children, the insane and wives whose husbands are away improving the world. Almost by reflex, she reached out and changed the wavelength of her windows. The garden faded; in its place, the city centre rose by her left hand, full of crowding people, blow-boats, and buildings – but she kept the sound down. She remained alone. An overcrowded world is the ideal place in which to be lonely.

The directors of Synthank were eating an enormous luncheon to celebrate the launching of their new product. Some of them wore plastic face-masks popular at the time. All were elegantly slender, despite the rich food and drink they were putting away. Their wives were elegantly slender, despite the food and drink they too were putting away. An earlier and less sophisticated generation would have regarded them as beautiful people, apart from their eyes. Their eyes were hard and calculating.

Henry Swinton, Managing Director of Synthank, was about to make a speech.

'I'm sorry your wife couldn't be with us to hear you,' his neighbour said.

'Monica prefers to stay at home thinking beautiful thoughts,' said Swinton, maintaining a smile.

'One would expect such a beautiful woman to have beautiful thoughts,' said the neighbour.

Take your mind off my wife, you bastard, thought Swinton, still smiling.

He rose to make his speech amid applause.

After a couple of jokes, he said, 'Today marks a real breakthrough for the company. It is now almost ten years since we put our first synthetic life-forms on the world market. You all know what a success they have been, particularly the miniature dinosaurs. But none of them had intelligence.

'It seems like a paradox that in this day and age we can create life but not intelligence. Our first selling line, the Crosswell Tape, sells best of all, and is the most stupid of all.'

Everyone laughed.

'Though three-quarters of our overcrowded world is starving, we are lucky here to have more than enough, thanks to population control. Obesity's our problem, not malnutrition. I guess there's nobody round this table who doesn't have a Crosswell working for him in the small intestine, a perfectly safe parasite tape-worm that enables its host to eat up to fifty per cent more food and still keep his or her figure. Right?'

General nods of agreement.

'Our miniature dinosaurs are almost equally stupid. Today, we launch an intelligent synthetic life-form – a full-size serving-man.

'Not only does he have intelligence, he has a controlled amount of intelligence. We believe people would be afraid of a being with a human brain. Our serving-man has a small computer in his cranium.

'There have been mechanicals on the market with minicomputers for brains – plastic things without life, supertoys – but we have at last found a way to link computer circuitry with synthetic flesh.'

David sat by the long window of his nursery, wrestling with paper and pencil. Finally, he stopped writing and began to roll the pencil up and down the slope of the desk-lid.

'Teddy!' he said.

Teddy lay on the bed against the wall, under a book with moving pictures and a giant plastic soldier. The speech-pattern of his master's voice activated him and he sat up.

'Teddy, I can't think what to say!'

Climbing off the bed, the bear walked stiffly over to cling to the boy's leg. David lifted him and set him on the desk.

'What have you said so far?'

'I've said –' He picked up his letter and stared hard at it. 'I've said, "Dear Mummy, I hope you're well just now. I love you."'

There was a long silence, until the bear said, 'That sounds fine. Go downstairs and give it to her.'

Another long silence.

'It isn't quite right. She won't understand.'

Inside the bear, a small computer worked through its program of possibilities. 'Why not do it again in crayon?'

David was staring out of the window. 'Teddy, you know what I was thinking? How do you tell what are real things from what aren't real things?'

The bear shuffled its alternatives. 'Real things are good.'

'I wonder if time is good. I don't think Mummy likes time very much. The other day, lots of days ago, she said that time went by her. Is time real, Teddy?'

'Clocks tell the time. Clocks are real. Mummy has clocks so she must like them. She has a clock on her wrist next to her dial.'

David had started to draw an airliner on the back of his letter. 'You and I are real, Teddy, aren't we?'

The bear's eyes regarded the boy unflinchingly. 'You and I are real, David.' It specialised in comfort.

Monica walked slowly about the house. It was almost time for the afternoon post to come over the wire. She punched the O.L. number on the dial on her wrist but nothing came through. A few minutes more.

She could take up her painting. Or she could dial her friends. Or she could wait till Henry came home. Or she could go up and play with David …

She walked out into the hall and to the bottom of the stairs.

'David!'

No answer. She called again and a third time.

'Teddy!' she called, in sharper tones.

'Yes, Mummy!' After a moment's pause, Teddy's head of golden fur appeared at the top of the stairs.

'Is David in his room, Teddy?'

'David went into the garden, Mummy.'

'Come down here, Teddy!'

She stood impassively, watching the little furry figure as it climbed down from step to step on its stubby limbs. When it reached the bottom, she picked it up and carried it into the living-room. It lay unmoving in her arms, staring up at her. She could feel just the slightest vibration from its motor.

'Stand there, Teddy. I want to talk to you.' She set him down on a tabletop, and he stood as she requested, arms set forward and open in the eternal gesture of embrace.

'Teddy, did David tell you to tell me he had gone into the garden?'

The circuits of the bear's brain were too simple for artifice.

'Yes, Mummy.'

'So you lied to me.'

'Yes, Mummy.'

'Stop calling me Mummy! Why is David avoiding me? He's not afraid of me, is he?'

'No. He loves you.'

'Why can't we communicate?'

'Because David's upstairs.'

The answer stopped her dead. Why waste time talking to this machine? Why not simply go upstairs and scoop David into her arms and talk to him, as a loving mother should to a loving son? She heard the sheer weight of silence in the house, with a different quality of silence issuing from every room. On the upper landing, something was moving very silently – David, trying to hide away from her ...

He was nearing the end of his speech now. The guests were attentive; so was the Press, lining two walls of the banqueting chamber, recording Henry's words and occasionally photographing him.

'Our serving-man will be, in many senses, a product of the computer. Without knowledge of the genome, we could never have worked through the sophisticated biochemics that go into synthetic flesh. The serving-man will also be an extension of the computer – for he will contain a computer in his own head, a microminiaturised computer capable of dealing with almost any situation he may encounter in the home. With reservations, of course.'

Laughter at this; many of those present knew the heated debate that had engulfed the Synthank boardroom before the decision had finally been taken to leave the serving-man neuter under his flawless uniform.

'Amid all the triumphs of our civilisation – yes, and amid the crushing problems of overpopulation too – it is sad to reflect how many millions of people suffer from increasing loneliness and isolation. Our serving-man will be a boon to them; he will always answer, and the most vapid conversation cannot bore him.

'For the future, we plan more models, male and female – some of them without the limitations of this first one, I promise you! – of more advanced design, true bio-electronic beings.

'Not only will they possess their own computers, capable of individual programming: they will be linked to the Ambient, the World Data Network. Thus everyone will be able to enjoy the equivalent of an Einstein in their own homes. Personal isolation will then be banished for ever!'

He sat down to enthusiastic applause. Even the synthetic serving-man, sitting at the table dressed in an unostentatious suit, applauded with gusto.

*

Dragging his satchel, David crept round the side of the house. He climbed on to the ornamental seat under the living-room window and peeped cautiously in.

His mother stood in the middle of the room. Her face was blank; its lack of expression scared him. He watched fascinated. He did not move; she did not move. Time might have stopped, as it had stopped in the garden. Teddy looked round, saw him, tumbled off the table, and came over to the window. Fumbling with his paws, he eventually got it open.

They looked at each other.

'I'm no good, Teddy. Let's run away!'

'You're a very good boy. Your mummy loves you.'

Slowly, he shook his head. 'If she loves me, then why can't I talk to her?'

'You're being silly, David. Mummy's lonely. That's why she has you.'

'She's got Daddy. I've got nobody 'cept you, and I'm lonely.'

Teddy gave him a friendly cuff over the head. 'If you feel so bad, you'd better go to the psychiatrist again.'

'I hate that old psychiatrist – he makes me feel I'm not real.' He started to run across the lawn. The bear toppled out of the window and followed as fast as its stubby legs would allow.

Monica Swinton was up in the nursery. She called to her son once and then stood there, undecided. All was silent.

Crayons lay on his desk. Obeying a sudden impulse, she went over to the desk and opened it. Dozens of pieces of paper lay inside. Many of them were written in crayon in David's clumsy writing, with each letter picked out in a colour different from the letter preceding it. None of the messages was finished.

MY DEAR MUMMY, HOW ARE YOU REALLY, DO YOU LOVE ME AS MUCH –

DEAR MUMMY, I LOVE YOU AND DADDY AND THE SUN IS SHINING –

DEAR DEAR MUMMY, TEDDY'S HELPING ME TO WRITE TO YOU. I LOVE YOU AND TEDDY –

DARLING MUMMY, I'M YOUR ONE AND ONLY SON AND I LOVE YOU SO MUCH THAT SOME TIMES –

DEAR MUMMY, YOU'RE REALLY MY MUMMY AND I HATE TEDDY –

DARLING MUMMY, GUESS HOW MUCH I LOVE –

DEAR MUMMY, I'M YOUR LITTLE BOY NOT TEDDY AND I LOVE YOU BUT TEDDY –

DEAR MUMMY, THIS IS A LETTER TO YOU JUST TO SAY HOW MUCH HOW EVER SO MUCH –

Monica dropped the pieces of paper and burst out crying. In their gay inaccurate colours the letters fanned out and settled on the floor.

Henry Swinton caught the express in high spirits, and occasionally said a word to the synthetic serving-man he was taking home with him. The serving-man answered politely and punctually, although his answers were not always entirely relevant by human standards.

The Swintons lived in one of the ritziest city-blocks. Embedded in other apartments, their apartment had no windows on to the outside; nobody wanted to see the overcrowded external world. Henry unlocked the door with his retina-pattern-scanner and walked in, followed by the serving-man.

At once, Henry was surrounded by the friendly illusion of gardens set in eternal summer. It was amazing what Whologram could do to create huge mirages in small spaces. Behind its roses and wisteria stood their house: the deception was complete: a Georgian mansion appeared to welcome him.

'How do you like it?' he asked the serving-man.

'Roses occasionally suffer from black spot.'

'These roses are guaranteed free from any imperfections.'

'It is always advisable to purchase goods with guarantees, even if they cost slightly more.'

'Thanks for the information,' Henry said dryly. Synthetic life-forms were less than ten years old, the old android mechanicals less than sixteen; the faults of their systems were still being ironed out, year by year.

He opened the door and called to Monica.

She came out of the sitting-room immediately and flung her arms round him, kissing him ardently on cheek and lips. Henry was amazed.

Pulling back to look at her face, he saw how she seemed to generate light and beauty. It was months since he had seen her so excited. Instinctively, he clasped her tighter.

'Darling what's happened?'

'Henry, Henry – oh, my darling, I was in despair ... But I've dialled the afternoon post and – you'll never believe it! Oh, it's wonderful!'

'For heaven's sake, woman, what's wonderful?'

He caught a glimpse of the heading on the stat in her hand, still warm from the wall-receiver; Ministry of Population. He felt the colour drain from his face in sudden shock and hope.

'Monica ... oh ... Don't tell me our number's come up!'

'Yes, my darling, yes, we've won this week's parenthood lottery! We can go ahead and conceive a child at once!'

He let out a yell of joy. They danced round the room. Pressure of population was such that reproduction had to be strictly controlled. Childbirth required government permission. For this moment they had waited four years. Incoherently they cried their delight.

They paused at last, gasping, and stood in the middle of the room to laugh at each other's happiness. When she had come down from the nursery, Monica had de-opaqued the windows, so that they now revealed the vista of garden beyond. Artificial sunlight was growing long and golden across the lawn – and David and Teddy were staring through the window at them.

Seeing their faces Henry and his wife grew serious.

'What do we do about *them*?' Henry asked.

'Teddy's no trouble. He works well enough.'

'Is David malfunctioning?'

'His verbal communication centre is still giving him trouble. I think he'll have to go back to the factory again.'

'Okay. We'll see how he does before the baby's born. Which reminds me – I have a surprise for you: help just when help is needed! Come into the hall and see what I've got.'

As the two adults disappeared from the room, boy and bear sat down beneath the standard roses.

'Teddy – I suppose Mummy and Daddy are real, aren't they?'

Teddy said, 'You ask such silly questions, David. Nobody knows what "real" really means. Let's go indoors.'

'First I'm going to have another rose!' Plucking a bright pink flower, he carried it with him into the house. It could lie on the pillow as he went to sleep. Its beauty and softness reminded him of Mummy.

That Uncomfortable Pause Between
Life and Art...

I'd visited the exhibition of paintings by William Holman Hunt at the Victoria & Albert Museum. Afterwards, I went to the cafeteria, sitting and drinking orangeade after orangeade. A woman of about fifty sat down opposite me, we exchanged a word about the beautiful summer weather, and she embarked immediately upon the story of her life, which had been full of trouble and three husbands; not to mention a spaniel that got run over on the Kingston Bypass.

In Hunt's work, we are meant to think of the surface of the canvas as non-existent – a conspiracy that no longer exists between modern painters and their audience. Each frame admits one to a little floodlit stage. Inside lies a diorama in bright colour. In a picture like *The Apple Harvest*, you look at the apples, rosily hanging between the girl's basket and the sack, and peer closer for the threads that keep them suspended so miraculously in mid-air. With Hunt, you never see the threads.

Her first husband was pretty rich. He was a tea-planter, with plantations out in Assam. She told me how many workers they employed. Even in the hills, the climate was too hot for her. Perhaps it was the hot London day that prompted her reminiscences. Anyhow, he died out in Assam, and so she'd had to come home alone. But on the boat back from Bombay, she had met Albert. She lit a cigarette and companionably blew the smoke at me.

My interest in Holman Hunt extends over many years. In some ways, he must have been like me – for instance, all that nonsense about actually transporting a goat to the shores of the Dead Sea to paint it! That is the sort of thing I might get involved in myself. But as a writer I also respond to what I diagnose as his dilemma. That novel of mine, *Report on Probability A*, the one that didn't cause such a fuss, centred round Hunt's best painting, *The Hireling Shepherd*.

I have been to Bombay too, but I didn't tell her that. By now, she needed no prompting. This chap Albert was apparently an authority on butterflies. Would anyone ever refer to me as 'an authority on Holman Hunt'? I tried to visualise my first wife chumming up with some fellow in a cafeteria, rattling off her tribulations, among which I imagine I would figure prominently, and saying, 'He was quite an authority on Holman Hunt'. No, that would be allowing me too much.

My intention was to write a review of the exhibition. Perhaps this is where the only parallel between Hunt and me comes in, and that is a fairly tenuous one. Hunt was right at the fag-end of one tradition, the Renaissance tradition of lining up acceptable objects in an ideal arrangement and painting them, allowing the spectator an essential role in completing the arrangement. And all the while, photography was creeping up on him; men like Degas and Toulouse-Lautrec were making what went on inside the frame its own reference; later still, the Cubists would explore the actual surface of the canvas.

On the other hand, Hunt was quietly revolutionary in his handling of backgrounds. ('I paint,' he said, 'direct on the canvas itself, with every detail I can see, and with the sunlight brightness of the day itself.) Some of his setting could come from Salvador Dali, and seem almost mescalin-influenced. The tremendous country round the Dead Sea is a case in point; Hunt embraced its surrealist qualities.

'Can I get you an orangeade? I'm going to have another myself.'

'I shouldn't really. I ought to be going. I'm supposed to be meeting my sister at Harrods.'

I bought it for her anyway. I hoped that while I was at the counter she would notice the book I was carrying about with me – Nigel Calder's *Technopolis* – but she was too involved in her own affairs to dwell on all my marvellous paradoxes. I should have said to her, 'Look, isn't it typical of the versatility of people today that I should be so fascinated in the uses or abuses of science, and so obsessed with the present unrolling into the future, and yet remain preoccupied with – well, frankly, not first-rate painters like Holman Hunt!' At times it is hard to see where such conflicting interests integrate. Hunt had the same sort of battle between religion (he was very High Church) and paintings. Perhaps the painting lost. Born a generation later, he might have been more successful.

Hunt was so misunderstood that he took to printing little pamphlets to accompany each painting, explaining what he was doing. He tried to make everything simple. In that respect, creators and critics are alike: all strive to make things either simpler or more complex. I only wish some of our critics could be humbler; one wants criticism and not autobiography, but surely it would be realistic if a critic occasionally said, 'My entirely derogatory judgements on Holman Hunt must not be considered in any way definitive, as I was distracted just after the viewing by a woman whose third husband is still alive but separated from her and now living, as far as is known, in a village eight miles from the centre of Torquay.'

As for *Technopolis,* I have been distracted in reviewing that. Calder is writing about ways in which society can control technology. He admits that a scientific policy is difficult to formulate, because the politicians can never look as far ahead in these matters as they need to do. Presumably this explains why nothing coherent is done about the population explosion, like phasing out family allowances, for example. But my mind keeps wandering off the subject; I have to confess I am curious about how the doctors cured her daughter Irene's harelip. She gives me plenty of detail but not the sort of detail I want. Like Hunt, in a way.

We are going to find it difficult to control the course of science and technology, which by now have got a bit set in their ways. We are still faced with problems that were already confronting the Victorians. When Hunt exhibited *The Hireling Shepherd* in the Royal Academy in 1852, the familiar ambivalent attitude to the machine was already established. Since there is no danger that any of my present readers have heard of *Report on Probability A*, I might as well say that one of my themes was a paralysis of time, which I pretended to detect and find exemplified in the anecdotalism of this canvas, and similar Victorian paintings. This poor woman sitting opposite me – she's not going to touch that orangeade I brought her – represents a personal paralysis of time. She's reliving her earlier days over and over. This whole package-deal of her life is no doubt trotted out to strangers every day. Her life may have become the fearful mess it is simply because she thinks backwards instead of forwards. Hunt kept thinking back to the Early Church instead of forward to the Impressionists. Isn't his sun breaking through the cypress trees in the Fiesole canvas of 1868 as fresh in its way as Monet's studies of light and shadow on the Seine, painted in the same year? I suppose the answer is, No, it is not. Just as this woman's remembrance of things past is not a patch on Proust's, though she may have suffered as much.

Here we sit, then: Hunt and she and Calder and me. Calder's in the best position; his time escape-route lies in the future, because his book is not even published till next week; nor does he exactly address himself to the denizens of the V & A canteen. But the rest of us are paralysed by time. So's her sister, stuck in Harrods waiting for her. And her third husband, down outside Torquay. As for me...has any critic before ever tried to arrive at an objective viewpoint in similar circumstances *and admitted it?* Critics ought to confide more, the way this woman does; we need to know more often what's in it for them.

What's in it for her? She didn't even go to look at the Hunts. She says she doesn't like paintings much. She did when she was a little girl. What the hell's she doing here anyway? I shouldn't have imagined she came to the V & A especially to revel in the delights of the cafeteria. Not with orangeade at one-and-three a carton. Perhaps she comes every morning – captive audience always on tap. I must break away. I notice she tells me everybody's name but her own. This hysterectomy she's telling me about now – would she be so liberal with the gruesome detail if we had been properly introduced? No painter has ever painted a hysterectomy, to my knowledge.

Some awful academic social realistic painter in Moscow – he must have done it. Glaring light; thick-set surgeons; anaesthetists in green overalls; devoted proletarian nurses, almost sexless; scalpels gleaming, the op nearly over; bust of Lenin in the background, surrounded by flags; the womb emerging; general moral uplift. Or perhaps the Russians consider it a decadent capitalist operation. The way she tells it, they're right!

Anyway, Hunt, William Holman. My review. Primarily a religious painter. More competent than his colleague Millais. The only one of the Pre-Raphaelite Brethren to stick to his principles. I came away from his canvases primed with the suspicion – no, confirmed in my opinion that, while he may be by no means the greatest of the Victorian painters, Hunt's place is assured – no, it is the colourist rather than the moralist that today – no, no, no... This woman's making more sense than I am. I came away still feeling a strong bond with Hunt. One of the great comic painters: comic-macabre, as *The Shadow of Death* proves. Born too late. Too early. Nothing but cliché... I must escape from this cliché of a life unrolling before me... Majorca to recover, indeed! There she met this rich Spaniard. If only one could suspect her of lying. That uncomfortable pause between life and art is not for her, any more than it was for Hunt.

She's on about sex all the time, you notice, without actually daring to tackle the subject head-on. Dear God, we all live out such muddled lives, and so many lives at once. Calder should write a book about controlling *us!*

Hurriedly, I swig down her untouched orangeade and make off with scarcely a farewell, heading towards Harrods, where my wife awaits me.

'Count on me,' I said simply. 'And don't forget – two-and-a-half per cent of the gross.'

We eyed one another in complete understanding. For sentiment's sake, I knew how I wanted to bid him goodbye; but there were people passing, and I was a little embarrassed. Instead, I grasped his worn frail hand in both of mine.

'Goodbye, Geoffrey!'

'Auf Wiedersehen, Brian, dear boy!'

Blinking moisture from my eyes, I hurried for the airport, the contract in my pocket.

Working in the Spaceship Yards

My first job of work as a young man was in the spaceship yards, where I felt my talents and expertise could be put to the greatest benefit of society. I worked as a FTL-fitter's mate's asistant. The FTL-fitter's mate was a woman called Nellie. As more and more women came to be employed in the yards, among the men and the androids and the robots, the men became increasingly circumspect in their behaviour. Their oaths were more guarded, their gestures less uncouth, and their care for their appearance less negligent. This I found strange, since the women showed clearly that they cared nothing for oaths, gestures, or appearances.

From wastebaskets round the site, I collected many suicide notes. Most of them had never reached their recipients and were mere drafts of suicide notes:

> *My darling – When you receive this, I shall no longer be in a position*
> *to ever trouble you again.*
> *By the time you receive this letter, I shall never be able.*
> *By the time you receive this, I shall be no more.*
> *My darling – Never again will we be able to break each other's hearts.*
> *You have been more than life to me.*
> *My love – I have been so wrong.*

It is very good of people to take such care in their compositions even in extremis. Education has had its effect. At my school, we learnt only how to write business letters. With reference to your last shipment of Martian pig iron/iron pigs. Since life is such a tragic business, why are we not educated how to write decent suicide notes?

In this age of progress, where everything is progressive and technological and new, the only bit of our Self we have left to ourselves is our Human Condition – which of course remains miserable, despite three protein-full meals a day. Protein does not help the Dark Night of the Soul. Androids, which look so like us (we have the new black androids working in the spaceship yards now) do not have a soul, and many of them are very distressed at lacking the long slow toothache of the Human Condition. Some of them have left their employment, and stand on street corners wearing dark glasses, begging for alms with pathetic messages round their shoulders. Orphan of Technology. Left Factry Too Yung. Have Pity on My Poor Metal Frame. And an especially heart-wrenching one I saw in the Queens district. Obsolescence Is the Poor Man's Death. They have their traumas; just to be deprived of the Human Condition must be traumatic.

Most androids hate the android-beggars. They tour the streets after work, beating up any beggars they find, kicking their tin mugs into the gutter. Faceless androids are scaring. They look like men in iron masks. You can never escape role-playing.

We were building Q-line ships when I was in the shipyard. They were the experimental ones. The Q1, the Q2, the Q3, had each been completed, had been towed out into orbit beyond Mars, and triggered off towards Alpha Centauri. Nothing was ever heard of them again. Perhaps they are making a tour of the entire universe, and will return to the solar system when the sun is ten kilometres deep in permafrost. Anyhow, I shan't live to see the day.

It was no fun building those ships. They had no luxury, no living quarters, no furnishings, no galleys, no miles and miles of carpeting and all the other paraphernalia of a proper spaceship. There was very little we could take as supplementary income. The computers that crewed them lived very austere lives.

'The sun will be ten kilometres deep in permafrost by the time you get back to the solar system!' I told BALL, the computer on the Q3, as we walled him in. 'What will you do then?'

'I shall measure the permafrost.'

I've noticed that about the truth. You don't expect it, so it often sounds like a joke. Computers and robots sound funny quite often because they have no roles to play. They just tell the truth. I asked this BALL, 'Who will you be measuring this permafrost for?'

'I shall be measuring it for its intrinsic interest.'

'Even if there are no human beings around to be interested?'

'You misunderstand the meaning of intrinsic.'

Each of these Q ships cost more than the entire annual national income of a state like Great Britain. Zip, out into the universe they went. Never seen again! My handiwork. All those miles of beautiful seamless welding. My life's work.

I say computers tell the truth. It is only the truth as they see it. Things go on that none of us see. Should we include them in our personal truth or not?

My mother was a good old sport. Before I reached the age of ten and was given my extra-familial posting, she and I had a lot of fun. Hers was a heart of gold – more, of uranium. She had an old deaf friend called Mrs Patt who used to come and visit mother once a week and sit in the big armchair while mother yelled questions and remarks at her.

Now I realise why I could not bear Mrs Patt – because everything I said sounded so trivial and stupid when repeated at the top of my voice.

'It's nice about the extra moonlight law, isn't it?'

'You what you say?'

'I said aren't you pleased about the extra moonlight law?'

'Pleased what?'

'Aren't you pleased about the extra moonlight law? We could do with another moon.'

'I can't hear what you say.'

'I say isn't it fun about the extra moonlight law?'

'What lawn is that?'

'The extra moonlight law. Law! Isn't it fun about the extra moonlight law?'

I used to hide behind the armchair before Mrs Patt came in. When she and mother started shouting, I would rise over the back of the chair so that Mrs Patt could not see me, sticking my thumbs in my ears and my little fingers up my nostrils so that my nose was wrinkled and distorted, waving my other fingers about while shooting my brows up and down, flobbing my tongue, and blinking my eyes furiously, in order to make mother laugh. She had to pretend she could not see me.

Occasionally, she would have to pretend to blow her nose, in order to enjoy a quick chuckle.

We had a big bad black cat. Sometimes I would appear round the chair with the tom dish on my head, mewing and wagging my ears.

The question I now ask myself, having reached more sober years – Mrs Patt visited the euthanasia clinic years ago – is whether I should or should not be included among Mrs Patt's roll call of truths. Since I was not among her observable phenomena, then I could not be part of her revealed Truth. For Mrs Patt, I did not exist in my post-armchair manifestation; therefore my effect upon her Self was totally negligible; therefore I could form no portion of her Truth, as she saw it.

Whether what I was doing was well-or ill-intentioned towards her likewise did not matter, since it did not impinge on her consciousness. The only effect of my performance on her was that she came to consider my mother as someone unusually prone to colds, necessitating frequent nose-blowing.

This suggests that there are two sorts of truth: one's personal truth, and what, for fear of using an even more idiotic term, I will call a Universal Truth. In this last category clearly belong events that go on even if nobody is observing them, like my fingers up my nose, the flights of the Q1, Q2, and Q3, and God.

All this I once tried to explain to my android friend, Jackson. I tried to tell him that he could only perceive Universal Truth, and had no cognisance of Personal Truth.

'Universal Truth is the greater, so I am greater than you, who perceive only Personal Truth,' he said.

'Not at all! I obviously perceive all of Personal Truth, since that's what it means, and also quite a bit of Universal Truth. So I get a much better idea of Total Truth than you.'

'Now you are inventing a third sort of truth, in order to win the argument. Just because you have Human Condition, you have to keep proving you are better than me.'

I switched him off. I am better than Jackson. I can switch him off.

Next day, going back on shift, I switched him on again.

'There are all sorts of horrible things signalling behind your metaphorical armchair that you aren't aware of,' he said immediately.

'At least human beings write suicide notes,' I said. It is a minor art that has never received full recognition. A very intimate art. You can't write a suicide note to someone you do not know.

> *Dear President – My name may not be familiar to you but I voted for you in the last election and, when you receive this, I shall no longer be able to trouble you ever again.*
>
> *I shall no longer ever be able to vote for you again. Not be able to support you at the next election.*
>
> *Dear President – This will come as something of a shock, particularly since you don't know me, but.*
>
> *Dear Sir – You have been more than a president to me.*

The hours in the spaceship yards were long, particularly for us young lads. We worked from ten till twelve and again from two till four. The robots worked from ten till four. The androids worked from ten till twelve and from two till four when I began at the yards as a FTL-fitter's mate's assistant, and they had no breaks for canteen, whereas men and women got fifteen minutes off in every hour for coffee and drugs. After I had been in the yards for some ten months, legislation was passed allowing androids five minutes off in every hour for coffee (they don't take drugs). The men went on strike against this legislation, but it all simmered down by Christmas, after a pay rise. The Q4 was delayed another sixteen weeks, but what is sixteen weeks when you are going to go round the universe?

*

The women were very emotional. Many of them fell in love with androids. The men were very bitter about this. My first love, Nellie, the FTL-fitter's mate, left me for an android electrician. She said he was more respectful.

In the canteen, we men used to talk about sex and philosophy and who was winning the latest Out-Thinking Contest. The women used to exchange recipes. I often feel women do not have quite such a large share of the Human Condition as we do.

When we first went to bed together Nellie said, 'You're a bit nervous, aren't you?'

Well, I was, but I said, 'No, I'm not nervous, it's just this question of role-playing. I haven't entirely devised one to cover this particular situation.'

'Well, buck up, then, or the whistle will be going. You can be the Great Lover or something, can't you?'

'Do I look like the Great Lover?' I asked in exasperation.

'I've seen smaller,' she said, and she smiled. After that, we always got on well together, and then she had to leave me for that android electrician.

For a few days, I was terribly miserable. I thought of writing her a suicide note but I didn't know how to word it.

> *Dear Nellie – I know you are too hard-hearted to care a hoot about this, but. I know you don't care a hoot but. I know you don't give a hoot. Give a rap. Are indifferent to. Are indifferent to what happens to me, but.*
>
> *As you lie there in the synthetic arms of your lover, it may interest you to know I am about to.*

But I was not really about to, for I struck up a close friendship with Nancy, and she enjoyed my Great Lover role. She was very good with an I-Know-We're-Really-Both-Too-Sensible-For-This role. After a time, I got a transfer so that I could work with her on the starboard cond-entister. She used to tell me recipes for exotic dishes. Sometimes, it was quite a relief to get back to my mates in the canteen.

*

At last the great day came when the Q4 was finished. The President came down and addressed us, and inspected the two-mile high needle of shining steel. He told us it had cost more than all South America was worth, and would open up a New Era in the History of Mankind. Or perhaps he said New Error. Anyhow, the Q4 was going to put us in touch with some other civilisation, many light years away. It was imperative for our survival that we get in rapport with them before our enemies did.

'Why don't we just get in rapport with our enemies?' Nancy asked me sourly. She has no sense of occasion.

As we all came away from the ceremony, I had a nasty surprise. I saw Nellie with her arm round that android electrician, and he was limping. An android, limping! There's role-playing for you. Byronic androids! If we aren't careful, they will be taking over the Human Condition just as they are taking our women. The future is black and the bins of our destiny are filling with suicide notes.

I felt really sick. Nancy stared at me as if she could see someone over my shoulder putting his thumbs in his ears and his little fingers up his nose and all that. Of course, when I looked round, nobody was there.

'Let's go and play Great Lovers while there's still time,' I said.